Celia Friedma[...] [...]om her earliest days and began writing at the age of thirteen. At university, she studied maths, then theatre before following her love of costume design to study and pursue a career in that field. She taught Costume Design at a northern Virginian university and has designed period dress patterns for a historical supply company. She now writes full-time and teaches a creative writing course at a local high school.

To find out more about Celia Friedman and other Orbit authors you can register for the free monthly newsletter at www.orbitbooks. co.uk

By C. S. Friedman

The Coldfire Trilogy
Black Sun Rising
When True Night Falls

Look out for
Crown of Shadows

WHEN TRUE NIGHT FALLS

The Coldfire Trilogy: Book Two

CELIA FRIEDMAN

www.orbitbooks.co.uk

ORBIT

First published in the United States in 1993 by Daw Books, Inc.
First published in Great Britain in 2006 by Orbit

A CIP catalogue record for this book
is available from the British Library.

ISBN-13: 978-1-84149-542-2
ISBN-10: 1-84149-542-5

Typeset in Granjon
by Palimpsest Book Production Limited, Grangemouth, Stirlingshire
Printed and bound in Great Britain by
Mackays of Chatham plc, Chatham, Kent

Orbit
An imprint of
Little, Brown Book Group
Brettenham House
Lancaster Place
London WC2E 7EN

A Member of the Hachette Livre Group of Companies

www.orbitbooks.co.uk

For Michael Whelan,
whose beautiful art
brings dreams to life.

The author would like to thank Todd Drunagel for saving chapter two from computer oblivion, and Mark Sunderlin for rescuing her from computer hell several times. (Sometimes a world without technology can be very appealing!) And very special thanks to Daniel Barr, for costuming above and beyond the call of duty.

PROLOGUE

I can't believe we're doing this.

Colony Commander Leonid Case lay full length upon the damp Ernan soil, his hands clenched into fists before him. This whole plan was insane, he thought. His furtive departure from the settlement, his midnight stalk through these alien woods, and now hiding in this gully like some forest-born predator, alert for the scent of prey . . . in fact, the only thing crazier than the way he was acting was the situation that had brought him here in the first place. And the man responsible for it.

Damn Ian! Damn his delusions! Didn't the settlement have enough problems here without his adding to them? Wasn't it enough that people were dying here – *dying!* – in ways that defied all human science? Did Ian have to add to that nightmare?

The blackness of despair churned coldly in Case's gut, and panic stirred in its wake. He couldn't let it get to him. He was responsible for this fledgling colony, which meant that the others depended on him – on his advice, his judgment, and most of all on his personal stability. He couldn't afford to let despair overwhelm him, any more than he could allow himself to openly vent his fury over his chief botanist's behavior. But sometimes it seemed almost more than he could handle. God knows he had signed on for better and for worse, well aware of all the tragedies that might befall a newborn colony . . . but no one had prepared him for *this*.

Thirty-six dead now. Thirty-six of his people. And not just dead: gruesomely dead, fearsomely dead, dead in ways that defied human acceptance. He remembered the feel of Sally Chang's frozen flesh in his hands, so brittle that when he tried to lift her body it shattered into jagged bits, like glass. And Wayne Reinhart's corpse, which was little more than a jellylike package of skin and blood and pulped organs by the time they found it. And Faren Whitehawk . . . that was the most frightening one of all, he thought. Not because it was the most repellent; Faren's corpse was whole, the flesh still pliant, the expression almost peaceful. But all the blood was gone from the body, impossibly drawn out through two puncture wounds in the neck. Or so the settlement's doctors had informed him. Christ in heaven! Looking down at those marks – ragged and reddened, crusted black about the edges with dried blood and worse – he knew that what they were facing here was nothing Earth could have prepared them for. Monsters drawn from Earth's tradition, their own human nightmares garbed in solid flesh and pitted against them . . . how did you fight such a thing? Where did you even start? When Carrie Sands was killed three nights later by some winged creature that had accosted her while she slept, he wasn't surprised to hear her bunkmate describe it as a creature straight out of East Indian mythology. Something that fed on nightmares, he recalled. Only this time it got carried away, and fed on flesh as well.

Jesus Christ. Where was it going to end?

Thirty-six dead. That was out of the three thousand and some odd colonists who had survived the coldsleep journey to this place, to stand under the light of an alien sun and commit themselves body and soul to building a new world. *His* world. Now they were all at risk. And dammit, the seedship should have foreseen this! It was supposed to survey each planet in question until there was no doubt, *absolutely no doubt,* that the colonists would thrive there. If not, it was programmed to move on to the next available system. In theory it was a foolproof procedure, designed to protect Earth's explorers from the thousand and one predictable hazards of extra-terrestrial colonization. Like rival predators. Incompatible protein structures. Climatic instability.

The key word there was *predictable*.

Case looked up at the starless night sky – so black, so empty, so utterly alien – and found himself shivering. What did a Terran seedship do when it had surveyed a thousand systems – perhaps tens of thousands – and still it had found no hospitable world for its charges? Would there come a time when its microchips would begin to wear, when its own mechanical senility would force it to make one less than ideal choice? Or was all this the fault of the programmers, who had never foreseen that a ship might wander so far, for so long, without success? *Go outward,* they had directed it, *survey each planet you come across, and if it does not suit your purpose, then refuel and go outward farther still.* He thought of Erna's midnight sky, so eerie in its utter starlessness. What was a program like that supposed to do when it ran out of options? When the next move would take it beyond the borders of the galaxy, into regions so utterly desolate that it might drift forever without finding another sun, another source of fuel? Was it supposed to leap blindly into that void, its circuits undisturbed by the prospect of eternal solitude? Or would it instead survey its last available option again and again, time after time, until at last its circuits had managed whatever convolution of logic was required to determine that the last choice was indeed acceptable, by the terms of its desperation? So that there, tens of thousands of light-years from Earth, separated by a multimillenial gap in communication, the four thousand colonists might be awakened at last.

We'll never know, Commander Case thought grimly. The bulk of the seedship was high above them now, circling the tormented planet like an errant moon. They had brought all the data down with them, each nanosecond's record of the ninety-year survey – and he had studied it so often that sometimes it seemed he knew each byte of it by heart. To what end? Even if he could find some hint of danger in the seedship's study, what good would it do them now? They couldn't go back. They couldn't get help. This far out in the galaxy they couldn't even get advice from home. The seedship's programmers were long since dead, as was the culture that had nurtured them. Communication with Earth would mean waiting more than forty thousand years for an answer – and that was *if* Earth was there to respond, and *if* it would bother. What had the mother planet become, in the millennia it had taken this seedship to find a home? The temporal gulf was almost too vast, too awesome to contemplate. And it didn't really matter, Case told himself grimly. The fact that they were alone here, absolutely and forever, was all that counted. As far as this colony was concerned, there was no Earth.

He shifted uncomfortably in his mossy trench, all too aware of the darkness that was gathering around him. It was a thick darkness, cold and ominous, as unlike the darknesses of Earth as this new sun's cold light was unlike the warm splendor of Sol. For a moment homesickness filled him, made doubly powerful by the fact that home as he knew it no longer existed. The colonists had made their commitment to Eden only to find that it had a serpent's soul, but there was no escaping it now. Not with the figures for cold-sleep mortality in excess of 86% for second immersion.

He heard a rustling beside him and stiffened; his left hand moved for his weapon, even as he imagined all the sorts of winged nightmares that might even now be descending on him. But it was only Lise, come to join him. He nodded a greeting and scrunched to one side, making room for her to crawl forward. There was barely room for both of them in the shallow gully.

Lise Perez, M.D. Thank God for her. She had saved his life a few nights back, under circumstances he shuddered to recall. She had almost saved Tom Bennet when that *thing* got past the eastern fence and launched itself into the mess cabin, and in any case she had prevented it from grabbing anyone else, until a cook finally brought it down by severing head from body with a meat cleaver. She was a competent officer, always collected, she had a nose for trouble – and she had been keeping tabs on Ian Casca for nearly a month now. God bless her for it.

'How long?' he whispered.

She looked at her watch. 'Half an hour.' And glanced up at him. 'He'll be here before that,' she assured him.

If anyone else had brought him out here – if anyone else had even *suggested* that he should come out here, making himself the perfect target for every nightmare beast in this planet's ghastly repertoire – laughter would have been the kindest of his responses. But Lise had suggested it and he trusted her judgment, sometimes more than his own. And Ian had to be dealt with. There was no way around that. Case should have jailed the man when this all started, but he had chosen to assign him to therapy instead, and now he was paying the price for that decision.

'Listen,' she whispered. 'Here he comes.'

He nodded, noting that though her jacket and pants were dark enough for cover her pale skin glowed like a beacon in the moonlight. They should have thought of that. Rubbed her down with charcoal, or lampblack, or . . . something. Made her dark, like him, so that they could creep through the night unseen. *Too late for that now,* he thought. He cursed himself for carelessness and motioned for her to keep low, so that the weeds might obscure her face.

True night was about to fall. Less than half an hour now. Case told himself that the term was a mere technicality, that even on Earth heavy cloudcover might obscure the stars and moon, leaving a man in total darkness – but he knew that there was more to it than that. He had tasted its true power once in the field, by turning off his lantern so that the darkness was free to envelop him – a darkness so absolute, so utterly boundless, that all the shadows of Earth paled by comparison. The mere memory of it made his skin crawl. By now the whole camp would be alight with beacons, bright floods fighting to drive back the shadows of the triple night. As if mere light would help. As if mere walls could keep the serpent out of Eden, or prevent it from reading their secret thoughts, from turning their fears and even their desires against them.

As he listened for the sound of Ian's approach, he remembered the night *it* had come for him, the serpent incarnate in an angel's form. Remembered how all his fear and his skepticism and even his innate caution were banished from his soul in an instant, as though they had never existed. Because what had stepped out from the shadows was his son – his *son*! – as young and as healthy as he had been ten years ago, before the accident that took him from Case's life. And in that moment there was no fear in the Commander's heart, no suspicion, not even a moment's doubt. Love filled him with such force that he trembled, and tears poured down his cheeks. He whispered his son's name, and the figure moved toward him. He reached out his hand, and the creature touched him – it touched him! – and it was warm, and alive, and he knew it by touch and scent and a thousand other signs. Christ in heaven, his son was alive again! He opened his arms wide and gathered the boy up, buried his face in his hair (and the smell was familiar, even that was right) and cried, let all the pain pour out in a tsunami of raw emotion, an endless tide of grief and love and loss . . .

And she had saved him. Lise. She had come, and she had seen, and she had understood at once. And acted. Somehow she'd killed the unnatural thing, or driven it off, and she'd dragged Case to MedOps. Barely in time. Later, when he had regained the where-withal to communicate, he asked her what she had seen. And she answered, steadily, *It was devouring you. From the inside out. That's what all these creatures do, one way or another. They feed on us.*

In the distance now he could hear the low rumble of a tram approaching, its solar collectors vibrating as it bumped over the uneven turf. Ian. It had to be him. The trams had proven to be dangerously unreliable – two had exploded while being started up, and three more simply would not work – but Ian was one of the few who seemed capable of making them run, and they gave him no surprises. Likewise the man's weapons functioned perfectly, while others jammed and backfired, and as for his lab equipment . . . the botanist lived a charmed life, without question. But at what price?

In his mind's eye Case could see the grisly stockpile that Lise had discovered one night, after following Ian from camp. Small mammals, a few birds, a single lizard . . . all beheaded or dismembered or both, and hidden beneath a thornbush at edge of the forest. When Case had confronted Ian about them the botanist had made no attempt to dissemble or even defend himself, but had said simply, *There's power in the blood. Power in sacrifice. Don't you see? That's how this planet works. Sacrifice is power, Leo.*

Sacrifice is power.

The tram was coming into sight now, and it was possible to make out the form of a man behind its controls. Lamp-light glinted on red hair, wind-tossed: Ian Casca's trademark. In the back of the tram was something bundled in a blanket, that might or might not be alive. Case felt a chill course through him as he gauged the size of the trapped animal, and he thought, *Might be human. Might be.* He couldn't see Lise's expression, but it was a good bet she was thinking the same thing.

The blood is the life, the Old Testament proclaimed. Lise had shown him that passage in Casca's own Bible, under-scored by two red lines on a dog-eared page. He wondered if Ian had made those marks before or after this horror began.

The tram had entered the clearing now, and after a few seconds of idling Ian braked and shut it down. The harsh purr of the motor died out into the night, leaving a silence so absolute that Case's breathing seemed a roar by contrast. Even the insects were still, as if they, too, feared the darkness that was about to fall.

Case tightened his hand about his gun. Waiting.

The old formulas will work, Ian had claimed. He was lifting a bag from the cargo section, a specimen case whose soft sides bulged when he set it down. From it he removed a long strip of red cloth and a canvas sack. *All we have to do is learn to apply them.* He hung the cloth about his neck so that its ends fell forward, brushing against his calves as he worked. Painted sigils glittered on its surface: geometrics bordered with Hebrew figures, ancient Egyptian hieroglyphs, something that might have been an astrological symbol . . . Case shook his head in amazement as the man reached into his sack and drew out a handful of white powder. The trappings of his madness were so precise, so deliberate, so painstakingly detailed . . . which made him all the more dangerous, Case reflected. A careless madman would have gotten himself locked up long ago.

Lise touched him on the arm. He turned back to look at her, saw the question in her eyes. But he shook his head. *Not yet.* He turned back to watch the botanist, who was now tracing a circle on the ground, dribbling powder through his fingers to mark its circumference. When he was done with that he began to sketch out more complex figures, his fingers trembling with fear – or excitement – as he worked. On the bed of the tram one of the bundles had begun to move, and Case heard a soft moan issue from it. *Human,* he thought. *No doubt about it.* His jaw tightened, but he forced himself not to move forward. Not yet. Erna had no jailhouse, and at the rate things were going wrong they might never get the time to build one. If Ian's madness had turned murderous, then for the sake of the colony he would have to be disposed of. Excised, the way one excised a cancerous tumor to save the flesh beneath. And as judge, jury, and executioner, Case had better be damned sure that what he was doing was justified.

The circle was finished now, and all the designs that the botanist had chosen to add to it. He poured the last handful of powder back into the bag, tied it shut again, and set it aside. Case tensed, ready to interfere the minute Ian went for his captives. But the man simply stepped back, so that he stood in the exact center of the circle he had marked, and shut his eyes. For a moment he was silent, as if readying himself. *For what?* Case wondered. What arcane operation did the man imagine would give him control over this violent, unpredictable world?

If only it were that easy, he thought bitterly. *Draw a few signs on the ground, recite an ancient incantation or two, and behold, all problems disappear . . .* for a brief moment he wished that he shared the botanist's delusion. He wondered if he, too, might not be willing to spill a little blood, if he truly believed it would help the colony survive. Human blood? It was a disturbing question, and not one he wished to investigate further. God save him from ever discovering that the shell of his morality was as thin and as fragile as that of Ian Casca's sanity . . .

The botanist stirred. Slowly, breathing deeply, he raised his hands up by his sides, and opened his eyes at last. The lamplight barely picked out his features, but even so Case could see the concentration that burned in his eyes, the sweat of tension that gleamed on his brow. He began to chant, in a manner that was half speech, half song. Case caught a few words of something that sounded like Latin, intermingled with bits that might be Greek, then Hebrew, then Aramaic. It was as though Ian had taken all the ancient tongues of Earth and sifted through them for words he needed, then mixed them indescriminately to create this custom-made ritual. *Words of power,* Case thought. For one sickening moment he wondered if Ian might not be right, if Earth's magical traditions might not wield some true power in this extraterrestrial forum . . . but a moan from beneath the blankets brought him back to his senses, and his hand tightened about his gun. *Even if it did work,* he thought grimly, *it's not worth the price.*

Then Ian stopped. Stared into the night. His whole body was taut, rigid with tension. 'Erna, hear me,' he intoned. 'I offer you this sacrifice. I offer you the most precious thing we possess: the lifeblood of Terra. In return I ask this: Take us in. Make us part of you. We tried to be aliens on your soil, and your creatures defeated us. Now make us part of this world, as those creatures are part of it. And in return . . . I offer you the heartsblood of Earth. The souls of this colony, now and forever.' He shut his eyes; Case thought that he trembled. 'May it please you,' he whispered. 'May you find it acceptable.'

His hands dropped down to his sides once more. For a moment he was silent; perhaps waiting for an answer? Case saw one of the bundles on the trams begin to stir, as if trying to free itself. Apparently so did Ian. The movement awakened him from his seeming trance, and he began to move toward the tram and its contents. Stepping over the line he had drawn, across the sigil-girded circle he had so carefully created. Drawing a slender knife from his belt as he moved.

That was enough for Case. He was on his feet in an instant, and Lise was right behind him. While she moved to intercept the man, to keep him from reaching the tram, he took up a solid position at the edge of the clearing and leveled his gun at the man's heart. 'That's enough,' he announced. 'Party's over, Casca. Stay right where you are.'

The botanist reeled visibly, as though Case's words had not only stopped him in his tracks but had awakened him from some kind of trance. He turned toward the commander and gaped at him, as if trying to absorb the fact of his presence.

'Leo,' he said at last. Starting to move toward him. 'How did you—'

'Stay where you are!' Case ordered. 'And keep your hands where I can see them.' He glanced toward Lise and nodded; she was kneeling on the tram's bed, inspecting its contents. 'No fast movements, you hear me? Just stay where you are and keep quiet.'

Lise had cut the tie on one of the bundles and was freeing its occupant. 'Well?' Case demanded.

'It's Erik Fielder.' She reached a hand in to take his pulse, and added, 'He's alive.' Quickly she moved to the other bundle and unwrapped its upper end. 'Liz Breslav. Out cold. I see bruises, some sort of impact damage to the side of the head . . . can't say how bad it is without Med-Ops. We need to get her back to the ship.'

It took him a minute to put the names in context; when he did, he darkened. Ian's choice of victims was all too practical. With true night coming, the colony's other members would have been huddled together in their makeshift cabins, seeking the dubious safety that could be found in numbers. It would have been hard for Ian to single out one or two of them, much less knock them out and drag their bodies from the camp without being seen. But Fielder and Breslav had drawn special guard duty for the night, which meant that they were already outside the camp, standing watch over the ship and its contents a good mile away. They would have been especially vulnerable, Case thought, if their enemy was not a creature of Erna, like they expected, but one of their own kind. A glib man who might talk his way into their company, and then strike at them from behind when they least expected it.

His mouth tightened into a hard line as he raised the gun. 'That's proof enough for me.'

Sudden understanding gleamed in Ian's eyes. Understanding . . . and fear. 'Leo, listen to me—'

'The charge is endangering the welfare of the colony,' Case said steadily. 'The verdict is guilty.' Something tightened inside him, something cold and sharp. Something that hated killing, even in the name of justice. It took effort to get the words out. 'The sentence is death.'

It's not a killing, he told himself. *It's an excision. A cleansing.* Ian had to die so that the rest of them could live. Was that murder?

Call it a sacrifice.

'Listen to me,' the botanist protested. 'You don't know what you're doing—'

'Don't I?' he asked angrily. With the toe of one boot he kicked at the nearer side of Ian's circle, erasing the chalk line. 'Damn it, man! This isn't some primitive tribe in need of a shaman, but a colony in desperate need of unity! I have enough trouble from the outside without having to guard against my own people—'

'And how many more deaths can you absorb?' the botanist demanded. 'You know as well as I do that the death rate is increasing geometrically. How many more nights does this colony have before it loses the numbers it needs to maintain a viable gene pool?'

'Two Terran months,' he answered gruffly. 'But we'll learn how to fight these creatures. We'll learn how to—'

'Erna will create new ones as fast as you destroy the old! And if you learn to kill one kind, then the next will be different. Don't you see, Leo, it's the *planet* you're fighting, the planet itself! Some force that controls the local ecosphere, keeping everything in balance. It doesn't know how to absorb us. It doesn't know how to *connect*. But it's going to keep trying.' With a shaking hand he brushed back a lock of hair from his eyes; it fell back down almost immediately. 'Leo, this planet was *perfect*. No drought, no famine, no cycles of surfeit and starvation like there are on Earth . . . think of it! A whole ecology in utter harmony – a true Eden. And then *we* came. And threatened that harmony by our very presence—'

'And you think these rituals will change all that?' Case asked harshly.

'I think they'll give us a tool. A means of communication. That's the challenge, don't you see? We have to impress the power here with Terran symbology, so that we have some way to reach out to it. To *control* it, Leo! If we don't manage that, then we may as well pack it in here and now. Because all our technology won't stop it from killing, when it controls the very laws of nature.'

'So you answer it with more killing? Feed it blood—'

'Sacrifice is the most ancient and powerful symbol we have,' Ian told him. 'Think of it! When primitive man sought to placate his dieties, it was that blood of his own kind that he burned on the altar. When the God of the Jews decided to test Abraham's faith, it was the sacrifice of his own flesh and blood that He demanded. Moses saved his people from the Angel of Death by smearing the blood of animals on their doorposts. And when God reached out His Hand to man with His message of divine forgiveness, He created a Son of His Own Substance to serve as a sacrificial offering. Sacrifice is a bridge between man and the Infinite – and it can work for us here, Leo. In time it can end the killings. I believe that.' When Case made no response, he added desperately, 'You can't understand—'

'I understand,' Case said quietly. 'All too well.' He gestured with the gun. 'Move away from the tram.'

'You can't stop it now. The offer's been made. The sacrifice—'

'Is canceled, here and now. Move back from the tram.'

For a moment Ian just stared at him; comprehension dawned at last. 'You thought I was going to kill them,' he whispered hoarsely. Incredulously. 'You thought I would kill my own people—'

'What the hell was I supposed to think?' Case snapped. 'You took them from the camp. You dedicated a sacrifice, then came at them with a knife. You tell me what conclusions to draw from that!'

The botanist opened his hand; the knife fell beside his feet. 'I was going to cut them loose,' he said. 'I brought them here so they wouldn't get hurt . . . Commander.'

Case shook his head sharply. 'You forget that we were here. We heard you. *I give you the lifeblood of Terra*—'

He stopped. Stared. Through the eyes of a man, into the madness that lay beyond.

And he knew.

He *knew*.

Oh, my God . . .

The sky to the east filled with light, with fire; he wheeled about to face the source of it, and the sound and the force of the explosion knocked the breath from his body as they struck. Flames were roaring upward from a point some five miles east of them, lighting the sky with a reflected blaze a thousand times brighter than lightning. He staggered back in despair as the hot wind buffeted him, laden with the smell of burning. 'You fool!' he hissed. 'You goddamn fool!'

The ship. He could see it in his mind's eye, not the proud ceramic shell of their landing capsule but a ravaged, blackened husk, a cloud of shrapnel and ash where there had once been a wealth of computerware, lab equipment, biostorage . . . and at the foot of the flames a sea of hot slag, a molten lake which was quickly dissolving all their hopes and their memories and their dreams . . . all their heritage. All gone now. All gone.

Eyes squeezing forth hot tears, he managed to regain his feet. A burning dust had begun to fall, fragments of metal and plastic charred black by that terrible fire. He shielded his eyes with one hand so that he could see where Ian Casca knelt – his hands clasped as if in prayer, a look of terrible ecstasy on his face – then he brought his gun hard about and fired. Once, twice, as many times as there were bullets, until the trigger clicked futiley against an empty chamber. And even then he kept firing. The fury in him had a life of its own, and even the sight of Ian's chest and skull peppered with bloody holes could not quell the storm of despair that was raging inside him.

At last it was Lise who took hold of his arm, who forced the gun from his shaking fingers. Her yellow hair was dusted with ash, and blood smeared one cheek where a chunk of debris had struck her.

'We've lost it,' he whispered hoarsely. 'We've lost it all. You realize that. Everything we had . . .'

Ever the pragmatist, she whispered, 'We still have the settlement. A few trams. Two generators—'

He shook his head. 'Won't last. Can't repair them. Oh, my God, Lise . . .' His hands were shaking. A cinder fell to the ground before him, extinguishing itself on the damp soil. He struggled to think clearly, to plan. Wasn't that his duty? 'We'll have to record what we can. All the data we can come up with . . . before people forget. Put it down on paper, write down everything we know—'

'They won't want to do that.' She said it quietly, but he knew as soon as she spoke the words that they were true. 'They'll want weapons first. Security. They won't want to waste time recording dead facts when there are things out there waiting to eat them.'

'It isn't a waste—'

'I know that. You know that. But will *they* understand?'

He shut his eyes. The sound of the explosion pounded in his brain, a heartbeat of loss. 'Then we'll lose everything we have,' he whispered. 'Everything we *are*.'

There was nothing she could say to that. Nothing she could do but hold on to him, while the sky filled with the black ash of their dreams. The fallout of Casca's sacrifice, the last shattered remnants of their Terran heritage.

In the firelight it looked a lot like blood.

THE PROMISED LAND

I

Report-in-absence from Damien Kilcannon Vryce, Knight of the Golden Flame, Companion of the Earth-Star Ascendant

To the Patriarch Jaxom IV, Holy Father of the Eastern Realm, Keeper of the Prophet's Law,

Signed and sealed this 5th day of March, 1247 A.S.

Most Reverend Father,

It is with a mixture of joy and trepidation that I write you on this fifth day of March, from the port city of Sattin. *Joy,* because I am able to report at last that our mission in the rakhlands was a success. The sorcerous tyrant who was draining that region of life and power has been sent to her final judgment, and the hordes who served her have likewise been dispatched. (Praise God, who makes such triumphs possible!) *Trepidation,* because I have come to believe that something far more deadly has finally turned its eye upon the human lands. And I fear that our recent victory, so hard won, may prove to be no more than a prelude to a far more bloody battle.

But let me record these things in their proper order:

We left from Jaggonath on October 5th of 1246, a party of three: myself, the Loremaster Ciani of Faraday, and Ciani's close friend and professional assistant Senzei Reese. You will recall that the lady had been attacked at her place of business by a trio of demonlike creatures, whose malevolent Workings had robbed her of her memories and her most precious powers. We had determined that these creatures came from the rakhlands and would be returning to that place. It was our intention to follow them to that secret land

and destroy them, thereby freeing the lady from their dire influence, and the human lands from further threat by their power.

You know that we set out for Kale, intending to hire passage to the rakhlands from that port. Such a journey meant five days of hard traveling, but nights could be spent in the relative safety of the daes. Since our quarry appeared to be night-bound, we anticipated little risk during this period. I served in my capacity as priest and Healer more than once along this road. And once, following a young boy's tragic death, I made the acquaintance of a man who shared our road, a traveler named Gerald Tarrant.

How shall I describe this man who later played such a part in our undertaking? Elegant. Forbidding. Seductive. Malevolent. Utterly ruthless. I enclose a drawing of his person, but no simple sketch can possibly capture the essence of the man. As for his purpose . . . let me say that I would not put it past him to have staged the whole thing – to have tormented a child until his spirit died, leaving an empty shell – simply because it amused him to watch a Healer flounder.

Despite his obvious power – or perhaps because of it – we chose to avoid this man for as long as we could. In Kale, however, that course was no longer viable. The fae-currents were too strong and too malignant for any of us to Work, which meant we could no longer use the earth-power to locate our enemy. In addition we were unfamiliar with local port customs, which proved a tremendous handicap. In the end we were forced to rely upon Tarrant despite our misgivings, and I must admit that he served us well in those areas.

Together the four of us traveled to the port of Morgot, where we hoped to be able to find a boat and a captain to suit our purposes. It was there that disaster struck. Our enemies ambushed us, their numbers doubled by reinforcements, and I give thanks to God that we were able to drive them off. But when the dust and the blood had settled, we discovered that the wild energies of Morgot had unleashed a far more deadly adversary, in the person of our dark companion. During the battle Tarrant had turned on Ciani, brutally stripping her of what little strength and memory she had left. When we tried to help her he struck us down, and while we were incapacitated he carried her off: into the wilds of the Forbidden Forest, the lair of the creature called the Hunter.

Senzei and I followed – wounded, exhausted, but desperate to rescue Ciani before she was given over to the master of the Forest. Into that dark land we rode, where the trees were interwoven so tightly that sunlight never reached the ground, where all living things – and semi-living, and undead – existed only to serve that land's fearsome tyrant. And at last we reached the citadel at the heart of the Forest, a black keep fashioned after Merentha Castle, home to the Hunter and his servants. There, to our dismay, we discovered our companion's true identity . . .

I wish that I had gentler words for this, Holiness, that could ease the blow of such terrible knowledge. I wish such words existed. But let me say it simply: the creature known to you as the Hunter, who tracks living women like animals for his amusement and designed this brutal realm called the Forbidden Forest, was known in another time by another name: the Neocount of Merentha, Gerald Tarrant. The Prophet of our faith.

Yes, Reverend Father, the Prophet still lives – if life is not a misnomer for such a corrupted state. The founder of our faith feared death so greatly that in the end he traded his human soul for immortality – and now he is trapped in that nether realm between true death and life, his every waking moment a struggle for balance. What manner of man might survive the ages thus, unable to participate in either death or life, earning his continued survival by practices of such cruelty that legend accorded him the status of a true demon? I sense a spark of humanity still in him, but it is deeply buried. And he believes – perhaps correctly – that to express that humanity is to court true death. The arbiters of Hell are not known for their compassion.

He had no further need for subterfuge but brandished his corrupted title proudly, glorying in our discomfort. He even claimed that he still served the Church, although in what manner he meant this I could not imagine. He told us that we would be permitted to leave the Forest, along with Ciani, to continue in our quest. And more. Our host announced that he would be joining our party, allying himself with our company until the lady's assailants were destroyed. He used words like *honor* and *obligation* to explain his motives, but the bottom line was this: the Hunter adheres to a code of behavior that is part fear, part vanity, and part Revivalist tradition — and he wields it like a shield to safeguard the last remnants of his human identity. By that code, he explained, he was now bound to us — against his will, it seemed — his dark power allied to our purpose until Ciani was freed. We were given no choice in the matter.

Alone, I might have defied him. Alone I might have chosen to face our enemies unarmed, rather than ally myself to such a malignant power. But I was not alone, and my companions did not share my revulsion. Never before had I been so acutely aware of the vast gap that exists between our nature, Church-nurtured, and that of the pagan multitudes. And I wished I had some way to explain to them that it is better to die with a clean soul than persevere through corruption. But my companions wanted that power supporting them more than they feared its nature, and in the end I was forced to acquiesce to the Hunter's will.

Together we four traveled eastward to the port of Sattin — journeying by night, because the sun was anathema to the Hunter's undead flesh. There, where the waters of the Serpent became so narrow that one could almost see across them, we found a captain willing to brave the rugged rakhland coast. But that was not the only danger facing us. There is a barrier about the rakhlands through which no Working may pass, a place where the power is wild, utterly chaotic, and even human senses lose their focus . . . suffice it to say that I am still haunted by images from that terrible crossing. We made it across and set down on the rakhland shore without incident, for which I give thanks to God; it was no small miracle that got us there.

We struggled westward along the rugged coast, to the mouth of the Achron River. From there we turned southward, into the heart of the continent. The terrain was harsh and traveling took its toll on us, as did the growing certainty that someone — or some*thing* — was watching us. Several nights later an earthquake struck, with devastating result: two of the horses were killed, and but for Tarrant's aid I would have drowned in the whitewaters of the

Achron. Even worse, it disarmed us at a crucial moment. For it was then that the rakh attacked.

Your Library has information on what these native predators once were; I have attached several drawings of what they now are. Though evolution has forced them to adopt a human shape, they are not human in nature; their intelligence, which rivals our own, seems at war with a bestial inheritance, making them unpredictable and often violent. They have never forgotten what humankind did to them – or attempted to do – and the memory of that holocaust is as fresh and as real to them as though the attempted genocide of their species occurred only days ago. In truth, the only thing which saved our lives was that their curiosity outweighed their anger – for the moment – and we were taken as bound prisoners to their camp. I have enclosed separate notes on their encampment and what little we could observe of their society. We tried to argue for our lives, our pleas translated into their tongue by the bilingual *khrast,* but how could we argue with such an ingrained hatred? In the end it was our purpose that saved us. For the demons we sought had struck here, as well, and the ravaged souls they had left behind gazed out at us through rakhene eyes, behind a veil of rakhene tears. In serving our own quest we would be serving the rakh as well.

We were given a guide from among their people, a *khrast* female named Hesseth. Ours was a tense partnership, made more so by an open display of Tarrant's murderous powers. But she led us across the great plains of the rakhlands, negotiating with various hostile tribes along the way, and we soon came to realize that we could not have made the journey without her. Not in the face of a hatred that had festered for so many centuries, with so many different tribes to appease.

We now knew that there was a human sorcerer allied to the demons we sought, and we did what we could to misdirect his Sight. For a time it seemed that we were successful – and then, amidst the snow-clad peaks of the rakhland mountains, he struck at us. Senzei Reese was tricked into going off alone and was killed, gruesomely; may his soul find peace in whatever pagan afterlife he created for himself. Tarrant was nearly killed as well, and in the end it was only our unity as a company and the strength of the holy Fire with which you had entrusted me that enabled us to reach our enemy's border alive.

There, on Hesseth's advice, we sought the aid of a rakhene tribe native to the region, whose ancestors had descended belowground during a period of inclement weather (possibly the Small Ice Age of the seventh century?) and remained there ever since. I append notes and sketches in quantity. You will note that they have adapted thoroughly to their dark environment, and now have few features in common with their aboveground brethren. It is a jarring lesson in how fast evolution works on this planet, when man is not present to interfere.

Using their underground tunnels we invaded the enemy's domain. There we learned that the leader of Ciani's assailants was human, a woman 'from the east' whose thirst for power drove her to imprison and feed upon the souls of adepts, filtering the earth-power through their pain. In the end it was her own madness that we turned against her, using her obsession to blind her to our purpose while we set loose the very earth that she had bound. The resulting earthquake destroyed her citadel and killed many of her servants, while the surge of earth-fae that accompanies all such upheavals drowned her in a mortal excess of the very power she lusted after.

By the grace of God and the power of the holy Fire, Ciani, Hesseth, and I escaped the ruins of the madwoman's citadel without further injury. The Hunter was not so fortunate. Forced to choose between certain death at the hands of our enemies and nearly certain death in the face of the sun, the Hunter chose to submit to the dawn – and thus freed our party, perhaps at the cost of his own life. May God grant me equal courage in my last moment, to embrace my fate with similar dignity. By his sacrifice Ciani was freed at last, and restored to all her former facilities. And we began the long trek home, back to the human lands.

I wish it ended there.

Even as I pen the words of this report the rakh are hunting down the last of the so-called *demons,* cleansing the land of their influence. Except that they were not demons, your Holiness. It was

Hesseth who discovered the truth: that our enemies were in fact rakh, warped by some malevolent will until they evolved to take this monstrous form. What manner of creature would deliberately alter a native species so, so that its natural vitality was suppressed and it was forced to feed upon the souls of others? And what purpose could it possibly have in binding these creations to the night, so that simple sunlight might destroy them? I fear the answers to those questions, Holiness. Something evil has taken root in the eastlands – something whose hunger spans the centuries, whose patience has allowed it to rework the very patterns of Nature – and we must deal with it swiftly, before it can learn from its losses here. Before it has a chance to respond.

I am going east to the ports of the Shelf, to seek passage across Novatlantis. Ciani tells me that in her native city there are mariners who will risk such a journey if the price is right, and backers who will provide the coin if they see a potential for profit in it. I believe that I can assemble a crew willing to try it. Five expeditions have attempted the crossing in the past, and it may be that one or more found safe harbor across those deadly waters. If so, I pray that God has protected them from the evil that has made its home there, and that they may see fit to become our allies. If not . . . then it will be that much greater a battle, Holiness. Was it not you who said that a single man may sometimes succeed where an army of men would fail?

Hesseth will be coming with me. It is her right, she says, and her duty. It is an awesome thing to watch the species altruism unfold in her – rakhene in its origins, perhaps, but utterly human in its expression. As for the fallen Prophet . . . he escaped true death by a slender margin, and I do not know whether to give thanks or weep that the living world must still suffer his presence. For if power such as his could be bound to our purpose, our chance of success would be increased a thousandfold.

Bind evil to serve a worthy cause, the Prophet wrote, *and you will have altered its nature forever.* I pray it will be so with him.

Thus it is, your Holiness, that as soon as I seal this letter (and find a reliable messenger, no easy task in this city) I will be leaving for Faraday. If luck is with me I will find a ship and a crew in time to sail with the spring tides, before the storm season threatens. But only if I move quickly. Holiness, I beg for your blessing. For my enterprise, if not for myself. It pains me deeply that I cannot return to Jaggonath to ask this in person, to kneel before you in the tradition of my Order and renew my vows before departing, but time does not permit it. Who can say what new evil may be spawned in a year, by a creature who feeds on crippled souls? I know that you would approve of my mission and sanction my haste if you could. Thus I seal this letter, and append to it all the information I have gathered in recent months, sending it to Jaggonath in my stead. May it serve you well. God willing, I shall return triumphant to add to it.

I remain, obediently,
Your servant and His,
Damien Kilcannon Vryce,
R.C.U., K.G.F., C.E.A.

A study in anger: speechlessly, restlessly, Jaggonath's Holy Father paced once from his desk to the window, then back again. Barely glancing at Damien before he began the course anew. Body rigid with tension, ivory robes rippling sharply with the force of his stride, snapping like pennants in an angry wind.

And then the dam burst. At last.

'How *dare* you,' he hissed. His voice was not loud, but the rage that it communicated was deafening. 'How dare you go off on your own, sending this in your stead . . . as if I would accept it as a substitute!' He slapped the package that lay on his desk with accusatory vehemence. Damien's letter. Damien's notes. A pile nearly an inch thick, made up of all his records from the rakhlands. All his notes on the Hunter. 'As if mere paper could excuse you from your duty! As if mere notes and pictures could serve as a substitute for proper procedure!'

'Your Holiness.' Damien swallowed hard, biting back on his own growing anger. It was a struggle for him to keep his voice calm, to keep from exploding in indignation. Right or wrong, he deserved better treatment than this . . . but he also knew that the fae which surrounded them was partly responsible for his response, that its currents had been altered by the Patriarch's rage so that its power was abrading his temper to the breaking point. *Not that knowing that makes it any easier to deal with,* he thought grimly. If he gave in and responded in kind – or even worse, dared to work a Shielding in the Patriarch's presence – it would be tantamount to vocational suicide. And so he forced his voice to be steady, low, even submissive. 'I beg of you, consider—'

'I *have* considered,' the Patriarch interrupted sharply. 'For weeks now. Since your message first arrived. Every waking moment, I have considered . . . and the situation looks worse each time.' He shook his head in mock amazement. 'Did you really think I wouldn't guess what you intended? Did you think I wouldn't understand why you sent this?'

'I felt there was a chance that I might not come back,' Damien said stiffly. 'I thought you should have all the facts you would need to deal with the Hunter, in case he returned without me—'

The blue eyes were fixed on him, their depths unforgiving. 'That's not the issue and you know it. The issue is your failure to return here. The issue is your summary dismissal of my authority. The issue is not whether you sent me a report, but the fact that you sent it *in lieu of* a personal audience. And I think we both know why you did that.'

Accusation, plain and simple. Damien's hands clenched at his sides; his heart began to pound, so loud it was hard to concentrate. He could lose it all here. Everything. All he had to do was say the wrong word, lie the wrong lie, and his whole life might come crashing down around him. The Patriarch had that kind of power.

'Time was of the essence,' he said at last. Choosing his words with care. 'I tried to explain that in my letter. What I intended—'

The Patriarch cut him off with a sharp gesture. 'What you *intended,* Reverend Vryce, was to avoid any personal contact with me. Do you think I don't know why? You were afraid that if you petitioned for leave to pursue this matter – as you *should* have done, as the hierarchy of our Church *demands* that you do – that I would have denied it. And rightfully so.' His gaze was fixed on the priest, as chill and as piercing as coldfire. 'Or perhaps you were afraid that I would permit you to go . . . but demand that you choose more suitable allies.'

Damien drew in a deep breath slowly, and thought: *There it is. That's what this is all about.* Not that Damien had failed to return to Jaggonath, not that his report was insufficient, not even that he had acted without sanction from his superior . . . but that he had chosen to travel with one of the greatest evils his world had ever produced. An evil so subtle and so sophisticated that it might corrupt even a priest's soul, a priest's dreams. And through that priest – just perhaps – the Church.

Was that possible? Had it begun already, deep inside him, where he refused to look? In his mind's eye he could see the Hunter grinning, a drop of fresh blood gleaming at the corner of his mouth. And he recoiled inwardly at the memory of that polluted soul, the touch of its malignancy against his own being. But Gerald Tarrant represented power, plain and simple, and they needed that kind of force. It was worth any price, he told himself, to have it. Even the risk of corruption.

Wasn't it?

We need his power on our side, he told himself. *Otherwise an even greater evil will take control of us all. Doesn't that mandate some kind of alliance?* But suddenly he wasn't sure of that. Suddenly he wasn't sure of anything. It was one thing to dismiss such a creature in mere words, especially as it had been months since he had last seen Gerald Tarrant. But the Patriarch's words, fae-reinforced, awakened memories far more direct, more horrifying. The Hunter's soul, caressing his own. The Hunter's vileness invading the deepest recesses of his heart, his soul, his faith. Leaving behind a channel that clung to him like a parasite, a reminder of the power that linked them. What would the Patriarch say if he knew about that? If he understood that Damien had submitted to a bond with the Hunter, which would endure for as long as they both lived?

'That was your real fear,' the Patriarch accused. 'Wasn't it? That I would recognize your lies for what they were—'

'There are no lies—'

'Half-truths, then! Evasions. Deceptions. It all amounts to the same thing, Vryce!' He slammed his hand down on the report. 'You write that Senzei Reese died, but never mention how! Never mention that in his last moments he destroyed a holy relic I had entrusted to you. That this treasure from our past was wasted. Wasted! And then there is the matter of the Hunter—'

'I can explain—'

'What? That fate flung the two of you together? That for the sake of your partnership he committed no sins while in your presence?' The cold eyes burned with condemnation, intense as the Hunter's coldfire. '*You saved his life,*' the Patriarch accused. 'When the enemy had captured him, and bound him, and sentenced him to destruction, you freed him. *You.* Did you think I wouldn't find out?' he demanded. 'Is that why you sent me this . . . this . . .' He struggled to find a suitable phrase, at last spat out, 'This *travesty* of a report? Hoping I would never learn the truth?'

He desperately tried to think of something to say – a protest, a plea, anything – but how could he answer such a charge? When he had written his report (agonizing over each and every word, analyzing every turn of phrase a thousand times over) he had never imagined that the Patriarch would learn the truth. Never. But now he realized that he had underestimated the man. The Patriarch was a natural sorcerer, even though he refused to acknowledge the fact. It stood to reason that the fae, altering the laws of probability in response to his will, should cause him to meet up with a source of information. Damien should have seen it coming. He should have prepared . . .

'You saved his life,' the Patriarch repeated. Utter condemnation, spiced with a more personal venom. 'In his name you betrayed your vows, your people. And God Himself, who sits judgment on all of us! Every evil which the Hunter commits, from now until the moment of his demise, will be because of you. Every wound the Church must suffer because of his influence, it will suffer because you freed him. Because *you* encouraged him to endure.'

He stepped forward, an openly aggressive move. Startled, Damien stepped back. The thick white wool of his ritual robe tangled about his ankles, an unfamiliar obstacle. About his neck the heavy gold collar of his Order pricked his skin with etched flame-points, sharp metal edges hot against the chill of his skin. Why had he worn these things? Had he thought that the regalia of his Order might shield him from the Patriarch's anger? If so, they had failed utterly.

'In the name of the One God,' the Patriarch pronounced, 'I have been given authority over this region – and *you*.' He paused, giving the fact of his absolute authority a moment to sink in. 'And in the name of God I now exercise it. In the name of those thousands who gave their lives to redeem this world, choosing death before corruption. In the name of the martyrs of our faith, who served the Church in its darkest hours – and never wavered in their service, though they faced more terrible trials than you or I can imagine. In their name, Reverend Sir Damien Vryce, in their most holy memory do I now divorce you from our service—'

Fear took hold of him as he recognized the ritual. 'Holy Father, no—'

'In their name I now declare you cast out from the society of priests, and from the Orders that initiated you—'

'*Don't*—'

The Patriarch reached forward too quickly for Damien to respond, and his hand closed tightly about the golden collar. '– Damien Kilcannon Vryce, I hereby dismiss you from our Church and from all its Orders, now and forever.' And he pulled back, hard, with the kind of strength that only rage could conjure. Metal cut into the back of Damien's neck as the decorative links strained to part, drawing blood as they finally gave way. The Patriarch pulled the heavy collar from him. 'You are unfit for our society.' He threw the collar to the floor, and ground his foot into the delicate metalwork. 'If not for *any* human society,' he added venomously.

For a moment Damien just stared at the Patriarch, unable to respond. Despair overwhelmed him, and a sense of utter helplessness. What could he say now that would make a difference? The Patriarch's authority was absolute. Even the Holy Mother, Matriarch of the westlands, would respect and honor such a dismissal. Which meant that he was no longer a priest. Which meant in turn that he was ... nothing. Because he suddenly realized that he had no identity that was not Church-born; there was no fragment of his psyche that did not define itself according to the Prophet's dream, the Prophet's hierarchy.

What could he do now? What could he be? The walls seemed to be closing in around him; the air was hard to breathe. Blood dripped from the wounds on his neck, staining his white robe crimson as it seeped down about his shoulders. It gathered in a stain that mimicked the spread of his collar. Why had he worn it here, this emblem that he so rarely donned? What had moved him to make such a gesture? Usually he scorned such regalia . . .

Usually . . .

His thoughts were a whirlwind. He struggled to think clearly.

It's wrong. Somehow. Wrong . . . He tried to remember how this meeting had come about, but he couldn't. His past was a void. His present was a sea of despair. He couldn't focus.

How did I get here? Why did I come?

Things began to swim in his vision: the collar. The Patriarch. The gleaming white robes he never wore. And some fact that lay hidden among those things, something he could sense but not define . . .

It's wrong, he thought. *All of it.*

And the room began to fade. Slowly at first, like a tapestry that was frayed at the edges. Then more rapidly. The collar shimmered where it lay, then vanished. The Patriarch's ivory silk became a curtain of light, then nothing. The chamber . . .

. . . became a room on a ship. His ship. The *Golden Glory*.

'Oh, my God,' he whispered. His heart was pounding with the force of a timpani; his throat still tight with fear. He lay there for a moment in utter silence, shaking, letting the real world seep in, waiting for it to banish the terror. Listening for sounds that would link him to the present: the creak of tarred timbers, the soft splash of ocean waves against the prow, the snap of sails in the wind. Comforting, familiar sounds. They had roused him from similar nightmares before, on similar nights. But this time it didn't seem to help. This time the fear that had hold of him wouldn't go away. The trembling wouldn't stop.

Because it hit too close to home, he thought. *Because this nightmare might yet come true*. What did the Patriarch really think when he read Damien's report? Did he take it at face value, or did he discern the subtle subterfuge with which it had been crafted? What kind of welcome would await Damien when at last he returned to Jaggonath?

I shouldn't have risked it. Shouldn't have dissembled. If he ever finds out . . .

Fear lay heavy on his chest, a thick, suffocating darkness. He tried to reason it away – as he had done so many times before, night after night on this endless journey – but reason alone wasn't enough this time. Because this fear had real substance. This nightmare might yet come to pass.

After a while he gave up, exhausted. And sank back into his fear, letting it possess him utterly. It was a gift to the one who traveled with him, whose hunger licked at the borders of his soul even now. The one who had inspired his dream, and therefore deserved to benefit from it.

Damn you, Tarrant.

Quiet night. Domina bright overhead, waves washing softly against the alteroak hull. Peace – outside, if not within him.

He went to where the washbucket lay and splashed his face with the cool desalinized water, washing the sweat of his fear from his skin. His shirt was damp against his body and the night wind quickly chilled him; he took down a woolen blanket from a masthook and wrapped it about his shoulders, shivering.

Drenched in Domina's light, the deck glittered with ocean spray. Overhead the sails stirred slightly, responding to a shifting breeze. For a moment Damien just stared out across the sea, breathing deeply. Waves black as ink rippled across the water, peaceful and predictable. He tried to Work his Sight, and – as usual – failed. There was no earth-fae on the ocean's surface for him to tap into.

We could be on Earth now, he thought. *For all this lack of power . . . would we even know the difference?* But the comparison was flawed and he knew it. On Earth they would be speeding across the water, abetted by the kind of technology that this planet would never support. Blind technology, mysterious power. Here on Erna it would have doomed them long before they left port, when the doubts and fears of the passengers first seeped into the waterproofed hull and began their disruptive influence. Long before they set sail the fae would have worked its first subtle distortions, affecting the friction of various parts, the microfine clearance of others. On Earth that kind of psychic debris had no power. Here, it would have doomed them before they even left port.

Wrapping the blanket closer about his shoulders, he headed toward the prow of the ship. He had no doubt that the Hunter was there, just as he had no doubt that the man was trying – yet again – to find some hint of earth-fae beneath the ink-black waves. The channel between them had become so strong that at times it was almost like telepathy. And though the Hunter had assured him that it would subside again in time – that it was their isolation from the earth-currents which made any hint of power seem a thousand times more powerful – Damien nursed a private nightmare in which the man's malignance clung to him with parasitic vigor for the rest of his life.

I volunteered for it, he reminded himself.

Not that there was any real choice.

Tarrant stood at the prow of the ship, a proud and elegant figurehead. Even after five midmonths of travel he looked as clean and as freshly pressed as he had on the night they set out from Faraday. Which was no small thing in a realm without earth-fae, Damien reflected. How many precious bits of power had the Hunter budgeted himself for maintaining that fastidious image? As he came to the prow he saw that Tarrant had drawn his sword, and one hand grasped it about the coldfire blade. Absorbing its Worked fae into himself, to support his unnatural life. Even from across the deck Damien could see that the malevolent light, once blinding, had been reduced to a hazy glow, and he managed to come within three feet of Tarrant before he felt its chill power freeze the spray on his hands. Whatever store of malevolent energy that thing had once contained, it was now nearly empty.

Tarrant turned to him, and for a moment his expression was unguarded: hunger whirlpooled in his eyes, black and malevolent. Then it was gone – the polished mask was back in place – and with a brief nod of acknowledgment the Hunter slid the length of Worked steel back into its warded sheath, dousing its light. In the moonlight it was possible to see just how much this trip had drained him, of color and energy both. Or was that ghastly tint his normal hue? Damien found he couldn't remember.

He took up a place beside the man, leaning against the waist-high railing. Staring out at the ocean in mute companionship. At last he muttered, 'That was a bad one.'

'You know that I require fear.'

'Worse than most.'

The Hunter chuckled softly. 'You've grown immune to most of my tricks, Reverend Vryce. In the beginning it was enough to plant suggestions in your mind and let them blossom into nightmares on their own. Now if I mean to make you afraid – and keep you dream-bound long enough for that fear to strengthen me – I must be more . . . *creative*.'

'Yeah. I know.' He sighed heavily. 'I just wish you didn't enjoy it so goddamned much.'

Below them the ocean was smooth and calm; only a gentle swell and a hint of foam marked the place where the prow of the *Golden Glory* sliced through it. The Hunter turned back to study the water, searching for some hint of power.

'See anything?' Damien asked at last.

Tarrant hesitated. 'A light so faint that it might be no more than my imagination. Or perhaps the first glimpse of a foreign current, rising to the surface. If I had to hazard a guess, I would say that we are now above the continental shelf, where the waters are shallower. Not shallow enough for Working,' he added. 'Not even for me.'

'But soon.'

'Soon,' he agreed. 'And if there are people here—' He left the thought unfinished. But hunger echoed in his voice.

You'll feed, Damien supplied silently. *Torturing and killing women here, as you once did in the Forest. How many innocents will suffer because I brought you here? Because I convinced you to come?*

But for once the guilt echoed emptily inside him, without its accustomed force. Because when he looked at the Hunter now, he saw not only a creature who fed on the fear of the living, but a sorcerer who had committed himself body and soul to a dangerous undertaking. And he remembered the storm that had overtaken them in mid-journey – hearing its winds lash the decks anew, seeing the storm-driven waves curl over the prow, angry froth cascading down forty, fifty, sixty feet to smash onto the deck with a tsunami's force – and he remembered thinking then that it was all over, that they had taken one chance too many, that this monster of the equatorial regions would surely devour them before nightfall. And then Tarrant had emerged. Daring the unnatural darkness of the storm, his skin reddened by the few spears of sunlight that managed to pierce the cloudcover. Fine silks whipped and torn by the wind, long fingers tangled in the rigging for support. And then his sword was drawn – *that* sword – and a Working born of pure coldfire blazed upward, into the heart of the storm. The next wave that struck the ship became a wall of sleet as it slammed into the deck, coating the planks with ice as it withdrew. Overhead a rope cracked with a sound like a gunshot, and fragments of it fell to the deck like shattered glass. To the Hunter they were mere distractions. Frost rimmed his hair like a halo as he forced the Worked fae upward, higher and higher, into the heart of the storm – seeking that one weak spot in its pattern which would allow him to turn it aside, or to otherwise lessen its fury. It was an almost impossible feat, Damien knew – but if anyone could do it, Tarrant could.

And slowly, incredibly, the storm abated. Not banished, by any means – a storm of such ferocity could hardly be unmade by a single Working – but altered in its course, so that the worst of it passed to the north of them. Icy waves no longer broke over the deck. Torn rigging hung limply, rather than whipping about in the wind. And Tarrant—

—Fell as the cloudcover overhead gave way at last, seared by a sudden shaft of sunlight. Damien struggled to his side, half-running, half-sliding on the treacherous ice. He used his body to shield Tarrant from the sunlight while he fought to disentangle his hand from the rigging. But the man's grip was like steel, and in the end Damien had to draw out his knife and slice through the precious ropes to free him. He dragged the adept belowdecks as quickly as he could, while overhead the sky slowly brightened with killing light . . .

He remembered that day now as he looked at Tarrant, and he thought, *But for you we would all be dead. Four dozen bodies rotting at the bottom of the sea, our mission in ruins. And our enemy would be unopposed, free to work his will upon the world. Isn't that worth the sacrifice of a life or two?* And he despaired. *Where is the balance in it? How do you judge such a thing?*

The pale eyes were fixed on him. Cold, so cold. Testing his limits. Weighing his soul.

'I knew what the price was when I brought you here,' he said at last. As the waves lapped softly at the hull beneath them.

God willing, I can come to terms with it.

2

Land. It rose from the sea with volcanic splendor, sharp peaks crowned in bald granite, tangles of vegetation cascading down the lower slopes like a verdant waterfall. There was no beach, nor any other gentle margin that the travelers might discern: sheer cliffs met the ocean in a sharp, jagged line, softened only by the spray of foam as waves dashed themselves against the rocks. Inhospitable to say the least . . . but that was hardly a surprise. Erna was not known for gentle beaches.

Land. Even at this distance it filled the air with scent, with sound: evergreens preparing their seeds, spring's first flowers budding, the cries of seabirds as they circled overhead, seeking a moment of liquid respite in which to dive for food. The passengers of the *Golden Glory* were gathered at the bow, some forty or more of them, and they squinted eagerly into the morning glare as they studied the features of the promised land. A few of them cradled the slender telescopes which Tarrant had supplied for the journey – and they handled them like priceless relics, if not out of reverence for the Old Science which created them, then out of fear of Tarrant. Their farseers had failed them months ago, along with many other ship's instruments; the lack of earth-power on the high seas had drained everything dry. It had surprised – and frightened – everyone but the Hunter.

How terrifying that must have been for the first explorers, Damien thought. *They'd have thought that because they disdained sorcery, their tools would function even here. Not realizing that even unconscious thought affects the earth-fae . . . and therefore no tool that man makes on land can be wholly free of its taint.* Was that why none of those ships were ever heard from again? Had they lost their way in mid-ocean, when their instruments failed them? Or staggered into some port by blind guesswork, perhaps, knowing that a return journey would be next to impossible? He hungered to know. Five expeditions, hundreds of men and women . . . and something had spawned an Evil here, more deadly and more subtle than anything the west had produced. He hungered to uncover it. He ached to destroy it.

Soon, he promised himself. *Soon. One step at a time*.

He stood in the wheelhouse of the *Golden Glory,* Tarrant's own telescope in hand. Beside him was a table overlaid with maps, the topmost a copy of one of the Hunter's. It showed the eastern continent as viewed from above, with elevations clearly marked in the neat mechanical printing of the colony's founders. A survey map, no doubt – or more likely a copy of one. Tarrant had lost enough things of value on the last trip to be wary of traveling with originals. On top of it were scattered the instruments which the pilot had used to establish their position, and Damien watched as she pushed aside a polished brass astrolabe in order to scrutinize a new section of coast. It said a lot about her current state of mind that she had chosen that tool over the more sophisticated instruments available; when Rasya was tense, she liked her tools primitive and simple.

At last she said, 'If we're where I think we are, then there's an island missing.'

'Ocean's risen,' the captain reminded her. His own eye remained fixed on the distant cliffs. 'Figure a lot'll be missing, from the time that map was made. Don't sweat it.'

'Thanks,' she said dryly. 'You're not the one whose job it is to see that we don't run aground.'

They were a study in opposites – so much so that it was hard to imagine them getting along, much less working together as closely and as efficiently as they did. Rasya Maradez was tall and lean, with clear blue eyes, sun-bronzed skin, and short hair bleached platinum by the unremitting sun. Smooth muscles played along her slender limbs as she moved, obscured only by a pair of cut-off breeches and an improvised halter top. Irresistible, if you liked the athletic type. Damien did. The captain, by contrast, was a swarthy man, dark-skinned and dark-featured, solid enough in his massive frame to act as a back-up anchor if they needed it. His face and hands were battle-scarred – from street brawls, Damien suspected – and though he handled his own gold-chased instrument with obvious reverence, his tough, lined fingers seemed more suited to a brigand than the person of an officer. Their temperaments were likewise mismatched but surprisingly compatible, resulting in a tense but efficient partnership that had successfully tamed Erna's most dangerous waters.

The captain turned slowly, scanning the length and breadth of the shoreline through his own instrument. Between his fingers delicately engraved figures adorned the golden barrel, studded with precious gems. Tarrant had given it to him as a gift when they first left port, and Damien remembered wondering at its design. He shouldn't have. Its message of value, tasteless but eloquent, had won the captain over in an instant. What good will the Hunter could not inspire in this crew, he clearly intended to purchase.

Carefully Damien studied the lay of the land beyond, breakwater and cliff face and an occasional rocky slope that might through some stretch of the imagination be termed a *beach* . . . he scanned the salt-frothed shoreline, wishing he had Tarrant's Sight. By now the Hunter would have analyzed every current in the region and picked them apart for the messages they carried. *Yes,* he would have said, *there's human life, just south of here. Unaware of our presence. Sail on with the wind* . . .

And then Damien drew in a sharp breath, as he caught sight of a pattern that wasn't wholly natural. It took him a moment to focus on it: a pale line, mostly straight, that wound upward from the base of the cliff to its summit several hundred feet above. *Artificial,* he thought. *Without a doubt.* His fingers tightened about the slender tube as he focused in on the line itself, on the rhythm of tiny shadows that peppered its length. Trying to identify them.

And for a moment he stopped breathing, as he realized what they were. What they had to be.

Dear God. That's it.

The captain turned to him. 'You see something?'

He nodded. His heart was pounding so loudly from excitement he was amazed that the others couldn't hear it. 'There.' He directed the man's gaze to the thing he had seen, then handed his own telescope to Rasya. Not wanting to say anything more until they had seen it for themselves. Until they had confirmed it.

The captain spotted it first, and swore softly. 'Vulkin' ninth messiah. Stairs?'

'Barely footholds,' Rasya corrected. 'Slope's too steep for more than that.'

'Humans carved 'em, though. That's for sure.'

Humans, Damien thought, *or something that looks human. Something that wears a human form and therefore uses human tools. Are we looking at the work of a possible ally ... or is this the mark of our enemy?* The uncertainty made him cold inside. He tried to work a Knowing, to settle his doubts, but the power that clung to the planet's surface was still too far below them. Inaccessible. Tarrant might be able to Work through this much water, but he sure as hell couldn't.

'Ras?' the captain prompted.

'Be bad for a landing,' she said quietly, 'even for a rowboat. And there's no place nearby to harbor the *Glory* – at least not that we've seen yet. That means we'd have to leave you here and move on, maybe ten, maybe a hundred miles down the coast. Not good.'

'But if you want it, we'll do it,' the captain assured Damien. 'That was the deal. Set you down wherever you want ... even if it is in the middle of just about nowhere.'

'And against our better judgment,' Rasya added.

Damien studied the coast for a long minute, as if somehow that could settle his unease. 'Can we wait here? Until the sun sets? That's—'

'Seven hours,' Rasya supplied, and the captain asked, 'Because of his Lordship?'

'I'd like him to take a look at this. Before any decisions are made.'

'Can't stay here,' Rasya warned. 'Not unless you want to be a sitting duck for the next smasher. Look there: that shore's been hit hard and often. Staying here is asking for trouble.' She ran a hand thoughtfully through her short hair. 'We could head out to sea for a while instead, come back in with Domina's tide ... risky at night, but if the wind holds steady I'd chance it.'

The captain looked to Damien for approval, then nodded. 'All right. Do it.'

She nodded, laid down the slim black telescope, and left them to give the orders that would adjust their course. Damien moved to follow her. But the captain's hand on his shoulder stopped him.

'Not yet,' he muttered. 'Not just yet.'

He gestured for Damien to retrieve the telescope. He did so, and focused once more on the distant shoreline.

'By the top of the stairs,' the captain directed. His voice was tense. 'About two hundred yards to the right. Back from the edge a bit.'

Shadows. Boulders. And a circular form that gleamed darkly in the sunlight, a ring of blue-black metal that looked out over the surf like a vast, nightbound eye. It was not hard to make out, once he had found it. It took him a while longer to make out the shape that was behind it. The long metal tube and its supporting frame, coarse timber fastened with heavy iron bolts. Iron balls beside it, stacked with geometric precision. Canisters.

He lowered the telescope. And swore softly.

'Now mind you,' the captain said, 'I haven't seen a lot of 'em ... but that damn sure looks like a cannon to me.'

Night fell, but it brought no true darkness. The cloudless sky was still half-filled with stars, a thousand brilliant points of light that twinkled in the cobalt heavens like diamonds on jeweler's velvet. Toward the west there were so many of them that their light ran together, pooling like molten gold along the horizon, crowning the sea with fire. Soon Erna's second sun would set – a false sun, made up of a million stars – but until then the Ernan colonists need have no fear of darkness. Only the creatures who feared true sunlight would call this time *night*.

Tarrant stood at the bow of the ship, his pale eyes narrowed against the Corelight. His gloved hands were tight about the railing, and Damien was sure that if he could have seen his knuckles they would have been white with tension. The man's whole body was rigid, his attention wholly fixed on the shore beyond. Trying to Know? At last he relaxed, and exhaled heavily. Frustrated.

'Still too deep,' he murmured. 'I had hoped . . .' He shook his head.

'You can't tell anything?'

The silver eyes flashed with irritation. 'I didn't say that.' He stared at the shoreline for a moment longer, nostrils distended as if to sift scents from the evening breeze. 'Life,' he murmured at last. Hungrily. 'There's human life there, in quantity. The currents are full of it. Rich with fear . . .' His lips tensed slightly. A smile? 'But that's not your concern, is it?'

'What else?' Damien asked stiffly.

'Civilization. But you guessed that, of course – from the cannon. They're organized enough to defend themselves, and disciplined enough to use gunpowder.'

'And they have something to defend themselves from.'

The pale eyes fixed on him, molten gold in the Corelight. 'Yes. There is that.'

'Our enemy?'

'Perhaps. But who can say what form that evil has taken, here in its native land? I would be wary of anything – even civilization – until we discover its foundation.'

'You can't tell?'

'All I can do now is look at the currents of power, and guess at the forces that molded them. If I could draw on the earth-fae, I might be able to conjure a more comprehensible image . . . but as of now, those are my limits. One might look at a river current and guess at its origins, based upon the sediment it carries, but one could hardly tell from that what manner of boat last sailed in it. These currents are no different.'

'We'll have to wait until we land, then. Damn.'

Tarrant glanced at him, then back out toward the shore. 'Yes,' he said softly. 'You will have to wait.'

Damien stiffened. He knew the Hunter well enough to become alert when his tone changed like that, and to listen very carefully to his exact choice of words. Five midmonths at sea had taught him a lot. 'You're leaving us?'

'That seems prudent,' he whispered.

'Not to me.'

'You need answers.' His voice was quiet, but hunger resonated in his tone. 'I need . . . food.'

He drew in a deep breath, slowly. Trying to sound calmer than he felt. 'You're going ashore to kill.'

The Hunter said nothing.

'Tarrant—'

'*I am what I am,*' he interrupted sharply. 'You knew my nature when you invited me to join you. You knew that I would kill, and kill often. That I require killing in order to sustain my own life. You knew that, and still you chose to invite me. Don't play at hypocrisy now,' he warned, shaking his head. 'It doesn't suit you.'

Damien's hands clenched into fists at his sides. He tried to force his voice to be steady. 'When?'

'As soon as we're out of surveillance.' He nodded toward the distant cliffs. 'They're watching us, you know. They've been watching us since we first arrived. By now there will have been messengers sent, defenses mobilizing . . . they will assume us to be a vanguard of their enemy, until proven otherwise.'

'All the more reason for us not to separate.'

'I'm no good to you here,' he said sharply. 'If a war fleet surrounded us tomorrow, I could do nothing to save us. On land I can follow your progress, Know the enemy, utilize the power of the earth-fae—'

'And feed.'

The silver eyes fixed on him. Diamondine, piercing. 'I am what I am,' he repeated. 'That issue is not open to debate.' He turned from the bow. 'And now, if you'll excuse me, there are things to be taken care of before I leave. I need to prepare.'

He bowed, a minimal gesture, and left Damien's side. A short walk took him past the wheelhouse, to the recessed midship section. There were people there, crew and passengers both, and they parted like a magicked sea at his approach. Some gazed at him in awe as he passed; others superstitiously averted their eyes, as they might do for a passing demon. He ignored them all. They had feared him once, as men will always fear the demonic, and some had even muttered that the ship would be better off if they exposed him to the sun and then scattered his dust upon the waves. But his performance during the storm had changed all that. Four dozen men and women who might once have turned against the Hunter now regarded him with a reverence just short of worship, and any who found that mode distasteful had learned to keep their silence.

If this were a pagan mob, they'd have turned him into a god by now, Damien thought darkly. He wondered if the Hunter's nature would allow him to accept that. Or did enough of the Church's philosophy still cling to his soul that even power, in such a form, would be abhorrent? *Thank God we'll never find out.*

He looked at the Hunter's retreating form – at the worshipful faces that surrounded him – and corrected himself grimly.

Pray God we never have to.

Tarrant's cabin was belowdecks, in the dark and crowded space normally allotted to cargo, livestock, and machinery. It had been by his own preference. Damien had originally provided him with a cabin alongside his own, whose tiny windows had been carefully barricaded against the sunlight . . . but Tarrant preferred a truly lightless demesne, where no living man might put his life in jeopardy by opening a single door. And Damien really couldn't blame him. If anything, the incident drove home just how vulnerable the Hunter was during the daylight hours.

Now an alteroak door guarded the jerry-rigged sanctuary, reinforced with iron bands and – Damien had no doubt – as much dark fae as the coarse wood could absorb. That power would have been growing down here since the light of the sun was first shut out, seeded by the darkness in Tarrant's own soul. Not a pretty thought.

He was bracing himself to knock when the heavy door swung open. The light of a single candle backlit the Hunter, its corona like a halo about his light brown hair. For a moment Damien thought he could feel the dark fae swirling about him, a hungry, malevolent power that drew its strength from darkness and isolation. Imagination, of course. He couldn't See that power – or any other – without first adjusting his senses.

'Come in,' the Hunter bade him, and for the first time since the chamber had been sealed months ago the priest entered.

The hold of the *Golden Glory* was a stifling place, its still air thick with the reek of animal droppings, stale smoke, and over-salted fish. Damien knew that such a stink was unavoidable – *you can only shovel shit so often,* the captain had assured him – but he had often wondered how Gerald Tarrant, normally so fastidious, endured it. Now, as he passed over the Hunter's threshold, he stepped into another world. Here, in this nightbound sanctuary, all was sterile. Here the power of the dark fae had been used to leach all the scents of life – and death – from the air. The Hunter might not have access to power that would serve him on the moonlit deck, but here in this carefully nurtured darkness he was lord and master of his own.

On the bed lay Hesseth, and the light of the single candle by her side was enough to illuminate a body rigid with tension, fur drawn erect like a cat's. A thin membrane had drawn across the interior corner of each eye, giving her face a truly alien appearance. Long, tufted ears were flattened tight against her skull, in terror. Or hostility. Or both.

'You okay?' Damien asked softly. She nodded, and even managed something that might have been intended as a smile. Her sharp, carnivorous teeth made the expression particularly feral.

Tarrant pulled over a stool to the side of the bed, and motioned for the priest to sit. As he did so he noticed that Hesseth's wrists had been tied to the sides of the bedframe. He looked up sharply at Tarrant.

'She has claws,' the adept reminded him. 'I considered such precautions . . . prudent.'

The slender furred hands were balled into fists, tightly clenched.

He could see the muscles inside her arms tense as she tested the strength of the bonds. 'You really think she'd strike at you?'

'I prefer to be prepared. For everything.' He glanced at Damien, and the priest sensed just how much was being left unsaid. *Her species is still primitive. Still possessed of a bestial soul. Who can say whether instinct or intelligence will rule, when she perceives herself to be threatened?* But there was more than that also: a darker under-current that flickered momentarily in the pale eyes, and then was carefully hidden again.

He still hates her, he thought. *All her people. They bound him once, and he'll never forget it.*

God help her if he ever decides she's expendable.

'Now,' the Hunter said softly. The familiar warning was all the more powerful for not being voiced: *Don't interfere.*

Tarrant sat by her side on the narrow bed, and for a moment was still. Gathering himself. Then he reached out and placed his hands on her face, slender fingers splayed out across her features like the legs of a hungry spider. She stiffened and gasped and a soft moan of pain escaped her, but she made no struggle to escape. Not that it would have done her any good. The dark fae bound her now, more perfectly than mere ropes ever could. Damien was sick-ened, envisioning it.

'Now,' the Hunter whispered. Coaxing the power. Seducing it. Meticulously manicured fingers stroked the sleek fur of her face with what seemed like loving tenderness, but Damien had seen the man Work often enough to know his power for what it was. Killing, always killing. The object of his attention might be a lone, fright-ened woman or a swarm of bacteria – or the follicles on a rakhene woman's face – but the pattern was always the same. The Hunter drew his power from Death.

Beneath his fingers the fine fur was coming loose, and it fell from her cheeks in a fine cloud of gold as he ran his hands across her skin. It was clear that the process was painful; Hesseth hissed as he Worked, her long claws biting deeply into the wood of the bedframe. Once she cried out, a keening note of suffering more bestial than human – and Damien knew Gerald Tarrant well enough to see the distaste flicker in his eyes. But she offered no pleas, despite the pain, and was clearly doing her best not to draw back from him. She had asked for this, after all. It had been her idea. And – as much as Damien hated to admit it – it was a damned good one.

It's not just fur she's sacrificing, he reminded himself. *It's her heritage. Her people. Because they hate humans too much to take her back like this.* It was, for her kind, the ultimate disfigurement. And he longed to take her hand, to squeeze it, to try to reassure her as he would reassure a human woman – but the inch-long claws that had already gouged deep furrows in the bed's frame made such a gesture impossible. And would she accept such a gesture? She had kept to herself for most of the voyage, disdaining the company of humans – even her own traveling companions – for many long months at sea. Would an offer of human contact comfort her now, or merely insult her?

Slowly, carefully, Gerald Tarrant remade her face. Ignoring her soft moans of suffering, ignoring the cries that periodically emanated from her, like the yelp of a wounded animal, pausing only briefly when a spasm of pain wracked her body – and then only because the motion made it hard for him to work – he stripped her face of its natural covering and laid bare the tender skin beneath. Cheeks. Forehead. Eyelids. Nose. The fur fell from her in patches, as though she were being skinned alive. And yet she made no complaint, though her arms had spasmed against the coarse rope bonds often enough and hard enough to draw blood.

Is that a bestial nature, you bastard?

At last it seemed that Tarrant was finished. He brushed a few loose hairs from her face and sat back to regard his handiwork. Hesseth lay still, helpless and exhausted, panting like a winded animal. And her face . . .

Was striking. Exotic. *Beautiful.* Tarrant had left behind thin lines of fur to serve as eyebrows and lashes, and they framed her eyes with graceful symmetry. The eyes were exotic, with a soft fold at the inner corner reminiscent of the human epicanthic. The hairline had been subtly graded, so that it appeared to give way not to fur but to long hair, thick and golden. The cheekbones were high and fine, the nose was more human than Damien would have thought possible, and the lips . . . Tarrant had done something to contract the muscles above and below them, so that they were pulled back into a human fullness. The result was perfectly balanced, breath-takingly beautiful. And awesome, in that its perfection had been sculpted in blood and pain. Even in destruction the Hunter was aesthetic. It was easy to forget that side of him, Damien thought. Just like it was easy to forget that beneath that brutal exterior lived the creative genius who had breathed life into his faith. God of Earth, if only that facet of him could be brought back to life . . .

'The hands won't pass,' Tarrant said shortly. 'Not with claws instead of fingernails. Best to count on gloves for that, and leave the fur to soften the effect if they have to come off. But there is one more thing . . .'

He placed his fingers upon her eyes, touching the inner corners. Her cry of pain was short and ragged, and it seemed to burst loose some dam inside her. When he withdrew from her, there was blood in her eyes in the place of the inner membrane, and tears also. She began to shake uncontrollably.

'That's all,' Tarrant assessed. Oblivious to her suffering. 'If she's careful she should pass.' He nodded, clearly pleased with his work. 'You may release her now.'

Carefully, Damien loosened her bonds. Gently he folded her bruised wrists across her chest and gathered her up in his arms, as he would a child. She moaned softly and pressed her face against his chest, burying herself in his warmth. He wished he had a third hand, that he might stroke her with. He wished he had something to say that could ease the pain, or lessen the humiliation of her disfigurement. But all he could whisper was, 'It's all right.' All he could think to say was, 'We'll get him, Hesseth. We'll kill the one who started all this. I swear it.'

Carefully, tenderly, he carried her out of the Hunter's lair, and up into the healing night.

It was midnight when Tarrant left. A bright night, with Domina's full disk and Casca's three-quarter face lighting the sky. A brisk night, with uneasy waves that trembled white at their upper edges, as if undecided about whether or not to break into froth. But Tarrant had assured them that the wind would grow no worse for an hour at least – although how he knew that without the earth-fae to draw on was beyond Damien – and so they were setting sail despite it. Or setting *oars,* more accurately.

Damien strained to make out the form of an island to the east of them, but could see only water. Which didn't mean it wasn't there, of course. He had the utmost faith in Rasya's observations, and if she said there was an island due east of them he wouldn't think to doubt it. Ever.

An island. That meant land, cresting above the waves.

Earth-fae.

Beneath them the lifeboat struck water, with the deep, resounding slap of a nuwhale's tail. Rasya swung herself over the side of the ship and began to clamber down toward it. Damien briefly considered insisting that he take her place, that he should be the one to transport the Hunter to shore . . . but they'd had that argument before, several times already, and he'd lost each time. Rasya wanted it this way and Tarrant had agreed, so who was he to interfere? What was he afraid of, anyway – that she'd see his power in action and instantly be corrupted? Give her more credit than that.

He felt strangely out of control, with Tarrant leaving. A curious feeling. As if he had ever really controlled the Hunter. As if anyone ever could.

At last the two men who had helped lower the lifeboat withdrew, leaving Damien and his dark ally alone on the deck. For a moment Tarrant just watched the sea, moonlit waves rippling like mercury beneath a haze of silver spray. Waiting. At last the men's footsteps were distant enough and faint enough that they could be certain of their privacy.

'You never asked why I came on this trip,' the Hunter said quietly.

'I assumed you had your reasons.'

'And never wondered what they were?'

Despite himself he smiled. 'You're not an easy man to pry information out of.'

'That never stopped you from trying.'

Damien shrugged.

Tarrant looked downward to where Rasya was waiting. Damien knew better than to press him. At last he said, in a voice hardly louder than the breeze, 'He came to me, you know. Our enemy's pet demon, the one she called Calesta. He came to me in the Forest, when I was done healing. I remembered him from her citadel . . .' Damien saw the muscles along the line of his jaw tighten momentarily. Remembering the eight days and nights of his captivity, when he had been at the mercy of a being even more sadistic than himself? 'It was he who'd revealed that his mistress had trapped me not with sunlight, as I'd perceived, but with simple illusion. A sorcerer's trick! It was my own fear that defeated me . . .' The pale eyes were narrowed in hatred; Damien thought he saw him tremble. 'He came to make peace, as demons will do when their masters die. I felt myself safe, being in my own domain at last, and made the mistake of listening.' He shook his head, remembering. 'He nearly caused me to betray myself. There in my own land, where the very earth serves my will . . . he almost bested me.' His expression was tight, but the emotion causing it was hard to read. Anger? Humiliation? The Hunter had never handled defeat well. 'I spent five hundred years making the Forest into a haven which neither man nor godling might threaten. It survived wars and crusades and natural disasters and was as much a part of me as the flesh that I wore . . . and he took me on there. There! Tricked me, and put my very soul in jeopardy . . .'

He drew in a deep breath, slowly. Trying to calm himself. 'If the Forest is no longer my refuge, then no place will ever be. I could hide myself away with my books and my conjurings for a month, a year, a century . . . but the threat would always be there. *Will* always be there, until I deal with it.' The pale eyes fixed on Damien. 'You understand?'

'I think so.'

'You've always distrusted me . . . which is appropriate, I assure you. But the day may come when that will be a dangerous luxury. Our relationship has been strained even here, on this ship, and I know you've had your doubts about the wisdom of our alliance. That'll only get worse as time goes on. Our enemy seems adept at reading our fears and turning them against us – perhaps even *feeding* on them – and so I thought it best if you understood why I was here. How much is at stake for me in this venture. I thought that knowledge would be worth more than anything I could say about trustworthiness, or loyalty.'

He could feel the power in those pale eyes as they studied him, weighing his soul for reaction. And for an instant – just an instant – it seemed to him that he could sense the uncertainty that lay hidden within their depths, the terrible vulnerability within the man. Because when all was said and done, the Hunter was no more comfortable with their alliance than he was. It was a sobering thought.

'I understand,' he said quietly.

I swore I'd kill him. He knows that when this is over I'll try. How fragile is the thread that binds us together? Even more important: how fragile does he perceive it to be?

With consummate grace the Neocount swung himself over the ship's railing and onto the narrow rope ladder beneath. *The natural grace of a predator,* Damien thought. As repelled as he was fascinated by the insight. When Tarrant's feet had caught a rung he paused, and looked at Damien. 'Expose my quarters,' he commanded. 'Tear down the walls that guard it. Bring my possessions into the daylight and expose them as well, so that nothing remains of my power.'

'I imagine we'll expose the whole ship when we reach port—'

'*Now,* priest. Before the locals contact us. Our enemies also shun the sunlight, remember? Best not to confuse that issue.' A hint of a smile, ever so faint, creased his lips. 'Trust me.'

'You once cautioned me never to do that,' he reminded him. 'But I'll take care of it.'

'At dawn.'

He winced, and counteroffered, 'Early. I promise.'

Tarrant chuckled. 'Good enough.' He began to make his descent – carefully, lest his ankle-length garments get caught between his feet and the rungs – but Damien stopped him.

'Tarrant.'

The Hunter looked up at him. And for a moment Damien saw in him not the cold-blooded murderer he was, but the man he once had been. A man of infinite vision. A man of faith.

That's still there, inside him. It has to be. But how to bring it out?

'Thank you,' he said at last. 'For telling me.' And he added, 'It helps.'

The Hunter nodded. His expression was grim.

'Let's hope it's enough.'

Rasya. He dreamed of her, and woke to find himself stiff with longing. They'd had such a good time together when the journey had first begun, what with his energy and her exuberance and a good bit of sexual know-how on both their parts. A perfect match, it had seemed. He'd hoped it would last. But then, as their navigational instruments began to fail, she grew increasingly restless. Tense. He made the mistake of thinking it was because of her work. By the time he realized the true cause, it was too late to salvage what they'd shared.

I've got wards to keep me from getting pregnant, she'd told him, *but what if they go, too? Hell of a time and place to be having kids, don't you think?*

And then there were the volcanos of Novatlantis and the flood tides of the Eastern Gate and the time never seemed quite right to suggest that there were more mechanical means they could resort to. Because they were beyond that, really. They'd fought enough over trivial things before her real fears came out in the open that recapturing those moments of intimacy would be all but impossible. Women were like that.

Too bad, he thought. It was good while it lasted. That's all you could really ask for, wasn't it?

He turned over to go back to sleep, half hoping his dream would pick up where it left off. Then a soft knocking on his cabin door reminded him of what had woken him up in the first place.

He fumbled for the lamp, managed to get it lit without setting himself on fire. Then bunched up the blankets where it mattered most and called out softly. 'What? Who is it?'

The door creaked open, ever so slightly. A slender figure slipped inside, draped in a coarse seaman's coat. With bare legs, he noted. Shorts, in this weather? How like her.

'You up?' Rasya asked.

It took all his self-control not to make the obvious wise-crack. 'I am now,' he managed. 'Tarrant gone?'

She nodded. '*Dissolved into night,* as the poet would say. Quite an impressive display.'

'Yeah. He's an impressive guy.'

Her blue eyes were fixed on him. Sparkling. Mischievous. God, he still wanted her. 'You up to some some company?' she asked softly.

'Why? Has something happened?'

'Not yet.' She smiled, somewhat tentatively. 'But I was thinking maybe it might.'

She came to the bed and sat down on it. By his side. Close enough that he could feel her warmth through the blanket.

'What about your wards?' he managed.

She grinned. 'His ex gave them a boost for me when we reached shore. Why else do you think I rowed him there?' The coat slid off one shoulder as she spoke; she wasn't wearing very much under it. Maybe nothing at all. 'The way I figure it, we've just about completed the second most dangerous voyage on the face of this planet, and so I'm about due for a little celebrating. Right?' She cocked her head and studied him. 'Of course, if you're not interested . . .'

Women. Don't even try to understand them. You're just not equipped.

'Hell I'm not,' he muttered, and he reached for her.

It was only later, in the depths of the night – much later, and after considerable exertion – that he thought to ask her, 'What's the *first* most dangerous voyage?'

It was too dark to see, but he thought he sensed her smile.

'Going home,' she whispered.

3

It was Sara's first time out.

Behind her, before her, all about her, the grim sentinels of the One God kept watch for faeborn dangers. As they did so they prodded her forward, pushing her when necessary, cursing her stubbornness under their breath even as they muttered the prayers of the Hunt. She was so afraid it was hard to move, the terror constricted her limbs, she found it hard to breathe . . . but that was good, she knew. Fear would draw the nightborn. Fear would manifest demons who were otherwise invisible. Fear would enable the Church to do its holiest work . . . and she understood all that, she understood the value of it, she just wished it didn't have to be *her* in the center of all this, marching numbly at the heart of this macabre procession while the faeborn gathered just beyond the reach of their torchlight, eager for the promised feast.

Her.

With a constant litany of prayers upon their lips, the hunters of the Church wended their way through the depths of the untamed forest. The thick darkness parted grudgingly before their light and closed up behind them, hungrily, as soon as they had passed. She had never seen such a darkness before, a dank, heavy blackness that clung to the trees like syrup, dripping thickly to pool about their feet. The mere touch of her feet against the nightclad ground made her shiver in revulsion. And in fear. Always, always fear . . .

At last the man in front signaled for them to stop. She did so, shivering. They had sent her out with only a woolen smock to guard against the evening's chill, and it was proving hopelessly inadequate. Perhaps they would have given her more had she asked for it, but how was she to know what she needed? She had never been outside before, save in the Church's sheltered confines. How could she possibly anticipate the rigors of such a journey – she, who had spent twelve sheltered years behind the high walls of the Church, who knew no more of nightborn dangers than the secondhand tales of cathedral matrons, whispered over the daily chores?

What does it matter? she thought despairingly. *What does any of it matter? I'm not coming back from this, am I?* Oh, they had told her otherwise. And she knew that some children did indeed come back from the Hunt, because she had seen them. Empty-eyed. Spirits bleeding. Souls screaming out in ceaseless horror, behind a glassy countenance that had lost all capacity for human expression. That was what these men hoped she might become some day. That was their true goal. They would have denied it had she asked them – had she dared to ask them – but she knew it nonetheless, with the absolute certainty of youth. And that thought frightened her more than all the monsters of the dark combined.

'This is the place,' the man in front announced. The others murmured their assent – their voices filled with hunger, she thought, a hunger for killing, a hunger for her pain – and urged her forward, into a clearing which Nature had provided for their sport. Suddenly the men at her side seemed far more terrifying than whatever evils the night might shelter, and in a sudden burst of panic she turned and tried to run from them. But strong, cold hands were on her shoulders before she could take three steps, and a chill voice warned her, 'Not now, little one. You just wait. We're not ready for that yet.'

They took her to the center of the clearing, where it waited. A low granite boulder. A steel ring, driven into it. A chain . . .

'Please,' she whispered. 'Please take me home. *Please.*'

They were too busy praying to listen. Prayers for the living, prayers to conjure wisdom, prayers to consecrate the Hunt. A heavy steel band was set about her slender ankle and snapped shut. It fit her, as it had fit a thousand girl-children before her; the measurements of the Chosen didn't vary much.

'Please,' she sobbed. Her voice and body shaking. 'Take me home . . .'

'In the morning,' one of the men uttered shortly, testing the strength of her chain. As if she could find her way out through some subtle flaw in the steel. 'All in good time.' The rest of them said nothing. They were forbidden to comfort her, she knew that – but it was terrifying nonetheless, to have the men she knew so well suddenly transformed into these emotionless statues. Statues who might curse the loss of a bolt or the escape of a night-wraith, but who would not blink an eye if she were torn to shreds before their very eyes.

Not true, she told herself desperately. *They have to care! They're my people, aren't they?* But it frightened her more than anything that suddenly she wasn't sure of that. She felt like an animal surrounded by strangers, being sacrificed for something she could barely comprehend.

Prey.

They had withdrawn to the shadows of the forest, black and concealing, so that she could no longer see them. The lantern which they had used to light their way through the forest had been hooded now, so that the faint stars of the rim and Casca's quarter-disk were the only illumination. Hardly enough to see by. Not nearly enough to drive away the hordes of monsters who took shelter in night's darkness, whose hunger she could sense just beyond those hardedged shadows . . .

'Please,' she whimpered. 'Oh, God, please. No.'

She heard them before she saw them. Heard them chittering among the trees while their forms were still masked by the shadows. Heard their scrabblings, as they fought for a prime vantage point. High above a vast shadow circled: razor-sharp wings, crowding out the moon. She sobbed, and jerked her foot against the chain, desperately trying to break free; the thick steel band didn't give.

'Let me go!' she screamed. As if the men would listen to her. As if they would care. 'Oh, God, please, let me go . . . I'll be good, I swear it. I'll do anything you want! Just get me out of here!' She jerked at the chain again and again, pulled herself along the half-frozen earth until the steel links were strained to their utmost – as if a child's strength could somehow break such a bond, if she only tried hard enough. And she prayed, with a passion born of utter terror. Knowing even as she did so that the God of her faith would never help her. The Hunt was His device – His plan, His ritual – and why would He set aside His plan for her, why would He break

His own rules for the comfort of one tiny soul? But to pray when one was frightened was a reflexive response, and so she muttered the ritual words of supplication even while her eyes darted from shadow to shadow, searching for movement.

At last she found it. She whimpered as the shadows opposite her stirred, as the liquid darkness coalesced into a long, scaled body. Something leapt at her. Long body, scaled flesh, horns set just above the eyes – it was upon her so quickly that she barely had time to scream before its claws raked her skin, its carrion breath choking her—

And then something struck it, hard. The creature made a noise that was half shriek, half gurgle, and fell back. She was dimly aware of a black shaft that transfixed its flesh, and of noxious blood that poured forth from it as it clawed at its chest, trying to pull the barbed shaft loose. Then another quarrel struck it, and another. It howled in pain and rage and fell back again, almost to the line of the trees. There were small things coming from the shadows now, faeborn parasites that thrived on dying flesh; they fixed their sharp teeth into it and began to feast, even while it thrashed about in pain. Even as she watched the blood that gushed from it slowed to a trickle, sizzling as it struck the ground. The desperate thrashing ceased. Only the tiny scavengers continued to move, and she could hear the gurgling sounds they made as they tore loose bits of the faeborn flesh and swallowed it.

She was shivering. Uncontrollably. Her face stung from where the beast's claws had raked her, and when she rubbed the spot with her hand her fingers came away bright red and sticky. That *thing* had almost gotten her. One more second and it might have ripped her throat out, or torn out her heart, or done something even worse, that left her alive to suffer. Suddenly mere death didn't seem so terrible anymore. At least it would end this suffering. At least it would quell the fear. She looked up at the sky, at the position of the moon, and sobbed. Mere minutes had passed since they had chained her here. Out of how many yet to pass? How many hours of fear and pain and utter despair must she endure, before the dawn released her? And if she survived this night – if her body survived, if some fragment of her mind retained the capacity to *fear* – how many more nights would there be, in which her God would use her to draw out the nightborn, in order that His servants might destroy them?

Suddenly she understood what had happened to the other children. And she envied them their utter withdrawal. Their peace.

Take me, she begged her God. *Take me away from this. I'll do anything . . .*

No response. Not from Him. But overhead a dark shape eclipsed the moon briefly; she glanced up in time to see black wings outlined against Casca's brilliance, talons that gleamed like rubies in the moonlight. Then, as if in response to her scrutiny, the dark thing which had been circling overhead began its descent. Sharp claws flexed in anticipation as the broad, night-black wings lowered it slowly to the ground. She was suddenly aware of how utterly still the night had become; even the faeborn demons who had been whispering in the shadows were silent now, as if they recognized something in this creature that even they feared. Then its eyes fixed on her – quicksilver, diamondine – and the hunger that was in them brought a soft moan to her lips. Of terror. Submission. *Desire.*

The chain no longer chafed at her ankle. The cuts on her face no longer burned. There was nothing in her universe but those eyes, those terrible eyes, and the cold burning hunger behind them. As the great bird scanned the surrounding countryside once more – taking the measure of its enemies, it seemed – she knew with utter certainty that the men of her city were as frozen as she was. Mesmerized by the force of this demon's presence.

'Take me home,' she whispered. No longer certain who she was talking to. No longer sure what she wanted.

Wingtips curled to catch the night air, it lowered itself with consummate grace to the boulder at the clearing's center. She caught the flash of ruby talons closing about about the thick steel ring, silver eyes scanning the woods for enemies. Transfixing them? Then a chill light seemed to rise up from about its feet, so bright that she had to shield her eyes or be blinded; silver-blue flames, that licked about the creature's flesh. She felt a thrill of pure terror as the mass that was within those flames melted, transformed, reshaped itself. Into—

A man. Or rather, a demon in man's form, whose flesh embodied the very chill of the night. The silver-blue power poured down from him like water, lapped at the base of the rock that supported him, ran outward in a thousand tiny rivulets that laced the ground like veins, until the whole of the clearing was caught up in the web of his power. The form he wore was breathtakingly beautiful, features as fine and as delicate as the numarble statues which flanked the great arch of the cathedral – but cold, as a statue's substance is cold, and utterly unhuman. She shivered, knowing that her fear had summoned something as far beyond the mere beasts of the Dark as the angels were above mere men. Wondering if the Church's hunters would dare to fire at such a creature.

Apparently one of the men had found his courage, for a dark, slim shape shot forth from the darkness. The demon did not turn to confront his attacker, nor otherwise acknowledge the assault – but power, brilliant, laced up from the ground like lightning, and sizzled as it struck the blessed shaft. A moment later the quarrel reached the place where he stood, but its course had been altered so that it missed its intended object by inches and continued onward, into the thick darkness of the forest beyond.

The clearing was silent now. Utterly silent. She could feel her heart pounding as the demon-man stepped down from his perch, coming toward her – and she knew that he could hear it, that its fevered rhythm drew him like sugar would draw an insect. Helpless, fascinated, she made no effort to flee, but lay frozen in a reverie that was as much yearning as it was pure terror.

Then something stirred at the edge of the clearing – and she nearly cried out, recognizing its source. One of the men was going to try to save her. She knew in an instant that his sword would be as ineffectual as his quarrels, that by entering the clearing he was opening himself up to attack . . . but her voice was frozen in her throat, and she lacked the power to warn him.

The demon's eyes never left hers, but they narrowed. Something in them flickered, and power shot up from the ground like lightning. It consumed the man in an instant, licking at his flesh like fire – and leaving frozen flesh in the place of ash, that shattered into a thousand glassy bits as he fell to the ground at the demon's feet.

All around her unnatural bonfires flared, leafless trees silhouetted against silver-blue unfire. She heard one of the men scream
out, another trying to flee – but the demon's power claimed them
all, and at last there was nothing left of the Church's special warriors
but a silver flicker that played across the ground, outlining bodies
as still as the earth itself.

Then, slowly, *he* came toward her.

His eyes were mirrors that reflected back at her all the terrors
of her childhood. His essence was hunger that drank in her fear.
His presence embodied the night, with all its special threats: The
faespawned. The undying. The Dark. And something else, that she
now hungered for as desperately as she had once hungered for
freedom.

Eyes shut, lips parted, she sank down into the sea of his hunger,
and the bittersweet ecstacy of dying.

4

Pounding. Rhythmic. Pervasive. It dissolved the dream from around
Damien and substituted reality, in all its claustrophobic glory. The
closeness of his cabin. The creaking of the deck. And a banging on
his door, too forceful to ignore.

'Time to get up, Rev!' Pounding. On the door, or in his head?
The dream fog dissolved slowly. 'Captain said to get you out here
if I value my hide, so rise n' shine! Time to go to work!'

With a muttered curse he grabbed his blanket from off the bed
and wrapped it around himself in an improvised toga. He'd just as
soon answer the door stark naked – it'd serve the man right if it
bothered him – but there were a few passengers on board who
wouldn't handle it well if they saw that, and diplomacy, as always,
won out. Sunlight streamed through the porthole, piercing through
the thick lawn curtain: early morning, he guessed, although he
couldn't have said whether it was the angle of the sunlight or its

hue which gave that away. He'd been keeping Tarrant's hours for long enough that even with the bastard gone he still missed the best of the daylight hours. *That's got to stop,* he told himself firmly, blinking the sleep from his eyes. *Soon.*

'Coming,' he muttered, even as he pulled the door open.

The first mate was stopped in mid-motion, his fist raised high. 'Good morn, Rev.' The fist opened slowly, as if only gradually becoming aware that the door was no longer within reach. He was wearing his uniform jacket, a stiff woolen shortcoat that smelled strongly of mothballs. And shoes. He was wearing shoes. Damien shook his head, trying to absorb that fact. When was the last time he'd seen the crew shod? 'He said to wake you up as soon as we were sure, and it looks like we're sure now, so you need to get on deck.'

'Sure about what?'

'Company.' A nervous grin betrayed two missing teeth. 'Just come into sight half a hour ago, but the captain said to wait until we knew what it was for sure—'

And suddenly it all made sense. The shoes, the uniform . . . *full port dress,* the captain would have called it. But there couldn't be a port on this stretch of coast, could there? If not . . . then what?'

'A ship?' he asked. Hearing the excitement in his own voice. And the tension. 'Another fortress? What?'

'Aye, all sails and steam and armed to the teeth. A ship, Rev,' he added, as though Damien hadn't just figured that out. 'You'd best come and look for yourself as soon as you're decent. Captain's wanting you now for sure. Up at the bow.' He nodded sharply toward the middeck. 'I got to go.'

A ship.

God in heaven . . . enemies, allies, what?

He pulled on the nearest pair of breeches – yesterday's, not really clean, but that couldn't be helped – and a fresh linen shirt that he'd laid out the night before. Not fancy, but it would do for the moment. In deference to the morning's style he pulled on a pair of soft boots as well, though he had long since adopted the crew's custom of going bare-foot on the rough wooden planks. Then the deck canted beneath his feet and for a moment he slid as the smooth leather soles fought for purchase; it took him a minute to steady himself, and then a few minutes more to learn to walk steadily again without the reassuring grip of ten toes to anchor him. Stunned, he managed to make his way from the cabin.

A ship!

The other passengers were gathered at the port rail, grouped predictably. In the long months they'd spent together, Damien had learned to recognize all their little cliques, and to draw voyeuristic amusement from watching how each little outbreak of emotion — a lover's spat, a partner's suspicion, even the fallout from a particularly ruthless game of poker — reshuffled the forty of them into new configurations, each with its own special stresses. The pettiness of it all was part of the reason he'd preferred to keep Tarrant's hours, feeding on the man's special knowledge as surely as the adept fed upon his dreams. And it was addictive, there was no denying that. He would never have thought of knowledge in those terms before, but Tarrant had taught him otherwise. A dangerous addiction, all the more so because it seemed so benign . . .

He wondered why all these men and women weren't crowding at the front of the ship, since the object of their scrutiny clearly lay in that direction. Perhaps the captain had threatened them back from the bow, to reserve that space for himself. If so, it served them right. He had once likened the *Golden Glory*'s passengers to a passel of kittens, who tended to be underfoot no matter where you went. Overhead, Damien caught sight of the *Glory*'s few sailors scurrying about like so many spiders, their hands and feet grasping the knotted rigging only long enough to get their bearings, then scrambling free across the hempen webs again. A figure clung to the mast itself, fingers and toes gripping salt-cured wood without visible support. He grinned, noting that Hesseth had found herself the best vantage point of all. White sails snapped in the wind all about her as the complex winch-and-wire system that controlled their position began to draw them in, denying them a grasp on the westerly breeze. Also giving her a clearer view. At moments like these he envied her the claws and agility that gave her such freedom. How much simpler and safer would his life have been if he had been armed likewise?

The captain was in uniform, and on him it seemed even more

alien. Woolen jacket, black breeches, high leather boots; the clean, formal line of his garments did nothing to refine him, merely made him look coarser by contrast. And yet powerful, doubly powerful, with a raw, unfettered agression that was its own authority. Little wonder he had managed to scare the passengers back from the bow.

'She's armed,' he said, as Damien came to his side. 'No doubt of it. Take a look.'

Did you expect any different? he wondered, remembering the cannon they had seen a few days earlier. He raised his own telescope up to his eyes and scanned the sea before them. By now they must be within . . . what, forty miles to the gateway of the inland sea? Fifty at the most. That made contact very likely. It surprised him, in a way, that it hadn't occurred before.

At last he found the object of the captain's attentions and focused his own lenses upon it. And gazed upon the face of their welcoming committee.

It was a ship, all right, and a damned big one. Even to his untrained eye it looked impressive; others would no doubt find it intimidating. He scanned its twenty-odd sails, wishing he knew enough of shiplore to read meaning into their various shapes and settings. He studied the deck, looking for things that he could interpret. There were columns rising from the middeck that might lead down to a furnace: steam power for backup? Few cabins meant it wasn't a passenger liner, which left at least a dozen possibilities. The smooth, sleek hull cut through the waves with fine precision, but was that any better or worse than his own ship's performance? He couldn't begin to judge. He had never liked sea travel, had assiduously avoided it most of his life; now he was paying the price for that.

Tarrant would have known. Wasn't Merentha a port in his time? He probably has every fact we'd need, right at his fingertips.

And then, scanning lower, he noticed the holes which pierced the ship's side: perfectly square, evenly spaced. Distinctly ominous, even to his untrained eye. He felt something inside him tighten as he recognized the only thing they could possibly be, as he finally voiced the impossible.

'Cannon,' he whispered. The word was cold on his tongue. Cannon, on a ship. 'Is that it?'

'Figure so,' the captain confirmed. 'Never seen 'em like that myself, but I imagine that's how they'd be placed. If one was going to fight,' he added.

Cannon on a ship. That one phrase embodied the impossible. Gunpowder might have limited use on land – mostly in the hands of those whose luck or power permitted them to control it – but it had no place on the open sea, not where a single mishap might doom a ship full of men and goods to a sudden watery grave. Misfires happened with the best of guns; the early wars had taught them that. Naval warfare had been rare and piracy all but unknown for how long now ... six hundred years? Eight hundred?

But not here, Damien thought. An unaccustomed chill began to take root in his soul. Any culture that armed its ships Earth-style must be very foolhardy, or very confident ... or both. And deadly. That was without question. And it had enemies. Powerful enemies.

He swung his sight upward, to the pennant that fluttered atop the mizzenmast, and waited for wind to favor him by stretching the fabric taut so he could see. The emblem of the foreign ship fluttered, folded ... and then snapped westward and held. Just long enough. His breath caught in his throat.

'Reverend?'

Two circles, interlocking. In one was a shape that might have been the Northamerican continent. An Earth-disk? In the other was a serpentine form that it took him a minute to identify. He struggled to remember the shapes on Tarrant's map, and tried to reconcile the distortions of the space-born probe with the viewpoint of land-bound cartographers. Yes. That was it. Without a doubt. He recognized it now.

This land. This continent. Bound to the Earth (if he read it right) by the same kind of symbol that his Church would use to signify the One God, the One Faith ... what else could that flag be, but a symbol of his calling?

A fervent prayer echoed in his soul, one he had never dared voice in all the long months of their travel. *Oh, God, let this land be Yours. Let its people be sanctified unto You, keepers of Your Law. Let them but serve the same dream that I do, and I know that we will prevail – we will triumph! – we will scour the evil from this planet so that Your followers may worship in peace and safety forever . . .*

'Father?'

'Might be Church-sign,' he murmured. 'Or might not.' Now that the first flush of optimism was fading, cold pragmatism took its place. *Our enemy has tricked us before. What if this sign is but another example of his scheming? Or if (it is possible) you're reading it wrong? Be careful, Damien. Don't let your own hope make you careless.* 'Can't be sure.' He looked up from the telescope, saw that Rasya had joined them. Against the deep blue of her pilot's uniform her sun-bleached hair burned like fire.

'It's a coastline vessel,' she informed him. 'Those sails'd give it good maneuverability, but it can't net the ocean wind like this can.' She nodded back toward their own square sails, now tightly reefed to their spars. 'Of course, here by the coast that's to their advantage. No way we could outrun them. And if I'm right about the engine . . .' She hesitated.

'What?' Damien asked, and the captain prompted, 'Go on.'

She glanced back at their own midship section, where two slender columns would serve to vent the turbine's smoke high above the deck. Only two columns. Slender. She gazed out at the alien ship, whose four thick columns seemed to dominate the entire deck. Was that fear in her eyes, or envy? 'I'd guess that it's more than a backup,' she said at last. 'In fact, judging by the design . . . I'd guess that sailpower is secondary.'

'Gods'v Earth,' the captain murmured. 'A true steamship? She's under sail now, sure enough—'

'The wind's with her,' Rasya supplied. 'But I'd venture a guess she doesn't slow down when it turns. Wouldn't have to.'

'Gunpowder over water,' Damien murmured. 'Dependable engines. Mechanized travel.' Tasting the words. Testing the concepts.

'It's like a different world,' Rasya agreed.

'A world your people hoped to create – eh, Reverend?' The captain's eyes, narrowed against the sun, were fixed on him. *Tell me these are your people,* they seemed to beg. *Tell me you know how to talk to them.*

'I don't know,' Damien whispered. Afraid to commit himself. Was it possible that in this isolated community the Church had finally achieved its goals, albeit on a limited scale? Or could their enemy fake those signs as well? 'I just don't know.'

'We're going to have to talk to them,' Rasya said quietly. 'On their terms, I'd say.'

The captain nodded. 'No doubt about that.' With effort he looked away from the distant ship, and back at her. 'How long ago were our signals standardized? Will they know our flags if they see 'em?'

'Not if they're from the first two expeditions. Too early.' Her eyes were narrowed in thought as she fought to recall the fine points of naval history. 'When did the third group set sail? Fifth century?'

'536,' Damien supplied.

'Might, then. I think it was all regulated by then. And, of course, Jansen's expedition—'

Her words were drowned out in the roar of an explosion. Damien tensed instinctively, felt himself reach for his sword – and then cursed himself for a damned fool, and a senseless one at that. What the hell was he going to fight? They couldn't even run for cover here, much less fend off cannonballs with their swords. That foreign ship could chew them up and spit them out without pausing to reset its sails. But he saw Rasya tense and glance back, as if wondering how quickly her own sails might be let down again. *Not quick enough,* he thought grimly. He braced himself for impact – and possibly death – as yet another explosion pounded from the foreign vessel. Never had he felt so utterly helpless.

A third, then. A fourth. A fifth. All perfectly timed, flawlessly executed. It reminded Damien of a nightmare Tarrant had once designed for him, of a world on which the fae didn't function. There, firearms were reliable. There they might be timed, and fired, with just such terrible precision . . .

Silence lay heavy in the air, thick with the smell of fear. Smoke curled upward from the holes in the foreign ship's side, wrapping about the masts like a pennant. Damien waited, tense, for the impact that was sure to come. Iron on water, or – God forbid – iron on wood, the splintering sound of the hull giving way as all their plans were nullified in an instant . . . but there was nothing. Nothing. He waited, breath held, praying silently. Nothing happened. The distant smoke coiled like serpents, then dispersed. There was no other sign. No other sound.

He looked at the captain – and saw a visage so transformed by fear that he hardly recognized it. Was this the man he'd met in Faraday, whose record bore witness to a fierce, indestructible courage? Was this the indomitable master of the wild seas, who had saved two ships from a smasher and killed a dockwraith barehanded, and God only knew what other exploits? Afraid?

And then he looked deep into the captain's eyes and saw something else there, too. Something more unnerving than mere fear. Something more powerful than terror.

Awe.

'Not a beat missed,' he whispered. 'Gods, can you imagine? If we tried to set off half a dozen guns like that – half a dozen *anything* – can you imagine?' He shook his head slowly. 'All five gone off right, and in perfect time . . .' His voice was trembling. 'Is it possible, Reverend? That men could do a thing like that?'

'We believe so,' he said. Choosing his words with care. He glanced back at Rasya, who seemed equally stunned. In the distance he could hear other sounds, coming from where the passengers stood. Whispers. Moans. Prayers. They knew enough of how Erna worked to recognize those five shots for what they were: a statement of utter control, indisputable power. If cannonballs had struck the deck, it could not have inspired more fear than this. 'The Church believes that such things would become possible, if enough souls devoted themselves to our cause.' Had that happened here? Had enough prayers, enough religious devotions, finally fulfilled the Prophet's vision? Was the fae and its constructs no threat to these people? It was almost too much to hope for. The mere thought made his head spin.

Careful, Damien, careful. You don't know anything yet.

'Talk to them,' the captain told Rasya. 'Tell them we come in peace.' She slipped away to see to it. After a moment, high overhead, signal flags blazed from the top of the mizzenmast. Red and black, precisely wielded. Damien watched the configurations for a moment, then – when they began to repeat – fixed his eyes on the distant ship once more. And held his breath, waiting for a response.

There was none.

'Someone's going to have to go over there,' the captain said at last. 'Face-to-face. It's the only way.'

'Dangerous as hell,' Damien muttered.

'Yeah. Tell me about it.'

Silence. Then: 'All right,' Damien said. 'I stand the best chance of speaking their language. Signal them I'm coming over.'

'They probably don't understand—'

'Or they do, and they're keeping their silence. Tell them anyway.' He looked down at his clothes, which seemed ten times as dirty as when he'd put them on. 'I'll need a few minutes to change, and . . . to prepare.'

'I'm going with you.'

'Hell you are.'

'It's my ship, dammit.'

'Which is why you need to stay. If anything happens to me—'

'Then we're all dead men anyway, Reverend, and it might as well be there as here. Now the way I figure it, I've got nothing to lose by going, right? And maybe – just maybe – these paranoid bastards'll soften up a bit when they see that we've put ourselves wholly in their power. – As if we aren't anyway, no matter what we do.' When Damien said nothing, he pressed, 'Make sense?'

'Yeah,' he said at last. And something cold deep inside him loosened its stranglehold on his heart at the thought that the captain would be coming. 'Rasya and Tor won't like it, you know.'

'That's why they take orders and I give 'em.'

He nodded meaningfully toward the distant ship. 'There are worse things than death, you know.'

'Trying to scare me won't work, Reverend.' A faint smile creased the sun-dried lips. 'I'm already as scared as I'm going to get today. Anything else?'

He looked at the man's scarred face, and wondered if all those marks were from simple barroom fights. Rumor said no. 'All right,' he said at last. 'You've got guts, Captain. I'll give you that.'

'Men with guts live hard and die young.' He managed a smile, not totally without humor. 'Let's hope it's the former in this case, eh, Reverend? I'll see to the ship. You go get dressed for company.'

Damien nodded and turned to leave. Then he hesitated. 'You might want to remind the crew—'

'That we're all Church faithful, from now until the day we leave this place? Don't worry, Reverend.' His dark eyes sparkled. 'I'll see that all the nasty pagans behave.' *Including myself,* his expression promised.

'Good enough,' Damien whispered. He hoped it was. The merchants were all of his faith, more or less, but it had been impossible to sign on a crew to match. He just hoped that they understood how much might be at stake if religious prejudice held sway here. Erna had been host to enough religious slaughters in her brief history that he didn't feel like adding another one to the list.

He started to leave, but the captain's voice stopped him. 'Father Vryce.'

Startled by his use of the more familiar title, Damien turned back. The captain had closed his telescope, and was now studying Damien in much the same manner that he had the foreign ship.

'I didn't ask your real business before we left,' he reminded the priest. 'Not in detail, anyway. I figured it suited me fine to sign on for the reasons you gave, and if you had some kind of personal crusade in mind once we landed, that wasn't my business. Right? And it still isn't. So I'm not going to ask. But it's clear to me that there's a lot not being said here, and as we head on over there,' he nodded toward the warship, 'I think you should mull over the fact that we'd all be a good bit safer here if I knew what the vulk was going on. It's hard to play the game right when you haven't been told the rules, Reverend. Think about that, will you?'

His robe was where he had packed it, underneath all his possessions in the bottom of a small steel-bound trunk. He uncovered it gently, reverently, not out of concern for its material substance – he had commissioned it out of wool, not silk, so that it would travel better – but in humble regard for its spiritual value. Carefully he unfolded it, laying it out across his bunk. Fine worsted, singed and polished, bleached to a creamy white: it caught the sunlight and held it, adding the blue glow of morning to its substance. About the neckline a wide band of embroidery proclaimed his rank with a pattern of overlapping flames, the mark of his Order. It wasn't the best workmanship, that was true, but it was the best that he'd been able to afford back in Faraday, when he'd paid for the thing out of his own pocket. He could hardly have sent to Jaggonath for his good robes without having to confront the Patriarch, and that had been out of the question. The gold was slightly tarnished now and a few of the threads had become unwrapped, betraying their yellow silk core, but the whole of it sparkled golden in the sunlight and it was doubtful that any onlooker would notice such details in the midst of formal ceremony.

He slid the robe on over his head; wool so fine it might have been silk whispered down over his hair, his shoulders, his linen shirt, his leggings. Its hem fell just short of his ankles, revealing soft kid boots. *Too long,* he thought, picturing the journey ahead of him, but he was hardly about to cut it. He took his harness down from the wall, sword and all, and considered it. It was traditional for members of his Order to be armed at all times – even when armaments would normally be forbidden – but they might not know that on board the other ship, and he didn't dare make a gesture that might be perceived as hostile. Finally he unlinked the baldrick from its anchoring belt and donned only the latter, folding the robe underneath it at his waist so that the hem fell no lower than his knees. Much better.

He drew out the Fire then, sliding it free of its worn leather sheath, closing his palm about it so that he might feel its heat. It was a precious talisman, a symbol of his Patriarch's trust . . . but no more than that, now. The crystal vial which contained the Worked fluid had cracked while he was in the rakhlands, and by the time he'd discovered the hairline flaw the few drops that remained had all but evaporated. He'd varnished the glass then, several times over, hoping to preserve what little was left – but all that he'd saved was a faint glow, a fleeting warmth, a mere ghost of the Church's most powerful Working. He held it for a moment, drawing strength from the memories it conjured – then put it away carefully, reverently, deep within the folds of clothing inside his trunk.

Then: clean hair, neatly brushed. Spotless fingernails. Fresh shave. He ran down the checklist in his mind, the do's and don't's that a man must observe when going from the field to the court. Damien had done it so many times now that he could no longer remember whether the list had been one of his own devising, or the parting gift of a well-meaning tutor.

At last he was finished. There was a crude mirror among his possessions, a polished flat of tin twice the length of his hand; he held it so that it reflected his face, then moved it slowly so that he might observe the whole length of his person. Which was as it should be: the person of a priest, not a warrior. He stood transformed.

Now, he thought, *Now I'm ready*.

With a prayer on his lips, he went to join the captain.

The ship was even larger than it had seemed from a distance, with a span that dwarfed the *Golden Glory* and made its small rowboat seem like a minnow flitting about its prow. *If they meant for it to impress us,* Damien thought, *it's working*. The graceful curve of the hull as it swept clear of the water hinted at structural dynamics more complex than anything the *Glory*'s designers had been familiar with; when Damien looked at the captain he saw stark envy in the man's eyes, and a cold calculation that said *if* they survived, *if* they were permitted to make contact with the natives, he was damned well going to get a look at the schematics for the thing.

A ladder was dropped from the starboard side, along with grappling lines of braided steel. The sailor who had rowed them across brought them in with such precision that it was no trial to catch the lowest rung, and no great challenge to affix the great hooks – foreign in form though they were – to the iron rings provided for that purpose.

'You first,' the captain said, holding the ladder taut.

'Don't you think—'

'I've done this more times than you have, Reverend. Go up while I'm bracing it and count your blessings.'

He did so, not mentioning that if he had climbed ice-clad ropes with his bare hands over Death's Gorge in Atria he could certainly handle this. It didn't seem a good time to argue.

They were waiting on the deck, a crowd of people as still and silent as the wood they stood upon. As Damien gave the captain and his crewmen a hand up, he studied them, trying to do it as unobtrusively as possible. Twelve guards, in meticulously tailored uniforms ill-suited to naval service; that meant Someone Important was probably on board, who had brought his soldiers with him. They were all armed, and ready for trouble. Four men and a woman, in uniforms not unlike that of the *Glory*'s crew: officers of this ship, perhaps? Three men and two women who could not be identified by their dress, save that it looked expensive; their stance proclaimed them to be civilians. Several figures moving in the background, swathed in dun robes that covered them from neck to wrist and ankle. And one man in the center of it all, whose bearing would have proclaimed his power even if his attire had not. Tall, proud, openly suspicious, he wore the robes of Damien's Church as if he had been born to them. White silk split open down the front to reveal close-fitting civilian garments, a mixture of priest's regalia and common attire that might have seemed blasphemous but for his attitude, which made it clear that everything he did and everything he wore was utterly correct. His skin was a rich brown, doubly dramatic against the white of his outer robe, and the sun picked out copper highlights along high cheekbones, a stern forehead, a strong jawline. His features were broad and well-formed and his black hair, closely cropped, did nothing to distract from them. Energy rippled from him in almost visible waves, and Damien guessed that he was the kind that was addicted to hard exercise – not for its own sake, or even to improve his flesh, so much as a need to give that energy an outlet, to channel it safely within a gym's controlled confines so that it did not consume him elsewhere. He was the kind of man who became a leader or destroyed himself trying – and in the former he had clearly succeeded.

'My name is Andir Toshida,' he said. His accent was liquid, strangely at odds with the harshness of his tone. It did little to hinder comprehension, for which Damien was grateful; given a possible eight hundred years of isolation, there was no telling what English might have become here. 'It is my duty to assess your origin and your intentions, and to render judgment accordingly. You will speak,' he commanded, and he looked first at Damien, then to the captain, 'and you will explain yourselves.'

There was no question of who should begin, and Damien did not hesitate. 'My name is Damien Kilcannon Vryce, Reverend Father twice knighted of the Eastern Autocracy of the One God.' He was watching the man for a reaction – any reaction – but the dark-skinned face was like stone. Utterly unreadable. 'This is Lio Rozca, Captain-General of the *Golden Glory,* and Halen Orswath, of his crew.' *We come in peace,* he wanted to say, but words like that meant nothing; they were cheap, they were easy, the legions of Hell could have voiced them with impunity. This man had too much substance to be taken in by empty platitudes. 'We came here from the west to determine if humans had settled here, to make contact with them if they had, and to establish trade with them when and where that was appropriate.'

One of the civilians whispered to another; a sharp look from Toshida cut the exchange short. 'A mercantile expedition.'

'Some came for that purpose.'

'Verda? Not to colonize?'

The captain exhaled noisily. 'We all have homes to go back to, if that's what you're asking.'

'We knew that five expeditions had already attempted the crossing,' Damien said. He saw neither surprise nor confirmation in Toshida's eyes, nothing that might say or unsay whether he knew about all five or not. How many had landed? How many were lost? 'We assumed at least one of them made it, and that therefore this land would be occupied. And since the most recent expedition was launched nearly four hundred years ago—' again, no hint of surprise in the man's eyes, '—we believed it likely that by now mankind had settled here. We hoped that you would welcome contact with your kin, and permit us to learn from your trials.'

'The crossing was made, verda. And mankind has . . . flourished.' A slight hesitation there, fleeting but eloquent. 'As to whether we

would welcome contact . . .' His expression hardened. 'That has yet
to be determined.'

He looked out toward the *Golden Glory,* now close enough to
the other ship that some details were apparent to the naked eye.
'You fly no flag,' he challenged.

'The ship's mine,' the captain said, 'and I'm an independent. The
crew's a mixed lot, from half a dozen cities at least. Likewise the
passengers.' He paused. 'I can run my initials up the mizzenmast
if it'll make you happy.'

If he heard the challenge in his tone, Toshida didn't react to it.
If anything he looked pleased, and nodded his head slightly as
though in approval. The woman nearest him gestured for his attention; he leaned down so that she might whisper in his ear, then
nodded again.

'My adviser says that you must be genuine. An enemy ship would
have presented itself better.'

There were smiles at that, albeit minimal ones. Damien allowed
himself the luxury of a long, deep breath, and wondered if it was
his imagination or if the atmosphere had just lightened measurably.
He decided to chance a question of his own.

'How many expeditions made it here?'

For a moment Toshida said nothing; he knew as well as Damien
did that once this inquisition turned into an equal exchange its
texture would have been altered permanently. At last he offered,
'Of the five ships that set sail with Lopescu, one reached these shores.
The Nyquist expedition arrived ten years later, entodo. Those were
our ancestors.'

'And the others?'

'No other westerners settled here,' he said smoothly. And then,
before Damien could question him anew, 'This land belongs to
the One God, as do all the people in it. Our land is governed by the
Prophet's Law; our politics are structured in accordance with our
faith. – May I assume that was the quera verda, Reverend Vryce?'

He bowed his head in affirmation. 'And the answer is what I'd
hoped for.'

Again the woman whispered to Toshida. He glanced about at
the other civilians – his advisers? – and took quiet council from

one of the men as well. Damien glanced over at the captain, noted that he was visibly calmer. Good. The man's instincts, unlike his own, would not be clouded by religious optimism. If he thought all was going well, it very probably was.

He could hear his heart pounding as he waited, and wished he had the fae to draw on for insight. This Toshida clearly had the power to grant them official sanction, or consign them to an ocean-bound grave. He would have given anything to Know the man better.

At last he spoke to them. 'I will see this ship of yours for myself, before I render my verdict. Verda?' He paused, as if waiting for a response. 'Unless you object.'

Without hesitation – because he had picked up enough of what was going on to recognize that hesitation would be damning – Damien bowed his assent. 'In God's Name.' And he added, 'We are your servants.' Just for good measure.

'But Your Eminence—' one of the civilians protested, and another began, 'Lord Regent—'

Toshida held up a hand in warning and the protests were silenced. 'The first trade mission from west to east deserves no less,' he said. '*If* that's what this is. I came out here precisely because I felt the situation merited it. Would you have me make my decision without seeing the truth for myself?'

The advisers were silent. They didn't look happy.

He turned to the captain. 'I'll need to inspect your vessel: its crew, its cargo, its passengers, every nook and cranny and packing crate within its hull. If you are what you say you are, then you have nothing to fear. If not . . .' He shrugged suggestively.

'The merchants won't be happy,' he warned.

'Merchants rarely are.'

'They'll want reassurance that their goods won't be fooled with.'

'If all we find are simple trade goods, then they have it.'

'On whose authority?' he challenged.

Far from being insulted by the captain's tone, Toshida seemed almost to approve of it. *The captain's protecting his own,* Damien thought. *That's a good sign in any decent company.* For some reason that exchange, more than any other which had preceded, reassured him as to their captors' intentions.

'On the authority of the Lord Regent of Mercia. Who is high priest and ruler enfacto of the capital city of this region, and therefore of its ruling center. Bien basta?'

The captain looked at Damien, who nodded slightly in approval. The exchange did not go unnoted. 'If they're at war,' Damien dared, 'they need to know we're not the enemy. You and I would do no less under the circumstances.'

The captain winced but nodded. 'Aye,' he agreed. And then to Toshida: 'You can tour the ship all you like, for that purpose. Just make sure it doesn't go beyond that, okay?'

'You have my word,' the Regent promised.

We are not at war, the Regent told him, as they rowed their way back to the *Golden Glory*. A half-dozen guards sat erect in each of the two boats, as tense and alert as if they feared something might leap from the sea to devour them. Damien was glad they were beyond the reach of the earth-fae, which might have created just such a creature for them. *We are not at war, but we have an enemy to the south. And sometimes the best way to avoid a war is by preparing to fight it.*

I understand, Damien assured him. And he did, more than the Regent could possibly know.

I understand exactly.

The inspection was precise, efficient, and ruthless. It was also – viewed from the Regent's perspective – absolutely necessary. Who could say what evil thing might not crouch hidden in a dark corner, might not nestle behind sleeping livestock, might not take up its shelter in a crate of canned goods bound for distant markets? Their enemy feared the sunlight, and therefore any place that might serve as a shelter against the light must be uncovered, opened up, searched.

They gathered the passengers together on the open deck, so that the Regent might see them. 'Is this all?' he demanded. Damien was halfway through a head count when Tyria Lester informed them that her brother Mels was laid out with a hangover, and had not managed to get out of bed that morning. 'Get him,' the Regent commanded, and Damien could almost hear the unspoken command that went with it: *Let me see him in the sunlight*. The man studied each of them in turn while the captain explained to all his rank, his power, his purpose. Damien could see the fear in their eyes, and he sympathized; since they didn't know what the Regent was looking for, how could they be certain that he wouldn't discover it in them? But his eyes passed over them quickly, one after another, and he nodded a curt approval to indicate that the lot of them had passed muster.

Then he turned to Hesseth.

She was dressed in her traveling garb, which is to say in layers that covered her from head to foot and then some. Only her face was visible – her altered face – and that was blistered from exposure to the sunlight, with angry red patches that ran across her cheekbones and down the ridge of her nose. It hadn't occurred to any of them at the time that her tender rakhene skin, normally protected by a layer of fur, would have no mechanism for tanning. He wondered what the Regent would make of such a burn. Was that one sign enough to condemn her in his eyes? He tensed, wondering if this was the moment when all their work would come to naught. Wondering what he could do to save her, if it was.

And then the Regent stepped back from her and bowed. Bowed! Deeply and reverently, as one might to an equal. She managed to maintain her poise somehow, but her frightened eyes met Damien's and begged him, *why*? To which he could only shake his head in mute response: *I don't know*.

The cabins were searched then, quickly and efficiently. The protests of the passengers and crew went unheeded. A phalanx of guards protected Toshida while he went through each room, while a handful more took up watch on the deck, to make sure that no people or weapons were shuffled from cabin to cabin ahead of him. He was as polite as he could be under the circumstances, but he was thorough. No living creature could have hidden from his scrutiny.

Then belowdeck, to the vast storage space within the hull. Every corner was searched. Every crate whose size or weight seemed consequential was pried open, to the accompanying protests of its owner. Gold ingots flashed in the lamplight, bricks of spices, flasks of perfume, books and gems and herbs and furs and bolts of silk, fine wool, silver bullion. It was the first time Damien had actually seen what his co-travelers were bringing with them, and he was stunned by its diversity and its value. No wonder they were terrified; Toshida could take it all from them if he liked, and claim some foreign law as justification. What could they do to stop him? How could they fight back? Whom would they turn to for justice?

But he had no interest in their baubles, nor in their complaints. Silently he continued through the ship, sparing a sharp glance for the space that Gerald Tarrant had so recently occupied. For a moment he paused, and Damien wondered if it was some structural anomoly that had caught his eye, or a whisper of power that had somehow seeped into the ancient wood, defying their ritual cleansing. He was suddenly very glad that Tarrant was gone, and even more glad that they'd brought down the ship's great mirrors and flooded this space with sunlight. If he had still been here, or his cabin still remained . . . he shuddered to think of the consequences. Thank God for the Hunter's foresight.

Last on the list was livestock. They went to the forward end of the hold where the horses were kept, and for a moment the Regent just stared at them; it was clear that to him they were totally alien creatures. Finally he motioned for one of his guards to inspect their space, and it said much for the man that despite his obvious misgivings he did so without hesitation. He needn't have worried. The horses' owners had fed them an herbal mixture designed to keep the animals docile while on the long journey, and to prevent the mares from coming into heat. Even the stallions were tractable.

'How very beautiful,' the Regent murmured. He turned to Damien. 'Pack animals?'

'Mostly,' he lied. 'But they'll carry a man.' For some reason he found that he wanted to keep the horses' true strength a secret. It was a minor advantage, but at least it was something.

'We brought breeding stock,' Mels Lester informed him. Five of the horses were his. 'Just in case.'

'Then I congratulate you on your foresight. Nyquist's expedition attempted to bring what they called "unhorses" with them, but more than half died enroute. Including all the males. A terrible loss.' He held out his hand to the nearest mare, who sniffed at it with passing interest. Damien could see the effect of the drug in her eyes, in her coat, in her mane, but to one who didn't know the species' natural state she must still have seemed a magnificent animal. 'These may prove to be worth more than all the rest of what you have on board,' Toshida told them. His guard had made the rounds of the enclosure, and nodded tightly toward the Regent. *Nothing there,* the gesture said. *Proceed as you see fit.*

The Regent turned to face them. In the shadowy closeness of the hold his gaze was piercing, the whites of his eyes glittering like polished gemstones against the darkness of his skin as he studied first one man, then another.

This is a man who could condemn us to death without a moment's hesitation, Damien thought. *And he would, if he thought we posed any threat to his domain.* God grant that he would prove an ally once this trial was over. God grant, above all else, that he not become an enemy.

'I see nothing on board this ship that would be a threat to my people,' the Regent said at last. A communal sigh of relief seemed to resonate from the westerners, and Damien could feel his own muscles unknotting. 'And I also see nothing to indicate that you aren't exactly what you claim. In which case . . .'

He smiled. It was an expression of genuine warmth, as different from his previous mien as night was from day. And yet it was equally natural to him, the flip side of a nature that must judge men as often as it must reward.

'Welcome to the promised land,' he said.

5

Black shapes scurrying across white sand, darting from boulder to boulder and dune to dune with predatory caution: the rhythm of invasion. Seen from up above, the creatures looked like rats or insects – anything but men. *Vermin,* the Protector thought, as he watched them swarm across his precious beach. *That's what they are: vermin.* The mere sight of them made him sick inside.

He stood by the wall at the top of the cliff and watched them as they made their approach, hands clenched tightly at his sides. It was the penance he had set himself, that he should stand here and watch the result of his treachery. Finally he could stand it no longer and he turned away, back toward the garden. All about him crystal tinkled, delicately crafted trees shifting in the night's chill breeze. It was his wife's creation, this wondrous place of wrought-glass flowers and etched leaves, and standing in it he imagined he could hear her voice. What would she say, if she were here tonight? *Why rush things, my love? Why not wait, and see what opportunity the future brings? There must be a better way.*

But we're running out of time, he thought darkly. *You can see that, Mira, can't you? It has to be done now, for all our sakes.*

Suddenly, from far below, screams resounded. Human screams. His men. Shadows of the invaders danced before his eyes. Demonspawned, nightborn, what was this battle to them? A chance to feed on their enemies' blood, to revel in the destruction of humanity's best. He winced as one particularly loud scream ended abruptly, and wished – not for the first time – that it could have been done some other way. But that just wasn't possible. There had to be blood shed. There had to be bodies – enough so that when the investigation came no one thought to question their numbers, or check to see whether the guards' weapons had been sufficient. Because they hadn't been. *He* had seen to that.

I did it for her, Mira. To protect our daughter. And he whispered – softly, as if she were standing there beside him – 'She has your eyes.'

When the screams at last subsided, he forced himself to move again. There was a low stone wall that guarded the cliff's edge, and this he followed until he was far from the manor house and its crystal garden, until the darkness had swallowed up all signs of human habitation. Only then did he come to the place where the stone wall ended, and a steep staircase – no more than shallow rungs and handholds, painstakingly carved into the cliff's steep surface – provided access to the beach beneath.

He could hear them scrabbling up the granite incline, sharp claws scraping against the unyielding rock. For a moment he thought how easy it would be to send them plummeting to their deaths, one by one as they reached the top . . . and then the first set of hands came over the edge, and a sleek body followed – catlike, wary. And the moment was gone forever.

Chalk-white skin, eyes as black as jet. Hair that seemed more like tangled fur, a mouth that was hard and cruel, without any lips to speak of. Like its face its body was human in form, utterly inhuman in substance. *This is the face of my treachery,* he thought. *This is what I've loosed upon the land.* He felt sick inside.

The creature grinned; sharp teeth glinted in the moonlight. 'You must be the Protector.' Its voice was a serpentine thing, sleek and sinuous. 'What – no armies to guard you? No weapons at hand?'

'We made a bargain,' he said shortly. His heart was pounding. 'I kept my end of it.' Another was climbing up now, sharp claws gripping the topmost step as it levered itself over the edge. Something thick and crimson dripped from the blade that it held between its teeth. Blood. Human blood. The blood of his men. 'I was told you would keep yours.' What were these things, anyway?

The creature said nothing. For a moment it merely studied the Protector, its dark tongue stroking the razor-sharp teeth. Then it looked toward the manor house and its eyes narrowed, as if it had seen someone approaching.

The Protector looked back that way – and something struck him from behind as he did so, something sharp and hard, that drove him to his knees in a shower of pain. He put his hands up to his head to protect it from further assault, felt something warm and sticky clinging to his scalp. Matting his hair.

'So sorry about your *bargain,*' the invader hissed. 'But there are things we need to do here, and leaving witnesses . . . *ssssst*!'

'My people,' he gasped. 'You promised! They know nothing . . .'

He saw it through a mist of blood and pain: the creature was changing. Its thin body gained in height, took on new weight. Its pale skin darkened. Its features, almost human, took on a more familiar cast – and as he looked into its eyes, as he recognized its chosen form, the sickness of pure horror overwhelmed him. He tried to cry out in warning – to his retainers, his soldiers, anyone! – but another blow, even more brutal, drove him to the ground. His moan of pain was smothered by dirt and blood. His vision was drenched in red.

'So sorry,' the invader crooned. Using *his* accent. *His* voice. 'But war is war, you understand. —Of course you do, Protector. And as for your people . . .' The creature chuckled; its tone was horribly familiar. 'I'm afraid we need them,' it whispered. His own voice. His own features. 'I'm afraid we need them all.'

I've failed you, Mira. I've failed us all. May God have mercy on my soul . . .

It was the sound of his own laughter that drove him down into the final darkness.

Deep within the Protector's keep, in a chamber with no windows, Jenseny played with the fringe of her gown and savored its rhythm with her fingers. She'd tried to explain that to her father once, how all the tiny threads hanging there together were a kind of music and how she could feel it through her fingers when she stroked them, but he didn't understand. He couldn't hear that and he couldn't hear the other things: the fall of rain on waxy leaves, the screech of living fibers as they were ripped from the earth, the beat of the spindle and the soft shuffle of the loom as it wove, wove, wove . . . Some days when the Light was strong she thought she could hear the marketplace, too, old women squabbling over prices while her father's hands stroked the soft cloth, drawing notes from it like it was a harp. She tried to share all that with him, but he couldn't hear it. Just like he couldn't hear so many things that were in her world.

Sometimes he would take her outside. Sometimes in the dead of night when his people were asleep he would come and wake her up and they would sneak outside, to stand in the moonlight with the soft wind blowing on their faces, listening to the music of the night. And he would tell her tales of the outside world, trying to draw pictures with his words so that she could see it all for herself. What he didn't know was that sometimes his words would make the pictures real, so that she had to fight not to reach out and touch them. And then sometimes he was sad and she could see the sadness, too, a thick gray stuff that clung to him like mud. Or black, like when her mother died. Black, like on that terrible day . . .

Suddenly she heard footsteps, and her heart skipped a beat in excitement. It was that time of night when her father usually came to her, just before he went to bed. Maybe he was coming to her now. Maybe he would take her outside again, and let her look upon her mother's world. She unwound her fingers from the silken fringe and made her hands lie still in her lap, paying no attention to the tinkling murmur of her dress as it fell back down to her knees. It upset him when she listened to things he couldn't hear. He said it reminded him of why she was here, of how the Church would kill her if they found out he had been keeping her hidden away all these years, so that she could grow up secretly. As always, she felt a quiver in her stomach at the thought of her father – a quiver that was made up of love and awe and excitement and dread and a thousand other things combined. For him, and the world he represented. Because she feared the outside world as much as she hungered for it, and he was its representative.

And then the heavy door swung open and he was there. Face beaming with love and pride and paternal devotion, his joy at setting aside the day's work so that they could have some time together at last. She ran to his arms and let him hold her tightly, the warmth of his body a shield against all danger. God, she loved him! She'd loved her mother, too, but now he was all she had left, and she hugged him for all she was worth. As if by doing so she was somehow hugging her mother, too.

But something was wrong tonight. She sensed it, without knowing how to define it. Suddenly his embrace seemed . . . wrong, somehow. As if *he* had suddenly become wrong.

Confused, she drew back from him. And then realized, *It's tonight*. With a touch of fear in her heart: *They must be here already*.

'What's the matter, pet? You all right?'

For a minute she just stared at him, not understanding the question. Did he think she wouldn't understand the danger in what he was doing? Did he think such an understanding wouldn't make her afraid?

She tried to make her voice strong with courage – like his always was – as she asked, 'Did they come?' Voice trembling only slightly. Eyes wide, searching his face for unspoken clues as to what was going on. Because *something* was going on, she was sure of it. Then he turned away, denying her that access. He turned away! As if he was afraid to confide in her. As if he didn't trust her. That thought hurt worse than any physical pain could. As if he hadn't told her all about his treaty with the invaders. As if he wouldn't trust her, his own flesh and blood, to keep such a secret!

'They came,' he said at last. Picking his way through the words with care, as if wondering how much to tell her. Jenseny got a funny feeling in her stomach as she watched him. Queasy and uncertain; she wished she knew where it came from. 'It'll be all right,' he assured her. 'Everything'll be all right. Don't worry about it.'

Don't worry about it.

I want to protect you, he had told her, on that terrible day when her mother died. *More than anything else, I want to shelter you from all of this – to shelter your spirit from all the evil in this world, all the knowledge that might cause you pain . . . but I can't do that, Jen. Not any more. It's a kind of make-believe, and it could hurt you someday. Because what would happen to you if something went wrong? What would happen if someday you did have to go outside, and I couldn't be there to help you? So I'm going to have to teach you things. Things that'll help you make it on your own, if you ever have to. Things that'll help you survive . . .*

He had shared everything with her since then. Everything! Even when it involved a treachery so terrible that the merest hint of it to her nurse could cause him to be imprisoned for life. He had trusted her then – no, even more, he had considered it his *responsibility* to confide in her. To never again pretend that she was a little puppy, who needed only the comforting hand of a master to make everything seem all right.

What had happened since then? What had changed him? Was it possible that a man might say something like that and then forget it? Or . . . pretend it had never been said?

The queasy sensation inside her turned cold and clammy, and she felt her hands trembling. What did you do when all the rules changed, and nobody told you why? When the person you loved most in the whole world – and the only one you really trusted – seemed to suddenly become a stranger, right before your eyes?

Maybe it was that thought which made the vision come. Or maybe the Light just happened to flash at that moment, making everything change. Or maybe . . . maybe she needed to know so much that she *forced* the Light to come, maybe it heard her crying out inside and therefore it came: a sudden rainbow brilliance that burst to life with blinding power. It was so bright that it hurt her eyes, and she heard herself cry out from the pain. It took a few seconds for her vision to adjust, longer than usual because this time she was afraid to look. Afraid to see.

And then—

And then—

Her father was gone. *No!* In the place where he had stood crouched something else: something hungry, something four-legged with glistening fangs whose eyes were deep, black pits of hate. Where its claws gripped the floor she heard screams – human screams – as if every person this thing had killed was being rent anew, to die in horrible agony. She put her hands to her ears and pressed them tightly to her head, trying to block out that terrible sound. She could hear its voice – no longer her father's, no longer human – but she blocked it out, she drowned it out with her own terrified keening, she refused to listen! Through tear-filled eyes she saw blood dripping from the creature's mouth, and something else:

a shred of cloth, horribly mangled. The rainbow Light had become a whirlwind of fire, a typhoon of brilliance, that swirled about her as she recognized the bloodied scrap. Her father's coat. That was her father's coat! This *thing* had devoured her father . . .

Suddenly it was too much for her, the Light and the vision and all the fear combined; she fell to the ground, the sickness swelling up in her like magma in a plugged volcano. She began to vomit helplessly, hopelessly, her body wracked by convulsions of terror – unable to crawl away, unable to cry out – overwhelmed by a sense of loss so terrible, so absolute, that she could barely comprehend its nature.

And then there were footsteps, running toward her. Her nurse. Strong hands gripped her shoulders from behind, forced her to a sitting position. Strong hands forced something into her mouth, that cleared her throat so she could breathe. Gasping, she shut her eyes. *Take it away,* she begged. *Make it go away.* Her body spasmed once more, but the convulsion lacked strength. Lacked fury. A warm hand stroked her hair. Hot tears poured down her face.

'What is it, Mira?' The creature that had eaten her father was speaking to her. *That's not my name!* she wanted to scream. Why did it call her by her mother's name? Then it took a step closer and she shivered. The arms about her tightened protectively.

'Give her a minute, Protector.' It was her nurse's voice. Jenseny drank in the familiar smell, gloried in the warmth and the comfort of the embrace. Buried herself in the familiar flesh. 'Let her recover,' the woman cautioned.

'What is it?' the creature demanded. Its voice sounded just like her father's again, but Jenseny wasn't fooled any more. Couldn't her nurse sense the falseness of it? Couldn't she smell the blood on its breath? 'What's wrong with her?'

'It's just a fit,' the woman said calmly. 'She has them now and then. You know that.' A soft cloth was wiping the tears from her eyes, the vomit from her chin. 'It's all right,' the old woman whispered. 'It's over now. Breathe deep. Breathe slowly.' Jenseny tried to. And choked. She tried again, with better success.

'Just a fit,' the nurse repeated. A mantra of comfort, meant to sooth. 'Happens all the time.' She tried to rise up, but Jenseny gripped her so tightly she couldn't. The nurse stroked the girl's hair gently, lovingly. 'It'll be all right,' she said quietly. To him. To *it*. 'I'll take care of her.'

There was silence then. Jenseny didn't dare look up for fear she would meet the creature's eyes. She sensed that she was in terrible danger now; what would happen if it realized that she knew the truth? But at last it seemed to take the nurse's words at face value. A heavy hand fell on her head and stroked it once, a caress more possessive than comforting. She shivered, trying to pretend the hand was her father's. Then at last the creature left them, its firm stride receding to the doorway and beyond, and the heavy thud of the alteroak door told her that she was safe. For now.

'It's all right, baby.' The nurse's voice was a soft murmur as she wiped her eyes, her mouth. 'It'll pass. It always does.'

It ate him! she wanted to scream. *It ate my father!* But she choked on the words, couldn't make them come out. All about her the room was growing cold with his absence, and the fabric of her dress . . . it cried out in mourning, because *he* had touched it, *he* had picked it out, and now he was gone . . .

'Jen?'

It was only a question of time before the creature became aware of the truth, that she knew. And when it did it would kill her – or worse. She would have to get far, far away from here before that happened. Far away, and—

Outside?

Outside was the real world. Outside was the untamed fae. Outside were the minions of a vengeful god, whose Church had doomed her to a half-life inside this windowless apartment. No one would take her in. No would help her. Outside meant going it alone, now and forever. She thought of what that meant, how terrible and dangerous it would be . . . and then, in her mind's eye, she saw that scrap of cloth again. The dripping blood. The hate-filled eyes. And she knew she could never pretend again. Not so that *it* would believe her.

'There,' the nurse whispered. 'Don't worry. You're safe here. You'll always be safe at home.'

Never, she thought, as the hot tears flowed down her face. *Never safe, never home, not ever again . . .*

6

They followed the Regent's ship to the south. The wind favored them all the way, and Damien couldn't help but wonder if that was Tarrant's doing. Wishful thinking. How comfortable it would be to imagine that the Hunter was expending his time and energy controlling the weather, instead of . . . other things.

Meanwhile there was nothing to do but keep to their course and speculate upon the place they were soon to visit. The merchants had been reassured to see signs of wealth on Toshida and his people – most of them had invested in luxury items, assuming that an eight-hundred-year-old colony would probably have all its necessities accounted for – and Mels was downright ecstatic about the Regent's response to his horses. An air of optimism prevailed overall, and if Damien and Hesseth now and then wondered how a land with all those good qualities could have spawned the kind of evil they'd fought in the rakhlands, they were the only ones who seemed to be worried. Optimism flourished in the cool, obliging winds, and the fear which had consumed them all seemed ready to disperse in the white southern sunshine.

Some thirty miles south of where they had first encountered Toshida they were joined by four other ships, smaller and less heavily armed than the Regent's, but still imposing to a westerner's eye. Without need for additional command from their leader's ship they flanked the *Glory* two to a side, herding her first toward the south, then to the east. An honor guard, the merchants insisted. Though Damien and the captain were less than certain about that, they realized that nothing would be gained by arguing the point now. Let the passengers indulge in blind optimism if it kept them quiet, the captain advised. There'd be time enough later to adjust their perspective if and when things went sour.

Thus far they had traveled out of sight of land, paralleling the rugged coastline. That said much for how dangerous the local tsunami were, for a seasoned captain would often risk a day or two of shallow seas to have familiar landmarks. Little wonder the coastline was only sparsely inhabited, Damien thought. He watched as Rasya fumed in impotence, unable to mark down a single landmark for future reference. She cursed Toshida while she worked. It wasn't just a question of making them helpless, she explained, by preventing her from compiling a detailed map that would help them navigate this course on their own; the changes which time and the rising seas had wrought upon this ragged coast would have given them priceless information about what to expect elsewhere on this continent. It was a legitimate concern, no doubt about it – but Damien sensed that what bothered her most was the fact that Toshida's pilots had detailed maps of this coastline and she did not. He had seen the members of her profession interact often enough to realize that beneath all their courtesy and cooperation was a streak of fierce competitiveness, and Rasya was no exception.

Then land came into sight at last. Two peaks, to the north and south of them. *The gates of the inland sea,* Rasya declared, and she showed them the place on the map where a narrow gap in the coastline mountain range permitted access to a body of water some six hundred miles long and fifty to one hundred across. A shallow, salty sea, she told them, and one that was bound to be even larger now that the waters of Erna had risen. They had guessed long ago that whatever civilization had developed in this region would be focused along the shores of such a sea. It seemed now that they'd been right.

It was with growing excitement that they gathered along the sides of the ship to watch the cliffs pass by. The sheer granite walls barely gave them room to pass, and mounds of rock that had been poured into the straits by centuries of earthquakes made their passage even more treacherous. The ships which were flanking them strung out single file, two behind them and two before, and they snaked through a maze of islets and breakwaters in the wake of Toshida's vessel. Rasya took notes furiously as she guided the ship through, and Damien noted darkly that if her hasty sketches failed her then the *Golden Glory* would be trapped here until the locals saw fit to help them leave. It was clear that the better part of these waters was not passable. And above them . . . he directed his gaze to the peaks which flanked them, and found them as heavily fortified as Toshida's ship had been. Fortresses built from granite slabs crowned the two mounts at their most stable points, and an impressive array of cannon was trained on the narrow waters between them. Which told Damien several things, not one of them reassuring. These people had a seaborne enemy. They expected attack at any time. And this deadly pass was the most likely point of access for anyone – trader, invader, or traveler – to the rich lands beyond.

They sent Toshida's ship out to us because if we'd reached this point on our own they would have had to blow us out of the water. No questions asked. No eulogies offered. The etiquette of war, ruthless and unapologizing.

Good for them, he thought grimly. Because if it turned out that their enemy was the same as his, there was no better way to deal with the bastards.

Night. The Core reflected brightly in the sea's mirrored surface, turning the water to gold beneath their bow. He leaned against the starboard rail, watching it, and then sighed. Time to go to bed. Time to try to sleep. There was no telling when they'd turn to land, and the sea was what, six hundred miles long? It was clear Toshida wasn't going to allow them to see the coast until they were ready to come into port, so he might as well relax. Or try to. Right?

He turned, only to find that Hesseth had come up behind him. Her head was still tightly wrapped, as it had been when Toshida and his people came on board. Best not to take chances when in view of strangers. The long robes she had affected since that meeting brushed against the deck as she leaned on the railing beside him.

'I'd never seen the sea, before I went to walk among the humans.' Her voice was soft, a thing of breezes and secrets; her sibilant accent rounded out the sharp edges of her English, producing a sound that was doubly soft, strangely beautiful. 'I still associate it with your species. These immense bodies of water, as vast as the land . . . not a human thing at all, but they seem that way to me.'

'Does it make you afraid?'

Her gaze flickered toward him, then away. 'I tasted real fear once, the day I realized that a force more powerful than all my people combined was set to devour them one by one. The day I realized I would have to fight alongside humans in order to defeat it. Next to that . . .' She shrugged. 'What's a little water? I can swim. Fur dries.'

'What about Novatlantis?'

She nodded tensely. 'That was frightening. I admit it.'

They were silent for a few minutes, side by side, remembering. A sky that roared in fury as it thundered black ash down upon its invaders. An ocean that boiled with the birth of a new island, so close to the *Glory* that a carpet of dead fish rippled in her wake. The stink of sulfur. The deadly nonstink of carbon dioxide. Sunlight blotted out by air-borne debris. Smoking pellets that fell from the sky, that probably wouldn't have set fire to the sails but they had to be ready, they had to have water and buckets and men in the rigging . . . six hundred miles of hell, Rasya had estimated, and while not all of it was that bad, there was the constant fear that it would become so. Not a pleasant trip, he mused. Not one he was anxious to repeat.

'Could I ask you a question?' she asked him. Hesitantly, as though the request might offend him.

'Of course.' He turned to face her, leaning one arm against the railing. Surprised, but not displeased by her query. It was rare she talked to the humans at all, and rarer still that she turned to one of them for help of any kind; species hostility still ran hot in her blood. 'Anything, Hesseth. What is it?'

'I was wondering . . .' Again a hint of hesitation, as if she didn't know the proper way to express herself. 'This is hard to put into words.'

'The simplest way is often the best.'

She considered it. And nodded, slowly. 'All right, then. Explain it to me. Your Church. Your faith. You talk about it like a religion, but it isn't just that, is it? I've seen human religions – I thought I understood them – but yours is different. When you and Tarrant get together . . . it sounds more like a campaign than a faith, sometimes. Not like I've seen in the others. Why?'

'Tell me first what you see in others, and I'll try to answer you.'

Her eyes, jet black in the darkness, narrowed as she considered. 'Your kind has a need to believe that its species is the center of the universe. Some religions address that. You have a need to control your fate; some address that, at least in theory. You want certain things from the world, and so you create gods who'll deliver them. You fear death, and so there are gods to administrate your afterlives. Etcetera. Etcetera.'

'And the rakh have no such needs?'

'The rakh are the rakh,' she said smoothly. 'Very different. *Assst,* how can I explain it to you? Our species is one small part of a very complex world, and we sense – and accept – our natural place in it. We see this planet as a living, breathing thing and we know ourselves an element of it. We understand what birth and death are to us, and we're at peace with that understanding. How can I explain? So many of these things have no words, because we never had a need to describe them. The world *is.* The rakh *are.* That's enough for us.'

'Humans struggle all their lives to achieve such acceptance,' he mused. 'And rarely succeed.'

'I know. When I'm not filled with fury at their destructiveness – or amazement at their stupidity – I sometimes feel sorry for them. Is that what human religions address?'

'In part.'

'And yours?'

'In part.' He shifted his weight so that he was more comfortable. 'How well do you understand the fae?'

'It's part of us. Like the air we breathe. How can I divorce myself from it enough to answer you?'

'I meant, how well do you understand what it is to *humans?*'

Her lips curled in a scornful smile. 'Your brains are a chaotic mess. That makes the fae a chaotic mess when it responds to you. Right?'

'Damn close,' he muttered. 'Look. If a tribe of rakh live in a land where water's been scarce, if they and their mounts go thirsty, if the plants themselves need rainfall to survive . . . what happens?'

She shrugged. 'It rains.'

'All right. Why? Because living things *need,* and that need affects the fae, and the fae alters the laws of probability, making rain more likely . . . are you with me?'

She nodded.

'Now, consider the human brain. Three distinct levels of functioning, myriad separate parts, each with its own way of reasoning – if reasoning it can be called – some by pure instinct, some by intelligence, some by methods so abstract we have no way of even describing them. All interconnected in such a way that a single thought, a single *need,* can awaken a thousand responses. Is there drought in the land? One part thirsts. One part wishes for rain. One part fears that rain will never come. One part thinks that if death by thirst is close by, it ought to indulge itself in every pleasure it can. One is angry at nature for starving it, and translates that anger into other things. One channels its fear into violence, in the hope that by redirecting its terror it need not face it head on. One is joyful because enemies are dying also, and another feels that death by dehydration is nature's just reward for some transgression, real or imagined, which it committed. All of that at once, inside one human head. Little wonder your people consider it chaotic. There's a type of doctor whose only purpose is to help humans wade through that mess and come to terms with who and what they are. An understanding your people take for granted.

'So the fae responds to us, just like it responds to you. But it doesn't recognize that all these levels are integral parts of the same being, it just takes the cue nearest at hand and responds to it. At least that's how we understand it. With some people the response falls into a predictable pattern – they can always control it, they can never control it, the fae responds to fears, or to hopes, or to hates . . . but with most people the response is utterly random.

'We do know that religious images are particularly volatile. So much so that over a hundred gods and messiahs appeared in the first twenty years after the Landing. Those were mere illusions; they had little substance and no power of their own. Reflections of mankind's need for divine reassurance, no more. But as generation after generation poured their hopes and their fears and their dreams into such images, they gained in strength. They gained in power.

They took on the personae that man ascribed to them, and came to believe in their own existence. We know that some of the colonists believed in a god-born messiah who would come and save them. The result was twenty false messiahs, each one more convincing than the last. Each one a construct of the fae, who blindly gave us what we wanted or feared the most. And of course they all fed on us, in one way or another. That's what constructs do: they feed on their source. That's why even the pleasant ones are so terribly dangerous.

'There was a time called the Dark Ages, when terror and havoc reigned. Fortunately, there were still a few men and women with clear enough vision to realize that *something* must be done . . . something to mold the human imagination so that it ceased to be its own worst enemy. Thus the Revival was born, an experiment in rigid social structure based upon traditional Earth-values. It was moderately successful. And the Church was founded. A small movement at first, barely of consequence, which taught that the God of Earth was the only divine creature worthy of worship. Because that one God was a concept so vast, so omnipotent, that not all the fae on Erna could mimic it.

'And then along came one very gifted man who said, what if we take this concept one step further? What if we mold this faith so that it channels our energies creatively, so that it *creates for us* the world we want? – You must understand, no one had ever thought on that scale before. No one had ever conceived of manipulating the fae as he planned to do: by manipulating humanity's collective consciousness, so that the fae was forced to respond. It was a brilliant vision, unparalleled in scope. It's the cornerstone of my faith.'

'You're talking about your Prophet.'

'Yes,' he whispered.

'Gerald Tarrant.'

He winced. 'In his life – his natural life – that's what he was to us. He took our prayers and rewrote them, until every word served his purpose. Every phrase. He redesigned every rite and every symbol – even dictated the relative lack of symbology which is the hallmark of our faith – so that with every prayer they voiced, with every breath they drew, the worshipers of the One God would reinforce the power of that vision. If there were enough believers, he taught, and if their faith were strong enough, the very nature of this world could be altered, in accordance with his vision.'

'Which was?'

He paused for a moment, arranging his thoughts. How long had it been since he had tried to explain his faith in language so simple? And yet if she were to travel safely among them she must have that knowledge. Toshida's manner had made that clear.

'The goal was threefold,' he said at last. 'One: To unify man's faith, so that millions of souls might impress the fae with the same image in unison. Two: To alter man's perception of the fae – to distance him from that power – thus weakening the link which permitted it to respond to him so easily. This meant a god who wouldn't make appearances on demand, nor provide easy miracles. It meant hardship and it meant sacrifice. But he believed that in the end it would save us, and permit us to regain our technological heritage. Three: To safeguard man's spirit while all this was taking place, so that when at last we cast off the shackles of this planet and rejoined our kin among the stars, we wouldn't discover that in the process we had become something other than human. Something less than we would want to be.' He paused, considering. 'I think in some ways that last one's the hardest part. But I believe it's the most important.'

'So what happened?' she pressed.

'Humankind learned the lesson too well. Because if man could make a true God in his image, why couldn't he create an obliging godling with even less effort? *What you worship shall come to exist,* the Prophet wrote. *The power of your faith will give your dreams substance.* And so it was. A thousand selfish men designed their own prayers and their own psalms and gave birth to a thousand godlings, each with its own petty domain, each feeding on man while serving his earthly desires. Even as the Church grew in strength, this trend continued, until there were over a hundred tiny states with their own pet deities, their own claim to power. So we went to war: man's final recourse when diplomacy fails him. It was a disaster. Oh, if it had been a clean and glorious conflict, filled with images of faith and capped by a clear-cut victory, it might have stirred men's hearts and won them to our side. It wasn't. It was a bloody mess that spanned three centuries, and it ended only when we bit off more than we could chew and tried to do battle with the fae itself – or rather, with the evil the fae had spawned. Our power base destroyed, our precious image sullied, we crept back to our churches and our pews to lick our wounds in private.'

'And now?'

He shut his eyes. 'We do what we can, Hesseth. We still serve the same dream, but defeat has taught us patience. We no longer see the Prophet's vision as the end of a neat progression that'll be consummated in our lifetimes, but as an ideal state that may not be realized for centuries yet. For tens of centuries. Except here,' he whispered, and he glanced toward Toshida's ship. 'Isolated, unified, devout . . . they may have accomplished what the west failed to do. By establishing a state free of pagan influence, by raising their children in unquestioning faith . . . what power, Hesseth! It could alter the world. It may already have begun to.'

'And Tarrant?'

He stiffened at the sound of the name. 'Cast out by his own creation,' he said sharply. 'The Church knew that it would never alter the fae's response to man until it had done away with private sorcery . . . and he couldn't give that up. Not even to save his own soul.' He drew in a deep breath of cool night air, exhaled it slowly. 'He tried to do away with Hell, you know. Excess philosophical baggage, he called it. Detrimental to our cause. He erased it from all the texts, expunged it from the liturgy. They put it back. The habits of Earth were too deeply ingrained, the image of divine judgment too comforting for the righteous. In the end he lost that battle.'

And so much more . . .

'And does he still believe in your Church?'

'He claims he still serves it. I fail to see how. I think that in the end he's unwilling to let go of what he created, or admit that it defeated him. He's vain, Hesseth, very vain, and the Church was his ultimate masterpiece. Sheer ego won't let him abandon it, even when it damns him with all its strength. Which is part and parcel of his madness.'

'And what about your own sorcery? How does that fit in?'

He shut his eyes. *Isn't that the question? How would Toshida answer it, I wonder?* 'Everything I do is done in the name of God, drawing on that Power for strength. Our Church – the western Matriarchy – believes that such a Working is compatible with our faith. Others disagree. And here . . .'

Here that issue never came up. Here they didn't have to compromise. It was a sobering thought indeed. And he felt a delicate chill run down his spine at the thought. *I've never drawn on the fae in my own name, or used it for my private benefit. But will that matter to these people? Will they recognize such fine distinctions?*

'We'll have to wait and see,' he whispered. Looking out at the foreign ship once more. Wondering about the land that had spawned it. The faith that drove it. Wondering . . . and worrying.

'You know,' Hesseth said quietly, 'I don't envy your species.'

Yeah, he thought. *Doesn't that say it all?*

They placed bets on the nature of Mercia: where it was, how large it was, how important it was in the scheme of things. Jones Hast made a crude copy of Tarrant's survey map and pinned it to the outer wall of the cabin section, along with a sharpened pencil. Passengers and crew were invited to mark their guesses and – for ten Faraday dollars or its equivalent – register them with the captain. Two dozen sets of initials now marked the crude reproduction, most of them clustered about the mouth of the inland sea, or fringing the two rivers that emptied their waters into it. Where was Toshida's capital city most likely to be located? With as little information as they had it was hard to say. He sought out Rasya's mark, found it sketched in darkly some miles south of a vast delta. The location seemed a little strange to him, but he knew Rasya well enough to suspect that her guess was founded on a sound understanding of what that shoreline was and what it might become. He even put ten dollars of his own on the line, betting that she was right.

As he handed his coinage to the captain, he remarked, 'I'm surprised you let yourself be put in charge of this.'

Rozca shrugged. 'They've got to work off their tension somehow, right? Might as well let it be harmless.' As he tucked the bills in his pocket, he added, 'I've seen worse than this, coming into an unknown shore. Much worse.'

Aye, Damien thought, *I'll bet you have.*

And then at last the lead ships turned east, heading toward land. Those whose wager marks adorned that portion of the map grinned and exulted as Rasya fought to make out some sign of land in the distance. At intervals she had a small pail let down to catch up a sample of water, which she tasted. Most of the time she spit her mouthful back into the sea with a frown that indicated she was searching for some clue in particular and not finding it. But then, on the fourth day of their escorted voyage, her ritual taste received a different response.

Damien and Captain Rozca were with her on the bridge; she handed the bucket to them and smiled. Damien did as the captain did, cupping his hand and scooping up a mouthful of water which he clumsily spilled into his mouth and tasted. Even as he spit it out the captain grinned and slapped Rasya on the back. 'Damned good call,' he congratulated her. 'Within ten miles, if I remember right. For my book you could smell out the currents in all ten hells and still have time for breakfast.'

Rasya turned to Damien, her blue eyes beaming. 'Well?' she demanded.

The water was cool and slightly murky but not unpleasant to the taste. Damien rolled the moist remnants of it about on his tongue, trying to sift it of meaning. But to him it was water, plain and simple. He swallowed the last few drops in silence, noting that the last few stages of the swallowing process were no more informative than the first.

'Tastes like seawater,' he said at last.

'The hell it does,' the captain swore. 'What, can't you tell at all?'

'No sea sense,' Rasya informed him smugly.

'There's no salt in it, man!' the captain informed him. 'Or vulkin' little, at any rate. That means a river nearby, and a damned big one. Water like that won't mix with the sea right out if the fresh current's strong enough. Hell, you can taste the river Vivia nearly a hundred miles out from its mouth; that's how they found it in the first place, you know.' His hands on his hips, he studied Damien, 'When you go into strange waters, you'd better be prepared to do so without a guide and without good charts, and that means learning to read the sea like a book. Gods know, the signs are all there for the seeing – or the tasting,' he amended with a grin. 'Rasya and I, we figure practice never hurts. Right?' When Damien said nothing he cocked his head, studying him. 'What's the matter, Reverend? Something's on your mind, I can see that. Speak up.'

'I was only thinking,' he said slowly, 'that maybe now I understand why my contacts in Faraday claimed you were the only two who could manage these waters.'

'The only two crazy enough,' Rasya agreed, and the captain grinned. 'Damn right,' he declared, displaying a cracked tooth. '*Damn* right!'

And I'm also thinking that this watery realm is as alien to me as outer space would be, and that I don't like the taste of my own helplessness. Whatever course we choose once we reach Mercia, it'll have to be overland. Unless there's no alternative.

Tarrant'll like that, he thought grimly. And he lifted the slender telescope the man had given him, to resume the search for land.

The great eastern river spilled its water into the sea with considerable vehemence, along with tons of mud that it had scoured from higher ground. The result was a vast delta of low-lying mud bars, some overgrown with reeds and marsh-brush, some nakedly transient. It was the kind of land that would slow down a tsunami, Damien noted, wearing the great wave down as it crossed mile after mile of shallows, until by the time it hit shore proper there would be little left to devastate man's settlements. *Hell,* he thought cynically, *it'd be no more than thirty or forty feet high by then. A baby.* He preferred the tangible safety of a cliffside perch himself, preferably above the two-hundred-foot mark. That, or a hundred miles of dry land between him and the shore. Or more.

Face it, priest. You just hate the sea.

They could see tiny shadows in the distance, dark spots drifting between the mottled islets. Maybe boats, the captain had ventured, sent out to harvest something from the marshland. He'd seen that once in the far west. And Damien watched as vast flocks of birds wheeled and dove and came up sputtering with fish in their beaks, while the captain described in vivid detail the hallucinogenic marsh-grass one could buy in Denastia City.

The breeze held steady. The guide-ships led them steadily north-east, skirting the freshwater current. Mile after mile of muddy green landscape passed by them on the port side, teeming with the life of the sea marshes. The smell of it was so thick on the breeze that it overwhelmed all their senses, so that even their hurried lunch of dried meat and grain cakes tasted of swamp grass and guano. Damien swallowed it quickly and moved to the bow, chewing on a bitter shoot he'd plucked from one of the garden boxes atop the wheelhouse. God willing there'd be real fruit soon, and greens that weren't watered by sea spray; this stuff might have saved them all from Sailor's Rot, but he'd welcome the day he never had to touch the stuff again.

Yet another joy of the sea, he thought dryly. He leaned on the bow rail and squinted into the sun, searching for land. The Core was just starting to rise, which was no help at all; between it and the sun he could hardly see.

And then something flickered on the surface of the water, which was neither marsh-grass nor land. He blinked, trying to focus. A jagged shape silhouetted against the rising sun – no, two – long and low to the water, with peaks that shimmered gold and white in the morning light.

I'll be damned, he thought, as he realized what they were. *Other ships*.

There were two of them, with more soon to follow: frigates and clippers and at least a dozen other types whose names he didn't know, who swept by the *Glory*'s starboard side with no more than a brief flash of red flags in greeting. All bore the same standard, that of the interlinked circles-and-continents, but some flew a lesser pennant beneath it. He counted them as they passed by, awed by the sheer number of them. Granted, the complex tides might favor travel at this hour – he knew they affected shipping schedules, wasn't quite sure of all the details – but to have such traffic in one place, all linked (he assumed) to one port . . . it spoke of considerably more sea travel than he was accustomed to, and he had been around. Was it possible that these people had found a safe harbor – a *truly* safe harbor – and that there were enough similar ports throughout this land that real sea trade was possible? The concept staggered his imagination. He was accustomed to the sea being regarded as an enemy, unpredictable at best, so that even a simple journey was fraught with peril. But here? He gazed at the great ships in amazement, noting that more than a few spewed the thick smoke of steam power from their central stacks. This was ... this was ...

Downright Earthlike, he thought. Awed by the thought. Jealous of the land that had prompted it.

A tiny shadow had appeared on the horizon that was neither ship nor swampland. The lookout, whose viewpoint bettered Damien's by some thirty vertical feet, was the first to recognize it. 'Land ahead!' the man announced, and he cried down specifics in the sea-code of the west. Damien watched through his glass as the shadow spread, lengthened, covered more than half the horizon with its craggy terrain. Coastline? Island? He wished that Rasya were with him so that he could ask her. But she was much too busy now to be bothered with a mere passenger's queries. And so he watched uninformed as the land drew nearer and nearer, and tried to read meaning into its form with his oh-so-limited skills.

A ragged, mountainous skyline spoke of a far more solid foundation than the mud islands they had passed, and a much older history. As they drew closer he could see that though its form was lost in the distance to the north its southern tip was clearly discernible, and the foreign ships that headed toward them seemed to be coming from around that point. And they were heading toward it. He watched as signal flags flashed from one ship to the other, bright splashes of red and white and black against the morning sky, and watched the distant shoreline shift to the port side of the ship as the *Glory* and its escorts made their way through the crowded seaway. Damien tried to guess how far away the land mass was or how tall those peaks might be, but he lacked any kind of reference scale; not for the first time, he wished the sea had mile markers.

A hand tapped his shoulder, interupting his reverie. It was Anshala Praveri, purveyor of . . . (he tried to remember) . . . spices?

'Pilot said to give you this,' she said, and she handed him a roll of paper.

Uncurling it, he discovered the map that had been pinned on the wall of the cabin section. Nothing had been marked on it since last he had seen it, and for a moment he was lost as to why it had been sent to him. Then his eyes traveled down to Rasya's mark, and the strange position it occupied. South of the river's mouth by several miles, her initials were entirely circled by a thin ring of land that jutted out from the coast. A few narrow channels gave access to enough water that the surveyors had labeled it a bay, but it hardly had the kind of access one would require for a major port. Unless time and tides – and earthquakes with their smashers – had resculpted that narrow arching tongue, opening wide one entrance to the sea . . .

And the seas have risen, he reminded himself. He felt the paper fall from his hands, heard the rustling of Anshala's clothing as she bent to retrieve it.

'What is it?' she asked him.

For a moment he couldn't respond. 'A safe port,' he said at last. His voice was hardly more than a whisper. 'A truly sheltered harbor.' How many were there in the human lands? He could remember only three, and each had become – for obvious reasons – a center of human commerce. If Lopescu and Nyquist had discovered one here, then their journey was truly blessed.

And then the *Glory* came around the southern point of the jagged land mass, and he saw.

Ships. They were scattered across the bay like so many thousands of birds just come to land, bright wings fluttering in the noontime breeze. Open-sea ships with rank after rank of weathered sails, coastland yachts with slender masts and peaked canvases, private boats that whipped about their more massive brethren with playful alacrity, some so tiny that a human weight against the spar was enough to shift their course. White upon white upon white upon white, all glistening in the dual skylight: silver from overhead, gold from the east, creating dual shadows that played upon the waters like nuporps, sporting in the multiple wakes. There was smoke as well, mostly from the numerous tugs that wove in and out of the traffic, guiding the larger ships to their safest route. But for most the crisp northeasterly wind was clearly enough, and sails bellowed full as ship after ship wended its way through the harbor's narrow mouth with no more power than Nature had provided.

If these are to be our allies, Damien thought in awe, *then we may yet triumph. But if they turn out to be our enemies . . . then we're in deep shit.* He did notice that few of the larger ships had any kind of visible armament, which was marginally reassuring. And certainly it was hard to imagine the creatures they had fought in the rakhlands – vicious and sun-sensitive, shadowbound and animalistic – having anything to do with this glorious display, or with the society that founded it.

But the Evil that we came here to fight is subtle, and its tools may vary. Don't give in to assumptions, he begged himself. Even as he felt optimism flood his body like fine wine, making his senses swim. Even as he tried to ignore the fact that a part of his spirit was souring like the wind itself, that a voice inside him rang with the force of a thousand chimes: *These are my people, oh God. Thy people. And see what wonders they have wrought, all in Thy Name!*

The coastline to the east of them rose quickly to meet a line of mountains which made it possible to see the city even from this distance. Immense and sprawling, Mercia carpeted the lower slopes in a tapestry of terra cotta tile, gleaming numarble, whitewashed brick. In the center of the city several buildings soared among the others, and sunlight glinted on their heights. One looked like a cathedral. The others could have been . . . anything. Damien raised his eyes above, saw a mountainside terraced for farmland, with the maize and sienna velvet of thriving crops already rippling along its heights.

The sound of winches tightening drew his attention back to the middeck – and up to the rigging, where sailors were scurrying to gather up the sails. Evidently Rozca had received some sign that they were to remain here, for the great anchors were released to fall into the sea even as the last of the sails were furled. Then, as if in response to the *Glory*'s actions, a small rowboat was lowered from the rear of Toshida's ship, to make its way across the waves to them.

Damien hurried to the head of the boarding ladder, where the ship's officers had already assembled. Rasya was gazing out across the harbor, and as Damien watched her study the foreign ships – as he noted the adoration and envy that filled her eyes – he wondered if any mere man could ever inspire such depths of emotion in her. Probably not. Which might be just what had made them so compatible as lovers, he reflected; both their hearts were given over to greater things.

The ladder shifted as it was grabbed from below, then rattled against the side of the ship as a single man climbed it. It wasn't Toshida this time, nor one of his advisers, but a guard whose uniform and bearing hinted at considerable rank. He climbed up onto the deck somewhat awkwardly, trying to manage the maneuver with a thick roll of fabric tucked under one arm. When he was finally on board he straightened himself regally and addressed them.

'His Eminence Toshida, Lord Regent of Mercia, bids you welcome to his port and to the Five Cities of God's Grace which bless these shores. He requests your indulgence and your patience while he sees to the details of your welcome. In that there has been no western expedition in centuries – and never one like yours – preparations for your disembarkation may possibly take longer than tired travelers would prefer. For this he apologizes.

'I am instructed to ask if there is anything he can send aboard which would make your wait easier. Mercia is eager to welcome its guests.'

For a moment there was silence, as each passenger and crew member digested his message. At last the captain ventured, 'Fresh fruit'd be welcome.'

'A damned relief,' one of the touchier passengers muttered.

'Fresh meat,' another dared, and the woman beside him added, 'but not fish.' That drew a chuckle.

'Soap,' Rasya offered. 'Lubricant.' She shut her eyes part way as she tried to remember what conveniences had run short in the last few weeks. A few of the sailors made suggestions of their own; half were for food items. One was for alcohol.

'That's it,' the first mate said at last. He looked at the captain.

Rozca nodded. 'We'll pay for it all. Keep a tally of what's brought on board and take care of all of it once we're settled in.'

'The goods are a gift of the city,' the officer informed him. 'A celebration of your arrival here against tremendous odds. His Eminence will permit nothing else,' he said quickly, forestalling Rozca's argument. 'Verdate.'

The captain swallowed his words with effort, then bowed his head. 'Like the man says.' Damien suspected he was secretly pleased, despite his token resistance. A gesture like that was an excellent omen.

'His Eminence asks that your crew and passengers remain on board until he contacts you again,' the officer said. 'He advises that there could be *complications,* if any of your people were to leave the ship prematurely. Tambia he asks that you fly this.'

He handed the bundle under his arm to the captain. With the first mate's help Rozca carefully unrolled it.

It was a flag – a pennant, more accurately – with a red band at the base and a long black tip that would flutter in the wind. On the red section was a series of seals, too small to be made out from a distance. Official markings, Damien guessed, for the benefit of the ship it guarded.

'What is it?' the captain asked.

'It warns other ships not to approach you,' the officer explained. 'You understand that we can turn the larger ships away ourselves, but the private boats sometimes go where they want . . . this will warn them off.'

'And if they do come on board?' Damien heard himself asking. 'What then?'

'They die,' the officer said coolly. 'As all men do, who defy the Regent's will. So you see, it would be best if the warning were raised as soon as possible. Verda?'

With those words for farewell he formally bowed his leavetaking and lowered himself once more over the ship's side. This time he had no difficulty with the ladder, as his arms were unencumbered.

For a moment there was silence, thick and uncomfortable. As each man wondered in his own way what manner of land they had come to, that combined hospitality and ruthless quasi-justice with such casual, numbing grace.

'All right,' the captain said gruffly. Breaking the spell. He handed the pennant to his first mate, who in turn handed it to a lesser crewman. 'You heard the man. Fly the vulkin' thing.'

7

Toshida never ran – he thought it lacked dignity – but he had long legs and a quick stride and he put them both to use with gusto. Thus it was that he walked from the harbor to the Matria's Sanctuary in record time, well ahead (he hoped) of any gawking voyeurs who might have anticipated his route.

The doors were open and he stepped inside. The guards spared him a sharp look – *do you belong here?* – to which he responded with a glare of his own – *what does it look like, you fool?* – and he continued on his way. His face had been in at least a thousand newspaper features, not to mention the Mercian five dollar credit note and an Octecentennial coin; if they didn't know it by now, he wasn't going to waste time educating them.

He found a Church attendant and didn't have to state his business; the boy simply nodded and led him upstairs. Thick velour carpet scrunched softly underfoot, a welcome alternative to the coarse planks of the ship. All about him the wealth of his nation welcomed him home: fine white numarble walls with crimson veins, elaborately carved fixtures plated with rose gold, stained-glass windows designed and executed by the most prestigious artists in the Five Cities. Gifts, all of them, and freely given; the house of the Matria would no more pressure its citizens to part with items of value than it would expect the tax department to pick up the tab for her decorating. Which was as it should be, he reflected. Exactly as it should be.

On the second landing there was a small waiting area, and the attendant indicated that he should make himself comfortable there while he announced him. He disdained to sit on the tapestried couch, but spent a moment studying the two engravings that adorned the wall behind it. One was of a sailing ship that had clearly seen better days; its sails were tattered and its mizzenmast had been split in a storm and black ash coated the standard that had been rigged to fly from a forward jib. That would be the First Holy Expedition, Lopescu's company. The second depicted a handful of ships coming into a primitive harbor; that would be Nyquist. The other walls featured paintings of nature, trees and flowers and a brilliant seascape that stretched across three large panels. *No pictures of the other expeditions,* he thought. *Is that a sign of our honesty, or of hypocrisy?*

Then the door before him opened and the attendant stepped out. 'She'll see you now, your Eminence. Please forgive the delay.'

With a gracious nod he passed the boy and entered the Matria's audience chamber. It was a large space, richly carpeted, whose narrow stained-glass windows cast jewellike shapes across the floor and walls. A broad desk of polished rosewood dominated the space, with matching chairs on either side. The Matria was seated behind it. As always, he felt strangely awed when ushered into her presence. And as always, that awe was coupled with a deep-seated resentment.

She nodded her welcome as he bowed. 'The newsmongers say there's a foreign ship in our harbor.'

'Then newsmongers can fly, your Holiness, because I came here as fast as a man can travel.'

She smiled. 'Actually, I like Raj's theory that each newspaper has only one common brain, and all those bodies who go running about are merely its limbs in disguise.' She rose from the desk and approached him, extending one slender hand. She was no longer a young woman, but age had been kind to her, and the features that had been striking in her youth had matured into something no less impressive. The white robes of her Order swept the floor as she came to him: narrow sleeves, full skirts, a tight-fitting coif that hid most of her hair from view. Her eyes were large and arresting, and for a moment – just a moment – Toshida was reminded of the Sanctified woman on board the foreign ship.

He took her hand and kissed it reverently, dropping to one knee as he did so. The fact that his station permitted him to remain standing made the gesture doubly dramatic and he knew it. 'I came to report to you as soon as we landed.'

'And?'

She returned to her seat behind the great desk and signaled for him to join her. He took a chair opposite.

'It appears to be a trading vessel,' he told her. 'Some four dozen passengers and crew with a good bit of merchandise. They claim to have set sail from the West, and I see no reason to doubt them. They all come from different cities, I gather. We'll get a list before we let them disembark.'

'Did you inspect the pilot's books?'

It took effort to keep from smiling. In all of his inspection there had been only one rough moment, inside the pilot's cabin. He remembered the woman – what was her name, Maraden? Marades? – seated atop the thick leather volumes, blue eyes flaring with indignation. *No,* she had said. *This is where I draw the line. I don't care who you are.* Her sun-whitened hair gleaming like silver, so oddly short, so strangely alluring. *Ask your own pilots what the custom is.* He had. And they'd told him. And since he wasn't ready to declare war on her ship, or to take her prisoner for personal reasons, he'd left the books alone.

'I saw the captain's log,' he responded evenly. 'It supports their story. And there were other signs. I believe them.'

Her golden eyes fixed on him. 'There's a lot riding on your judgment.'

'Verda, Matria. I was thorough, I assure you.'

'And their cargo? Did you check that?'

'Luxury goods for the most part. Some livestock. I counted seven crates that contained dried vegetable matter in one form or another; we'll check them for narcotic content before they unload. Nothing else of any concern.' As an afterthought he added, 'It's a rich load, and they brought no guards. Security may be a problem. What courtesies may I extend to them?'

She narrowed her eyes, considering. 'A dozen of your private guard for the first week, compliments of the city. After that, supply them with a reference for suitable independents. It sounds like they're carrying more than enough to pay for it.'

And then her eyes met his and he had the dizzying sensation of falling; for a moment his vision clouded and he could see only soft shapes, red and blue and amber shadows and the hazy outline of what must be her desk. It took effort to pretend that nothing was wrong, to keep from reaching out to take hold of the desk's edge to stabilize himself. But he was damned if he was going to let the Matria – or *any* Matria – unsettle him that much. He had come too far and dealt with them too often to quake in the face of their power now.

'The nightborn,' she said quietly. 'What of him?'

He didn't speak until he knew he had full control of his voice again. 'I saw no sign of any nightborn creature, human or otherwise.'

'Did you search?'

His vision was returning to normal, but the giddyness remained. He articulated carefully. 'I inspected everyone on board in the light of day. Some were pale, a few were burned, but no one seemed worse for the experience. I searched every cabin, with special attention to possible hiding places. I opened every crate on the ship and walked the length and breadth of every level . . . and I saw no nightborn creature there, nor any space that might have sheltered one. I'm sorry.'

She turned away from him; the room snapped suddenly back into normal perspective. 'I had a vision,' she said softly. 'A ship would come from the West, just as this one did, at just this time . . . and he would be on it, accompanied by a priest. He's dangerous, Andir, an enemy of our Church and our people. If you tell me there was no man on that vessel who fit his description, I believe you. If you tell me there was no place on that vessel for him to hide, I believe that, too. But what are the odds that this one ship – the only merchant-ship ever sent from the West – would arrive at our shores at just this moment, fulfilling my prophecy in every detail but that one? God warned me of this man for a reason, Andir. We would do well to heed His warning.'

'He wasn't on the ship, Holiness, and there was no sign of him. I swear it. But there was a priest, as you say, and a Sanctified woman tambia.'

She looked startled. 'Sanctified? But that's impossible. The West doesn't have—'

And then she stopped herself, and chose her remaining words with care. 'The last expedition gave us no reason to believe that the West had developed such an Order.'

'I saw her, Holiness. Verdate.'

She stared at him for a long while in silence, digesting that information. 'All right,' she said at last. 'It may be the ship I foresaw. Maybe not. Either way, I want the priest and the woman followed whenever they're on shore. Discreetly, verda? And as for the others . . . what would you recommend?'

'I think we would profit from the trade they offer, your Holiness.' A vision of horses flashed before his eyes; with effort he suppressed it. 'There are some things we need to take care of before they disembark, of course. The health issue concerns me; they may carry diseases we're no longer immune to. I would like to feel secure that their cultural expectations are harmonious with our own, so that they don't disrupt our society too much. And we presently have no import taxes which would apply to such a vessel . . . it might be well to get a couple on the books before we assess their cargo.'

The Matria smiled, displaying pure white teeth. 'I've always liked your style, Andir. See that it's done.' She offered him her hand again, and he stretched forward to kiss it. 'I thank you for a thorough job, my Lord Regent. As always.'

'To serve you is to serve the Church,' he responded. His tone was one of absolute reverence, devoid of any political resentment. The latter had no place here – or anywhere, for that matter, save deep within his heart. There it coiled, like a venemous serpent. Undying. Unforgiving.

He pushed his chair back and stood. Then hesitated. He had another question, but wasn't quite sure how to voice it. 'Your Holiness . . .'

'You may speak freely,' she prompted.

'When this is all done . . . when they've made their rounds and traded their goods and packed up to go home . . . are you going to let them leave?'

It seemed to him that her smile faltered. Certainly the humor went out of her eyes. What took its place was hard and cold, and strangely predatory.

'When that time comes,' she promised, 'we shall see.'

8

On the first day after the *Glory* dropped its anchor the inquisition began. It started at noon, when Lord Toshida arrived to 'ask a few questions.' There were, of course, considerations of where to speak, whom to speak with first, questions of rank and protocol and, certainly, efficiency . . . and before anyone quite realized what was happening he had managed to maneuver the travelers in such a way that it was impossible for anyone he had questioned to make contact with those still awaiting interview. It was all very quietly done, all most politely managed, so much so that many of the passengers seemed not to realize the implications of Toshida's strategy. Damien did, and he wasn't happy. Not happy at all.

'Shit,' he muttered. Whispering the oath, lest Toshida's guards – ever present, ever alert – should hear him. Hesseth looked sharply at him, and despite the tight-fitting coif which masked her head he had the distinct impression of furred ears pricking forward, to fix on his speech.

'Bad?' she whispered.

Very bad, an inner voice insisted. But for her sake he muttered, 'Maybe.' Forcing the words out. 'Let's hope not.'

He had prepared the crew for a trial just like this. Hadn't he? He had explained to the pagan crew members why it would be important for them to pretend to be of his faith, had given them the basic information they would need to persevere in that role . . . but would it work? If the Regent's questions turned to religion, could they answer him safely based on what little knowledge they had? And what about Hesseth? Would the merchants remember that she was supposed to be human? Would they care enough to maintain that lie, if Toshida became suspicious? There was so much that Damien's small company stood to lose if anyone made even a tiny slip – one passing reference to Hesseth's fur, or Hesseth's claws, or Hesseth's alien nature. Or even worse, to Damien's sorcery. Was the Regent listening for hints of such a secret? Was that why he had come on board?

And then, of course, there was Gerald Tarrant.

A cold wind gusted across his soul as he thought of the man. *Tear down my walls,* he had said, *expose my belongings. See that nothing remains of my power*. Damien had taken it one step further. He had asked the passengers and crew to pretend that the Neocount had never been on their ship at all. It had seemed like a good idea at the time, and they seemed willing to play along. But would it be enough? If Toshida came to suspect that something was wrong, if he asked the right questions – perhaps threatening them openly, perhaps maneuvering them into a rhetorical corner where it was hard to maintain the lie – might not one of them slip up? It would only take one word, Damien reminded himself, one wrong, careless word . . .

And then the guard was standing before him and waiting, and it was clear from his manner that Damien's time had come. With a prayer on his lips he followed the man, across the deck to the small cabin which Toshida had commandeered for his interviews. Ushered in by the guard, he entered. The shades inside were drawn, so that none might look in on them; even the sea view was shuttered. Two oil lamps cast cool golden light about the room and its occupants; its hue lent an eerie cast to the Regent's dark skin, like that of an ancient bronze statue.

'Reverend Vryce.' The Regent's tone was cool but cordial. 'Please sit.'

He took the chair opposite Toshida's own. Damien glanced down at the desk between them, noted several bills of lading, shipping specs, one map. Then they were gone, gathered up by Toshida's dark hands and set far to one side, out of the lamplight.

'My government has some concerns,' Toshida said quietly. His voice was utterly neutral in tenor, as befit one whose power was beyond question. 'Would you mind clarifying a few issues for me?'

'Of course not,' he responded. Trying not to let his uneasiness affect his tone.

Would it matter if I did?

It began with simple questions, the kind that a government official might be expected to ask of a foreign ship in his harbor. Damien answered those simply and honestly, and when he lacked information he referred Toshida to those who would be able to answer. Then came questions that probed into Damien himself. Was it he who had organized this expedition? Why? Damien answered those questions with care, honestly wherever possible but preferring occasional vagueness to an outright lie. No one on board but Hesseth knew his true motives, thus it was unlikely that Toshida would be able to entrap him. Still he was careful, remembering always that twenty of his co-travelers had already talked to Toshida – possibly about him – and that he was being measured against that template.

At last the Regent seemed satisfied with that line of questioning, and turned to another. 'Tell me about the health of the crew.'

'What would you like to know?'

'You were in charge of that facet of the journey, verda?' The dark fingers steepled, casting dual shadows. 'Tell me about your preparations.'

It was impossible to tell from Toshida's expression whether he knew just how revealing this ground might prove. How much had the others told him? Damien cursed his own lack of knowledge, in particular his ignorance of the status of sorcery here. Would the others have thought to protect him? Would they even have realized that such protection was necessary? He chose his words very carefully. 'I felt that there would be considerable risk making contact with a colony that had its own disease profile. So I made sure of two things as I signed on my people: that each of them had a good history of resisting illness, and that no one was presently carrying anything which might infect your people. We took every precaution possible,' he assured him. Hoping it would be enough.

'So you relied upon interviews, verda?'

He shook his head. 'Everyone was examined. Passengers, officers, crew.'

'By whom?'

He answered without hesitating, because hesitation would be damning. 'By qualified professionals.'

I Healed them, you son of a bitch. With my Church-sanctioned powers I Worked the fae and used it on each and every one of them, to make sure that when we got to this precious city of yours we wouldn't spread eight hundred years of bacterial evolution among your people. I did that. I. And I used the fae to strengthen their immune systems so that they could survive your diseases, and took a few other precautions as well, whose names you wouldn't even recognize. That's what I do, Regent. That's what I am.

He drew in a deep breath, faked a cough to cover it. God, the man was getting to him. That was bad. That was dangerous.

Toshida jotted a few notes on the topmost piece of paper; the light was too poor for Damien to make out what they were. 'Reverend Vryce, I've been directed to ask you a question which you may find offensive. If so, I apologize. The circumstances we find ourselves in are most unusual, verda? Sometimes that makes for uncomfortable questions.'

'Please go ahead,' he said quietly.

The Regent's eyes fixed on his, commanding his gaze. They were deep sable brown, Damien noted, nearly black, so dark that in the dim light it was impossible to make out iris from pupil, or tell where the two might be divided. Disconcertingly like Hesseth's in the darkness.

'Have you ever used sorcery?' he asked. And then added, 'For any purpose?'

For a moment there was silence. Utter stillness. *How much does he know?* Damien thought desperately. *What did the others say?* To be caught in one lie, no matter how small, meant admitting to the possibility of others. And that meant an endless barrage of questions, with certain condemnation at the end of it.

The dark eyes were fixed on him. Demanding an answer.

'I was ordained in our western Matriarchy,' he said at last. 'The Holy Mother taught that sorcery worked in God's name was a holy enterprise. Later I traveled to the east, where I served that region's Patriarch. His views were somewhat different, and in accordance with my vows I served his will while I was there.' He drew in a deep breath, choosing his words with care. 'My vows demand obedience to the hierarchy of my Church, whatever that may be. That means obedience to your laws, your Eminence, and respect for your customs. The vows of my Order permit no less.'

The Regent's reaction was strange. He stiffened slightly – but not in response to his words, Damien thought. Perhaps in response to something they implied.

There was something odd in his tone that Damien couldn't quite define. Something almost . . . hungry.

'Your Patriarch, you say.'

'Yes, your Eminence.'

'A man,' the Regent mused.

Puzzled, Damien nodded.

'Is he your autarch? Is that what the title means?'

He nodded again. 'The Church was unified under one leader late in the third century. But the natural barriers between east and west were too great for one man to govern both realms effectively, so it was decided to have an autarch for each region.' And he ventured: 'As you would have your own in this region.'

'Each city has its own Matria,' the Regent responded. There was a tightness in him that was almost animal in nature, a tension that belied his smooth, even speech. *There's something in him waiting to explode,* Damien thought. *Something that's been ready to explode for a long, long time.* 'Their communal word is our law.'

'And the Regency?' he dared. 'Where does that fit in?'

For the first time since the interview began, the Regent looked away. 'The Matria are our visionaries, our oracles. They hear and interpret the Voice of the One God, and live eternally Sanctified in His Name . . . which lifestyle is not particularly well suited to governance, Reverend Vryce. Verda?'

'So you rule in fact?'

'In some things. Always subject to the Matria's will.' He turned back to face Damien. There was an intensity in his gaze that was hard to meet, an almost predatory alertness. Damien was acutely aware that he was watching him for his reaction. 'My rank is as high as a man can aspire to in these lands. But I'm surprised you didn't know that, Reverend Vryce. Wasn't it the Prophet himself who established that pattern?'

Was he hearing him right? Was it possible that in this place the autocracy was reserved for women, and this man – this energetic, ambitious man – had been reined in by no more than a perverse sexist custom? He was suddenly very glad that he had played poker as often and as well as he did; he had never had more need of a dispassionate expression. 'Customs differ,' he said carefully. 'And even the Prophet's words are subject to interpretation.' He didn't dare address the question any more directly than that. Not now. Not until he had more of a handle on who and what these people were. To do otherwise would be like throwing a match into a keg of black power, just to see what would happen. Madness.

For a few seconds the Regent was silent. Considering his words. Sifting them for all the messages they contained, voiced and unvoiced.

'You understand,' he said at last, 'some of what we've discussed here would be . . . upsetting for my people. Verda? This talk of foreign hierarchy, disparate customs . . .' His dark eyes narrowed. 'And sorcery. All these things are sensitive issues, best kept to a private forum. Don't you agree, Reverend Vryce?'

He found that he had been holding his breath; it took effort to speak. 'What about my people?' he chanced. *In other words, how much is my silence worth to you?*

'I see no further need to question them,' the Regent responded smoothly. Which said it all.

Was there anything other than religious faith that could have kept this man from demanding his own long ago, from toppling kingdoms to achieve it? Was there anything that could succeed in holding him down now, once he fully understood his options? Damien felt like he had indeed thrown a match into a powder keg. And that keg was sitting on an arsenal.

The Regent pushed back his chair and stood. 'It's clear you prepared well for this voyage, and I see no reason why you should remain under quarantine. I'll inform the Matria of that decision.' As he spoke his ruler's title there was just a trace of hostility in his tone, almost imperceptible – but Damien was sure that if he Worked his vision he would see the fury inside him seething like a demon, screaming its indignation. 'My aide will give your people a brief tour of the city tomorrow, so that they know their way around. After that, you're all free to come and go as you please. I anticipate the merchants will be able to unload their cargo by the end of the week, or move on with it as they desire.'

'Thank you,' Damien said. 'I'll tell them.'

The Regent nodded, his dark eyes narrow. Piercing gaze, oh, so piercing. What future world was he gazing upon, that made his look so fierce? What secret potential had Damien's words unveiled, which had previously been unspeakable?

'No,' Toshida said softly. 'Thank *you*.'

If Damien had been concerned that there would be any further investigation of his role on board the *Glory,* he was quickly reassured. Their tour of the city, attended by most of the passengers and all the lesser crew, went without a hitch. There were the predictable swarms of reporters, of course, who flanked them like hunting dogs throughout their journey. *Is it what you expected? Was it worth the crossing? How have we surprised, disappointed, impressed, intrigued, appealed to you?* And of course the inevitable queries from tabloid artists regarding ghost islands, sea monsters, and western sexual practices. At one point their guide made a point of gathering them together and explaining to them in simple words and an almost decipherable accent that their stories were worth quite a bit to these people, and they shouldn't part with too much information without getting paid for it. To which Anshala responded, in a tone that was equally patronizing, 'We're not brainless savages, you know.' And they were left to conduct themselves as they saw fit.

On the third night a celebration was declared in honor of the travelers, to include a display of fireworks when the Core set after dusk. The invitation to attend was hand-delivered by the captain of Toshida's guard to Rozca himself, no doubt in recognition of his stubborn refusal to leave his ship the day before. Despite the fact that Rozca loudly refused to attend that gala display or any other until he was satisfied with the security of his ship, he appeared to be pleased by the attention. And later, when that same officer returned at dusk to take personal charge of the *Golden Glory,* Rozca allowed himself to be talked off his bridge and across the dock and into town itself.

Fireworks: controlled small-scale explosions, performed for entertainment. *An old Earth custom,* the Regent's man assured them, and Damien was amazed at how casually the phrase rolled off his lips. Damien's own people had been struggling with the basics of survival for so long that they had all but forgotten what true Earth custom was, and used the phrase only rarely to denote a ritual whose roots were so ancient they could no longer be remembered. Here, where relative stability had been achieved a mere three centuries after the Landing, oral tradition had preserved much more of Earth's heritage. The West might have recorded Earth's facts in its struggle to preserve its scientific heritage, Damien reflected. But the East alone remembered Earth's spirit.

Impressive. Like everything else about this land. And, like everything else, utterly alien.

They were led to a vast park in the center of the city, bounded at one end by the Regent's Manor and at the other by the Governance Center. The central portion of the park was immense, acre upon acre of meticulously landscaped terrain that seemed to Damien a living symbol of the carefully controlled order of this land. No plants grew at random. No weed would dare to sprout. Pink blossoms bloomed exactly where pink blossoms ought to be, and the rows of towering trees that flanked the sides of the central lawn were a living testament to man's dominion over Nature in this one tiny corner of the universe. Damien wondered if the children who now sported about those trunks would ever understand that fact, or if they took their power for granted. In much the same way that Earth once had, to the detriment of all its inhabitants.

The numbers gathered in the great square were already too great to count, but to Damien's untutored eye it seemed that the whole city must be present, and then some. Some had clearly come to see the fireworks, and they spread out their blankets on those sculpted hillocks where the view promised to be the best. Their children sported merrily across the crowded plain, as excited by the prospect of staying up this late as they were by the coming spectacle. Others had clearly come to see the strangers, and they crowded about the reviewing stand in ranks so thick that their children could not run, but resorted to playing hide-and-seek behind the bodies and between the legs of strangers. Until some well-meaning relative caught hold of one of them them and tried to imprint upon that child's brain the importance of the night's display. Damien smiled as he watched, and estimated the message would remain with them for about five minutes, if that long. He had been that age. He remembered.

The sun had set nearly three hours ago, but the Core had only recently followed. The sky was that curious shade of blue which was neither sun-cold nor Core-warm but that in-between shade, twilight. A fine mist had gathered over the city, hinting at the imminence of rain. Toshida said not to worry, that the fog would only make the fireworks more enjoyable. Damien couldn't begin to explain to him how utterly alien such a reassurance seemed. If the same thing had happened in Jaggonath, the nervous uncertainty of ten thousand viewers would have stopped the performance dead, or at least made it very dangerous to proceed. Fear had a way of feeding on itself and then altering the fae, which in turn was capable of affecting any physical event. Did these people have such faith in their leaders that they no longer questioned their decisions? Or had centuries of faith finally weakened the link between *fearing* and *being* – as it had been meant to do, as the Prophet had designed it to do, so many years ago? The thought was almost too awesome to contemplate.

Today fireworks, Damien mused. *Tomorrow the stars*.

The reviewing stand had been erected near one end of the great lawn, within the shadow of the Regent's Manor. *No accident there,* Damien observed, as he watched the Governor and his retinue make their way to their seats. Damien glanced over toward the Regent, found him in animated conversation with Rasya. Toshida seemed to be fascinated with the *Glory*'s pilot, although whether or not that interest was mutual remained to be seen. Damien wondered if he might not be put off by her total lack of regard for landbound authority . . . or whether that might not be the attraction. Certainly there were at least a hundred women here who made it clear, by their dress and their gaze and their constant proximity to the reviewing stand, that they were his for the asking.

Maybe he needs a break from that, Damien thought dryly.

Then there was a murmur at one end of the platform, and a wave of motion as the tightly packed crowd rearranged itself to make way for someone. Damien made out the form of a woman, middle-aged, dressed in dun-colored robes that concealed her from wrist to ankle, loose folds obscuring whatever details of her figure might otherwise have been visible. He recalled men and women on Toshida's ship who had been dressed similarly, and the Regent's strange response to Hesseth's presence on board the *Glory* suddenly became clear. Indeed, as the woman approached them, Toshida stood so that he might bow deeply, a gesture redolent with genuine respect, perhaps even with awe. No ritual obeisance, that. Even Damien felt its power.

'The Matria sends her regrets,' the woman announced. Speaking to them all. Wisps of pale hair misted about the edges of her coif, giving her face an ethereal appearance. 'She won't be able to attend tonight.'

Again the Regent bowed, this time in acknowledgment of her message. 'Will you do the honors?' he said. Indicating the speaker's platform at the front of the platform.

'In her name,' she agreed, and stepped up on to it.

A hush fell over the crowd, as one by one the people closest to the stand realized that an Important Moment was about to take place. It spread across the great lawn like a wave, heads turning one by one as voices died down, to gaze upon the spectacle. The robed woman held out her hands as if in welcoming, and waited. At last – when the silence that greeted her was absolute, the aura of anticipation almost tangible – she began to speak.

'Praised be the One God, Creator of Earth and Erna. Praised be the Holy Progenitor of mankind, whose Will gave us life and whose Faith gives us strength, whose Hand protects us from the faeborn. Praised be the Lord our One Protector, who in His infinite Wisdom protects us from the damned. Praised be His covenant with our ancestors, which decreed that for so long as we serve His Will, so long as we keep His Law, this land and the seas and the sky and all that is between them shall be ours to cultivate. As it was for our forebears on Earth, as it shall be forever for our children. Amen.'

And the crowd murmured, *Amen*.

Very neat, Damien thought. Despising himself for his cynicism, even as his brain analyzed the facts. *In other words, this is God's show and nothing – not your fears and not the fae – is going to spoil it. A specific targeting of mob faith to the issue at hand. Nicely done.* He remembered the robed figures on Toshida's ship, and suddenly understood what they'd been doing there. A timely blessing on each cannon, on the ammo, on the act of ignition . . . so that the soldiers believed, with all the passion of religious fervor and on every level of their being, that the cannon would work exactly as planned. These people knew the Prophet's theories, all right. And had taken them one step further than the Prophet ever did. Damien wondered if those selfsame prayers would abort a 'natural' misfire. Hell . . . was anything really 'natural' on this world?

And then, without warning, the fireworks began. Explosion after explosion split the night in rapid succession, leaving the visitors no time to catch their breath between them. Artificial stars burst into life across the darkening sky, blossoms and streamers and spirals of them, diamonds and spheres and waterfalls of stars that lit the sky like a second Core. As if that spectacle was not enough, the fog captured the light of each starburst and reflected it across the city, illuminating the crowd with wave after wave of eerie color, like the light of a second sun. And through it all, though band after band of shooting stars expired in darkness just above their heads, not one drop of fire touched the earth. Not one gleaming bit swooped low to singe flesh. Not one person in the crowd seemed to quail at the thought that it might. It was a grand symphony of creation, not only of light but of faith. Damien found himself overcome by awe. Not at the display itself – miraculous as it seemed – but at the people who had gathered to watch it. At their utter confidence in the technology they had tamed. Men and women who gazed at the sky without fear, without awe, merely a measured appreciation of the night's entertainment. And if they broke into applause now and then, it was for the lights, for their makers, and not for the faith that had made this night possible.

They take it for granted, he thought. The concept was so alien it made his head spin. *Across nine-tenths of this world such a display would be all but impossible, and yet to them it's just one more night's entertainment.* Had he ever even imagined such a thing? Had anyone? His ancestors had dreamed of resculpting this world to suit Earth's parameters, but did they really understood what that meant? No more than Damien had, and he had devoted his life to that subject. But this was it, here and now, the essence of Earth incarnate: not only science, not just technology, but a life founded in utter confidence, in the absolute surety of things and people – a faith in physical causality so deeply rooted that it was given no thought at all. Just lived.

He shut his eyes, trembling. This was his faith. Not the mapping of a world, not the workings of a steam engine, not even the half-dozen warning shots that had been fired across their bow. This confidence in the common people. This utter joy, and the abandon it engendered. This innocence, and the freedom it implied . . .

I've worked for this all my life . . . and I would work a dozen lifetimes more, if that time were given to me, and die willingly a thousand times over if it would bring Erna one step closer to this kind of unity.

It ended. Sometime. He watched it through eyes that were brimming with tears – of joy, of faith, of humility. The entire sky was filled with light, with stars, whose combined glare lit the city brighter than a sun . . . and then it was over. The last sparks died. The mist gave up its colors and faded into the night, a mere veil between man and the stars. And Damien felt himself breathe steadily at last.

'Well?' It was the Regent's voice from beside him, measured and even but with just a trace of tension. 'What did you think?'

He met the man's eyes and thought, *The question's not casual, any more than this 'celebration' was. He meant to communicate something, and he has.* 'Rarely have I been so impressed,' he told Toshida. Using his tone and manner to make it clear that the answer was no more lightly stated than the question had been; this night had shaken his soul to its roots. Toshida nodded his approval, and might have spoken to Damien again had it not been for the *Glory*'s captain, who chose that moment to come up beside him and shake his hand and declare that in all his travels – which had been many and various, he assured him – he had never seen a public display to rival tonight's fireshow. Then he was pushed aside by another of the travelers, who in turn gave way to Rasya (and was that flirtation in her eyes?), and Damien watched them take their turns one after another until it was clear that the Regent was well and truly occupied for at least an hour.

Unnoticed, he made his way to the back stairs and descended from the reviewing platform. The Regent's Manor loomed behind him, and he skirted its carefully sculpted lawns by Domina's moonlight, searching for a road that would take him where he wanted to go without running into a thousand tourists. At last he found it, a narrow path whose entrance was masked by hedges. He made his way along it to the north, trying to remember the layout of the city. A few people passed by him – teenage couples arm in arm, a group of loud-voiced men, a family of five with two children walking and one, the youngest, slung over his father's shoulder – but for the most part the narrow street was quiet, an unlikely conduit for the thousands that would be heading home after the night's celebration.

And at last he came to the building he sought. It stood in the center of an immense circular lawn, whose manicured gardens and precisely aligned trees all drew one's attention to its gleaming portals, its Revivalist grandeur. He knew from the maps he had seen that this building stood at the true center of Mercia, that though other buildings might rival it in physical grandeur its geographic position made it clear that it was the life and the soul of that miraculous city.

Slowly, reverently, he approached Mercia's great cathedral.

He expected there to be a guard on duty. There was none. He guessed that they had seen him coming and, observing his robes, had elected to be discreetly absent. For which he was grateful. He would have found it difficult to talk to anyone now, save the One he had come to address. The One whose Presence breathed from the stones of this building like a living essence, drawing Damien in.

With a prayer on his lips, his heart pounding, he pushed open the great doors and entered.

The sanctuary was empty, and utterly silent. The stillness of it was so absolute that it invaded Damien's soul, quieting the roar of his blood, the whirlwind of his emotions. Domina's light filtered through stained-glass windows five times the height of a man, spreading a shifting mosaic of colored light across the polished stone floor. The ceiling overhead was so high it was lost in shadows, as intangible as the night itself. The sheer vastness of the space seemed to dwarf him, impressing upon him the ultimate humility of human existence – and at the same time it forced him to expand, to fill its vaulted emptiness with the fire of his human spirit. In here, one could believe there was a God. In here one could believe that man could commune with Him.

He walked quietly to the head of the aisle, listening to his footsteps resound in the emptiness. Faith curled about him like an evening mist, centuries upon centuries of unquestioning devotion that had left their mark upon the floor he trod, the altar before him, the very air he breathed. Earth-fae: utterly tamed, utterly tractable. He had dreamed of it without understanding. Now he knew. Now he understood. He put out his hand, knowing that it curled about his living warmth like a flame. No need to See it; faith was enough.

Silently he knelt on the plush velvet carpet, his white robe gathered beneath his knees. In his eyes the afterimage of the fireworks still burned, sparks that shimmered and died in the shadow of Mercia's great altar. How unimpressive those lights seemed now, when compared to the triumph of faith that had made them possible! And they knew that, he thought. Not the common people, perhaps, but the leaders. They knew.

Trembling, he bowed his head. And tried to voice a prayer so deeply embedded in his soul that for a moment no words would come. For a moment he did no more than pour his hope, his joy, his love of the Church into the boundless reservoir of faith that surrounded him.

And then the words came.

Thank You, Lord, for giving me this day. This joy. Thank You for letting me taste that beauty of the human spirit which is the core of our faith. Thank You for giving me even one moment in which human greed, uncertainty, and aggression receded from concern, and the Dream that is our faith stood revealed before me in all its terrible splendor. Help me to hold that moment within my heart forever, a source of strength in times of trial, a source of faith in times of questioning. Help me to be a vehicle through which others may glimpse what I have seen, and a tool by which the future may be fashioned in its image. In Your most holy Name, Lord God of Earth and Erna. Always and forever in Your Name.

There were tears on his face, running down his cheeks. He left them alone. They, too, were a kind of prayer, too precious to disturb: a psalm of pure emotion.

Strangely, in my joy I find I feel terribly alone. The priests of my homeland may devote their lives to a vision of such perfection, but they know it will never be fulfilled in their lifetime. The people here may reap the rewards of their unity, but how can they begin to understand its true value when they have nothing less perfect to compare it with? Only in stepping from one world to the other can one see so clearly the borderline between the two, and the fragile balance necessary to maintain it. Help me to keep hold of that most precious vision, Lord. Help me to serve mankind the better for having known it.

There was a sound behind him. It took a moment to sink into his consciousness. It was as though he floated in another world, halfway between this planet and something that was beyond all definition. Something so painfully beautiful that he could hardly bear to look upon it, much less turn his eyes away to seek out the source of a simple sound.

'Father?'

The realm of the Infinite loosed its grip upon his soul, and gently returned him to the present. He got to his feet slowly, with effort, and turned; his eyes, well-adjusted to the darkness, had no difficulty in making out the speaker's identity.

'Captain Rozca,' he whispered. Not a little surprised. More than a little confused.

The man came toward him slowly, stepping from shadow into ruby-colored light, then into shadow again. A heartbeat of illumination. 'I didn't mean to disturb you, Father. If it's a bad time—'

'Not at all,' Damien managed. The captain's expression seemed strained, as if reflecting some inner turmoil. Best not to address that directly, he thought. Best to let him express it in his own way, in his own time. 'How did you find me?'

'I followed you from the fairgrounds. I hope you don't mind. I thought, that is I felt, that is . . . I wanted to talk to you.'

'I'm here,' he said softly.

'When I saw . . . I mean . . . They couldn't have done that at home, could they?' He was closer now, close enough that Damien could watch his face as he struggled to find the right words. 'The fireworks, I mean.'

'No.' He shut his eyes for a moment, remembering. The brilliance. The joy. 'Maybe priests could manage something like it, maybe adepts could mimic it . . . but not like that. Not on such a scale.'

'You talked to me about it on the *Glory,*' he said. 'How if enough people worshiped your god it would make a real difference. Not just in matters of faith, you said, or in religious things, but in the way we lived. I didn't really understand. Not then. But here . . .' He looked toward a window, helplessly. 'I've seen things here I didn't think a god could do. And you know what gets to me? That they vulking take it for granted! It's just one more show of pretty lights to them, or one more smoking cannon, or one more bustling steamship . . . they don't even know what they've got here, Father. Do you feel that? Am I crazy?'

'No, you're not crazy. You have vision, and that's very rare. Very precious.' *Hold onto this moment,* he wanted to say. *You may never have one like it again.*

'It's just that I . . . damn it, this is hard.' He turned back to Damien, but couldn't meet his eyes. 'I don't say things like this too good, you know. Words don't come easy to me. It's just that I've been thinking all night, all through the firelights, and I . . .' He drew in a deep breath, shaking. 'I want you to take my oath, Father.'

For a moment Damien had no words. Speech seemed an alien concept; words that he might have spoken jumbled in his brain, caught on his tongue. He forced them out. They weren't the words he wanted to say, but words that he was bound to. Because fairness was part of his duty, too. Perhaps the most important part.

'What you've seen here is very impressive, I understand that. But when our business is done here you'll be leaving, and this night will be no more than a memory. In the world we came from, will that be enough? Mine isn't an easy faith, captain, or a popular one. Are you sure it's what you want?'

'Father,' he answered, 'The way I see it, you go through life in stages. First you're young and ambitious and you think nothing's going to get in your way, not ever. Then you get to the point when you realize that the world's a damned hard place to live – downright nasty on occasion – and it's hard enough to keep your head above water all the time, much less come out on top like you want. At that point you figure if some god can make it all a little easier, why not? What's a prayer or two to you, if it gets you what you want? But then,' he said, 'when you get older, you realize there's something else you want, too. Something that's harder to put a name to. Something a man gets when he writes a song that'll be sung long after he's dead, or paints something that his great-great-grandchildren will hang on the wall . . . or helps change his world. Do you see, Father? There's a lot of things this world might become, and before tonight I didn't much bother to think about it. My own little piece of the present was enough, and the rest could take care of itself. But now . . . I've seen what the future could be, Father. I've seen what this world can become. And I want to help make it happen. Even if it's just a little bit. I want to do my share.' He hesitated. When he spoke again there was genuine humility in his voice, a tone no man could counterfeit. 'Will you take my oath?'

Damien nodded.

The captain knelt before him; it was clearly a position to which he was not accustomed. After a moment's hesitation he lifted his hands, clasped palm to palm, before him. Damien folded his own about them, his pulse warm against the callused skin. And he spoke the same words that had been said to him so very long ago, so very far away, at the birthtime of his soul.

'This is the way of the Lord the One God, who created Earth

and Erna, who led us to the stars, whose faith is the salvation of humankind . . .'

And as he intoned the words that would bind yet another soul to his mission, he whispered silently, *Thank you, God. For giving me this moment. For showing me that I wasn't alone tonight. For showing me that none of us are alone, not ever. Not in Your service.*

And thank You for touching this man's soul. For letting him taste of our dream. There is no more precious gift.

'Welcome to God's service,' he whispered.

9

A study in silence: the jagged peak of Guardian Mountain, granite-clad and still. No life stirred on those harsh slopes, nor anything that might attract life. No breeze swept across the bare rock, though winds had gusted strongly up to half an hour before. The storm which had been headed this way had been turned aside, for no better reason than the one with the power to do so had no patience left for storms. The peak was as still as death itself, reflecting the mood of the one who stood upon it. Reflecting his soul.

And then there was movement. Not visible to most, perhaps, but visible to him. A tremor of earth-fae; a whisper of foreboding. The power that was near him thickened, focused, began to coagulate into solid form. Flesh. A woman's body at first, and then – as the body became more solid – it shifted to a man's form, draped in a man's attire. Velvet robes, priceless jewels, fur collar that rippled as if in the wind, despite the lack of breeze. As he changed form, so did the surroundings. The cold peak disappeared, to be replaced by a palace interior. Rich silk tapestries, frescoed walls . . . the fae-creature waited a moment for the man on the peak to react, then shrugged. The tapestries gave way to trees, the walls to a brilliant Coreset. Still no response. He let that fade to a church interior. When even that image failed to stir the man's interest, he let it fade as well, and replaced it with a scene out of nightmare. A vast field of skulls stretched for miles before them, and in its center – at the feet of the man – an offering cup of blood. About its brim was engraved a ribald limerick in ancient Earth-script. He saw the man glance down to read it, then turn slowly toward him. His expression made it clear he was not amused.

'You really have no sense of humor tonight,' Karril said.

'I Called you five nights ago,' Gerald Tarrant pointed out.

'You did. And someday when you're in a better mood I'll tell you just how much fun it wasn't to cross Novatlantis. My kind rides the earth-currents, remember? Do you know what they're like in that region? If a horse did to you what the fae did to me, you'd unevolve the whole species.' With a short wave of his hand the demon banished the nightmare images. Black walls took their place, dressed with crimson curtains and golden sconces: the trappings of the Hunter's palace. 'You want to tell me what's eating you, or you want me to guess?'

'I thought you could read my soul.'

'I can't read pain. You know that.'

'Is it that?' he murmured. 'Already?'

'You tell me.' When the Hunter said nothing he pressed, 'You Called me for a reason.'

'I Called you to see if I could Work through to the west from here.'

'Well?' He spread his hands generously. 'I heard you. Here I am.'

'Yes,' he said quietly. 'With you it worked.'

For a moment the demon studied him. Then, very softly, he ventured, 'I wasn't your first effort, was I? You must have tried other times, without result. Tried to call up some power from your western reservoir, and it wouldn't respond. Is that it?'

The Hunter nodded tightly.

'I suppose it makes sense, you know. Summon a demon who has a will of his own, and maybe he'll choose to make the trip. Summon the power of the Forest, which has no independent spirit . . .'

'I couldn't,' he whispered. 'The distance was too great. And Novatlantis—'

The demon shuddered dramatically. 'I understand.'

'You know what that means, don't you?' His voice was quiet but strained; evidently his self-control was being pushed to the breaking point. 'I can't go home. Not the same way I got here.'

'I thought your priestly friend was willing to support you.'

'Yes. He fed me his blood and his nightmares for half a year . . . and I starved, Karril. I *starved*. Even now the hunger still resonates within me. Why? It's never been like this before. Never been something I couldn't master. Until now.'

'You fed, I take it.'

He shut his eyes, remembering. 'As soon as we landed, and many times since. Fear so rich it made me giddy to taste it, blood so hot with terror that leaching it of warmth should have cooled my hunger for a decade. This land is ripe for me, Karril, and its people are unprotected. And yet . . . I feel empty again. Desperately empty. The scent of a victim makes me tremble with hunger . . . even though I know that my physical need has been satisfied. Why? It's never been like this before.'

'You never starved yourself for that long before.'

'Why should that matter? You can starve a vampire for centuries, but within a night after he's fed—'

'You haven't been a mere vampire for centuries now. Remember?'

'It shouldn't make a difference.'

'Of course it does! You have a complex soul, my friend. A *human* soul, for all its hellish trappings. Such a thing takes time to heal. Hells, even a housecat that's starved for five months will hoard its food for a while. Give it time.'

'I haven't got time,' he muttered. Turning away. His hands, clenched into fists, trembled slightly. 'Our enemy must know we're here,' he whispered. 'I have no time for weakness.'

'I would help if I could,' the demon said softly. 'You know that. But my powers are limited.' He indicated the room that surrounded them, as if to say, *this is it*. 'I can give you illusion. I can intensify the pleasure of killing, perhaps even offer a brief euphoria of forgetfulness. But escapism's never been your style, I know that. What more can I offer?'

'You can give me information.'

The demon chuckled softly. 'Ah, now it all comes together. Is that why you called me here?'

'It's why I chose you, as opposed to half a dozen other spirits who might have made the trip. For all your shallow posturings you're a good servant, Karril. And I know I'm not the only adept who's felt that way.'

The demon grinned. 'How much effort does it take, really? The most precious thing in an adept's world is knowledge. And what is that to me? How hard is it to part with a simple fact or two? And being demonic myself, I do have an advantage in research. So tell me what you need, Hunter. If I can help, I will.'

The Neocount turned so that his eyes were on Karril's; black fire stirred in their depths. 'There was a demon we fought in the rakhlands. He came to me later and . . .' He shook his head sharply, banishing the memory. 'Simply put, he tried to destroy me. And almost succeeded. I'm here to keep it from happening again.'

'A worthy crusade.'

'I can't Know him without increasing the power that binds us together, and that would make him even stronger. Too risky. Yet I need to know who he is, *what* he is, what his parameters are . . . can you tell me that?'

'If I know him. If not . . .' he grinned. 'Let's say that for an old friend I'd do some research. Did this creature of darkness have a name?'

'He called himself Calesta.'

The demon's face went white. Utterly white. Not the fleshy pale color of human surprise, in which blood leaves the face and all else remains, but the total colorlessness of one whose face is but an illusion, responsive to one's moods on a much more primal level. 'Calesta?'

'You know of him?'

A long, strained pause. 'I know of him,' he said at last. 'But I didn't know . . .' He left off helplessly.

'I need information, Karril.'

'Yes. You would.' He turned away. 'But I can't help you, Hunter. Not this time.'

'Why?'

A pause. The demon shook his head. 'I can't answer that either.' he whispered. 'I'm sorry.'

'You're playing games with me—'

'No. I'm not. I swear it.'

'Then help me! – or tell me why you can't. One or the other.'

The demon said nothing. The brightness of the walls about them faded; it was possible to see the lights of a nearby city through one curtain.

The Hunter took a step toward him; his pale eyes flashed in anger. 'He tricked me, Karril. He meant to destroy my soul, and he almost succeeded. Now I've crossed half a world so that I can have my vengeance, and I will. And you will help me.' When the demon failed to respond, his expression darkened. 'If I suffer in this because you refused to help me, so help me God, I'll bind you to my pain—'

'I can't!' he whispered fiercely. 'Not this time, Hunter. I'm sorry.'

'Why?' he demanded. 'You've never failed me before. Why is this time different?'

'It's just ... I can't.' If he were human, he might have been sweating heavily; as it was, his gaze flickered nervously from side to side as if trying to escape Tarrant's own. 'I'm forbidden to get involved. Forbidden to interfere. All right? Is that enough?'

The Hunter's voice was like ice. 'Forbidden by whom?'

'No one you would know. And not for any reason you would respect. But it's binding, I assure you.'

'I can fight it—'

'You can't.'

'I could Banish—'

'Not this! Not this time. I'm sorry.'

'And I'm supposed to just accept that?' he demanded.

Karril said nothing.

He grabbed him by the shoulders, turned him to face him. 'My life is on the line here, demon. I must use the resources that are available to me. *You* are one of those resources.' He paused, giving that a moment to sink in. 'I've always valued our relationship. Since the moment you first came to me, centuries ago, I've dealt with you honestly and openly. And you've always returned that courtesy.

Until now.' Earth-fae began to gather at his feet, ready for Working. 'For the last time, Karril. Will you tell me what you know of your own accord, or do I have to Summon it out of you?'

For a long moment the demon just stared at him. At last he said, in a low voice, 'You can't, you know.'

'Can't what?'

'Summon me. Force the information out, in any way.'

'Are you claiming some special protection?'

'No. But I'm telling you that my kind isn't affected by such things. Never has been.'

'Your kind ... you mean your sub-type?'

'Yes, my sub-type. My family, if you will. The demons you call *Iezu*.'

'I've Summoned Iezu before. I've Summoned *you,* in fact—'

'And I played along. Because those are the rules of the game as humans define it. I know my place. We all do. But the truth is that your sorcery can't control any of us. Never could.'

The Hunter's face was a mask of fury, and something else. Fear? 'You're bluffing,' he accused

'Have I ever bluffed with you? Is that my way? Summon me, if you like. See for yourself. Humans need the illusion of control, but maybe you're the one exception. Maybe you can handle the fact that your precious Workings won't affect me. Go on, try!'

Tarrant turned away from him. His hands were shaking. Black fire burned in his soul.

'There's nothing I can say or do to make a difference in this conflict,' the demon told him. 'There's nothing you can ask me for that I can give you if Calesta's involved. I'm sorry, old friend. More sorry than you can imagine. But the laws that bind me are older than you or I, and stronger than both of us combined. I wish it were otherwise.'

'Go,' he whispered hoarsely. 'Get out of here! To the west, if you want, or feed on these people for a while. God knows they're ripe for it. Just get out of my sight.'

'Gerald—'

'*Go!*' His shoulders were trembling, the motion slight but eloquent. In all the time that Karril had known him – nearly nine centuries now – he had never seen him this upset. Never seen him this close to losing it.

It's the lack of control, the demon thought. *The one thing he can't handle. The one thing he could never handle.*

'I didn't know you meant to fight him,' he said. Softly, oh so softly, hoping that the words would reach him through his rage. 'I would have tried to warn you. I would have tried to talk you out of it . . .' *And why?* he thought. *Because I care? That's not supposed to happen at all. You see, I break the rules just by knowing you.* The thought that he was causing pain ran counter to his every instinct. The knowledge that he could do otherwise with a few simple words was almost more than he could bear.

'Be careful,' he whispered suddenly. 'He can read you like I do: see into your soul, uncover all your weaknesses. Trust nothing that you see or hear; remember that the senses are flesh-born, and flesh can be manipulated.' He looked about himself nervously, as if checking for eavesdroppers. 'Gods of Earth! I've said too much already. Be careful, my old friend. The price of defeat is higher than you know.'

Tarrant whipped about as if to confront him, but Karril was already gone: sucked into the night along with all his illusions, dispersed on the evening breeze. For a moment Tarrant just stared at the space where he had been. Then, mastering his rage with effort, he worked a Summoning. To force Karril to return. To force him to respond to him.

Nothing happened.

Nothing at all.

He looked back toward the city lights below, and felt an unaccustomed rage stab through his flesh. Anger, hot as brimstone, set his blood to burning.

'Damn you,' he muttered. 'Damn you to Hell!'

He started down the mountainside, toward the city and its innocents.

10

The Consecration of the Faithful took place on the fifth day after Damien's arrival, the evening of the local sabbath. He was invited to participate. Toshida had supplied him with full sweeping robes in the local style, emblazoned with the golden flames of his Order. Hurriedly made, he guessed, but no less opulent for it. He tried to get Hesseth to attend, but the mere mention of his Church brought a hiss of distaste to her lips. She had been playing Sanctified Woman for several days now – the role forced upon her by her costume – and the continual stress of faking an identity she didn't understand was beginning to take its toll on her nerves. Damien wished they could find a safe forum in which to ask for information about the Sanctified, but neither he nor Hesseth thought it would be wise to admit their ignorance. It was simply too valuable to have such a role, which permitted her to cover her alien body without raising suspicion; they dared not do anything that would put it at risk.

She was in their rooms when he left her, poring over maps of the region. They had yet to locate anything which might be termed a *stronghold of the enemy*, although several locations were suspect. Whatever game their nemesis was playing here, it was clearly more subtle than the one he had played in the rakhlands.

If he could ask Toshida openly about it ... but no. For some reason that thought made him uneasy, and he had learned over the years that his instinct was a thing to be trusted. Maybe it was Toshida's rank that made him anxious, his obvious power over their situation. But that had never stopped Damien with Jaggonath's Patriarch, had it? No, it was clearly something more than that. And the thought that there might be something wrong here – subtle enough and unpleasant enough that he had not yet acknowledged it in his conscious mind – was doubly unnerving.

By the time he arrived at sunset the cathedral was full, and he gazed at the assembled faces of the Mercian faithful with wonder. They were darker than his own people on the average, with few blonds among them; no wonder Toshida was so fascinated by Rasya. Tarrant would stand out like a sore thumb, he realized, with his light brown hair and melanin-deficient skin clearly declaring him a stranger. He hoped the Hunter had the wherewithal to notice that, and to compensate. Wherever the hell he was.

The assembled faithful stirred as Toshida made his entrance. Resplendent in the robes of his Church, he was the living image of authority, both temporal and ecclesiastical: a flawless synthesis of power. Against the copper-toned darkness of his skin the white robes gleamed like a beacon; it was impossible for the eye not to be drawn to him, impossible for the soul to resist his mastery. As he raised up his arms in a gesture of benediction the full sleeves spread like wings, and Damien felt rather than heard a hush come over the assemblage.

'May God protect us from the faeborn,' he intoned. 'May He defend us from the assaults of the nightborn, the darkbound, the ones who would devour us. May He safeguard our bodies and our souls, so that we may live to praise His Name.'

And the assemblage responded, as one voice, *Amen*.

Even as he listened to the rest of the service, Damien found himself appreciating its flawless design. The faith of thousands had been harnessed here, not only to worship the One God (or perhaps to create Him, some theologians might argue,) but to turn each city into a fortress, impregnable to demonic assault. In this it had succeeded, utterly. He had been on land two nights now, had already witnessed the unheard-of-freedom that these people enjoyed. Because no demon made it past the city gates. Not ever. There might be a few faeborn dangers spawned inside the city itself, but the kinds of horrors that the west endured – vampiric spirits who went from city to city in search of sustenance, who withdrew to the solitude of the great forests in order to escape the sunlight, then returned again at nightfall – were all but unknown here. Any faeborn wraiths that left the city could not come back. Period. Which made the odds of being attacked by something nasty on a parallel with the odds of being mugged. Not very high, in this carefully policed region.

'Humble we stand before You,' the Regent pronounced, 'obedient to Your Law.'

Amen.

He had yet to meet the Matria. He had thought he understood her position in this city, but the more he learned the more uncertain he was of that. If anything, she seemed to be a creature of utter mystery, who came and went with such unpredictability that she was more a symbol-in-absence than a vital part of this thriving theosystem. Which was strange. Very strange. And not like the Church he knew at all.

At last it was time for him to speak. He heard the Regent introduce him as he came to the pulpit, felt the gaze of the assembled fixing on him with an almost palpable force. He drew in a breath, gathered his thoughts . . . and then froze, as the communal gaze shifted elsewhere.

Behind him.

He turned, and felt his own heart skip a beat.

The Matria.

Her body was slight, but her presence was not; as she came forward to take her place beside Toshida, he was struck by just how much presence that slender form could command. Layered robes of fine silk whispered about her legs and ankles, hinting at the form beneath; her veil was anchored by a heavy crown that adorned her hair without fully concealing it. She was not a beautiful woman, but in that costume and role she embodied all the beauty and power of his faith, and when Toshida bowed in greeting, there was no question of who really controlled the reins of state.

She sat beside Toshida, in one of the ornate thrones that flanked the podium. *Go on,* her gaze said to Damien. *Continue.* And it seemed that she smiled slightly as she settled back onto the cushions.

It took effort to turn away from her and pick up where he had left off. It took even more effort not to mold the earth-fae into a Knowing, to discover more of who and what she was. But that would be rank stupidity in front of this many witnesses, plain and simple.

And so he addressed his attention – and his words – to the congregation. Presenting something that was not quite a sermon, not exactly a history lesson . . . but it had elements of both, as he used words to sculpt a bridge between their disparate worlds.

He wanted to respond to what they had accomplished. He wanted them to see it through his eyes. He wanted to give them the gift of his vision, to help them draw back from their day to day life and see – really *see* – how great their triumph was.

And more. He wanted to put all that in context, so that they knew how hard western man was struggling to find a similar peace. And – most of all – he wanted them to know what it would mean to the west when he brought home word of their triumph. For word of their success would surely spread, until all of Erna was inspired to devote itself to the Prophet's dream. At last.

When he was done, he bowed to the multitude, deeply and formally, and then stepped down from the podium. Toshida nodded his approval as he took up his place once more, and the regular service resumed. When Damien was seated, he looked over toward the Matria, meaning to acknowledge her presence. To his surprise, he found that she was already gone.

What—?

She had come to hear him speak, then. That was all. She had come to hear what the foreign priest had to say – to take the measure of his faith – and then she had left before there could be any more intimate contact between them. Had he displeased her with his sermon? No, he thought. That wasn't likely. Was it possible she simply wanted to leave before chance or protocol brought them closer together? Why? The question plagued him all through the service, and into the hours beyond. What was there about him that the Matria would feel a need to avoid?

The hour was late when he finally returned to the Regent's Manor, and he was glad Toshida had been unable to accompany him. He needed to think. The Manor had a guest wing for visiting dignitaries and Toshida had insisted that he accept a room therein. For his comfort, or so he could be watched? Probably both, Hesseth had said. Damien had insisted that she be housed there also, and though Toshida clearly found the request more than a little strange – didn't she want to stay in the House of the Sanctified with the others of her Order? – in the end he'd agreed. The two of them shared a parlor, and as Damien climbed the vast circular staircase that led to the guest wing he was certain she would be there, waiting for him.

She was.

So was Gerald Tarrant.

For a moment Damien just stood in the doorway. Coming from the church service into the Hunter's presence was like having a bowl of ice water suddenly splashed in his face; it took him a moment to catch his breath.

Then, very carefully, very quietly, he shut the door.

'Were you seen?' he asked.

'By guards? No.'

'At all.'

The Hunter shook his head. 'No one knows I'm in the city. No one knows I'm on this continent, for that matter. I thought it best to keep it that way.'

He nodded tensely in agreement. 'They searched the ship, you know. Pretty thoroughly. Just like you said they would.' *Looking for you,* he wanted to say. But he didn't know that for certain, did he? 'Looking for something nocturnal,' he said at last, and Tarrant nodded.

He forced himself to walk into the room, to overcome his revulsion enough to ask the necessary question. 'You feel better?'

'I fed,' the Hunter responded dryly. 'If that's what you're asking. Nothing that a gourmet would brag about, but let's say I've recovered from the journey here.'

The words were out before he could stop them. 'How many?'

'You really want to know?'

The pale eyes were fixed on him. Cold, so very cold. After a moment he managed to look away, and muttered, 'No. I guess not.'

'My strength isn't what it once was . . . but that won't improve for some time, I regret. Not without the Forest's power to draw on.' His slender hand fingered the hilt of his sword, as if reminding Damien that it, too, had been drained of strength. 'However, my knowledge base is undiminished. And Mes Hesseth has done a fine job of accumulating maps.'

It was only then that he noticed that the floor – the whole floor – was covered with renderings of the land they had come to. Street maps, road maps, nautical charts, maps of landmarks and state monuments and political divisions . . . most were the fold-out type that was sold at newstands and on street corners, but some were in Hesseth's own hand, painstakingly copied from library references. While he had been playing priest, the rakh-woman had been assembling a cartographer's wet dream.

'Any luck?' he asked. Trying not to meet that frigid gaze. Trying not to ask where Tarrant had been, or what he had been doing.

The Hunter walked to where one map lay and crouched by its side; like all his movements this one was fluid, catlike in its grace. 'Three possibilities. You won't like one of them.'

Damien glanced at Hesseth – who had taken her place by the side of that map – and then lowered himself to the floor opposite. 'Go on.'

'There's a region here—' he indicated a point some two hundred miles south of them, nestled between two mountain ranges, '—about which the locals know little. But they speak of monsters there, horrible malformed creatures who trap and then devour unwary travelers. That could be meaningful.'

'Or just a legend.'

'Or just a group of faeborn creatures loosely banded together, not at all related to the ones we seek.' *Trap and devour unwary travelers* could be said of half the things that roamed the night. 'It's worth noting that there are few travelers in that region. Not enough to feed a horde of demons.'

'And ours were a horde,' Damien said softly. Remembering that their enemy had kept a stockpile of humans and rakh underground, milking their souls of enough vitality to sustain an unholy army. 'Doesn't sound right, does it?'

The Hunter shook his head.

'Second possibility?'

Hesseth was closest to that part of the map; she spread it flat with long, gold-furred fingers so that Damien could study it.

'The southern continent,' Tarrant explained. 'Separated from this one by very little water . . . and possibly none at all when the first expedition arrived.' He looked up at Damien. 'There's a settlement down there, Reverend. One that the locals are very much afraid of. That's what the cannon are for. That's why the coastline is guarded. If this region has an enemy, its stronghold is here.' A meticulously manicured finger tapped the map. 'And that may be our enemy as well.'

Damien considered it. 'And the third possibility?'

'You won't like it,' he warned.

'You said that already.'

Tarrant stood. Taking care not to step on any of the maps, he walked to the window. Damien saw his eyes narrow as he Worked the fae, probably in some form of Obscuring. That precaution concluded, he pulled the heavy curtain aside. The city that was spread out before them was well-lit even at midnight.

'The roots of it are here,' he whispered.

'The roots of what?'

'Our enemy's power. Can't you see it?' He nodded toward the city lights. 'It's here. All around us.'

It took him a moment to find his voice. 'You're crazy.'

'I said you wouldn't want to hear it.'

'These people have a more sane society than any I've seen on Erna. They live without fear, without despair. Their life is full of wonder, and their faith is—'

'Is that all you've seen? Faith and prayer, safety and order? I'm disappointed, Reverend Vryce. I thought you'd be a little more discerning than that.' His hand on the curtain tightened as he gazed out into the night. 'There's something wrong here. Something so terribly wrong I can't even put a name to it. But the symptoms are right there in front of you, there for the seeing . . . unless you don't want to. Unless you prefer dreams to reality.' The Hunter turned back to him; the silver gaze was piercing. 'Do you?'

It took effort to keep his voice from resonating with the anger he felt. 'Just because your eyes are more attuned to corruption than mine doesn't mean this land is polluted. Maybe it's you who sees what you want to see . . . *Hunter*.'

If Damien had expected Tarrant to respond with anger – or with any human emotion – he was wrong. The slender fingers released the curtain, which fell back into place. The pale gray eyes fixed on him, their depths cool and confident. 'Ah. So very confident. You must know a lot about this land, to be so quick to defend it. So tell me, Reverend – if you can – what happened to the last three expeditions that were sent here?'

He tried to remember Toshida's exact words, but for some reason they eluded him. 'They never arrived.'

'So. You have bought their propaganda.' He glanced at the rakh-woman. 'Hesseth?'

'Two of them made it,' she said quietly.

'They were slaughtered,' the Hunter informed him. 'Man, woman, and child. The first time only the pagans were killed, and the Church's faithful were allowed to settle here. But that led to problems – social, political – so the next time a ship made it through they killed everyone on board. In the words of an old Earth philosopher, "God will know His own."'

'It's in the library,' Hesseth told Damien. 'They set fire to it while it was still at sea. Any who jumped ship were killed in the water, before they could swim to land.'

'As they would have done to us,' Tarrant assured him. 'That's what Toshida's ship was prepared to do – what it was *sent out to do* – and if you're alive today it's only because you had enough foresight to coach the crew in its lies long before we got here.'

Damien said nothing. His hands clenched silently, then unclenched. Again.

'Shall I guess what you're thinking, Reverend Vryce? *That all happened four hundred years ago. These people are different now.* Maybe so. So let's consider something else.' He walked to where Damien was and crouched down opposite him again; only the map was between them. 'Fact: there's an Order called the Sanctified. You know what they do. But do you know how they purify themselves for doing it? With a vow of chastity, Reverend. For three years, for five years, or for life. Now, another man might applaud that – purity of the body equals purity of the soul – but you've read my writings. You know how destructive it is to build into any religion an assumption that natural, healthful urges are *unclean*. For every Sanctified man in this region there are at least ten who wallow in guilt each time they have an unplanned erection. Is that the kind of emotion you want the fae responding to? Not to mention the repressed energies of the Sanctified themselves.'

'So they made a mistake,' he growled.

'Did they? I wonder. The people who came here from the west had no such tradition. So where did it come from? When did it start?' He leaned forward. 'And the Matria. Haven't you wondered about that? Doesn't it strike you as odd that only women can head the Church here?'

'Why should it?' Hesseth demanded. 'Division of labor according to gender is part of your human heritage. What makes this so significant?'

'First, because the colonists who were chosen to come to this world had no such tradition. Each colony had its own socio-psychological profile, and that was part of ours. Second, because there are real biological differences between men and women, and those *should* serve as a template for any division of labor which develops. It did in my own time, when we resurrected the so-called "traditional" roles as part of the Revivalist experiment. Men competed for the reins of power and women adopted roles of protection and nurturing. That arrangement worked because it was compatible with our biological heritage; this one isn't.'

'Toshida said they were seers,' Damien told him. 'Oracles.'

He shook his head, dismissing the thought. 'Neither clairvoyance nor prophecy is strictly a female venue. No, I see no *natural* cause for this system. And that makes me question its source.'

He gazed down at the map as if remembering; his pale eyes flickered from city to city, all along the eastern coast.

'And then there are the wards,' he said softly. 'Religious symbols marked on every pillar and gate, surrounding every city. Emblems placed on buoys throughout the harbor, so that even the closer ships are protected. They outline a sphere of protection so powerful, so perpetually reinforced by religious fervor, that not even a high-order demon can get by them. I know. I watched several try. No horror that this world has spawned can get into the northern cities, not by any means.' He turned back to Damien. His pale eyes were blazing. 'And yet I can. For me there's no resistance, none at all. As if the wards didn't even acknowledge my existence.' He shook his head tensely. 'In Jaggonath no ward could stop me, but that didn't mean I didn't feel them. Sometimes with the good ones I actually had to unWork them partway to get past. But not here. Never here.'

'Are you sure?' Damien asked.

The Hunter nodded. 'My nature is demonic, Reverend. Plain and simple. And if I didn't struggle every waking moment to maintain my human identity, I would become a demon in fact as well as essence. Yet the power which guards this land doesn't even recognize me as a threat, or make any attempt to keep me out. If so, what else doesn't it recognize?' he demanded. 'And who engineered such a weakness?'

'And why,' Damien muttered.

Tarrant nodded.

'Good God.' He reached up and rubbed his forehead. It was too much to absorb; his head was pounding. 'Is that all?'

'Isn't it enough?' the Hunter asked softly.

Damien looked up at him. 'Is it all?'

Slowly Tarrant shook his head. 'No. There was a child outside Penitencia, chained to a rock as an offering to the monsters of the night. There are children raised in every city for that very purpose: to serve as bait for the faeborn, so that men can destroy whatever comes to feed on their fear. They die very young. Or suffer a fate far worse than death. This one recognized what I was, and what I wanted . . . and welcomed me.'

Damien was silent. He could feel his own hands trembling – with the force of frustration, of rage. Of betrayal. The dream had seemed so perfect . . . What had fouled it? Or *who*?

'Listen to me,' the Hunter said sharply. 'I don't know how all these facts connect, but they do. There's no question of that. And whoever or whatever caused it isn't going to be out in the open, that's certain.'

He forced his eyes to look at the map. 'South, you think?'

Tarrant looked at Hesseth, who nodded. 'Best bet.'

He drew in a deep breath, tried to still the shaking of his hands. *A young girl chained to a rock, bait for demons* . . . 'We need more information. First.'

'*Listen to me.*' Tarrant's words were reinforced with earth-fae, and they adhered themselves to Damien's brain like fire. 'Don't talk to anyone. Anyone! Do you understand? Our enemy is subtle, and his strategy spans centuries. Even men and women who mean well may serve his purpose without knowing it. Isn't that what we're seeing here? Good intentions twisted to an evil purpose?' He stood; dark silk rippled about his calves. 'I let my guard down once in the rakhlands – for less than a second – and endured eight days of burning hell as a result. Our enemy is subtle, Vryce, and that's what makes him so dangerous. If he weren't, don't you think these people would have fought him? Or at least acknowledged his influence?'

'He must know we're here,' the priest muttered. The vision of the chained child was still before his eyes. 'If his influence is as far-reaching as you say—'

'All the more reason to move quickly,' he agreed. 'Since we don't know how far his power extends, or how many people are under his control. Best to move now.'

He walked to the door, carefully avoiding the maps that surrounded it. Before he left, he turned to look at Damien – and something in the priest's expression must have displeased him, because the pale eyes narrowed.

'I killed eight times in the cities,' he said. Nostrils flaring as he spoke, as if he were recalling the scents of the kill. 'Eight women. And each time the wards let me pass by with not even a murmur. You remember that, if you start to have doubts. If Mercia starts to look good again. You ask yourself what kind of power would welcome the Hunter into its stockyards.'

And then he was gone, quickly and silently. Not pausing to work an Obscuring to hide himself, but wrapping the fae about him for that purpose even as the door closed behind him. Damien felt the sudden urge to throw something after him, but the only things at hand were fixtures of the apartment: not his, and far too valuable. At last he saw a shoe peeking out from underneath a couch, that he had kicked off the day before. He grabbed it up and launched it at the door. Hard. It hit with a resounding thwack and slid to the floor, dispelling a small part of his rage. Only a small part.

'Was that because he killed the women?' Hesseth asked. 'Or because he told you about it?'

'Neither.'

He sat on the edge of a couch and rubbed his temples; beneath his fingertips he could feel his blood pounding. 'Because he's right,' he whispered hoarsely. 'God damn him. He's right about all of it.'

II

It was midnight. True midnight, when the forces of dawn and dusk were perfectly balanced.

There was a cold front moving out and a warm front moving in; the turbulent line between the two was just crossing the Five Cities district.

Domina was overhead, Casca low in the east, Prima below the western horizon. In accordance with the complex mathematical dynamics of their positioning – which took into account their mass, gravity, and position relative to the planet – they were just coming into perfect geometric alignment.

The upper current in the Straits of Preservation had been flowing east all night. Now it was still, preparing to flow to the west.

Water condensed in the clouds overhead, transforming from vapor to liquid.

Unseen, unfelt, the Diangelo Fault moved slightly.

The wind began to shift.

—And power shot out across the land, a power born not of moonlight or earthquakes or the motion of the sea, but of the combination of all those things and a thousand, a million more. A power which was as much a part of Erna as her tides, her seasons, her rhythms of day and night. A power which lanced out in gleaming strands across the length and breadth of the continent, shimmering rainbow threads connecting city with city – cathedral with cathedral—

Matria with Matria.

In the far north, where the Teachers waited, one mind reached out to touch the fragile strands. The rainbow web shivered as its message was read, analyzed, considered.

Tides shifted. Power surged across the continent in waves, like bands of spectral light.

The mind reached out again. Its message, a consensus, was placed in the flickering web.

And then the moment passed. The moons moved out of alignment. The wind held steady. Dawn gained in dominance over dusk, and rain began to fall. The upper current in the Straits of Preservation flowed west, as it would until morning.

The power dispersed as quickly as it had appeared, so that no sign of it remained. Whatever message it had carried was likewise dispersed into the night, swallowed by the shadows of oblivion. But not before it had reached its destination. Not before its meaning had been deciphered.

'I understand,' Mercia's Matria whispered. 'Yes. I understand exactly.'

And she promised, 'First thing in the morning, I'll take care of them.'

12

He couldn't bring himself to tell Captain Rozca the truth. Couldn't bring himself to take that newborn faith, so very precious, so utterly fragile, and make it bear the weight of his foreboding. And why should he? The captain had made his covenant with an ideal, with a God, not with any one city or socio-political schema. Let him dream on a little longer in his innocence, Damien decided. Let him taste as much of the sweetness as he could, before the bitter undercurrents of this paradoxical land rose to the surface and fouled his perspective.

He did tell him other things. All of it. He couldn't expect the man to take a risk for him without knowing what the stakes were; he couldn't expect him to be convincing in his assigned role without being thoroughly grounded in the details of Damien's quest. Rozca took it all calmly enough, asking questions only when a turn of phrase was unclear to him; otherwise he absorbed the tale of rakh and demons, torture and vengeance, much as he might any seafaring story told over tankards of ale in a cliffside tavern. He'd heard crazier tales before, he told Damien, though never before had he been thrust into the middle of one. He seemed to handle it well enough. Maybe a man who had devoted his life to dodging smashers and cruising volcanic rifts had partaken enough of life's risks to put this one, however deadly, in its context.

It was all very reassuring for Damien. And when he asked the captain what he had come to ask – the reason he had been up at the break of dawn to make his way down to the harbor, and out to the *Glory* – the captain simply nodded and said it would be no problem. Or it would be a problem, sure enough, but he figured he could handle it. And he grinned, in a manner that left no doubt that Lio Rozca was up to any challenge this foreign shore could throw at him.

I hope so, Damien thought grimly. Praying that the man's courage wouldn't have to be tested too soon.

A tug had brought the priest out to the ship; a rowboat of the *Glory,* manned by a yawning crewman, took him back. At this hour there was business aplenty in the harbor – the minor tide would be turning in an hour, with Domina's tide soon to follow – but the crowd of tourists and newsmongers who so often clogged the port was blissfully absent. Everyone working in dawn's early light had his or her own business to take care of, which meant that as Damien wended his way through the crowds along the shore he could be fairly certain of remaining unobserved. Which was good. Reassuring. And he needed all the reassurance he could get right now.

The scene with Tarrant the night before had shaken him badly. He had hardly slept at all, and what little sleep he had managed to snatch in bits and pieces was riddled with fragments of nightmares, all too familiar in their tenor. It wasn't what Tarrant had said, or even the way he had said it. It was Damien's sudden acknowledgment of how careless he had been. How trusting. It was the sudden revelation of how greatly he had put them all at risk by focusing on his religious rapture rather than on the mission at hand. Not that he would have traded those precious moments for anything in the world, he thought. They were part of who he was now, a core of faith for him to draw on. But he should have kept his eyes open. He should have been asking questions. He should have done . . . oh, so many things.

No regretting it now. He could only hope that it wasn't too late. Five days had passed since their quarantine had been lifted, which was a very short time in the scheme of things. Or long enough to mobilize an army, if soldiers had been ready and waiting . . .

He had done the best he could, given his sleepless state. When the first light of dawn showed over the mountains, he had gone down to the harbor to find Rozca. Now that part of his plan was taken care of, and he felt marginally safer. Later he would talk to Mels and Tyria Lester and see if they would agree to help him – a far less risky role than the one the captain would be playing, but equally important – and then, if all went well, Damien and his companions would be covered. They could leave Mercia on a moment's notice without anyone being the wiser, and any pursuit which sought them out would inevitably be delayed.

Paranoia in action, he thought. The only reasonable course.

Tarrant would have been proud of him.

It was still early morning when he made his way back to the Regent's Manor. He eschewed the more obvious route for one that circled around to the west, through the farmer's market. Wagons full of fish and game and freshly plucked poultry had been there since first light, and already the restauranteurs and specialty buyers of Mercia's better districts were picking their way through the heaps of slaughtered flesh, squeezing and sniffing and doing God knows what else to ascertain the value of their wares. The air was thick with the smell of brine and a sweet undercurrent of blood, and for a moment Damien found himself back in the rakhene mountains, a cup of Ciani's blood in his hand. Knee-deep in ice and snow, feeding blood to the Hunter. He shook his head, banishing the memory with effort. He would have been dead if not for Tarrant, several times over. And vice versa. It was a good thing to remember as they prepared to plunge into this unknown land, with nothing but faith and a tenuous alliance to sustain them.

The market road took him around the back way, so that he approached the Manor from behind. Perhaps if he had come around the front he would simply have entered the great hall, so lost in his musings that he would fail to notice subtle differences around him. Perhaps. But something about the rear walk prodded his attention toward the building and its guards, and what he saw made him stop for a moment, uncertain.

Something was different.

He stepped into the shadow of a tree, wondering why he couldn't put a finger on what it was that bothered him. *Paranoia in action* he chided himself, but the feeling of *wrongness* refused to go away. *It's not paranoia if they're really out to get you.* He studied the grounds, the building itself, the guards who were stationed by the gate—

The guards.

He felt his heart skip a beat. The guards, their uniforms . . . he tried to remember what they had been wearing when he left the Manor. Red fitted tunic, sword just so, insignia of rank . . .

Insignia of rank.

He couldn't remember exactly what it was before. He had never looked that closely. But this was surely different: more ornate, more elaborate. As if the guards who now watched the Manor's gate were from the same source as the others, but of a considerably higher rank.

The others had been the Regent's private guard. There was only one rank any higher than that. And only one reason he could think of, short of revolution, why the Matria's elite soldiers would now be guarding this building.

Shit.

He stepped back onto the pathway, careful not to move too quickly. Careful to let his own pace match that of the people around him, brisk but unhurried. He let the currents of humanity carry him away from the building, until the gleaming white walls were out of sight. Only then did he dare to stop. Only then did he try to think.

Everything he had seen and heard in this place indicated that Toshida and his Matria were in perfect accord, personally and politically. Whatever private bitterness the man might harbor about the limits of his rank, Damien gathered it had never been expressed openly. Indeed, the man had all but sworn him to silence on the matter. So why would the Matria send in her own guards to take the place of his? What service would she require that the Regent could not – or would not – fulfill?

The more he thought about that the less he liked his conclusions. He remembered Tarrant's accusations, some of them aimed at this Matriarchy. Was it possible that Mercia's leader was somehow allied with their enemy? Certainly Tarrant had believed that to be possible. If so, and if her guards had come at the break of dawn to surround the Regent's Manor ...

Where was Hesseth? he wondered suddenly. Panic flaring suddenly in his gut, at the thought that she might have been taken prisoner. Damn it, how could he find out?

He took a deep breath, and tried to think clearly. Weighing his options. At last he turned about and began to walk again, this time toward the east.

There was no true wilderness available to him, not within the city walls. And there was no other privacy he could have, unless he dared to rent a room in some hotel or hostel. But that meant having to show his identification, which entailed its own special risk. He decided against it. There were several parks in the city, replete with trees and myriad garden paths, and if he headed toward the largest one he stood a good chance of finding some green little nook that would shield him from prying eyes.

He was in luck. The park was nearly deserted, with but a few hardy joggers and one nursemaid with a gaggle of children to avoid. He chose a lesser path whose loose, rocky surface would be inhospitable to sportsmen and followed it until all other roads were lost from sight, whereupon he was fairly certain that no one would disturb him.

Carefully he lowered himself to his knees, and tried to make himself relax. A short prayer served to focus his consciousness, and a simple Working to summon his Sight. Now he could see the earth-fae as it flowed about him, a power as of yet untamed by any human will. It was flowing west, which was hardly ideal; he would have to work against the current to get any information from the Manor. But he had done that kind of thing before, under far worse conditions than this. He let the words of a Knowing shape themselves upon his lips, traced its unlocking patterns with his mind's inner eye, and saw the fae begin to gather in response. Forming a picture that only he could see, sounds and sights and meanings placed within his mind by the rich power of the earth.

Hesseth, he prompted it. *Where?*

He saw her awakened at dawn by the sound of movement within the Manor. Saw the almost animal alertness with which she moved, clawed hands grabbing up a few valuable items and wrapping them in a blanket, which she then belted to her person. There were voices in the corridor now, very close, very wrong. He could feel her tension building, could smell her fear as she grabbed up a pile of folded maps and tucked those into her belt as well. Balancing need against risk as the voices drew ever closer. Mere whispers, really. Damien wondered if a human ear could have heard them. Perhaps they considered themselves safe from discovery, not knowing of his sorcery or her rakhene senses. Too late now. She pushed upon the piercedwork window and with feline agility leapt up to the sill; even as her door was thrust open, she dropped down beneath the window, strong claws digging deep into the thick wood frame.

Voices in her room, speaking in foreign accents. He heard her breathing softly, was aware of her scanning the side of the building for danger. Nothing yet. With care she lowered herself, sharp claws biting into whatever wooden fixtures were within reach. Once she had to tuck herself behind a column as a guard passed by beneath, but no one thought to look up at the building itself. Damien watched as she gained the ground, scaled a broad tree by the gate, navigated branches that no human could have traversed to make her way across the iron fence, and from there, via trees, gained the ground once more . . .

He felt something unknot inside him, to know that she had gotten away from them safely. If the forces of the Matria were indeed being mobilized against them, then they were in serious trouble. Thank God Tarrant had upset him the night before, so that he'd been unable to sleep. Thank God he'd been gone before first light, so that the soldiers had missed him.

He took a minute to breathe deeply, willing his panic to subside. It was all right now. The Matria didn't know about his sorcery or Hesseth's skills, which gave them an initial advantage. By the time she learned to compensate, Rozca would make his move, and that should distract them for just long enough . . . he felt the pieces of his plan coming together like fragments of a jigsaw puzzle, forced their shapes into alignment. First he had to find Hesseth. Then he had to finish what he had started. Then, when all his preparations were complete, when he had compensated at least in part for his carelessness in the five days preceding . . .

It was time to get the hell out of here.

Toshida didn't like being roused at daybreak by the Matria's guard. He didn't like finding out that his own men had been dismissed, to make way for hers. Even less did he like being summoned to her presence within minutes of awakening, so that the time he might have spent composing himself and preparing for an audience was instead spent trekking to her chambers in the presence of four of her guards.

At least she didn't keep him waiting. *Thank heaven for small favors,* he thought, as one of her attendants ushered him into her audience chamber. He tried to compose himself so that his anger wasn't visible; years of practice in that art permitted him perfect control over his countenance, so that only the emotions he wished to communicate were mirrored in his expression. Not rage. Not rank indignation. Not all the things he truly felt.

'Your Holiness,' he greeted her. Bowing ever so slightly. Kissing her hand with less than perfect enthusiasm. Let her see in this small way that she had insulted him. Let her see that this time she had gone too far.

If she noticed the subtle signs of his displeasure, she made no sign of it. 'You have two guests in your Manor,' she told him. 'The priest from the western ship, and his *Sanctified*.' She spoke the word in a manner which made it clear she did not consider the title justified. 'I want them.'

'They're guests of the city,' he said evenly. And then added, ever so quietly, '*My* guests.'

She dismissed his words with a wave of her hand. 'They pose a danger to us, my lord Regent, and therefore they must be taken into custody. I'm sure you can understand the necessity of that.'

He kept his voice calm, his face carefully neutral. It wasn't easy. 'What I understand is that you've already gone after them, your Holiness. Your guards have taken over my home and office; are you telling me you need my permission before going any further? A curious time to be drawing that distinction.'

'We did what was necessary,' she said curtly. 'No insult was intended. We had to move quickly so as not to alarm them.'

'In which I assume you succeeded?'

Uncharacteristically, she hesitated. 'No,' she said at last. 'Both of them were out when my people arrived. I was hoping you knew where they might be.'

'They're free to come and go as they please,' he reminded her. 'Or were, until this morning. Nor did they usually inform me of their plans.' *They were guests, not prisoners.* He felt anger surfacing; he did his best to fight it back. 'I'm afraid I can't help you.'

For a long moment she stared at him. He expected to feel the dizziness he associated with her power, but for once he was spared that ordeal. 'All right,' she said at last. 'Their possessions are still in the Manor, which means they'll most likely come back there. I want them apprehended. You ken? Your guards or mine, as long as they're taken.'

'On what legal pretext?' he asked calmly.

Her eyes narrowed to amber slits. 'A vision from God, Andir. A revelation. These people are evil, and they mean us great harm. They must be arrested immediately, so that the Matrias can deal with them. Pick whatever law you want to support your action, as long as you take them. *Soon.* That is the Will of the Lord. I—'

She was interrupted by a gentle rapping on the door. 'Yes? What is it?'

The attendant entered the room. 'Begging your Holiness' pardon, this message just came.' He stepped forward and handed a folded square of paper to her, then bowed deeply as he exited. She took it and unfolded it quickly; Toshida made out the scrawl of hurried writing on its face.

Her expression of anger was more a hiss than a curse. 'Two sailors from the *Golden Glory* came to the Manor to collect the priest's and the woman's possessions. They claimed to know nothing of their whereabouts, were merely responding to instructions given some time ago. The guards, having no orders to the contrary, let them proceed.' She looked up at Toshida. 'If they're on that ship, I want them. If they're not on it yet, then take them when they get there. Ken verda?'

He bowed ever so slightly. A minimal gesture. 'As you command, your Holiness.'

'I know this is an unusual order, Andir. But these are unusual circumstances. We took a chance letting the foreigners land here, and perhaps we moved too quickly.' *Perhaps you moved too quickly,* was the unspoken criticism. *It was your decision to let them live.* 'Just get those two into custody, whatever it takes. We can work out the legalities of it later, when they're no longer capable of harming us. Free, they threaten . . . *everything.*'

'Yes, Matria.' His tone was humble, but inside his thoughts were seething. *A Sanctified woman and a priest. What harm could they possibly do? Unless you fear the knowledge they bring with them, of places where leadership is based on deeds, not visions. Is that it? Is it not them that you fear, but what they may do to your people? What they may awaken in me?*

'As you command,' he told her. Because there was nothing else to say, no other way to proceed. For now, his duty was to serve her will. Even when he didn't fully understand it. Even when he might not agree.

For now.

The captain of the *Golden Glory* was annotating his log when the crewman came to him.

'He's here,' the man said simply.

He closed the leather-bound book and locked it. 'Toshida?'

The sailor nodded.

With a sigh he rose up, muttering a prayer to his new-found God. Not that this one was likely to help him; wasn't that the whole point? He noted with some curiosity, as he left the wheelhouse, that it didn't really bother him. In fact, it was oddly reassuring to think that his fate was totally – and permanently – in his control.

Toshida was waiting by the boarding ladder, just as Damien had said he would be. Whatever guards or aides-de-camp he might have brought with him were still down in the boat, out of sight and hearing. That was good. Men who had to save face in front of their inferiors were a lot more dangerous.

Rozca made sure that none of his own people were nearby, then greeted the Lord Regent. 'Your Eminence. This is an honor. What can I do for you?'

'I'm looking for two people. I believe they may be on board.'

'Two of my passengers? Or crew?'

'A priest named Damien Vryce. And a Sanctified woman who accompanies him. Have you seen them?'

Then again, Rozca thought, *sometimes it's nice to have a god help out. Just to smooth things over a bit.*

A man could get himself killed on his own.

'No,' he said at last. Committing himself. Knowing what the result would be. 'No, I haven't.'

'But you sent for their things. Verda?'

He shrugged. 'His Reverence asked me to. Said they might want to travel. I didn't ask for details.'

'So you're expecting them.'

He shrugged again.

He could feel the anger rising from the man, like heat off a sun-baked sidewalk. 'Yes or no, Captain Rozca.'

'Lord Regent. With all due respect, Father Vryce and his friends are free to come and go as they please. Without reporting to you, me, or anyone else. Isn't that the case?'

'Yes or no, Captain Rozca.'

He met the man's gaze head-on, coarse bravado versus polished stubbornness. A lifetime at sea and in coastal barrooms had taught him how to stare a man into the dirt, and he applied that skill now with relish.

'Sorry,' he said curtly. 'Can't help you.'

'You're making a serious mistake,' Toshida warned.

'Maybe,' Rozca agreed, shifting his weight from one leg to the other. 'But it's my right to make it.'

'I could search the ship, verda? I'd get my answer then.'

Rozca spat on the deck; not because he felt the need to, but because it seemed an appropriate gesture. 'Yeah. You go ahead and do that. But before you start, make sure I get a copy of your Writ of Search and Seizure – that is the right document, isn't it? – because now that we have visas proper we're subject to all your laws, aren't we? Including protection of privacy. At least that's how I understand it.' He paused. 'And if I remember your constitution aright, not even the Lord Regent of the Five Cities is above the law of the land. Verda?'

The narrowed eyes fixed on him, dark with fury. It might have driven back a lesser man, but Rozca stood his ground. Praying, as he did so, that Damien had guessed right about their legal system. If not . . . well, then they were all in really deep shit now. Starting with him.

At last the Regent snapped, 'I'll be back.' And without further word he lowered himself down over the side, and onto the boarding ladder.

Rozca felt himself breathe a sigh of relief as he watched the man descend to his waiting boat. Not that it was over yet, but at least the worst part was done with. The part he had dreaded the most.

When the small boat was safely in the distance, he turned to look for his pilot and first mate, only to discover that they were already beside him. Waiting.

He turned to Tor first. 'Crew on board?'

The first mate nodded.

'Supplies?'

'Believe so. Enough for a month at least, what with no passengers on board. I'll check.'

'Do that.' He turned to Rasya. 'You find out the range?'

'Mercia claims ten miles,' she responded. 'After that it's free water.'

'Then I want us eleven miles out, as fast as we can get there. Faster than that man can dig up a writ and get back to us. You understand?' She nodded. 'You know what's riding on it.' Again she nodded.

'All right, then. We'll sail the kind of route we would if we had two people on board who needed to go south, very quickly and very quietly. Understood?' Rasya nodded. The first mate muttered, 'Aye, sir.'

He gestured a dismissal and the two went off to work. The thought of setting out to sea again was not unwelcome to any of them; he only wished the decision had been made under better circumstances.

With a sigh he turned back toward the shore and leaned against the ship's rail. 'All right, Vryce,' he muttered. 'There it is. What you wanted.' He sighed again, deeply. 'I just hope you know what the vulk you're doing.'

Mels Lester wasn't a particularly brave man. If asked to describe himself, he probably would have come up with a list of adjectives that included *nervous, hesitant,* and even *downright cowardly*. But when a friend asked you to do something and said that it was a matter of life or death – and when your sister said she'd lock up the liquor cabinet and smash any bottle you brought into the house if you didn't help him out – well, then, you just did it. And tried really hard not to think about the consequences.

Thus it was that he found himself at the city gate along with Tyria and eight horses, showing his papers to the guard there and praying that no one would look too closely at what they were carrying or how they were carrying it. Not that a local would know the difference. Mercia's pack animals were too small for riding, so how would they know that the heavy leather saddles strapped to one of the horses didn't have to be resting on four woolen blankets? And maybe they wouldn't notice that the windbreaker Mels was wearing was over a considerably heavier jacket, and that over a thick woolen sweater. (All assuming the sweat rolling down his face didn't give him away). As for Tyria, she had a pack slung across her back that was big enough to be carrying not only the gear they needed, but a month's worth of camping supplies as well. Add to that a staff here, a hunting knife there, and it was nothing short of a miracle that the guards didn't stop them. But Father Vryce had said they wouldn't, and after all he was a priest . . . so maybe it was a miracle after all.

'You see?' Tyria whispered as they led the horses through the gate. 'That was all right.'

So far, he thought unhappily. At least the Regent hadn't come. He had sent Toshida a note to come join them, inviting him to see the horses put through their paces. He had been sure the Regent would be here, despite Damien's assurance that the man would have 'other things to do.' And while Damien could possibly have kept up a pretense in the face of such a man, Mels would surely have folded. So thank God the Regent had been busy.

They set up a temporary camp just out of sight of the city gate, far enough from the main road that few travelers would notice them. There he was able to disrobe at last, piling his excess garments alongside Tyria's collection of smuggled bits and their own equestrian equipment. They took turns then, one of them walking several horses while the other stood guard over the supplies. The animals were still stiff from their travels, and it took a long while for the natural grace of their gait to return to them; Mels judged it would be some time before they were ready for a more demanding workout. Still, it was good to see them out here, and he took comfort in the healthy sheen of their coats, their obvious pleasure in being outdoors at last. Soon enough their strength would come back to them, and the thought of what a man like the Regent would pay once he saw the animals galloping full out was enough to make his head spin.

He had taken his second turn out in the fields when Tyria said to him, 'Come on. It's time.' And she nodded toward the west, where the sun was rapidly setting.

They bundled the clothing and extra provisions on three of the horses: a sleek black creature with crescent-shaped hooves whom Mels coveted desperately (but Gerald Tarrant had refused to sell), a dun-colored mare whose mane extended down exotically about her shoulders, and a powerful dappled gelding with massive triple hooves and a thick, coarse coat.

Between the city and the terraced farms there was a narrow road, and they followed this southward until they came to a place where trees obscured their view of the city. There they rested, and permitted the horses to take water from the narrow stream paralleling their path.

'Maybe they won't come,' Mels worried.

'Shhh.'

The light surrounding them began to fade, shadows lengthening about the trees. Soon the creatures of the night would come out. Soon the gates of the city would be locked. Hell, where *were* they?

And then there was a rustling behind them and Hesseth stepped out. Not Hesseth as they had seen her in Mercia, all hidden behind long robes and mock-human mannerisms, but Hesseth as she had traveled in the west: tightly clad in layers that fit her like a second skin, colored like the earth that surrounded her. Her eyes were black, wide open to the coming night; her ears, tip-tufted, pricked forward as she saw the horses.

'I'll take them,' she said, and she gathered up the reins of the three laden mounts.

'We brought what we could,' Tyria told her. 'Damien said not to go near your own stuff, or ask anyone else about supplies, so we had to guess a lot . . .'

'You brought the horses, which was the most important thing. We couldn't have gotten near them without being seen.'

'Why'd you have to sneak out?' Mels demanded. 'What happened?'

The rakh-woman looked at him, then shook her head. 'The less you know, the better off you'll be.'

'Damien said that,' Tyria agreed.

'Where is he?' Mels asked.

'Checking out the currents,' she said smoothly. 'He'll be here soon.' A merciful lie. She didn't want to tell them how badly shaken Damien was by the events of that day. Oh, he had held himself together long enough to Locate Hesseth, and had mastered enough fae to keep the two of them Obscured while they climbed the city's circumference wall. But afterward? It was like a dark cloud had descended on him. Mourning for the corruption of his faith, perhaps.

Or guilt over having waited so long to prepare for flight. Maybe both at once, she thought; humans were like that.

She glanced back over her shoulder, toward the distant city gate. 'They'll have changed the guard by now. No one should notice that you're coming back with fewer horses than you left with, or minus some supplies.' She paused. 'We can't thank you enough.'

'We stand to make a fortune here,' Tyria said frankly. 'That's Damien's doing. Tell him thanks from us.'

'And good luck,' Mels added. 'Wherever you're going.'

If that was a hint for more information, it went unnoticed. 'Thanks,' Hesseth said simply. Offering nothing more. It was safer for all of them that way.

As Mels and Tyria led their horses back toward the city gate, Hesseth went over the situation in her own mind. The city's research facilities were lost to them now. Any day the Matria might see through their little deceit and launch a pursuit in earnest, which could involve other cities and even the southern Protectorates. They had some supplies – thanks to Mels and Tyria – but most of the bits and pieces that Damien had packed for traveling were somewhere between the Manor and the *Golden Glory*. The priest was in a dour mood. Tarrant was clearly on edge about something. And it was a good bet that their enemy knew they were here.

'Good luck?' she whispered, with a bitter laugh. 'Assst! We're going to need it.'

13

Jenseny ran. South at first, because she figured they wouldn't be as quick to search for her there. North were the farms, the flatlands, all gentle terrain and shallow rivers, a far more welcoming land than that which she had chosen. She imagined they would be searching for her there, expecting that a child, like water, would naturally flow toward the point of least resistance. South were the mountains, harshly forested, a tangle of cliffs and trees covered over in places with matted vines that clung to the canopy and blanketed the landscape in half-lit gloom. But there were few faeborn creatures in the great woods – most preferred to hang about the northern cities in the hopes of catching unwary travelers, or of breaching the warded walls through sheer force of numbers – and she was more than a little afraid of the sunlight anyway, so the southern woods were good enough for her. Good enough for now.

There were other Protectorates to the south, she knew, strung out like beacon lamps at intervals along the rocky shore. At first she thought she might find sanctuary in one of them, but the concept of dealing with strangers – any strangers – chilled her to the core. In her newborn terror it seemed that such men were not individuals, but mere fragments of a greater whole which had cast her out, condemned her, and now sentenced her father to die a gruesome death for having dared to shelter her. They were Other, and she was . . .

Alone.

So alone.

She dreamt of her father. Some nights the dreams were good, bits of their life together replayed in all its loving intensity. But waking up from those dreams was a little bit like dying, because it meant rediscovering that he wasn't there, he wasn't going to be there, not now and not ever again. More often the dreams themselves were bad. Some were nightmares proper, gruesome replays of her confrontation, distorted imaginings of what his death must have been like. Then there were others, even more frightening – dreams in which her father was his normal self but she was not, dreams in which she screamed at him, screamed at him for leaving her and for not being there for her and for daring to die when she needed him so badly, oh so very badly . . . Those were the dreams that upset her the most, and she lay afterward on the damp loam shivering with guilt and shame, feeling like she had somehow betrayed his love without quite knowing how.

Sometimes the creatures of the night would come after her. She was usually aware of their approach long before she could actually see them, though she couldn't have said how she managed that.

Maybe it was the Light. It didn't make the truth visible exactly, not like it had with her father's killer, but sometimes when the air lit up really brightly with its colors she would get a crawling sensation up along her spine, and then she knew that something was coming. Then she would run and run and pray (to the gods of this world, which her father said was a safe prayer) that it would go find some other prey, forget about her, not notice if she stopped to hide ... and as often as not it did. Maybe the Light did that, too. It had never been more than a diversion to her, something that made the voices around her seem stronger and all the colors brighter, but maybe here in the Outside it was a more active force.

She should have asked her father about that while she had the chance.

She should have asked him so many things ...

She slept during the day because she knew that was the safest time to let her guard down, and tried to find a cave or a crevice or some other sheltered space to do it in. Once she had tried making a lean-to out of her blanket and some fallen branches – her father had taught her how – but the noise from the sunlight was so terrible that she couldn't sleep, not even with her head wrapped up tightly in her jacket. Why hadn't he warned her about that? He had tried so hard to make her ready in case she had to go Outside someday, why hadn't he ever told her that the sun came into the sky at dawn with a crash like a thousand cymbals being slammed together all at once, that the slender beams which poked down through the canopy at noontime struck the ground with such explosive force that when she lay on the ground she could feel it shake beneath her? Was it possible that he'd never heard these things himself? Like he'd never heard so many other things that were likewise a part of her world?

Oh, dad. She mourned for his limitations even as she mourned the loss of his life, mourned the barriers that had been between them even when they were closest. There was always so much he couldn't see, couldn't hear, couldn't feel ...

But you loved me. You always loved me. So much ...

Why couldn't I have saved you?

Day passed slowly into night and back again, over and over,

exhausting and endless hours filled with a bleak despair. Once when the Light was strongest (it had cracked across the valley like a bolt of cloud-to-cloud lightning, rainbow colors flashing in the clear night air) she had dared to ask the unaskable, namely if the creature that had killed her father was actively trying to find her. The way she figured it, maybe since the Light would help her see and hear so many other things it would help her with that, too. She held her breath, waiting. And suddenly it seemed to her that the woods were very still, very quiet, oh so empty . . . like nothing big was moving except for her. Then the Light was gone, and she was left wondering if she'd gotten her answer or not. Or whether it was just her own loneliness reflected back at her, like in some giant mirror that reflected not your face but the essence of your soul.

She needed her father. Or someone. Anyone. As long as it was someone she could trust. But who was that? Members of the Church would kill her on sight, and the creature who had murdered her father must have allies . . . With sudden horror she realized that if they could eat her father and take his place, they could probably do that with anyone – which meant that *anybody* might be one of theirs. Even her old nurse. Even the other Protectors. All eaten and replaced, with . . . *them*.

Shivering, she fell to the ground and wrapped her arms about her knees. Her pants were threadbare, ripped by thorns and rough bark and too many days of sleeping on the ground; her shirt was so muddied and dusted with clay that it nearly matched her skin. Suddenly the dirt and the scratches and the tiredness and the fear were all too much for her, and she lowered her head into her arms and sobbed helplessly, wishing it would just end somehow. Wishing her father hadn't raised her to always keep on fighting, because you never knew (he used to tell her) how the future might be a better place, so long as you got there to see it. Only now she couldn't imagine any better future, couldn't envision anything but more of the same forever and ever, running and hiding and forcing herself to eat berries from the brush even though she could hear them screaming as she pulled them loose . . . and being alone. Utterly. Now, and forever.

Tears weren't enough, but they were all she had. *Think of them as prayers,* her father had once told her. That was back when her mother died. *Think of every tear which falls as a message to your mother, wherever she is, that you love her very, very much.* Because people couldn't cross into the land of the dead without being dead themselves, he explained, but prayers and love could make the crossing. She always thought of that when she cried, even when it was for some other reason. So that something in her tears was always good, no matter how upset she was.

There was nothing good now. Only a loneliness so terrible that it drained her of the last of her strength, a feeling of helplessness – and hopelessness – so absolute that she didn't see how she was going to survive the next hour, much less make it through the next few days. Why did it matter, anyway? What future was there for her? Why had her father invested so much time and energy into seeing that she could take care of herself, when in fact the best she had to look forward to was a quasi-animal existence, homeless and companionless and living off berries until the snow came and there were no more of those, and then it would be freezing cold and there would be no food unless she hunted and no one at all to be with her, no one to help keep her going . . .

I want you, dad. She prayed it desperately in her heart. She whispered it into the night. *I need you. Come back to me. Please.*

There was no answer. No one came.

Given the nature of Erna, that was probably fortunate.

She was sleeping when the Light came, so it invaded her dreams. Rainbow filaments that dissolved her current fantasy and drew her high, high up, so that she was looking down onto the mountains like a bird might. There was her own body, sheltered under a granite overhang, jacket balled up over her ears to cut out the noise of day. There was the crevasse that had turned her aside from her chosen route, deep and ragged and filled with shadows. And there, in the distance—

She awoke. Suddenly. The vision was still with her, framed by shimmering filaments.

People.

People.

She should get up. She should greet them. No, she should hide. They could be enemies. They could be *the* enemy. They could be . . .

But they weren't.

They were children.

The vision was fading now, along with the Light; she struggled to maintain it. Five, six, seven children – no, even more than that – she couldn't see how old they were, the vision was fading too fast, damn damn *damn!* She sobbed in frustration as it faded out entirely, her hands shaking.

Children.

The enemy? No. That thing had killed her father because he was *important;* on some visceral level she understood that. It wouldn't want mere children. They must be from some nearby city, or maybe a Protectorate . . .

Only there weren't any of those near here. She knew that.

So who were they? Where were they from?

Shivering, she waited. Terrified of meeting them. Terrified that they might pass her by. The loneliness in her was screaming so loudly she was amazed they couldn't hear it . . . or maybe they could. Maybe that was why they were coming for her.

Children. Like her. They wouldn't hurt her, would they?

There was a sound above her, farther up the hillside. She dared to peek out from under her shelter. And then she stepped out, there in front of them, and let her jacket fall. No shelter now. No safety. Only a terrible need, and the barest ray of hope inside her. More than she had felt in days.

There were twelve of them, arrayed along the hillside. The oldest few were armed with crude spears and leather-hilted knives, and some carried bows across their backs. The youngest only had knives. All were dressed in a motley assortment of garments, some clearly woven in the fashionable cities, some crudely cut from untanned skins by less experienced hands. Rought-cut fringes and tiny shell ornaments adorned every edge, and here and there some dye had been painted across a shirt or pants leg in coarse zigzag patterns. It took no trick of the Light to see that though many of them had come from well-off homes, they had been on their own for some time now.

The tallest among them – a pale boy with dark straggly hair – held out his hand toward her. An offer. A welcome.

She started forward toward them, trying to ignore the painful cymbal-crash of sunlight about her feet. The pale boy nodded encouragement. A few of the younger ones grinned openly. Though she couldn't hear their words of welcome – the sunlight's noise was too loud, their words were lost in the chaos of it – she saw in their expressions that they were glad to have found her. Almost as glad as she was to be found.

And she knew, then and there, that it was going to be all right. *Everything* was going to be all right.

She climbed up the hillside to join them.

The Light wasn't strong again for nearly two days. So she couldn't see what they really were, not until then.

By then it was too late to run.

VALLEY OF MISTS

14

The Hunter didn't join them right after sunset. He didn't join them after Coreset either, though the setting of the luminous galactic center took place more than two hours after the sun was gone. A bad omen, Damien thought. But what could they do?

They had traveled a few miles along the rock-lined gully in which Mels and Tyria had found Hesseth. It was hard going, what with the loose ground and a stream they sometimes had to wade through, but it seemed to be the only path available. In this region all the comfortable terrain had been claimed by the cities or the farms; land that would favor fugitives was by definition unpleasant. Damien cursed as he pried the third stone from between his horse's hoofed toes, knowing even as he did so that he was being unfair. They should be grateful for the scraggly trees that sheltered them, and for the landscape that had dropped them below the eye level of any casual observer. And they should be doubly grateful that none of the demons who clustered about the city's gates had taken notice of them. Yet.

They finally made camp during Coreset. The process was not one of pitching tents and tending a fire as much as going through the assorted bits and pieces that the Lester siblings had brought them and seeing what they had. The collection included a good bit of blanketry and warm clothing, an assortment of knives and small tools, rope, some food, a few cooking aids, and first aid supplies. Damien blessed them for the first aid; he hadn't thought to mention it. The food consisted of the kind of things noncampers might purchase for a camping expedition – mostly sugared snacks and mixes for soups – but there was some dried meat and cheese and a flat, hard bread that promised to travel well, as well as several pounds of feed for the horses. *Could have been worse,* he thought, repacking it. *Could have been much worse.*

They lit a very small fire and heated some water, while he scanned the skies for any shape that might be Tarrant. But the same twisted trees that gave them partial cover also hid most of the night sky, and at last he gave it up.

'You think they'll come after us?' Hesseth asked.

He broke open a package of crackers – *Honey Ginger Nugrams,* the wrapper said – and handed one to her. They were chewy and sweet, the kind of thing good parents wouldn't let their kids eat too often. He had planned to put cheese on top of his, but the taste dissuaded him. 'I think we'd know it by now if they did,' he answered. 'We're not that far from the city gates, and there weren't a lot of paths to choose from. If they look this way, they'll find us.'

'Would they leave the city after sunset?' she wondered aloud.

'Let's hope not.'

They'd have to move quickly in the morning, just in case the Matria's hordes did indeed come after them. Their horses would be an advantage in the long run, but only on open ground, and only after they had worked the stiffness out of their legs. Damien wondered how long it would be before Toshida had a mount of his own and learned how to ride it. Not long at all, he suspected. Not nearly long enough. If he decided to come after the fugitives himself, it could be a close pursuit. They needed open ground in the very near future if they were to make the most of their current advantage.

And then Hesseth looked up sharply at the sky. Her soft hiss was one that Damien had come to associate with sudden alertness; his hand went to his sword as he followed her gaze. For a moment he saw nothing. Then the broad sweep of a predatory wing blacked out a line of stars, and he felt his own breath catch. Something with very large wings was circling overhead, just above the tops of the trees. The form was familiar, but he didn't relax his guard. Nor would he until the Hunter – if that was indeed who it was – proved his true identity.

The great bird circled twice more, as if surveying the surrounding land, and then swooped down into the gully. For lack of more suitable turf it came down in the water, its broad wings nearly touching the two stony banks. Something was in its talons, Damien observed, soft white feathers in the grip of crimson claws, but it was thrust underwater too quickly for him to make out what it was.

Coldfire blossomed in the stream bed. It was the first time Damien had seen the Hunter transform in water, and it was well worth the vision; ice speared out from the point of contact with a suddenness that was audible, crackling and splitting as it expanded against the sides of the narrow gully. Two of the horses, tethered by the bank, whinnied unhappily and pulled at their reins; Tarrant's merely snorted as if to say, *What took you so long?* Blue flames – intense but unilluminating – seared the stream bed with a cold so intense that Damien's breath fogged in the cool spring air, and frost rimmed the scraggly plants closest to the stream.

When the coldfire died, it left Tarrant on hard ice, and he quickly stepped to the shore. Frost shivered from his boots as he climbed to where the two had made camp, and ice crystals glimmered in his soft brown hair. It might be early spring in the eastern lands, but the Hunter traveled within his own private winter.

He looked at the two of them, at the horses, and at the camp. Damien could see the pale silver eyes taking it all in, sifting through what he saw for the information he wanted. At last he nodded, more to himself than to them. 'You move quickly when you have to.' He threw something to Damien: soft and white and spattered with blood. 'Here. I brought you dinner.'

Damien looked at the dead bird in his hands, dimly aware that Tarrant had thrown another to Hesseth. For a moment all that occurred to him was how utterly unlike Tarrant it was to hunt for them. Then he saw the harness. With reddened, sticky fingers he undid the tiny catch, pulling the leather contraption from the bird's cooling body. Knowing in his gut what it was, what it had to be. Not liking that knowledge one damn bit.

'Carrier birds,' he muttered.

Tarrant nodded. 'They were released at dusk to travel south, and crossed my path soon after. I killed the first because it seemed suspicious; after I realized what it was, I hunted down its companion.' He walked to a dry bit of ground and lowered himself onto it; the thickness of his mantle protected him from the dusty earth. 'I searched for more, but there were none in that portion of the sky. Which doesn't mean that no more were sent.'

'Yeah,' Damien muttered, pulling the message vellum free of its container. With care he unrolled it. 'A good hundred or more, the way our luck's running.'

The Matria's seal was on the bottom. Even though deep inside he had known it was going to be there, it was still a shock to see it. It was even more of a shock to read the instructions outlined in the message: where, when, and how he and Hesseth were to be disposed of. Not *why,* he noted. Was that because the Protectors would understand her motives, or – more likely – because no one around here dared to ask questions? The procedures outlined in the letter were more typical of a police state than a thriving theocracy. He wondered how far that went. He wondered how the hell it had started.

'God in Heaven,' he muttered. 'She's a vicious one, that's for sure.' He turned it so that he could read the heading by the fire's light. 'To the Kierstaad Protectorate.' He looked up at Hesseth.

'To the Chikung Protectorate,' she read from hers.

'Shit.' He read it again, wincing at the detailed instructions for disposing of the two travelers after capture. 'Not much room for compromise here. It's a good bet she's warning all the Protectorates, and in that case . . . shit. It'll mean the shore's off limits all the way down the coast.'

He offered the letter to the Hunter, who read it. If he had any reaction to its source – or its tone – he didn't show it. 'Clearly they mean business.'

'That's an understatement.'

'Our enemies are thorough,' he said coolly. 'Did you expect any less?'

Damien glared. 'I thought they'd want to capture us, yes, question us to find out who we really were, what we wanted—'

'They know who you really are,' Tarrant interrupted, 'and they know what you want. These documents are no less than a declaration of war.' When Damien said nothing, he pressed, 'Do you doubt their purpose? Do you question who sent them?'

'No,' he muttered. Fingering the seal of the Matria which was affixed to the last inch of the missive. Leaving a smear of crimson on the golden wax. 'No. You were right. Whatever's wrong here, the Matrias are part of it. And that means...' He couldn't finish. The thought was too painful.

That means that the Church is involved.

'At least they think we're coming by ship,' Hesseth said. 'That'll buy us some time, if nothing else.'

Damien looked again at the letter in his hand, seeking out the line that made reference to that. *It is believed they may be traveling south on a Western ship named the* Golden Glory. *All ports should be alert.* 'We shouldn't count on it,' he warned. Then added, thoughtfully, 'Rozca'll have a nasty time thanks to this.'

'Rozca can handle it,' Tarrant assured him. 'All he has to do is let his ship be searched and he's in the clear. Correct? Meanwhile he's bought us what we needed most: time.' He nodded approvingly. 'It was well planned, Vryce. Considering how quickly you threw it all together, it does you credit.'

'Thanks,' he muttered. He felt strangely uncomfortable receiving praise from the Hunter. 'What now?'

Tarrant looked back toward the city. 'The next step is to choose our destination.'

'South,' Hesseth said quickly.

The men both looked at her.

'If, as you say, the Matria is allied to our enemy... and if she knows our purpose... then by her own words, our enemy is to the south of here.' She held up the letter in her hand.

'Just so,' the Hunter agreed. 'And I have some information that may bear on our route...' His gaze fixed suddenly on Damien; the gray eyes narrowed. 'But I think there's a need even more pressing than that,' he said softly. 'How long since you've slept, priest?'

'Since dawn,' he muttered. He had been trying not to think about sleep, had tried to just keep going for as long as it took and deal with the need for rest when time and circumstances allowed, but the Hunter's words were fresh reminder of just how long it had been. And once named, the specter of exhaustion could no longer be denied. 'I didn't sleep more than an hour or two last night, if you must know.'

'You probably owe your life to that,' he said dryly. 'Hesseth?'

'I could go on if we had to,' she said. 'But sleep would be welcome.'

He nodded. 'We need to move on a bit farther, until we find safer ground—'

'You think they'd come after us tonight?' Damien asked sharply.

'No. But I do think that the walls of this gully were sculpted by water, and it would be a shame if all our plans were laid to waste by a flash flood. It is that season, you know.'

He gained his feet in a single fluid movement, like the uncoiling of a snake. 'When we find higher ground, I'll stand watch for the two of you. So that you can sleep in safety. Until dawn, at least.'

It was a good thing he was too tired to really think about their arrangement, Damien reflected as he helped Hesseth pack up their gear. Otherwise it might really scare him how comfortable he was with the thought of placing his safety in Tarrant's hands.

Hell, he thought. *You can get used to anything.*

It took them nearly two hours to find a suitable campsite. By then they were truly exhausted, and even the horses looked drained. Five midmonths of confinement had taken their toll on the beasts, and Damien guessed that it would be a long time before they exhibited the strength and endurance that was the hallmark of their species.

They found a patch of ground that was reasonably smooth and threw their blankets down upon it. The bulk of the galaxy had set some time ago, leaving the sky mostly black. Damien muttered something about how long would it be until the first true night occurred? Did anyone know? Tarrant said something back which involved calendars and timetables and a whole list of details . . . but at least he knew when it was coming. Which was all Damien really needed to know tonight. Certainly all he could absorb.

He was asleep as soon as his head touched the ground.

And dreamed.

. . . the cathedral is dark, so dark, not even a glimmer of moonlight breaking through the colored windows, nothing to illuminate the cold stone vastness but the glitter of one tiny candle, flickering like the light of a distant star . . .

. . . and he walks down the aisle toward it as one might walk toward the light of God, feeling its warmth in the breezes of the aisle, drawn to it with palpable force . . .

. . . scent in the air, sweeter than incense, stronger than perfume, musky and compelling. A thick, caressing aroma that warms his throat when he breathes, that tingles in his lungs like cerebus smoke and spreads outward in his blood, outward with every heartbeat, outward to every cell of his body, warming, caressing, inviting . . .

At the altar is a figure. Wraithlike, it is veiled in layers of fine white silk that ripple with each breath it takes. The light of a single candle is captured by one layer, then another, then by the flesh beneath. It is a woman's body, Damien notes, round and well-formed and infinitely pleasing. The curve of a breast catches the light, the darkness of a nipple, the shadow of an inner thigh. Only the face is darkness in shadow, so that Damien cannot make out who it is. But the invitation is clear in her posture as well as her scent.

A slender hand reaches to the neck of the gauzy robe, unfastens it. Silk whispers downward over smooth flesh, layer after layer until all are puddled on the floor about her feet. Her breasts are full, heavily rounded, and a sheen of sweat is on her thighs. The musky aroma envelops him, and he feels his body stiffen in response. It is not so much pleasure that drives him now, but need; a primal hunger that has no name, that ceased to have a name millennia ago when humans learned to dilute their animal drives and thus control them. This has no control. This has no trappings of civilization, or of intellect. This has no possible end but the utter submission to a drive so deeply embedded in his flesh that a million years of species denial could never fully conquer it.

He reaches out to her. The flesh is dark beneath her breasts, with a line of small brown spots beneath each one. Something is wrong about that. His head throbs as he tries to think, as he struggles to remember. That and the smell and the touch of her body, silk-soft, more like fine fur than like human skin . . .

He feels a coldness stirring deep inside, even as he moves toward her. Something is wrong, so very wrong . . . his head is spinning. He struggles to orient himself, even as his body responds to her invitation. No: to her demand . . .

And then he looks at her face. The flickering light illuminates her features in spurts of amber, a strobe of recognition.

Golden eyes.

Golden fur.

The Matria's crown ...

He awoke suddenly. Breathless. Shaken. It took him a minute to remember where he was, to make out Tarrant's outline in the shadows. The Hunter was watching him. He shuddered once, uncomfortably aware of the stiffness in his groin. Not hot now, nor expectant, but tight with dread. And fear.

He let the blanket gather in his lap as he forced himself to a sitting position. And breathed the night air deeply, trying to calm himself.

'Bad dream?' the Hunter asked softly.

'Yeah.' He looked up at him. 'One of yours?'

Tarrant smiled faintly. 'There's no need for that now, is there?'

He rubbed his temples. The dream's afterimage was rapidly fading from his mind. It was important to remember ... what? The thoughts wouldn't come together. Something important. Something he had almost understood.

'You need help?' Tarrant asked softly.

He noticed that the Hunter's sword was thrust into the ground not far from him. Absorbing the earth-fae? He could feel the cold of its power through his blankets. 'I dreamed of the Matria ... I think. Only it wasn't her, it was a rakh ...'

Rakh.

He was remembering now. The rakhene women who'd been in Hesseth's camp. Some of them clearly in heat – or its rakhene equivalent – their naked hunger distracting every male within reach. Clearly that image had etched itself upon his brain, along with attendant hormonal messages.

He was remembering other things, too. Things he had learned on their last journey together. The facts came together, impacted, almost too fast to absorb.

'The rakh women—' he whispered. 'Oh, my God ...'

Somehow he managed to sit up. He was shaking badly. Tarrant's face was lost in shadow, but even so the priest could sense the intensity of his scrutiny.

'You asked why would only the women be the seers – the Matrias – when women have no more prophetic power than men. But they do. You said it yourself, back in . . . hell, I don't remember. Soon after I met you. You said that only women could use the *tidal fae*. Remember?'

'I said that women could sometimes *See* it,' the Hunter said coolly. 'No human being has ever Worked it. It defies that kind of control—'

'Are you sure of that?'

'I tried it, Reverend Vryce. I nearly died. Later, assuming my failure to be a consequence of my gender, I tried to manipulate one woman who could See it.' He shook his head stiffly. 'Not even my will can tame such a power. And if not mine, then whose?'

'The rakh,' he whispered. Knowing the craziness of the suggestion even as he voiced it. 'That's the fae they draw on. Remember? And a few of them know how to control it consciously.' He looked over at Hesseth. '*She* does,' he whispered. 'We found that out after you'd been captured. The rakh females use sorcery. *All* of them! Not human-style, not with the earth-fae . . . but it's sorcery all the same.' He felt suddenly breathless. Suddenly afraid. 'Do you understand? *Only the females*.'

The Hunter's voice was very quiet. 'Are you saying the Matria is rakh?'

'Am I?' He shook his head, as if to clear it. 'Is that possible? It seems insane . . . but so much is in this place. You asked it yourself: why would men be banned from Church leadership? It doesn't make any sense at all if they're human. But if they're rakh . . .' He looked down at Hesseth. Fully asleep, probably dreaming, her claws twitching slightly as if in response to an unseen threat. 'She said they used the tidal fae. Can humans do that?'

Tarrant hesitated. 'The women I've known who could See that power were very rare . . . and usually quite mad. The tidal fae's inconstant, unpredictable, often violent. Anyone tapping into it—'

'Would be equally unpredictable. Yes? Especially if they relied upon it for disguise. They'd have to hide when the power waned, come out only when it was stable enough for Working. Don't you see? My God!' He shut his eyes, trembling. With excitement? With fear? 'That's what the Matria did. They never knew when she was going to show up, or when she'd suddenly cancel an appearance.' He looked at the Hunter. 'You were in other cities. You tell me. Was it like that in all of them?'

Tarrant considered it. 'Yes,' he said at last. 'That seems to be the general pattern here. I attributed it to an eccentricity of their Order, but if it's not . . . if you're right . . .'

'It would mean a lifetime of subterfuge. Years spent among the enemy. Hesseth says that even humanity's smell is intolerable to her—'

'It would also mean the Church here was in rakhene hands,' Tarrant reminded him. 'And has been for centuries. Toward what end?'

'You said they hunted human children,' Damien said softly. 'Considering how the rakh hate our species, wouldn't that make sense?'

'I said they used human children to hunt the faeborn.'

'Is that so very different? As far as the children are concerned?'

For a moment Tarrant just stared at him. Then he looked away.

'There's something else I didn't tell you,' he said quietly. 'It didn't seem important at the time. But maybe it is.' Though the man's face was turned away from him and half in shadow, Damien thought that his expression darkened. Something hard and cold came into his voice, which had not been there before. 'These people kill adepts,' Tarrant told him. '*All* adepts. They catch them in the cradle when their senses are still so confused that they can't protect themselves – not even reflexively – and they murder them. Every time.'

'What if it wasn't obvious—'

'You can't hide something like that,' he said angrily. 'Not in the first few years. Not when a child responds to things that no one else can see or hear. An adept lives in a world five times as complex as that of his parents, and must struggle to sort it out. That can't be hidden. Trust me. People have tried. Back in my day, when they feared it as a sign of possession, when it meant that a child might be put to the torch . . . it can't be hidden, Reverend Vryce. Not ever.' He shook his head; his expression was grim. 'There's no living adept in this region at all. I know. I used my power to search the currents, to find some sign – *any* sign – but there's nothing. Nothing! Man's greatest adaptation to this world – his *only* adaptation – and these people have wiped it out, child by child.'

For a moment Damien couldn't find any words. At last he managed, 'You thought that wasn't important?'

The Hunter turned back to him. His eyes were black, and cold with hate. 'I thought it made perfect sense,' he snapped. 'Don't you? A land ruled by the Church's iron hand, that tolerates no philosophical disruption . . . a utopia in name and substance, as long as no one challenges its central doctrine. As an adept would have to do, in order to survive.' He laughed shortly, a bitter sound. 'Of *course* this land kills its adepts, Reverend Vryce. I predicted that it would as soon as I understood who and what these people were. Didn't you?'

'No,' he said softly. 'No, I . . . never.'

'You realize their sancity is all an illusion, don't you? The ultimate in self-deception. They've learned to control the fae, all right, but it's been at the cost of their own souls.' His eyes were focused on a distant point; perhaps in the past. Perhaps in his own soul. 'Exactly what I feared would happen,' he whispered. 'Exactly what I warned them about.' He shut his eyes. 'Why wouldn't they listen? Why don't they ever listen?'

Tarrant reached out and put a hand on his horse's shoulder; Damien was amazed to see the pale flesh tremble. He was afraid to say anything, afraid that the fragile moment might shatter like glass at the very sound of his voice. Something deeply buried and very private had come to the surface in Tarrant, perhaps for the first time in centuries. He had the sense of a door cracking open ever so slightly, admitting a brief glimpse of the Prophet's soul. But he felt that if he said the wrong thing – if he tried to say anything at all – that door would slam shut again, with the finality of a tomb. And the brief glimpse of humanity which echoed in those words would be lost again, perhaps for a second millennia. Perhaps forever.

At last the Hunter lowered his hand from the horse; a shudder seemed to course through his body. 'None of that matters now,' he said softly. 'Not even their motives. The end result is that there are no sorcerors in this land, with or without the Vision. Which means that these people are helpless. Whatever evil our enemy plans . . . we're the only ones who can stop him.'

'It also means that our enemy isn't prepared for opposition. Right? If there's no human sorcery here, then he's not used to dealing with it.' He spoke slowly, carefully, trying to keep the fear out of his voice. 'That could work to our advantage.'

The Hunter looked at him. And suddenly it seemed to Damien that the pale eyes were mirrors, reflecting more centuries than any one man should have to endure. Reflecting more horrors than any human soul, however corrupt, should have to witness.

'Let's hope so,' the Hunter whispered.

15

The Protector's keep was dark when Istram Iseldas approached it, which struck him as odd. But then, so much was odd this long-month. First there were the reports of an invasion force moving up the coast – thanks be to a merciful God that nothing ever came of that – followed by an extremely cryptic message from the Matria of Mercia. Followed closely by last night's trespass and arrest . . . most disturbing. Most disturbing indeed.

He lifted up the great knocker (in the shape of a stelf-hound, the symbol of the local Protectorate) and struck it against the heavy wooden door several times. The sun was nearly down, he noted, which meant that he probably should stay here overnight. God willing, he and his neighbor Protector could get things squared away well enough to make that possible.

The heavy door opened. A servant he had never seen before studied him with dark, uncommunicative eyes. Considering Istram's rank and familiarity with this keep, it was a jarringly cold welcome.

'Protector Iseldas,' he told the man. 'I'm here to see Leman Kierstaad.'

The man stepped back wordlessly to allow him to enter. Dark eyes in a pale face, black hair above, dark clothes below: unwholesome looking, Istram decided. Downright unhealthy. He'd have had the man out in the sunshine long ago, nursing a respectable tan. 'If he's in his study, I can find him.'

'Follow me,' the pale man said.

He was led through the keep in silence, his footsteps ringing eerily in the empty halls. Despite the gloom of the afternoon few lamps had been lighted, and the shadows that gathered in corners and beneath the heavy furniture were almost nightlike in their substance. To be sure, the Kierstaad abode had been gloomy since the death of its mistress – whether because Leman lacked the energy to brighten it up, or because he actively preferred it that way as an expression of his mourning, Istram couldn't say – but its atmosphere had never seemed so dark as today. So downright oppressive. He shivered as he followed the servant, wondering what his old friend's state of mind must be. Had the joint pressure of a Protector's responsibility and a widower's heartache finally proven too much for him?

But when at last he was shown into Leman Kierstaad's presence it was in a chamber that was brightly lit, amber lamplight flooding the walls like sunshine. He noted that the shutters were closed here as elsewhere, but what did that matter? The lamplight was cheery enough, and he felt his dire mood evaporating in its warmth.

The Protector was seated in a broad carved chair, a woolen blanket across his lap. He rose slightly in greeting, then sat again. 'Istram. This is a surprise. Sit down.' He waved toward a chair opposite his own. 'Can I get you something? Coffee, perhaps? Or a drink? Name it.'

'Iced water will be fine,' he said. Somewhat surprised that his old friend had forgotten that preference of his. 'With a sour rind, if you have it.'

Protector Kierstaad passed on the order to his dismal-looking servant, who withdrew to fulfill it. It gave Istram a chance to study his long-time neighbor. It seemed there were more lines on his face than before, or perhaps the old lines were harsher. Little wonder. The last six years had been rough on him, and if not for the responsibility of his Protectorate he probably would have called it quits long ago. The strain of the forced endurance was showing.

We'll have to find a replacement, he thought. *Can't have this part of the coast unprotected, not even for a day.*

'So,' Kierstaad said, rearranging his blanket. 'It's been a long time, Istram. How's the wife?'

'Shopping up north. Her yearly trip.'

'Mercia, this time? Felicida?'

'Paza Nova, I believe.'

'Ah.' He chuckled. 'That'll cost you.'

'It already has.' He hesitated. 'And you? Are you well?'

A shadow passed over the other man's face. 'As well as can be expected,' he said quietly. 'I don't ask much any more, you know that. God's strength to keep this land secure, and enough memories to make life worth living.'

'And is it secure?' he asked. Hearing the edge in his own voice.

'Why do you ask?'

He sighed. He had meant to bring up the matter gradually, gently, but the words had just come out. Now it was too late to take them back. 'Your men were on my land, Leman. Skulking about like a band of nightborn. It's a miracle they weren't killed when my own guards found them.'

Kierstaad frowned. 'You captured them?'

Istram spread his hands helplessly. 'I didn't have much choice, did I? Half a dozen unknown men, prowling the borders of my Protectorate like stelves in search of prey ... that's how my men described it, Lee. Even allowing for the exaggeration of the moment, it's still rather odd.'

He waited. When Kierstaad said nothing he pressed, 'I thought you might like to tell me about it.'

'About what?'

'What do you think?' he said irritably. 'I've got my land to protect, just like you do. Something strange happens, I need to figure out what it is. Even if it comes from you.' He shrugged. 'That's my job, you know. Same as yours.'

The servant was back again, a tall glass in hand. Istram took it from him and drank deeply.

'They were hunting,' Kierstaad told him. 'Some large beast attacked the villages. Mauled a child in Nester, just two days past. I sent them out to find it.'

'They weren't armed like hunters.'

He shrugged. 'They took what they thought was necessary. I didn't supervise their choices.'

'At night?'

'Istram. Please.' He spread his hands wide; it was the kind of gesture a man might make to show that he had no weapons. 'They were hunters. I'm not. They said the beast would be holed up for the night, would be well-fed and slow to respond then. It was their job, not mine. I trusted them to do it. All right?'

For a moment he just stared at the man, wishing he could read what was in his eyes. At last he sighed. 'All right, Lee. If that's all it was. But let me know next time, all right? God knows, if there's a maneater at large I should be mobilizing, too.' *Especially when we have warning of a possible invasion fleet,* he almost added. *Especially when I have to account for everything that moves and breathes within my territory.*

'I'm sorry, Istram. I really am. No insult meant. Really.'

He forced himself to relax. 'All right. None taken, I guess. I'll have them released in the morning.'

'Good. Thank you.'

'I guess I'm just a little jumpy, what with the invasion warning and all. It's the first one since I became Protector, you know.'

Kierstaad smiled faintly. 'It'll pass without incident, I'm sure. They all do.'

'And now this with the westerners. I guess nothing's wrong, it's just . . . it seems extreme. I . . . what's wrong?'

'*What* with the westerners?' Kierstaad demanded. Suddenly tense. 'What are you talking about?'

'The message that came from Mercia. You were sent one, weren't you?' He reached into his jacket and pulled the tiny scrap of paper out. 'Here it is.' He scanned it for the part he wanted, then nodded. 'She wrote that all the Protectorates would be contacted. You should have gotten something by now.'

'Let me see.' He leaned forward to take the paper from him. It rolled up slightly in his hand, still set from its hours in the bird's harness. His lips pressed together as he read it, and his eyes narrowed.

'No,' he said at last. 'No, I haven't gotten anything.'

Istram hesitated. 'Doesn't it seem a little . . . well, extreme to you? Immediate death upon capture? Not even a questioning?'

'The last pagans from the west were dealt with mercifully. And some of them escaped, to found the very nation that now threatens us. Isn't this a safer course?'

'But these aren't pagans. These are two of our own. A priest and a Sanctified woman, the letter says. I don't—'

'Are you questioning a Matria's judgment?'

Istram blinked. 'No. It's just that I . . . no. Good God. Of course not.'

'Well, then.' Kierstaad reached down to the table at his side, a fine piece with slender legs and tiled top. There was a cup sitting on it, with some pale brown liquid inside. Tee? As Istram watched his old friend sip from the fragile china cup, he remembered that the man had never cared for hot drinks. But perhaps his tastes had changed when Miranda Kierstaad died; so much about him had. 'It seems that's settled, then. I'm glad you came to me. I hear stories of other Protectors, you know, as suspicious of each other as they are of the enemy. I'd hate for that to happen to us.'

Despite himself he smiled. 'I can't imagine that it would.'

The china cup was replaced; it made a faint *ting* on the hand-painted tiles as he set it down. There seemed to be something tense about the Protector, something that belied the warmth of his tone and the casual grace of his gestures. Was he hiding something? The thought was not a welcome one, but it worried at the edges of Istram's brain as he watched the older man rise from his chair. Was it possible there was something to hide? Or was Istram just seeing the first clear signs of a breakdown that had been six long years in the making? The death of a man who had lost his love of life six years ago, when his wife had gone to sleep one winter night and never awakened?

If not for the Protectorate, he wouldn't have lasted this long, Istram thought. *What else is left that matters to him?*

Kierstaad cleared his throat noisily. 'You're welcome for dinner, of course. And to stay the night if you want. If your people won't worry . . .'

'I was on a tour of the border,' he told him. 'They don't expect me back for days.'

The clear gray eyes fixed on him then, with a suddenness and an intensity that were unnerving. Uncomfortable, he looked away. 'Indeed? Then we must make doubly sure you're safe.'

He called out a man's name; not loudly, but the clear voice carried. A moment later the same servant returned.

'Will you excuse me for a few minutes, Istram?' His tone was apologetic. 'I had some duties this evening which I can cancel, but I'll need to sit down with Sems here and discuss a few things before dinner.'

'Of course.' He gestured toward the outer door. 'I'll wait outside if you like.'

'It won't take long,' he promised. Gray eyes glittering in the lamplight. 'I'll call you as soon as we're done.'

The western terrace of Kierstaad's keep was a place of wonder and beauty, and Istram could never set foot in it without being awed anew. A garden of crystalline structures shimmered and shivered in the slightest breeze, tinkling like glass bells each time the evening air shifted in its course. Standing in its center was like being inside a musical instrument while some exquisite hand plucked notes upon its strings. You could close your eyes and feel the music inside you, or open them and gaze upon the visual symphony that surrounded you. A thousand etched-glass leaves that captured the Core's golden light. Delicately blown stems that glistened like icicles, refining the light into rainbow strands. A garden of miracle workmanship, a place of true magic and absolute beauty. And the last living work of Miranda Kierstaad, before the lung disease that had plagued her since birth had claimed her final breath.

Here he could share something of Leman's sorrow, surrounded by the work of the woman his friend had adored. Was it better to have a place like this, which captured the essence of one's love, or did it only serve as a reminder of his terrible loss? Since the garden was still intact, he assumed the former; Kierstaad was a decisive man who would surely have pulled down the crystalline trees if they had added one fraction to his pain.

The doors to the keep – glass-paneled, now thickly curtained – swung open. With but a moment's hesitation at the doorstep, Leman Kierstaad came out onto the terrace. 'Beautiful, isn't it?' His eyes were on Istram as he walked toward the western wall, with its delicate glassy ivy. Drawing Istram's gaze along with his own, until the visitor faced into the setting Core. 'And so very fragile.'

He reached out a hand to the nearest hand-blown vine and pulled. A yard-long segment snapped into pieces; splinters of glass fell to the earth like glistening, sharp-edged rain. The motion was so quick, so unexpected, that for a moment Istram couldn't even react. Then he stepped forward, meaning to do – what? Stop the man? It was mindless instinct that drove him, a gut response to witnessing such beauty ravaged. Even as he moved he saw Kierstaad's eyes focus on a point behind his head. And he knew that he had been distracted for a reason.

He tried to turn. Pain burst in his skull as something struck him from behind, driving him down to his knees. He tried to cry out, but a second blow silenced him, leaving only a gasp that poured from his lips like blood. Again. He tried to raise up his arms, to protect himself, but something had been crushed that was needed to make them move; they fell limply down by his side, streaked with crimson blood, and stayed that way as he fell. Again the blow fell. He heard the crunch of bone splitting as fresh blood filled his throat, choking him. His breath was a gurgle that watered the ground with red foam. All about him was darkness.

And then, as if from a distance, Leman Kierstaad's voice: 'Are you ready?'

He could barely hear the answer over the roaring in his ears. The blazing pain. 'Do it now?'

'The imprint's best at the moment of death. Trying it later . . . that's tricky.'

He tried to move his fingers. Couldn't. Tried to feel his legs. No. 'How's that?'

He was dying.

'You'll leave in the morning, as he would have done. Go directly to the keep. If anyone asks why you cut the tour short, say it was based on classified information that I gave you. No one questions a Protector.'

'And then?'

Betrayed. They were all betrayed. The land had already been invaded, by creatures that hid behind human faces. No boats had to land. Not now. No armies would ever be seen. Nothing would be noticed . . . until it was too late.

'I want all your men out in those woods, searching. We have to find that girl. Turn the villages inside out if you have to, check every path, search every stream . . . she's only a child, and she's never been outside before. She can't elude us forever.'

'But if she's just a child—'

'She *saw* me,' the Kierstaad-voice hissed. 'I don't know why, I don't know how, but she knew that something was wrong. Why else would she run away that very night, when she could never hope to survive on her own? I want her captured. I want her alive. I want to know what special power she has, that his Highness failed to anticipate . . .' The voice trailed off into a true hiss, too soft for Istram to hear. His blood was a roar in his ears, a hot flood in his throat. The sounds of the world outside were fading. 'Go north into this man's lands' – something kicked him hard in the back and his body jerked, smearing blood on the floor – 'and do what it takes to find her.'

'And if the villagers object to our search?'

'What do you care? They're human.' The voice had become a predatory hiss. 'If they get in your way, then kill them.'

Istram tried to cough. Failed. There was no room left for air in his lungs; everything was filled with blood.

'Just make sure you leave no witnesses,' the Kierstaad-voice cautioned. It was a voice filled with hate. A tone filled with hunger. It seeped down into the darkness that surrounded him, a last flicker of red in the gathering mists. Enough to inspire terror in the throbbing remnants of his soul.

I have to warn them, was Istram's last thought. The Protector in him still clutched at life – insane, obsessed – even as his body shuddered in its dying. *Have to get word to the others. Somehow* . . .

And then even the terror expired, and there was only darkness.

16

They followed the stream bed south, though at times the footing was so bad that they had to lead the horses through the water, feeling their way through soaked leather soles. *At least it isn't winter,* Damien thought, remembering their frozen trek through the rakhland mountains. What he tried not to think about was the fact that a few hundred miles closer to the southern ice cap and ten thousand feet higher up it might be every bit as unpleasant as it had been in the far north. And so when they spread out the maps – Tarrant's, as always, and the few which Hesseth had managed to salvage from their ill-fated room in the Manor, he studied the geography every bit as carefully as the Hunter did, with an eye for the weather.

For a few nights they concentrated on putting as much distance between them and Mercia as possible. The horses gained energy quickly – much more so than Damien had expected – and to their relief the animals seemed happy to supplement their limited grain supply with a few grassy plants that grew on the banks of the stream. It wasn't necessary for Tarrant to point out that without a reliable supply of travel feed they were going to have to limit their journey to regions that would support an equine appetite; Damien had thought of that the first day out. At least for the moment that seemed to be no problem. They would have to be careful when they chose their route, and keep a close eye on the vegetation.

One more thing to worry about.

They didn't have many weapons, and that made the priest nervous. Hesseth had managed to rescue his sword and a few knives, and Tarrant still had his coldfire blade, but that didn't mean much in a land where every citadel had firearms and even farmers might be armed with some kind of projectile weapon. On their second day from the city Damien tried to manufacture a bow from some supple saplings by the waterside, but though he tried every combination of wood and string that was available to him – short of gutting the horses for their sinew – he could achieve no combination that was satisfactory. At last in frustration he cast the bits of wood aside. They would have to purchase arms somewhere – a risky enterprise at best – or steal some, which was even less savory. Their prospects seemed darker and darker. If only they'd had time to prepare. If only he'd known when he spoke to Rozca how soon they would have to leave the city, so that he could have arranged a way to meet up—

Stop it. Now. You did the best you could. Deal with what you've got.

The gully deepened as they traveled south, and at last they thought it best to climb to higher ground while that was still possible. The scraggly trees flanking the stream had given way to a forest of sorts, but it was far from a healthy system. Stunted trees were spaced far enough apart that sunlight could seep down between them, which meant that every inch from the dirt up to the canopy had given rise to some sort of plant life. Which meant thick underbrush, often studded with thorns or coated with irritant. It was rough going, what with hacking through the under-brush to make way for their horses, and they had to stop often to rest. More than once Damien looked back the way they had come and winced; they were leaving a path so clearly marked that an army of blind men couldn't have missed it. They would just have to hope that the many miles they had put in concealing their tracks in the stream's running water would be enough to slow their pursuers down.

And, of course, their ruse with Rozca. God, there was so much riding on that . . .

At night Tarrant joined them. He had insisted that Damien and Hesseth continue traveling through some of the daylight hours, which meant that he spent the first few hours of evening searching them out and catching up. Damien tried to ignore the twisting in his gut in those hours. It was hard to forget what had happened in the rakhlands, when Tarrant's failure to join them on time had resulted in days of torturous travel and nights of pain and fear. But there were no caves along their path, Tarrant had told them, which meant that he didn't have the option of taking shelter with them. For once Damien didn't question him. They seemed to have grown past petty questions of trust and annoyance into a relationship that was firmly rooted in their common need.

I trust him, Damien thought, studying the Hunter's lean profile. *Under the right circumstances I would trust him with my life*. It was a new and not wholly comfortable feeling.

It was Tarrant who studied the currents of earth-fae that coursed about their feet, Tarrant who read meaning into their depth and their direction and a thousand other elements that Damien couldn't begin to guess at. Sometimes he Worked his vision and tried to See as the Hunter did, but though he could observe the silver-blue currents he could not decipher their mysteries. As Tarrant explained when he voiced his frustration, a man who looked at the sky once a longmonth, and then only for a moment, might see that it was blue, but the man whose eyes were open twenty-four hours a day for a lifetime could distinguish a thousand hues in the very same heavens. So it was with them. And when Tarrant announced that the currents were shifting, that their response to his own malevolence was subtly changing, Damien took his word for the fact that someone or something must be causing it. He sure as hell couldn't See the difference.

At last the scraggly woods gave way to forest proper, and they knew by that sign that they were now south of the inland sea, and past the last of its cities. Damien breathed a sigh of relief. In the lands of the Protectorates the Matrias' word was still law, but sparse population and limited lines of communication made the risk of active pursuit considerably less. Or so he tried to convince himself, as they entered the depths of the Protectors' woods.

Here there was a canopy proper, rich in verdant foliage. The light which filtered down to the ground was less than ideal for growth, which limited the number of plants that could take root in the shadowed earth. The horses trod this land with ease, and for the first time since leaving Mercia, Damien felt they were making good time.

To where? he thought. *Toward what?*

Near dawn each day they gathered around a minimal campfire and laid out their maps. Tarrant had begun to sketch in the patterns of power that he was observing, so that his own map of choice had begun to resemble the fae-charts back home. Tremors had struck three times while they traveled, and the surge of earth-fae which accompanied all earthquakes had given the Hunter even more information about the southern terrain. One of them had occurred so soon after sunset that Damien had had a vision of Tarrant trapped in mid-transformation, burned to a crisp by the untamable power of the earth. The Hunter had merely smiled when he spoke of it, but it seemed to Damien that he, too, was less confident, and before he transformed himself each morning the priest could see him carefully studying the currents, searching for that ever-so-slight irregularity which would warn of a quake in the making.

Southward, the maps said. Southward along the spine of a narrow, serpentine continent. Southward in a narrow channel between where the Protectors ruled and where barren mountains held sway. Or over those mountains at one of three passes, and into the lands of the Terata. Monsters, ghouls, or demonkin, they hunted mere humans for amusement and then rendered them down for meat. Or so the legends said. Damien – who had seen enough monstrosities in Tarrant's cursed domain to last him a lifetime – had no desire to test them.

Southward to where the continent that sheltered them pointed like a slender finger to the islands beyond. On one of those – an immense land, the size of three landbound nations combined – Mercia's enemies were said to shelter. An unholy army, gaining strength against the day when it would be ready to attack at last. The Church folk feared them enough to fortify the length of the coast with citadels, so that even in the most dismal, inhospitable reaches some Protector was waiting with his guards. The terrain itself had worked in their favor; there were so few places along the coast where an invading ship might harbor safely that it really was possible to guard it all. As long as the cities on the southernmost tip kept their own walls strong, and were ever vigilant . . .

That was where they were headed, that southern tip. Tarrant

insisted. They must have more information on their enemy before making any move, and that was the best place to garner it. Though the cities there were linked to their northern neighbors by the Church, they were nominally independent, which meant that with a little luck – and a lot of careful Workings – the party might be able to supply itself with food, information, and weapons without getting killed in the process. Even more important, the currents which coursed northward in this region would be free from interference there, and Tarrant might be able to work a Knowing of considerable power. He was quick to remind them that while the currents had worked against them in the rakhlands, bringing their fae-scent to the enemy while hindering their own efforts, here they were downcurrent of the enemy. Information would flow to them like a scent on the wind, and they need exert no special power to interpret it. All they had to do was get upcurrent of the cities, so that the patterns were clear.

About damned time something worked in our favor, Damien thought. As he strapped his all-too-limited supplies onto his horse's back, and settled his one weapon between his shoulders. *We need all the help we can get.*

Evening. The sun had set a while ago and the Core was too low for its light to make much difference; the forest air was a gloomy gray, and their tiny campfire did little to brighten it.

'Something's coming,' Hesseth whispered.

They had found a stretch of clear ground to camp on, where no trees obscured their view of the night sky. The ground was hard and cold and uninviting, but being out from under the canopy meant Tarrant could find them that much faster. Now Damien wondered how wise that choice had been. It meant little that Tarrant found them quickly, if the enemy found them first. The rocky promontory gave them high ground, but the trees surrounding them would hide any attackers. Bad combination.

He brushed some loose dirt over the fire as he whispered to Hesseth, 'Where?'

She shook her head. He saw her straining forward with her long, tufted ears, as if trying to focus on some distant sound. He listened as hard as he could himself, but heard nothing amiss. Which didn't mean anything, of course. His human senses were considerably less acute than hers.

At least the rustlings and chirrupings which surrounded them hadn't ceased. That meant that no large animal was prowling nearby, which might have frightened the forest's smaller inhabitants into a wary silence. Damien took his sword in hand and tightened his fingers about the grip. If the smaller animals weren't scared, that meant that nothing large was nearby . . . or that whatever was on the prowl had no flesh of its own for them to sense. How long had it been since they'd encountered anything demonic? The faeborn of this region had chosen to cluster about the city gates, leaving them thus far in peace. But there would come a time when they were far enough from the cities that whatever creatures man's fear spawned might look closer to home for sustenance . . .

He drew in a deep breath and Worked his sight. For a moment the gray mist resisted, refusing to give way. Then the currents began to glow about him, the cool silver-gray of the earth-power—

And he cursed. Loudly. Rising to his feet with his sword in hand, feeling his fingers spasm fearfully about the grip. Hesseth rose beside him, and before she could ask what he had Seen, he told her, 'Something very dark. Very hungry. It's coming this way.' The last time he had sensed a power like this had been in Tarrant's Forest, where the man's own murderous instincts had tainted the earthfae. Here the threat was more specific, but every bit as unwholesome. And as terrifying.

—Speaking of Tarrant, where was he when you needed him?

'There.' He pointed to the south, where it seemed to him that the current was changing. Dark threads floated in the low-lying mist, pulsing as if in time to some inner heartbeat. He could smell its dark pollution, not with his nose but with his inner senses, and the reek of stale blood and rotting flesh made him want to vomit. He fought the sensation, even as he gathered himself to Work. Knowing as he did so that all his skill and Hesseth's combined couldn't stop something that powerful, not if it was truly intent upon devouring them.

They burst from the forest's cover as the last words of the Shielding passed his lips, and by the time the earth-fae surrounding him had thickened in response, the first one was upon them. It was a horrible thing, a mockery of human shape with half its skull caved in and one arm dangling by a thread of flesh. He caught a glimpse of cracked bone as the creature came toward them, the green of rot rimming its many wounds. Damien reached out and pulled Hesseth toward him as the monster charged; the smaller his circle of influence was, the stronger he could make it. He heard her hiss as the creature charged, felt her stiffen against his side as it was caught in midair as if in gel, as it struggled to get through the thickening boundary to claw at the two of them. Behind it rushed others – so many others! – an army of horror, a veritable battalion of death incarnate that howled in anguish and hunger as it poured through the clearing, filling every inch of space within the trees. The horses squealed in terror as the faeborn creatures filled the clearing, but the monsters had no interest in equine souls; the stink of rotting flesh enveloped Damien as creature after creature thrust itself against the priest's defensive Working, shredded flesh and maggot-ridden limbs scrabbling over the shell of earth-fae like so many insects. The priest had seen more frightening things in his life, but never anything more horrible; it took all his self-control not to close his eyes to shut the vision out.

There must have been hundreds of the creatures. Thousands. The sea of them seemed endless as it pounded against his hastily Worked defenses, each blow requiring one more bit of strength from him to balance it. He felt himself tiring, and fast. Could Hesseth help? he wondered. Was the power she used available at this moment, and could she Work it into some defensive pattern? *If she could, then she would have,* he told himself grimly. Streaks of blackened blood hung suspended in midair inches before his face, defining the limits of his power. Where had these things come from? What did they usually feed on, that would support so many? His sword-arm tensed as the wall of fae seemed to give before him, gritty claws raking the air no more than an inch from his face – and then he forced it back and it held, the black blood smoked and the monsters screamed and the reek of it, the terrible reek of it that

came near to overwhelming him utterly, the stink that filled his
nose and his mouth and burned his lungs when he breathed it in,
so that it was all he could do not to gag and lose his concentration
utterly . . .

'Look,' Hesseth said hoarsely. 'They're going!'

He dared a glance behind him in the direction she indicated.
The creatures were indeed leaving the field of battle, disappearing
among the trees on the far side of the clearing as quickly as they
had arrived. Caught in the current of exodus, the ones who
surrounded Damien and Hesseth screamed as they were swept
away. In moments they, too, were past the tree line and into the
forest, leaving only their blood and a fragment or two of flesh as a
witness to their feverish attack.

For a long minute Damien stood still, his heart pounding against
his rib cage, Hesseth pressed against his side. The warm musk of her
scent, familiar to him after months of travel, helped clear his head.
After a moment he dared to breathe deeply, and loosened his hold
on her shoulder. After another moment – a very long, very tense
moment – he dared to let his Shielding disperse. Bits of flesh and
flakes of blood fell to the ground as the fae which he had shaped
resumed its natural course. All demonic stuff, of course; he probably would cease to see it as soon as he let his special vision fade.
But for now he needed all his senses. No telling when the creatures
might return. No telling when something worse might follow.

They weren't after us, he thought numbly. *Or anyone in particular.
We just happened to be in their way.* He thought of the soldierfish of
the Lower Arterac, the army spiders of the Cameroon Delta. It
didn't matter to either of those species what stood in their way,
provided it was edible and stood in one place long enough to be
eaten. But both those species lived in rich ecospheres, where food
existed in abundance. What would thousands of demonlings do for
sustenance in the wilderness, where human abodes were few and
far between?

And what brought them into existence in the first place? he
wondered.

A shadow fell over their campsite as something passed overhead.
He didn't have to look up to know what it was. Tarrant circled

several times before coming to earth, as if he were uncertain about trusting his flesh to transformation. Or perhaps he was just scouting for enemies.

As soon as he had landed and regained his human form, Damien told him, 'We were attacked—'

'I saw,' Tarrant assured him.

He pictured the Hunter soaring comfortably overhead while the creatures attacked them and glared. 'You could have helped.'

'It's no easy thing to Work the fae while in a nonhuman form, Reverend Vryce. Nor is there much earth-power to manipulate at that height. But rest assured, if your own defense had failed, I would have attempted . . . something.'

'What did you see?' Hesseth asked.

Tarrant considered for a moment. What the rakh-woman had asked for was not a recap of the obvious, but his interpretation of what had gone on. 'They were newborn,' he said at last. 'Still riding on the force of their creation, not yet accustomed to feeding off humankind. One night old, I would guess. If not younger than that.'

Something in his tone made Damien look up sharply at him. 'You've seen this kind of thing before?'

The Hunter nodded. 'Several times. Ulandra comes to mind, right after the tsunami broke through her sea wall and drowned the entire city. And the fields of Yor, when Hasting's fortress fell at last and the invading army slaughtered everyone within. And I seem to recall a particularly nasty horde being created when the Neoduke of Moray snapped under siege and slaughtered his entire court for the cookpot.' He smiled darkly. 'Unfortunately, his Grace had no idea that the constructs birthed by his victims' dying screams devoured every soldier outside his gates, and he killed himself in the morning. Which rather negated the point of the whole exercise.'

For a moment Damien just stared at him. He struggled to find his voice. 'Mass murder?'

'That, or some natural disaster. Just as the terminal terror of one man can give birth to a demonling, so can the anguish of a thousand souls give birth to . . . what you saw. And you were very fortunate,' he added. 'They weren't yet crazed with hunger, as they will be in a few nights. Nor have they developed real intelligence yet, as the faeborn are wont to do.'

'They came from that direction.' Hesseth pointed. 'Does that mean—?'

The Hunter nodded. 'The source will be there. Less than a night's journey from us, if I read things correctly.' He looked at Damien and said dryly, 'I suppose you'll want to go to it?'

He hesitated. 'It's along our route,' he said at last. 'If there's some danger there—'

'As there certainly will be.'

'Then we need to find out what it is. Right?' When the Hunter didn't answer, he pressed, 'Don't you agree?'

The Hunter smiled faintly. It was a tense expression, but not without humor.

'If I didn't,' he asked dryly, 'would it make a bit of difference?'

The village was deserted—

Or so it seemed.

They entered the main gate silently, leading their horses behind them. There were no faeborn predators fluttering about the gate-wards, as there would have been outside any city. It was wrong, terribly wrong. As he passed the warded lintels he noticed that the very air seemed leached of sound, eerily silent. No insects chirruped in the under-brush, nor was there the rustling of any tiny herbi-vore. In the still night air he could hear himself breathing, and the sound seemed unnaturally loud.

'Can you smell it?' Hesseth whispered. The place demanded whispering.

He lifted his nose to the air and tested the breeze for content. At first he smelled nothing worse than a vague miasma, the kind of damp unwholesomeness common in swamps and mires. Then the wind shifted slightly, and he caught a whiff of something else. Decaying meat. Drying blood. Death.

They moved into the village warily, senses alert for any sign of movement. There was none. The breeze blew a few loose leaves across the street, then stilled. Nothing else.

'Tarrant?' he whispered.

The Hunter looked about, his pale eyes narrowed in concentration. 'No life,' he said at last. 'No life at all. Nor *unlife,*' he added quickly. An acknowledgment that his own unique state reminded them of questions they might otherwise not think to ask.

Damien looked at the buildings which flanked the narrow street. Simple wood and brick construction, painted long ago in colors that were neither too bright nor too dull; it was hard to tell anything about the people here just from their facades. 'We should look inside.'

Hesseth hissed a soft agreement.

'If you want,' the Hunter said softly, 'I'll stay with the horses.'

Damien looked up sharply at him, wondering if there was something here he didn't want to see. But no, his eyes were fixed on the earth-fae before him, and the silver intensity that glittered in their depths told the priest that he had every intention of finding out what had happened.

Taking two of the small lanterns with them, Damien and Hesseth entered the nearest house.

The door was unlocked, and swung open at their touch. Two feet back it jammed against something, and Damien had to press his weight against it in order to force it open.

A chest. Someone had pushed a heavy chest up against the door, hoping to keep it shut.

Which meant someone was probably still inside.

His first instinct was to call out some reassurance, in case someone was still alive. But while the Hunter might be wrong in other things, Damien trusted his judgment utterly in matters of death. And so he picked his way carefully through the house's sitting room, over bits of furniture and decor that seemed to have been scattered by some violent movement. The smell grew thicker as he moved toward the back of the house. At the far end of the room was a heavy wooden door, slightly ajar. He walked warily up to it and peeked inside.

No life, the Hunter had told them.

There were five bodies in the bedroom, strewn about like damaged and discarded toys. One lay on its back across a window seat, and Damien could just make out the look of tortured horror on the young man's face. That, and the reek of urine and fecal matter which filled the small room, told Damien that death had been neither slow nor secretive in this place.

He looked at them a moment longer, but couldn't determine the cause of death. Let Tarrant discover that with his Knowing. He backed out of the small room and shut the door gently, feeling his gut unknot just a little as the powerful stench was closed away. Flies buzzed past his face as he forced himself to breathe deeply. Once. Twice. Again.

He looked about for Hesseth. He didn't see her in the sitting room, but there was another door open at its far end. As he made his way toward it he heard her hiss softly; the sound was more anguished than hostile.

He found her in a back room, kneeling in a narrow doorway. Looking beyond her Damien saw the fixtures of a primitive bathroom, the walls and floor awash with blood.

'What happened?' he whispered.

She pointed to where a pile of bodies lay in the far corner, huddled together like a pile of broken dolls. Four children, all pale and lifeless. By their feet lay another body, that of an older woman.

He squeezed his way into the small room, casting his lantern light on the bodies. There was a dark gash visible on the neck of one of the children, and he pushed the small head gently to one side in order to get a better look. The cut was deep and long and there was no question about its being the cause of death. Another child was positioned so that its neck was also visible; he studied that also, nodding to himself as the grisly pattern made itself clear. Then he stopped by the woman's body long enough to see the two deep cuts that grooved her wrists, the blood-covered knife in her hand. And he ushered Hesseth out.

'She killed them,' he said quietly. 'Most likely they were her own children, and she killed them to save them from . . . *that*.' He nodded back toward the room he had inspected, not willing to put the horror into words. Not just yet. 'A cut to the carotid artery is a quick and almost painless death. She knew what she was doing.'

'What happened here?' the rakh-woman whispered.

He shook his head. 'I don't know, Hesseth. But it didn't happen quickly, that's for sure.'

The relatively clean air of the streets was a welcome relief after the poisoned closeness of the house's interior; he breathed deeply when they exited, trying to clear his lungs.

Then he looked up at Tarrant, a question in his eyes. The Neocount said nothing, but nodded toward a building across the street from them. *Meeting Hall,* the sign over the door said. 'In there,' he directed them. His tone communicated nothing.

Filled with more than a little misgiving, Damien and Hesseth moved toward the building. The smell was stronger there, sick and forbidding. His stomach was tight with dread as he turned the worn brass handle and pushed it open, as he stepped forward to look inside—

Oh, my God.

He was back out on the street again, reeling as though something had struck him in the face. The afterimage of the meeting hall's contents was burned into his vision, shadows and highlights of utter horror sculpted by the lantern's light. Bodies that were nailed to the wooden floor and gutted. Intestines wound about a desk leg, their owner still attached. More brutal, malevolent destruction than he had ever seen in one place before. And on every face, in every staring eye, a look of such utter horror that there was no question in Damien's mind that these people had been alive while they were eviscerated. Perhaps being tortured in a careful progression so that future victims could see their coming fate, writhing terrified in their bonds as body after body was vivisected . . .

It was too much. Too much. He leaned over and vomited in the street, bitter fluids surging from his gut in violent revulsion. Again and again, until his stomach was more than empty. Still it spasmed, and his mouth burned with the fluids of his revulsion.

He didn't look at Tarrant. He didn't want to see those eyes – so cool, so utterly inhuman – fixed on his helplessness. He didn't want to acknowledge what he knew deep inside, which was that even a horror such as this would fail to move the Hunter. Had Gerald Tarrant not done a similar thing to his own wife and children? Would he not gladly do worse in the future, if he felt that survival demanded it?

Instead Damien looked for Hesseth. She was nowhere to be found. He was just about to start worrying when she staggered out of the meeting hall doorway, one hand clenched shut about something. Under the angry red patches of her perpetual sunburn her face was drained of all living color, and her mouth hung slack as if she lacked the strength to shape whatever words she needed.

She walked to him. Slowly. Like him, she refused to meet Tarrant's eyes. When she was no more than two feet away her hand uncurled, slowly. Flakes of blackened blood clung to her palm, making it hard to see what she held. A thin, curving object with shreds of flesh still adhering to its wider end. As if it had been torn from some living thing so violently that the flesh itself had given way.

It was a claw.

She gave him a moment to study it, flexing her own claws so that he might compare. The curve was the same, the composition, the proportion – everything but the size, which was slightly larger. There was no question what manner of creature it had come from.

'My people did this,' she whispered hoarsely. 'Rakh.' Her hand started to tremble so violently that she had to close it again, rather than drop the grisly thing. 'Why?' she whispered. 'Why?'

He drew her to him because she seemed to need it, and carefully, delicately, folded his arms around her. For a moment he was afraid that she might respond badly, that her natural aversion to humankind might overpower her need for comfort. But she buried herself against his chest and shivered violently, so he held her tightly. No tears came from those amber eyes; the rakhene anatomy did not allow for it. But she trembled with a grief that was every bit as genuine and as passionate as that which a human woman might know, and he did his best to comfort her.

'Let's get out of here,' he whispered.

Tarrant stirred. 'Let's collect some weapons and *then* get out of here.'

Damien looked up at him. The pale eyes contained neither disdain nor impatience, but something that in another life might have been called sympathy. 'It may be our only chance,' the Hunter pointed out.

After a minute Damien nodded. He disentangled Hesseth from his embrace, gently. 'Come on,' he said softly. 'We need supplies. Let's find them and then we can get out of here.'

'What if they come back?'

He looked up at Tarrant, then back toward the meeting hall. 'I don't think they will,' he said quietly. 'There's nothing here for them. Not anymore.'

And because she could shed no tears, he did so. A few drops squeezed from the corners of his eyes, a monument to her grief. He hated himself for showing such weakness in front of Tarrant – and hated Tarrant for not doing so himself, for being so far removed from the sphere of human emotions that not even this outrageous slaughter could move him.

'Come on,' he muttered. Forcing himself to move again. Forcing himself to function. 'Let's get on with it.'

Hours later. How many? Time and distance were a featureless blur, each minute blending into the one that followed, each step shrouded in a fog of mourning. Perhaps yards. Perhaps miles. Perhaps half a night. Who could say?

At last they dismounted. The chill light of dawn was just stirring in the eastern sky; not enough to make Tarrant take cover yet, but enough to give him warning. They made their camp mechanically, pitching the tent that Hesseth had pieced together from their extra blankets. Not using the camping supplies that they had picked up in the village. Not ready for that yet.

When the small fire was burning and the horses had been tended to and water had been gathered from a nearby stream, then the words came. Slowly. With effort.

'Why?' Hesseth whispered.

'Your people are known for a fierce hatred of humankind,' Tarrant offered. It was the first time he had spoken since they'd left the village. 'Is it so incredible that their hatred has found an outlet here?'

She glared at him. 'My people aren't like that.'

Tarrant said nothing.

She turned away. Her furred hands clenched. 'My people would happily kill all humans. Just like they wanted to kill you, when you came into our territory. But that's different. That's . . .'

'Better?' the Hunter asked dryly. 'Cleaner?'

She turned on him; her amber eyes were blazing. 'Animals kill for food, or defense. Or to rid themselves of something undesirable. They don't torture other creatures for the sheer pleasure of seeing them suffer. That's a human thing.'

'Maybe your people have become more human than they know.'

'Stop it,' Damien snapped. At Tarrant. 'Stop it *now*.'

For a moment there was silence. The crackling of the fire. The soft breathing of the horses.

'We knew we were fighting something with the ability to corrupt men's souls,' the priest said. 'Didn't we see that in Mercia? Men and women who meant well, who had devoted their lives to a beneficent God . . . yet who would murder their fellow humans without a moment of remorse, and consign helpless children to a ritual of torture.' God, it hurt to remember all that. He fought to keep his voice steady. 'I think what we've seen tonight is that he – or she, or it – has done the same to your people.' He watched as Hesseth lowered her head, trying to make his voice as gentle as it could become. 'He did have something to start with, after all. How much work would it be to twist a rakhene soul, so that the desire to kill one's enemy became the desire to torture him to death?'

'It isn't a rakh thing,' she hissed softly. 'It isn't the way we work.'

He waited a moment before he answered. 'That may have changed,' he said gently. 'I'm sorry, Hesseth. But it's the truth. God alone knows how long he's had to operate, but it's clear that he's had enough time to influence your people. To influence *both* our peoples,' he added quickly. 'God alone knows why . . .'

'Yes,' Tarrant agreed. 'That's a good question, isn't it? A demon might feed on that kind of hatred, or on the pain it engendered, or on any other emotion that was a consequence of the system . . . but only with humans, not the rakh. Why corrupt a native species? No demon could gain strength from that.'

'Are you sure?' Damien asked.

'Absolutely. The faeborn draw their strength from man because he creates them; they rely on him for sustenance. What good is a rakhene soul to them? Its nature is as alien to demonkind as we are to Erna. They can't digest it.'

'So the purpose is something else.'

Tarrant nodded. 'And you forget something else.'

Hesseth stiffened. Damien looked up sharply at him.

'The rakh who came to this continent must have done so over ten thousand years ago, when the land bridge in the north was still intact. Nothing else can explain their appearance on both continents. And it's clear that when the fae began to alter them, making them more like humanity, both groups were affected. Why not? This planet is a unified whole; the same currents course over all of it. But the hatred?' He shook his head, his expression grim. 'That wasn't a physical change, but a social response to the Crusades, a western phenomenon. Why would the rakh who lived here – who had not even come in contact with humankind at that point – share such feelings? Why should the masters of their own continent hate a species they had never even seen? It makes no sense.'

'What are you suggesting?'

'That the rakh here were taught to hate. It's all part of some greater plan, designed to corrupt those who live here. Human and rakh alike.'

'Why?' Hesseth demanded, her voice shaking slightly.

Tarrant shook his head in frustration. 'I wish I knew. Tonight's discovery raises so many questions . . . and I don't know where to begin answering them. I'm sorry.'

He stood. The sky was light enough now that it illuminated him from above, casting a shadowy halo about his hair. 'What we do know is that the enemy's cause is more complicated than we at first suspected . . . and likewise his tools are more varied than we anticipated. We should be very wary.' He looked at the graying sky with regret. 'I hate to leave you now—'

'We understand,' Damien said.

'Keep careful guard. I don't think anyone will bother to come back to the village . . . but it's dangerous to anticipate our enemy when we don't understand the game he's playing. I wish now that we had obliterated our tracks,' he murmured, 'at least through the town. But it's too late for that now.'

Damien turned to Hesseth. 'Can you—'

She shook her head. 'Not from this distance. I'm sorry.'

'We need clear currents,' Tarrant said. 'I need to get farther south, so I can Know him with nothing standing between us. Without understanding his motives . . .' He shook his head. 'Our only hope lies in comprehending what he wants, what he's done here.'

'And what he is,' Damien supplied.

'Yes,' the Hunter agreed. Stepping back so that he might transform himself without the power of his coldfire Working hurting his companions. 'What he is. That, most of all.'

The dawn sky was gray now, with a hint of pale blue at the lower edge. Tarrant looked at it once as if gauging the sun's progress, then studied the earth-fae at his feet for any warning of imminent seismic activity. Evidently there was none. The Hunter stood up straight, bracing himself for the painful effort of transformation.

And then the coldfire flared, and the broad wings rose into the sky. And there were only the two of them left, and the dawn, and the silence.

17

'Protector Iseldas?'

The creature who wore that form looked up, noted the arrival of one of his own kind, and nodded. 'Come in. Close the door. Carefully,' he added, indicating with a glance the hallway outside.

The other looked carefully up and down the corridor, testing its privacy with more-than-human senses. At last he grunted in satisfaction and entered the firelit chamber. The heavy double doors swung shut with a soft thud and the lock dropped noisily into place

'Did you find her?' the mock-Iseldas demanded.

'Not yet.'

'Well, then? What?' His nerves were on edge from dealing with the Iseldas clan all day. Petty human underlings, with petty human concerns. Someday they would all be gone. Someday this region would be wiped clean of them forever, so that a more worthy species might take their place. 'I told you to stay out until you find her.'

'We found something.' He hesitated before stepping forward, as if unsure of the protocol. He had been far more comfortable in Kierstaad's domain, where all the house staff had been replaced; here, with only a few of them amidst two dozen true humans, the constant strain of his disguise was wearing his patience thin. 'We thought you should see it.'

He handed the imposter – *call him Iseldas,* he chided himself, *learn to do it* – the paper in his hand. All folded and dirty and covered with blood, as befit a drawing from the village.

Ah, the village. He savored the memory with glee. So much of their life was spent pretending to be human, pretending to be civilized, that it was good to let one's animal soul rear its head at last. The Prince would not understand, perhaps, nor condone such wholesale slaughter – on grounds of efficiency, of course, rather than compassion – but these creatures here who made the rules, these men of his own race who lived and breathed the lives of humans, they understood. They knew that the price of such a grand subterfuge was an occasional indulgence.

Leave no witnesses, Kierstaad had said. They hadn't.

He watched while Iseldas – the new Iseldas – unfolded the travel-worn paper. Watched while he scrutinized the crude ink drawings on its surface. His brow furrowed in concentration, but he said nothing. At last he held up the paper. 'What are these?'

'Tracks, we believe.' He pointed to the first drawing – a precise reproduction of the street outside the Meeting Hall – and then the sketches below, which divided up the cryptic shapes into something resembling hoofmarks. 'Three animals, all similar. *Very* large.'

The first set was crescent-shaped, sharp-edged, deeply incised into the earth. The second had been made by feet with three-clawed toes, the center digit slightly larger than the other two. The third might have been of their offspring, with a half-moon shape flanked by two deep scratches. Figures indicated how far apart the marks were.

'What are they?' Iseldas demanded.

'We don't know. But they were accompanied by human footsteps.'

Iseldas looked up sharply. 'You said all the villagers were dead.'

'All of them were. These must have come from elsewhere. You see that their animals are foreign—'

'And large,' he hissed. The reaction was not one of human reason, but of animal uncertainty; the thought of the foreign beast's size and bulk was as unnerving as a hostile odor. 'Any other signs?'

He shook his head.

'You're sure the human footsteps came after?'

There was no need to ask him *after what*? They both understood what he meant. 'I can't swear they weren't there when we cleansed the town. Why stop to check a dirt road for mere footsteps? There must have been thousands. But these flanked the animal tracks exactly, and I'm fairly sure those *weren't* there before. They're odd enough that we would have noticed.'

And threatening enough, Iseldas thought. An animal which left tracks like that could weigh over a ton. That was rare in these parts, and decidedly dangerous. The hooves looked deadly, too, large enough and solid enough to crush bone. All in all, the thought of such a beast free in the woods – his woods – made him feel like his fur was standing on end.

'I want you out after this,' he commanded. 'Find out where these tracks lead, what's making them—'

'What about the girl?'

He hissed as he breathed in. What about the girl? Kierstaad said she would have gone north, but he frankly doubted it. Most likely the local carnivores had gotten to her, and all that was left for them was to locate her bones. If they hadn't been buried somewhere for a winter snack.

But duty was duty. The Undying Prince had taught them that.

'Keep searching for her,' he growled. 'But get at least two or three on this trail, too.' He looked down at the paper in his hands, at the odd shapes that could not be – but clearly were – some animal's tracks. 'I'll send this on to the Matrias. See what they make of it. Do we still have birds?'

'For Mercia and Penitencia.'

'Mercia. That's where the last letter came from. Maybe this has something to do with the westerners.' A sudden spark of excitement stirred within him. What if these tracks were connected to the outsiders, somehow? What if the western-born fugitives hadn't gone by sea after all, but by land, and he was able to capture them? There'd be reward aplenty for that move, once the northern lands were taken. He growled softly in anticipation, considering it. 'Send the question to Mercia.'

'Right away.'

'And also . . . do we have a bird for Kierstaad?'

'Why not send a messenger? It's right across the—'

'I don't want to waste the people or the time. Do we have a bird?'

He blinked. 'I think so. Why?'

'Send word that we need more support. Send word that I want enough people to replace Iseldas' staff. Totally. This business of having to be on guard against eavesdroppers, of the constant pretense . . . it wears. It wears badly. I want the support to establish myself here properly, before the Protector's wife comes home.' And he muttered, 'That'll be challenge enough.'

'You going to mate with her?' he hissed softly. There was an undercurrent of challenge in his voice.

Iseldas' fur began to rise. Or rather, it *would* have risen had he still possessed any true fur. But all he had now was a sparse covering of human hair, useless for protection or display. How did the humans stand it?

'Watch yourself,' he warned. Making his voice as much a growl as the human speech apparatus would permit. 'I'm in charge here. You want to fight, let's get on with it. Otherwise watch your tongue.'

The other male growled low in his throat, and for a minute Iseldas thought he might indeed make a move toward him. All his masculine instincts were afire, but despite his best effort he could manage no physical display. The fur wasn't there to stand erect. The claws weren't there to be bared. Even his teeth had been transformed, so that his snarl was shorn of its visual display.

How he hated this transformation! They might as well cut his balls off as make him wear human flesh. The result was much the same.

But the other male was likewise handicapped, and Iseldas could see him struggling with his uncooperative body. Though he might have continued the challenge in his native form, he was clearly not comfortable with doing so on human terms. At last he stepped back ever so slightly, and delicately inclined his head. The gesture was awkward, but it communicated.

'Now get to work,' Iseldas snapped. 'And spare me your insults in the future.'

The other male growled softly, but he did leave as ordered. Iseldas was glad of it. He had no doubt that an out-and-out battle for dominance would have revealed their nature to the true humans, no matter what story they made up to cover it. Humans might be stupid, but they weren't blind.

You'll have to face him someday. Either that, or let him form a pack of his own. He's too strong willed to play the second male forever.

He smiled slightly, remembering his own rise through the ranks. The fever of ambition that had burned within him like a fire, consuming all reason. The heady sense of invulnerability that accompanied each new combat. He had dominated most of the males in the Kierstaad domain – usually by intimidating them, sometimes by actual combat – and he might have taken on Kierstaad himself, if not for this new assignment. Little wonder that the mock-Protector had chosen him for this role. He hoped that when his time came he could make a similarly wise decision.

It's never easy being the prime male, he consoled himself. As he sipped from the wine in the goblet at hand, and dreamed that it was human blood.

18

They divided up their new supplies the following evening. It was hard for Damien to handle the village items without feeling somehow that he was also grasping their tragedy. It was hard not to remember those twisted, tormented bodies as he sorted through the items that had once belonged to their owners.

You would approve of our mission, he promised them silently. *With these weapons we can perhaps destroy the evil that brought you down. With these we can keep it from killing others.*

Dried food in quantity, and grain for the horses. Knives for hunting, skinning, and killing. Several small handguns and their ammunition. Three versions of a larger, more primitive weapon that was unlike anything Damien had seen before. He hefted one to his shoulder, noting that its stock was not unlike that of a spring-bolt, his projectile weapon of choice. But instead of a smooth, barreled head it had a construction resembling a bow in miniature, set perpendicular to the line of fire. An awkward construction, Damien noted, but it seemed to work; the few practice shots he and Hesseth took with it launched the smooth, metal-tipped bolts across a clearing and inches deep into the bark of a tree. Not bad. It didn't have the balance of a springbolt, of course, and one could eviscerate oneself trying to use the butt as an impact weapon, but it was immeasurably better than what they'd had. They checked all the working parts twice, divided up five boxes of bolts, and felt considerably safer than they had the night before.

Then there were the guns. Tarrant had brought them, along with the ammunition and priming agents they required. Damien would just as soon have left them there. Only three houses in the village had had them, which indicated to him that the firearms were rare outside the great cities. For good reason. He watched as Tarrant cleaned the fine metal parts with the hooks and wire brushes he had also gathered, until he seemed satisfied. It was the kind of care a normal man might give such a weapon: not only to make sure it worked, but to make sure the user *knew* that it would work. On a world where doubt too easily became disaster, anything less would be suicide.

'Can't you just Work it into efficiency?' He demanded of Tarrant. Anxious to be moving again, to put the devastation of last night's discovery even farther behind them.

'I could Work the metal parts,' the Hunter assured him. '—and indeed, I am doing that. But as for the rest . . .' He blew at a touchhole softly, spraying fine black powder across the stock. 'I think you forget my limitations. I have no power over fire, or anything that manipulates fire – and this falls into that category.'

'You mean you can't stop it from misfiring?' Hesseth asked.

What an incredible concept! That this man who could move mountains, who could and did shift whole weather systems in an instant – who had redefined the very parameters of death, at least as they related to his own person – could not assure that a simple mechanical instrument would function as it should, any more than your average man in the street.

'I can't,' he agreed, confirming the incredible. 'But nor will I *cause* it to misfire, as the doubts of so many might do.' He brushed off the last of the guns and laid it down beside the others. They gleamed golden on the dark grass, reflecting the Corelight. 'They're not my weapon of choice – as you well know – but if our enemy is armed with guns, then we should at least have the option of meeting him on similar ground.' He looked at Damien. 'Have you ever used one of these?'

'Once.' He still remembered the kick of the carved wooden grip in his hand, the dread feeling – just for an instant – that something he had sparked off was too fast and too secretive for him to control. His master had *tsk tsked,* and announced with solemn finality, 'Some men are born to handle firearms. You, Vryce, are clearly not one of them. But with practice and knowledge I have every confidence that you can bring this weapon under control, so that it's deadly only to your enemies.'

Practice and knowledge. Only there were so many other things to see and learn and do at the same time, and besides, he liked the sword. It was a pleasing sensation to launch an attack at an enemy and feel the heavy swing carry through like an extension of his arm, the sharp steel resonating with triumph as it cut through living flesh, blood dripping along its edge . . . or so he imagined. The truth was that he'd been just fifteen at the time, and the most he'd done was batter a jousting block with hardwood blades, and once – just once – helped dispatch a low-order ghoul that was cruising the visitor's dormitory. Which he'd done with a knife, not with a sword, but the theory was much the same. The point was, steel he understood. Steel he *trusted*. Black powder was more like . . . well, like magic.

'They're all yours,' he assured Tarrant, and he thought he saw the Hunter smile.

There was a slight tremor then, but the Hunter declared it to be of no consequence. *Harmonic tremors,* he explained, which felt like small-scale earthquakes but didn't disturb the earth-fae nearly so drastically. Damien did note that there had been five distinct tremors since they'd started traveling south, and doubtless many more too subtle to them to detect. Neither he nor Tarrant had said it in so many words, but the truth was clear to both of them: this wasn't a safe region to Work in. Tarrant was taking a chance with his transformations, but at least that was after careful study of the currents. They'd better be careful in the heat of battle, though, lest the energies unleashed by a shifting planet burn one of them – or both – to a crisp. Damien had already seen the fae sear through a woman's brain in the rakhlands, and he had no desire to experience it any more directly.

They loaded the horses and began to ride. Damien and Hesseth had allowed enough time for resting that both felt somewhat refreshed, though nightmares had made sleep a touch-and-go affair. They were lucky that Tarrant was with them, Damien reflected; otherwise the powers at large might well manifest their fear and their horror right back at them. But the Hunter's presence seemed to discourage fear-ghouls from forming, and most of the region's extant terrors preferred to stay a good distance away.

They continued south. The horses were stronger now, and the terrain more obliging than it had been; considering the near-darkness that Tarrant's schedule resigned them to, they made good time. Once they neared a village – its presence was proclaimed not only by its lights and its sounds but by the dozens of silent wraiths who flitted about its gates, hunger curling from them like tendrils of black mist – and they remained in the vicinity just long enough to read the currents that flowed through it, to see that no horror had just taken place or was just about to. But the village was peaceful, its people contentedly sequestered for the night, and Damien had to fight back his urge to warn them. In truth, what could a stranger say to them that they would believe? And what would he warn them about? They didn't really know what happened, did they?

Once soon after, when the moonlight flashed down upon them, he gazed upon the Hunter's profile. *He knows what happened,* the priest thought. *He Saw.* And it made a cold shiver course up his spine, to think that one of them had actually witnessed the slaughter.

I wouldn't share that Knowing for anything.

The next village was directly in their path; they had to circle to the east to avoid it. That course led them down a rocky slope to a river, perhaps an extension of the stream they had followed so long ago. Had the night been dark they might have waited until morning before crossing, but Casca was full overhead by that time and Prima's crescent added its share of light from the east; they waded their horses through what looked like the calmest stretch of water, and outside of riding calf-deep in the ice cold mountain runoff made the crossing without mishap.

They stopped at the first likely site they found and toweled themselves and their mounts dry. The night breeze was cool but not unpleasant, at least not when one was dry. As he wrung out his boots, Damien noticed Tarrant studying the land before them.

'What is it?'

'The currents,' he murmured. 'They're . . . odd.'

His tone was enough to make Damien tense up; he saw Hesseth's ears prick forward. 'Odd how?'

The Hunter held up a hand to silence him. Damien could see his pale eyes focusing on some point just beyond them, perhaps where the earth-fae surged over some promontory and became particularly Workable. After a moment he stiffened. A soft hiss escaped his lips.

'We're being followed,' he said quietly.

He heard Hesseth curse in her rakhene tongue. For himself, he muttered angrily that it had all seemed too good to be true. The Hunter waved them silent again, his eyes fixed on fae-wrought pictures that only he could see. His companions waited.

'They found the tracks. They're following them. They're not sure who we are, or what we're mounted on . . . *damn,*' he hissed. 'They have information. *Real* information. And they're organized.'

'Villagers?' Damien dared. Feeling a cold churning in his gut as he asked. He knew what the answer would be.

'We should be so lucky.' The Hunter's expression was grim. 'Not villagers, no. And I think . . . maybe not human.'

For a moment the words hung between them, impaled upon the stillness of the air.

'You're not sure?'

He shook his head, frustrated. 'They're north of us, which means I have to fight the current to read anything. In addition there's some extra unclarity, perhaps an Obscuring of some kind, perhaps . . .' He shook his head, clearly frustrated. 'They don't seem to have Workers with them. Yet I sense power. Something quiescent . . . maybe a Warding? Hard to say.'

'Which means what?' Hesseth demanded. That the fine points of human sorcery meant nothing to her was clear from her tone.

'It means we move.' Soft hair glimmered in the double moonlight as he turned to face her; his eyes were shadowed, unreadable. 'We move fast. It means we think about some way to Obscure our presence, even though they already know where we are – which makes such a Working very difficult,' he added. 'It means we think about the obviousness of our route, and finding a defensible shelter, and the possibility of ambush—' He let the last sentence hang in the air unfinished, with all its threat intact.

'It means the good times are over,' Damien said dryly.

'*Assst!*' Hesseth's eyes sparkled darkly. 'Is that what they were?'

'Perhaps we should consider crossing the mountains,' Tarrant told them. 'Precisely because it is a more difficult route.'

'They're behind us,' Damien responded. 'They haven't got horses or any near equivalent, so if we make good time—'

'You're not listening,' the Hunter said softly. The threat in his voice was all the more powerful for being so delicately voiced. 'I said they have *information*. That means they got it from somewhere. That means that some kind of network is operating.'

It took him a minute for the implications of that to sink in. 'Shit,' he muttered. 'Shit.'

'We know this coast is lined with Protectorates, whose only

purpose is to seek out and destroy enemy forces. If they've truly been alerted, do you think we can outrun them? Every border we pass means a new army poised in waiting. I don't like it,' he told them. 'Even with all of us together it's too dangerous, and with the nights as short as they are . . .' There was no need for him to continue. The thought of facing the Protectorates' legions was bad enough; the thought of facing them in the daylight hours, without Tarrant's power beside them, was truly daunting.

'What do you suggest?' Hesseth asked.

He gestured toward the south. 'For now, continue as we've been doing. We won't have another option for a while. Between your skills and mine we can probably Obscure our trail, but it wouldn't hurt to stick to rocky ground. It's always hard to Obscure something once it's been noticed.'

'And then?'

'The map indicates a pass some forty miles to the south of here. That could be anything from a true break in the mountains to a single ridge which is slightly less daunting than its neighbors. I suggest we take it. It would be easier for me to leave signs that we had continued south than it would be to simply make our tracks disappear. By the time they catch on and backtrack we'll be out of the Protectorates and truly Obscured. Of course, if we decided to kill whatever was following us – or even just take a look at it – such a region would be ideal for entrapment.'

'That works both ways,' Hesseth reminded him. 'What if they anticipate us?'

'Unlikely,' the Hunter responded. 'Think about it. They can't be sure that we know about their pursuit, and the route just west of the mountains – which we've been taking – is quick and easy. Why would we change? Also . . .' He glanced at Damien. 'There are the Terata. What small party of humans wouldn't prefer the threat of a simple pursuit to a land filled with bloodthirsty demons?'

'That's a very good point,' Damien noted.

A faint expression – it might have been a smile – flashed ever so briefly across the Hunter's face. 'I'm far more comfortable with the concept of demons than with an armed pursuit. Demons at least are unlikely to attack in the daylight.'

'So you're comfortable with demons,' Damien snapped. 'What about us?'

The pale eyes gleamed in the moonlight. 'Do you see a viable alternative?'

He bit his lip, considering. At last he muttered, 'No, dammit. But I don't like it. I don't like it at all.'

'He's right, though.' Hesseth's voice was low. 'He can handle demons. And most of them won't care about me. Besides—'

'And I'm lunch. Thanks. Thanks a lot.'

'We'll protect you,' she promised. Smiling just a little.

He looked at her, then at Tarrant. Surely it was his own imagination that perceived an expression of smugness on that aristocratic visage. Or was it challenge?'

'I don't know.' He directed his words at Tarrant. 'The last time I made a decision like this I wound up getting stuck with *you*.'

With a sigh he hooked his foot into the stirrup and hoisted himself onto the horse's back. Already the saddle felt natural to him, as if he had spent the last half-year riding, not sailing. A marked improvement.

'What the hell,' he muttered. 'I was getting bored anyway. Let's do it.'

19

The figure coalesced out of the midnight air, drawing its very substance from the darkness. All about it crystal tinkled, the delicate wrought-glass leaves of Miranda Kierstaad's last creation. The figure heard nothing. In the west, where it gazed, Domina's slim crescent was being swallowed by an ink-black roofline; stone crenellations cut into the lunar brilliance like a hundred tiny bitemarks. The figure saw nothing. Inside the keep there was commotion now, as the guard who had first seen the apparition searched hastily for his master. The figure knew nothing. Nor did it stir when the mock-Kierstaad entered the crystal-line garden, for its maker had not known which of the many males it sent out would achieve supremacy by invasion time, and therefore could not tailor its Sending to respond to a particular presence. It only waited long enough, in its maker's opinion, for whoever ran the Kierstaad Protectorate to make his way to the crystalline garden. And then a few minutes more, just to make sure.

Suddenly the figure seemed no longer a simple image, but a living man. Blue eyes looked about the garden, then fixed on the invader standing closest. It was difficult for the mock-Kierstaad to make formal obeisance – he now lacked most of the parts that needed to be smoothed, or flattened, or drooped – but he did the best he could with his inadequate human flesh. It would have to be enough.

The Prince's image had aged, he noted. The pale skin was no longer perfectly smooth, its blush no longer resonant with perfect health. There was a streak of white in the yellow hair, and lines where no lines had ever been. That was the way of it, he recalled. The chosen flesh of the Undying Prince remained youthful for decades, but once it began to age its decay was swift and dramatic. The soul inside that slender, graceful body would be preparing itself for Rebirth now, and neither man nor rakh could hope to predict what form the Prince would take next time, nor even what gender he might adopt.

Briefly, the mock-Kierstaad wondered what the Prince's first flesh had looked like. Briefly. He was a rakhene warrior, bred for the Prince's purposes, and as such did not have either the capacity or the inclination to philosophize at length.

The figure drew in a deep breath and spoke. 'Word reaches me that two of the Protectorates have fallen. You are to be commended. I hear of no outcry from the humans, so clearly you managed to keep your presence in the north a secret from them. Excellent. I know that this job is difficult for you, that you would far rather kill than hide, far rather take vengeance upon your human enemies than pretend to be one of them . . . but have patience. That time will come. I promise it.

'Remember: strike now, and a handful of humans will fall. Strike later, in force, and you may cleanse the entire region of their stink forever.

'On to other matters: You know that the foreigners we seek may now be traveling through your lands. No doubt you've sent out teams to search for them, in accordance with the Matria's request, and established watch posts at the most likely points of passage in your realm. All very good. But the Matrias don't know who and what these people are, and therefore their instructions were limited. So listen closely, and act upon my words; the fate of our entire project – as well as your own life – may well depend upon it.

'Of the three humans who are traveling south, at least two – the males – are sorcerors. What this means is that if you try to entrap them they'll probably see it coming, and the power that they wield may well give them the advantage in battle even if your people outnumber them. But though they are powerful they are also human, and human power is bound to the earth. When the earth shakes and for a brief time afterward, the fae they rely upon will be too hot to handle. Only then can you strike at them. Only then will they be helpless.

'I realize that the motion of the earth cannot be predicted, which makes it hard for you to plan. Nevertheless, the advantage of such a move is worth the inconvenience. Your region is seismically active, and rarely does a week pass without a handful of tremors. Be patient. Be careful. Wait for Erna to give you your cue, and the enemies of our purpose may be dispatched to the hell of their own creation. I myself will launch a Working that should distract them; you may use that cover to move in silence and safety.

'I am confident in your ability to make this kill and safeguard our great project. Surely the scent of triumph will be strong upon you, so that when you return home your women will be aroused by its power.'

The apparition faded. Eyes first, dissolving into pools of blackness, and then the rest of the figure. For a moment Kierstaad's conqueror stood very still, absorbing the essence of the message. He hadn't ever thought in terms of what this project would do for his mating precedence. That was a concept worth savoring.

But he hadn't come to a position of power through hormone

balance alone – though that was certainly part of it – and even as
he turned back to the keep he was mentally scouring the lands in
his Protectorate, searching for a way to prepare a mobile ambush.

The travelers would have to avoid the villages there, and also
there . . . the closeness of the mountains meant there was only one
safe path open to them, so they must take that . . . they would make
choices based on secrecy at every point, so their route could
be predicted . . . yes. He began to visualize the emplacements, the
preparations. Yes. It could be done. Wait for the earth to move, wait
for the humans to be helpless, then attack . . .

He could almost smell the triumph on his fur.

20

It would have been easy back home to watch for an ambush. In
Jaggonath a simple Knowing would have been enough to untangle
the secretive patterns of the fae, to reveal where and when the subtle
malevolence of entrapment had made its mark. Tarrant could
have done it with little effort, maintaining such a Working for hours
at a time. Even Damien could have kept it up for a reasonably long
stretch of time, providing he kept repeating the mental patterns
which sustained his Sight. But here, where repeated earthquakes
made any long-term Working perilous, where the surge of earth-
fae that accompanied all such tremors would burn his mind or
Tarrant's to a crisp before they had time to cry out a warning, such
a sustained Knowing was out of the question. And so they had to
rely upon intermittent Workings, short little bursts of information
that they plucked from the fae whenever the currents looked safe.

It clearly distressed the Hunter to restrain himself this way, and
Damien could understand why. As an adept Tarrant had lived
immersed in the earth-fae since his first conscious moments; to grasp
hold of that power and mold it to his will was as natural to him as
breathing was to Damien. It took effort for him to keep himself

from Working the fae, an effort that was clearly taking its toll on him. Periodically the priest would see the man stiffen in his saddle, or mutter angrily to himself, as if he had just restrained himself from some unconscious act of Knowing.

How could he have coped as a child, if he'd been born in this region? Damien suspected he wouldn't have made it past adolescence, if that long. Little wonder there were no adepts here, nor anyone capable of a real Working . . .

And then he remembered the real reason for that, and his face flushed hot with shame and fury as he kneed his horse to a faster pace. If he was driven onward in this quest for no other reason, it was to avenge all those children. Generation after generation of helpless, innocent souls, sacrificed on the altar of intolerance . . . and they were all guilty of it, he thought. Every human being who participated – by cutting a tiny throat, by staking a frightened child out as bait for demons, or even just by sitting back and making no protest while others did the dirty work – every one of them was guilty, every one of them would answer before God for all those terrible deaths. And he, Damien Kilcannon Vryce, would see to it that the monster responsible for causing it all would burn in Hell forever. If he did nothing else of value in his life, that alone would be sufficient service to his God.

When dawn came and Tarrant left them, Damien and Hesseth made camp, but they lit no fire and raised no tents. They took the supplies they needed from their saddlebags and then refastened the leather packs; they fed and watered the horses and brushed them vigorously, then resaddled them. Though neither of them voiced their concern, it was clear that both of them wanted to be ready to move on a moment's notice. Even the horses seemed to sense their inner tension, and made no protest when the bulky saddles were returned to their backs. Maybe danger was in the air. Maybe they could smell it.

They slept restlessly in turn, the slightest sound out of the ordinary rousing them in an instant. How much sleep Damien lost to the chattering of birds and the twigs broken by foraging rodents he didn't want to know. But though his nerves were wound up tighter than a watch spring, he neither saw nor heard anything to indicate that trouble was coming, and when he dared to look at the currents he likewise perceived no immediate threat. Good enough for now. There was a strange flavor to the earth-power, he thought, but it was so faint that he couldn't focus on it for a Knowing; they would have to wait for Tarrant to return before they could determine its source.

They had found a good campsite – close by the river but not visible from it, on firm rocky ground that hid the horses' tracks, easily defended – and decided to stay where they were until night-fall. Damien was loath to risk travel again without Tarrant by his side, and though Hesseth wasn't about to admit to such a senti-ment, he suspected she felt the same way. Whatever personal revulsion she felt for the Hunter, it was, like his own, overweighed by a pragmatic appreciation of the man's power.

God knows, if they're on our trail, we need all the help we can get.

Promptly at sunset the Hunter rejoined them. His transforma-tion was quick and businesslike, and as soon as the coldfire had faded from his flesh he dropped to one knee and placed the flat of his hand against the ground, as if testing the temperature of the earth. The delicate nostrils flared like a cat's. After a moment he stood again, but his eyes were still fixed on the ground before him.

'The currents are very strange,' he muttered. 'I noticed it when I awoke, and hoped it was no more than a passing anomaly . . . but it appears not.' He looked at Damien. 'Did you sense it?'

'I sensed something,' the priest answered. 'I couldn't identify it.'

'Almost as if there were a foreign presence in the current . . . yet nothing so precise as that. I worked a Knowing when I first noticed it, but I couldn't get a fix on it. That might mean that it's nothing important, some natural occurrence which has no deeper meaning . . .'

'Or that something's been Obscured from us,' Damien said grimly.

'Just so,' he agreed.

Tarrant held his hand up for silence. The pale eyes narrowed in concentration once more, and Damien could almost feel the raw power coalesce about him. The priest Worked his own vision, and he watched in awe as the silver-blue ripples of earth-fae gathered about the Hunter's feet, in a pool so deep and so intense that he could no longer see the ground through its light. The very power of the earth obeyed the Hunter like a household pet, coming to heel upon command. And yet even that was not enough to serve his need. Tarrant reached out his hands as the power thickened, intensified, rose about his legs until waves of raw power, blue-burning, lapped at his knees. And then came the Knowing. Damien could see it taking shape, ghostlike, between his outstretched arms. A hint of form. A shadow of meaning. And then ... nothing. The wraith-like image collapsed, its substance rejoining the pool of power at his feet. Then even that faded, until the earth-fae that attended Tarrant was no more brilliant than any other. The eddies and ripples which made up the current drew back from the Hunter and returned to their regular course. And Tarrant shook his head in frustration, acknowledging to himself – and to his traveling companions – that he had failed.

'If something was Obscured from us, it was well done.' Damien could hear the frustration in his voice, and something else. Fear? If something had been Obscured so well that even the Hunter couldn't make it out, didn't that imply a Working of tremendous power? Didn't it speak of an enemy at least as powerful as Tarrant himself?

Not a nice thought. Not a nice thought at all.

'Well?' Hesseth demanded. 'What do we do now?'

For a moment Tarrant said nothing. Damien could guess what was going through his mind. Enemies behind them, and now this foreign trace ahead ... Even the Hunter, for all his arrogant confidence, had to be less than happy about their situation. Had to be considering their alternatives.

Only there weren't any. That was the problem.

'It could be someone trying to Know us against the current,' he said at last. 'Someone reaching out to establish an initial link with us. If so, I've turned it aside.' *For now*. He didn't say it, but Damien could hear the words. *This one time*.

'Our enemy?' she asked.

He hesitated. Damien imagined he was thinking of the hundreds of miles between them and the supposed home site of their enemy, of the mountains and the cities and God alone knew what else that divided them, all of which would wreak havoc with such a Working. A Knowing worked across such a distance, across myriad obstacles and against the current, was almost doomed to failure.

'If so,' he said at last, 'he has phenomenal power.'

'So what do we do?' Damien asked. Not liking the darkness in his tone at all.

The Hunter looked south. What did those eyes see, which were always focused on the earth-power? For once Damien didn't envy him his special Sight. 'We go on. It's all we can do. Perhaps once we cross the mountains we'll be beyond his scrutiny . . . perhaps.'

They mounted up once more and continued south along the bank of the river. The ground was becoming more and more rocky, which helped to obscure their trail, but it was bad for the horses' footing. More than once, Damien had to dismount to dig out a sharp rock from his horse's hoof, and once they had to stop long enough for him to Heal the sole of Hesseth's mount, where a stone chip had gashed deeply into the tender flesh behind the toe-guards. Several times they had to lead the animals down to the river – no easy task in itself – and make their way warily through shallow water that ran black as ink, obscuring any dangers that might lie underneath. Their fear of earthquakes meant that Damien dared not use Senzei's trick, using the glow of the earth-fae through the water to detect irregularities beneath the surface, but Tarrant led them forward with his own special Sight and thus they proceeded without mishap.

Periodically Tarrant would signal for them to stop, and he would study the earth-power anew. Not just for signs of ambush now, although that was still a concern. The foreign trace he had failed to interpret clearly worried him, and he began to stop more and more frequently in an attempt to fix on it. Damien wondered if he had ever before been so completely frustrated in his attempt to Know something.

'Is it getting stronger?' he asked him once. The Hunter's expression grew grim, but he said nothing. Which was in itself a kind of affirmation.

'Let's say I don't like the feel of things,' he muttered at last. 'Not at all.'

'What about our pursuers?' Hesseth asked him.

He looked about, studying the earth-fae carefully. 'Those who follow are still some distance behind us,' he said at last. 'But those who lie in wait are closer than I would like. And it's strange . . .' He bit his lower lip, considering. 'In the other Protectorates I had the distinct impression that there were men scouring the woods for us, a general but unfocused effort . . . but here the feeling is different. Much more focused.' He looked back at them. 'I think it's crucial for you two to get safely across to the east before the sun rises. That'll put you in a different current, safe from whoever's trying to reach us.'

'Is there something specific you're afraid of?' Damien asked him.

The Hunter's expression darkened. 'I'm wary of anything that has the power to defy me.' For a moment he sounded tired; it was a strangely human attribute. 'The foreign trace muddies the current enough that it's hard for me to tell just how far ahead our enemies are. I don't like that. And I don't like the thought that it might get worse as we continue going south.'

'You think it's some kind of attack?'

'I don't know what it is. I'd prefer not to have to find out.' He pulled his horse about so that it faced to the south once more, and urged it into motion.

'Let's just hope the pass comes up soon,' he muttered.

It was more a gap than a pass proper, more a wound in the earth's rocky flesh than anything which Nature had intended. Some quake in ages past had split through the mountainside, and centuries of wind, water, and ice had worried at the resulting crack until it was wide enough – barely – for a mounted man to pass through at the bottom. Its walls were riddled with parallel faults that slashed diagonally through the rock, and erosion had worn at the varying layers until the whole of it looked like a bricklayer's nightmare. It was easier to imagine that vast, trapezoidal slabs of stone had been affixed to the walls of the gap, and that the mortar between them had been washed away, than it was to envision the whole as one solid piece which time and the elements had carved up so drastically.

They stared at it for some time in silence, each traveler cocooned in his own misgivings. At last Damien gave vent to their joint response.

'Shit,' he muttered.

'Hardly encouraging,' the Hunter agreed.

He urged his horse a few steps closer – the animals didn't seem to like it any more than they did – and took a good look at the walls of the crevasse. And cursed again, softly. No doubt Tarrant was examining it for flaws, tracing the lines of earth-fae as they ran through the channels in the rock, seeing where it might give, seeing where it might be solid. To Damien it just looked bad.

'Should we—' he began, but as he turned back toward Tarrant and Hesseth, the Neocount's expression silenced him.

'Don't Work!' the Hunter warned, in a tone that was becoming all too familiar.

He pulled his horse sharply around and got away from the crevasse, fast. Even as he rejoined his party the earth began to tremble. He saw Tarrant assessing the terrain with a practiced eye, checking for immediate dangers, and he did the same. Hesseth, who had grown up on the plains, didn't share their instinctive reaction, but she was sharp enough to move with them when they forced their mounts – now skittish and hard to control – a few yards back to the north, where the ground looked more solid.

To the east of them the mountains rumbled, the earthquake's roar magnified in the hollow chambers that riddled the ancient rock like sound in a musical instrument. The horses stepped about anxiously, trying to keep their balance as the ground bucked and twisted beneath them. A granite slab overhead came loose with a crack and hurtled down into the river just ahead of them. Then another. Spray plumed up in white sheets and fell over them like rain. The animals were frightened enough that they might have bolted, but even they seemed to know that there was nowhere to go, and the party managed to keep control of them. Barely. It was, as Damien had feared, a Bad One. Not their first on this trip by any means, but that didn't make it any less frightening.

At last the rumbling faded, and the ground about them settled down. There was a gash in the earth just south of them which hadn't been there before, and they had to jump the horses across it to get back to the mouth of the pass. The broken walls looked twice as imposing as before, Damien thought. As if Nature herself had seen fit to give them a reminder of what havoc she could wreak, once they were committed to that narrow space.

The Neocount pulled up alongside Damien. His horse was still jumpy, and for once he was unable to calm it with a touch; the earth-fae was still running molten from the earthquake's outpouring, and not even an adept dared make contact with it.

'Well,' the Hunter began, 'I see no real alternative—'

Shots rang out in the crisp night air, three distinct explosions that split the night with a crack. One of them hit the rock beside Tarrant, so that chips of granite flew at him. One scored the ground by the feet of Hesseth's mount. And the third—

Damien's horse squealed in pain and terror and bucked. It happened so fast the priest barely had time to react. His hand closed about the pommel of his saddle with spastic force as he pressed his knees into the horse's flanks, desperately trying to keep his seat. He was aware of Hesseth's horse wheeling to the north of him – also wounded? – and of Tarrant crying out orders which he had no way of hearing. Shots rang out again, but he had no way of knowing if any of them had hit their mark; his entire world had shrunk to the limit of a horse's reach, and every fiber of his being was focused on its motion, its terror, and his own mounting danger.

It went down on one leg then, and he knew with a fighter's certain instinct that it was going down for good. As the massive weight of the animal fell to the ground he pushed himself free of it, hitting the ground with a force that drove the breath from his lungs, rolling to his right, away from the animal, away from the gunfire, sharp pain in his left arm where he struck a rock – but keep rolling, keep moving – he heard the thud of his animal hitting the earth, the terrified squeal of its dying, and he suddenly understood that they hadn't missed him like he thought. They had been shooting for the horses, they understood that once the great beasts were out of the picture it was man against man, a party of three against an army . . . Dazed, he lay still for an instant, trying to get his bearings. Hesseth was by the mouth of the crevasse, her weapon raised to her shoulder, ready to return fire as soon as the enemy was visible. Tarrant – where was Tarrant? He looked up and found the black horse not a yard from his face. The Hunter's face was a mask of fury as he kept the animal moving, gesturing for Damien to get to his feet even as his other hand braced a stolen pistol for firing.

Another shot rang out from the woods, and this time Tarrant answered with gunfire. The sharp report rang in Damien's ear as he staggered to his feet. In the distance he heard someone cry out in pain and surprise, and a crashing that might be the fall of a body. Hesseth's bolt whizzed past them as Tarrant reached out a hand for him. Damien grasped him tightly about the wrist, felt Tarrant's ice-cold fingers close like a vise about his own wrist as the Hunter's booted foot kicked out of its stirrup, freeing the metal ring for Damien's use. Pain shot up his damaged arm like fire as he caught it with his toe and vaulted up onto the black horse's back. The back edge of the saddle rammed into his crotch, but he stayed there, stayed there despite the blinding pain, afraid to slide back for fear he would fall off, unable to slide forward. Praying like he had never prayed before.

The black horse followed Hesseth's past the mouth of the crevasse and into the darkness beyond. In the distance Damien could hear his own horse squealing, and he hoped that in its dying madness it would at least provide an obstacle for the armed men who were sure to follow. The walls of the crevasse scraped against them as the horses struggled along its jagged bottom. Damien had gotten a firm enough knee-grip on the horse's flanks that his crotch was no longer slamming down onto the saddle with every step – thank God for that – and he watched the chasm walls pass by all too slowly, as the horses picked their way in near-darkness over boulders and crevices and water-filled potholes. Damien was painfully aware of how precariously those tons of rocks overhead seemed to be balanced, of how very close the looming walls were pressed against them. If there were an aftershock now . . . but no, he mustn't think of that. Just keep riding. Just hang on. They were committed now, for better or for worse, and there was nothing they could do one way or the other to save themselves if an earthquake did come. Not without being able to Work.

If it shakes, it shakes. If we die, we die. Better come to terms with that now.

It seemed they rode for eternity like that, but in fact it could have been no more than mere minutes. Damien's chest and arms were chilled from contact with the unearthly cold of the Hunter's body, but he managed to hang on to the man. Behind him the priest could hear cries of pursuit; they were not nearly as far behind them as he would like. *We're not going to make it,* he thought. Fear churned coldly in his gut. *The horses just can't do it.* Then, to his immense relief, the chasm floor evened out somewhat. Hesseth's mount bolted forward, and Tarrant's horse followed suit. But though they were able to pull ahead of their pursuers for a time, so that their cries no longer echoed behind them, Damien knew that the change was only temporary. And when the horses pulled up short before a veritable obstacle course of fallen boulders, he knew with dread certainty that they weren't going to make it through fast enough. They were going to have to take a stand and fight.

But Tarrant had other plans. As his horse nervously pawed the rocky earth, he scanned the walls of the crevasse above them with meticulous attention, and Damien could just imagine what he was seeing. Molten power pouring from the clefts like lava, cascading down the walls in sheets of fire to boil about their feet. Too hot to handle. Too hot to use. It would cool off soon, now that the quake was over, but not soon enough. Not for them.

Then the Hunter swung one leg forward over his horse's neck and dismounted. As Damien slid forward, he put the end of the reins in his hand and instructed them, 'Go on, the two of you. Go as far as you can, as fast as you can. Get out of this trap if that's possible, and then make camp. I'll see that there's no pursuit.' Despite the moonlight which illuminated his face, his expression was unreadable. 'Go!'

He struck the black horse sharply on the rear and it bounded forward, clearing the nearest obstacle by inches. Damien just had time to see Tarrant take hold of the rock wall as if he meant to climb it, and then a protrusion cut off his sight-line. For a few seconds he could do no more than cling to the horse as it made its way along the rockstrewn ground; then he reined it in and motioned for Hesseth to pull ahead of him.

'What are you doing?' she demanded.

'I'm going back to him.' He swung his leg back over the horse and dismounted; fire shot through his groin as he landed. 'I think he's going to do something very stupid. I want to make sure he doesn't do it alone.' He noticed that there was blood on her arm, a crimson smear from elbow to wrist. But since she had chosen to use that arm to guide the horse, he assumed it wasn't a serious wound. 'Take this.' He unclipped the lead line from his saddle and threw it over to her. Tarrant's horse snorted impatiently as she pulled it into line with her own.

He met her eyes for a moment. Amber, alien, and so very worried. 'I'll be all right,' he promised her. 'Go as far as you can. I can Locate you later, when the fae cools down.'

'Be careful,' she whispered. Then, with a fearful glance back over her shoulder – but their pursuers hadn't caught up with them, not yet – she urged her own horse forward. The black horse snorted once in indignation, but when the lead grew taut it followed, and soon the two of them were out of sight, swallowed by the harsh shadows of the crevasse.

Damien turned back the way they had come and retraced the last few yards quickly. It hurt to walk, it would hurt even more to climb, but he had seen what Tarrant might not have noticed: a perfect half-moon directly overhead, harbinger of the dawn. Maybe the skies hadn't started growing lighter yet, maybe Tarrant's special senses hadn't yet reacted to the threat of the coming sunlight, but Damien had traveled with him long enough to know how acute the danger was. Especially if he couldn't Work. Especially – and this most of all – if the Hunter was doing something as foolhardy and dangerous as Damien suspected he was.

He ran back to the place where Tarrant had left them and studied the southern wall. When he found sufficient handholds to support his weight, he hoisted himself up. Pain shot up his damaged arm as he shifted his weight onto it, but if it wasn't broken outright it was just going to have to work for a living. He moaned softly but kept climbing. The wall of the crevasse was rife with fault lines, but they all angled downward; he had no trouble finding a place to dig in with his fingers or feet, but it took all his rock-climbing skill to keep from sliding out as he shifted his weight, ever so carefully (but not too slowly, there were enemies soon to follow), jamming his fingers and sometimes his fists into the cracks so hard that they were forced to support him. Briefly he considered how much danger he was in if Tarrant got to the top before him. *Damned unlikely,* he thought. The Hunter might be unequaled in sorcery, but it was unlikely he had much experience in rock climbing. If he managed not to fall at all, it would be damned slow going.

Twenty feet above the chasm floor. High enough that their attackers might not notice him if they passed beneath. Thirty. He found a horizontal ridge large enough for his feet to fit into and eased his way west along it, back toward where he figured Tarrant must be. Relatively easy going . . . and then a chunk of granite broke loose from beneath his foot and plummeted down to the floor so far below. Its impact was like an explosion in the moonlit silence, the sound of which echoed for long minutes afterward. He hugged the cold rock, his heart pounding. His arm throbbed with such pain that he could hardly move it, but move it he did: one foot to the right where a deep chink beckoned, and a hand to follow. Move after move, his practiced eye struggling to make out forms in the darkness. On the floor of the chasm the moonlight had been helpful, but here it merely taunted him, shining its light upon smooth, useless surfaces and casting the areas he needed most into deep black shadow. He made his way more by feel than by sight, hoping that Tarrant's superior vision wouldn't give him *too* much of an advantage—

And then he saw him. Dark silk whipping out from the rock, pale skin against cold granite, the glitter of gold threads on his scabbard. He had found a ledge some two feet in depth and nearly ten feet across, and he was standing on it with his back to the chasm wall, studying the terrain beneath him. He looked over in surprise as Damien's fingers caught at the ledge, and stern disapproval flashed in his eyes as the priest levered himself up on to it, and eased his way over to him.

'You shouldn't have come,' the Hunter whispered.

'Yeah. That makes two of us.' He looked down at the rocky wall beneath them, but all he could make out were jagged shadows. Too damned many jagged shadows. In the distance he could hear voices, now, and the sound of men running. 'I thought you might do something stupid like trying to bring the wall down.'

The pale eyes glittered. 'I might.'

'What about the fae? Is it workable yet?'

'Almost,' he said softly, his voice no louder than the wind. 'Not quite.'

'Then what—'

In answer he pulled out his sword. It wasn't nearly as bright as it had been back in the west, but clearly he had been reWorking it. Its cold light spilled across the rock with viscous luminescence.

'You can't do that,' Damien whispered. The voices from below were closer now; any moment they might see their pursuers. 'Even if you use that for power instead of the earth-fae, you'll still be making contact with the currents—'

'You see an alternative?' the Hunter demanded.

An instant of silence, night-chilled, eloquent. He looked into those eyes – so cold, so inhuman – and saw in them the truth of what he already knew: that the Hunter feared death more than any living man he knew. So much so that he was once willing to sacrifice his humanity in the name of continued existence. So much so that now, with all the denizens of Hell licking their lips at the thought of his imminent demise, he could commit himself to a mission like this as coldly and dispassionately as if there were no risk at all. Because there was, as he said, no real alternative. If the pass stayed open, their enemies would catch them; it was only a question of time. And he could neither flee to safety nor Work the earth-fae to save them while that power still surged.

This way . . . it was a slim chance, but it was all he had. And therefore it was the only path the Neocount of Merentha could possibly choose.

Tarrant turned toward the spot he had chosen, and slid his sword into one of the cracks in the rock. He angled it carefully. Blue sparks played around the lips of the crack as he moved it, and once Tarrant cried out sharply in pain, as if something had burned him. Could he Work the sword's power on the earth itself without opening himself up to the raging force of the earth-fae? Damien reached out to him—

—and then the channel between them came alive and he saw as the Hunter saw, saw the hot power cascading down over the rocks, saw it surging into the chasm where it boiled, it fumed, its steam came up and licked the chasm walls, burning, boiling . . . he could feel it through his arm as if his own hand grasped the coldfire sword, a power so terrible that his flesh was seared where it touched him, a power that transformed his cells more quickly than they could ever hope to heal themselves, a power that killed, a power that burned, a power that swallowed the whole of the world in blinding white light . . .

And there. In the center. The point of a sword. The chill of expanding ice. He heard the rock explode, felt the shock drive him back against the granite wall as the chosen fault line gave way and a whole section of wall came loose. It ripped free with a roar like a cannonade and thundered down into the chasm. Striking the far wall with deafening force, shattering into a brittle tonnage of raw granite that bounced and split and fell again, filling the narrow cavity beneath. Each boulder enough to crush a man, each one followed by a thousand more, a veritable sea of rockfall, a tidal wave of granite. Damien felt the ledge shiver beneath his feet, and for a moment he was afraid that it, too, would give way. He moved toward Tarrant defensively, just in time to see him fall. Just in time to reach out with all his strength and slam the man back against the rock, hard enough to keep him there. He could feel the pain raging through him, the fire, the glittering spears of heat. 'Gerald!' he yelled. Trying to get his attention. Trying to break the contact. But the Hunter was lost in his own Working, was drowning in the raw power of what he had conjured. Was losing his battle.

Only an idiot Works the fae right after an earthquake, Ciani had once said. Or was it Senzei? Damien leaned over as far as he could and tried to get hold of the Hunter's other hand, the one clasped about the blazing sword. Its light was blinding now, a cold blue unsun that seared his vision to icy blackness if he looked at it directly. *Have to break the link, somehow. Have to get him loose.* The narrow ledge was trembling beneath his feet and he knew that it was now or never, that if he waited for an aftershock to hit they would both be dead. And then what would happen to Hesseth? 'Come on,' he muttered, and he reached across Tarrant to get hold of his far arm. For a moment he lost his balance and began to fall backward, then – with an effort that caused him to cry out in pain – recovered his stability. Only one more foot to go. His arm could hang in there. It wasn't broken. Was it? Now several inches. Now one . . .

His hand closed about the Hunter's wrist and he pulled back on it, hard. He had hoped that the sudden movement would break the link, but clearly it would take more than that. 'Come on, damn you! Come out of it!' He could feel the cold power surging through his hand, chilling his flesh to immobility. And beyond it – behind it – the power of the earth itself, waiting to surge through him as it had clearly surged through Tarrant.

He tried to focus on the sword. His arm was numb now, and the coldness was spreading. He tried to remember how hungry that steel was for death, how eager it was to consume any human soul that touched it. 'Come on,' he whispered to it. 'Come and get me.' Gravel trickled from somewhere above, raining down into the chasm. The world was filled with dust. 'You want my life? Come get it.' He was trying to focus the sword on him, not the earth, in the hope that would break the link between the two. The cold power licked at him, and spears of ice shot through his veins. 'That's it,' he whispered. 'Come to me.'

And then he was slammed back, hard. The breath left his lungs in a short burst and he was gasping, swallowing the rock dust that his motion had dislodged. He was aware that he no longer held Tarrant's wrist, but it was hard to say just where his arm was; that whole side of him was numb with cold, unfeeling.

He managed to get his eyes open. The first thing he saw was that half the ledge was gone; Tarrant's blast must have weakened it enough that it finally gave way. Then he looked up and saw Tarrant. The man's face was white, utterly colorless, and his eyes were flushed red. But he was conscious. Safe. Alive, in a manner of speaking.

'That was a very foolish thing to do,' the Hunter gasped. The hand that held the sword was shaking; he seemed to lack the strength to sheathe it. 'Very foolish,' he whispered.

'Yeah.' Damien wiped the dust from his eyes. The feeling was coming back into his arm, but not as fast as he would have liked. Not with dawn coming. 'I had a good teacher.'

And then he saw a faint smile on Tarrant's face – only a flicker, but a smile nonetheless – and he knew deep down inside that they were going to be okay. Both of them.

'Can you climb?' he asked. Flexing his frozen arm. It would move now, though it was still stiff. He didn't like to think about how close he had come to losing more than an arm. He could still feel the chill power of the Worked steel, even from a distance. 'It's not too far to the top.'

The Hunter looked up. Damien thought he saw him shudder.

'Not much choice, is there?'

'You could always transform yourself.'

Instead of parrying with a dry retort, Tarrant leaned back against the granite wall and shut his eyes.

God in Heaven. He's in bad shape. Damien tried to gauge the rock above them – no easy feat at that angle – and wondered if he could get them both up to the top. Probably so, he decided. But not before dawn. Already the sky was lightening in the east, which meant they had, what? Half an hour? Not long enough, he thought, assessing the rock face above them. Not nearly long enough.

He turned to find Tarrant's eyes also turned toward the east. 'I guess it's time to climb,' he whispered hoarsely.

'Looks like it. Up or down?'

'Up.' He didn't even look at the rock face before committing himself. 'There's no shelter down there. I checked.'

'And above?'

'One can only hope,' he whispered.

He moved to sheathe the coldfire blade – and almost dropped it, his hand losing strength as it struck against the edge of the ledge. Damien grabbed for it quickly, and for a moment he almost lost his balance. But compared to some of what he'd climbed, a two-foot ledge was practically a luxury accommodation; he managed to keep three points on the rock while he closed his hand about the icy grip, and after a moment he regained his security. He straightened up slowly, caught his breath, and eased the long sword into Tarrant's scabbard.

'Try to hold onto that thing, will you?'

The Hunter managed a faint smile. 'I promise.'

'You going to make it?'

He glanced again at the east, and this time Damien did see him shiver. 'I have to, don't I?'

Damien pulled a knife from his belt and tore a ragged strip from the bottom of his shirt. Then two more. When he knotted them together, they made a strip some eight feet long; it was far from ideal, but it would have to do. 'On your belt,' he ordered, handing one end to Tarrant. The other end he affixed to his own. It was good linen, tough fabric, and it might make the difference if one of them slipped.

If he slips, he corrected himself. It would take all his skill to cling to the rock face if the weight of a grown man suddenly jerked him back; how well could Tarrant, so obviously wounded, manage such a feat?

They started to climb. The rising sun at least gave them some measure of light, so that Damien was able to pick out a reasonably workable course. Tarrant climbed well enough, but his hands were shaking from weakness; how long would he be able to keep it up? Damien tried not to look at the sky as they struggled upward, but he couldn't help but notice that the bumps and crevices surrounding him were becoming more and more visible.

Then there was a crumbling ledge and a slip and Damien grabbed his companion, flattening him back against the rock. He could feel Tarrant's growing weakness through the contact, and it frightened him. How badly had the earth-fae hurt him? How long would it take him to heal? He hauled him up to the next step, helped the pale hands grasp hold of a helpful protrusion. *Would* he heal? The next few yards were easy enough. He was beginning to think they would make it. The sky was blue now, and the stars of the rim were no longer visible. They fought for another yard, then another. His hands were bleeding, and Tarrant's own were scraped raw. One more little bit . . .

And then they were over, they had made it, they pulled

themselves up onto the coarse dirt of the mountain's face and lay there for a minute in sheer exhaustion. Damien rolled up onto one elbow and studied his companion. Tarrant didn't look good. He didn't look good at all.

'We need shelter,' he told him. 'You tell me where to go, I'll get you there. But I can't find it myself.' When Tarrant didn't move, he whispered fiercely, 'We've only got maybe half an hour left!'

'Less than that,' the Hunter gasped. 'Far less than that.' He made a move as if to rise up, but clearly lacked the strength. Damien hooked an arm about his shoulder and helped him. With effort, he got him to his feet. It seemed to take forever.

'Can you See?' Damien asked. 'Can you find something?'

The Hunter nodded weakly. Damien supported him as he studied the surrounding terrain, as he tried to read structure into the black earth and scraggly foliage that surrounded them. 'There,' he whispered at last. Pointing east. 'Something that way.'

Together they struggled toward the east. Occasionally Tarrant would study the ground again and then point in a new direction. Damien took him where he wanted to go. If he stopped to think about things, it would probably terrify him how very weak Tarrant had become. He could no longer even stand alone, much less manage the exertion necessary to forge forward across the rough terrain.

Has he finally pushed himself too far? Damien wondered. *What if this is beyond his healing?*

The Hunter fell to his knees; it took Damien a moment to realize that he'd done it deliberately. 'There,' he whispered. Pointing to a shallow depression in the earth, where a thornbush was rooted.

Damien knelt by the depression. The bush made it impossible for him to see the bottom, so he grasped it by the base and pulled it forcibly from the ground. He could feel the thorns pierce his hand as he wrenched it loose, but that was just too bad. He didn't have the time to be more careful.

What was revealed when the last of the roots pulled loose was a hole some two feet in diameter, like that an animal might make. He pushed at the edge of it with his hand, and then, when he saw what it was, repositioned himself so he could kick at it. The earth gave way beneath his feet, tumbling down into darkness. He could feel cool air beneath his face as he finally hit rock at one edge, then another. Animals might have used this hole, but they sure as hell didn't make it; Tarrant had found the opening to a natural cavern.

With care he lowered the Neocount's body down into blackness. The pale skin was already reddened from contact with dawn's early light, the eyes swollen and bloodshot. He hoped it wasn't too late. When Tarrant's body had fallen through, he followed it, lowering himself down into the cavern's depths.

It was a drop of perhaps twelve feet. He managed to avoid landing on his companion, which was an accomplishment all on its own. Tarrant lay limp and unconscious, and for all he knew might have been dead. Time enough later to figure that out. He dragged his body away from the opening, until sunlight no longer shone directly on him. The cavern was floored with mud, and by the time he found a dark nook to serve as shelter they were both covered in it. But darkness meant safety. That was all that mattered, right?

He unclasped Tarrant's cloak and managed to get it off him, then used it to cover his body like a blanket. The Hunter's skin was cold, utterly unlifelike, but that wasn't necessarily a bad sign. He took care that the man's hands and face were safely covered, then leaned back at last and drew in a deep breath. Another. Something cold and scared finally unknotted in his gut. Even the pain in his arm began to subside.

They'd be all right. They'd find Hesseth when night fell, and Damien would Heal the living, and . . . they'd be all right. The worst was over.

Secure in the darkness of their muddy haven, Damien Vryce slept.

21

The Hunter didn't awaken at dusk. Even though the cave was black, even though the sun outside had long since set behind the mountains, still his body did not stir. Damien tried the taste of blood to bring him back – not a hard thing to supply, as his hands were scored with scratches and puncture wounds – but even that didn't work. He tried not to worry. He had seen the Hunter recover from worse – that is, from what he *assumed* was worse – and somewhere deep inside he did have faith that the man was going to make it, that it was just some idiosyncracy of his alive-but-not-alive flesh that had kept him asleep this long. He extinguished the tiny fire he had lit inside the cave, just in case total darkness was what the man needed. How did he heal himself, anyway? He had already said that the Workings he used were unlike those of a true Healing. What manner of power did he require? And did he have the strength to conjure it? Those were the thoughts that ran through Damien's mind as he waited in the inky blackness, listening to the trickle of rain aboveground and the occasional rustling of insects. What was it the Hunter had said to him? *I have no power over fire, or light, or life.* Did the earth-fae count as fire? Did the images of magmal heat and searing light that accompanied its surge the night before reflect its true essence, or was that just a visual trapping which his own human mind applied?

Damn it, Hunter, wake up. We've got work to do.

Coreset passed. He knew because he climbed up to check on it, using the linen strip he'd knotted together for their dangerous ascent. It had taken him a good half hour to get it into place; dark caverns were far easier to drop down into than they were to climb out of. But he'd had nothing to do with the daylight hours besides collect firewood, look for food, and arrange for an easier way out of the cave. And pray, of course. So very hard. So many times.

God, there's so much wrong in this land. So much pain and grief and suffering I don't know where to start. I never felt like I was overwhelmed before, but this time I do. Give me strength, please. Renew my faith in this mission. Help me protect my companions, because without them I am nothing. The evil in this land is too vast, too firmly entrenched, for a single man to defeat it.

After Coreset, at last, the Hunter stirred. The first thing Damien heard was a moan from underneath the cloak. He was up in an instant, and managed to feel his way over to where the Neocount lay. There was the rustling of fabric as the Hunter freed himself, then a long, laborious breath.

'You all right?' Damien asked.

'I've been better,' the Hunter whispered. Hoarsely. Weakly.

'If you need blood—'

'Not from you,' he said quickly. Then added, 'Not tonight, anyway. I'll make it.'

The shadows stirred as Tarrant struggled to his feet. 'What time is it?' he managed.

'I don't know. The Core set a while ago.'

'Ah,' he said. 'The darkness. Of course.'

He walked over to where the linen strip hung. He seemed to have no trouble seeing in the dark, but his step sounded unsteady. Hesitant. 'I'm not sure I can do this.'

And that said it all. Because on any other night the Hunter could simply have changed form and flown out, or crawled out, or whatever else it took to get up there. To be trapped in his human flesh . . . that meant that he was far from healed. Not a good sign at all.

'Here,' Damien said. 'I'll help you.'

He felt his way over to where the Hunter stood. He'd had plenty of time to explore the small space during the day, so the darkness was only a small hindrance. He cupped his hands and braced himself, fighting for traction in the mud. When he was steady, he felt a cold hand on his shoulder, and the instep of a muddy boot slipped into his grip. He held it tightly as the Neocount stepped up, trying to time his support with the man's rise so that together they might gain as much height as possible. It wasn't quite enough to get him to the opening, but when he had gotten a secure grip on the linen strip Damien shifted his position and pushed him higher. There was a scrabbling on the dirt above then, and the weight was gone.

He stopped a minute to catch his breath, then climbed up himself.

The Hunter was standing to one side of the hole, waiting. As Damien gained the top, he saw him looking about, taking in the lay of the land. Damien wondered how much he remembered from the night before.

'Where's our rakh friend?' Tarrant asked. His voice was raspy and harsh, as though his throat had been wounded. And perhaps it had. Who could say what damage the wild fae had caused, when it burned its way through his flesh?

'Gone east through the gap.' Damien brushed at the mud on his breeches. A useless gesture. His whole body was encrusted with dark brown muck, and the only thing that made it tolerable was the fact that Tarrant was likewise covered. It shouldn't have pleased him that the man was dirty, but it did. It seemed so . . . well, *human*.

'And our pursuers?'

The Neocount's words startled him. *He doesn't know*, he realized. *He doesn't remember*. 'You stopped them,' he said shortly. 'You brought the wall down right on their heads. Even if others try to follow us, you made the gap impassable. They'd have to climb the mountain to find our trail again.'

He considered that. 'I remember . . . planning that,' he said at last. 'I remember . . . fear. And fire. And climbing – that dimly, as though it were a dream. No more.'

'You tapped into the earth-fae after the quake. Not right after, but soon enough. It almost killed you.'

'Yes,' he said quietly. 'I can see that.'

'You going to be all right?'

'Nothing's damaged that won't heal. It will take time, though, and—' He stopped himself, but not before Damien had finished the thought in his own mind. *Fresh food,* he thought. *Fear. Blood. Human suffering*.

'We should regroup first,' Tarrant said quietly.

'Yeah. I thought we should parallel the gap as long as possible, since that's the way she went. It'd be hard to work a Locating for her on this side of the crest.'

The Hunter nodded. 'The ridge most likely divides the current. Once we cross that, it should be easy.'

'Can you walk that far?'

'I'm standing, aren't I?'

'But if your strength—'

'Did you bring the horses?'

'No. Of course not.'

'Then I have no alternative, have I? Strength or no strength.'

Damien bit back a sharp rejoinder. He should be glad that Tarrant was irritating him once more. It showed the man was recovering.

'This way, all right?' He started across the rocky ground.

'One moment.'

He stopped, and then after a second turned back. The Hunter was standing with his eyes shut, his brow furrowed as if in intense concentration. One hand was on the hilt of his sword, and though the powerful blade had not been drawn it clearly served as a necessary reassurance.

Cool silver flame spurted up from the ground around his feet. Not with its usual force, but still cold enough to chill the air around him. The unfire licked at his flesh with silver-blue tongues, conjured flames twining about his flesh until the whole of his body was immersed in it. A chill wind swept over Damien, and the scent of winter ice.

And then the flame was gone. A thin frost rimmed the Hunter's body, that shivered free of him when he moved. Fine white ice crystals cascaded to the ground, along with something else. Something brown. It took him a moment to recognize it.

Damn your vanity, he thought, as the Hunter nodded his readiness and began to walk. There was no mud on him now, nor any sign of dirt or blood. What little moonlight there was gleamed on smooth silk and on spotless hair, perfectly arranged. Even the man's leather boots were clean. *Why did I know you'd do that?*

'Come on,' he said. Brushing back his own sweat-slicked hair. 'Let's find Hesseth.'

They found the rakh-woman's camp soon after midnight. The gap hadn't taken her far, but it had taken her there safely; she and the two horses were gathered around a minimal campfire about a half-mile from the crevasse's eastern end.

Two horses. That meant fewer supplies, missing maps, and one less animal to ride. Damien wondered which of the two remaining saddles would best allow him to ride double with Hesseth; his groin had no desire to repeat last night's experience. Of course it would be Hesseth and him together, and Tarrant would ride alone; he never questioned that. He couldn't picture the aristocratic sorcerer sharing his saddle with anyone, even if it would be the most practical distribution of weight. Some things you just didn't ask.

There was a bandage on her arm, he noticed as they came into the small camp, and a patch of smelly ointment on her mare's flank. Thank God the animal hadn't bolted when it was hit. Tarrant's black mount seemed unharmed and unflustered. *I guess if you come from the Hunter's Forest,* Damien mused, *even a place like this looks good.*

There was no surprise on her face when they came into camp – armed and wary, she had probably spotted them coming some time ago – but the joy that suffused her face was a welcome greeting after hours of painful hiking. She came up to Damien and put a hand to the side of his face, rubbing gently. Sharing her scent, he realized; it must be a rakhene custom. He grinned at her in turn, not quite knowing how to respond. She even vouchsafed a minimal smile for Tarrant, a rare and precious gesture. He responded with a nod that said yes, he knew just what she meant by it, and yes, he was appropriately moved.

They traded their tales over the campfire, while Hesseth brewed warm tee and dug out the freshest of their rations. Damien could have eaten a horse. As for Tarrant, he stood apart from them while they ate and talked, scanning the darkness for danger. It was not a role Damien would have chosen for him in his current state, but he glad to have him do it. He was so stiff by now that it was all he could do to lower himself to a sitting position and take the food that Hesseth offered. It was going to hurt like hell in the morning, he thought miserably, as he bit into a strip of dried meat.

He was acutely aware of Tarrant listening to him as he described their exploits of the night before, rediscovering his own actions through Damien's words. A strange concept. How much they had come to depend on each other on this trip!

Danger makes strange bedfellows.

When he had told her everything, and when she had shared her own journey through the narrow gap, he set his food aside and applied his attention to their wounds. His groin ached like hell as he stretched forward to reach her arm, but thank God physical infirmity didn't affect one's Working. His own arm throbbed hotly as he studied her rakhene flesh, then used the fae to knit the broken cells together once more. After that he applied his skills to himself, and though his concentration was less than perfect, the currents were strong in this region; half an hour later, when he was secure that all the serious damage had been repaired, he relaxed and let the Working fade. His body still hurt like hell, but that was something he couldn't fix. *Pain is the brain's way of signaling that something is wrong,* his master had taught him. *Alter that system and you're messing with the brain itself.* In time his throbbing nerves would figure out that the source of the problem was gone, and would quiet down.

It was partly his own fault, of course. He hadn't Healed himself completely. But when earthquakes were as frequent as they were here, you didn't waste precious time cleaning out a leftover hematoma; it was just too risky to Work that long. And besides (he told himself, wincing as he shifted position), no one ever died from a black-and-blue mark. Right?

When they were done with all that, Tarrant rejoined them. He looked slightly better than before, but that might have been the lighting; the warm light of the campfire was kinder to him than the moonlight. Certainly he was still weak, and when he lowered himself to the earth beside them, Damien saw his balance wavering.

'We're still far from the valley,' he said. His voice sounded better, at least. 'The map shows another two ridges between us and it, although what that translates to in terms of real-life mountains is anyone's guess.'

'It's a climb,' Hesseth agreed. 'What about pursuit?'

'Unlikely, I think. They can't follow your trail through the gap; I saw to that. And I've Obscured ours since dusk, so that it will be next to impossible to find.'

Given his condition, Damien was surprised. 'Did you?'

The pale eyes fixed on him. 'I only make a mistake once, priest.'

'Then we should get moving as soon as night falls.' Hesseth rewrapped the dried meat so that it would keep. 'By then we should all be rested enough, anyway.'

The Hunter seemed to hesitate. 'You can move when night falls,' he said quietly. 'Or even before that, if you like. But I would reco-mmend not entering the valley until I'm with you again; the Terata are said to hunt there.'

'What—' Hesseth began. Though she was clearly surprised by his intentions, Damien wasn't. He'd been expecting something like this since Tarrant had climbed out of the cave.

'He needs food,' he said. He could hear the edge in his own voice. 'That means humans. And there aren't any where we're going.'

'I could hold out for long enough to make it down south,' Tarrant explained, 'but not in this condition. Nor would I be of any use to your – or to our communal – purpose without substantial healing.'

'Which requires killing,' Hesseth challenged.

Tarrant didn't answer. No words were necessary.

'You'll have to be careful,' Damien muttered. 'They're looking for us.'

'They won't expect me to return, least of all on wing. I can fly right over their traps and their armies, into villages where no one lies in wait for me. The land is full of people,' he said evenly. His eyes were fixed on Damien, daring him to protest. 'I'll be safe enough.'

'How long?' the priest managed. Not meeting his gaze.

'At least a day or two. I'll want to go far enough that no act of mine is linked to our presence; it would be a shame to escape their clutches now, only to inspire them to new pursuit later. I'll be careful. Trust me.'

'Like you were in the cities?' Damien said sharply.

'Like I was in the cities,' he answered coolly. Not missing a beat. 'Cover what ground you can in the next few days. But don't go into the valley without me. If you get to it before I come back, then stop and rest. The horses will be grateful for it.'

He stood, then, and Damien could see by the motion how weak he was. How stiff. How much blood would it take to heal a weak-ness like that? How many deaths? He tried not to think about it.

You hire a demon to fight a demon, and this is the price you pay. 'Where will you go?' he asked. Hating himself for his curiosity, even as he wondered which Protectorate would surrender its women to sate the Hunter's appetite. God, if there were only an alternative.

'North,' the Hunter told him. 'The way we came. Some place

large enough to harbor an army . . . or a sizable raiding party. Some place that already smells of blood.'

He heard Hesseth draw in her breath sharply as she realized what he meant. Who it was he meant to kill.

Damien thought of the village they had passed through. The bodies, the blood . . . the children huddled in the bathroom, their necks cleanly slit. Whoever had killed them, their crime would taint the currents for miles. For one with the Hunter's sight, they would be easy to find.

Easy to kill.

'The least I can do for the man who saved me last night is choose suitable prey,' the Hunter said. Standing back now, so that the shadows of the night might enfold him. So that the darkness might lend him its power. For a moment Damien was afraid that he wouldn't be able to summon the power he needed, that his strength was too far gone. Hadn't he once said that transformation was the most difficult of all workings?

Then the coldfire flared, blindingly bright, and from its pyre arose a great black bird. It beat the night air with its wings – once, twice – and then rose up into the air, where the night obscured its motion. Garnet talons glittered in the moonlight.

'Be careful,' Damien whispered. Watching as its great wings tamed the night wind. Watching as it rose yet higher, until distance and darkness hid it from sight.

Only later, when he knew for a fact that it was out of hearing, did he add – very quietly – 'Good hunting.'

22

It took them four days to cross the mountains. They could have made better time if they'd tried, but there was no reason to rush. Knowing after Knowing made it clear that none of their pursuers had followed them, which gave them the luxury of leisure time for the first time in their journey. And after what they had seen and done in the Protectorates they needed it, both to regain their strength and their composure. Fortunately, the fertile silence of the wooded slopes was a perfect balm for human and rakhene soul alike. Even the horses seemed grateful for a few easy days.

Damien tried hard not to worry about Tarrant. Tried not to remember that once in the past the Hunter had left their company and then not returned. It seemed so long ago that he'd been captured, almost in another life . . . but the enemy was the same. In the rakhlands it had taken the form of a woman, here it might be a man or rakh or even a true demon – but there was no question in his own mind that the two powers were linked. And so Damien worried about Tarrant's safety, and Hesseth no doubt worried about Tarrant's safety, and they tried hard not to inflame each other's fears by talking about them. That would only make it worse.

How much I've changed, he mused as they made camp one night. *Once I would have stood back and let him die. Once I thought that nothing could be worse than freeing the Hunter to feed again. Now I protect him without a second thought, and calmly wave good-bye while he goes off to murder countless innocents.* But the situation was different now and he knew it. Tarrant had saved his own life several times, and while he understood that it was always for a selfish purpose – the Neocount never did anything except to benefit himself – the fact remained that he had done it. That changed how you looked at a man, whether you wanted it to or not. And the people he'd be killing weren't innocents this time, were they? Murderers deserved to die. Since the justice of the Church couldn't touch them, let the Hunter provide their punishment. Whatever he did to them, it couldn't possibly be worse than what they did to that village. Could it?

Be honest, he chided himself. *We can't succeed in this mission without him. That's the bottom line. You need him, and so you must endure him. Protect him, even. It's all part of this dark game we're playing.*

Use evil to fight evil, the Prophet wrote. If you're lucky, they'll destroy each other. Is that what I want? That Tarrant should die in combat, delivering the world from two evils at once?

He shut his eyes. His hands were shaking.

I don't know. I'm not sure anymore. Not sure of anything.

He said that his presence would corrupt me. Has it begun already? Is this what corruption feels like?

God, protect my spirit, he prayed. *The enemy can have my body, my life . . . but preserve my soul, I beg You. I've placed it in such jeopardy with this alliance. But there was no other way. You can see that, can't You? No other way to succeed.*

At night, while they set up camp, he tried to explain to Hesseth about the earth-fae. Though she manipulated it unconsciously – as all native species did – she didn't really see it, at least not in the sense that Tarrant did. And so she listened to his descriptions in rapt wonder, like a child listening to fairy tales. He tried to explain it all. How the earth-fae surged up from beneath the planet's crust with enough force to kill. How it settled down soon after and then flowed like water over the land, in currents that could be mapped and harnessed, from the strongest tide down to the tiniest ripple. Since humans used the earth-fae for their Workings, he explained, then all their Workings must flow with the currents. Thus Tarrant or he could attempt to Know their enemy – in other words, interpret the effect of his presence upon the earth-fae – but it would take tremendous power to launch an active assault against the current. For their enemy, of course, the opposite held true. It would take almost superhuman force to draw information upcurrent for hundreds of miles, but any message or assault which was launched from the south would naturally flow toward them. That's what had worried Tarrant so much about the foreign touch in the currents near the crevasse, he explained; if it was an attempt to focus on their exact position, it might mean that something very big and very nasty was on its way.

And then, when he was done, he dared to ask her about the tidal fae. It was the first time since the rakhlands that he had broached the subject directly. He wasn't sure she would take it well – in the past she had responded to such questions with downright hostility – but though she was silent for a moment, he sensed that it was not because she was offended by his question, but because she was trying to find words for something that was beyond all language.

'It's like a heartbeat,' she said at last. 'Like the whole world has a heartbeat, very slow and very resonant. Sometimes, when I want to Work, it's as if I can feel the blood of the planet surging through everything, through the land and the sky and through me, and I can shape it with a thought . . . and sometimes the world is silent, and there's nothing to shape. Nothing at all. There's no telling which it will be, either. No predicting any given moment. Because I say it's one heartbeat, but it's really like a thousand, and the rhythm between them is what matters . . . including my own pulse. And all the rhythms of my body. Do you understand? It's so hard to explain something you don't think about. Something that humans never sense.'

'Do you see it in any form?'

'Sometimes. A flash of light, when several beats come together. As brilliant as a lightning strike when a lot of power is involved. Sometimes the whole sky will light up – just for an instant – like the whole world was a piece of shattered glass, with light glistening along every flaw. Light broken into a thousand colors. So very beautiful . . .' She shut her eyes, remembering. 'It can be dangerous, though. I know of at least one *khrast* who was hunting when the tidal fae pulsed, and when the light blinded her, the quarry turned and charged . . . so we try not to see it, we train ourselves not to look. It's a matter of survival, you understand.'

He asked her gently, 'Do you succeed?'

'Mostly,' she smiled. 'But it is very beautiful. And that's part of what we learned from your species: how to hunger for beauty.' She sketched a pattern in the dirt with a claw while she spoke: circles within circles within circles. 'And it's part of what stands between us and our males. The defining difference, you might say.' She looked up at him. 'Your women don't see it?'

'Tarrant says that a few can, with effort. Occasionally a man gets a glimpse, but no more.'

'More sorcery.' She shook her head sadly. 'You're such strangers to this world, you humans. You come here and redefine our very world, you sculpt our native species as though they were clay, you spawn a thousand monsters each time you draw a breath . . . but you never really *belong* here. Not even after all these years. You live on this planet, but you're not part of it.'

'Yeah,' he muttered. 'Tell me about it.'

Days of traveling, nights of rest. A luxurious schedule, which he could indulge in only because of Tarrant's absence. On the third night there were five minutes of true darkness, when the sun, the stars, and all three moons were hidden behind the bulk of the planet, and he wondered if Tarrant was taking advantage of its power. The true night might be a time of terror for most men, a time when humanity's darkest imaginings borrowed substance from the night and came calling, but for the Hunter it was a time of unequaled power and potential. Maybe (Damien thought as he severed the spine of something gruesome which the dark fae had conjured) Tarrant could use it to get a handle on who or what they were going after. God knows, they could use information.

On the third day they came over a ridge and saw the valley at last. Vast, dramatic, forbidding, it was unlike anything he had ever seen before. He was accustomed to valleys that lay comfortably in the cradle of their surrounding mountains, flat plains which were a cohesive part of the mountain range which flanked them. This was a whole different creature. It was as though the earth had folded crisply in two, so that between the rocky hills they had just crossed and the soaring granite peaks of the eastern coastal range there was a deep crease – perhaps sea-level deep – with walls so steep that climbing them would be all but impossible, and a bottom that was lost in a sea of tree tops and mountain shadows. A white mist seemed to fill the whole of the valley, twining about the tree-tops like hazy serpents. The late afternoon sun did little to illuminate it, but cast its light instead on the sheer granite cliffs opposite them, so that the peaks seemed crowned in fire, and the depths were doubly dark by contrast. There would be precious few hours of the day in which the sun would rise high enough to shine directly down into the vast gorge, and even then the thick mist would protect the gloom that blanketed the miles like a shroud.

Despite the relative warmth of the afternoon, Damien found himself shivering. 'That's the route, huh?'

'The one he wanted.'

He stared at it a while longer, taking the measure of its gloom. As if by doing so he could somehow alter it. 'It's that or climbing mountains all the way south.'

'Or going back to the Protectorates.'

'Yeah.' A breeze drifted up to them, damp and cool. 'No thanks.'

He braced himself, drew in a deep breath, and patterned a Knowing. For a minute the fae didn't respond, and he was afraid that he was too far from the valley's current to access its secrets. Then the familiar patterns appeared, and he dissected them carefully for information. He found no evidence of anyone watching them, or of anything lying in wait. Not yet. But there was a feeling about the area that he didn't like, and he was almost disappointed when the Knowing failed to define a specific threat. Better an enemy you could give a name to than a cold, clammy ignorance crawling up your spine.

'Is it all right?' she asked.

He sighed, and let the Knowing fade. 'For now.' He looked back to where the horses were waiting, saw Tarrant's black mount grazing on a nasty-looking weed. Hesseth's mare, as usual, was more circumspect. 'I think this is as far as we should go without Tarrant. We'd better make camp and wait for him.'

She nodded.

He went to the black horse and gathered up its reins. 'Come on,' he muttered. 'Time to move.' Beside him Hesseth urged her own mount back, until the two animals faced away from the daunting panorama, back toward the mountain's crest.

Without a word. That was the eerie part. Neither of them saying a thing, but moving in silent and perfect concord. Both of them knowing that the thing to do was to cross over the crest again and descend partway down the mountainside, so that they might pitch their camp out of sight of the dismal valley.

Not a good omen, he thought. Not good at all.

Tarrant returned on the fourth night, and it was clear that whatever slaughter he'd indulged in had renewed both his flesh and his spirit. His pale eyes gleamed with the subtle malevolence that Damien had learned to know and hate in the rakhlands, and his movements were a flawless admixture of arrogance and grace. But for all that he despised the Hunter's facade of dark elegance, Damien was glad to see it back in place. The change meant recovery and recovery meant power – possibly more than Tarrant had wielded since landing in this twisted realm – and power was what they needed right now, pure and simple.

He took his place among them as though he had never been gone, and made no attempt to explain how he had passed his absent nights. Nor did Damien ask. If he had learned nothing else in his months with the Hunter, it was that there were some things he didn't want to know.

The Neocount looked about the camp with discerning eyes – and looked about the currents as well, with hardly more effort – and then said, 'You've been here a good day at least. I assume that means you've found the valley.'

'Over the ridge.' Damien nodded toward the east. 'Not a pretty sight.'

The Hunter went where he indicated, and was soon lost from sight. Damien took the small pot of water from over the fire and placed it to one side, dropping in a few tee pellets. It could be a long wait.

The tee was fully brewed and he'd drunk down half of it by the time the Hunter returned. Tarrant reentered the circle of the fire without a word and sat, lowering himself with a grace and ease that Damien hadn't seen in a long time.

Damn him. He must have killed a lot.

'What do you think?' Hesseth asked him.

'First tell me what you two saw.'

They looked at each other; at last it was Damien who answered. 'A nasty, damp, dismal place with little sunlight and a host of terrain unpleasantries. You'd probably like it,' he added.

'Actually, I do. There'll be fewer hours of direct sunlight in those depths – if any at all – which means that I can stay with you longer. If the mist holds steady throughout the day it might even be possible – in an emergency – for me to walk abroad at noon. That's no small thing, you know.'

'I hadn't thought of it,' Damien admitted.

'There's no scent of our enemy in the currents, which either means that he hasn't anticipated our taking this route, or that the new current doesn't afford him access to us. Hopefully both. Given the force and the direction of the flow, I should be able to Obscure our progress from his eyes with little effort.'

'What about the Terata?' Hesseth asked him.

He seemed to hesitate. 'I saw no trace of any creature I could label as such ... but I'm bound by the same basic ignorance that you are. Until we either get closer to them or have better knowledge of what to look for, I don't think my skills will be much help. I did catch the scent of human life, however.'

'Human?' Damien was startled. 'I thought there were no people here.'

'So did I. Apparently we were wrong.'

'What kind of people?' Hesseth demanded.

'Hard to say at this point. But it's a sizable group, I do know that. Several dozen at least.'

'Living down there?'

'It would appear so.'

'That implies that the Terata can't be as terrible as we'd heard.' Hesseth's tone was one of reason. 'If they were, the humans would be dead or gone.'

The Hunter's eyes fixed on her. In the darkness, pupils distended, they were black. Utterly black. Not merely a color, but a manifestation of emptiness.

'You saw what your people became here,' he said softly. 'You witnessed what they did. Are you saying that whatever force molded the rakh couldn't also mold humans, if it wanted to?'

'Do you think that's the case here?' Damien asked him.

'I think that something is very wrong in this region, and to pass early judgment on anything – even our own species – is a mistake. I saw signs of faeborn creatures in the currents, but what does that mean? Any group of humans will create its own monsters in time. How can we assess their nature from here?'

'You sound more curious than afraid.'

The Neocount chuckled. 'Does that surprise you?'

'No.' Despite himself he smiled. 'I guess not.'

'We are what we are, Reverend Vryce. And I was a scholar long before I became ... what I am.' A faint smile creased the corners of his lips. 'Scholar enough to know what you fear most of all, Reverend. Tonight I'll Work the weather as best I can, so that tomorrow the valley mist is lifted. If that's possible,' he amended. 'That will make it better for you, won't it? If you have clear sight of your enemy's turf?'

'I'd prefer it.'

'You should start toward the valley well before dusk. It will take you some hours to find a safe path down, and then time to descend. I'll meet you at the bottom.' Though he was speaking to Damien, his eyes were fixed on Hesseth.

For a moment he was silent. The insects about them chirruped softly, to the accompanying crackle of the flames.

'The Kierstaad Protectorate,' he said at last, 'is controlled by rakh.' His voice was soft, ever so soft, as though somehow he felt that excessive volume might wound her. 'As is the one to the north of it. They're nearly human in form, but their soul is clearly rakhene; the fae responds to them as it never would to a man.'

Damien thought he saw her shudder.

'Their disguise is supported by human sorcery. I don't know the mechanics of it – I didn't dare get that close – but the scent is unmistakable. And I think . . .' He hesitated. Glanced at Damien. 'It was very similar to what I sensed by the crevasse. The same foreign touch.'

Hesseth drew in a quick breath, hissing. 'Why?' she demanded. Of the air. Of no one. 'What's the purpose of it all?'

'Clearly they mean to control this continent,' the Hunter mused.

For a moment she just stared at him. Trying to absorb what he had said, with all its implications. 'Maybe in the south,' she admitted. 'Maybe . . . although that shouldn't have turned them into monsters. But what about the north? What about the Matrias? They have control of the Church hierarchy, but what good does it do them? They still have to live among humans, hiding their own identity. Is that really power?'

'Power enough to affect human society,' Damien pointed out. 'The Church here has its own record of atrocities. Maybe by a slow manipulation—'

'Are you saying that my people are responsible for the crimes of humans?' Her amber eyes flashed angrily.

'I'm saying that in addition to rakhene power, the one pattern we've seen here – over and over – is degradation of spirit. Does it really matter which species serves as a tool, if some master hand is at work? We're all equally vulnerable.'

She sat back, and forced her bristling fur back into place. Damien thought he heard her growling softly.

'An interesting concept,' Tarrant mused. 'It may give us our first real insight into the nature of our enemy.'

'You think he feeds on degradation?'

He shook his head. 'The rakh have been affected, and faeborn demons don't feed on that species. No, it's got to be more than that . . . but this is a start. Any common link must be a clue to our enemy's purpose.'

'And therefore to his identity,' Damien added.

'And therefore how to kill him,' Hesseth hissed.

The sheer venom in her voice startled Damien. Not because it surprised him, or because he hated their unknown enemy any less than she did, but because for the first time he was hearing her hatred in the context of other patterns. And what he heard disturbed him.

Are we changing also? Is that the price we pay to come here? Are we allowing this place to degrade our spirits as surely as it did with the rakh, and with my Church?

What happens if we reach the enemy at last, only to discover that in the end we are no better than his other puppets?

'Damien?' It was Hesseth.

'I'm all right,' he managed. But he wasn't, and he knew she could hear it in his voice. 'Something personal.'

'Indeed,' the Hunter said softly. He didn't need to look at Tarrant to know that the man's eyes were fixed on him, and that he was studying Damien with more than mere sight. 'A night of prayer would do you good, Reverend Vryce. It would cleanse your spirit.'

He looked up sharply at Tarrant, expecting to see mockery in those pale eyes. But to his surprise there was none. Instead he saw something that might, in another man, be called *compassion*.

Was that possible? Had so much of the Hunter's veneer been stripped away by their recent experience that he was capable of such an emotion? His cruel persona had been forged and tempered in the solitude of the Forbidden Forest, where his only companions were demons and wraiths and a few carefully chosen men who had likewise sacrificed their emotional birthright. Was it being worn so thin by the constant presence of humanity that a hint of the original Neocount could begin to peek through?

We're making you more human, he mused.

The thought was strangely chilling.

He took out the Fire near morning, when the skies were a muted gray and Tarrant had left them in search of a daylight haven. The thick layer of varnish that protected the crystal vial had dulled, cataractlike, to a milky finish; the light that shone from within was hardly enough to illuminate his hand, and its miraculous warmth was nearly intangible even when he closed his palm around it.

But it was faith. Pure faith. Faith distilled into material substance, that had witnessed centuries of conflict. The faith of a million souls in the mission of his Church. The faith of a thousand priests in their last battle against evil. The faith of a single Patriarch in the one priest he sent east, believing – in his own words – that a single man might succeed where an army of men would fail.

May you be right, Holy Father. May I be worthy of your trust.

He prayed.

Rain fell in the morning, a brief thundershower. Soon after that the wind shifted direction, gusting with enough power that Damien felt uneasy about riding too near the edge of the steep granite drop. Whatever that combination amounted to down in the valley, it did manage to thin out the mist until it was no more than a translucent cloud. Through it, between the treetops, Damien could make out brown-black earth and an occasional clump of green. A gap in the trees revealed water – a river? – that snaked along the valley's floor, gleaming blackly between the evergreen branches. Not a pleasant land, but not overtly threatening either; after they had spent a good hour studying it through Hesseth's telescope, Damien felt immeasurably better about what lay ahead.

Getting down there was another matter. As they rode along the upper edge of the valley wall – hundreds of feet above the valley floor – Damien realized that descent might well prove impossible. The steep slope was mostly rock, which offered no sure footing for man or horse. Occasionally there were sections that sloped down more gently, or hills that abutted the valley wall from below, but none of those extended more than half the distance they needed, and all of them ended in steep granite inclines that would have been a challenge to a skilled mountain climber. Not to mention a skilled mountain climber with a horse.

But there had to be a way. The maps convinced him of that. The gap they had ridden through was labeled a pass, and what was a pass but a way through the mountains? If this course was useless, if it truly dead-ended, then no one would have assigned it that designation. Right? Logic said there had to be a way through, close enough that they could find it. Right?

He worked hard on believing that. It gave his mind something to focus on besides the terrain, which offered an unpleasant choice between heavily wooded slopes and sheer granite flats. More often than not they chose the latter, which meant riding dangerously close to the edge of that vast chasm. The horses seemed to prefer it to the woods, though, and Damien decided to indulge them. Trust the animals to know their own capacity.

At last, in the late afternoon, they found what looked like a moderately safe descent. Crumbled earth and fragmented granite offered a slope that was daunting but not downright suicidal, and they decided to try it. Half-sliding, the horses struggled for balance as they negotiated the treacherous slope. Their movement set rockfalls in motion that sculpted the mountainside anew even as they descended, and more than once the animals nearly went down. At one point the black horse began to limp and Damien had to stop to Heal it, knitting its damaged tendon together while gravel trickled past him like a river. All in all, he thought, the only thing worse than trying to descend this slope would be trying to climb it. Thank God that whatever happened they would not be coming back this way.

It took them more than an hour to reach the halfway point. By then the sun was already sinking below the crest of the western mountain, and the Core was right behind it. At least there would be stars for a while to guide them. By the light of the galaxy they fought for their descent, sometimes riding the horses and sometimes leading them. Finally, exhausted, they came to solid ground at last. By then even the Core had set, and Damien breathed deeply as he cast a last glance back toward the deadly slope, now cloaked in deepening shadow.

Tarrant was waiting for them.

Wordlessly Damien dismounted and handed him the reins of the Forest steed. He glanced up at Hesseth to see if there was any need to explain the arrangements – or to argue them – but clearly she had come to the same decision that he had. He swung up behind her with considerably more care than he had with Tarrant. She was small and fit easily in the slope of the saddle before him. There was a scent about her fur that was musky and warm and not unpleasant; he hoped that she found his own human odor at least tolerable. Between her acute sense of smell and his own semiclean state he had his doubts – he had done the best he could under the circumstances, but it was hard to stay truly clean when your changes of clothing were buried in a saddlepack more than fifty miles back – but in the name of diplomacy she made no comment about it. God bless her for that.

Silently, filled with foreboding, they descended the last mossy slope and entered the misty forest.

The valley mist wasn't as bad as it might have been, thanks to Tarrant, but combined with the midnight's darkness it had the effect of isolating them from the world outside. The few stars which were left were hidden from sight, and even the treetops overhead were thoroughly obscured by the drifting shroud of fog. Damien lit a lantern, which illuminated the ground about their feet but also the mist itself, so that it was impossible to see more than twenty or thirty feet in any direction. It was as if a shell had been erected around them, a perfect sphere of translucent substance that glimmered pale amber, reflecting the lamplight. It was uncomfortably claustrophobic, and dangerously limiting.

And if it's this bad now, he thought as they rode, *just wait till Tarrant's conjured weather passes. This is probably heaven by contrast.*

In silence they made their way, slowly and ever so carefully. Though normally Damien didn't worry about mere predators – most larger animals shied away from humans, unless hunger made them desperate – their lack of visibility made him feel particularly helpless. He noticed that Hesseth was tense between his arms, and her ears pricked forward at the slightest sound, their tufted tips scanning the path ahead, beside, behind them. Only Tarrant seemed to be taking it all in his stride, but Damien knew him well enough now to guess at the tension that lay coiled tight inside him. The Hunter hated what he couldn't control.

At last Tarrant signaled for them to stop. When Hesseth's horse had pulled up alongside his own he dismounted, then knelt to touch the ground with one slender finger. Testing the currents. Tasting the earth-fae. Damien Worked his own sight and saw a powerful northerly flow, sparkling with alien secrets. He didn't attempt a Knowing, but drank in the vision in its pure, uninterpreted form. Was this how adepts saw the world? Or was the richness of abstract power somehow translated into meaningful form in their brains, so that no formal Knowing was necessary?

'Odd.' Tarrant stood; his eyes were still fixed on the ground. 'Very odd.'

'I'm not sure I like the sound of that.'

'I'm not sure you should.' The Neocount bit his lip as he studied the currents; Damien could see his pale eyes tracing the earth-fae's motion, again and again. 'There's something there. Sorcery, I think. The trace is very faint; I can hardly make it out. And yet . . .'

When he didn't finish the thought, Damien prompted him, 'What?'

'By sorcery I mean that someone is consciously altering the fae. And yet, the patterns are not what I would associate with Working.' He looked up at Damien. 'Not with a normal Working.'

'Rakh?' Hesseth demanded.

He shook his head. 'No. The flavor of it is decidedly human.'

'Or demonic,' Damien said quietly.

'Yes,' the Hunter whispered. 'That is the other possibility.'

'I don't understand,' Hesseth protested.

Tarrant studied the currents again as he spoke; it was almost as if he were addressing the earth-fae, not her. 'Demons are born of humankind. They feed on humans, they manipulate human fantasies, some even define themselves in human terms. Their fae-signature is therefore very similar to that of humans . . . sometimes so much so that it's hard to tell the two apart.'

'But demons don't do sorcery, do they?' Damien struggled to remember exactly what the textbooks said. 'They don't Work the fae like we do. Right? So their signature would have to differ in that respect.'

For a moment the Hunter said nothing. Then he said, very quietly, 'There is one kind that does. I think. The trace might look like that, if one of them were active here.'

'One of who?'

The Hunter seemed about to speak, then shook his head instead. 'Not until I know for sure. But if it is that . . .' There was an odd tone to his voice, that Damien was hard put to identify. 'It would . . . complicate things.'

And then he realized what the tone was. Fear. The Hunter was afraid.

'You want to go on?' he asked. Suddenly not so sure himself.

Tarrant nodded. 'It's still far off. Perhaps if we get closer I can read its source. Let's hope.'

He swung himself back up onto his horse's back. Damien expected him to move his mount forward, and prepared to urge his own horse to follow. But Tarrant turned back to them instead, twisting about in the black leather saddle.

'There's something else,' he told them. 'Something I don't understand at all. I sensed very clearly that there was human life in this valley, somewhere to the south of us. That trace should be growing stronger as we travel toward it. A simple Knowing should reveal it.' He shook his head in frustration; his fine hair, mist-dampened, glistened in the lamplight. 'It's not there now,' he muttered.

'What? The trace?'

'Anything. Any sign of humanity. It's as if no other humans were in these woods — as if no other humans have *ever* been in these woods. But I know that's not the case. It simply can't be.'

'An Obscuring?' Damien asked. 'If a band of hostile humans wanted to hide themselves—'

'No.' He shook his head sharply, almost angrily. 'Even that would leave a trace. A kind of echo, which should still be discernible. No, it's as if . . . as if they *ceased to exist,* somehow. As if they ceased to ever have existed.'

'Are you sure of that?' Hesseth demanded.

He glared at her. 'Do you doubt my skills?'

'You were misled in the rakhlands,' she reminded him.

The Hunter's expression darkened. 'I'm not a fool, you know. I do learn from my mistakes.' Anger flared coldly in his eyes. 'I'm not saying there isn't more to this than meets the eye. If human sorcery were a simple affair, then any idiot could guard himself against it. Obviously, anything I see in the currents might have been put there for our benefit. But all Workings leave some mark, even a mis-Knowing; now that I know to look for such things, I'm hardly likely to miss it.'

'I'm sorry,' she said. By the tension in her body Damien could tell just how much those words were costing her. 'Is there anything I can do to help?'

'Obscure us if you can,' he said shortly. And he kneed his horse into sudden motion, so that it practically leapt ahead into the mist.

They traveled for over an hour through the fog-shrouded woodland, until their hair and their clothing and the horse's flesh beneath them were all damp from the omnipresent moisture. With the day's miserly warmth long gone from the earth the air grew more and more chill, the mist more and more icy. They moved at a slow but steady pace, and Damien and Hesseth took turns walking so as not to push their communal horse past endurance. If the day had been pleasant, the exercise would have been welcome; as it was, he was glad when at last Tarrant signaled for a break.

He brushed the horse down a bit, more to reassure it than for any other reason; there was no real hope of getting the animal dry. It was more a ritual of normalcy than anything else, a chore so automatic that his mind could wander while his muscles worked. Trying to untangle Tarrant's words in his own mind, to come up with an explanation of who or what might be ahead of them . . . but if the

Neocount of Merentha couldn't come up with a plausible explanation, how could he hope to?

We need more information, he thought. And he prayed that the information would come to them before the danger with which it was surely allied.

They rested and ate in silence, and in silence they remounted and resumed their course. Tarrant led the way. Damien sensed a growing unease in him – dare he call it fear? – but he had no way to address the issue, no safe way to draw him out on it. They would just have to function in ignorance until the Neocount decided that it was time to share his fears.

The forest changed as they traveled farther south. Subtly at first, one species of tree giving way to another, one type of clinging vine giving way to its cousin. It was hard to say exactly where or when the flora began to seem threatening, or to pinpoint what was wrong with it. All the elements of a normal forest were in place, along with the smell of rot and a hundred varieties of mold that the omnipresent mist fostered. If anything, it should be a surprise that plant life growing under these conditions should seem so normal.

Now vines proliferated, and they were not the healthy green vines of home. Thick ropy stems twined about the trunks of trees, sprouting spongy leaves that looked like some kind of fungus. They were not even green, these vines, but a kind of ghostly white that shimmered wetly in the party's lamplight. Damien went out of his way to see that the mare didn't touch them. In some places they had grown so thick that a mat of tangled vines hung between the trees like sheets, and small mantled insects scurried in between the knots and the funguslike leaves. Toward the treetops the vines took on a green cast, but that was because they had sucked the color from their hosts; dead branches swayed in the chill night breeze, moldy bark fingers with white leaves at their tips. The whole of it reeked of rot and decay, and Damien had no doubt that thousands of tiny scavengers were eating their way through the dying trees' flesh, so that all that was left in the end was a ghostly shell, a husk of dead bark, a grotesque trellis for the clinging vines.

It's just nature, he told himself. *Species have adapted to meet the special demands of this place.* But that didn't seem right, somehow.

Tarrant's Forest had been horrible, but all the elements were inter-
locked in perfect biological harmony; you could sense that balance,
even though you were repelled by its tenor. But here ... there was
too much death, he decided. Too much decay. It was as if Nature's
precious balance had somehow been overburdened, as if something
had been introduced or removed – or *changed* – that threw the
whole system out of kilter. What would the vines feed on when all
their hosts were dead? They rode past dense mats of tangled vines,
that covered their trees like a blanket. What happened when that
growth became so thick that sunshine could no longer reach the host
tree's leaves? If one listened closely enough, could one hear the
sounds of a forest dying? The moans of an ecosystem in collapse?
The thought of it made him shiver, so that Hesseth twisted around
to see what was wrong with him. Her expression was grim, and
the thin ridge of scar tissue which was all that remained of her inner
eyelid was drawn in as far is it would go. So. She felt it, too. There
was some comfort in that, at least.

They rode for hours, with brief stops so that he and Hesseth and
the horses could eat, and so that Tarrant could study the currents.
The rotting forest seemed to close in about them as soon as they
stopped, for which reason Damien and Hesseth ate as quickly as
they could, and took no more rest than was absolutely necessary.
Even Tarrant seemed uncomfortable in this place. And when you
really thought about it, Damien reflected, didn't that make sense?
The Hunter was a creature of order and precision, whose creative
genius had embraced not only man's faith, but nature in all her vast
complexity. Was there any greater ugliness than this, an ecosystem
corrupted past saving?

After a time – no telling how long, he had lost all sense of mea-
suring the hour – the Hunter turned east. They followed him
without question, trusting in his sense of purpose. Overhead the
vine-blanket thickened, and spongy tendrils hung down low enough
to brush their hair as they passed. The sour smell of decay was nigh
on overwhelming, even to Damien's merely human senses; he could
only guess at how much Hesseth was suffering. Lower and lower
the tangled masses hung, until at last Tarrant had to draw his sword
and cut a path through them in order to continue. The coldfire

light of the Worked steel was reflected by the mists about them, turning the whole world a cold silver-blue. Tendrils of vine shattered like glass as he cut through them, tangled mats becoming shards of ice in an instant, glittering like stars as they fell.

And then they were in the open again. Tarrant cut a tunnel through the last thick tangle – a veritable wall of white vines and fungus, with mold clinging to every available surface – and then the vines were behind them, and the trees also, and the party looked out upon an expanse of water so clean and fresh that just looking at it made Damien feel renewed.

Tarrant nodded toward the water. 'I thought that under the circumstances the river might offer you the best campsite.' His choice of words made Damien glance up at the sky. No good; there was still enough mist to keep him from seeing how exactly dark the sky was. But Tarrant's manner made it clear that dawn was coming, and in this place it would take him some time to find a suitable shelter.

'You sure you wouldn't rather stay with us?'

He hesitated. 'There's no shelter for me here. I regret.'

He chose for some reason of his own not to transform on the spot, but made his way back toward the midnight confines of the forest. Damien watched as the vine-tunnel swallowed him, then reluctantly turned his attention to making camp. He was worried. Very worried. He had made the offer more as a gesture than as a serious suggestion; he knew the Hunter well enough to know how much he valued his daytime privacy. If Tarrant would actually prefer to stay with them, if he would prefer Damien's presence to whatever was *out there* . . . that was a sobering concept, indeed.

Daylight. Sort of. The mist turned a deep gray, then a dingy half-gray, but got no lighter. Between the steep walls of the valley and the fog that attended its floor, the sunlight was hard pressed to penetrate. At noon the swirling fog turned white at last, but it was only a brief respite; within an hour the world was gray once more. It reminded Damien of the false dawn of the arctic region, where the late autumn sun teased the eye once a day but never fully rose. It was depressing there, too, he remembered.

There were things that came out of the fog, faint wisps of faeborn life that drifted through the airborne miasma like some ethereal fish. They had no solidity, these creatures, and their forms were as changeable as the mist, but lack of material substance made them no less dangerous. Evidently Tarrant's presence had kept them at bay during the night, but now – with the light so dim that it could barely hurt them – they drifted toward Damien with the blind instinct of demonic hunger, sensing in his flesh and his human vitality a feast beyond all measure. God alone knew what part of him they wanted; he didn't stop to figure it out. When two strokes of his sword convinced him that solid weapons were of no use in this case – they passed through the fog-wraiths with little more effect than a wire passing through smoke – he resorted to a Working. He drove them back as far as he could with the threat of a Dispelling, then crafted crude wards to keep them from coming back. His hands shook as he Worked, for he knew how risky it was to spend so much time immersed in the currents; an earthquake now would fry his brain before he knew what hit him. But at last he was done, and he took the eight stones he had chosen and placed them about the circumference of the camp in a rough circle. The coarse rocks were far from ideal for ward-making – the best ward hosts were carefully inscribed, precisely made, symbolically powerful items – but they'd have to do for now. Each of them had been bound to a pattern that would tap into the earth-fae if one of the demonlings tried to approach, and would use that power to drive them away. Since rocks had no brains, the earth-fae could surge all it liked and not do them an ounce of harm.

Hesseth watched him in some amusement, but spared him any derisive comment. Which was good. Because the damned things hadn't gone after *her,* had they?

Only when he was done and had rejoined her by the fire did she venture, 'He must have been right, you know.'

'Who?'

'Tarrant. About there being humans here.'

He looked back toward the forest, where the last of the fae-creatures had fled. 'There'd have to be, wouldn't there? And a lot of them, too. It takes more than a single mind to manifest numbers like that.'

Now that the creatures were gone it was hard to visualize them, but he tried. How odd they were ... and how utterly logical that they should exist. 'It's fear of the mist,' he reflected aloud. 'That's what spawned them. Fear of the mist and what it hides. The humans here must have come from outside this valley, and they found the mist threatening. So that when their negative emotions began to sculpt the earth-fae, it took that form. Foglike. Amorphous.' He looked back at the fire, and tried to think. Tried to make it all come together. 'There are no more traditional demons here, are there? At least none that we've seen yet. Yet most human communities produce a folkloric repertoire – vampires and succubi, human distortions – long before they come up with anything as abstract as this. Strange,' he mused. Something foggy with bright red eyes began to drift in from across the river; when it reached his nearest ward, it shivered and stopped. 'I wonder what caused it?'

'Tarrant will probably know,' she murmured. Watching as the demonling turned away, drifting into the mist beyond the wards.

Tarrant didn't know.

When he returned that night he paused briefly at the outer boundary of the campsite, and gazed upon the wardstones one after another. Only when he was done, did he join them by the fireside. 'These aren't strong enough to matter,' he said to Damien, 'but you should bear in mind that the power I draw on is demonic in nature. Your wards define me as an enemy.'

Damien winced; he should have anticipated that. 'Sorry.'

As they doused the fire and saddled the horses, Damien and Hesseth told him about the strange demonlings. He shared with them his own growing frustration at being unable to get a fix on the humans who must be somewhere in these woods. 'It's not an Obscuring,' he insisted. His tone was almost angry, it seemed to Damien. 'But what, then? What could make a dozen or more humans vanish from the currents, so that the earth-fae didn't acknowledge their presence?'

There was no answer for that, and no other option but to go on. They rode back into the strangling forest, and for once Damien was glad for its closeness. It was comforting to see something besides a wall of gray fog, even if it was this twisted flora.

They spent the night in silence, riding through mile after mile of the alien forest, trying to make out its features by lamplight. Tarrant could see by the fae-light, of course, and Hesseth's nocturnal eyes worked well in the dark, but for Damien it was a constant strain. Add to that the fact that the forest was changing, and that each mile was stranger than the last, and it was no surprise that by the time Tarrant declared it a night he was exhausted.

Vines strangling trees. Then vines in shreds, white sap dripping from their ravaged ends. Then black things that scuttled up and down the tree trunks, carrying bits of vine and spongy leaves in their mouth. Then larger things, spiderlike, that ate those. Rodents that fed on the spiders. They weren't intermingled, as natural species would have been, but existed in waves so populous that each new life-form devastated the forest anew, leaving a wasteland of dead trees and shriveled vines and bones. So very many bones. They littered the ground like dead leaves in autumn. Piles so thick that they cracked beneath the horses' hooves with every step. The smell of decay, of rotting flesh, was so overwhelming in places that Damien wrapped a strip of cloth over his nose and mouth and Worked it to act as a barrier. Hesseth looked so nauseous that he offered to do the same for her, and to his surprise she accepted. Whatever Tarrant did to deal with the smell was private and undiscernible, but Damien was sure he did something. The Hunter was too fastidious a man to put up with that kind of stink for long.

And then, at last, they were back at the river. It was wider now, and the water gleamed as it rippled over a rocky bed. Damien started forward toward it, meaning to gather some river water for their dinner, but Tarrant's hand on his arm stopped him.

'What is it?'

'The pattern of this region. Think about it. One species takes root, then overbreeds and destroys the environment. So another is introduced which establishes balance for a while, until it, too, overbreeds. And then another. And another.'

It took him a minute to realize what the Hunter was driving at. 'You think someone *evolved* those life-forms?'

'Nature is infinitely complex, Reverend Vryce. Who knows that better than I? A natural ecosystem is a delicately balanced creation, with all sorts of checks and balances that are continuously evolving in tandem. Nothing like this. The simplicity of it, and the waste . . . I sense a human hand behind it. Very inexperienced, limited in understanding, perhaps overwhelmed by its failure to control. Because in order to establish a new species properly, you have to make sure it comes equipped with counterspecies: predators, parasites, diseases, degraders. That wasn't done here. Such power, without understanding the consequences of applying it. No wonder there was such destruction.'

'Each life-form had its own territory,' Hesseth pointed out.

'Perhaps. Or perhaps instead each life-form was created at some central point, and then allowed to spread. The vines first, and then the animals that fed on them. Predators for them, when they were out of control. And again. Each species spreading out from that central point, like waves across the region. So that as we travel—'

'We're heading toward that center,' Damien said suddenly.

The Hunter nodded. 'That, and we're due for the next creation. The last was rodents, and large ones. Anything feeding on them would also be a threat to humankind, and thus to their creators.'

'Insects could kill them off,' Hesseth offered. 'Or even diseases. Those wouldn't have to endanger humans.'

'Correct. And I would have used the latter, if this were my game. But whoever's playing God with this ecosystem lacks that kind of subtlety. So what would be a safe killer, from our sorcerer's point of view? Another small creature? Too inefficient. Something large? Too dangerous. Perhaps something large but rooted down, so that it isn't free to roam. Then it could be avoided. But you can't just scatter these killers at random, can you? The animals would learn to avoid them. They would have to be in hiding, and concentrated some place where all the animals would have to go . . .'

He studied the ground for a moment, then bent down and picked up a rock. It was flat, Damien noted, very thin, and about the size of his hand. With a flick of his wrist he launched it out toward the water. It hit the surface hard near the shore and then skipped several times, and was swallowed by the fog before they could see it sink.

'Very neat,' Damien said. 'But I don't see how—'

The water erupted. From beneath the spot where the stone first struck the surface something burst upward in a spurt of foam. It was green, and glistening, and it whipped about wildly in search of the cause of the commotion. Damien saw green leaves and slender tendrils, with something sharp and white at their center. Hungry. God. He could *feel* the hunger, could feel it freezing his limbs, making him unable to fight, unable to struggle . . .

He shook his head violently and forced himself to turn away. It wasn't easy. After a moment the noise subsided. After another moment the feeling of helplessness did also. He turned back to the water, saw nothing but smooth ripples on its surface.

'Good God,' he whispered. 'What was that?'

'Our sorcerer's last gambit, I assume. What will happen when this one goes out of control is anyone's guess. Fortunately, the next creation will probably be a river creature also. It should mean easier traveling for a while.'

'If you're right,' Hesseth said, 'if this is all the work of humans . . . then how far are we from them? Can you guess that?'

'Pretty close, I would imagine. How many more steps in the food chain ladder are possible before something decides it likes the taste of human flesh? I think we should be very careful from now on,' he warned. 'These things are getting larger each time, and far more dangerous. In the end it may not be the humans here who are the greatest threat, but these creations.'

'You still can't Know anything about the humans here?' Damien asked.

The Hunter turned cold eyes on him. 'I can't. I've tried. It's as if they disappeared.'

'Or were eaten?' Hesseth offered.

'I'd have sensed that,' he responded shortly.

Be careful. That was what Damien thought as they rode along the shoreline and looked for a place to camp. Be careful. As if they hadn't been before. As if the Hunter had to tell them a thing like that.

He's worried, he thought. *Possibly even frightened. Has anyone ever defied his power before, in quite this way?*

And if he's frightened . . . where the hell does that leave us?

They searched for a safer campsite along the rocky shore.

'Damien. Damien. Get up.'

The whisper invaded his dreams. It took him a minute to realize whose it was, and why it sounded so urgent.

'*Damien*. Wake up. Please.'

Then he understood. The dream shattered into a thousand fragments. Sleep was gone in an instant.

'What is it?' he croaked, sitting up. His throat was dry. 'What?'

He saw that Hesseth was armed. 'Someone's coming,' she whispered. Her ears were flattened against her head and her fur was bristling. 'I can smell them.'

As he quickly got to his feet, he looked for cover, someplace safe to shoot from. But they had chosen this spot because it was out of the forest but far enough from the river, and not for its martial features. He damned himself – and Tarrant – for that shortsightedness.

'Where?' he whispered.

She nodded toward the south. And hesitated.

'Many,' she breathed at last.

Damn. Damn. Damn. He chose an outcropping behind them which offered limited cover. No way to hide the horses. No time to obliterate the camp. He motioned for her to crouch down beside him, behind the low ridge.

He could hear them now. Rustling. Voices. An odd mixture of caution and carelessness, low voices and heavy footfall. And damn, there were a lot of them. You couldn't make that kind of noise with only a handful.

They came closer, moving from up the south, and then their direction shifted. West. That meant they were encircling the camp. The voices were silent now, wary of being heard by their quarry.

So they knew where the camp was, and most likely knew what they were hunting. Damn. In another few minutes he and Hesseth would be surrounded, and then there would be no way out but through the river. Could they sneak away quickly enough, going far enough north that they escaped the deadly circle . . . but no, that meant leaving the horses behind along with all their supplies. And there was no way they could travel all the miles they had to with neither mounts nor gear.

He felt desperation grab hold of him – that, and a cold calculation, as he realized where their only chance lay. He reached out for Hesseth, met her eyes, nodded toward the horses. *We grab them,* his expression said, *and run for it.* North. They could stay by the river – but not too close – where the terrain would allow a horse to gallop, and maybe they could just break out of this. They'd make noise all right, lots of it, but no human feet could outrun a horse. It was a long shot, to be sure . . . but he figured it was the only chance they had.

But as he sprinted forward toward his mount the vines at the edge of the forest parted, and he knew that it was too late; if they were coming into the open, it meant that the camp was already surrounded. There was no time to get back behind the ridge now, for what little shelter it provided. And besides, if he did that, he'd be revealing Hesseth's position. Let her have a chance.

Heart pounding, he braced his weapon against his shoulder and waited for the enemy to reveal itself.

The first thing he saw was a face. A horrible visage, with slashes of red above and below distorted human features. He was so on edge that it took him a minute to realize what it was. Beside it another appeared, equally grotesque, crudely painted. They were the faces of his childhood nightmares, the masks that his unconscious mind had assigned to demons of the night long before he had actually seen any. And masks they were, in a very real sense. He watched in amazement as more and more armed figures came out of the woods, until the campsite was surrounded. They were fierce, these warriors who wore the demon-masks; their dirty bodies were painted with the colors of blood and death, and bones were tied to their weapons. Their wooden spears and crude arrows were all stained brown or black about the tip, and Damien had no doubt that it was blood of many kills which had seeped down into the wood.

He should have moved before they were in position. Or gone back to Hesseth. He should have done *something*.

But he couldn't. He just stared.

They were *children*.

More then twenty of them surrounded the camp now; he didn't dare turn his head to count. Few stood higher than his chest. At least a handful were small enough that they couldn't have been more than seven or eight years old at the most, and the rest seemed little older. Though it was hard to make out their shapes between the grotesque masks they wore and the leather vests and breeches which had been similarly painted, Damien would have wagered that not more than one or two of them had reached their teens yet.

How bizarre. How utterly, horribly bizarre.

They were all armed, and though their weapons were crudely made they were undoubtedly effective. As they came slowly into the clearing, Damien realized that he had only two choices. He could try to cut them down, using his size, his strength, and his experience as an advantage to counteract their numbers. Or he could surrender, bide his time until Tarrant returned. The latter went against his every instinct, and he found himself bracing for battle, calculating just how and when he should move against so many . . . but they were children. Children! How would it feel, to cut down those tiny bodies? Could he do it? Suddenly he wasn't so sure. His hands, clasped about the weapon, trembled slightly.

Prodded from her hiding place, Hesseth joined him. He heard her growling low in her throat as she scanned the crowd surrounding them, as unhappy as he was about the choices.

'Who are you?' he demanded of them. 'What do you want?'

It was a lean boy – one of the tallest – who responded. 'You come with us. Now. Put down your weapons and come—'

'Or we kill you,' another one interrupted. She was a tiny thing, with bedraggled bits of blonde hair hanging down about her shoulders.

'Do it fast,' the lean boy commanded.

Damien looked at Hesseth, and saw in her eyes a reflection of his own inner turmoil. Perhaps a moment ago he could have pretended that they weren't human, could have managed to close his eyes and mow them down with sword and with sorcery . . . but not now. Not now that they'd spoken. All his human instinct cried out against it. Children were to be protected, not murdered.

If they had moved against him, he could have fought. If they had threatened his life. If they had seemed so angry or irrational that he thought they might kill him outright rather than take him prisoner. If . . . anything.

But they didn't. And they weren't.

He lowered his weapon. The children waited. He looked at Hesseth – her ears were still flat against her head and she was hissing softly, but she nodded – and he laid the weapon down. And stepped back. It was little more than a gesture; between his strength and Hesseth's claws they were far from helpless in this crowd. But it seemed to be what the masked children wanted.

He watched while they moved into the clearing, gathering up the supplies and taking hold of the horses' reins. They didn't move like children, Damien thought. Too awkward. Too stiff. It was hard to watch them closely, he discovered. Hard to focus on one for any length of time. Was that the remnants of an Obscuring? It was an odd sensation.

At last the camp had been gathered up, except for those few items the children didn't value. Damien's weapon had been taken up, along with Hesseth's. A slender girl with a predatory mask carried his sword in its harness; it was taller than she was.

'Who are they?' Hesseth whispered. '*What* are they?'

The tall boy heard her. As the children drew close about them, preparing to herd Hesseth and Damien back into the forest and to God knows where, he took a stance opposite them with his feet spread wide and his spear planted firmly in the ground by his side. A challenging stance. A triumphal stance.

'Terata,' he told them. And though a mask obscured his features, Damien had the distinct impression that he was grinning. 'We're the Terata.'

23

They tied his hands behind his back. It went against his grain to allow it, but he saw no other option. He had already surrendered, after all. As they bound the coarse rope tightly about his wrists he did what he could to tense his arms, to thicken his wrists, and they seemed not to notice. That should net him some slack later. When they left him to work on Hesseth, he pulled at his bonds in several directions, testing the sophistication of the arrangement. He was pleased to feel it give slightly, which meant that although he had been tied tightly, he had not been tied well; between that and the small slack he had earned, he should be able to work himself free later.

When they were satisfied that their prisoners were bound, the Terata led them into the forest. Spears prodding their backs to keep them moving, they forced Damien and Hesseth through the thick brush that flanked the river, then into the shadowy realm beyond. Once Damien fell, and the sharp point of a weapon stabbed between his shoulder blades; he had to bite his lip to keep from cursing them aloud.

They're children, he reminded himself. Struggling to his feet without benefit of his hands. He could feel blood trickling down between his shoulder blades, adhering his woolen shirt to his back. *Self-indulgent by nature, not yet sophisticated enough to value self-control . . . you anger them now, and there's no telling what they'll do. Be careful, Vryce.*

Where had they come from, these painted infants? What chain of circumstances had brought them to this place? He could only wonder as he stumbled through the shadowy forest, trying to keep his footing for fear that some fledgling warrior might run him through if he didn't. Hesseth seemed to be doing well enough, though the set of her ears and the soft hiss of her breathing made it clear she was far from happy about the turn their travels had taken.

Yeah, he thought darkly. *That makes two of us.*

The Terata led them south. Through a forest that had been stripped of its lower leaves by some gnawing creature – another sorcerous creation? – and past trees that had been girdled by tooth-marks, robbed of their sap so that the upper limbs dried out and died. Long bark fingers scraped down from the heights above them, brushing their hair as they passed. Now that Tarrant had pointed out the pattern of life here, Damien could see it clearly. And if the Neocount had wondered what type of mind would create such crea-tures, now Damien understood. Limited minds. Untested, untrained. Minds that could not yet encompass the awesome complexity of Nature, nor make allowances for her excesses.

Children.

That meant at least one of them was a sorcerer, he reminded himself. If not more than one. And the power required to Work an entire species was no small thing; these Terata might lack adult sophistication, but in raw power they could probably hold their own with any mature sorceror. A sobering thought to consider as he fought his way across beds of dead twigs, pulling loose from the thorns that snagged his clothing as he passed.

Then something loomed ahead of him that brought him to a stop. For once no spear-point prodded him onward. He gazed at the wall of tangled brush before him and wondered how they meant to hack their way through it with nothing more than spears and arrows and a few short knives. Had the children traveled this route before? It seemed unlikely—

Light flared brightly to one side of him. He turned and saw one boy holding a torch, whose smoky flame illuminated the woods and the mist surrounding them. Then he reached down and tore up some grasses, which he thrust into the flame; black smoke coiled upward, thick and choking. He then passed the torch to the lean boy at the front of the pack, the one who had spoken to Damien. With a quick glance at the prisoners the boy moved to where the barrier-brush began, and for a moment stood still, studying it. The light of the torch glinted on the tips of vast thorns, as long as a man's hand and as thick about the base as a finger. Liquid glistened on the needle-sharp tips, and something about the way it gleamed made Damien very uneasy about coming in contact with it. It seemed to him that the brush seemed to rustle slightly as the boy drew near – or was that his imagination working overtime? – and then the lean Terata thrust the torch forward so that smoke billowed into the brush, obscuring the nearer branches—

The brush shuddered. Thorns twitched. Damien watched in horrified amazement as branches which had seemed dry and brittle drew back like arms, their glistening thorns trembling as if in rage. The boy thrust the torch even farther forward, and tangled limbs whipped back as if trying to escape him. There was a hole in the tangled wall now, and the boy worked at it – moving the torch from one side to the other, threatening back whatever branches seemed to be returning to their place – until the opening was nearly as wide as a man. Then another child, a small girl, came forward with a second torch and lit it from his; with her help he managed to enlarge the opening until it formed a crude tunnel perhaps six feet in height, and wide enough for a horse to pass through.

'Go!' he ordered. The Terata moved quickly. The nearer limbs of the thornbush shook as they passed, and Damien had no doubt that if the smoke thinned for a moment the branches would close in upon the travelers. But the girl and the lean boy held the thorns at bay with practiced skill, and even enlarged the opening enough that when the horses passed through their manes hardly brushed the nearest branches. Damien dared to work a Knowing as he entered the thorny tunnel, and what he learned nearly caused him to stumble. But then a number of small hands pushed him and he was through, falling to his knees on the rocky earth a safe distance from the grasping branches.

When they all were through, the girl and boy followed. With them gone, the smoke cleared in an instant. The branches which had drawn back snapped toward them with sound like a whip cracking, but the children had gauged their distance well; the longest thorns fell inches short of their target, and all the convulsions of branches which followed were incapable of getting them any closer.

As he watched the vast plant writhe in frustrated hunger, Damien wished that Tarrant were with them. And not just because his power would have been so welcome.

You were wrong, Hunter. They didn't put their killer in the river at first. They didn't have that much foresight. They rooted their creation in the ground and let it grow, until the animals it fed on had learned to avoid it and the only prey left to it were the Terata.

He could hear the branches twitching as he got to his feet. Struggling for food. Starving, in the midst of plenty.

But these children do learn from their mistakes, he thought grimly. Watching as the Terata extinguished their smoking torches. *Something to remember.*

The miles fell behind them with painful slowness. It was hard for Damien to match his stride to that of the children; for all of their youthful energy, their legs were so much shorter than his own that every step was a struggle to match their pace. When he moved too quickly a spear-point in his back or a knife-point in his side reminded him to slow down; he didn't look down to check but would have bet that his body was spotted with blood from the treatment. Hesseth seemed to hold her own, moving with feline grace among the children, like a sleek predator among awkward browsers.

And their movement was all wrong, he thought. Watching the three leaders of the group ahead of him, the others out of the corners of his eyes. For all that they were children, for all that their bodies were still growing and therefore awkward, there was a wrongness to their motion that went beyond that. He couldn't put his finger on what it was – when he tried to focus on them his vision grew hazy, until he had to focus his attention straight ahead to bring his eyes under control once more – but some deep-set instinct warned him that it was wrong, that something about these children was even more strange than it appeared, and that he'd damned well figure out what it was before his life depended on that understanding.

Half a day later. Well past noon. Exhaustion numbed his limbs, his mind, his hopes. The dismal forest thinned at last, leaving only the serpentine mist curling above muddy earth. He could smell the river, though he couldn't see it. Hesseth looked bedraggled. He felt no better. The awkward pace had drained them both.

At last they came to a place where the river spread out before them, glistening coldly in the filtered sunlight. It was no longer a free-moving stream of water that gushed over rocks and through tree-lined channels, but a vast lake whose still surface rippled softly as far as the eye could see. Trees had fallen into the water at various points and lake plants had taken root in their bark, sprouting branches that covered the water's surface like a web. Green fronds waved softly in the current as small animals scampered across the tangled branches, as comfortable inches above the water's surface as they had once been in the treetops. Here and there Damien could see a sandbar peeking through a bed of reeds, mountain mud carried down from the heights by the swift-running river. And in the center . . .

An island arose some half-mile in the distance, that was clearly their destination. The base was a vast mound of boulders, sparsely covered with greenery. Flood waters had left their mark a good ten feet above the current water line, and only above there did trees and larger bushes flourish – but those were twisted creations, whose gnarled trunks and contorted branches seemed grimly well suited to serve as the Terata's home. Damien wondered if the children had sculpted these life-forms as well, or if they had learned enough of a lesson from their other attempts to leave this island in its natural state.

They started toward the water, prodding Damien forward. He regarded the lake's surface with some trepidation, remembering the waterborn predators that lived upriver. But though it seemed that there was no solid land ahead of them, the children led them through a matted path in the rushes to a mud bar that stretched some ten yards into the water. He stepped out upon it gingerly, glad that the horses weren't intelligent enough to understand the risk. But the ground beneath his feet was quite solid, not like mud at all – so much not like mud that he paused for an instant to Work his sight, wondering what it was that he truly walked upon. And his Working failed. No, not *failed* exactly; it was more like *slid off*. As if the space he was trying to focus on was made of the slickest glass, and his Sight had gone skittering off its surface.

Strange. He had never experienced anything like it before, could come up with no explanation for the odd effect. Tarrant had once turned his Workings aside, back when they had first met, but the sensation was nothing like this. Was this how the Hunter had felt when his best attempts at a Knowing had netted impossible results? Ominous.

The lead boy had reached the end of the mud bar, but though water seemed to lap at his ankles the ground was as solid as ever. He turned slightly to the left as he stepped off into the water, and the others were careful to follow. Damien braced himself as he came to the end of the bar, knowing that if these children were willing to wade in the cold mountain water, then it was probably quite safe—

And then he stepped down, and didn't get wet. Nor did the ground beneath him feel like it now looked: a treacherous surface of pitted gravel and water-polished stones, slicked by slime and algae and sported about by thousands of tiny fish. No, it felt more like . . . wood. Was that possible? Old wood, weatherworn and mist-dampened. He tried to Work his sight again – nearly stumbled doing so – but if the water beneath his feet was some kind of illusion, he damned well couldn't See through it. Nor could he See any sign of the region having been Worked, although there should have been something. *Every Working leaves its mark*, Damien thought, as he followed carefully in the children's footsteps. *Without exception*. But if there was a Worker's mark on this, he damned well couldn't see it.

Tarrant could make it out. Tarrant could make sense of this. He glanced up at the sky – or rather, up at the mist overhead – and judged it to be very near nightfall. A sense of relief flooded his nerves at the thought, and he felt his muscles relax a tiny bit.

All we have to do is make it till he gets here.

At the end of the unseen bridge was a visible line of stairs, crudely cut into the base of the island. Damien climbed them carefully, knowing that his bound hands would be unable to afford him balance should anything go wrong. Behind him he could hear the children struggling with the horses, who were clearly unhappy about the route. But in the end the animals were coerced into climbing – with sorcery, perhaps? – and soon they had all gained the top of the island, to gaze out upon the Terata camp.

It was, as the Terata themselves were, fragmented and ill-executed. Skin tents betrayed by their shapes that the staffs upholding them were less than perfectly arranged, and indeed several had collapsed; there were children working on them even as Damien watched. A foul smell came and went with the breeze, from skins that were less than perfectly tanned, and the odor of long-dead meat seemed to hang about the camp like a haze. And the children! There were at least two dozen here, in addition to Damien's band of captors, including several that were mere babes, hardly able to walk. Without their masks and fierce weapons they looked strangely vulnerable, and though their flesh seemed healthy enough, Damien thought he caught a hint of past abuse in their eyes, the haunted look of bruised souls.

When they saw his party, the children turned and cheered, and gathered about them every bit as gaily as youngsters begging candy from adults. The little faces were dirt-smeared and sunburned, but they looked healthy enough. If you didn't look in their eyes.

Flanked by cavorting youngsters, the prisoners were led to the center of the rocky isle. There a cave mouth gaped, its root-fringed darkness leading down into the depths of the island. The children pushed Damien forward, and clearly meant for him to enter it. He glanced back at Hesseth. She wasn't any more happy about it than he was, but she seemed reasonably confident. At last he nodded and ducked through the opening, to the accompaniment of blows. The ground was slick beneath his feet and he almost fell, but he managed to stay upright and get out of the way before Hesseth slipped down into the darkness. When they were both inside, a thick grate of wood was put into place over the opening, and Damien heard some kind of latch being fixed in place around it. Thick tree limbs, bound together with coarse rope. Hard to break through, but not impossible. He was glad that the children hadn't taken up metalworking.

'Turn around,' Hesseth whispered softly. When he did so, he felt her lean down to where his hands were bound; the damaged skin of her face rubbed against his wrist as she gnawed him free of his bonds. He untied her then, and rubbed some life back into his hands. Good enough for now. It would only be hours before Tarrant returned to them, and he felt confident they could protect themselves that long.

By the fading light of the sun which filtered down through the grate, he studied their prison. It was a rough space, muddy, replete with the nooks and crannies that nature delighted in. For a brief moment he considered crawling into one of those narrow passageways in the hopes that it would lead to freedom, but then he remembered the children. Tiny, lithe, and insatiably curious, they would have followed every path to its end long before declaring this space a prison, and if there were an opening they would have sealed it long ago. So much for that. He shifted slightly so that his own shadow didn't blacken the rock face before him, turned to the left—

And saw eyes.

Hesseth must have seen them at the same time that he did, for he felt her sharp intake of breath beside him. For a moment he thought that the two gleaming points were the eyes of an animal, but then he remembered the size and scale of his hosts. And yes, it was a child. No doubt about that. A frightened child who scrabbled backward as he approached, keening terror low in its throat. A girl? Hard to say in this darkness, but the voice sounded female.

'Get away from me!' she shrieked. Her voice was hoarse and broken, as if she had bruised it by screaming too much. 'Get back! I know your God. He can't have me!'

He froze where he was. The cave was suddenly so silent that he could hear his heart pounding. Then, slowly, he took a step backward. The eyes didn't move. Another step. When there were perhaps twelve feet of distance between himself and the owner of those eyes, it seemed to him that she relaxed somewhat.

'Who are you?' he asked gently. Her strange accusation still ringing in his ears. *Your God can't have me*. 'Why are you here?'

'Keep away!' she gasped. 'Keep them away from me!'

Them.

The children?

What was going on here?

He looked at Hesseth. The rakh-woman's face – and thus her expression – were lost in shadow. But he thought he saw her nod.

'All right,' he said gently. 'We won't come near you.' He chose a spot on the muddy ground that was smoother than most, and sat. A cool wind blew in through the grating, chilling his sweat. He could sense those eyes fixed on him, studying him, but he tried not to meet them. Animals sometimes needed time to accustom themselves to the smell of a newcomer; perhaps in her fear she was subject to a similar instinct. Let her take her time, then. Time was one thing they had.

After many long minutes of shadowy silence, a rustling from outside the gate alerted Damien to someone's approach. It was a young boy, maskless but coated with war paint and mud, carrying a carved wooden spear. He came over to the grate and stared inside the makeshift prison – and something burst from the far corner, something small and filthy and very, very scared, moving with a suddenness that made Damien jump. The small girl ran to the grate and fell to her knees before it, clutching its bars, her whole body shaking with terror. 'Take them away,' she gasped. 'Please! He's a priest, can't you see? They'll kill you all!'

'The god of the cities don't have no power here,' the boy reminded her. 'Remember? As for *them*—' and he nodded toward Damien and Hesseth, '—they'll just be here till sacrifice.' His eyes glittered hungrily. 'I expect old Bug-eyes'll eat 'em for a snack, don't you? Eat 'em up whole, and spit out the bones for us to play with. So don't you worry.'

Sacrifice. Damien didn't like the sound of that. How long till night fell? They needed Tarrant, badly.

It was Hesseth who kept her head together and thought to ask, 'When is this sacrifice?'

The boy looked at her. If her strange ears and hands aroused any curiosity in him, it didn't show. 'Tomorrow,' he told her. 'Whenever *he* says it's time.'

He nodded back as he spoke, not the way that Damien and Hesseth had come, but down another path. One half of a circular clearing was visible, and in its center a statue. Black stone – obsidian? – crudely carved into a man's shape. Only not a real man. The body was human enough, allowing for the crudity of the carving, and its arms were outstretched as any carved figure's might be, but the face seemed . . . wrong, somehow. The eyes were too large, and they were not of a human cast. Strangely familiar, it seemed to him. He waited until the fog shifted, until enough light came through the mist to illuminate the features . . .

And then he remembered. That face. Those eyes. They had mocked him from over a woman's shoulder, once. In the crystalline tower in the rakhlands, just minutes before Tarrant's conjured quake had surged through those walls.

Faceted eyes, like a fly's. Mirror-perfect. They seemed to turn toward him as the sunlight shifted, sparkling with amusement. But that was his imagination. Wasn't it?

'Who is that?' he gasped. Barely managing to get out the words.

The boy grinned. 'That's our god, city-man. And you'll meet him soon enough.'

He pushed some small packages through the bars, followed by a crude wooden cup. Food of some sort. The girl grabbed up one of the tiny bundles – half-cooked meat wrapped in a large green leaf, it looked like – and ran to her corner, where she tore into it like one starving. Her eyes never left Damien. After a time, Hesseth went over and got the two remaining packages, which she sniffed and then presented to Damien.

The priest didn't move. His eyes were fixed on that statue, on the terrible visage that was all too familiar. The dusky air about it had taken on a gray cast, and the sky overhead – where he could see it – was tinted with the gold of the setting Core. The sun must be gone by now. Night had fallen. Where was Tarrant? Couldn't he sense Damien's need through the link that bound them? Didn't he know to rush?

Calesta. That was the demon's name, he recalled. Tarrant's tormentor. Servant of the House of Storms. The one who had stood behind the shoulder of Damien's captor in that terrible place, encouraging torture as the ultimate means of dominance. Even after all these months the memory made him shiver, and the name was enough to turn his blood to ice. They had known that he might be here, that he might be connected with the enemy they had come to fight . . . but this?

If they believe in him enough, they can make him a god. They can give him that kind of power.

Two dozen mad children, and a god who delighted in pain. No wonder the city-folk were afraid of them. No wonder they embraced the distancing power of legends, preferring to believe that the Terata were animals, or fae-wraiths, or perhaps even demons themselves ... anything but human. Anything but *this*.

'Come quickly,' he whispered. As if Tarrant could hear him. 'As soon as you can. We need you.'

24

The Hunter flew over the valley fifteen times – or was it sixteen? – and still he couldn't find the others. He sifted through the earth-fae with meticulous care, but still could discover no trace of them. He even conjured up a wind to scour the valley clean of its omnipresent mist, but despite the increased visibility he still found nothing.

Which was patently impossible. If they had ridden on, if they were in hiding, even if they had died, there would have been some sign of their passing. Even an Obscuring would have left its mark, a faint echo of power that would be discernible in the currents. But there was nothing. Nothing! It was as if they had simply disappeared. Or ... as if they had never existed.

Just like the other humans here, he thought grimly.

He came to a stop on a barren peak and exchanged his feathers for human flesh. The wind whipped his long tunic around his calves as he stared down into the valley, his fists clenched tightly in silent frustration. They had to be there, he thought. They *had* to be. And if he couldn't locate them, there was only one explanation. Not a pleasant one, but he was prepared to deal with it.

He drew in a deep breath to brace himself for Working – the mountain air was cold, and left a film of ice in his lungs – and then he patterned the earth-fae into a Summoning. It would have no real power over the one he was calling, he understood that now. But he wanted something that was more than an invitation, something that communicated not only his desire for an audience but his power, his determination.

If he's still in the east, he thought.

The demon came. It took him half an hour to arrive, but Tarrant was ready for that; he was prepared to wait another five days if he had to. Karril brought with him no decorative backdrop this time, no false panorama. Perhaps he sensed Tarrant's mood. Perhaps he knew that Iezu illusion was the one thing that might push the Hunter over the edge, toward unfettered violence.

'So,' Tarrant said, when the familiar form had solidified. 'You did stay in the east, as I thought.'

Karril looked about quickly: at the mountain, at the chill night sky, at the hills in the distance ... but not down into the valley, Tarrant noted. Not that.

'What is it you want?' he asked quietly.

'Reverend Vryce and the rakh-woman have disappeared. I need your help to find them.'

Karril stared at him in astonishment. 'You know I can't get involved in this. Did you think just asking again—'

'Perhaps I should explain the circumstances.' His voice uncoiled like a serpent, slick and venemous. 'Three nights ago there were humans there.' He pointed down into the valley, to where they had been two nights ago. 'Now they're gone. One night ago Hesseth and Reverend Vryce made camp beside that river. Now they're gone.' Ice-cold eyes fixed on the demon, black with hate. 'Not dead. Not deserted. Not even Obscured. *Gone.*'

'So what?' Despite the demon's tone of bravado, there was nervousness in his eyes. *He can sense the rage in me,* Tarrant mused. *He knows how close I am to directing it at him.* 'What do you expect me to do?'

'Find them.'

Karril was silent.

'Then tell me how to.'

The demon turned away from him. Afraid to meet his eyes? 'I told you, I can't ever—'

'Get involved? Don't fool yourself, Karril; you *are* involved. This isn't the work of some human sorcerer; I'd smell that a mile away. And it isn't the work of a simple demon either, I know that.' He took a step closer to Karril, was pleased to see that the move made him nervous. In some ways the demon was remarkably human. 'It must be illusion. What else? A veil of false reality, obscuring their movements. But there's only one kind of creature on this planet that can create an illusion so perfect, so utterly undetectable. Isn't there, Karril?'

'I know nothing about sorcery,' he whispered.

'But you can change the world's appearance with a thought, can't you? Create images of material objects so real that the human mind, accepting their existence, finds them utterly solid. You can even kill with such illusions – though I doubt you ever tried.' He paused. 'All the Iezu have that power, don't they? Isn't that part of what defines your kind?'

Karril said nothing.

'Only the Iezu are capable of such artifice. Only one of that kind could cloak a valley so completely that no human sorcery could defy it – and leave not even a mark upon the currents, to testify to his interference. Only the Iezu, Karril.'

The demon said nothing.

'You hear me?'

'I hear you,' he whispered.

'I want answers, Karril. I want them now.'

'And if not?' the demon challenged. 'What then? Will you Bind me? Disperse me? I told you, we can't be controlled like that.'

'Ah, yes. That was an unpleasant surprise. But I've given the problem a lot of thought since you told me that . . . would you like to hear my conclusions?' He waited for a response; when there was none he continued. 'All human Workings involve a mental formula. One has to define the Worker – oneself – and one's subject, and the form which the earth-fae will take to link the two together. So I thought, what if some part of that formula were flawed? Not the linkage, obviously, but something less noticeable. Perhaps the supporting definitions. In short, might a Summoning fail – or a Binding, or a Dispersing – because my understanding of its recipient's nature was flawed?' He wasn't sure, but he thought that Karril was trembling. 'I could correct that,' he said quietly. No need for volume; the threat was inherent in his tone. 'I could focus all the power I needed by drawing on my negative emotions – my anger, my indignation, hate, fear, *pain* – and then direct it at someone I knew, without trying to define who or what he was. Such as you, Karril.' He gave that a few seconds to sink in. 'What do you think? Would it work?'

'I don't know.' The demon's tone was miserable. 'No one's ever tried that.'

'Perhaps it's overdue, then.'

He watched as Karril struggled with himself – with his conscience? – in silence. At last the demon muttered, 'What is it you want?'

'I told you. The lifting of the veil that masks what's in the valley. You don't have to help me beyond that; just let me see the enemy's work, and I'll fight my own battles.'

The demon shut his eyes tightly. 'I can't,' he whispered.

'Karril—'

'I can't! It's not my doing. I don't have the power.'

'But it is a Iezu Working,' the Hunter persisted.

The words came slowly, squeezed out of him one by one. 'Yes. That's why I can't get involved, don't you see? We're forbidden to fight one another.'

'By whom?' Tarrant demanded.

Karril turned away. Staring down into the valley, he whispered. 'By the one who created us. Our progenitor.'

'*Progenitor?* Are you telling me that the Iezu were *born*?'

The demon nodded.

'That's impossible. The very definition of a demon—'

'That's how I understand it,' Karril said quickly. 'It's how we *all* understand it. So maybe we're wrong. What difference does that make? If we *believe* ourselves to be a family – if we function as if we are – does it change anything to have you question our origin?' He turned back to Tarrant; his voice was shaking. 'I'll tell you another thing. The same force that gave birth to us can kill us, just as quickly. We all know that. And I'm no more anxious to die than you are. Consider this: do the Iezu, being born, have souls that will survive death, or do they simply dissipate into the currents like other demons do? I'm not anxious to find out, Hunter. And I will, if you force me to get involved in this. That's the truth.'

For a moment there was no sound but the wind, slowly dying. Then the Hunter's voice, as quiet as the night. 'The valley has been cloaked by one of the Iezu.'

'Yes.'

'And you can't dispel his Working.'

The demon shook his head.

'Then offer me an alternative, Karril. I'm desperate, and that means I won't hesitate to kill you, if necessary. You know that. Tell me what you can do.'

The demon drew in a deep breath, trembling. It was a human gesture, not necessary for either life or speech. His flesh was only an illusion, after all. 'I can talk to him. I can . . . plead. That's all.'

'And what are the chances that will work?'

'Very slim,' he admitted. 'But if the alternative is open conflict between us . . . we'd both die, then.'

'Good. I suggest you remind him of that.'

'And if it doesn't work?'

The gray eyes narrowed. 'That would be unpleasant for both of us, wouldn't it?'

'There's an understatement,' the demon muttered.

'Just do that one thing for me. I'll take care of the rest.'

'Do you think you can?' Karril asked sharply.

'What?'

'Destroy him. The one responsible for this. That's what you intend, isn't it?'

'Do you think I can't?'

The demon sighed. 'If any other man had asked me that question . . . then I would have said no. No human power could defeat him. But you, Hunter? If the years have taught me nothing else, it's never to underestimate you. And none of your enemies have survived, have they? So who am I to judge the odds against you?'

The Hunter's expression softened slightly, into something that might almost be called a smile. 'You flatter me.'

'Hardly.' But the demon's expression softened as well, as he bowed his leavetaking.

It would have been hard to define the exact moment at which Karril's chosen flesh began to fade; one minute he seemed as solid as any natural human, and the next he seemed transparent, so that the distant stars shone through him. A perfect illusion, Tarrant mused. The greatest talent of the Iezu demons – and their most potent weapon.

Before the demon's form completed its dissolution – when the ruddy flesh and opulent attire had not yet faded into the shadows of the night – Tarrant ventured, 'Karril?'

The figure remained as it was, half flesh and half mist. The translucent eyes were curious.

'I'm . . . sorry. That it has to be this way.' The words came hard to him; regret was an uncomfortable emotion. 'I wish there were an alternative.'

It seemed to him that Karril's ghost-flesh smiled slightly.

'Yeah,' said the demon. 'Same here.'

And as the last of his form dissolved into the night, he whispered, 'Take care, old friend.'

25

The night passed slowly. Tarrant never came. Damien tried hard not to think about what might have happened to him, but images from the past refused to be put down. The Hunter in fire. The Hunter screaming. The Hunter's flesh in his hands, so charred and tortured that the skin came off when he pulled, displaying smoking red meat . . .

It doesn't have to be that way. He might not even have been captured. Maybe the strange sorcery of this place is keeping him away. Maybe any minute now he'll learn to break through it.

Maybe.

Demonlings arrived with the night, wispy bits of malevolence that crowded about the bars of their prison like so many starving animals. He worked a simple Repelling to keep them out of the cave itself, but they hung about its border with unnerving persistency. Periodically he had to reinforce his work, and while he did so memories of the quakes of this region ran through his mind. Once there was a slight tremor just after he was done, and he shook for many long minutes afterward. How long could he keep it up before sheer chance defeated him?

Through it all the little girl watched him. She had squeezed back into the farthest corner of the cell, a water-carved alcove so tiny that Damien couldn't have pried her out if he'd tried. That she was mortally afraid of the priest was obvious; it only took one accidental step in her direction for her to cry out, and try to wedge herself even farther back into the rock. And the accusations she cried out at him! *Your God can't have me. I won't bleed for him.* As if the One God would collect children. As if He would hurt them.

But then he remembered the children of the cities, chained up as bait for the faeborn. And the adepts, all the helpless adepts, murdered in their cribs for the crime of being able to See. And all the others there must have been as well, babies who couldn't See but who seemed a little strange, the children of hysterical parents who were all too ready to sacrifice their own to keep humanity pure . . . yes. Whether or not this little girl had suffered at the Church's hands, she had every right to fear men of his calling.

How terrible. How unthinkable, that the seeds of his faith had garnished such a dark harvest. If he thought about it too long he would surely weep, like he had for so many nights after they'd left Mercia. Secretly, of course. In silence. Such tears were a very private thing.

It's not just the Church that's gone wrong here. This whole land is wrong, from start to finish.

He took out the Fire. Gently, carefully, wary of breaking its container yet again. So little was left. Even in the darkness of the cave it hardly glowed at all, and the creatures who fluttered about the thick wooden grate merely paused to take note of it, then resumed their fluttering. He closed his hand about it, could barely feel its warmth. So much power gone, he mused. So much wasted. If only the faith of those thousands could have been focused where it was needed. Here. If only it could have been used for a Cleansing.

It was Hesseth's soft hiss that alerted him. He glanced first at the gate, then toward the back of the cave. The girl. She had moved. Crouched forward on all fours, alert as a beleaguered animal, prepared to bolt back to her hole should danger threaten. She froze when he looked at her, but when he didn't move – he made very sure he didn't move – she inched forward. Slowly, one hand in front of the other, flexing her weight on her fingers like a stalking predator, her body low to the floor. Her eyes seemed twice as large as they caught the dim Firelight, and amber highlights played along lengths of black, matted hair.

He held himself utterly still as she approached, hardly daring to breathe. When she came within an arm's length, she reached out to him, slender fingers oh so delicate in the darkness, short nails underscored by dirt. He could see the hunger in her now, sunken cheeks and deep-set eyes half-masked by dirt, the hollows at the base of her neck and the deep channels along her muscles that spoke of weeks of starvation, a body stressed almost beyond endurance. Then the thin fingers stretched out toward his hand, then hesitated; he could see her lower lip trembling.

Slowly, carefully, he opened the hand that held the Fire, until the crystal vial was cradled in his open palm. Only then did she reach out to it, tiny fingers struggling toward its light like a plant seeking the sun. Her index finger made contact then, and she gasped; it took all his self-control not to move toward her, away from her, not to do *something*. But he sensed that any movement on his part might shatter the fragile moment, might send her scuttling back to her muddy den to starve alone in silence once more.

'Damien—' Hesseth whispered, but he shushed her. The girl's hand closed about the crystal vial. Tiny, and so very fragile; she couldn't be more than thirteen or fourteen at the most, probably younger. He could feel the girl's eyes on him, but he didn't meet them; he sensed that whatever she might read in his expression would only drive her away.

And then she lifted the vial, and took it from him. Small hands clasped tightly about it, bright eyes fixed on its secrets. He thought she moaned softly, but couldn't tell if it was from pleasure or pain. Or both. By his side Hesseth was crouched tensely, ready to move if the precious vial was threatened. But Damien wasn't afraid. He knew the power that was in those few drops of moisture, and he was willing to bet that the girl could see it somehow. Or feel it. Or . . . something.

Then she knelt in the mud and clasped the vial to her, whispering something too low for Damien to hear. She clutched the Fire to her stomach and doubled over it, her whole body shaking. Sobbing in utter silence; weeping without a sound. His heart went out to her and he nearly moved forward, nearly took her in his arms – but how would she take that? Might it not undo whatever this fragile moment had accomplished? He sat back on his heels and waited, hurting inside. Wanting to help. Daring to do nothing.

And then the shaking ceased. Like an animal she curled up about the Fire, hiding it from sight. Her head, tucked beneath one arm, was invisible. Only her long hair trailed out from the compact bundle, matted black strands mixing with the mud until it was impossible to tell where one began and the other ended. Exhaustion hung about her like a pall of smoke.

After many minutes, Damien dared to move. The girl didn't stir.

'Asleep?' Hesseth whispered. As she, too, shifted position.

He dared a Working. There was a chance it would awaken her, but he tried to be very careful. He gathered up the earth-fae as though it were the most delicate silk, and bade it weave a picture for his eyes. A Knowing. But what he saw was half as much sound as vision, and a thousand more elements he couldn't begin to define. A symphony of meaning that he had no way to interpret. No experience.

But one thing was clear and he voiced it. Softly. 'She's sleeping. Peacefully.'

There were songs on the hillside, glorious songs of sunlight and optimism and energy, the endless music of faith. She could see them arrayed along the gentle slope, warriors whose armor gleamed Core-golden in the light of noon, soldiers whose banners were strung with bits of glass so that as they moved their standards sparkled, and as the wind beat on the richly woven cloth there was the sound of bells, of sparkling water, a thousand glassy chimes that rang out the song of God's One Faith across the Darklands. Young men, old men, women astride their horses, soldier-priests so young they were nearly children – all helmeted in silver and gold and pennanted in brilliant silks, lining up for battle. The very air about them rang with their faith, their sacrifice, their passion. The very daylight was a song of triumph.

She floated through their ranks like a fae-wraith, touching, seeing, hearing all. Shields that flashed like fire in the sunlight. Swords that sang of perseverance and hope. She touched one blade and could hear all the hymns that had gone into its making, the thousand and one voices that had lent it power. Years of chants, years of prayer, years of utter faith . . . she moved to where another soldier stood and gazed at the crystal flask in his hand. The liquid within glowed with a heat that she could feel on her face, and its music was a symphony of hope.

They were riding into death, she knew. All these brilliant soldiers, all these priceless weapons, were about to ride into a darkness so terrible that it would snuff out all their songs forever. She could feel their place in history taking shape about them, not a beginning of hope but an ending, the extinguishing of a time of untrammeled dreams in exchange for one of cynicism and despair. She wanted to cry out and warn them, but what good would her words do? They knew the odds. They knew that the Evil they had decided to fight might well prove more powerful than all their prayers and charms and spells combined . . . and still they gathered. Thousands upon thousands of them, knees clasped tightly about their anxious steeds, hands closing restlessly about their sword-grips and their springbolt butts and their polished pistols. And the Fire. It glistened in a dozen crystal orbs, in a thousand crystal vials. So very beautiful that it hurt her to look upon it, so rich in hope that she cried out to hear its song. Faith. Pure faith. She could drink it in all her life and still hunger for it. She could drown herself in it and never have enough.

You'll die! she cried out to them. Not wanting the music to end. You'll all die, horribly! The Forest will eat you alive! What good is that to anyone? Go home while you still can!

And then it seemed to her that one of the soldier-priests turned to her.

Eyes of liquid flame, brilliant as the Holy Fire, fixed upon the space she occupied. His shield and sword were molten gold, and his banner-glass tinkled in the wind. He was too bright to look upon, too beautiful for her to look away. His voice was like the wind.

Some things, he whispered, are worth dying for.

And then the music became sunlight became peace, blissful peace, and she felt the vision fading. Melting into warmth. The gentle warmth of a mother's arms. The loving warmth of a father's eyes.

For the first time in many long nights, Jenseny Kierstaad slept.

26

In the realm of black lava
    In the citadel of night
    In the throne room of the Undying Prince
    Calesta waited.

The form which appeared before him did so without fan-fare, without flourish. He hissed softly as it solidified, a sound like finger-nails scraping on slate. Recognition was instant.

'Karril.' The sharp black lips shaped sharp words, harsh to the ear and mind. 'To what do I owe this dubious pleasure?'

When Karril's eyes had fully manifested, he looked around, taking in the rich trappings of the throne room: gilded chairs, crystal lamps, a wall of black glass through which the whole realm might be glimpsed. 'You seem to be doing well for yourself.'

Calesta bowed his head. 'My patron is wealthy.'

'And powerful?'

'Of course.'

'No doubt you see to that.'

'We each have our own ways of bonding with humans.' The black mist that drifted about his glassy form coiled around his neck like serpents. 'Why are you here? There's no love lost between us.'

'No,' Karril agreed. 'And never will be, I'm afraid.' He took a few steps toward Calesta, running his finger along the edge of a gilded chair. When he spoke again, there was an unaccustomed hardness in his voice. 'You trespass, Calesta.'

The black figure snorted. 'Hardly.'

'You trespass,' Karril repeated. 'Nine centuries ago I bonded with a human, and now you interfere.'

Understanding glistened in Calesta's faceted eyes. 'Gerald Tarrant.'

Karril nodded.

'If that's what you came about, you're wasting your time. Tarrant's *mine*. I swore it the day he destroyed my project in the rakhlands. Him and that oversized priest of his—'

'The priest is no concern of mine. The Hunter is.'

The black face smiled; obsidian teeth glinted in a lightless gash. 'So sorry you had to come all this way, then, just to be disappointed. The matter isn't open to debate.'

'I think it is,' Karril insisted. 'I think it bears on the very rules we live by. Or would you like to have the matter arbitrated?'

The faceted eyes flashed angrily. 'You wouldn't dare,' he growled.

'Try me.'

'On what basis? Noninterference? This war began long before you got involved in it.'

'He's been mine for nine centuries, Calesta. That predates any claim of yours and you know it. Remember the rule? No one of us may interfere where another has staked his claim.'

'Yours? He's been *yours*?' The black figure laughed harshly. 'Come off it, Karril! When did the Hunter ever submit to you?'

'I've fed on him—'

'I've fed on thousands – millions! – and it doesn't make them mine. Not in the sense you mean. No, your precious Neocount values his independence too much to truly bond with you – or any of the Iezu – and because of that the rules don't apply here. So sorry, brother. If that's what you came for, you may as well leave now.'

'If I do,' Karril said calmly, 'it will be to go straight to our maker.'

The obsidian body stiffened. 'You wouldn't dare. I have the right—'

'Shall we let *her* decide that?'

The black figure drew itself up; the sharp edges of its flesh glittered dangerously. 'You little fool! Petty god of sweaty couplings, patron prince of masturbators . . . don't you see what you're interfering with? Can't you see how many years I've put into this, how much planning is behind it? I'll *change* this world, Karril. Not just its outward appearance; I'll change its fundamental laws. I'll alter the fae itself! In time the entire planet will resonate in harmony with my aspect. Isn't that worth the death of a piddling sorcerer or two? Think of it! Our natures are so very similar, Karril; you can feed where I do. You often have. Think what it will be like when this whole planet exists only to indulge us—'

'You don't have to call off your precious project,' Karril said icily. 'You don't even have to let Tarrant go free. Just lift the illusion from the Terata's domain. That's all I came to ask.'

'Why don't you join me instead?' Calesta asked softly. 'We're so very alike, you and I. Together we could tame this human species, and reshape it to suit our will. Why won't you do it?'

Karril shook his head. 'You disgust me, you know that?'

'Your answer never changes, does it?'

'Did you really think it would? We were born to be symbiotes, not predators. And you're pushing that line. What would our maker think?' When Calesta didn't answer, he pressed, 'Lift your illusion from the Terata camp so that Gerald Tarrant can see your creations for what they are. Or else I'll go before our maker and let *her* decide the merit of my arguments.' A pause, threat-laden. 'I'm willing to take that chance, Calesta. Are you?'

'You're bluffing,' he accused.

'I've never been more serious.'

'She'd kill us both.'

'Very possibly.'

'You haven't got the nerve to chance it!'

'Is that your final answer?'

Calesta was about to respond when a third voice broke in. 'Go ahead, Calesta. Indulge him. It might prove amusing.'

The two demons turned. In the doorway stood a man, tall and blond and perhaps fifty years of age. Though he wore no coronet to proclaim his rank, it was obvious in the way he entered the chamber. This room had been designed to please him. The whole world existed to indulge him.

'Lift the illusion,' he urged. 'What does it matter? We'll have him in the end, all the same.' He came near to where Calesta stood – the demon's chosen body was rigid with tension – and looked Karril over with eyes that missed nothing. 'Friend of yours?'

'Hardly,' Calesta growled.

'So.' He chuckled. 'The faeborn have their own wars. I thought infighting was against Iezu law.' When no one responded, he asked, 'What's this one's name?'

Neither of them answered. There was power in the name of demons, which made their silence a defiant gesture. The prince's expression darkened.

'As you wish.' He nodded toward Karril. 'You came to speak for the undead sorcerer?'

'I came to ask Calesta to lift his illusion,' he said through gritted teeth. How could he threaten this man? How could he coerce him? The prince was human, and thus immune from the kind of threats one would use on a demon; as for human threats, he had already conquered death. What tool was left for manipulation? 'So the sorcerer could fight his own battles.'

'Sounds reasonable to me,' the Undying Prince assessed.

Calesta said nothing.

'I would like to see him confront the Terata,' the Prince mused. 'It would be interesting to see if he makes it to my realm, and in what condition. In fact . . .' His piercing gaze wandered to Karril. Fixed there. 'I'm thinking he might be put to a better use than a target for Iezu vengeance.'

Calesta hissed.

'Think. How many men are there of that caliber? Perhaps one a generation is born with that ability, and so many die, so many make fatal mistakes . . . Here is one who's survived the centuries – the most challenging art of all – and crossed land and sea against all odds . . . and come here. Why waste that power? Why discard that unique intellect? Between us we could tame a planet.'

He turned to Calesta. 'Lift the illusion.'

'But my Lord—'

'*Lift it.*'

The demon took a step backward; anger flashed in his mirror-bright eyes.

'I'm not one of your mindless puppets, Calesta. Remember that. And I'm not that woman in the rakhlands, whom you twisted over the decades. I know your power and I know your limits and I won't hesitate to use that knowledge. Those are the terms of your service here. I've never seen fit to interfere in your hobbies before – not even when you took that woman from my lands, along with half an army – but this time there's something I want, and I'll damn well have it. Lift the illusion. *Now*. Let the Hunter see what kind of power he's dealing with.'

The demon's glassy form blazed in the lamplight. 'You command this?' he demanded.

'I do.'

The tendrils of smoke agitated about him, forming a thick black cloud. 'I'll give him the eyes to see through it,' he hissed. 'No more. The others will just have to suffer.'

'The others aren't my concern.' The Prince turned to Karril. 'Is that sufficient?'

Karril managed to nod.

'There's a service you'll do for me in exchange. Tarrant's too far away for me to contact him directly against his will. You'll take him a message. Ask him to receive it.'

'And if he doesn't?'

The blue eyes glittered. 'That's his choice. But he might regret it later, I think. Mention that.'

'I won't do anything that causes him to be hurt.'

The Prince chuckled softly. 'Loyalty in a Iezu is so refreshing. Isn't it, Calesta?' He waved expansively. 'It'll be no more than a message. You can view it yourself if you like. He won't even have to open a channel to me to listen to it . . . although he might choose to do that, in time. Yes. I think that he will.'

He turned and left then, as silently as he had come. Not until he was gone – and safely out of hearing – did Karril whisper, 'Strange game you're playing here, Calesta.'

The black face cracked; the foggy tendrils twisted. It might have been a smile.

'Not strange at all,' Calesta assured him. 'Merely complex. So stay out of my way, will you? Because as you said, the price of open conflict would be high.'

And his faceted eyes glittered as he added sweetly, *'Brother.'*

27

The one thing he wanted almost as much as freedom, Damien decided, was a bath.

Morning light illuminated all too clearly their current state. Hesseth was clean enough, having started the previous day in fresh clothes, and while rakhene fur had its own distinctive odor it lacked the foulness of stale human sweat. Damien had supplied the latter in abundance. It was hard enough trying to keep clean with only one set of clothes to his name – the rest having been lost a small eternity ago, back at the gap – but when the only available river was seeded with nasty carnivores, and then their juvenile captors decided that the only water necessary was a single cupful for the three of them to pass around . . . he wanted a bath. Badly. And he suspected that his cellmates wanted him to have one.

They were all covered in mud, of course. And God alone knew what else that mud contained. Thus far his only need for biological relief had been satisfied by urinating into a corner, but it occurred to him that if they stayed here much longer they'd be adding more solid substance to the mucky chamber as well. And what about the girl? He got the impression she had been here some time already. Did they let her out for a toilet break now and then, or had she grown adept at hiding her own waste beneath the muddy cover? His nose was so numbed by the reek of mold and rotted meat which seemed to hang about the Terata island that he could no longer sort through the foul odors surrounding him to analyze their source.

Hesseth must be suffering quite a bit, though. Thank God his sense of smell was only human.

The girl. What was she? When he awakened in the gray light of dawn – surprised to find that he'd fallen asleep at all in this dismal place – he found the Fire by his side, set one end upright in the mud. Sometime during the night the girl had crept back to her tiny hole and curled up there like an animal, head tucked down by her knees. After a moment he took the vial up and put it back in its protective pouch. What had she been doing with it? Why the strange reaction? And come to think of it, how the hell had she known that he was a priest? Without his sword there was no obvious sign of his profession, and he hardly looked like a clergyman.

A priest of swamps, he thought, rubbing a coating of grime from his chin. Stubble raked his hand. *Serving a god of mud.*

Gently, very gently, he worked a Knowing. He didn't know how sensitive she was – or even what form her sensitivity would take – but he did his best not to wake her. The currents were sluggish, but at last they responded. He felt Hesseth drawing near beside him as the pictures formed, ghostly tableaux that were nearly as confusing as the girl herself. Could the rakh-woman see his Knowing for what it was, or did she merely sense the flow of power? He had never thought to ask.

Images misted through the gray morning light, fading one into the other like fae-wraiths. Contrasting images that seemed to come from different worlds, even different realities. Warm scenes from a secure home. A garden of crystal leaves, shimmering in the moonlight. A coat drenched in blood. The darkness of a cavern. A young girl running. The face of a priest contorted in hatred, the downstab of a ritual sword . . . he felt her almost awaken as that image formed, and had to dim down his Knowing until sleep once more claimed her. Then: Religious images, drenched in blood. A mother's smile. A predator's grin. A woman so twisted by age and neglect that her joints had thickened like tumors, her eyes tearing blood and pus. Malformations. Unhealed wounds. And running, always running; that image surrounded all the others, flanking them, creating a fragile web of unity that bound them all together.

Terror. That's what all those pictures were born of, he thought, as he let the Knowing fade. He had no way of guessing how many of the images were real, and how many were the result of terror feeding on itself. Imagination could do terrible things in a place like this, especially to a young mind. Especially to one so infinitely vulnerable as this.

He longed to go to her. He hungered to comfort her. It went against all his training – against his very nature – to see such suffering and not move to heal it. But the priest's face that he had seen in his Knowing loomed large in his mind, radiating a hate that was almost palpable. Real or not, it was real to *her,* and that was all that mattered. Maybe that was the face she saw when she looked at him. Maybe it was what she had learned to expect from his kind.

He prayed for her quietly. And mourned within, that he could not conjure a balm for her soul half so easily as he could Heal her flesh. Was that not the ultimate irony of his calling?

Food. It was brought to them in small bundles, inexpertly cooked. He tasted his dubiously, then downed a small bit of it. Hesseth studied hers, then decided against it; perhaps its mildly sour smell warned her of contents that her rakhene stomach couldn't assimilate. His own body had fought off food poisoning often enough that he thought he must have calluses on his stomach lining by now, but even so he ate little. Just enough to keep up his strength. Weakness could be as dangerous as food poisoning in a place like this.

The girl still wouldn't come near them, but waited until they withdrew to the far corner of the cave before she would claim her share. Even then her movements were strained, and it was clear that she was prepared to bolt the instant that either of them moved. Neither of them did. To Damien's surprise she didn't return immediately to her tiny shelter, but sat where the food had been left for her and gulped it down quickly. Her eyes left them only once, and that was when she looked for the cup of water. She gulped from it thirstily, her gaunt throat trembling as the water went down. She hadn't gotten her share from the night before, Damien recalled, which meant she was probably desperate for fluid. Oh, well. He and Hesseth could manage without for a day if they had to.

But to his surprise she stopped before the small portion was finished, and slowly lowered the bowl. It was clear that she was still thirsty, and that the movement took effort. She glanced down into the cup, as if making sure that there was enough left over, and then placed it in front of her. Pushing it toward them. Then she moved slowly back to her own corner of the cavern, her eyes never leaving Damien.

After a minute he crept forward and took up the bowl. He passed it to Hesseth first, then drank from it himself. The girl hadn't left them much, but considering how hard it must have been for her to keep from drinking it all it was practically a feast.

'Thank you,' he said. Very gently. Willing his voice to be as soft as it could become. 'Thank you very much.'

The girl stared at him, but said nothing.

'Do you have a name?'

Still no response.

'I'm Damien Kilcannon Vryce,' he told her. 'This is Hesseth sa-Restrath. We came from the western continent, to explore this land. To see if anyone had settled here.'

For a moment there was no response. Then, in a voice no louder than a whisper, the girl said hoarsely, 'Jenseny.'

'Jenseny.' He said the name slowly, let her hear how very gentle it sounded on his tongue. 'Are you from here, Jenseny? From the valley?'

'You're a priest,' she accused.

For a moment he said nothing. Then he nodded.

'A priest of the One God.'

'Yes,' he said. Trying to remove all possible threat from his voice.

Her wide eyes blinked; was that a tear on her lashes? 'Priests *kill*,' she accused.

He drew in a deep breath. Remembering the contorted face in his Knowing, the vicious downstab of a Church sword as it sliced into . . . what? A child? Yes, that was the image. And here she was, only a child herself. No wonder she was afraid!

He couldn't bring himself to tell her that priests didn't kill. Children had an uncanny ability to tell when you were lying, and he sensed that if he lost her trust now he'd lose her forever. So he said very gently, 'Priests kill sometimes. But where I come from, they only kill the faeborn. So that people don't have to be afraid all the time.'

He could see her trembling as she considered that. 'Never children?' she breathed.

'No, Jenseny. Never. My people would rather die themselves than ever hurt a child.'

He saw her tremble then, and she bit her lower lip so hard that there was a bead of blood there when she spoke again. '*They* do it,' she whispered. 'All the time.'

'Yeah.' He could hear the shame of it resonate in his own voice as he whispered, 'I know.'

Her eyes moved from Damien at last, and fixed on Hesseth. 'She isn't human,' she accused.

'No,' Damien agreed, and Hesseth said quietly, 'I'm rakh.'

She shivered then, and nearly withdrew to the safety of her bolthole. Damien thought it said much for her innate courage that in the end she stayed where she was.

'Rakh killed my father,' she said. Tears started to flow down her cheeks, etching ravines into the mud on her face. She simply drew her knees up and clasped them tightly to her. 'They *ate* him,' she whispered feverishly. 'They ate him and took his place.'

'Not all rakh are like that,' Damien told her. Willing utter calmness into his voice. Hoping that it would affect her.

But her head snapped up in rage. 'Yes they are! They're all the same! My father knew! My father was there! My father saw . . .'

And then it seemed to hit her all at once – the loss, the fear, the utter hopelessness of her plight – and she sobbed helplessly into her arms. 'He was there,' she whispered hoarsely. 'He said they were all the same. All monsters of the dark—'

Damien looked at Hesseth.

'It's daylight now,' the rakh-woman offered.

But the girl was past all hearing. Her body wracked by sobs, she wept into the mud that coated her arms with a passion Damien ached to heal. But what good could he do, when she clearly feared him so? And when she perceived his traveling companion as one of the tribe that had 'eaten' her father? Best now to keep his distance, lest he frighten her even more. Maybe later he could work on increasing the fragile contact between them. Maybe later he could earn her trust.

And maybe later, he thought, he could find out just where this strange girl's father had been, and what it was that he saw.

Footsteps approaching. He heard them before he could identify their source; the mist had thickened so much that it was hard to see more than ten feet past the prison gate. The glassy black statue was lost in the distance, swallowed up by the gray veil of fog.

Would Tarrant come tonight? he wondered. Or was the Hunter gone for good? Much as he didn't like the thought of that, it was certainly possible. At any rate they were on their own until night-fall, and that was hours away.

A delegation of eight diminutive warriors approached the makeshift prison. Damien noted that these were all somewhat older, as Terata standards went, and armed with long spears that would permit them to threaten Damien and Hesseth without getting within hand-to-hand combat distance. A bad sign, he decided; it meant they anticipated trouble.

The bolts that supported the heavy grate were pulled back, and then the two tallest boys removed the grate itself. They had painted their faces, Damien noted, in a parody of the masks they had worn off the island; another bad sign. The whole day was looking downright ominous.

'It's time,' one of the painted warriors announced. A girl. A boy's voice ordered, 'Get out.'

Damien looked at Hesseth, and at the girl. At last, though he was less than happy about the order, he began to move. The minute he cleared the cavern entrance four spears were lowered and pressed against his chest; not only couldn't he run away, but if he moved too quickly in any direction he would skewer himself in an instant.

His hands were tied behind his back once more, and a nooselike rope was slipped over his head to serve as a leash. When they had him thus trussed up, they signaled for Hesseth to come out, and she was subjected to similar preparations. Testing his bonds, Damien noted that they were tighter than the last time. Yet another bad omen.

Two of the adolescent warriors had to go in after Jenseny. Since Damien had seen her run to the grate to plead with them at one point, he was surprised to see the utter terror that suffused her face when the Terata actually approached her. Maybe it had been enough for her then that the grate had been there, protecting her from close contact. Maybe. More likely it was that she feared the Terata, but had feared Damien even more. Enough to send her running to the children who so clearly terrified her, who even now grabbed hold of her with bruising strength and dragged her, struggling, from the prison.

They were led like leashed animals along the muddy path, toward the clearing where Calesta's statue stood. The noose about their necks would tighten at the slightest provocation, and once when Damien stumbled it nearly choked him. But the child who was leading him reached into the hemp collar and loosened it for him. He had to stand on tiptoe to do it – no, he *should* have had to stand on tiptoe, but in fact he didn't. How odd. The touch of his fingers was cold, and . . . something odd. Something Damien couldn't put a name to, but when the flesh made contact with his own he couldn't help but shiver. For an instant the boy's face seemed to fade, to be forming into something else . . . and then the moment was gone, and everything was as it should be.

Or as it *seemed* to be, Damien thought.

The clearing surrounding Calesta's statue was already filled with children, and though Damien couldn't count them he guessed there were at least three or four dozen. The Terata came in all ages and sizes, from lanky preteenagers to children so small that they could hardly walk. But no one older than that, he noted. No one who had gone through puberty. What happened to them when they aged?

Their leashes were tied to a squat tree that sat at one edge of the clearing. At first he thought that the children would leave them together, but that was too good to be true. A young girl scrambled up amidst the twisting branches and affixed their leashes to opposite ends of the tree; the rope was taut enough that if they tried to move they would probably hang themselves. Great. Jenseny was released nearby, and she darted for the cover of the great trunk behind them. Out of the corner of his eye Damien could see her huddled beneath a tangle of twisted branches, staring with wide eyes toward the clearing.

From where she sat she could see his hands, and Heseth's; would she betray them if they tried to free themselves? He didn't think so. He began to flex his hands, testing the knots that bound him for strength. There was a little slack, and he struggled to get it around to where it would do him the most good. Hard to do all that without moving his body, but the noose about his neck gave him no choice. He just hoped the children wouldn't notice.

But their minds were on other things now. They were heaping small items about the base of the statue. Food, spears, bits of shining metal . . . offerings, Damien decided. One child brought forth a handful of glittering gems and broken bits of jewelry and dropped it on the pile. Another offered up a torn silk shirt. He heard Hesseth gasp as several of their own possessions were added to the pile. Either these children had captured other travelers or they raided the villages themselves, he thought; there were too many valuable items here for any other explanation.

When the pile was at last complete, the children gathered around the statue. Some stood utterly silent, waiting. Others began to sway impatiently, fidgeting with the restlessness of youth. He could feel their expectation filling the clearing with volatile force, and he worked all the harder at getting himself free. Whatever happened here, he didn't think he was going to like it.

At last one of the boys stepped forward, and the small crowd hushed. His face was fierce behind the war paint, and his skinny chest had been bared to the wind. He faced the statue and raised up his weapon – a bow – and then announced:

'My name is Piter. Five days ago I led a band down to the southern cities. We found a girl chained up by the Holies, and we set her free. We had to kill five men to do it. I want to thank you for helping us sneak up on them, because they were much bigger than we were and I don't think we could have killed them without your help.' He reached out to the crowd, toward one small girl in particular. She was wearing a cotton shift, now torn and muddied, and her face was streaked with tears. 'This is the girl,' he announced, as she made her way to the statue. 'Her name is Bethie.' When she came up beside him, he indicated that she should lay her hands upon the statue. It was hard for her to reach, given the pile of stolen goods that surrounded it, but at last she did so. When he nodded that she could let go, she did so, and regained her balance.

'Thank you,' she whispered.

'His name is Calesta.'

'Thank you, Calesta.'

The two of them returned to the circle. Another girl stepped out. She was tall and slender and carried a long spear, which she flourished as she spoke.

'My name is Merri. I went into the Protectorates, and found a baby being exposed. I know there were guards in those woods, but none of them saw me, and I took the baby. I want to thank you for your protection, and also for helping me find the baby. She can't thank you yet, so I guess I have to do it for both of us.' She reached out and touched the black statue, slender fingers splayed across its icy flesh. It seemed to Damien that she trembled for an instant as contact was made, but he couldn't be sure. He was too busy struggling with his bonds to concentrate on such tiny details.

Four other children followed. They, too, had tales to tell, but the endings were not nearly as triumphant. Two had discovered exposed infants too late to save them. One had gone to free a child chained by the Holies, but there were too many men guarding the girl for even a surprise attack; he had retreated. One brave girl had even ventured as far as the northern cities, but when the forest gave way to farmlands she had lost her nerve and come home again. All of them thanked Calesta for keeping them safe from their enemies. All of them touched the black statue as well, and it seemed to Damien that more than one of them flinched as they did so. What did they expect might happen?

Religious sacrifices. Adepts left to die. No wonder there's power here. No wonder it's so chaotic. A tribe of rejected children, dedicated to rescuing other children from the abuses of eastern society. It made sense in a way. But why did it seem so unwholesome? Why did some of the children seem so ... well, so *odd,* as they approached the base of the great statue? Why was it that Damien couldn't seem to focus on some of them?

He worked a loop of rope over one hand and paused to draw a deep breath. Once you had that much slack it was only a matter of time. He wanted to be free so badly he could taste it.

The children had begun to move now. All but one began to circle about the statue, beating their feet upon the earth. Some closed their eyes as they moved, lost in the rhythm of it. Some began to chant tunelessly, their voices rising and falling with the stamping of feet.

One boy faced the statue. He raised up his hands and addressed the black figure, one hand clasped about a crude stone ax. 'You gave us safety,' he told it. His voice, though loud enough, barely carried over the noise that surrounded him. 'We thank you with sacrifice. Tell us who you want. Tell us what to do.' Then he, too, joined the circling crowd. The children were moving faster and faster, gradually working themselves up to a frenzy. The chanting had become shouting, and children thrust at the air with their spears and knives.

Then one small child broke free of the ring and ran toward the statue. He was small enough that he had to scramble up on the offerings in order to reach the feet of the figure. Bits of gold and jewelry cascaded to the ground as he placed his hands on the statue's feet. 'My name's Keven,' he told it. He kept his hands in place for perhaps a minute, then let go of the statue and slid back down to the ground. 'Keven!' he screamed. He ran back to the others, repeating his name over and over again like some sacred mantra. It seemed to Damien that there was joy in his eyes, and something else also. Relief?

He turned his head to look at Jenseny. But she had turned away, hiding her eyes from the spectacle before them. He could see her shaking.

One more loop, now. The rope about his hands was loosening, almost enough that he could slip one hand out. Almost ...

One by one the children did as Keven had done. Some approached the statue quietly and reverently; others shrieked and laughed and danced their way to its base, scattering the offerings in their utter abandon as they reached up to clasp the feet of the statue. The whole inner circle was littered with bits of food and pillaged treasure, and the air inside the fogbound clearing was stiflingly hot, and rang with the frenzied screams of the children as they danced in faster and faster circles.

And then, just as Damien managed to get his hands free, the children stopped. Not all at once, but in a wave, as if each took the cue from his neighbor. Within a minute the screaming circle was silent, and all eyes were fixed on the child in its center.

It was a girl. Screaming. She must have just had her hands on the statue, for even now they gripped the edge of its base. 'No!' she screamed. 'Not me! Not me!' A strange rippling seemed to course though her flesh, something Damien felt more than saw; her outline became fuzzy, difficult to focus upon. 'Not me!' she begged, as she tumbled to a heap amidst the scattered offerings. 'Please, no!'

She was beginning to change. It was hard to make out the details as she thrashed about in her terror, but Damien thought that her body was growing longer. Bending. The spine hunched up behind her shoulder blades, and twisted in its lower portion so that her hips were wildly canted. Her arms and legs grew longer and then thinned, the flesh drawing tight about her bones until she looked like a living skeleton. Her eyes had sunk deep into her skull, and the screaming mouth was no more than a gash in a creased-parchment face, her white skin mottled by brown spots that ranged from the size of freckles to the livid swell of a fertile tumor just beneath her jaw. Another tumor just beneath it had broken open, and dark fluid glistened in its surface.

And then the children moved. Yelling and screaming they fell upon her, their weapons raised. He could no longer hear her cries at all, nor see her, but as the weapons were thrust downward one after the other he could imagine her pain. Her terror. For a moment he was frozen, as the full horror of the situation struck him like a blow to the face; then, more desperate than ever, he slipped himself free of the restraining rope. Spear after spear was thrust down into that trembling, magicked flesh as he freed himself from the noose about his neck; he tried not to think about her, but it was impossible. What had Calesta done? Aged her? His brain felt numb as he ran to where Hesseth stood, and slipped the noose up over her head. Too much horror. Too many questions. He had to get them both free before the children turned on them. He had seen killing frenzies before, knew just how dangerous such a mob could be. Even children, he thought, as he worked loose the knots that bound her hands. No; *especially* children.

Then at last they were both free to move, and just in time. The tallest of the children had broken free of the group, and as he scanned his tribe his eyes fell upon the visitors. A shout brought several of the other children around, though most were far too involved with their grisly slaughter to acknowledge any stimulus outside their own circle. The gray fog drew in close, like a cocoon, as face after bloody face turned toward Damien and Hesseth. Spears were lowered; knives were flourished. For a split second Damien wondered if it might not be better to stay and fight than to run – which was their only other option as he saw it – but he never had time to make a decision. Even as the children began to move, a cold wind swept down on them. The mist itself seemed to darken over their heads, like a stormcloud about to deluge the earth with rain. Bloodthirsty children looked up from their kill, small eyes wide with fear, faces streaked with blood.

And then it came. Not a fae-wraith, though at first it seemed to be. Broad white wings beat back the mist, fanning it into fevered twisters about the border of the clearing. Diamondine claws reached for the statue's shoulder, then shut closed about it; obsidian crumbled like ash at the contact. It was an immense creature, and though it wore a bird's form it was clearly much more than a bird. Its white feathers smoked as it sat on the statue, their tips turning black and then crumbling to ash as it fanned the gray mist with its wings. At times Damien thought he could see the faint spark of golden flames between the snow-white layers.

And maybe that was what gave it away. Maybe it was the image of burning, so deeply rooted in his memory, that awakened him to who and what the great bird was.

'Tarrant,' he whispered. Gazing at him in awe. He couldn't even imagine what kind of courage it must take for the Hunter to leave his shelter while the sun was still high in the sky. The mist might help, but it was only temporary; a few gusts of wind from the right direction and the Neocount would be totally exposed.

As if in answer to his thoughts the great bird screeched out its challenge, and more of Calesta's statue crumbled beneath his grip. Coldfire began to pour down the black surface, spurts of unflame that fell from its shoulders like tears. The children began to draw back, and Damien could just make out the form of their prey on the ground. A shapeless mass of flesh, now, with half a dozen spears embedded in it. The coldfire reached the corpse, sizzling as it consumed both flesh and blood. A few of the children started to move away. One of them turned to run. Damien himself took a step back, and saw that Hesseth moved with him. Whatever power Tarrant was conjuring here, it was nothing he wanted to mess with.

—And then the silver-blue power shot out like a tongue of flame, licking at the face of one of the children. Whatever scream the girl might have voiced was frozen in her throat as she went down, and she died in eerie silence. The unflames licked at another, then another, and bodies began to fall about the circle. Some children screamed. Some turned to run. Damien wanted to turn his eyes and look away, but his conscience wouldn't permit him to do it. *You brought this man here,* he told himself harshly. Forcing himself to watch. *Never forget what he is. Never forget what he can and will do.* As all about them children screamed, children ran, children tripped over piles of bodies and struggled for balance as the silver-blue flames licked out at them, consuming the very heat of their lives in an instant. All about lay the dead, the fallen, their lips a cold blue, their eyes frozen and empty.

Then the last of the living children had fled, and the circle was lifeless. With a vast stroke of its wings the great bird came down to land. No sooner had it touched down than the coldfire flared up and consumed it, but the power was far from pure; looking closely, Damien could see the sparkle of golden flames – true fire – polluting its substance. *Damn. That must hurt.* When the Hunter was human once more, he quickly drew a fold of his cloak over his head like a hood, but not before Damien caught a glimpse of what the filtered sunlight had done to him.

'You know where the horses are?' Tarrant demanded. Scanning the clearing as he approached them. Studying the dead.

It was Hesseth who answered him. 'No.'

He was still for a moment, then he pointed. The finger that poked out from under the cloak was sun-reddened and peeling; it seemed to Damien that its condition worsened even as the motion was completed. 'That way. Get them and then keep going, to the end of the island. I'll meet you there.'

Then it seemed from his posture that his eyes fell on something behind them. Damien whirled about, only to find that the girl from their prison was still with them. Too frozen with fear to move, she was cowering behind the inadequate shelter of a tree trunk, her dark eyes wide with terror. Even without Working the fae Damien could sense her slipping under, giving way at last to a barrage of fear too terrible for a mere child to resist.

It was Hesseth who moved first, covering the ground between them even as Tarrant began to react. 'No!' she cried. She pulled the child to her and wrapped her arms about her. 'Not this one! Not like that.'

For a moment it seemed that the Hunter would move against her anyway, with or without Hesseth in the way. But at last he turned back to Damien, and in a hoarse voice whispered, 'I haven't the strength to argue now. Take the horses. Meet me where I said. I'll be there as soon as I've finished things.'

He turned to go. Damien grabbed his arm through the cloak. 'It's finished. Let them go. They're just children, Hunter. They won't—'

'Children?' he snapped. 'Is that what you think they are? You fool!' A hand shot free of the protective cloak and closed about the back of his neck; the Hunter's skin was hot against his own. 'Look at your precious children now. Share my vision and See!'

The power struck him like a hot iron, driving the breath from his body. For a moment he could see nothing but the hot sun, the blazing sun, whose killing light penetrated the fog and reflected from every surface. Then, element by element, he began to pick out details of the carnage. Bodies of children, wracked by coldfire. Only . . .

Only they weren't really children.

He staggered toward the nearest clump of bodies, aware that Tarrant was moving with him. Heat lanced up through his arches as he walked on the sunlit ground, and it felt like his head was on fire. He knelt down by one of the bodies and stared at it in horror and amazement. What had seemed the body of a child was transformed through Tarrant's vision into something twisted, something grotesque, a creature whom the years had tortured even while it played at childish games and believed itself to be truly young. The limbs were skeleton-thin, the torso so emaciated that ribs could be counted. Its joints were swollen with thick calcium deposits that must have made each movement a torment, and a yellow discoloration had begun to envelop one arm.

He staggered to another body, and another. Not all of them were as old as the first, but all stank of age and neglect. Cuts which had been left undressed had ulcerated, leaving one body a mass of open wounds. Cancer, untreated, had consumed a middle-aged woman. From one gashed leg he could smell the stink of gangrene, and another had broken his foot only to have it heal into a crooked, twisted mass.

Numbly he moved from body to body. Sorting through the carnage for understanding, for acceptance. A few of the fallen had been real children, but even those were in bad shape. Whatever Working had maintained the illusion that these poor creatures were children, it had also blinded them to their own infirmity. It had kept them drunk on the vitality of false youth even while age and infection ate away at their true bodies. Little wonder so few of them had survived to old age. Little wonder they had fallen upon their unlucky comrade with such savage glee. Once the concealing illusion had been stripped from her, she was a reminder to them of what they would themselves become. No wonder they feared and hated her. No wonder they killed.

Then the vision faded, and the ground was littered once more with the bodies of dead children. He lowered his head and shuddered, overcome by the awful power of what he had learned.

'We don't want them following us,' the Hunter whispered hoarsely. His voice echoed with the pain of his exposure; how much longer could he go on like this? 'You get the horses and see if you can find our supplies. I'll see there's no pursuit.'

'You're going to kill them,' he whispered.

The Hunter said nothing.

'Some of them are real children, you know. And none of them understand what's happening.'

'They're all *his,*' The Hunter said sharply. Gesturing back toward the statue. 'Do you want that behind us? Do you want to be hunted down again as soon as I turn my back?' He strode toward the wall of fog; it seemed to part at his approach. 'I'm not arguing with you this time, priest. There's a time and place for mercy. This isn't it.'

He said it quietly but firmly. 'Not the children, Gerald.'

For a moment the Hunter stared at him. Then, with a muttered curse, he strode into the wall of mist. The gray veil closed behind him, hiding him from their sight.

With effort, Damien rose to his feet. His body ached as though he had fought all night. He looked at Hesseth, at the small child huddled in her arms, and thought, *At least we've saved one.* What was her name, Jenseny? At least she was still a real child, he mused; Tarrant surely would have killed her otherwise.

So many deaths. So much destruction. What force was responsible for all this? He remembered the statue of Calesta and shivered. What was his motive?

'Come on,' he muttered. Trying not to think. Fighting not to feel. 'Let's find the goddamned horses.'

The horses were tired and edgy and not in the best of shape but they could walk, and right now that was all Damien cared about. Jenseny stared at the huge creatures in amazement as Hesseth and the priest gathered up what few stores they had left. Their food was untouched, as were their camping supplies, but many of the small items were missing. At least the weapons were still there, Damien thought. Thank God for that.

They led the horses to the edge of the island, where Tarrant was waiting. In silence he led them down the rocky slope, and out onto the water. Though he knew that what appeared to be part of the river was really a bridge, Damien had trouble getting the horses to brave the route a second time; in the end he had to blind the animals with strips of linen and force them to follow.

When they were across, Tarrant turned back toward the hidden bridge. His movements were stiff, Damien noted, and he sensed that the man was in no little pain. Thus far the thick mist had held, but if it thinned out even for a moment . . . he shuddered to think of it.

Then the Hunter reached out his hand, and the water exploded. Pieces of wood and ice went flying up and downstream, and a tree trunk which had been near the bridge shattered into a thousand glassy fragments. Splinters of frozen wood rained down upon the party like hail.

'That should do it,' Tarrant said shortly, and he turned back to lead the party into the woods. Damien felt something tight in his gut loosen up just a little bit. If the Neocount had taken time out to destroy the bridge, that meant that he hadn't killed everyone on the island. The real children were still alive.

Later, when he managed to pull up beside Tarrant, he whispered softly, 'Thank you.'

The Hunter didn't answer. But Damien knew that he heard.

They walked their horses into the forest. After a day and night in the cramped prison, Damien and Hesseth both needed the exercise. As for the girl, she was hard-pressed to match their pace, and at last her strength gave out. Damien called for Tarrant to stop, and together he and Hesseth lifted Jenseny's limp form up onto the mare's back. He could feel Tarrant's eyes boring into his back, his rage at indulging such a delay. *Tough luck,* he thought, as he strapped her firmly into the saddle. *Deal with it.* But when they were done and had begun to move again, he did take a minute to let Tarrant know that the girl might have information they needed. It was only half the reason she was with them, but it was the half that Tarrant would care about. No doubt he had used up his limited quota of human compassion when he spared the children's lives.

When they moved into the depths of the forest, where foliage conspired with the mist to shield the party from sunlight, Tarrant seemed to relax somewhat. Soon after, when the last of the dim light began to fade, he pushed the makeshift hood back from his head. The skin of his face was raw and crusted, and Jenseny – who had caught only a glimpse of him before – stiffened in her saddle and gasped. But Damien and Hesseth's reaction (or lack of one) seemed to calm her, and after a moment she was slumped in her seat once again, dozing as they went.

'You'll be all right?' Damien asked. Not really doubting it.

The Hunter nodded; a bit of singed skin fell from his temple. 'True night falls for half an hour tomorrow; if I'm not whole by then, that will heal me.'

He stopped and turned and regarded Jenseny. The tired girl was sound asleep. 'Does she really have information?' he challenged. 'Something useful?'

Damien hesitated. 'She might. And she seems to have Vision of some kind.' *She knew I was a priest. Who knows what else she Saw?* He looked sharply at Tarrant. 'Why? Did you think I said that just to save her?'

Tarrant's lips tightened, loosening bits of burned skin. It was hard to say if his expression was a smile or a sneer.

'I wouldn't put it past you,' the Hunter muttered.

They made their camp long after midnight. Damien could no longer remember how many miles they'd traveled, or how long they'd been moving. He remembered passing the thornbushes, Hesseth holding the girl tight against her while he drove back the branches with smoke, as he had seen the Terata do. They weren't quite as efficient as the children had been, having had less practice, Tarrant's horse was badly scratched going through. But it was almost a pleasure to Heal again, a kind of cleansing, and Damien took care to make sure he had cleaned the wound of poison before he used the forest's earth-fae to knit it safely shut again.

Throughout it all the girl watched them. She was still wary of Damien, though her initial terror seemed to have subsided somewhat. Tarrant seemed to both fascinate and repel her. For his part the Hunter attempted to ignore her existence, and when he did look her way it was with great irritation, as if to say that his life had enough complications without a crazy child being dropped in the middle of it. Damien sensed that as soon as they were alone, or as soon as the girl was safely asleep, Tarrant was going to let him have it for bringing her.

But she could be useful, he thought to himself. *She could have information.* And behind that lay another thought, even more compelling. *I just couldn't leave her there.*

By the time they made camp his whole body ached, and he thought that once he sat down he would surely never move again. For which reason he saw that the girl was down from her mount and working at unpacking the horses before he even tried it. They had lost a lot. Not the large items, the important ones, but all the hundred and one tiny items that he had packed against the day of their unexpected need. Oh, well. On a trip like this you prepared as best you could and then made do with the cards that fate dealt you. At least they had blankets and the crude tent which Hesseth had assembled. At least they had food.

When those were in place – and a fire had been started, and water gathered from the stream nearby to be heated over it, and the horses brushed down and hobbled for the night, and Jenseny huddled inside the tent for some much-needed sleep – he finally allowed himself to ease his weary flesh down to the ground and rest. Hardly a moment after he had done so, Tarrant sat down opposite him.

He met those eyes, so pale, so cold, without wondering what was in them. He knew.

The Hunter spoke first. 'You don't know who she is. You don't know *what* she is. The danger of having her with us—'

'In this forest? What's she going to do?' With a weary hand he wiped a crust of dirt from his forehead. He could taste the salt of sweat on his lips. 'She's a child, Hunter. A very tired, very frightened child. I want to get her out of this dismal place. When we get to the coastal cities, then we can talk about alternative plans.' He rubbed his hands one against the other; his fingernails were dirt-encrusted, his skin little better. 'Not here. Not now. Not when I'm so tired I can barely think.'

'She's not just a child and you know it. If she has Vision – of any kind – then she may have power. She knew you were a priest, Hesseth tells me. Don't you realize what that implies?'

'I know. I know. But even if she were a full adept—'

'Not all adepts are sane,' Tarrant reminded him. 'In fact, very few are. Even in a normal environment the pressures of such a life are almost beyond bearing, and here . . .' He shook his head. 'And she is, as you say, a *child*. Unstable to start with, even more so under these circumstances. Who can say what goes on in the darker corridors of that brain, or how and when madness might manifest itself? You're playing with fire here.'

'Then let's just say I'm prepared to be burned.'

He could see the Hunter's jawline tighten; reflected fire-light burned in his eyes. 'Maybe you are, Reverend Vryce. Brave and foolhardy man that you are. But I'm part of this expedition, too, and so is Mes Hesseth. And our mission here is far too important and dangerous for us to take chances like this – even to satisfy your nurturing instincts.' With a fluid motion he stood, and settled his cloak more comfortably about his shoulders. 'Think about it.'

'You going somewhere?'

'I have business to attend to.'

'I'd have thought you killed enough for one night.'

The Hunter's expression was frigid. 'The currents will move in their course whether you choose to notice them or not. We're far enough south that there's a chance I can read them now, get some kind of bearing on the enemy. And I'd prefer not to Work too close to your guest, if that's all right with you.'

Damien wondered just what it was about the tone of his voice that set him on edge. The words were certainly no more arrogant and condescending than Tarrant's usual ripostes, but the tone was . . . odd. Too subtle in its difference for him to pinpoint, but the difference was definitely there. For some reason it was unnerving.

'Yeah,' he managed. 'Sure. Go ahead.'

As the Hunter left the camp he thought: *He's hiding something*.

In the darkness of the forest, in a small clearing sheltered over by trees so thick that even the moonlight was dim, Gerald Tarrant stopped. He took a moment to gather himself, then whispered a Iezu name. As he had anticipated, no formal Summoning was necessary. Even as the last syllable left his lips the demon came to him, drawing its substance from the night.

'So,' Karril said. 'You've decided?'

His mouth set tightly, the Hunter nodded.

The demon held out a hand to him. In his palm was cradled a tiny star, a bit of Worked light that glimmered and pulsed against his illusory flesh. 'Kind of tasteless, given your preferences, but he said it was the best he could do without a physical ward to contain it. And I couldn't have carried that back with me.'

'It'll do,' the Hunter said shortly.

He held out his own hand to receive it. The tiny star moved from Karril's palm to his own, shimmering brightly against the whiteness of his flesh.

'You want me to go?' the demon asked.

'I want you to stay.'

Slowly he closed his fingers over the thing. Power pulsed out from it, fanning out along the current. None of it went to the south, he noted, which was a good sign. Or at least a safe sign. He was still wary of a trap.

Slowly an image formed in the clearing before him. First the shape of a man imprinted itself upon the darkness: not quite as tall as Tarrant, not nearly as young. Then color spilled from its shoulders, became crimson robes. Silk, Tarrant noted, unadorned but finely woven. Jewelry glittered on age-weathered hands. A crown took shape above graying temples.

When the image was complete, it portrayed a man perhaps fifty years of age, light-skinned, mildly athletic. A man who had taken care of his flesh. The figure waited a moment before beginning to speak, perhaps to give Tarrant a moment in which to study it. Then it began.

'Greetings, Neocount of Merentha.' It bowed its head ever so slightly, a gesture of carefully measured respect. 'My servant brings me word of your history and your exploits. May I say what a pleasure it is to have a man of your power come here.'

Tarrant said nothing, but his eyes betrayed his impatience.

'By now you are no doubt wondering whom and what you face. Permit me to enlighten you. My name is Iso Rashi, and I serve as Prince of this region. My parents came here some five hundred years ago as part of the Third Expedition. No doubt you know the fate of those ships. The warriors of the One God are fond of bragging of their exploits, but they aren't quite so eloquent when it comes to their failures. Nearly one hundred men and women survived the slaughter of the Third Expedition, and made their way to the south. Their descendants are my subjects. Ours is a nation birthed in violence, and its currency is hate – for the cities of the north and for all they represent. I make no attempt to hide that fact, or to make apologies for it. We are what the followers of the One God have made us.

'I reach out to you now because I believe that you and I are much the same, Gerald Tarrant. And because there are so few others capable of claiming that distinction. I perceive in your power echoes of my own; I sense in your determination and your ruthlessness the kind of drive that maintains this throne. And we have both conquered death. There is a very special distinction in that. Surely the scale of our lives is different than that of the common man. Surely our vision must be that much more ambitious.'

The figure paused; it reached out one hand toward Tarrant. 'I've come to offer you an alliance. The undead allied to the undying. My demons have told me of your power; you've seen enough evidence of mine to judge it. Can you envision a more perfect match than this? Power allied to power, enough to shake a world.

'What's in it for me, you ask? The chance to spare my nation what could be a devastating attack, and avoid a conflict that might kill one or both of us. The spirit of Death has a marked distaste for immortals, as you must surely know; I prefer not to tempt him. And for you, Neocount of Merentha? What price would be sufficient to turn you away from battle? What power could tempt you away from your isolation, after so many centuries?'

The figure smiled; the cold eyes gleamed. '*I can make you a god.*' it pronounced. 'My people control the reins of faith in the north. I can put them at your disposal. You can conquer the north in an instant – a vengeful deity whose arrival makes the priesthood of the One quail in terror – or you can play a more subtle game. After a decade of careful propaganda, the Prophet could live again. Within two decades, he could be deified. Within a century . . .' He gestured broadly. 'But I hardly have to describe to *you* what the power of the popular imagination can accomplish. Think about it, Neocount. The power of a god. The options of a deity. What will the patrons of Hell think of you then, when you raise yourself up out of their clutches forever?'

The figure paused; its arms fell back down to its sides. 'That is the substance of my offer, Gerald Tarrant. A true alliance between self-declared immortals, as befits their power and purpose. My mission demands that I subjugate the north, but it doesn't demand that I destroy it. There's enough wealth in this region for two men like us, and I propose that we share it. As for any demons who might come between us, perhaps the Iezu . . . the faeborn were created to be servants of man, and not his master. Servants are replaceable. Yours *and* mine.' He smiled coldly. 'I think you understand me.'

'Think about it, Neocount. Think about it carefully. I await your reply.'

Its message completed, the figure faded slowly into night. The last thing to fade was the glitter of its crown.

Tarrant opened his hand. His palm was empty.

The night was very quiet.

'Will you answer him?' Karril dared.

'Yes.' He shaped the words carefully, deliberately. It was clear he was deep in thought. 'I'll answer him.'

His eyes were unfocused, fixed on landscapes and possibilities that were visible only to the mind. Wisps of intentions sparked to life about him, only to be swallowed up once more by the darkness of the Hunter's soul.

'When I've decided,' he said quietly.

28

Jenseny awakened in a strange place.

For a moment she just lay huddled in the darkness, unable to remember where she was, or even what day it was. Then, slowly, it all came back to her. She felt strangely numb, as if she had been afraid for so long that something inside her had finally snapped and she just couldn't be afraid any more. Or maybe, instead, she felt safe. Maybe this was what safety felt like in the Outside.

Slowly, as if her newfound sense of security was something that might be dispelled by movement, she raised herself up on one elbow and looked around. She was in a dark space whose irregular walls were made up of woolen blankets, crudely stitched together; some kind of makeshift shelter. There were a few holes through which sunlight shone, and a triangular opening in the far wall that was propped open with a stick. In the far corner there was a pile of supplies, too much in shadow for her to make out details. Opposite where she lay was another pile of blankets, with the rakh-woman curled up warmly inside them, sleeping.

Silently, with the care of a frightened animal, she crept from her own bedding. Even in sleep the rakh-woman's presence was reassuring, and she wished she were awake so that she might crawl closer to her and curl up by her side. That she had feared her once seemed so distant now, so unreal, that it might have been in another life for all it affected her. Because in that moment when Hesseth had pulled Jenseny away from the white-feathered sorcerer she had blazed with such protectiveness, such searing maternal ferocity, that Jenseny could no longer think of her as one of the southern rakh. She had become something different, a species all her own, so replete with warmth and protective strength that Jenseny ached to hold her again, to drink it in anew. When the rakh-woman held her she felt *safe* again, like she could nuzzle herself into that warm fur and just forget that the rest of the world existed, because the rakh-woman would take care of her. No matter what.

When she was very quiet and very still she could hear the voices in that golden fur, the songs of a life lived far away from mistborn jungles and human sorcery. Sometimes if she was very, very still and the Light came on strong enough, she could see a camp filled with rakh like this one, with tinkling ornaments and painted tents and golden-furred children who ran from tent to tent, squealing with delight as they tumbled and raced like kittens. She liked the rakh children. She was sorry when the Light faded, taking that vision with it. Doubly sorry, because when they were gone she felt so lonely. Her father had been good to her, and the few servants who'd cared for her had been gentle and kind, but what was it like to run with other children? What was it like to laugh and yell with no care for who might hear you, safe in the knowledge that you *belonged* in your world, that nobody was going to show up suddenly and take you from the ones you loved because you had screamed too loud, or because someone had seen you running... It hurt, watching those children. It hurt to want what they had so very much, and to know she could never have it.

But at least she was away from the Terata. And the rakh-woman was here. And the strange priest also. She didn't yet know if she should be afraid of him or not. Her father had said that all priests were the enemy, and that if any of the One God's servants ever found out about her they would take her away and kill her, and probably kill him also for having protected her. But this priest couldn't be like that, could he? When he'd told her that his kind would rather die than hurt children, it had seemed to her that he really *believed* that, and even though the Light was pretty strong then, she could hear no false note in his voice to warn her that he was lying. What an incredible thought that was! That a servant of Erna's most vicious god could be so very gentle. Maybe it wasn't really the same god that he worshiped. Maybe his people called it by the same name, but it was a different god altogether. Yes. That would make sense.

Slowly she crawled to the flap of the tent, where a crooked stick held the wool covering to one side. Warily she peeked out. The mist outside was thin and sunlight had trickled down to the forest floor, its noise muted to a dull clatter. She looked around for danger, but couldn't seem to find any. There was a low fire burning some ten feet from the tent, its glowing embers surrounded by a circle of stones. A cookpot hung from a tripod arranged over the flames, and whatever was in it smelled good. Hunger stirred in her belly, and she wondered whether she dared take some of the food. Surely it would be all right. The priest and the rakh-woman would hardly rescue her and then not feed her, right? Especially since she was so very hungry.

She had just started toward the cookpot – timidly, like a skerrel braving open ground – when a footfall behind her set her heart pounding so hard against her rib cage that she could hardly breathe. She jumped up and was about to run when a kindly voice said, 'Easy, girl! The camp's warded tight, and Tarrant says there's nothing within miles to hurt you.'

She whirled around to find the priest behind her. He was half naked and dripping wet, and over one arm he carried a load of soaking wet cloth. 'Give the stew a few minutes to cool so you don't burn yourself. Here.' He came over to the fire and lifted up the pot by its hook, setting it aside on the stones to cool. She carefully kept her distance. 'There's a stream if you want to get clean,' he told her, nodding back the way he had come. He began to take the pieces of wet cloth from his arm and hang them on the tree branches surrounding the camp, so that the wind would dry them. One was a shirt, she saw, and an undershirt, a jacket, leggings . . . she watched while he laid out all his garments of the day before, except the woolen breeches that he was wearing. *He kept those on for me,* she realized. *So that I wouldn't feel uncomfortable.* The thought quieted alarm bells that had been ringing in her head, and she relaxed a tiny bit. The priest must have seen it, for he grinned.

'Feeling better, are you?' He knelt by where the cook-pot was and picked up a tin cup that was lying beside it. With a wooden spoon he began to ladle the hot stew into it. 'I thought a good night's sleep might do it for you. Here, try this.'

He handed her the cup. Her first instinct was to try to avoid coming in contact with him, but then she bit her lip and just reached out and tried not to worry about it. Her hand brushed against his as she took the warm metal cup from his grasp . . . and it was all right. He *felt* just as gentle as he sounded. She relaxed just a tiny bit more, and studied him as she blew on the hot stew to cool it.

He was a big man. Not merely tall, the way her father had been, but thick and solid. His face and arms were a leathery brown, but where his body had been protected by clothing it was a lighter shade, not unlike her own. Wet hair curled on his chest and arms, but not enough to obscure the half-dozen sizable scars that marked his barrellike torso, or the multitudes more that had healed enough to become no more than faint ridges along his flesh. There was one particularly bad gash along his left arm, a ridge of angry pink that ran from his elbow halfway down to his wrist. He saw her looking at it and smiled. 'That's from the last expedition. Skin takes a long time to get its natural color back, you know.' There were parallel ridges along his rib cage on one side – claw marks? – and a welter of stripes across his back that she couldn't begin to interpret. She was almost grateful that the Light wasn't strong just then, because then she would have seen even more, and there would have been too much to make any sense of it. Best to take these things slowly, she thought.

He handed her a wooden spoon and she scooped up some of the cooling stew. The scent of cooking vegetables and some aromatic meat tingled her nose. 'Hesseth went hunting,' he explained as she tasted it. Hot. Very hot. But, oh, it was so good . . . The heat and the smell of it blossomed within her as she ate; she felt more alive than she had since leaving home.

He rubbed his jaw as he sat down opposite her, somewhat self-consciously. 'I guess they gave my razor to Calesta. Hope the bastard cuts himself with it.'

She shivered at the sound of the demon's name. He was scooping some stew up for himself, and didn't notice. Or so she thought.

'You all right?' he asked softly.

She managed to nod.

'Were you there very long? With the Terata, I mean.'

His voice was so very gentle. Like the rakh-woman's touch. Hard and strong but infinitely tender.

'Three days. I think. I'm not sure.' Again she shivered, remembering. Following *them* through the forest. Trying to run when she realized what they really were. Driven forward at spearpoint . . .

'Easy,' he murmured. 'That's over now, Jenseny. You don't have to go back there, ever.'

'I was so scared,' she whispered.

'Yeah. Truth to tell, so were we.' He spooned up some of the stew and tasted it. 'Even Tarrant, I think. Though he puts on a damned good show.'

Tarrant. That was the third one in their group, the pale-skinned sorcerer. He didn't like her at all. His gaze was like ice, and when he looked at her she could feel her very blood freeze up. But he was also fascinating, in the way that dead things could be both terrible and fascinating. She remembered an animal she had found in the forest, the first day after she had left her father's keep. It was a small thing, golden and furry, and it must have been killed in a territorial fight because although its neck was torn up it hadn't been eaten, just left there for the scavengers to find. When she had come across it, the body was still warm, and the blood-spattered eyes were closed as if in sleep. She remembered putting her hand on it, driven by a terrible fascination, feeling its warmth like the heat of a living thing. For long moments she knelt there, her hand on its tiny body, waiting. For a heartbeat, maybe. An intake of breath. Anything. It seemed incredible that anything which felt so alive could be so utterly dead. So perfectly silent.

Tarrant was like that, she thought.

The priest had gotten himself a portion of the stew as well – his own tin cup was battered and bent, and had clearly seen better days – and he ate in easy silence, glancing at her occasionally but never looking at her for so long that she felt uncomfortable. She found that she was able to relax a little, for the first time since leaving home. This man wasn't going to hurt her, and certainly the rakh-woman wouldn't. Tarrant, now . . . that was another story. But Tarrant wasn't here. She drank in the sunlight and the safety and the warm fullness of her meal with a grateful heart, while the knots in her soul slowly began to untangle.

The next time the priest looked at her – kind, his eyes were so kind, it was hard to imagine a man like that killing anything – she nodded toward the tent. 'Doesn't she want breakfast, too?'

The priest smiled, and took a deep drink from a cup by the fire. 'It's her sleep time now.'

'Don't you sleep at the same time?'

'Not while we're traveling. This way one of us is always awake, in case there's trouble. She'll have her turn later.'

'Why don't you sleep at night?' she asked. *Night* was only a vague concept to her – in her rooms at home lamps might be lit at any hour, and all *night* meant was that her father was more likely to come – but now she had seen the sunlight and the twilight and midnight's darkness, and was struggling to sort them out into some kind of order. 'Don't most people do that?'

The priest hesitated. Only for an instant – but she heard it in the music of his voice, a faint sour note amidst the comforting glissando. 'Most people do. Certainly it's easier that way. But Tarrant . . . the sunlight hurts him. So we move at night.'

Something inside her knotted up again, something cold and afraid. For a moment she couldn't speak.

'Jenseny?'

'They were like that,' she whispered. 'The rakh. They could come out in the sun if they had to, but it burned them. That's what my father said.'

For a moment there was silence. She was afraid to look at him. Afraid to listen.

'You don't have to be afraid of Tarrant,' he said at last. 'He's a violent man, and he does a lot of bad things, but he won't hurt you.' His tone was gentle but firm, not unlike her father's. She lowered her head, feeling tears start up in her eyes. The priest's tone awakened so many memories . . . she tried not to see her father's face, tried not to hear his voice. It hurt too much.

'Jenseny?'

'I'm okay,' she whispered. Wanting to be brave for him.

'We came here because of those rakh,' he told her. 'To stop the killing.'

'They ate him,' she whispered. Choking on tears. 'They ate him, and took his place . . .' Eyes squeezed tightly shut, she fought not to cry. She tried not to remember. But there was enough Light in the camp that the visions came unbidden, and with them a sense of loss so terrible that she could hardly choke out the words. 'I can't go home . . .'

He didn't come over to her then, but he did something. Because the vision slowly faded, and with it the hurt. It wouldn't have faded on its own, she knew that. How had he made it stop?

'Jenseny.' His tone was gentle. 'We came here to stop that from happening. We can't help your father now, but we can stop them from hurting others. That's why we're here.'

A new fear took root in her, which had never been there before. Would they do that to others? Would all the Protectors die like that – eaten by monsters and then replaced – and would all their children have to cry away the nights, pretending that they didn't know? It was almost too terrible to think about.

'We need your help,' he said. Very softly. 'We need to know what your father told you about the rakh. We need to know what he saw. Jenseny . . . it'll help us fight them.' When she didn't answer – *couldn't* answer – he whispered, 'Please.'

What if they ate not only the Protectors, but their families and children as well? What if they went into the villages along the coast and ate the people there, too? She could almost hear the screams as those people died, mothers and fathers and children, too, children just like her, eaten up by things that looked like people but that weren't really people. Rakh-things from the Black Lands, eating their way through the One God's country.

'*Jenseny.*' He had come to her side so that he might take her in his arms. His skin was cool and damp, but his arms were strong, and she shook violently as he held her. 'It's all right,' he murmured, stroking her hair gently. 'You don't have to talk about it if you don't want to. I'm sorry I asked.'

She wanted to help them so much. That was the part that hurt worst of all. She wanted to help them more than anything, but she was afraid to. What would they think when they found out that her father was responsible for all this? What would they think if she told them that the Protector Kierstaad, whose job it was to keep the rakh-things out, had opened wide his gates and welcomed them in? Would they understand? Would they let her explain why he had done it? Or would they hate her, too, for having been a part of it?

She couldn't risk that. Not now. Not when these people were all she had.

'I can't,' she choked out. Hoping he would understand. Not knowing how he possibly could. Choking on guilt because she knew she could help them, and yet . . . if these people came to hate her then she would have no one. No one at all. And she didn't want to be like that again, not ever.

'I'm sorry,' she whispered. Hot tears dripping down her face. 'I'm so sorry . . .'

And he held her while she wept. Just like her father would have done. Just like her mother used to do. He held her in this strange place, with dangers all about them, and whispered words of hope and safety. And even more important words, in response to her apology.

'It's all right,' he whispered to her. Stroking her hair. Soothing her fears. 'You don't have to talk about it if you don't want to. It's okay.'

'I can't . . .'

'Shh. It's all right.'

And he held her, just held her, while she wept away her sorrow. While the sunlight – the beautiful sunlight – washed away all signs of mourning, and left at last only peace.

'Our enemy is Iezu,' Gerald Tarrant pronounced.

The mist had grown thicker with nightfall, blocking out what little Corelight still shone down into the valley. The air was damp and heavy, and at moments the mist felt more like rain than fog. They had left the tent pitched because of the wetness, and Jenseny was tucked away inside it, presumably sleeping. God knows she needed it.

Jenseny Kierstaad, Damien thought. Remembering that family name from their maps. Guessing at the horrors which her young eyes had seen, in the Protectorate where rakhene invaders had tortured dozens of people to death. No wonder she wasn't up to talking about it yet. God alone knew if she ever would be. It was miracle enough that she was still alive, and as sane as she was.

'Which means what?' Hesseth asked.

'Trouble.' There was something doubly dark in Tarrant's tone tonight, Damien thought, as if the news he had brought was disturbing on a personal level as well. He seemed . . . well, *edgy*. Which wasn't like him. Another thing to worry about? 'The Iezu have never been enemies of man, but that may be changing. And if it does . . .'

'Assst!' the rakh-woman hissed in exasperation. 'Some of us haven't spent a lifetime obsessed with human demonology, you know.'

'And some of us haven't been as obsessed as others,' Damien added. 'Who and what are the Iezu?'

For a moment the Hunter was still. The dying fire reflected gold sparks in his hair and eyes as he studied them both. At last, ever so slightly, he inclined his head.

'All right. I'll explain what I know – but I warn you, it isn't much. The Iezu have been around a long time, and most sorcerers have interacted with them, but they've always been obscure about their origins. Nevertheless – for the sake of the unschooled – I'll do my best.

'The Iezu are a sub-group of demons. That is – by modern definition – faeborn constructs with enough intelligence and sophistication to communicate on a human level. Like all true demons they feed on man, and manifest solid flesh only when they require it, but there the similarity ends.

'All demons feed on man in one way or another, and most prefer the role of *predator* to that of *parasite*. Even the low-order types who feed on renewable resources, such as semen or blood, prefer to suck their victims dry. Very few have the desire – or the self-discipline – to spare their victims' lives. And they give nothing in return for what they take, except for those fleeting illusions which might be required to seduce a man or woman into their clutches.

'The Iezu aren't like that. They rarely kill. As for how they came into being . . . no one really knows. Those few Iezu who speak of such things refer to a Maker, or Creator, who chose to bring their kind into the world. One of them even claims to have been *born,* rather than *manifested.*' He paused for a moment, as if reflecting upon that concept. 'How curious,' he murmured. 'And how ominous, for what it implies about this world.

'Most of the Iezu never take on human form. Most of them never appear to humans in any shape at all, or interact with them except in the course of feeding. It's doubtful if their victims are even aware of their existence. But a few, skilled in the arts of illusion, create bodies and voices and mannerisms with which to communicate, and seem to delight in human-style intercourse. The first of these appeared in the early fourth century, and more followed soon after. In my library back home I have files on nearly three dozen, and that's by no means a final figure. None have ever died that we know of.

'If I assumed that you knew of them—' and here he was speaking to Damien, '—it was because so many sorcerers do. The lady Ciani consulted several, and when an enemy's attack robbed her of her facilities it was a Iezu who tried to help her.'

'Karril,' Damien recalled. 'I think that was the name.'

Tarrant nodded. 'Perhaps the very first of his kind; certainly one of the oldest. Karril is worshiped as a god in some regions, as many of the Iezu are; their nature makes them particularly compatible with that role. And he seems to enjoy interaction with adepts, which not all of them do. I, too, have relied on him for information. Sometimes even for guidance.'

'You would trust a demon?'

'The Iezu aren't common demons, Reverend Vryce. Many pride themselves on their interaction with man. And even when they feed, they don't take anything from man that can't be replenished. Their hunger is for emotional energy, and they seem to be able to feed off that without weakening their prey. In fact, the bond between Iezu and human can even intensify the emotional experience for both.'

'Karril was worshiped as a god of pleasure, wasn't he?'

Tarrant nodded. 'And the men and women who couple in his temples not only feed him with their passion, but draw on him for intensification of their pleasure. It's a true symbiosis between man and the faeborn – or as close to one as Erna is capable of providing.'

'So what's the catch?' the priest demanded. 'There has to be one, or the whole damn planet would have set up Iezu shrines.'

'A lot of them have, Reverend Vryce. Of the ninety-six pagan churches in Jaggonath, more than forty are dedicated to Iezu. Not that they know it, of course. The lady Ciani was trying to catalog them when events . . . *distracted* her.

'As for the "catch," it's both simple and deadly. Obsession. Addiction. Dependency. And not all of the Iezu hunger after pleasant emotions. Some lust after varieties of pain, and bond themselves to men and women who delight in self-torture; others have needs so complex or abstract that their victims expend all their vital energy trying to define just what it is they hunger for. Obsession can kill, remember that, and even when it doesn't, it always deforms its victims. That's the price of a true Iezu bond, for those who choose to embrace it.'

'So why would a sorcerer chance it?' Damien asked. 'Surely they understand the risk.'

'Some think they can handle it. Some see it as a challenge. Most – like myself – perceive in the Iezu a valuable tool. Those who are willing to appear in human form – perhaps a tenth of their total number – are eloquent, sophisticated, and often amiable in nature. They have considerable knowledge about demonkind in general, and can tap sources of information that humans have no access to. And they recognize their own dependence upon humankind. That's what really sets them apart from common demons: they may feed on man, they may delight in seducing him into symbiotic bondage, but in the end they do recognize that it is they who will be the losers if humankind fails to thrive.'

'So what does it mean that our enemy is Iezu?' Hesseth demanded. 'To us, and to this mission?'

'You've seen it for yourself,' he said quietly. 'The one power that all the Iezu have. The skill that defines their kind.'

It took Damien a minute to realize what he meant. 'Illusion.'

The Hunter nodded.

'You mean those children—' Hesseth began.

'Illusion. That's all it was. That's all it had to be. The Iezu have no other power than that. But isn't that enough?' he demanded. 'A Iezu cloaked the valley so thoroughly that all my sorcery couldn't see through his work. The children rotted to pieces even as they worshiped their Iezu patron, unable to see the truth of their own flesh.'

'You saw through it,' Hesseth challenged.

He turned to look at her. 'I bargained with a Iezu for that right,' he said quietly. 'Which may not work again. We would do well not to count on it.'

'Still,' said Damien, 'If they have no power beyond that—'

'Don't underestimate the danger of illusion,' Tarrant warned. 'Remember the power of human belief. In the rakhlands I was captured by an enemy who wielded sunlight against me. Was that real or illusory? In that moment I believed it, and so it burned me. It could have killed me. We're not talking about some parlor conjuration, which you can Banish with a little concentration, but a total warping of natural perception, manipulated by an enemy who knows its power. And you can bet he'll use it carefully, in circumstances where we aren't prepared to resist. It was surprise as much as anything which defeated me in the rakhlands.'

'So is it this Calesta who's one of them?' Hesseth asked. 'Is he your Iezu demon?'

The Hunter's expression darkened. 'Most likely. And we can expect him to be allied to some powerful human, as he was in the rakhlands. That's not uncommon with demons in general, but it's standard operating procedure for the Iezu.' Something dark seemed to flicker in the back of his eyes then, something cold and uncertain. Whatever it was, he didn't choose to share it. 'It will make our campaign more difficult,' he said quietly, 'and far more dangerous.'

'You sound afraid,' Damien challenged him.

The Hunter hesitated. 'Maybe I am. Maybe we all should be. If you told me that I would have to face a horde of demons unarmed, with nothing but my Workings to support me, I would be reasonably confident that my power was up to the challenge. But the Iezu? No man has ever killed one. I wonder now if any man has ever *controlled* one. Many of the laws of demonkind seem to be suspended in that family, which means that the techniques mankind has developed for dealing with such threats may well be inoperative here. Isn't that reason enough to fear?'

'What about the atrocities we've seen?' Hesseth asked him. 'Do you think this Calesta's responsible?'

Tarrant seemed to hesitate. 'Without knowing exactly what emotion he feeds upon, I couldn't answer that. But my instinct says no. Not him alone. When a Iezu feeds, there's usually a clear pattern. An emotional theme, if you will. I don't see that here.'

'What about pain?' Hesseth demanded. 'What if he fed on human suffering? Wouldn't that explain a lot of what we've seen?'

'Pain may indeed be part of it,' he agreed. 'But it isn't enough. The inhabitants of the Proctectorates were suffering, but what aboutthose in the northern cities? Except for a few frightened children, those regions were remarkably peaceful. No, if a Iezu were responsible, his mark would be visible there also.'

'What about degradation?' Damien offered. 'You mentioned that as a pattern.'

'Yes – but rakh were also affected. The Iezu can't feed on the rakh – or any other native species – so why waste effort corrupting them? No, it has to be something else. Possibly something that reflects Calesta's human alliance.'

'You know for a fact that he's allied with someone?'

A strange, dark emotion flickered in the depths of the Hunter's eyes. 'I think it's likely,' he said quietly. 'And why not? He served a human master in the rakhlands; why not do the same here? In time such a human would have no choice but to serve the demon who had bonded with him, regardless of their original relationship . . .'

His voice faded into the night, into silence. For a moment he shut his eyes.

'No human being who accepted such a bond could ever be free,' he said softly. 'He might think that he was, but that would be just another illusion. There is no surer way to lose one's soul than to ally oneself with a Iezu demon.'

Something in his tone made the hair on Damien's neck start to rise. He was about to say something – more to break the mood than to question the man – when a rustling behind him reminded him suddenly that they were no longer a party of three.

He saw Tarrant's eyes shoot open as he turned back toward the tent, and he could feel the chill of the Hunter's scrutiny on his back. He hoped that Jenseny didn't see it as she stood at the edge of the firelight, her dark hair haloed by fog.

'I heard voices,' she said weakly. Her dark eyes flickered toward Tarrant, then away again quickly. As if she feared even to look at him. 'You said we'd leave when it was dark, and it looked dark, so I came out . . .'

'Quite all right,' Tarrant said softly. His tone was like velvet, silken and cool. 'Come to the fire. Sit down. Join us.'

Damien whipped about to confront him, but the Hunter didn't meet his eyes. Instead his gaze remained fixed on the girl. As she walked somewhat slowly to a place by the fire, and gradually lowered herself to the earth, her eyes rose to meet his own. She seemed to be trembling.

'If you hurt her—' Hesseth began.

'Shhh.' He was utterly still, utterly focused. The power pouring forth from him was palpable. 'I know what I'm doing. Our guest has nothing to fear if she cooperates with us. You know that, don't you, Jenseny?'

The girl nodded dully. There was a flicker of panic in the back of her eyes. Her breathing was slow and heavy.

'You have no right!' Damien protested.

'I have the right of one who's risking his life on this miserable quest – and I'll not let you get in my way, priest, I warn you.' He leaned forward slowly, his eyes still fixed on the girl. 'She won't be hurt. Not if she obeys me. She understands that. Don't you, Jenseny?'

The girl nodded slowly. Something glistened in the corner of the eye nearest Damien. A tear? He ached inside to help her, but was afraid to interfere. He had seen Tarrant's power work often enough to know that trying to break in now would put the girl at risk. Behind him he could hear Hesseth hissing softly, and he knew that she had come to the same conclusion. He could only guess how much it was costing her.

Damn you, Tarrant. Damn you for what you put us through. Damn you for what you force us to condone.

Helpless, bitter, he watched while the girl's eyes glazed over, her mind consumed by Tarrant's hypnotic power. And he remembered all those other times that he'd had to sit back and do nothing while innocent souls were forced to submit to that malignant will. Senzei. Ciani. A frightened rakhene girl. Now this fragile child. His heart ached to see the fear in her eyes, to imagine the terror that was in her soul.

'If you feed on one drop of her fear,' he muttered, 'so help me God, I'll rip out your heart with my bare hands.'

Though the cold silver eyes remained focused on the girl, a hint of a smile curled those thin lips. 'Now now, priest. No need to get violent. Everything's under control . . . isn't it, Jenseny?'

The girl trembled, said nothing.

'You are so very relaxed,' Tarrant told the girl. His low voice musical in the darkness, rich with silken malevolence. 'So very safe. Isn't that right?'

The girl hesitated before nodding. Damien's heart twisted.

'No one's going to hurt you. No one's going to hurt you at all. The things you fear are far away, and we're here to protect you. No reason to be afraid. No reason at all.'

A tear squeezed from the girl's left eye. She said nothing.

'Reverend Vryce told me you were afraid to talk to us. But there's no reason to be afraid, is there? Because we can protect you. We can keep you safe.'

The girl was still. Her face was drained of color.

'You want to talk to us, don't you? Because that would help us protect you. That would help us keep the things you fear away from you.'

She shook her head stiffly, fearfully: No.

'You want to talk to us,' he insisted, and Damien could sense the power behind his words. The raw force that towered like a wave over his cool, even pronouncements. He wondered if she could see it, if that was why she was so afraid. What were the parameters of her special vision?

'Go easy,' he whispered to Tarrant.

If the Hunter heard him, he gave no sign of it. With increasing firmness he told the girl, 'You want to tell us what you know. You want to tell us what your father said about the rakh. About the place they came from. You want to tell us everything.'

Beads of cold sweat broke out on the girl's forehead. She shook her head again, more weakly this time. Clearly she was losing ground.

The Hunter's eyes narrowed. Though his voice was carefully controlled, Damien could sense the growing impatience behind it. *Talk to him, Jenseny. Please. Tell him what he wants to know. It's the only safe course.*

'Tarrant.' It was Hesseth. 'Maybe you'd better—'

'She'll talk,' he snapped. 'Secrecy is a luxury in times like these, one we can't afford. She needs to understand what will happen if she *doesn't* help us, and then the words will come.'

Sensing his intention – its tenor if not its form – Damien lunged forward toward the girl. Not quickly enough. The Hunter's power engulfed her like a whirlwind, and she screamed – a shrill, terrible sound. As Damien reached out for her, he Worked his vision so that he could see what Tarrant was doing, what vision he had conjured for her eyes to see—

And he was back in the village, where the slaughter had taken place. No. He was back in the village *while* the slaughter was taking place. Dark figures coursed the blood-soaked streets, holding parts of human bodies aloft like trophies. Arms. Legs. Entrails. The screams that came from the houses were deafening, broken only by the beastlike howls of the invaders as they gloried in their grue-some indulgence. Then the scene shifted, as the Hunter's Knowing focused his vision even more finely: he was seeing the inside of the meeting hall now, where a man and a woman had been nailed to the floor, and two of the invaders moved forward with blades that were clearly intended for disemboweling—

And he attacked. Not Tarrant, nor the girl. The vision. Though he knew he lacked the strength to stand against the Hunter – though he knew that to anger the man now might well be suicidal – he couldn't stand back and let this happen. Not to that fragile soul. He leaned forward and grabbed hold of the girl – her limbs were like ice – and pulled her against the living warmth of his body, even while he gathered himself for a Working. The power was like a fire within him, scalding fury and compassion and raw indignation all mixed in together, fanned by months upon months of frustration into a conflagration almost too hot to contain. Months in the rakhlands. Months at sea. Months in this place, holding his peace while the Hunter tortured, the Hunter killed, the Hunter remade this land in his own malign image. Choking back on his conscience until it bled, until all his dreams ran red with guilt. No more.

It all poured out of him like a flood tide, too much power for one man to contain. It Worked the fae into a wall of fire, which no undead sorcery might pierce. It wrapped Tarrant's malignant vision in a scalding cocoon and seared, one by one, the fine strands of its construction. Images melted like wax and dissipated into the still night air. Bodies and blood evaporated into dust. Cradling the girl in his arms, Damien beat back the last fragments of the Hunter's assault, trying not to think about the power that lay behind them. Trying not to consider the fact that when the vision was finally gone there would be only Tarrant and himself, and the hate which he had conjured between them.

And then the full force of the Hunter's fury struck him. A power born of darkness, of death, of ultimate cold. It roared in his ears as it whipped about him like a tornado, tearing his fiery wall to shreds. Rage, pure rage; the feral fury of a man who was so powerful that no living creature dared to defy him, no man or beast had ever interfered with his plans ... until now. Damien heard the girl in his arms cry out as the sorcerous hate enveloped them, and he realized to his horror that she was sharing his vision of the assault. *God lend me strength,* he prayed desperately. Not for himself, but for the girl. *Help me protect her.* The thought of her innocence laid bare before Tarrant's assault was so horrible that he struck out in sheer desperation – but his Working was a twisted thing, warped by the force of his despair, and it couldn't stand against the man. Darkness invaded his vision, his mind, his soul. He felt the girl shiver in his arms as he made one last attempt to summon power. Pouring all the force of his despair into one last prayer, making the very heavens ring with his plea, the currents resonate with his need—

And something responded. A power. A Presence. It was sunlight to Tarrant's night, peace to his fury, water to Damien's flames. It soothed and commanded and smoothed and cleansed, washing away the debris of Tarrant's Working like a spring shower might cleanse the land of dust. The heat of Damien's rage turned to cool, soothing rain, and he felt the girl relax in his arms as the power washed over her as well. Utter tranquillity. Consummate peace. It unknotted his defenses even as it unmade Tarrant's assault, casting the dust of their conflict upon the currents. Its power was not force but quiet, like the rippling of lake-water in the moonlight. Damien's anger dissolved into the night, and with it all his fear. Tarrant couldn't hurt him now; he knew it, and so did the girl. Nothing fleshborn could hurt either of them.

He saw the forest trees as if through a rippling glass, their edges softened and made wondrous by the power that still filled the clearing. Color shimmered about their bark and among their leaves, and it seemed to him that the branches stirred as if in an unfelt wind. In his arms the child was peaceful, breathing steadily, and he knew that she, too, was possessed by a preternatural peace, an utter confidence in their safety. As for Tarrant . . . the pale gray eyes were narrow and cold, and for once in this journey – perhaps for the first time in his life – Damien had no trouble reading what was in them.

Fear.

Their eyes locked for a moment, then the Hunter turned and moved quickly toward the forest. Damien tried to call out to him, but for a moment no words would come. His body was numb, stunned by the force of what it had absorbed. Slowly, with effort, he regained control of his flesh. He wasn't aware of how completely the power had filled him until it was gone, or of how blissfully *complete* he had felt in its presence. Now it was no longer there, and his body ached with regret. He wondered if the girl felt the same. He wondered what Hesseth had experienced. And he wondered about Tarrant's fear.

'Take her,' he whispered, and Hesseth moved forward to take the trembling child from his arms. Somehow he knew that she wasn't shaking from fear now, but from awe; in a way that was even more affecting. 'Take her,' he repeated – with more strength this time – and Hesseth gathered up the girl in her arms and held her, murmuring rakhene endearments to her as Damien somehow managed to get to his feet.

The ground felt strange. The air tasted strange. The act of speaking was an alien act, that he managed only with effort. 'Tarrant . . .' He couldn't finish the thought. But Hesseth nodded, understanding. And he somehow got his legs to move, to carry him across the encampment to the place where Tarrant had disappeared. A minimal Working, whispered, served to make the Hunter's path visible, and silently he followed it. Committing himself to the woods, to the currents, and to whatever faeborn mysteries this strange night might have conjured.

But there were no fae-wraiths abroad tonight, and for once Tarrant had made no effort to disguise his trail. Damien found him in a clearing perhaps half a mile from the camp. So dark was the Hunter's form, so still, that he very nearly passed him by. But something moved him to look again at one of the many shadows which the trees had etched into the Corelight, and there he found him.

He was leaning against a broad, twisted tree, his pale hand resting on its ragged bark. Above him and about him the shadows of leaves fluttered like so many birds, underscoring his utter stillness. His head was pressed against his upraised hand, forehead and palm against the tree's broad trunk. Wisps of power, night-black, appeared like tiny flames around him, only to be swallowed up by his own darker substance an instant later.

Knowing that the Hunter must have heard his approach, Damien stopped where he was. The strange peace which had possessed him back at the camp had evaporated into the night, but even in its wake the fury of battle did not return. Another emotion – not quite fear, not exactly awe – was taking its place.

At last the Hunter spoke to him. Not opening his pale eyes, nor turning toward the priest. Nor lifting his head from where it was bowed.

'What you tapped into,' he said hoarsely. 'Have you ever done that before?'

Slowly Damien shook his head, somehow certain that Tarrant would be aware of his response. The Hunter's presence seemed to fill the whole clearing, seemed to reach out into the forest and beyond, as if questing for something. No, not *questing* exactly. More like . . . *hungering*.

'Do you know what it was that you conjured?' Tarrant demanded. The words seemed to choke him.

He hesitated, at last offering, 'A power born of faith.' The description seemed hopelessly inadequate, but he had no better way to describe it. Some things couldn't be reduced to simple language.

Slowly the Hunter turned to him. His face was pale and hollow in the dim Corelight, as though some terrible disease had ravaged both flesh and spirit. Though Damien knew that Tarrant's appearance was as much the result of mist-filtered shadows playing across his face as anything, still it was a wrenching, tortured visage. The priest shuddered to look at him.

'Nearly one thousand years ago,' the Hunter muttered hoarsely, 'I conceived of a plan to change this world. Wielding human faith like a sword, I meant to remake the very power base of Erna. For years I pored over holy text after holy text – those few which had survived the Sacrifice, as well as others which were written afterward – crafting my weapons word by word, phrase by phrase, sentence by sentence. It was my life's greatest work, compared to which all else was mere accompaniment. If there was a God of Earth, I reasoned, then we must mold the fae with our faith until our pleas could reach His ears. If there was a God who ruled the entire universe, then we would craft such a message with our prayers that He must surely respond to us. And if there was no One God in either place, nor any being who might adopt that role . . . then the faith of man would *create* one. A sovereign god of Erna, whose power would be so vast that all the currents of earth-fae would pale in significance before Him. That was my dream. No, more: that was *my purpose in existing*. And if in the end I chose to barter my soul for a few extra years, it wasn't so much out of fear of death as a fear of what death implied. Ignorance. Blindness. An inability to see the seeds of my work take root and grow, and to observe what manner of fruit might be harvested from it. Survival for me meant the chance to see the centuries unfold, to watch mankind take what I had given him and add to it, develop it, make it his own, until by his faith he could tame the fae itself. It was a plan so vast that no one human lifetime could contain it, and I burned to see it through to completion. Do you understand, priest? That was what I sacrificed my humanity for. That was why I smothered in blood the core of my mortal existence. Because I wanted to *know*. Because I wanted to *see*. Because the concept of dying in ignorance was terrifying to me, and I lacked the courage to face it. Do you understand?'

The intensity of his speech – and his pain – flooded Damien's mind; it was hard to focus on mere words in the face of such a deluge. But slowly understanding came, and with it the power to voice it. In a voice that resonated with awe, and not a little fear, he whispered, 'You looked upon the face of God.'

For a moment the Hunter just stared at him. The hollowed eyes were haunted, and it seemed that he trembled slightly.

'No,' he whispered. 'I saw . . . No.'

He turned away again, and leaned his weight against the weathered bark by his side. His eyes fell shut, and slowly – painfully, it seemed – he drew in a slow breath. 'Without doubt we have created something,' he whispered. 'The faith of millions has finally reached that critical point where it's capable of manifesting something greater than itself. Perhaps there was a God here to start with; perhaps the will of man created Him. Does it matter how it happened? Something is now active in our world that wasn't before. You felt it. You *saw* it. A power so vast that the human imagination can hardly encompass it. A power capable of remaking this world . . .' He drew in a ragged breath; Damien thought he saw his shoulders tremble.

'Shall I tell you what I learned tonight?' the Hunter whispered. 'There is indeed a God of Erna. And because of what I am – because of the bargain that I struck so many years ago – I can't even look upon His Face. This is the fruit of my labors, Reverend Vryce. That I can never gaze upon the result of all my labor. I sold my soul for knowledge of the future, only to have that very pact render me forever ignorant.'

He leaned heavily against the bark of the tree, as if in pain. Silence gathered about him like a cloak, like armor. For a long while Damien dared not compromise it, but at last he said, very softly, 'You know as well as I do that pact doesn't have to be permanent.'

The Hunter turned to him, slowly. Strands of pale hair were fanned across his forehead like a spider's web. Incredulously he asked, 'Are you trying to sell me on repentance? Now?'

'You know that it's never too late,' Damien said gently. His heart was pounding like a timpani, but he managed to keep his voice steady. 'Your own writings proclaimed that.'

For a moment Gerald Tarrant just stared at him. The look in his eyes said clearly that he thought Damien was mad, or worse. Then he blinked, and asked hoarsely, 'You really believe that?'

'You know I do.'

'Do you realize what repentance would mean for me? Do you understand the price?'

'I know it means going against the habit of nearly a thousand years. But even so—'

'It means death, Reverend Vryce, plain and simple! My body is nine hundred years older than it has any right to be; what do you think will happen to it when the pact that sustains me is broken? Return magically to the condition of its youth, so that I can pick up where I left off? I doubt it, priest. I doubt it very much.'

'Would death be so terrifying if Hell were out of the picture?'

He shook his head. 'It isn't out of the picture, priest. It never will be.'

'Read your own writings,' Damien reminded him. '*The nature of the One God is Mercy, and His Word is forgiveness. The man or woman who truly repents*—'

'Do you know what repentance means, for me? Do you really understand it?' There was anger in his voice now, but it had a desperate edge. 'Repentance means standing before God and saying, I'm sorry. For everything. All the sins I ever committed, I wish they could be undone. I wish I could to go back to that time and do it all over again, so that Death could take me in my proper hour. I wish I could have died at twenty-nine, without ever seeing the future. I wish I could have died before my dream took hold, before mankind had time to interpret my works. I wish I could have died in ignorance of what this world would become, severed from the world of the living before I could begin to untangle the mysteries that surrounded me. I can't do it, Vryce. Not honestly. I could say the words, but I could never mean them. And my last dying thought would be of all that I had yet to see, which God's forgiveness had cost me.' He laughed shortly, bitterly. 'Do you really think that would work? Do you really think such an attitude would save me?'

Now it was he who shut his eyes. He could hear the pain in his own voice as he spoke. 'You're trapped by your own intelligence, you know. A simpler man would have found his way back to God long ago.'

'Don't you think I know that?' he whispered. 'Don't you think that knowledge is part and parcel of my damnation?'

He lowered his head, aching to say something that would help, that would heal. But if a man of the Hunter's intellect could see no way out of this terrible trap, what manner of salvation could Damien offer? At last he muttered, inadequately, 'I wish there was something I could do to change things for you.'

'No one can,' he whispered. 'But I knew the risk, you see. I knew when I made my bargain that there would be no backing out. I understood it then and I understand it now. It's just . . . this whole thing took me by surprise. That's all. After nine hundred years, living beyond the reach of the Church . . . I wasn't ready. For this.' After a moment he added, 'I suppose you were.'

'No one is ever prepared to meet God,' Damien said quietly. 'We may think we are, but that's only because we don't understand Him.'

Eyes shut, the Hunter nodded. 'The girl is safe from me, you realize. I don't dare Work her again. If even some tiny portion of that Power remained within her, even a faded vision of it—'

'Do you really think you can avoid death forever?' Damien asked softly.

A strange expression flickered across the Hunter's face. Almost a smile. Almost a tremor.

'I'm sure as hell going to try,' he assured him.

When Damien returned to the campsite Jenseny was asleep, curled up tightly in Hesseth's arms. For a long time he just watched her, listening to the rhythm of her breathing, feeling the warmth that rose from their close-knit bodies. Hesseth stroked the long black hair gently, separating its knotted strands with her claws. The girl's face was streaked with tears, but for now it seemed peaceful.

At last he whispered, 'Is she all right?'

'She will be, I think. What about Tarrant?'

He shook his head. 'I don't know. I hope so.'

And because he offered nothing more, Hesseth didn't press him for an explanation.

How well we've come to know one another, he thought. *Aliens to each other in every sense of the word, and yet we've discovered a common etiquette.*

If only our peoples could have done the same, so much death might have been avoided.

He settled himself down on the opposite side of the fire, and felt exhaustion settle over him like a shroud. Too much for one night, he thought. Too much for *any* night.

God, show me how to help Gerald Tarrant. Teach me how to reclaim his soul without destroying his humanity in the process. Show me the path through his madness . . .

When sleep began to dull his senses, he made no attempt to resist it. Because sleep was forgetfulness and sleep was peace, and that was what he needed more than anything else right now.

In the stillness of the forest clearing, Gerald Tarrant waited. The first of morning's sunlight had filtered down through the omnipresent mist, turning the air a filmy gray. It warmed his skin, but not so painfully that he had to leave to find shelter. Not yet.

A figure formed in the space before him, drawing its substance from the mist. As he watched, the Iezu manifestation took on form, color, and at last life. When it was complete, the Hunter nodded in acknowledgment and addressed it.

'It's nearly dawn, Karril. I called you hours ago.'

'Your pain kept me away,' the demon said softly.

Tarrant shut his eyes. It seemed to Karril that he trembled. 'Then I'm sorry,' he whispered. 'Thank you for coming despite that.'

'Are you all right?'

For a moment he just stood there, as still as the trees that surrounded him. At last, without answering, he held out his left hand. A small spot of darkness quivered like a flame in the center of his palm. 'Will you take this to the Prince for me?'

'What is it?'

'An answer. To his offer.' He shook his head. 'No more than that, I promise you.'

The demon held out his hand beneath Tarrant's, so that the Hunter might pour the unflame into his own palm. It flickered there like a malevolent star, jet black against his own illusory flesh.

'Can I ask what your decision was?'

'I thought you didn't want to get involved.'

'I seem to be involved despite that, don't I? So how about filling me in?'

Grim-faced, Tarrant turned away. He said nothing.

'This isn't like you, Hunter.'

He whipped back to face him; his eyes, sun-reddened, blazed with anger. 'Who are you to judge what is and isn't *like me*? Who is any demon to judge me? If I thought for one moment—'

Then he shut his eyes as if in pain, and raised a hand to rub his forehead. 'I'm sorry, Karril. That wasn't fair. It's been a rough night, but I shouldn't take that out on you. Your service deserves better.'

The demon shrugged. 'Every friendship of nine hundred years has its moments of strain. Don't worry about it.'

'You served me well all those years. Even though I now understand that you didn't have to.'

A faint smile softened the demon's expression. 'The first human being I ever spoke with will always have a warm place in my heart. Even if he does pride himself on his lack of humanity.' He closed his hand about the black flame, wincing as its power bit into him. 'Couldn't you have chosen a more pleasant form for this?'

The Hunter's expression darkened. 'He sent me true fire. Whether it was meant as a warning or a display of power, the gesture deserves to be returned.'

'Ah. Ever the diplomat.'

'You can carry it, can't you?'

'There are several hundred things I'd rather be carrying, but I'll manage. Is that all?'

The Hunter nodded.

'Then I'll be on my way. Dawn beckons, you know. Take care, Hunter.'

The Iezu form began to fade, its colors seeping out into the fog.

'Karril . . .'

The demon paused as he was and waited.

He whispered it, 'Thank you. For everything.'

The demon nodded. Then his flesh became translucent, transparent, and slowly dissolved in the misty gray light of dawn. The black star in his hand was the last thing to fade, and that went out suddenly, like a snuffed candle flame. The smell of conjuration was sharp in the damp air.

Gone to its destination, Tarrant thought. Gone to deliver its message of death and betrayal.

Alone in the light of the early dawn, the Neocount of Merentha shivered.

THE BLACK LANDS

29

There it is, Damien thought. *We made it*.

The cities of the coast lay nestled in a crescent-shaped valley whose broad, curving mouth opened to the sea. To the east and west loomed the bald granite peaks of the continent's two mountain ranges, which curved like pincers about the cities' bounty and then extended far out into the water. There they became two diminishing lines of weather-worn ridges and jagged islands which stretched southward as far as the eye could see, providing the crescent shore with a vast harbor that was sheltered from storm and from foreign tsunami alike.

Clearly humankind had thrived here. Looking down upon the cities of the south – there were three that he could make out by moonlight, and probably more that would be visible in the light of day – Damien saw all the signs of successful settlement. Lush farmlands hugged the mountains, and a system of roads was visible that spanned the valley like a web. The fact that it was all at sea level, or very near to it, spoke volumes for the natural safety of this fertile niche; if the harbor waters had ever spawned any smashers of their own, man would have sought higher ground.

He stood on a ridge some two hundred feet above the valley floor and gazed at their destination. Some hundred yards to the east of them the waters of the valley – now a sizable river, formidable in current – plunged headlong over the rocky edge, roaring like a hurricane as they smashed themselves upon the rocks below. From there it was another drop, and then another, as the vast waterfall plummeted in stages to the floor of the harbor basin. Damien gazed down into the mist-filled lower valley and thought he saw figures milling about the foaming lake below. Fae-wraiths? Real people? Perhaps lovers, braving the dangers of the night in order to spur on their passion. Or perhaps even tourists, from the Protectorates or beyond; who could say what manner of commerce these thriving cities supported? One thing was certain: after weeks of traipsing through cold forests and over bare granite plateaus, Damien was overjoyed to see people again. Any people. He felt muscles unknot that had not been relaxed for weeks, and even though he knew that the dangers in those cities might be every bit as deadly as those without, he couldn't help the sense of optimism that filled him at the sight of this thriving human metropolis.

Jenseny was something else again. She wouldn't even come near the edge of the cliff, but stayed back by the horses, cowering close against their flesh. *Humanity* meant danger and betrayal to her – how quickly the young learned to fear! – and clearly she dreaded the coming descent. But at least she had stayed with them this long. That was something Damien hadn't expected, and if he had failed to sketch out plans for her in the past few days it was mostly because he hadn't really thought she'd still be with them. For a while it had seemed that she might bolt from them, animal-like, at the first sign of danger, disappearing into the brush like a frightened skerrel. Now she seemed somewhat more stable, if no less terrified. Somewhat more human.

How ironic, that the rakh-woman should prove the humanizing factor with her. He wondered if Hesseth had noticed the change. He wondered if she had caught the humor of it.

Love is a universal language, he reminded himself. Then he glanced back at the girl – still terrified, still cowering, but Hesseth had gone to comfort her – and thought, *So is loneliness.*

With a sigh he looked about for Tarrant. At last he spotted him some hundred yards away, standing by the edge of the river, gazing down upon the valley beneath. He made his way to where the tall man stood and offered him the telescope. But Tarrant shook his head, his pale eyes fixed on the panorama below. Studying the southern cities, with all the special senses available to him. Damien waited in silence. At last the Hunter nodded shortly and stepped back from the edge; fine mist sparkled in his hair like diamonds.

'Our enemy isn't here,' he said quietly. Despite the roar of the compound waterfall beside him, his words carried easily to Damien's ears. 'Although his people have been to this shore, without question.'

'As invaders?' he asked. He had to shout to make himself heard. Not for the first time, he was jealous of Tarrant's easy power. 'Spies?'

The Hunter brushed back a lock of hair from his forehead; water dripped from it like a tear. 'I'm not sure. The traces are complicated, and layered about each other like the rings of a tree; it's hard to sort them out. But I would say from the fortifications here—' and he waved an eloquent hand out over the valley, '—or rather, from the *lack* of them, that whatever conflict now exists is diplomatic rather than martial. Hardly what one would expect,' he mused.

He turned to look at the river by his side, whose chill water rippled and foamed as it gushed over the edge. It gave Damien a rare moment in which to study the man unobserved. There had been a change in him recently, and not for the better. Damien would have been hard-pressed to capture it in words, but he could sense it clearly enough. *Maybe it's hunger,* he thought. He thought of the cities before them, nestled in the lower valley, and shuddered. He considered how many nights had passed since they'd left the Terata camp, long nights spent traveling in an empty land. Though Tarrant hadn't talked about his needs, it was clear what the cities must mean to him. Fresh food. Rejuvenation. Maybe even – with the right luck – a hunt.

Damien felt sick inside, and turned away. *You never get used to it. Not ever. You never learn to accept it.*

God help me if I ever do.

In recent nights Tarrant had avoided Jenseny, and the rest of the party as well. He no longer rode with them but flew overhead as they traveled, keeping pace with them far above the thick canopy of treetops. Which was just as well, Damien mused. God alone knew how he would have reacted if they'd asked him to ride double with someone, or how Hesseth's mare would have handled it if they tried to put three people on her back. There was a limit to what even strong horses could handle. No, it was best that they travel as they did. He just wished he didn't feel in his gut that this was just another facet of the strange darkness which now hung about the man like a shroud, which seemed to grow as the long days of travel progressed.

He stood in the presence of God, he reminded himself, *and was rejected. He's faced the truth of his own damnation head on. Wouldn't that change a man?* Shouldn't *that change a man?*

Repentance meant death, the Neocount had told him. And death, in his philosophy, meant eternal judgment. Was there any way out of that intellectual trap which the sorcerer had crafted for himself? Was there any path he would accept? The thought of saving that twisted soul instead of destroying it was a heady concept, and not one that he had considered before. He wasn't yet sure it was possible.

'We'll need to get rid of the horses,' the Hunter announced.

'What?' It took a second for him to get his conversational bearings. 'Why?'

'Because they'll give us away. There's no creature native to the east that's even remotely like them, and the Matrias know that. If they've sent any warning to these people, it'll include a description of our mounts. In the mountains we could hide them, but down there?' He gestured toward the city lights below them.

Damien considered it. He hardly relished the thought of traveling south without the beasts, particularly in the unknown lands of their enemy . . . but the Hunter was right. Even if they could hide the animals in the midst of a city – a dubious enterprise at best – they could hardly book sea passage without revealing their existence. And if the Matrias had indeed alerted this region, they might as well emblazon their coats with bright red targets as go down to the coast with two horses in tow.

Damn the luck. Damn it to hell.

'What's the alternative?' he asked gruffly.

'Kill them,' he said easily. 'Or set them free here, before we descend.'

'That would just be a slower death, wouldn't it?'

A faint smile curled the Hunter's thin lips. 'Mine's a resourceful beast, Reverend; he'll survive well enough. And Hesseth's mare might choose to stay with him, which would give her a better chance.'

'Yeah. What are the odds of that?'

'The ancient xandu mated for life. Some of that instinct no doubt still remains in their descendants. I'm sure that between your skills and mine we would have no trouble reawakening it.'

Damien stared at him, incredulous. 'Haven't you forgotten something?' When the Hunter didn't respond, he pressed, 'What about the *mating* part? Isn't that kind of important?'

'My horse wasn't gelded,' he pointed out.

'Sure. He isn't exactly a raging stallion either. If he was, don't you think with a mare present—'

'I didn't say he wasn't *altered,* Reverend Vryce. I stopped up the flow of certain hormones to render him tractable in mixed company. That can be undone easily enough. Given a few months of normalcy . . .' He shrugged. 'I imagine the old patterns would reassert themselves soon enough.'

'In which case . . .' He looked back at the horses. 'They might breed.'

He sensed, rather than saw, the Hunter's smile. 'Very probably.'

'How successfully?'

'It's hardly an ideal gene pool, but I'd say they stand a chance. Certainly more than they would if we took them with us.'

Wild horses. Not xandu. Not some tamed equivalent. A truly wild gene pool, adapting itself to this hardy terrain. The concept was intriguing, he decided. God knows, this valley needed some new input.

And then another thought struck him, and he looked sharply at Tarrant. 'Are you doing this for their good, or for yours?'

He shrugged. 'The species was wild once, and might be wild again. How much of its survival instinct survived the process of forced evolution? I would be lying if I said that the experiment didn't appeal to me.'

And that's the heart of it, Damien thought. *Once you've started a project, you can't let go of it. This whole planet is no more than a vast experimental laboratory for you, a testing ground for your pet theories. And nothing else really matters to you, does it? Ten thousand men might be slaughtered in front of you and you wouldn't bat an eyelash, but if anyone threatened one of your precious experiments you'd move heaven and earth to destroy him.* What manner of dark vanity could produce such a finely honed selfishness? It was almost beyond his comprehension.

'Well?' the Hunter pressed. 'What's your judgment on the matter? Since I'm so biased,' he added dryly.

Damien resisted the temptation to glare at him. Narrowly. 'Don't you think we ought to ask Hesseth what she thinks? There are three of us,' he reminded him.

Only there were four of them now, he realized with a start, not three. How long would the girl stay with them? He had given passing thought to the concept of finding her a home in one of the coastal cities, but how likely was that? And what about the information she had hinted at, but never dared reveal?

'Let's ask Hesseth,' he repeated quietly.

He didn't just mean the horses.

What made you want to be a priest? the girl had asked him.

So hard to answer. So difficult to choose the right words. So hard to explain to this child what the Church was to him – what God was to him – when he knew that in the back of her mind were all the atrocities the Holies had committed. All the years she had spent locked away from light and life, for fear of his God.

And yet she asked him. Eyes wide and bright, with only a flicker of fear in their depths. Compelling an answer.

What made you want to be a priest?

Was there a moment of revelation he could share with her, one single instant which turned him away from secular courses and fixed his heart on this most difficult of paths? It seemed he had always been a priest, had always wanted to be a priest. But the decision had to come sometime, didn't it? Certainly he hadn't been born to the priesthood.

There was one incident he did remember clearly, and he shared it with her. He had been young, very young, and they were studying Earth History in school. He remembered the teacher tying together facts and fragments into a narrative that breathed life into the mother planet, unlike the usual dry recitation that graced those schoolroom walls. And that night he dreamed. Fantastic dreams, terrifying dreams. Dreams of what Earth might have been like, a chaos of energy and ambition and hope, almost too intense to absorb. He remembered gleaming tubes of metal that darted across the earth without a horse to pull them, capsules of painted metal that soared through the sky with effortless grace, words and pictures flying across the length of a continent in less than the time it took to draw a breath. And of course the greatest accomplishment of all: the Ship. Vast as an ocean, powerful as an earthquake, it stood ready to tame the wastelands of the galaxy, to spread man's seed throughout the universe. Those visions were so bright, so solid, that when he awakened his heart was pounding, and his breath was dry in his throat. And he understood about Erna at last. He *understood*. Not in some little pocket of his brain, which memorized Earth-facts only to spew them out on a standardized test and then forget them, but in his heart. In his soul. He understood what Earth had been and what Erna could be, that awesome and terrible birthright which was the very core of man's heritage. And he understood, for the first time in his young life, just what the fae had done to his species. To his future.

Life was pointless, he understood that now. All that mankind was doing on Erna was marking time, fighting for survival on a day-to-day basis while the planet grew in power and malevolence. Man's doom was inevitable, and in the shadow of such a judgment his life, his dreams, even his few accomplishments were leached of all meaning. So why go on? Why keep fighting?

It was a terrifying revelation, almost more than his young mind could handle. For months he struggled with it, while all around him others succumbed to the power of similar awakenings. Four of his classmates started seeing counselors as a result, and one – he heard this years after the fact – tried to kill himself. The others blocked it out, or failed to understand, or in some other way avoided the issue. In time they would adapt, begetting children of their own to face this damned and damning planet. In time, perhaps, some of those might become sorcerers.

Why did he become a priest? Because the One God was a living expression of man's optimism. Because his Church was man's greatest hope – if not his *only* hope – on a wild and hostile planet. Because only by devoting his strength and his passion to God did Damien feel he could justify his own existence. Any other profession would have been an exercise in futility.

He didn't say it in those words. He didn't want to frighten her the way he had been frightened back then. And most of all he didn't tell her about the Prophet, whose brilliant vision had given his life a focus. Because that might lead to other questions, which might have lead to certain answers . . . and he didn't want to have to explain to her that the murderous demon who traveled with them was all that was left of that illustrious figure. Not yet. The truth was hard enough for him to come to terms with, and he had spent nearly a year traveling with the man; he didn't want her newborn understanding – so precious, so frail – contaminated by such knowledge.

And then there was the night that he and Tarrant had fought.

He wondered how much she had seen that night. He found to his surprise that he couldn't bring himself to ask her. It was as if his memory of the Peace which had filled him was a fragile thing, no more substantive than a dream, which the wrong words might disperse. *Any* words. And yet it was there between them, always. The answer to all her questions. The core of his lifelong faith.

He looked at her, nestled against the warmth of Hesseth's fur in much the way that he had seen rakhene children snuggle against their parents, and an unaccustomed warmth suffused his soul. The bond between them truly amazed him. From Jenseny's viewpoint it made sense, of course; lonely and terrified, robbed of home and hope, she would of course cling to the first nurturing soul who welcomed her. But Hesseth? She hated humans and all that they stood for, even (he guessed) human children. So what special chemistry had taken place between the two of them, which permitted such closeness to develop? He didn't dare ask about it, for fear he would disturb its precious balance.

But he wondered. And he admired. And sometimes – just sometimes – he envied.

They decided to let the horses go. No one was happy about it, but it was clear to all that there was no alternative Tarrant Worked his own steed so that its hormonal balance would be what nature intended, then stripped it of its saddle and gear and set it loose. He Worked Hesseth's mare as well – a process that the rakh-woman was clearly not thrilled about – and in the end expressed equal satisfaction with that work He even tried to instill an instinctive avoidance of such thorned flora as the Terata had created, in the hope that would keep them safe from the worst of those nightmare experiments.

And then they let them go.

Thus have we altered this ecosystem, Damien thought as he watched them canter off – hesitantly at first, then with increasing confidence. The last sight he had of them was the stallion tossing its head in the wind, black mane rippling in the moonlight *Forever* If anyone else had suggested such a move, he would have been worried about the possible repercussions, but in this one area he had utter faith in the Neocount's judgment. The Hunter's Forest might have been a fearsome place, but it was also a perfectly balanced ecosystem. And if Tarrant had loosed fertile horses here, then the local environment could handle it; Damien didn't doubt that for a moment.

Their descent had to wait until the morning. Once the Core had set there simply wasn't enough natural light for them to negotiate the terraced cliff face safely, and Tarrant was loath to light the lanterns. They didn't dare be seen descending, he cautioned them, lest some city guard be sent out to greet them. Damien agreed. And so they waited until the sky grew pale with sunlight and the shadows of the peaked islands stretched westward across the water before they moved, packing their camp even as Tarrant took his leave to seek out a more secretive shelter.

'What about the saddles?' Hesseth asked, and after a brief discussion they decided to bury them. It would hardly do to have some sportsman climb that slope and discover their equipment scattered along the ridge. Only when the equestrian gear was well underground, and the earth over it had been tamped down and camouflaged, did Hesseth draw out her linen coif once more and bind it over her head, hiding her tufted ears from sight. *Time for disguises again,* Damien thought darkly. For once he was glad that Tarrant wasn't with them; one less person to hide. As for Jenseny . . . they would have to leave her, down there. Somewhere in those cities. They would have to find her a home, or at least a means of survival, so that they could leave her safely behind when they moved into the enemy's territory . . .

And what if she has information that we need? What if her power could help us? He shook his head, banishing the thought. Too many ifs. Too many unknowns. The walls of her trauma were high and strong, and if they'd had a long month to work on them in safety, perhaps they could have convinced the girl to open up, to share her precious knowledge with them . . . but not in a week's time, and not under these conditions. And there was no way that he would permit her to be broken, not by Tarrant's power or his own careful lies.

Bound together by a length of rope, they descended. It was a tricky descent but not an impossible one, and the one time Jenseny slipped he managed to pull her up short by the rope before she had dropped more than a yard. That was the only mishap. Freshwater spray cast rainbows in the air about them as they sought out the dryer handholds, and by the time the Core rose over the eastern mountains they were standing on firm ground, the fertile southlands spread out before them. Golden light played over the slopes as they packed away their climbing gear, and the waterfall's spray shivered into spectral drops as it fell. It was hard to connect such panoramic beauty with the places they had just been, hard to reconcile where they were today with the horrors of their communal yesterdays. Then he looked at Jenseny, sensing the aura of desolation that hung about her like a dank cloud, and he thought, *Not so hard.* Because they had brought a bit of the valley with them, in her eyes. A link to where they had come from, and where they were going. A reminder.

God grant that we never forget it, he thought grimly. As he coiled the last rope and fitted it into Tarrant's pack. As he hoisted the black leather up on his shoulder, preparing to hike onward once more.

'Come on,' he muttered, as he urged his party forward. 'Let's get there.'

Jenseny tried hard not to be afraid.

Maybe if it was still night she could have managed it. She had gotten used to the night. When the Core was up, it meant that the whole world gleamed with golden highlights, as if some giant lamp had been lit, and the shadows were warm and gentle. The Core didn't make noise like the sun did, and its light wasn't nearly as piercing; if she closed her eyes and tried hard, she could almost imagine that she was back in her own rooms, the steady flame of an oil lamp her only illumination. And when the Core went away, it was even better. The night enfolded her with its darkness, making her feel that she was not out in the open but in some small enclosed space, safe and comfortable. Sometimes the moons would rise and they had their own sounds – a faint clatter from Domina, a dull buzz from Prima, a bare whisper of a hum from Casca – but their light didn't fill the heavens like the sunlight did, and still she felt safe.

And then it was day.

And they came to the city.

It was a terrible place, a fearsome place, a place that made her feel dizzy and weak and terrified all at once. The houses were thick and tall and set so close together that as they walked down the street it seemed she was back in Devil's Chasm, wending her way over rubble and across pits while praying that the earth wouldn't suddenly shift beneath her feet. The houses had voices, too – loud voices – and though she tried not to hear them she couldn't shut them out. Sometimes she would brush up against a wall accidentally and then the voices would become a scream, as if the whole history of the house had been compressed into one noisy instant. Contractor squabbles and rent wars and once the forcible eviction of a man who took up a sword and started hacking at his neighbors ... it was terrible, too terrible, and she couldn't even stand before the force of it, much less hope to contain it. Once the passing crowd pressed her against the pillar of a butcher's shop, and the sense of raw animal pain was so overwhelming that she fell sobbing to her knees, unable to go on. Damien picked her up then and carried her for a while, and she was content to lay huddled in his arms and drink in the comfort he was offering. Trying to shut out the terrible voices, and all the pain they embodied.

She had to be brave for them, she knew that. Though she didn't understand the details of their journey she knew that these people had come here for a vital mission, and that her presence among them might threaten their success. She tried hard not to be a burden. But the crowds! The voices! The narrow streets seemed to focus the sunlight, magnifying its light and its sound until she almost couldn't stand it. Sometimes she just couldn't seem to make her legs move at all, but froze up in the middle of the street and shook while the hurrying crowds parted like a river around her. Then Hesseth would come and whisper words to her, rakhene words she couldn't understand, but she knew that they were meant for children, that back in the rakhene homeland young girls like herself would be comforted with just such sounds. She loved those sounds. Sometimes when the Light was strong she would stop and just listen to them, not even try to go on walking, and it took the priest's gentle touch on her shoulder to get her moving again. And even then the sounds stayed with her, like a whisper of rakh-children playing in the high grass. A comfort to both her fear and her loneliness. If she could have curled up in Hesseth's arms forever, she would have been happy, just listening to those sounds. Shutting out the horror of the city that surrounded.

At last, on Damien's cue, they approached a stocky building and stopped. It was an old building, and though its owners had dressed it up in bright, gaudy colors, its paint was now chipping from its pillars and its front steps were sagging. She huddled close to Hesseth, trying hard not to hear the voices that were resident in that wood.

'You think?' the rakh-woman asked.

The priest nodded grimly. 'Unpleasant enough, that's for sure.' Then he raised up one hand and quickly sketched a shape in the air in front of him; Jenseny felt a shock, as if thousands of needles had all pricked her at the same time. Hesseth looked at her in concern.

'They'll keep secrets,' Damien muttered. And he led them inside.

The big room inside the building was as worn and weathered as the outside. The rugs were painful to walk on, but though she would have preferred to go around them Jenseny didn't want to leave the rakh-woman's side. Once she stepped on a dark brown stain and was nearly overcome by a stabbing pain in her side; Hesseth's arm held her upright. 'Kasst,' the rakh-woman whispered, and she drank in comfort from the sound. One step after another, forced and hesitant. And then she was beyond the rugs and the floor was much better, it didn't hold the pain so badly. She shivered as she stood, waiting while the priest negotiated with a stocky man. At last a few precious treasures changed hands: from the priest, a small handful of coins. From the other man, a pair of tarnished keys. The stocky man turned to go then, but Damien put a hand on his shoulder to stop him.

'No questions,' the priest said quietly, and Jenseny felt the needles prick her again. For a moment the man looked dazed, and then he nodded.

Worked, she thought. Tasting the alien word, struggling to understand it. *He Worked him.*

They went upstairs.

The hallways were grimy and narrow and close, but for Jenseny they were a welcome change. She huddled in the center of the corridor while Damien fumbled with the keys, testing them both. At last the door before him swung open, and he waved his companions inside.

Hesseth sighed as she let the heavy pack slide off her back. 'Assst! I miss the horses.'

'Ditto,' he grumbled, as he did the same. 'But there's no way around it.'

Jenseny looked up at him. 'Isn't it bad for you to control people like that?'

For a moment there was silence. She heard him draw in a deep breath, slowly, and then he asked – ever so quietly – 'What do you mean?'

She struggled to find words for what she wanted to say. The concepts were alien, and defied definition. 'You told me that your God doesn't want you to use the fae to control people, only . . . to heal and such. But didn't you control that man down there?' When he didn't answer, she added in explanation, 'When you told him "no questions."'

For a moment he said nothing. But she could hear the words, as clearly as if he had spoken them. They were in his eyes, and his body, and the breath that he exhaled.

How did you know that?

After a moment he came to her, and crouched down before her so that he was at her level. It was good to look directly into his eyes like that. Brown eyes, so very warm. She could feel their heat on her face.

'What we've come here to do is very important,' he told her. His voice was soft and carefully controlled and he was choosing his words with obvious care. 'If we don't succeed, a lot of people will be hurt. Like your father. Remember? We came here to stop that kind of thing from happening again, so no one else is ever hurt like that again. And sometimes, to do this . . . sometimes we have to do things we don't like. Things we wouldn't do at any other time.'

'Isn't it still wrong?' she asked.

For a long, long moment he didn't answer her. She could feel Hesseth's eyes upon them both, the long ears pricked forward to catch his answer. Had she asked something bad? She just wanted to understand.

'My Church thinks it's wrong,' he said at last. 'Sometimes I'm not so sure.' He stood up slowly, one knee popping as he did so. 'In the name of this quest we've done a lot of things we didn't want to do, Jenseny, and I guess we'll do a lot more. That's how it goes, sometimes. You make the best choice you can.'

'Tarrant would be proud of that argument,' Hesseth said softly.

The priest looked over at her — and something passed between them that Jenseny couldn't interpret, but it was sharp and was hot and it was filled with pain.

'Yeah,' the priest muttered. Turning away from them both. 'Who the vulk do you think it was taught it to me?'

They were going to leave her here.

They didn't say it. They didn't have to. It had been clear enough on the journey here that they weren't going to take her past the cities, and that didn't leave a whole lot of options. Oh, they would try to provide for her, they would try to prepare her for it, maybe they would even try to find a home that would take her in . . . but it all meant the same thing, in the end. They would leave her here. In this place. With the voices. Surrounded by buildings and people that virtually screamed with pain, abandoned to a life of such unremitting fear that they couldn't begin to guess at it.

The rakhene children would be gone then. So would Hesseth. And so would Damien, and with him the last vestige of that fragile Peace which she had experienced in the forest. A Peace so sweet and so warm that she would give her very life to feel it again. Part of it was still here, inside him. She sensed it when he held her. And if he went away . . . then she would lose that Peace. Forever.

Alone. She had been so alone before, so full of pain. Then these people had rescued her. She still mourned her father's death, still woke in the night quaking from terrible nightmares of loss and desolation – but the priest and the rakh-woman had eased her suffering, and the Peace had numbed her grief. Now she would lose all that. It was more than she could stand to think about.

Sometimes when she thought about her father she got angry, and that frightened her. *Why?* she demanded of him. *Why did you leave me?* Even as the words came, she was shamed by them, but they flowed from the heart of her too fast and too hard to stop. *Why didn't you protect me better? Why did you go and die and leave me alone? What am I supposed to do now that you're gone?* She felt that by blaming him she was somehow betraying him, but the anger was too real and too intense for her to stop it. *Where are you, now that I need you? Didn't you know this would happen?*

Tears pouring down her cheeks – body trembling with fear and shame – Jenseny gazed out through the grimy window at the crowds and the sunlight and tried hard not to think about her future.

30

The church was small, and the strip of land that surrounded it was narrow and muddy. Houses and storefronts crowded close about its walls on all four sides, casting its thin strip of lawn into shadow, robbing it of vitality. If not for a low wrought-iron fence – more show than substance, as its height was easily scaled by any thief – and that narrow band of green and brown, the church might well have shared its very walls with the businesses that clustered claustrophobically in the city's low-rent district, so well did its facade of faded brick and mildewed mortar match their own.

No doubt there were finer churches in the better neighborhoods, and perhaps a great cathedral or two in the city's center. Perhaps, as in Mercia, city life revolved around a central cathedral, and rich lawns and costly ornaments framed a building whose gilded arches gleamed in the Corelight, drawing the faithful like flies. Such a building would be beautiful, breathtaking in both its scope and its upkeep. It would also – Damien was willing to bet – be heavily guarded.

A wagon rattled to the left of him as he approached the rusted iron fence, drawn by the short, stocky animals that this region used as beasts of burden. There was a sharp cry off to his right, followed by the crash of glass; a domestic dispute, he guessed, spawned by the humid closeness of this district. He took advantage of the double light – a rosy mauve from the early sunset, Core-gold from the galaxy overhead – to study the sanctified building. A modest church to start with, it had clearly seen better days. Its few stained-glass windows were protected by thick wire mesh, and bars reinforced those on the lower floors. But despite its humble design and defensive hardware, the small church was clearly used, and used often. The steps were well-worn, the brass-fitted doors polished to a bright finish by the caress of a thousand passing hands. Even as Damien watched, more than a dozen men and women traversed the broad stone stairs, some in pairs or chatting groups, one or two alone. And their faith would have left its mark. The prayers of thousands, day after day, would have seeped into the ancient stonework and the deeply carved wood, leaving their mark upon the building's substance as clear and as readable as any bars or iron deadbolts. The faith of these people, and all that it implied. Which meant that whatever corruption the Matrias had engendered here, that, too, would cling to this building. Easy to read, for one who had the Sight. Or at least so he hoped.

He braced himself to Work . . . and then hesitated. It wasn't that he was afraid of being found out. He had come to this dismal corner of the city precisely for that reason, afraid that if the servants of the local Matria were watching for his arrival they might well have staked out the better-known cathedrals. There was anonymity in these garbage-strewn streets, and with his travel-stained and clumsily repaired clothing he was perfectly suited to take advantage of it. No, no one would notice him here. And in this land, so utterly bereft of human sorcery, it was unlikely that the Matrias or their servants would think to focus in on his Working to locate him, or would even know how to do so. He was as safe here as he was going to get in this warped and corrupted land, and it wasn't the thought of capture which made him tremble in the church's dusky shadow. Not exactly. It was more like . . . like . . .

I'm afraid to Know, he thought. Fear wrapped cold tendrils around his heart. *Afraid to See. Afraid to know the corruption for what it truly is, and to witness how far it's progressed.*

He hadn't been near a church since their flight from Mercia. Which meant that up until now he'd had no chance to See for himself what changes had been worked among these people, to analyze what effects the secret rakhene matriarchy had had upon their faith. Not yet. And as he stood beyond the gates of the modest church, as the inhabitants of the city shuffled and clattered past him, he realized that he didn't want to see. Didn't want to know. Not ever.

His hands closed tightly about the cast iron bars, squeezing them until his knuckles went white. *Knowledge is power,* he told himself. *You need it. You can't fight the enemy without it.* Doubts assailed him, made doubly powerful by the force of his fear. He had thought that if he Worked his sight near a church he might see the corruption here for what it was, might be able to read some pattern into the degradation of his faith, some purpose . . . but what if he couldn't? And what if he succeeded in conjuring such a vision, only to find that he couldn't bear to absorb its message? The corruption of this region struck at the very heart of who and what he was; did he dare experience it directly?

I have to, he thought feverishly. *That's all there is to it.* And he braced himself for Working. Wishing that it were as easy to brace himself for revelation. Wishing that his heart could be made invulnerable, just for an instant.

With care he reached out and touched the foreign currents – they were rich and strong, all that a sorcerer could ask for – and he tapped into the earth-power to remake his sight, so that it would respond to the fae's special wavelengths. For a moment he didn't dare look at the church, but fixed his eyes upon the ground. Silver-blue fae rippled across the rutted concrete in patterns of moire complexity, obscuring the muddy cracks beneath. Then, slowly, he raised up his eyes.

And he Saw.

Oh, my God . . .

For a moment he was simply stunned, incapable of accepting what his senses proclaimed. Then, slowly, it sank in. The church was clean. Clean! Its aura glowed warmly with faith and hope and the prayers of generations, just as one would expect in another time, another place. Its music was not the dissonance of earthly corruption, but the delicate harmony of true devotion. He stared at it in amazement, not quite believing. He shook his head, as if somehow that would clear his Sight. Nothing changed. The aura of the building was bright and pure, as befit a true house of worship. The currents which coursed about those worn foundations sparkled and glittered with the fragments of human hope which they had absorbed, as pure as the Corelight which fell upon them. The fae that poured forth from the building itself . . . that was as sweet and as reverent as any which flowed from the great cathedral in Jaggonath, and as he listened he could hear the whisper of prayers that it carried, and catch the faint, sweet smell of human faith.

Impossible.

Simply impossible.

He stared at it aghast, struggling to understand. Why would the eastern rakh invest so much time and effort in taking control of his Church, and then do nothing to alter it? What was their ultimate purpose, if not an assault on the human spirit? And what about the force that seemed to be guiding them? He could understand a demon who fed on human degradation, an Enemy whose goal it was to twist human faith toward a darker purpose . . . but that wasn't happening here. Not at all. These people were steadfast in their faith, and it showed. The very earth glowed with their dedication.

What is it you want? he demanded silently. Of all of them: the Regents, the Matrias, the unknown enemy who grew closer each night. *What game are you playing here?* Until this moment he'd thought that he understood the pattern here, at least on a visceral level; now even that basic assumption was in doubt. If mankind had made an enemy here, its nature was so alien that Damien couldn't begin to guess at its motives; or else its plans were so long-sighted that in the context of a single year – or even a century – the greater pattern was all but invisible. And that made Damien afraid. Very afraid. It made him fear in a way he never had before, and it made him wonder – perhaps for the first time – if he might not have taken on a task that no one human could accomplish. Even with Tarrant's help. Even with Hesseth's power, and the girl's.

What are you? he demanded. *What is it you want?* But there was only silence to answer him, and the sibilant whisper of faith. Pure. Righteous. Terrifying.

Heart cold, hands shaking, he turned back toward the grimy hotel, to await the dusk and Tarrant's return.

31

Night fell slowly in the harbor cities, accompanied by a sunset the color of blood. Long after twilight's darkness had shadowed the city streets it was still possible to see sunlight in the distance, breaking in between the peaked islands and glimmering across the water. When that had faded, the Core remained: light without warmth, a false golden sheath for the city. How long would it be before that faded as well? The Core had been two hours behind the sun when they'd landed in Mercia; how long had it been since they'd fled that city?

With a sigh Damien let the curtain drop from his hand, falling back into place of its own accord. The strong northerly current here meant he couldn't use the earth-fae to access information about the Matrias' plans, or Know the details of their pursuit. He could test the fae that was coming up from the south, use it to Know the enemy . . . but Tarrant was better at that kind of thing than he was. Tarrant was better at interpreting the strange and often cryptic visions that a long-distance Knowing was wont to conjure. Let him do it.

Damien looked over at the rooms they had rented, one bedroom and a small parlor connected by a curtained archway. He would sleep in the parlor tonight, on its well-worn couch, and leave the bedroom for Hesseth and the girl. A semblance of privacy. After their weeks together in the woods it seemed almost a frivolous arrangement – God knows, they had seen each other naked more than once – but it pleased his sense of propriety that they now had this option. A token civilized gesture. And of course, there was the girl now to consider.

The girl . . .

She was nestled against Hesseth's side like a kitten, the two of them intertwined on the couch. How peaceful she looked, now that there were walls between her and the outside world. But how real was that barrier? Damien didn't have to Know the room's interior to tell that it had seen its share of violence and misery. Why didn't that affect her? Why could she fight off the empathic images here, but not out in the streets?

Because this is her territory now, he mused. Watching as she snuggled her way even deeper into Hesseth's embrace. *She's defined it as such, therefore it doesn't bother her.* What did that imply about her Vision? Was her reaction in the streets a symptom of true power, or of mental instability? He was all too aware that it could be both. In which case she really might be dangerous. He had tried to Know her once or twice, to no avail. Whatever power she drew on eluded his own Sight, and he had to assume that the same was true for Tarrant. And that, all by itself, was a daunting concept.

Sensing his scrutiny, Hesseth looked up at him. 'Tarrant?'

He shook his head. 'Didn't see him.' He unhooked the swag of the ceiling lamp and lowered it down to where he could reach it more comfortably. 'And it's well into night,' he muttered, lighting the four wicks. They were dusty, and sputtered as they caught fire. 'Core's almost gone. So where the vulk is he?'

Her amber gaze was reproachful. 'You know that.' With one hand she stroked Jenseny's long dark hair, separating the strands with her claws. 'Don't you?'

He exhaled heavily. 'Yeah. I guess so.' For a minute he just stared at the tiny flames, four stars behind grimy glass panes. Then, with a sigh, he hitched the lamp back into place overhead. 'It usually doesn't take him this long.'

How many will he kill tonight? He tried not to think about that. Again. The ache in his conscience translated into a sharp pain between his eyes, which he rubbed with dry fingers. He needed the sanctity of a church tonight, the cultured tranquillity of formal prayer. Needed it badly. But if the Matrias were watching for him in this city . . . he dared not risk it. Standing outside a church was risky enough; entering one would be downright suicidal.

He was startled suddenly as the door creaked, and his hand went instinctively for the sword at his shoulder. But the weapon was in its harness, resting on the bed a good ten feet away. He didn't need it anyway. It was Tarrant, at last. Damien bit back on his anger as the tall man entered, quieting the rusty hinges with a glance. The Neocount looked about the room, peered through the curtain to the bedroom beyond, and his pale eyes narrowed in distaste. Suddenly the place seemed twice as dingy, the air twice as stale. Damn him for noticing! And damn him twice for disapproving. He hadn't been here when they'd been searching for a safe haven, had he? So he'd damn well better not criticize their choice.

Easy. Easy. Don't let him get to you. Don't let this whole damned trip wear down your nerves.

Without a word Tarrant walked to the room's small table and pulled out a chair for himself. Damien nodded to Hesseth, who followed suit, disentangling herself from Jenseny's embrace with gentle care. When they all were seated, Damien pulled over the table lamp and lit it; light sputtered resentfully into being behind tinted glass, etching human and rakhene features in hard yellow highlights. The color made Tarrant's eyes look feral, inhuman. More like his true self, Damien thought. It was a disquieting vision.

Sensing that the Hunter was about to make some deprecating comment about their lodgings, Damien said quickly, 'It was safe. The first safe place we found.'

'The girl was having trouble—' Hesseth began.

'Ah, yes. The *girl*.' The pale eyes narrowed, fixed on that sleeping form. A thin frown of distaste curled the Hunter's lips. 'Do we know what she is yet? Has she chosen to share her precious knowledge with us? Or is she still just a parasitic cipher—'

'Don't,' Damien warned. He felt his hand edging up toward his shoulder, toward where his sword would normally be harnessed; an instinctive gesture. 'Don't make it worse than it has to be.'

The Neocount's expression was unusually cold, even for him. In recent days he had avoided the young girl's company entirely, cutting short any discussion which centered on her. Now the hostility in him seemed more intense than Damien remembered from before, and the priest didn't quite know how to account for it. When they'd first rescued the girl, Tarrant had been angry, yes, and justifiably suspicious, but not this openly hostile. Not this much like a snake with its fangs bared, ready to strike. It had all changed that night in the woods, he thought. The night Tarrant had dared to attack the girl, and Something had intervened. Could one brief incident change a man so drastically?

She saw his God, he reminded himself. He knew that instinctively for the truth, though he and the girl had never discussed it. And Tarrant knew it, too. He must. What a terrible thing that must be for him, to watch a stranger be granted the ultimate Vision while he was forbidden communion. And jealousy could spawn hatred, Damien thought. A uniquely vicious hatred. No wonder he had been on edge since then.

He forced himself not to address that issue, tried to steer the conversation onto safer ground. 'The city has a safe harbor—'

'Closely guarded, no doubt.'

'You think the Matrias are looking for us this far south?' Hesseth asked.

'Without question,' Tarrant assured her. 'I can see it in the currents. I can smell it in the winds. The whole city stinks of ambush.'

Damien felt his heart sinking in his chest as the words hit home. Not until this moment had he realized how much he'd been hoping that Tarrant would prove his suspicions wrong. 'What, then? You have a suggestion?'

'We need to move quickly. Book passage across the water before the local Matria realizes we're here. With a good enough Obscuring we might be able to hire a ship before—'

'Hold on,' Damien said sharply. 'Just a minute. We were talking about collecting information when we got here, weren't we? Trying to take the enemy's measure before we decided what to do next. Wasn't that the idea? I don't like the concept of rushing over to the enemy's turf before we even know—'

'Time is a luxury here,' the Hunter snapped. 'And one we can't afford. Do you think that the soldiers of the Matria will sit back and indulge us while we gather our maps and our notes and our courage? There's a price on your heads—'

'You don't know that—'

'I do,' he said coldly. 'I know it for a fact. And I know the amount that's been offered, as well, and it's high enough to make every local contact suspect. Do you really want to stay here, under those circumstances? Do you really think you can accomplish so much here that's it's worth throwing your lives away?'

'The alternative doesn't sound much better,' Hesseth challenged. 'Blind flight . . . toward what? For what?'

'We need to get off this continent. We need to get beyond the reach of the Matrias' network before it finds us. I understand that you're uncomfortable with such a move—'

'That's putting it lightly.'

'—But I assure you, remaining in this city is the most dangerous thing we could do right now. Or in any city on this coast, for that matter.'

Damien shook his head. 'The Matrias' lands don't trade with the southern kingdom, did you know that? They may not be technically at war, but they're hostile enough. Travel between the two is strictly forbidden.'

'Yes,' the Hunter said dryly. 'All commerce with the southern kingdom is forbidden.' His smooth voice dripped with disdain. 'Do you think that stops it? Rule one of history is that *trade goes on*, priest. Always. It may give way for a time, say during a war – if a strong enough blockade is established – but as soon as there is a crack in one's defenses, even a tiny flaw, traders will smell it out. Profit is every bit as powerful a motivator as patriotism, Vryce. Perhaps more so.'

'You're saying there'll be transportation.'

He nodded. 'Without question.'

'Any suggestions on how to find it?'

'As a matter of fact, I have a name for you.' He withdrew a folded paper from his pocket and handed it over; Damien unfolded it carefully, angling it so it would catch the light. *Ran Moskovan*, it said. *Licensed port Angelo Duro, #346-298-J*. Beneath that was the name of a local bar, a street address, and a time. 'Free merchanter by day, black marketeer by night. He's got his own ship – stream-lined and swift – and it's got enough secret cubby-holes to make any smuggler green with envy. According to my Divining, he's the safest bet we've got in this town. You'll have to meet with him tomorrow and talk price.' He leaned back in his chair. 'I suggest you be generous. Gold's the only master such men pay heed to.'

'Easier said than done,' Damien muttered. He looked at Hesseth, who caught his meaning and reached into her pocket. A thin handful of coins was all she had, and she scattered them across the table. 'I have about fifty left, that was on me when my horse went down. The rest is with my supplies – wherever the hell they are.'

'And it's all northern coin, or foreign.' Hesseth pointed out. 'A dead giveaway, if anyone knows to watch for it.'

The Hunter seemed undisturbed by the news. 'Which is why I collected these.' He reached into his pocket and drew out a small silken pouch. Mud-stained, Damien noted, or perhaps crusted with something worse. Wordlessly the Hunter pulled open the mouth of the pouch and spilled out a stream of gems across the tabletop, mud-covered and blood-splattered but undeniably precious.

'Where—' Hesseth gasped.

It took Damien a moment to make the obvious connection. 'Terata?'

Tarrant nodded. 'It occurred to me then that we might need capital. I must admit that the thought of using Calesta's offerings—'

There was a moan from the couch. Low, barely voiced, but so resonant with pain that even Tarrant fell suddenly silent, and twisted about to look that way. It was the girl. She was awake now, and her eyes were wide, her body trembling. It was hard to read her expression. Fear? Surprise? Confusion?

'What?' she whispered. Sensing their eyes on her. 'What is it?' She struggled to her feet, her eyes fixed on them. No, Damien thought. Not on *them*. On the table between them, and what lay on it.

Slowly she walked toward them, her eyes never leaving that spot. Damien didn't have to See to know that she was radiating fear, or that the Hunter was feeding on it. 'What is it?' she whispered. 'What did you bring?' Her voice was shaking now, and her hands seemed to tremble as she reached out toward the table. For a brief moment Damien considered sweeping the gems away from her, out of reach – and then the instant was gone and she had seen them, she was touching them, she was rubbing her tiny fingers over the pile of gems as if searching for something, moaning in pain even as she did so. He remembered her reaction to the city, to its walls and its pillars and people, and he ached to pull her away, to protect her from this new source of pain. But like his two companions, he was paralyzed by curiosity. Curiosity and dread.

She gasped as she found something in the pile, and moaned softly as she raised it up. A ruby or a garnet, Damien assessed, that gleamed a dark red from beneath its crust of dried blood and dirt. Her shaking fingers stroked its surface, caressing it free of the dirt that caked its surface. Her breath came in shorter and shorter gasps as she absorbed whatever pain the small stone carried. Damien ached to help her, didn't know where to start.

'It was his,' the small girl gasped. Choking out the words. A tear squeezed out of the corner of one eye, glistening like a diamond in the lamplight. 'His!'

It was Hesseth who first made the connection. 'Her father,' she whispered. 'He must have owned it.'

'But how—' Damien began.

A cold hand on his shoulder warned him to silence. He glanced at the Hunter, saw the man's eyes fixed on the center of the table. No: above it. He followed his gaze – and felt his breath catch in his throat, as he saw what was happening there.

There was a shape forming in the air between them, a slow swirling of light and color that seemed to draw its strength from the pile of dirty gems on the table. At first it seemed formless, as insubstantial as a cloud of dust motes reflecting the flickering lamp flame. But as they watched it gained in substance, until it seemed to Damien that an object was now suspended in the air before them. No. Not an object. A *hand*. Medium brown in coloring, lightly scarred along one side, with nails that were short and clean with just a hint of silken fabric wrapped about the wrist. Even as they watched it flexed, and the glint of the red stone set on one finger was unmistakable. He didn't need to see the one Jenseny was holding to know they were one and the same; the knowledge seeped into his brain like a Knowing and stuck there, spawned by the same power that had conjured this vision.

'How?' he whispered. And though the answer was obvious, he could hardly accept it. *Jenseny?*

—And then, suddenly, the vision was gone. Extinguished in a rainbow cascade of light, dissolved into the air once more. The girl's hand trembled, clutched about her treasure; tears ran freely down her cheeks.

'It was his,' the girl whispered. Her voice was shaking. 'He gave it to one of his people, he said.'

'Someone who later ran into the Terata,' Tarrant supplied.

She nodded wildly and sobbed, 'I can feel how he died . . .' She gasped suddenly and one hand twitched; Damien guessed that the ring had not been stolen gently, but severed from a living hand.

'It's not earth-fae she's drawing on,' Tarrant mused aloud. 'Something stronger. Wilder.'

'They killed him,' the girl whispered. 'They killed him and they killed my father, and they'll keep on killing if you don't stop them!'

Damien saw Hesseth reach out for the child. 'If it's really stronger than the earth-fae—'

'But *wild,* priest. Remember that. There are forces in this world that can never be tamed—'

'—And humans can't use them because you only think in terms of *taming,*' Hesseth retorted. 'The rakh know that sometimes using a power means submitting to it.' She looked down at Jenseny, now nestled in her arms; her expression was one of awe. 'I think she knows that, too,' she whispered.

The girl looked up at them. Her face was streaked by tears and her lower lip was trembling, but her voice was strong as she challenged them, 'Take me with you.'

Damien could feel the fury gather about Tarrant like a storm cloud. 'Out of the question,' he snapped.

'They killed my father!'

Tarrant ignored her, turned to glare at Damien. 'This is your doing, priest. I suggest you find a solution.'

'I want to help you!'

Tarrant stood. He seemed twice as tall in that dusty space, looming over the girl's head like some spectre the night had conjured. His expression was dark.

'She's unstable,' he said shortly. 'Utterly undisciplined. And I see nothing to indicate that she has any control over the power she uses, or even an understanding of what it is.'

'I know where the Black Lands are!' Jenseny cried out. 'And I know the traps there! If you don't take me with you, you won't see them, and he'll kill you!'

For a moment there was silence – a terrible silence, filled to bursting with suspicion and fear and yes, a faint flicker of hope. At last Damien found his voice once more and managed, 'What are the Black Lands?'

'Where the Prince lives. The one they call the Undying.' Her tone was defiant now, her wide eyes fixed on Tarrant. Daring him to stop her. 'Inside the Wasting. I've seen it, I tell you. I could take you through.'

'How?' Tarrant demanded. His voice was like ice. 'How do you know all this?'

'I saw . . . pictures.' She was clearly struggling for words now, trying to describe something that defied the confinement of language. 'He used to tell me stories, and there would be pictures.'

'Your father drew them for you?' Hesseth asked.

'He didn't know they were there,' she whispered. 'He never saw them.' The tears were running freely now, as grief broke through her air of defiance. 'Sometimes when he talked they would be there, and I could see what he was saying. Like I'd been there myself. The Black Lands, and the Wasting, and all the places in the south . . .' Her words trailed off into silence as she lowered her face onto Hesseth's shoulder. Weeping into the warm golden fur. 'I could get you there,' she sobbed. 'I could help you make it through!'

'Out of the question,' the Hunter repeated coldly.

Damien was less certain. 'If she knows the way—'

'Think about it, priest! Two nations are at war here. The whole coastal region is fortified against invasion. And one Protector goes and visits the heart of the enemy's territory, right in the midst of all that. Why don't you ask yourself *why*, Reverend Vryce. Better yet – why don't you ask the girl?'

Jenseny pulled away suddenly from Hesseth; her light brown face had gone sallow with fear. 'He didn't mean it!' she cried out. 'He wanted to help. He thought he could save them!'

It all came together then in Damien's mind – her father, the rakh, the bloody invasion . . . The Protector of Kierstaad had bargained with the enemy, and had paid for that treachery with his life. Which meant that inasmuch as any one man could be said to bear the responsibility for the recent invasion, Jenseny's father was clearly guilty.

My God, thought Damien. Watching as the small girl cringed, clearly in terror of their judgment. *What a terrible weight for a young soul to bear.*

'I won't put my life in the hands of a child, priest. Valuable or not, we leave her here.'

'No!' the girl cried out, suddenly panicked. 'Not here! Not with the voices!'

'*Quiet,*' the Hunter breathed, and his words, powerlaced, made the very air shiver. '*Now.*'

Choking, she swallowed back on her fear.

'Look at her!' he demanded. 'Do you doubt my judgment now?

There's no place in this mission for a child. You should have known that from the start.'

'I couldn't leave her there.'

'No? So now what? Do you suggest we start interviewing nursemaids? Every time we stop to talk to a local we increase the risk of detection! Perhaps we should approach an adoption service.'

'Then what do you suggest?' the priest demanded. 'You tell me.'

His gaze was like ice as it centered on the girl. 'You know what I suggest,' he said coldly. There was death in his voice. 'You know what my answer is.'

'No,' the rakh-woman hissed, as his meaning struck her. 'You have no right—'

'Ah. Are we back to morals again? Have we so soon forgotten the lesson our enemy taught us – that if we hope to succeed, we must be willing to sacrifice everything? Even that?'

'I don't remember learning that,' Damien growled. And Hesseth protested, 'She's just a child—'

'And you think I don't know that? I had children of my own, Mes rakh, have you forgotten? I raised them and I nurtured them, and when they got in my way I killed them. Children are expendable—'

'*Two,*' Jenseny interjected.

Startled, the Hunter blinked. 'What?'

'Two of them,' the girl said. Her thin voice shaking. 'You only killed two.'

For a moment he stared at her in amazement. And in fear? Then he whipped about and caught up his pouch, shoving it into a pocket of his tunic. 'You found her,' he spat at Damien. 'You get rid of her.' It seemed to Damien that there was something else in his tone besides anger now, something far less confident. Was it possible the Hunter was afraid?

And then he was gone, and the door slammed shut behind him. Dust coiled thickly in the yellow light.

'Is that true?' Hesseth asked him. 'What she said.'

He looked at the girl – and discovered that he, too, was afraid. Was it truly her power that was wild, or was that a manifestation of her own unstable nature? Was there any safe way to distinguish between the two?

'About what?'

'His children. Not killing them all.'

He squeezed his eyes shut. 'I don't know. The Church says . . . I don't know, Hesseth.' Then he looked toward the door, so recently shut behind the Hunter, and muttered, 'I'd better go after him.'

'Damien—'

'He's right, we can't waste time here.' *And we can't let our party fall apart now, not when we're almost within striking distance of the enemy.*

He grabbed up his jacket and started toward the door, but her voice stopped him.

'That was tidal fae, Damien.'

He turned back, aware that his expression was one of utter disbelief.

'Are you sure?'

She nodded.

'But humans can't—' He couldn't finish. The mere thought of it was too incredible.

'Maybe now they can,' she said quietly. She had drawn the child to her again, was stroking the long dark hair with half-sheathed claws. 'Maybe your species is adapting to this world at last. Once upon a time your people couldn't see or work the earth-fae at all; now human adepts take those skills for granted. Maybe the fae *can* alter humans, after all – but only slowly, over the course of generations.'

A chill ran up his spine. If the fae was capable of changing humanity like it changed the native species . . . he looked at Hesseth's half-human form, at her oh-so-human features, and shivered. What if *adaptation* to this world meant giving up the very things that made them human? What if the price of universal Sight was the loss of their human heritage?

He couldn't afford to think about that. Now now. That was a whole new domain of fear, and he had enough to deal with. He reached for his sword, then decided not to take it. Too conspicuous. He grabbed up a hunting knife instead and tucked it inside his sleeve, where no stranger would notice it. 'Keep her in here,' he warned. 'Keep her quiet.'

'Don't leave me,' the girl whispered.

He looked at her – and knew then and there that Tarrant was right, that the risk involved in taking her with them was incalculable, that she might well cost them all their lives . . . but she knew the way. She had seen the Black Lands. Wasn't it less risky to take her along than to go on that journey blind, feeling their way along trap by trap, danger by danger? Suddenly he didn't know. Suddenly he wasn't sure of anything.

'I'll be back,' he muttered. And he shut the door firmly behind him as he committed himself to the Hunter's trail.

Cool night. Heavy air, dank with the smell of fish and mildew and human refuse. He breathed in deeply, as if somehow he could catch the Hunter's scent. A whore stumbled past him, muttering a drunken apology as she banged her shoulder against a brick wall. A young man came over to help her and they moved off together, laughing at some crude sexual innuendo he had improvised. *The life of the city,* Damien mused. Any city. In the end they were all the same.

He leaned back against the coarse brick of the hotel's facade, all too aware of how well he fit in with the natives here. *I'll buy a clean shirt first thing in the morning,* he promised himself, fingering one spot on his elbow where the heavy linen was wearing through. *Clean pants. A change of underwear.*

God! What a sad luxury . . .

When he was sure that no one was watching him, he relaxed against the building, half-shutting his eyes as he fought to concentrate. Although there was a channel established between him and Tarrant, he had never before tried to access it, or to use it for his own purposes. On a certain level it bothered him to do so, for there was certainly an unspoken agreement between himself and the Hunter that neither of them would use that channel for a Working except by mutual agreement. *To hell with that,* he thought grimly. He tried to sense that tenuous link, tried to grab hold of it with his mind and lend it some real solidity. It wasn't easy. A channel wasn't a thing in itself, simply a path of least resistance for the fae to follow. It took him some time to figure out what it felt like and an even longer time to become sensitive to its messages. *Where is he?* he demanded of it. Trying to sense its strength, its direction, its tenor. *How far?* He received no answer in words, nor in images as such, but had a vague feeling of which way to go. Good enough. He started off down the narrow street, and just in time; a head peeking out of a third-floor window warned him that he had been noticed, and no doubt if he had stayed in place a few minutes longer some kind of local policeman would have stopped by to see what he wanted. And that . . .

Would have been the end of it, he thought. Chilled by the image the Hunter had raised, of a whole city primed for ambush. If they didn't get out of here soon, he realized, they might never get out of here at all.

He followed Tarrant's trail through the heart of the slums, feeling the flow of earth-fae along the channel that bound them and guiding his steps by its direction. Past the crowded slums of the city's center, past the tightly packed houses of its outer districts, past the wider lawns and white-washed walls of a richer residential neighborhood at its border . . . at first he was afraid that the Hunter might have gone out to kill, to slake his fury in a brutal bloodletting, but now he knew better. If Tarrant had gone this far without feeding, then he was after something else. Escape. Solitude. Silence within and without him, in which to gather his thoughts. In which to regain control.

There were wraiths outside the city borders as well as more solid demonlings, enough of the latter to make him sorry that he hadn't brought his sword along. The price of traveling with Tarrant (he thought as he dispatched one particularly nasty winged thing, which had managed to dig its claws into his shoulder before he gutted it with a backswipe of the hunting knife) was that you tended to forget such things existed. They sure as hell didn't manifest in the Hunter's presence.

Which was how he found Tarrant, eventually. Like a child playing warm-and-cold, he went in the direction where the creatures seemed most scarce, until he came to a place where there were none at all. A few steps more brought him over a broken ridge, to a place where a steep mound of boulders lay piled against a vertical wall of sheer granite. Tarrant stood at the pinnacle of the mound, his dark nature devouring the night's power before any wraith or demonling could make use of it. In the distance, barely visible from that vantage point, the sea cast white-capped waves against a jagged granite island; in the stillness of the night it was just possible to hear the surf.

When the Hunter made no move to descend, Damien sheathed his knife and climbed up after him. When he reached the top, the Hunter didn't look at him, or otherwise stir to acknowledge his presence, but he said – very softly – 'Your shoulder is infected.'

With a soft curse Damien sat, and he worked a quick Healing to cleanse and close his wounds.

The delicate nostrils flared, sifting the night air for scents. 'The rest of the blood?'

'Just scratches,' Damien assured him. Then: 'There's a lot of nasty stuff in this region.'

'Local constructs can't feed inside the city. Therefore they gather outside the gates and wait for food to come to them.'

His eyes remained fixed on the south. Looking for signs of the enemy, or simply watching the sea? His profile, outlined against the moonlight, was a chill and perfect mask. So utterly controlled, Damien thought. Every hair in place. Every inch of skin spotless and smooth. And cold, so cold. No wonder mere sunlight could kill him.

'Is it true?' Damien asked quietly.

'What?'

'What she said about your children. That you didn't kill them all.'

His voice was a whisper, hardly louder than the breeze. 'Don't you know?'

'I thought I did. Now I wonder.'

'What do the Church's texts say?'

'That you killed your family. Murdered your children and dismembered your wife. Just that.'

'*Just* that,' he repeated softly. As if the phrase amused him.

'Is it?' he pressed.

The Hunter sighed. 'My oldest son was gone that night. Staying at a neighbor's, as I recall. I didn't consider his presence important enough to justify my going after him.'

'The other deaths were enough for you.'

The pale eyes fixed on him, sparkling like cracked ice in the moonlight. 'They were enough to establish my compact,' he said. 'That was all I required.'

'And that's it?'

He looked away again, gazed at the distant sea. 'That's it, priest. The whole story. You may add it to your texts, if you like. No doubt the Church will benefit from the correction.'

For a moment he could hardly respond, just stood there in amazement. Then: 'You're full of shit, you know that?' When the Hunter said nothing, he pressed, 'You're asking me to believe that one of your children *just happened to be elsewhere* that night? The most important Working of your whole damned life and you didn't plan it well enough to keep all your victims together?' He spat on the stony ground. 'How gullible do you think I am?'

The Hunter chuckled darkly. 'So you tell me.'

'I think you wanted him alive. I think that vanity is your one weakness, and this time you couldn't let go. The Tarrant line was something you'd created and you couldn't resist the temptation to see what he would do with it all – the land, the power, the title – once you were gone. No mercy involved, Hunter – just another one of your precious experiments, to add to all the others.' When Tarrant didn't respond, he pressed, 'Well? Am I right?'

The silver eyes fixed on him – disdainful, forbidding. 'Why did you come here?' he demanded.

He answered quietly, 'Hesseth says the girl's using the tidal fae.'

He heard Tarrant's response, an indrawn hiss. 'So. Humanity adapts to that power, at last.'

'You don't sound very surprised.'

'Longevity gives one a special perspective, Reverend Vryce. I was born in an era when adepts were rare, and I've watched their ranks increase with each new generation. Yet few of us have children of our own, and the Sight is rarely inherited. So what other explanation is there? This planet is changing us, bringing us in line with all the native species. But the tidal fae . . . that's something else entirely.'

He shook his head, folding his arms across his chest. It was a strangely human gesture. Strangely vulnerable. 'That night . . .' he whispered.

Damien didn't have to ask which night. There was only one that mattered.

'I thought that night . . . if our enemy were Iezu . . . dear God.' Tarrant's self-embrace tightened as he leaned back against the rock behind him. Remembering? 'We had no chance, you understand. Not against one of that clan. Not against a demon who could turn our own senses against us.' He drew in a deep breath, slowly. 'So I thought . . .'

The words trailed off into silence. In the distance surf rumbled, and the distant roar of thunder warned of a storm closing in. Or passing by.

'No good,' he whispered. 'It's no good.'

'What?'

Tarrant shook his head. Lightning shot over the ocean, a distant spark. 'I thought there wasn't a demon I couldn't handle in open combat, but a Iezu . . . that changes all the rules.'

'What you're saying is that we need the girl.'

Slowly, as if every word were being weighed and considered before it was spoken, he answered, 'Her vision is extraordinary, and seems to pierce through Iezu illusion. I suppose that if we were to continue our intended course, then one might believe we could benefit from that.'

'Which means what?' he demanded. The compound conditionals made his head spin. 'She comes, or no?'

'If you wish,' the Hunter whispered.

And that was so unlike him that Damien just stopped speaking altogether and stared at the man. Wondering why his sudden complacency scared him more than all the threats, all the anger. Wondering why he suddenly had the sinking feeling that the very rules he'd been playing by had been changed, only no one would tell him what the new rules were. Or when they had been instituted.

'Your call, Reverend Vryce.' Lightning flashed across the southern sky. 'It's your expedition, your quest . . . your call.'

Thunder rumbled across the sea.

'All right,' Damien said. 'We take her with us. And since it's the tidal fae she's using, maybe Hesseth can teach her how to control it.'

'The rakh can't Work for strangers,' Tarrant reminded him. 'Otherwise Hesseth could serve us herself, and we wouldn't need the child at all. As I recall, the plains rakh can only Work for their own kin.'

He thought of the small girl nestled against Hesseth's fur, of the long claws cleaning and combing her hair with loving precision. 'Somehow I don't think that'll be a problem.'

More lightning flashed. Damien counted eight seconds, then thunder rumbled. The storm was moving in.

'I told you where to find Ran Moskovan,' the Hunter told him, 'and I can tell you what the odds are that he'll help us, without turning us in. Not much more than that.'

'The time you wrote down. That's for tonight?'

'That, or tomorrow. Your choice. After that he'll be gone.'

For *gone,* read *south.* The enemy's turf.

'Two days,' he muttered. Already it seemed too long to be staying in this place. He looked up at Tarrant and asked him, 'Alone?'

'Your call, Reverend Vryce.'

The priest sighed. 'You know, you were a lot easier to deal with when you were nasty.'

It seemed to him that the Hunter smiled. 'You'd better start back now, priest. There's rain coming, in quantity.' As if in illustration of his point a bright spear of lightning cut across the sky. Thunder followed almost immediately.

'Gerald.'

Startled by his use of the familiar address, the Hunter looked down at him.

The words caught in his throat; he had to force them out. 'If you really think we can't win here . . . if you think there's *no chance at all* . . . then tell me. In those words.'

'And then what? You'll give it up and go home?'

'I came here to risk my life for a cause. Not to waste it away in some suicidal exercise. That benefits no one.' He waited for a response, but when the Hunter was not forthcoming he pressed, 'I may not care much for your lifestyle, but I do value your judgment. You know that. So if you tell me that we don't have a chance of success here – not any chance at all – I'll reconsider our mission.'

'And turn back?'

'Well . . .' He coughed. 'Let's say I'd look for some other way to attack this mess.'

Silence.

'Well?'

'There is a chance,' the Hunter whispered. 'A very slim chance, but it's there. And the girl's presence might cost you dearly, but it will also confound your enemies. Only time can tell whom that will serve most in the end.'

He felt something unknot deep in his gut, something cold and hard and – yes – scared. For the first time in several long minutes he dared to draw in a deep breath. 'That's enough, then.' Who would have thought such a tenuous judgment could give him such a sense of relief? 'Thank you.'

A cold drop hit him on the head then, and another on his arm. The faint patter of raindrops sounded from nearer the shore, coming their way.

He almost didn't ask it. Almost.

'How much did they offer?'

A raindrop splattered on the light brown hair. 'Ten thousand for you, Reverend Vryce. Five thousand for Mes Hesseth. Two thousand for any other poor soul who happened to be accompanying you at the time the reward was claimed.'

He thought of the child and his stomach tightened. 'Dead? Alive? What?'

'Only dead,' the Hunter said quietly. 'They have, as you see, no interest in detaining you. Only in removing you from the picture.' The pale eyes fixed on him. 'You'd better start back now. It's a long walk, and there's rain coming.'

'And you?'

'I can take care of myself,' he assured him. And added, somewhat soberly, 'I always do.'

But Damien didn't move right away. For a moment he just stayed where he was, watching the man. Wondering at the past that Tarrant had revealed to him.

His descendants may still be alive, he realized. *A whole Tarrant clan, sired by this demonic pride, baptised in sacrificial slaughter. Dear God! To live and die under such a shadow . . . What would that do to a child, to come home and face such a thing? What mark would it leave on the generations that followed? I shiver just to think of it.*

Then the rain came down in earnest, and he quickly scrambled down the slippery rocks to more solid ground. Tarrant was invisible behind a veil of water, lost in the glistening darkness. If he was there at all. If he hadn't somehow found shelter in that last dry instant.

Like I should have done, Damien chided himself, as he started the long, wet walk back to his companions.

32

The Matria of Esperanova didn't like to keep her Regent waiting. The other humans were only so much flotsam to her – she would leave them waiting for hours without a second thought – but this Regent was a special case. She had carefully nurtured their relationship down through the years, and now she had no doubt that if a puddle suddenly appeared in front of her, he would throw himself down bodily in the mud and the water so that, by treading on his back, she might keep her silk shoes dry. She even felt a vaguely maternal protectiveness toward him sometimes, like one might feel for a starving kitten, a puppy lost in the rain . . . or a pet. Yes, that's what Kinsei Donnel was. A pet.

She hated to keep him waiting, but the tides weren't being cooperative today. She had already tried twice to put on her disguise, but the sluggish tidal force wouldn't vouchsafe her enough power to whip up half a human nose, much less a whole convincing face. For many long minutes she struggled with it, and then, just as she was ready to throw up her claws in frustration, the power flickered into existence briefly in the air surrounding her. Not much, but it was good enough. She molded it with a practiced touch, and used it to weave a mask over her features that no human could see through. There wasn't enough power to mask her rakhene scent as well, but that was all right. The humans never noticed it anyway.

Frustrated by the delay, she walked quickly to her receiving chamber to welcome the Regent. Like most Matrias she kept the better part of her body hidden, swathed in the robes and headdress of her calling, and that kept the effort of disguise down to a minimum. Nevertheless, there had been times when the power had failed her utterly and she had been forced to slough her illusory features before the appointed time. Usually she had managed to get to some private space before that happened, but once a human servant had been with her and she hadn't thought to send him away until the change had already begun. She'd had him killed, of course. Some religious excuse. Heresy? Possession? She couldn't remember. The man had seen her true self emerge, and so he had died. Finita.

Human religions were so useful.

Some of the Matrias went so far as to cultivate a quasi-human appearance, tinting their facial fur to a more human shade or even shaving it off entirely. The closer you came to looking like a human in fact, the easier it was to conjure an illusion to complete the facade. But this Matria had never been able to bring herself to do it. Humanity was a repellent species, and sometimes the only thing that got her through the day was knowing that at night – in her secret locked chamber, where no human being had ever set foot – she might cast off that hated visage along with her robes and truly relax, resplendent in fur and the features that Erna had blessed her with.

And the smell, she thought, as a human servant passed by her in the hall. The sharp, sour stink of his species stung her nose, and she grimaced in distaste. *Don't forget the smell.*

Reception chamber. Small and informal, with a minimum of

religious clutter. The kind of room you used when you wanted to communicate to someone that his relationship with you had taken on a truly personal air, that he was – in your eyes – a Special Person. It was the kind of gesture that humans reveled in, and she had used it time and again as positive reinforcement for her well-trained Regent.

Stupid animals, she thought, as she opened the alteroak doors.

Kinsei Donnel was inside waiting, and as usual there was no surprise involved in greeting him. Familiar eyes in a nondescript face, faintly bovine. Limpid expression, also bovine. A faint aura of excitment about him today, which she could have read if the power were stronger. That intrigued her; Esperanova's Regent rarely got excited.

'Kinsei,' she purred.

He came to her and dropped to one knee, that he might kiss her hand in adoration. 'Your Holiness.'

'This is an unexpected surprise.' He got to his feet slowly and clumsily, not unlike a cow who had been knocked over in its sleep. 'What brings you here?'

The limpid eyes glittered with rare animation. 'They found them,' he told her. 'Here. In Esperanova.'

'Who?'

'The strangers. From Mercia. The *westerners,*' he clarified, voicing the title with awe.

She felt her heartbeat quicken, and her claws unsheathed reflexively; she was glad that the same illusion which guarded her face would mask that extremity as well. 'Tell me.'

'Selkirst found them. You remember him, freelance out of Justa? Seems he staked out the moneychangers and a couple of jewelers, figuring if the westerners came here they'd need some local cash. Because they'd lost a horse in Kierstaad, he explained, and maybe a third of their supplies with it. So he had his men staked out by those places, told them what to look for but not why.'

Of course, she thought dryly. *Wouldn't want to share the reward with them.* 'Go on.'

'He saw the priest. That is, one of his men did. He fit the description and all, real travel-worn, bearded but otherwise just like your posting said. The man followed him from a jeweler's to a hunting supply, then to a grocery. Checked up on his purchases later, and they all fit the profile. Dried stuff, high-cal nutrient supplements and such. Vitamins.'

'Weapons?'

He shook his head. 'Clothing, mostly. Mess kit, field razor, canteen. Travel gear.'

With effort she made her claws retract. 'Verda,' she whispered. 'So it's our city, is it? Verda ben. We're ready for them.'

'Do you want me to pick them up?'

'Was the woman with him?'

His brow furrowed deeply as he thought about that. 'No. I don't think so.'

'What about the horses?'

He hesitated; clearly neither he nor his informant was too sure what a *horse* was. 'I don't think so, Holiness.'

She managed to suppress her growing irritation. 'Where is he now?'

'Selkirst said he was staying at a hotel in the tenderloin. *Budget Hourly*. His men are watching the place. But . . .'

He seemed to hesitate then, so she urged him, 'Go on.'

'It's just . . . he said they questioned the proprietor. To find out if the woman was there, to confirm it. But it was odd, he said. Like the man didn't even know who was staying there.'

'Given the establishment,' she said dryly, 'that's no great surprise.' But even as she spoke the words, she felt something deep inside herself tighten – something primitive and bestial and very, very hungry. *Our prey is a sorcerer,* she told herself. And: *That makes the hunt more interesting.*

She had hunted a human once, in the Black Lands, long before she came north for this assignment. Sometimes she sorely missed those days. The freedom. The exhilaration. The sharp scent of hatred stirring free her rakhene blood. And now the fugitives were here, in Esperanova. Her city. It was a pale shadow of that former hunt, but it was the best she was going to get. Her claws flexed at the thought.

'All right,' she said. 'Get your people on it. Have them put the building under watch, twenty-four hours a day. But no move is to be made while the man's inside, ken verda? It's vital.'

'I understand,' he said. His expression said that yes, he'd obey, but no, he didn't really understand.

'We need them *both*, Kinsei. The woman, too. If we take the man now and she isn't with him . . .' *You can't break a sorcerer for information,* an inner voice warned. *Not with claws.*

No, she answered. *But you can have fun trying.* 'If she's not with him, then follow him. Discreetly. I want them both.'

'And if she is?'

'Instruct your men to wait until they're out in the open. I don't want any innocent bystanders hurt. Wait for open ground, then strike.'

'You want them taken?'

'I want them *killed,* Kinsei. I want their bodies brought here. I want to see proof of their death with my own eyes.'

He coughed raggedly. 'What if . . . there are others?'

'Besides the priest and the woman?'

'Yeah. What if there's someone else with them?'

She smiled then, remembering an Earth saying that she had once heard. From one of Earth's many religious wars. It had stuck in her mind ever since, a sterling sample of human reasoning.

'Their God will know His own,' she purred. 'Let Him sort them out.'

33

They left before sunset. The tides wouldn't be right for travel until well after dusk – so Moskovan assured them – but Damien wanted to get moving while the daylight crowds were still in the streets. This city might be relatively free of faeborn dangers, but its people generally still kept to a daylight schedule. Human instinct. It would certainly play in their favor now; crowded city streets offered a cover that no mere Working could rival. No matter how well it was worked, an Obscuring was only as effective as the environment allowed. And as Damien's teachers had never ceased to stress, it was far easier to get yourself lost in the multiple distractions of a crowd than it was to conjure up invisibility when there wasn't a distraction in sight.

Not that he'd been able to Work much anyway. There had been tremors only an hour ago, barely strong enough to feel – but the fae had been like wildfire when he'd tried to use it, and he'd had to back off before the job was really perfect. If only they'd had another hour to let the power cool down, to resume its accustomed course . . . but there was no point in complaining about that now. You made do with what you had when you had it, and tried to be grateful for all the times that the fae had been workable when you needed it most.

Tarrant could have Worked it, he thought. But there was still enough light in the sky that Tarrant couldn't possibly join them yet. God alone knew where he was, or what manner of shelter he currently occupied. Damien found himself praying that the Hunter was safe. Without shame this time, and without regret. Because while they had little chance of success in their mission as things stood right now, they would have no chance at all without the Hunter's power behind them.

They hurried down the narrow streets, trying to match the pace of the crowd, anxious to get where they were going. The girl struggled along beside them, her hand entwined in Hesseth's, her face pale and drawn. It said much for her courage that she was doing as well as she was; Damien knew that the sounds and sensations which accosted her were nigh on overwhelming, and that it took all her strength to shut them out and keep going. So far she was doing well enough. Soon they would be out of this crime-ridden district and in a quieter quarter, and perhaps that would help. He hoped so, for her sake. He could almost feel her pain.

Then he heard Hesseth hiss softly beside him, a sound meant for his ears and his ears only. Without breaking stride or looking directly at her, he whispered, 'What is it?'

'Footsteps. Behind us. Matching our pace. They've been there for a while,' she added.

Damien took a minute to listen. The noise of the crowd about them was chaotic – workers traipsing home for the night, mothers screaming at dawdling children, conversational snippets appearing and disappearing on all sides of them – and he found that his merely human ears couldn't focus on the one noise he wanted. He braced himself and muttered the key to a Working. Power surged up through his body with such force that he wondered if he might not have taken on more than he could handle, but a moment later it subsided; the earth-fae released by the tremors was quieting down at last.

He made sure that his feet kept moving while he fashioned the Knowing, careful not to break his stride. Such a Working did not require total immersion in the currents, which gave him some hope of managing it. Carefully, gingerly, he touched his will to the surging earth-fae. Barely brushing its surface with his thoughts, but that was enough: the power was like wildfire. He tried to Work it, focusing on sound rather than vision, to detect that one special rhythm which Hesseth had noted. He heard Jenseny gasp as the Working took shape – clearly she could feel it happening – but a hand on her shoulder was enough to warn her to stay quiet. She was learning.

Now he heard it. Not one pair of footsteps but two, perhaps ten yards back from them. His Knowing broke down the rhythms of the crowd into several ordered patterns, and he could hear how much those two stood out. Too fast. Too hard. Too determined, for this meandering crowd. He slowed down a bit, motioned for Hesseth to follow suit. The footsteps kept their distance. He speeded up – gradually, hoping they wouldn't note the deliberate pattern in his movements – and they speeded up also, so that they were neither closer nor farther behind. At last he exhaled heavily and let the Knowing fade.

'Damien?' the rakh-woman whispered.

'We're in trouble,' he whispered back.

They were coming out of the tenderloin district now, into an area of nicer housing and wider streets. It was a good bet the crowds would thin out here, leaving them without that precious shield. That's what their pursuers were waiting for, he realized. An open field, devoid of innocent targets. A clean line of fire.

'God of Earth,' he muttered. And he steered them eastward, even as he prayed.

Not now, he thought feverishly. *Please. Not like this. We have too much to do. Please don't let them stop us now.*

If he had prayed to a pagan god, perhaps it would have answered. Perhaps, for a favored son, it would have staged a truly divine rescue, complete with pyrotechnics and a choir of demons. Certainly Tarrant's Iezu seemed to have the power and the temperament to stage such a thing. But the price of changing the world through faith was that one had to forgo such convenient spectacles, and it was with heavy heart and a trembling hand that Damien steered his companions away from their intended path, into the heart of the factory district.

Here long, featureless buildings housed the manpower that had made Esperanova a city to be reckoned with. Here young men and women – and sometimes children, despite the labor laws – picked among baskets of freshly prospected gems, choosing those whose color or brilliance held especial promise. Here slender hands refined the stones one by one, not only the larger, prouder specimens but rubies as fine as dust, diamonds as delicate as powder. For some techniques only a child's hand would do; those of an adult were simply too large and clumsy to manage the requisite manipulation. In other buildings precious metals were melted, blended, and cast into myriad decorative forms for sale in the northern cities. Fine steel blades were forged and whetted. Wood was whittled into furniture as smooth as glass. Esperanova's wealth was based upon her labor force, and the western quarter of the city was a maze of factory complexes, large and small. All of which, without exception, would soon be closing for the night.

The streets were almost empty when they arrived, which was good cause for panic. He had taken a chance in coming here – a big one – and for a moment he feared he had gambled too much. He could almost feel Hesseth's eyes on him as he guided them through the labyrinthine district, questioning his purpose in bringing them to such a place. Maybe even questioning his sanity. For a short while he wondered about that himself, as he herded his party from street to street, trying to avoid those streets and alleys which were truly deserted. It was getting harder and harder.

And then, without warning, a whistle split the dusky air. He felt Jenseny's hand tense up in his own, and he squeezed it once in reassurance. For a moment he could only wait, praying that his assessment of the situation was sound. The people surrounding them had thinned out long minutes ago, which meant there wasn't much cover left. Already he could feel the back of his neck begin to crawl, as if in response to some springbolt or firearm which was aimed at that spot—

Then they came. In twos and threes at first, and then in a herd. A swarm. Women and children and young boys and older men, red-eyed and tired and anxious to wend their way through the maze of factory streets, until they got to wherever home might be. A boundless, shapeless mass of people, who comprised by their mere presence the greatest Obscuring of all. He exhaled heavily in relief as the crowd enveloped them, sensing the potential for safety in their numbers. He felt Jenseny tense as all those new psyches battered her, as she shared their memories and their fears and . . . who knew what else? He made sure he had a firm hold on her hand and dragged her forward, muttering a key under his breath as he did so. It was hard to concentrate in the midst of such a stampede, but he had no illusions about the task: his very life depended on it. And so he wove a Working even while strangers shouldered into him from the right and the left, even while he had to pull Jenseny close against him to keep the flood tide of humanity from sweeping her away, even while he had to watch for Hesseth's coiffed head and make sure that it, too, was within safe distance.

He needed an Obscuring. A powerful Obscuring, that drew on the very nature of human distraction for its strength. For while a single grain of sand might be observed upon a granite plain (his teacher would have argued), in the midst of a sand dune it was all but invisible. So it would be with them, now. If Damien could hold onto the power – if he could channel it right – they should be able to distract their pursuers long enough to lose them. *Nothing obscures a clear trail,* Damien's teacher would have insisted, *better than a thousand other footprints.* He hoped to hell the man was right.

The earth-fae was still hot, shrill to the touch, hard to mold. He felt an unaccustomed sweat break out on his forehead as he plunged into it, struggling to break it to his will. It would have been difficult under the best of curcumstances; done while walking, knocked about by this indifferent crowd, it was all but impossible. Once Hesseth had to urge him forward with a touch in order to keep him moving; he had instinctively turned inside himself as sorcerers were wont to do, shutting out all awareness not directly connected to his Working. Such behavior was a luxury here and now, and he was glad she had awakened him. Already several of the people nearby were looking at him strangely, which was the last thing he needed. He picked up his pace again, letting the motion of the crowd carry him along. No time now to focus on footsteps, or wonder where those two pair were; it took all he had to concentrate on the flow of the earth-power, to wrestle it into subservience. And then . . . yes. There it was. The current shifted itself beneath his touch and began to reform. He held his breath, trying to stabilize it. A child running through the crowd barreled into his legs, but he barely felt it; his Working was the only thing real to him, the hot earth-fae and the dripping sweat and the pain that lanced through his limbs like needles as he struggled to tame the wild power that flowed about his feet. He no longer even knew if he was walking, and he barely knew where he was; only the power mattered now, the surging flow which the quakeling had released. Only the Obscuring mattered.

And then it was done. He let his Vision fade – and staggered for a moment, blinded by its afterimage. Hesseth tried to pull him along, but he put out a hand to stop her, and he caught up the child before the crowd could sweep her away.

'It's done,' he gasped. He nodded toward the nearest wall. 'Get out. Now.'

She understood immediately, and together they managed to get themselves and the child over to the wall, and away from press of flesh. Jenseny was shivering, clearly terrified, but at least she was still with them. Still standing. That was something, wasn't it?

Damien leaned against the brick wall and breathed deeply, trying to calm himself. It was done. It had worked. Any minute now their pursuers would be passing them by, eyes fixed firmly on the crowds ahead, unaware that their prey had turned aside. And then they would be safe for a while. Maybe long enough. One could only hope.

'What did you do?' the girl whispered. Frightened to speak but too curious to remain silent. 'What happened?'

'I caused them to be distracted,' he whispered back. He probably could have spoken aloud in utter safety, but why push his luck? 'When they try to see us, they'll wind up watching other people, until it's too late.'

'How long will it last?' Hesseth asked.

He sighed, and rubbed his temples. 'Long enough. If we keep to crowded areas, we should be able to make it to the harbor unnoticed; that much'll stay with us.'

'And then?'

He shut his eyes and allowed himself the luxury of a long, deep breath. An Obscuring like this was a touchy thing, and a thousand and one variables affected it. But one thing mattered more than any other. One single element could be their undoing.

'That depends,' he said quietly, 'on if they're expecting us.'

Night falling. Harbor shadowed. Perfect time for an ambush.

'There they are.'

From behind the bulk of a storage shed – corrugated tin, mottled with rust – the Regent's soldiers took the measure of their prey. Tucked away in the shadow of the shed they were nearly invisible. Perfect.

'Now?' A soldier whispered, but their leader shook his head: No. Not yet.

There were few enough people on the wharf now that it was possible to make out the strangers clearly. The priest, coarsely dressed, with no sign of rank or vocation other than the sturdy sword harnessed across his back. The woman, lithe and mysterious, swathed in such layers of wool as were reserved for church tradition. And a child, thin and fearful, whose dark eyes swept over the piers again and again, as if searching for something to be afraid of. Her thick dark hair coiled like snakes over her shoulder, and she twisted its ends in her fingers as she gazed at shadows of the harbor.

'Who's the kid?' Charrel demanded, his voice a hoarse whisper in the darkness.

'Doesn't matter,' their leader told him. 'You know our orders.'

They began to move. Slowly at first, like pack animals testing the ground for solidity. Slipping from shadow to shadow, silent as men could be, their dark clothing all but invisible in the thick, gloomy dusk. Their quarry hadn't seen them yet, which was good. If they could manage to surround them before they responded—

And then the child looked at them. Straight at them, her dark eyes piercing through the shadows like lances. Her mouth fell open and she trembled violently, momentarily unable to respond to what she had seen. It would only last an instant, the leader guessed, and he was gesturing for one of his men to fire just as a family group wandered across the wharf, fouling the line of fire. He cursed under his breath and hissed, 'Fan out! Contain them!' Even as the girl moved. Even as she warned her companions about the danger that was closing in on them, and they began to run.

Damn! The officer thought, holding his weapon close to his side as he moved out into the open. Running now, his hand clenched tightly about the pistol's grip. *Damn!* The people on the wharf got out of his way when they saw him coming – as they'd damned well better – but it wasn't soon enough, it couldn't possibly be soon enough, the fugitives were running toward the nearest crowd and would soon be lost among them, damn it!

And then he saw one of his men cut them off, herding them back into the open. The child stumbled, and the priest caught her up in his arms. That slowed them. They were approaching a part of the harbor where business was slow, and the crowds that had served them as shelter were thinning. The leader pushed his way by an old woman, nearly trampling a child in his haste. The Regent had said that the fugitives would be boarding a free merchanter, but that wasn't the direction they were heading in now; he could only assume that the Regent's source of intelligence had been mistaken, that they hoped to make it to one of the great passenger ships docked at the west end of the harbor, now drawing in their gangplanks to catch the departing tide. *Well, you won't get there,* he swore silently, and he pushed for even greater speed. *You won't get past this harbor alive.*

And then there was an opening. Charrel had the clearest shot, and fired first; a crossbow quarrel lanced across the space between them and speared through the child's thigh. She spasmed in the priest's arm and screamed, and for a moment it seemed to her pursuer that a brilliant light, blood-red, enveloped her body. Then an elderly couple moved out of the way – at last! – and he fired, he held up the pistol and pulled on the trigger and felt the explosive power take root in his hand, to send death plummeting through the air with a force no crossbow could rival. The soft lead pellet missed the priest by inches but took the woman in her side, and she fell; red blood exploded across the white of her robe as she fell to her knees, and

—and—

—and—

His vision wavered. He staggered as though struck, dimly aware that sorcery was the cause. Trying to fight the effect. It seemed to him that the three figures were blurring, as in a drawing whose edges had been erased. Giving up their color, their form, to meld into the twilight. He shook his head desperately, hoping that his men were holding on. He couldn't lose them now, not when they were so close to triumph. He squinted into the shadowy air as he lined up the second pellet in the gun's chamber, as he aligned the second priming. It wasn't that they were becoming invisible, so much as ... changing. Yes. That was it. The girl's dark hair becoming a tangle of blond curls, the priest's formidable bulk shrinking to the middle-aged potbelly of a henpecked bureaucrat, the woman's robe becoming mere housewife's garb, blood-spattered ...

'My God,' he whispered.

And he lowered his gun.

And he stared.

They were cringing now, terrified of him and his men, but they needn't have been. Not now. Because he knew in his gut as he gazed at them that these faces were the real ones. Not what he had seen before. Not what he had fired at.

He looked about wildly, as if somewhere on the wharf an explanation would be waiting. What he saw, in the distance, was a merchanter setting sail. White canvas leaves dropping to catch the wind, angled sails billowing in the stiff southerly breeze. He struggled to make out the flag that topped the mizzenmast, and when he did he cursed. He knew that symbol, all too well. He had studied it in the Regent's chamber only hours before.

'What is it?' came a voice at his shoulder. One of his men. 'What happened?'

He turned back, saw one of his soldiers tending to the wounded. Trying to comfort the innocent victims, in a voice that must be shaking with fear. He felt that fear himself, like a knot in his gut.

'We vulked up,' he muttered. 'We vulked it up good.'

In the distance, safely out of reach, the *Desert Queen* made for the open sea.

Not until they were safely out of the harbor did Damien feel the knot in his own gut loosen up. Not until the lights of the city were so low on the horizon that a passing wave might swallow them up, and the granite arms that reached out from the mainland to the harbor were all but invisible in the fading light, did he feel that he could relax.

Soft golden Corelight washed over the deck as he made his way to where Tarrant stood and it picked out jeweled highlights on the water beyond. About and above them the sailors scurried to make the most of what the wind had to offer, and Damien had no doubt that if the wind held in their favor the *Desert Queen* was capable of outrunning – and probably outmaneuvering – any possible pursuit. Wasn't that the one capacity a smuggler needed most?

'I can't believe we made it,' Hesseth was saying as he joined them. The girl was by her side, her arm around the rakh-woman's waist. 'I can't believe there was no one watching for us.'

'They were watching,' Tarrant said quietly.

Damien looked up at him – delicate profile haloed in gold, eyes as dark and as secretive as the sea – and demanded, 'So what happened?'

The Hunter shrugged; his eyes remained fixed on the sea. 'They must have been misled, somehow.' A faint smile ghosted across his lips, then was gone. 'Perhaps they followed the wrong trail. Perhaps they attacked the wrong people.'

A cold, sick feeling stirred in Damien's gut. He had to force the word out. 'Simulacra?'

'Perhaps,' the Hunter murmured.

Sickness transmuted into sudden anger. He grasped the man by the arm, closing his finger angrily about flesh no warmer than ice. 'Do we have to leave a trail of blood behind us?' he demanded. 'Does every victory have to cost some innocent his life?'

The dark eyes turned on him with gentle disdain. 'You've made your feeling on that point rather clear, Reverend Vryce.' With his free hand he plucked Damien's own from his arm, handling it like one would a child's. 'As it happened, I didn't kill them. Nor do I think that our enemies will. I gave them, as you would have wanted, a fair chance. Even though that increased the risk to us all.'

For a moment Damien was utterly speechless. 'But . . . if the enemy thinks they're us—'

'That illusion faded as soon as we were safely under sail, priest. Not the safety margin I would have preferred, but obviously it will have to do.'

He turned to go then – to seek out some private niche on the tiny vessel, no doubt, some shadow he could claim for himself – but Damien challenged him, 'You spared their lives?'

The Hunter turned back to him; a sparkle of dry humor glinted in his eyes. 'In all probability, yes.'

'For what reason?' He couldn't imagine Tarrant motivated by human compassion.

'For the best of reasons,' the Neocount assured him. 'Because I knew that if they died I would have to spend the better part of this voyage hearing about it.' And he added, with gentle maliciousness, 'Verda?'

34

The Sea of Dreams, it was called.

It was dark. It was cold. It was turbulent and deadly. Eastern and western waters met with a clash above a sea floor studded with mounts and mountains, driven by a system of tides that revealed new hazards with every passing hour. Or concealed them, just as swiftly. In places there were obstacles so close to the surface that the currents parted around them, rippling with whitewater ferocity. In others there were pools where chance had turned the currents aside, so that in the midst of chaos one might find a circle of water as smooth as glass, a surreal arrangement that might last only seconds, or perhaps as long as hours. It was rumored that somewhere in the midst of the Sea of Dreams lay a vast pool of untroubled water, where even the wind had ceased to blow. After more than an hour on board the *Desert Queen,* Damien was ready to believe it.

Here the Novatlantic Ocean, fifty feet higher than its eastern neighbor, plunged through the rocky gap which nature had supplied, dashing its waves upon numerous obstacles as it churned its way east. Here the cold currents of the antarctic region met the warm waters of the tropics with whirlpool ferocity, raising a mist that gathered about the peaked granite islands, hiding them from sight. Here there was a path from north to south that might be sailed, but only by men who knew these waters like the back of their hands. And then only with luck, and only when the tides permitted.

Much to his surprise, Damien found that he had been afraid for so long now that even the sight of rocky obstacles passing mere yards from the bow wasn't enough to upset him. In the face of what they were up against – and how long they had been fleeing – it just wasn't enough to upset him. Besides, he had been through

Novatlantis, which was a journey ten times longer than this and easily ten times as turbulent. If he had made it through that terrible trip without panicking, he could certainly manage to make it through this one.

Moskovan had given the option of remaining below, but not one of them had taken him up on it. Now they watched as barren islands, knife-edged in the moonlight, passed mere yards away to port and starboard. They watched as the sea gathered itself into an impromptu whirlpool between two islands, then suddenly dispersed. As the Novatlantic Ocean poured over some unseen obstacle to create a waterfall not ten yards high, but nearly two miles in length. It was a wondrous and terrible sea, and Damien was grateful that the man Tarrant had found to take them across it seemed eminently capable of doing so. God alone knew how many ships had been lost in those rocky depths.

If the Sea of Dreams seemed strange to the travelers, the sailors of the *Desert Queen* were even more so. Silent and somber, they maneuvered the sleek vessel through its passage with no more than short whistled signals passing between them. To Damien, who had grown accustomed to the shouts and banter of the *Glory*'s crew, their behavior seemed even stranger than the sea itself. But though there were at least a dozen questions he would have liked to ask Moskovan, the ship's owner was not available for questioning. He might take on passengers for a price, but he clearly had no interest in catering to their curiosity.

And then the last of the great islands fell behind the stern, swallowed up by mist and darkness. Ahead lay somewhat calmer water, and a promise of smoother sailing. Damien let loose of the rail he had been gripping, and as the blood rushed painfully back into his hands he acknowledged just how tightly he'd held it. God in Heaven, what he wouldn't give to be back in Jaggonath right now! Or any inland city, for that matter.

Moskovan had told them of a safer route, had even given them the option of choosing to take it. Nearly four times the length of this one, it involved sailing west into the Novatlantic, and circling wide round this turbulent sea. That course took longer but entailed little risk, and most black marketeers preferred it. As did he,

Moskovan assured them. And then he looked pointedly at Damien and added: *When I'm not being hunted*.

Whereupon Damien had made the only choice possible.

He looked back the way they had come and tried to imagine one of the Matria's ships making it through that maze of islands and whirlpools. No. The choice they'd made had been the right one, and if it cost them more money and rubbed their nerves raw, that was just the price of freedom. Money well spent, in his book.

A firm hand on his shoulder startled him; he turned around to find one of the sailors beside him. The man stepped quickly back so as not to offend and muttered, 'Captain said to stay with you.' A glance back to where Tarrant stood showed a sailor beside him also – though the adept's response looked anything but cordial – but when Damien looked for Hesseth and Jenseny, he found them nowhere to be seen. One hand moved instinctively toward his sword as he demanded, 'Where are my companions?' Suddenly aware that their greatest danger might not come from the sea.

The sailor, who had turned away to regard the sea, didn't respond. He repeated the question again, more loudly, and this time the man seemed to hear it. 'Back in the cabin. Captain suggested. Not good waters for the young, you see? Verdate,' he added, for Damien's benefit. Assuming him to be a northerner, no doubt.

The priest was about to respond when something in the distance caught his eyes. Hard to say exactly what it was; it disappeared as soon as he looked directly at it, and thus was glimpsed more by memory than by sight. A glimmering, ever so faint, that seemed to shiver beneath the waves. He had barely drawn in a breath to question the sailor when another one flashed on the sea's glassy surface – like a star this time, that glittered and bounced as it rode the waves, then disappeared from view.

'What is it?' he demanded. The sailor didn't answer, but his expression was grim. He held out something toward Damien, two small objects nestled in a weathered palm. Damien picked them up, holding them up to the moonlight so that he might see them better. Small rubber bits of irregular shape, their base perhaps as wide as his thumb. They looked like . . . earplugs? He glanced up at the sailor, saw the dull sheen of similar bits resting in the man's own ears. Yes. That explained the whistling, anyway. And the men's silence. They must all be wearing them. But why? It seemed an inconvenient accoutrement for a voyage like this.

And then one of the silvery lights came near the ship and took up station there. Perhaps five yards from the *Desert Queen*'s hull, just below the surface of the water. Another joined it. It was hard to make out their shapes through the water, hard to see them past the sheen of moonlight on the rippling surface. At times they seemed almost human in form, at others almost eellike. Their images shivered through the water like quicksilver, defying his interpretation.

'What are they?' he whispered. Forgetting that the sailor couldn't hear anything less than a shout. Two more creatures joined the first, and the four spaced themselves out along the hull with silent and perfect precision. More were coming. He could see their strange light glittering along the waves as they made their way toward the ship, eerie and beautiful beneath the glassy surface. Fascinated, Damien worked a Knowing – and only then remembered where he was. There was no earth-fae accessible here, not for him and not for them. Which meant that whatever they were, they must be wholly natural.

Incredible.

One of the creatures rose up through the water then, its silvery head rising above the glassy surface, strands of hair coiling about the waves as it rode. *How bizarre,* Damien thought, as it turned its face toward him. *And how exquisitely beautiful.* It had eyes and lips and cheekbones and nose all of a human cast, but made of a substance that rippled like mercury in the moonlight. Its eyes glistened like diamonds and strands of its long hair, cast loose upon the waves, rippled with eerie phosphorescence. They were all rising up now, some two dozen of the creatures – and perhaps there were more on the port side of the ship, who could say? – and their faces were wondrous things, delicate human sculptings that were sometimes female, sometimes male, sometimes magically androgynous. Breathtaking, all of them. Utterly mesmerizing.

They began to sing. Not with mere voices, as humans might do, but with their bodies. With their flesh. Chimes flowed from the silver skin, jarringly discordant, strangely beautiful. The thin floating hairs quivered like harp strings, and each stroke of the creatures' arms and legs – or fins? – added one more glissando to the weird harmony. Though he was dimly aware that this must be the danger the sailors were guarding against, Damien found himself unable to put the plugs in his ears to shut the sound out. It was too beautiful. Too . . . compelling.

Visions began to dance before his eyes. Wispy images at first, which became more solid as the strange music took hold in his brain. Slowly they became faces he knew, visions from his past. His mother. His brother. His Matriarch. His first lover. Ciani of Faraday, humor sparkling in her bright eyes. The *khrast*-woman Hesseth, hostile and proud. Images that had once seemed commonplace to him, but now were infused with a rare and perfect beauty. The strange sounds swam in his head, awakening his most precious memories, granting them new and vital substance within his soul.

Come to us, the voices sang. Inhuman, but somehow comprehensible to him. *Come to us, and we will give you more.*

Ciani reached out to him. Not the Ciani he had left in the rakhlands, proud and hungry and distant. The Ciani he had known and loved in Jaggonath, filtered through the veil of his longings, *needing* him in a way the new Ciani never would. 'Come to me,' she whispered. Suspended in the air just beyond the deck, but he knew that the air would support him, too. Knew that in this place, in this time, he was no more solid than she. 'Join us,' she whispered. And he felt his feet moving forward moving, his fears giving way . . .

The sailor grabbed him, jerking him back. It shouldn't have been necessary. He knew how to guard against a demon's wiles, had been drilled in the proper defensive Workings so often they should have come as second nature. *Only there are no Workings here,* he realized suddenly. The sailor was helping him put the plugs in his ears, which was good; his arms so heavy that he could hardly move them. 'Come to me,' Ciani whispered. 'Let me show you what I've found . . .' When the rubber bits were finally in place, the strange music faded abruptly, and along with it the dreamlike images. *No Workings, therefore no defense.* He wondered how Tarrant had fared. Could one demon seduce another? He glanced toward the bow, saw the Hunter standing rigid with his sword half-drawn;

icicles hung from the railing before him as the coldfire glow of a recent Working faded into the night. Which meant that he had felt the music's power. Which meant that he had feared it. Which meant that there was still enough humanity about him that some demons might consider him fair game. That was an interesting thought – and a frightening one. It certainly didn't bode well for their mission.

He could no longer hear the silver swimmers, but now he could see them clearly. What he had taken for arms and legs were slender tentacles, serpentine fins; they mimicked the rhythm of human movement in much the same way that a bit of flesh on the lip of a clam might mimic the movements of a fish. Their phosphorescence filled the water as they gathered close about the hull, frustrated and angry now that their pet enchantment had failed. Their faces, upraised, were anything but human, and their expressions were far from amiable.

He felt the footsteps without hearing them, and turned instinctively; it was Ran Moskovan, with a heavy package hoisted up onto one shoulder. The sailor who had saved Damien moved to help him, and together they lowered the bulky burden and unwrapped it. Red meat, not altogether fresh; its odor drifted to Damien on the breeze and soured his stomach as he breathed it in. Hard to say what the cut was, or what animal it had come from. But given the size and the shape of it—

'Human?' he whispered.

Artificially deafened, the two neither heard nor answered him. Together they hefted the dead weight up to the railing – and yes, it could have been a human torso once, a body that someone had sliced and gutted and then sewn shut again – and without ceremony they shoved it over into the water. It hit with a splash, and the sea-demons gave it no chance to sink. In an instant all twenty of them converged on it, and the water became a bloody, foaming mass as they ripped it to shreds. More creatures were coming now, from the far side of the ship, and fights ensued as the newcomers demanded their share. As the ship began to pull away from the seaborn battle, Damien thought he saw silver flesh being torn as well, and a dark fluid that was not human blood stained the froth in the *Desert Queen*'s wake.

They watched the fight for some minutes, until it was clear that all of the creatures were involved. Then and only then did Moskovan and his man remove their earplugs, and signal that it was safe for Damien to do the same.

'That'll hold them for a while,' Moskovan told him. 'Maybe long enough for us to make deep water.'

'What were they?' he demanded.

Moskovan shrugged. 'Who really knows? They call them sirens, after some singing demons on Earth. I call them a pain in the ass. Plugs are all right for a while, but sooner or later the music gets through. You want to keep your crew intact, the only way is to feed them.' He saw Damien's expression go dark, and easily guessed at its cause. 'Medical school leftovers,' he told him, nodding toward the spot where the meat had been thrown overboard. 'Costs a pretty penny – and it's damned hard to get hold of between semesters – but there's no other way to do it. Fish'll eat anything, but the faeborn'll only eat humans. That's a fact.'

'How can they be faeborn?' he demanded. 'How can anything faeborn live here?'

'Water's shallow in spots. Shallow enough that the power comes through – and where there's power there's demons. First law of Erna.' He gestured toward the plugs in Damien's hand. 'Next time you see the lights, you get those in fast. Or go inside and let my men lock you in. Understand?'

'No problem,' he assured him. Wondering what kind of visions the little girl had seen. Wondering if Hesseth had been affected. Wishing he had the nerve to go up to where Tarrant stood – still and silent, utterly alone – and ask what visions the sirens had awakened in him. As if the Hunter would confide in him . . . or in any man.

He sighed, and turned back to study the water. Dark now, and cleansed of blood. Cleansed – temporarily – of enchantment.

The Sea of Dreams, he mused. *Apt name.*

He'd be glad as hell when they were out of it.

The galley was narrow and low-ceilinged, which meant that for a man of Damien's size – not to mention Tarrant's height – it was markedly claustrophobic. But it had the amenities they needed: a place to sit, a modicum of privacy, and heat. In the far corner a wood stove with one burner drove back the worst of the sea's chills, and the coffeepot set atop it promised a more direct application of warmth. The coffee was bad, very bad, but at least it was hot. Damien was on his third cup.

He was seated by the stove alongside Hesseth; Gerald Tarrant stood opposite, as if disdaining their need for heat. Jenseny was at the table playing with toys the Neocount had given her: a set of playing cards with heavily decorated face cards – not Jack, Queen and King, Damien noted, but Protector, Regent, and Matria – and a small pile of twisted metal bits, each one a puzzle requiring her to join or unjoin their knotted elements. Tarrant had apparently purchased them in Esperanova for the purpose of keeping her young mind occupied, and in that way they had succeeded admirably. Damien was torn between being grateful to him for thinking of such a thing and feeling vaguely shamed that the Hunter had shown more proper paternal instinct than he had. Never mind that the Neocount had once been a family man. It was still embarrassing.

'Well?' Damien prompted. 'What next?'

'We land in the south,' Hesseth offered. Ever the practical one. 'We settle in, take our time and do some research, find out where the enemy is.'

'And *what* he is,' Damien reminded her. 'Not to mention what his connection is with the Iezu.'

Tarrant said nothing.

Quietly, setting down the coffee cup before he rose, Damien went over to where Jenseny was and sat down beside her. If he had been watching only her face, he would have thought she didn't notice him. But he was watching her hands, and he saw them tremble.

'Jenseny.' He said it gently, willing all the softness into his voice that it could possibly contain. Praying that it would be enough. 'You said you knew something about the Prince, and about the Black Lands. We need to know about those things. Will you tell us?'

She said nothing. Her hands, shaking, closed into fists. Her eyes shut tightly, as if in pain.

'*Kastareth*.' Hesseth voiced the rakhene endearment gently as she moved to join them. 'You're part of our team now, remember? We need your help.' Her gloved hand reached out and touched Jenseny's; a graceful gesture, delicate as a butterfly landing on a flower petal. 'Please, *kasa*. Help us. We need you.'

The child looked up at her, and Damien could almost feel her drawing strength from the rakh-woman's soul. Then she looked at Damien, her dark eyes searching his face for some quality he couldn't begin to define. Then, last of all, she turned to Tarrant. For once the sorcerer refrained from making an inflammatory comment. God bless him for it.

'Jenseny.' Hesseth's tone was liquid, soothing. Was there tidal power woven into those words, lending them subtle force? Damien wouldn't have been surprised if there were. 'What did your father tell you about the south? What did he see there?'

The girl blinked heavily; something that might have been a tear glittered on her lashes. 'He didn't want to hurt anyone,' she whispered. 'He thought he was doing good.'

'We know that,' Damien said gently, and Hesseth said, 'We understand.'

'He said that they'd attack the north sooner or later, and if it didn't happen for a long time, then there would be too many of them, and we wouldn't be ready, and no one would be able to stop them.' She drew in a long breath, shaking. A tear shivered free at last, and wended its way down her cheek as she spoke. 'He said the way things were going they would just take over and we wouldn't be able to do anything about it. And they would hurt us, because of how much they hated us.'

Damien asked quietly, 'And was he going to change that?'

The dark eyes fixed on him. So very frightened, Damien thought. Of their rejection, as much as of the enemy. It pained him deeply to see her like that. It pained him deeply to see any child hurting that much.

'He said,' she whispered slowly, 'that if a few of them came north – only a few – that maybe the Matrias would get scared. Maybe they would see how much danger there was and do something about it.'

'Controlled invasion,' Tarrant said quietly. 'He must have gambled that an attack on his Protectorate would motivate the northern cities into providing a more stalwart defense. Or perhaps even an offense. Perhaps he wanted to force a true war here and now, before the south was ready for it.'

'Either way he failed,' Damien said bitterly. 'How could he know that his country was already controlled by the enemy? All they needed was a place to start the invasion proper . . . and he provided that.'

'He didn't want to hurt anyone,' the girl whispered. Hesseth moved closer to her, and with a gentle arm drew her close. 'He said he had made a good deal with the Prince, and everything was going to be all right . . .'

'As it should have been,' Damien assured her. 'But evidently our enemy doesn't keep to his bargains.' He reached out gently and took one of the child's hands in his. Her skin was damp, and cool to the touch. 'We understand what your father was trying to do. And it wasn't his fault that it didn't work, Jenseny. We're not blaming him for what happened.' He wished that the fae was Workable here so that he might give the words extra weight, extra power. As it was, he had only his voice for a tool, and limited physical contact. 'He went south, didn't he, Jenseny? He went and met with the Prince to arrange all this. Did he tell you about that? Did he tell you what he saw there?'

The girl hesitated. After a moment she nodded.

'Can you tell us about it?' When she still didn't answer, he encouraged her, 'Anything you can remember.'

'Please, *kasa*,' Hesseth murmured.

The girl drew in a deep breath, shivering. 'He said that the Prince of the south never dies. He said that the Prince is very, very old, but you can't see it because he makes his body young again whenever he needs to. He said that he'll do it again soon. He'll make his body young, but he'll also make it different so that he looks like a different person every time, but he's really still the same.' She looked up nervously at Damien, desperately seeking reassurance. The priest nodded, even as he hoped that Tarrant was absorbing these facts. Of all of them, the Neocount was the most likely to understand the Prince's Workings.

'Go on,' he urged gently.

'He said . . . that's how the Prince keeps his power.' She glanced up at Tarrant, then shivered and looked quickly away. 'He can be all different kinds of people, so all kinds of people obey him. Even the rakh.'

Hesseth hissed softly, but said nothing. It was up to Damien to prompt the girl, 'Tell us about the rakh.'

She hesitated. 'They're like people, but they aren't really people. They have marks on their faces, here.' She ran a finger up along her forehead, then down again. Paint? Tattoos? Or animal markings? Damien glanced over to Hesseth, wondering. Did the original rakh have markings like that, before the fae humanized them? If not, was it possible their foreign brethren did? But Hesseth shook her head ever so slightly, indicating that she had no helpful information. Damn.

'Do the rakh obey the Prince?' he asked Jenseny.

She hesitated, then nodded. 'Most of them. Because one time he made himself into a rakh, so they act like he's one of them. Not really one of them, because he's human now, but . . . kind of half-and-half.'

'Which explains a lot,' Tarrant said quietly. 'Few rakh would accept the authority of a true human.'

'But how could he become a rakh?' Hesseth said sharply. She looked up at Tarrant. 'Is that possible?'

The Hunter mulled over her question for a long minute before answering. 'One could shapeshift into that form,' he said at last. 'Although such a change would be difficult to maintain, and also dangerous. But there is an easier way.'

It took Damien a moment to catch his drift. 'Illusion?'

He nodded. 'Just so.'

'But . . . that perfect? That lasting?'

'A mere human couldn't do it,' he agreed. 'But remember, there are other forces involved here.'

The priest whispered it: 'Iezu.'

The Hunter nodded; his expression was grim.

'Would they be willing to do that? Maintain an illusion for so many years – generations, it sounds like – just to keep one man in power? Do the Iezu do things like that?'

'Not usually. One must therefore assume that if they did, they are being well paid for it.'

'Or well *fed*,' Damien muttered.

The Hunter nodded. 'Precisely.'

Either the girl had picked up enough details of their business here to understand what they were discussing, or the sheer grimness of their tone must have frightened her; Hesseth felt her stiffen, and she tightened her arm about the girl protectively. Sharp claws flexed in their sheaths, as if ready to do battle with her fears.

'Tell us about the rakh,' she urged softly.

She shut her eyes, trying to remember. 'He said . . . they don't like the sunlight. Most of them. I think. He said that they called themselves the *People of the Night*.'

'Not surprising,' Hesseth noted. 'Our common ancestors were nocturnal creatures.'

'But your cousins in Lema were truly nightbound,' Tarrant reminded her. 'So much so that they were taken for real demons, and when they were exposed to sunlight it killed them, as certainly as it would kill any ghoul or vampire. I doubt that your ancestors would have suffered such a fate.'

'No native species is that sensitive,' she said quietly.

'Of course not. Nature may be quixotic, but she isn't stupid. It takes a human mind to sculpt such a deadly weakness, and human motivation to bind it to a thriving species.'

'But why?' Damien demanded. 'If they're his servants, why disable them? And if they're his enemies, why stop there?'

'Maybe he's not done with them yet,' the Hunter suggested.

Damien was about to say something more when the galley door swung open suddenly. The tall, lean figure of the ship's owner came into view feet first as he descended the short staircase into the galley.

'Feeling a need for heat, are you?' Moskovan grinned as he made his way toward the coffee pot. 'You'll be glad to know we're out of the dreamsea at last. No more obstacles between us and Freeshore except a few well-charted islands and maybe the occasional spring storm.'

He pulled down a wooden cup from its hook and poured the thick coffee into it. The cup was halfway to his lips before Damien fully registered what he said.

'Freeshore? I thought we were heading toward Hellsport.'

Moskovan glanced at Tarrant. A brief communication seemed to flash between them, subtle and wordless. 'That was the original plan, yes. But Mer Tarrant and I've discussed things, and we decided on a course adjustment. Freeshore'll get you where you're going much sooner.'

'And just where are we going?' Damien demanded.

It was Tarrant who answered him, his voice as level and cool as always. 'Freeshore offers access to the Black Lands, and thus the Prince's domain.'

Damien stared at him. 'Are you out of your vulking mind? The *last* place we want to be is on the Prince's doorstep.'

Moskovan chuckled. 'Oh, it's hardly that.'

'And who gives you the right to alter our course just like that? Without asking anyone, or even telling us?'

'You were occupied,' Tarrant responded coolly. 'It was left to me to arrange the details—'

'Bullshit.'

With a dry smile Moskovan drained the rest of his coffee and put the mug back on its peg. 'I'll leave you alone to work this out.' As he walked past Tarrant, he said to him, 'Let me know if you need me.'

When he was gone, and the thick door had swung closed behind him, Damien demanded, 'What the vulk is going on here?'

Tarrant shrugged. 'Mer Moskovan suggested an alternate route. It seemed reasonable to me.'

'Don't you think you should have consulted us?'

'You weren't there at the time.'

He somehow managed to keep his fury out of his voice. It took a hellish effort. 'All right. So tell us about it now.'

In answer he took a folded map out of his tunic pocket, came to where they sat, and laid it out on the table before them. It was folded so that the Sea of Dreams was at the top, with the slender mass of the southern continent visible beneath it.

He gave them a moment to get their bearings by finding Hellsport, at the northernmost tip of the continent. Then he indicated a point some hundred miles farther down the coast, marked by a large star and far bolder lettering. FREESHORE, it proclaimed. HUMAN CAPITAL.

'Where'd you get this?' Damien muttered. 'No, don't answer that. Moskovan, of course.' He perused the detailed map, so obviously of southern manufacture, noting that the same river which ran through the Black Lands made its mouth at Freeshore. Which meant that any trade ship supplying the Black Lands would use that river for access. Which meant that for all there were nearly a hundred miles between Freeshore and the Black Lands, in terms of travel the one was indeed as good as on the doorstep of the other.

'And you thought this was a good idea?' he said sharply.

'I thought it had its merits.'

'Did you?' he demanded. 'Did you really?' He pushed his chair back and stood. It was easier to speak that way, now that he was angry. There were some things you couldn't say cramped into a small chair behind a smaller table. 'Let me make one thing clear to you, Tarrant. The *last* thing I want to do is march into this man's stronghold before we even know who he is, what he is, or what the vulk he's doing here. You understand that? You may have forced that strategy on us in the rakhlands by getting yourself captured, but I'm damned if I'm going to chance it again. We've got the luxury of time and distance this time around, so let's use a little caution, all right? Lema wasn't all that pleasant an experience that I'm anxious to repeat it.'

He said it quietly, in a voice as smooth and as chill as ice. 'You don't understand all the variables, priest—'

'The hell I don't!' he snapped. 'What about the currents? In Hellsport they'd be running north – straight from the Prince's domain to us. An ideal situation on every front. In Freeshore we'd be off to the west, which means we'd have to work that much harder to Know the enemy, while he wouldn't have to work nearly as hard to get at us.' When the Hunter said nothing he demanded, 'Well? Isn't that worth something?'

'Of course it is,' he said evenly. 'And don't you think our enemy's aware of it? Don't you think he gets news from the north – directly from the Matrias, most likely – and therefore knows every detail of our flight across that nation? Including our departure from

Esperanova, priest. You think about that. You think about what it means to head straight for the one place he'd most expect us to land. And then if you can come up with a good argument for landing there anyway, let me know. I'd be interested in hearing it.'

There was a long, uncomfortable silence. At last Damien turned away.

'Shit.' He sat down heavily. 'You should have said something. You should have told us.'

'I apologize for that,' the Neocount said evenly. 'If it's any consolation, I would have much preferred the Hellsport landing. We could have made that port soon after midnight, but as for Freeshore . . .' He shrugged; the gesture seemed strangely artificial. 'That'll take longer.'

'Will we make it by dawn?'

'If not, there are enough hidden corners on this vessel to shelter me. I made sure of that before I committed us to this voyage.'

Damien looked over at Hesseth; her expression was grim, but she nodded slightly. 'All right,' he muttered. Rubbing his forehead as if it pained him. 'We'll do it your way. But from now on we're in this together, you understand? No more bargains struck behind our backs. No more surprises.'

'Of course.' The Hunter bowed ever so slightly. It was a polished gesture, precisely executed. It made Damien want to strangle him. 'And I assure you, this is the better course. For all of us.'

'Yeah,' Damien muttered. Closing his eyes again. Trying hard not to think about the future. 'We'll see.'

Jenseny slept.

The sea is black, blacker than ink, blacker than night's deepest shadows, and it stirs restlessly in the evening wind. There's a storm off to the west, but it won't come in this close; all that the shoreline will taste is a brief fit of ozone and a few wintry gusts. The rest will blow itself out over the deep ocean.

Jenseny dreamt.

The ship pulls into harbor, cutting through whitecaps like a finely honed blade. Freeshore's piers are crowded with boats of all sizes, but not with people. Like all southern cities it fears the night, and the only people abroad at this dark hour are those who must be, those whose livelihoods depend on it.

And others.

She smells it first on the icy wind: a sourness tainting the midnight air, a wrongness fouling the offshore breeze. She tries to make out something that might serve as a source — anything at all — but the wooden piers are empty of all but a few night watchmen and a drunkard or two. Nothing she can see would make such a smell.

Water laps at the hulls of anchored ships, and she can hear the creaks of the smaller boats as they rub against the docks, rising and falling with the waves. Isn't there something else also? A whisper perhaps. A soft rustling, like cloth against wood. She struggles to make it out, but there are too many distractions. Sails being winched. Orders being shouted. A thousand and one petty noises that drown out . . . what? What is it that she can almost, but not quite, hear?

A hand falls on her shoulder: she turns to find the priest behind her, Hesseth and Tarrant beside. They look strained and tired, but happy to be landing at last. 'Ready to go?' the priest asks, and she manages to nod. Should she tell them what she senses? Or will Tarrant just chalk it up to a child's imagination and insist they all ignore her? What if it really is her imagination, finally driven out of control by emotional exhaustion? Suddenly she doesn't know what to do. Suddenly she isn't even sure of what she smelled or what she heard or what she expected to see, there on the docks. But the sense of dread is so cold within her that she can hardly move when they urge her forward, so tightly is it cramping her stomach.

She watches as the sailors tie up the ship, then bridge the choppy water with a narrow gangplank. The priest urges her across it, gently. For a moment she almost turns back and runs, so suddenly does terror overwhelm her, but the priest's hand is firm on her shoulder and Hesseth is a warm presence behind her and from somewhere she finds the strength to move forward. The piers are wet from a recent rain and the damp wood makes her footsteps sound more heavy and more certain than they are. A guard comes over to them as they disembark, but the smuggler Moskovan is ready for him; he shows the uniformed man their travel papers and at last the guard nods that yes, all is in order, they may proceed with their business.

Again – in the distance – come the whispers. Again comes the certain feeling that things aren't right, that things aren't going to be right until they get out of this place. They should turn around and run away as fast as they can – to their ship, to a different one, anywhere! – before those whispers find them.

'Jenseny?' The priest stops walking and kneels down beside her. He senses that something is wrong. 'What is it?'

She doesn't know how to tell him. She doesn't know if she should. Didn't he explain to her that the voices in Esperanova were only memories of things that had happened there, no more worthy of notice than a display in a storefront window? That's what he'll think these noises are, too. How can she possibly convince him they're any more than that?

'I'm okay,' she whispers. Not because the words are true, but because they're the only ones she can bring herself to voice. How can she make them understand the danger?

They go on. The pier is long and walking on solid planks feels strange after so many hours at sea; Tarrant says that's normal. She's shivering, but from more than the cold, and the fear inside her is so tight and painful that she can hardly stand upright.

And then they come. Black figures, swift and silent. They come from beside the travelers and before them and even from underneath the pier itself, so that in an instant the company is surrounded. Jenseny hears the whisk of steel against steel as the priest's sword is drawn, but the gesture of defiance is doomed to failure even before it is begun. There are too many of them and they are everywhere, and their own swords glitter in the moonlight along with tiny stars that are arrow-tips and worse, as the blustery wind begins to move in from the sea—

She awakened with a suddenness that left her breathless; it took her a minute to get her bearings. The lamp in the galley had been turned down so that shadows reigned in the narrow space, and she shivered as she fought to make out shapes in the darkness. The rakh-woman was by her side and she stirred as Jenseny awoke, alarmed by her sudden tension. '*Kasa?* What is it?'

I had a bad dream, she wanted to say. But it wasn't just a bad dream. She knew that as surely as she knew that the Enemy was waiting for them in Freeshore, not Hellsport. The same Enemy who had killed her father, and who would kill her too if he had half a chance. He was in Freeshore. Now. Waiting. She knew it as surely as she breathed.

'It's a trap,' she gasped. Fighting her way to her feet. She was shaking so badly she could hardly stand upright, and the motion of the ship wasn't helping. 'They're waiting for us!'

The rakh-woman looked at her strangely for a moment, then said – very quietly, very calmly – 'Wait here. I'll get the others.' Jenseny did so, shivering in the chill of the galley while Hesseth ran to get Tarrant and the priest. There was Light now, but not much of it, and it did no more than exacerbate her fear. What was the Light but a window that opened onto terrible things, a way of seeing the truth when illusion was far, far preferable? In that single instant she would have shut it out of her life forever if she could have. So powerful was the force of her revulsion that she doubled over with it, and was retching dryly when the others came to her.

The priest was by her side in an instant. 'Easy now. Easy.' With gentle words and gentle touch he eased her through the last of the spasms, and though she knew that he could work no Healing in this place she felt better for his being there. The cramp in her stomach eased up a little bit and after a few seconds she was able to stand up straight. After a few seconds more, with his help, she managed to sit down on a chair and breathe again.

'Freeshore. Trap.' She gasped the words, shaking so badly she could hardly speak. When she shut her eyes she could see the black figures rising up again, oh so many of them ... the Light was stronger now and it silhouetted them, making their outlines burn like fire. 'They're waiting for us there,' she breathed. Half-sobbing as she forced the words out. 'It's a trap!'

She saw the priest look at his companions, but her vision was too blurred by tears for her to see what passed between them. At last Hesseth volunteered, 'She was asleep.'

'Probably dreaming,' the Hunter offered.

'Which doesn't mean she's wrong,' the priest snapped.

He knelt before her then, so very gentle in his voice and in his manner, so tender and loving in every way, and he asked her to tell him what she had seen. So she did. Haltingly, hesitant, not quite sure how to capture the terrible vision in words. When she was done she lowered her face into her hands and whimpered softly, and the rakh-woman came over and sat by her side and held her close, so that the voices of all the rakh children could comfort her.

'It's a dream,' Tarrant said derisively. She could hear the scorn in his voice. 'Forged by the mind of a frightened child, manifesting her fears. Nothing more.'

'I don't like it,' the priest muttered. 'I don't like any of it.'

The Hunter snorted. 'Are we to be ruled by dreams now? Not just our own, but those of a half-crazed child?'

'She's more than that,' he growled. 'You know that.'

'What I *know* is that I chose Freeshore because it seemed the best port for our purposes. And so it remains, despite all dreams to the contrary.'

'But it wasn't even your idea in the first place. Was it? As I recall, it was Moskovan who suggested—'

'Please, priest! Do you think I'm stupid? Before I sent you to meet with Ran Moskovan, I subjected him to such a thorough Knowing that I could write his autobiography for him – and then I added a few extra Workings just in case, to keep him in line. That man could no more betray us now than he could sail this sea without a ship.'

There was a long-drawn silence, cold and hostile.

'Look.' Tarrant's voice was like ice. 'You do what you want with the child. But if there's an ambush waiting anywhere for us, it's probably in Hellsport – and I for one have no intention of meeting it. Dreams or no dreams.'

His footsteps were hard and angry on the cold wooden stairs, and when he had passed through the galley door it slammed shut behind him, as if underscoring his mood. Jenseney cringed deep into Hesseth's warmth, where the hate and the rage couldn't reach her. The rakh-children whispered to her, words of comfort in an alien tongue. *Go to Hellsport,* they whispered. *Hellsport is safe. Freeshore is a trap.*

I know, she thought to them. The Light swirled about her, brilliant now. *What can I do? How can I change things? Tell me,* she begged. But the voices faded into a dull rumbling, not like speech at all. More like distant thunder.

'What now?' Hesseth asked.

The priest exhaled heavily as he dropped down onto the bench beside them. 'What, indeed? I can't turn the damned ship around by myself, can I?'

'Would you if you could?' she asked quietly.

Jenseny heard him catch his breath. There was a long pause.

'Maybe,' he muttered. 'It doesn't matter, does it? The decision's been made for us. It's not like you and I can start off to Hellsport on our own.'

She could hear something else now, a new kind of whisper. Like a wind blowing toward them, sweeping across miles of open water. With it came the delicate percussion of rainfall, the timpani of distant lightning. Too soft yet for other ears to hear; it was the Light that brought it to her, spanning the empty miles for her ears alone.

'God damn it,' the priest muttered. 'I hate sea travel.' And then he was gone and the galley door slammed shut behind him also, leaving Jenseny and Hesseth alone.

In the darkness.

With the Light.

With the music of the coming storm . . .

For all his months at sea, Damien had never gotten a firm grasp on sailing. Oh, he knew that a wind from behind them was good, that a wind from head-on was bad, and that no wind at all was a pain in the ass since it meant either waiting until the breeze kicked in again, or stoking up the furnace with appropriate prayers and meditations so that steam power hopefully would get them moving. But he had never really gotten a sense of the fine points in between: when it was best to gather up some of the sails (but not all of them), why an angled wind was sometimes the best wind of all, and what subtle hints the wind and sea provided when trouble – *real* trouble – was on its way.

What he had learned to interpret were the people around him. By the time they'd been at sea a month he could tell by the lowering of Rasya's brow when rain was coming, and he'd learned that the best barometer of the sea's condition was the relative coarseness of

Captain Rozca's manner. After four midmonths at sea he could tell when a storm was on its way by the way the first mate swore, and how fast it was moving in by the portions that the cook doled out at evening mess.

Now, though these sailors were unknown to him and their whistled code was wholly incomprehensible, that same sense told him that something was wrong. He didn't have to see Moskovan make repeated trips to check his instruments to know that conditions were changing quickly; that was clear in the men's manner as they worked, in the first mate's face as he scowled at the sea. He remembered the squalls they had struggled through in Novatlantis – one of which had forced them to land for repairs, at an island so new that parts of its shoreline were still steaming as it cooled – and he felt a cold knot form in his gut at the thought of facing one here.

Moskovan said before we left that the weather looked good. He said it should stay good for a day or two. But he knew that weather prediction was a chancy art at best. Even Earth, it was rumored, had never fully mastered it.

He located Tarrant, moved to join him. But the Hunter shook his head ever so slightly as he approached, as if to say *No, I have no more information than you do.* Damn, he missed Rozca. And that whole crew. They never would have gone on like this without someone telling the passengers what was happening.

At last – when the last of the sails was set and everything on board the deck had been firmly fastened down – Moskovan vouchsafed them a few words. 'Wind's shifted,' he told them. 'And the pressure's dropping fast. That's a bad sign in any waters, but here . . .' He shook his head grimly. 'Most likely it's coming straight up the coast. That means right smack into us, if we keep on going the way we are.'

'Then I assume that's out of the question,' Tarrant said evenly. 'What are our options?'

He looked out at the waves surrounding them, white-capped and angry. 'We're going in,' he said shortly. 'No other way. We can make the cape inside an hour, and that should be good enough. Hellsport's got a sheltered harbor that'll keep us safe and sound, if we can get there in time.' He looked up sharply at Tarrant. 'Unless you've got something that'll turn this aside. If so, now's the time to use it.'

Tarrant gazed out at the sea in silence, for so long that Damien wondered if he had heard. But at last he said quietly, 'No. I can't Work this. Do what you must.'

When Moskovan had left them, Damien asked, 'Not enough power available?'

He put a hand on the pommel of his sword, rested it there. 'There's enough.'

'Don't want to use it up?'

The Hunter turned to him; in the mist-filtered lamplight his eyes were as pale as ice. 'I can't Work this storm,' he said evenly, 'because it's already been Worked. And not by a power I care to spar with.'

'Our enemy, you mean?'

He turned away. 'Don't be naive, Vryce.'

It took him a minute to realize what the Hunter meant; when he did so, he was stunned. 'You think the girl—' He couldn't finish.

'I checked the weather before we left. Even allowing for typical meteorological surprises, it shouldn't have become . . . this.' A sweeping gesture encompassed it all: the white-capped waves, the rising wind, the slap of ocean foam against the hull. 'There's no question in my mind that the storm was altered so that it would come in closer to shore. And likewise no question that the tool used for that alteration was not earth-fae, or any earth-bound sorcery.' He glanced back meaningfully toward the galley. 'Hesseth doesn't Work the weather. That leaves only one possibility I can think of. Unless you have another suggestion.'

It seemed too incredible. He could hardly respond. 'You once told me weather-Working was so complicated that most adepts can't even do it.'

'No, Vryce. Moving a storm is easy, provided it already exists. *Controlling* it is hard. Anyone with enough raw power can yank a few clouds into position, or draw in a respectable wind. But very few can alter an entire weather system, so that the storm thus changed stays under control.' He gazed out at the foaming waves, now casting sheets of spray about the ship's hull. Thin rainbows hung before the ship's lanterns. 'Merely raising a storm, without thought for consequences? That's not so very difficult. Under the right circumstances, even a child could do it.'

'A scared child,' Damien muttered. 'One who thinks we're all going to die if we land in Freeshore.'

For a moment the Hunter said nothing. The look in his eyes was strangely distant, as though his thoughts were not fixed on this time and place at all, but on some internal vista. 'It would seem,' he said at last, 'that the matter is now out of our hands.'

'Not necessarily. When the storm passes—'

'Then there will be another. Or something worse. The girl is afraid of Freeshore, and Nature responds to her fear; do you want to tempt that power? This time it was only a storm. Let's be grateful for that.'

'You were worried about Hellsport,' Damien reminded him. 'Do you think we can deal with whatever's waiting for us?'

The Hunter gazed out over the sea, where foamy waves were breaking into spray. The rising wind was audible in the rigging, a whistling that rose and fell with each gust.

'Let's just hope we make it to Hellsport in time,' he said quietly. 'That's enough to worry about for one night, don't you think?'

They made it.

Just barely.

The wind was shrieking through the rigging by the time they rounded Hellsport's sea wall, and the foaming waves that beat against the hull filled the air with cold, salty spray. It was hard to stand on the swaying deck with the wind that strong, so Damien had gone below, where he waited with Hesseth and Jenseny. Tarrant alone remained above. Watching for the distant light of the earth-fae, Damien guessed. Searching for land as only he could see it.

The girl was sick and miserable, but she had managed not to throw up thus far. A major accomplishment, Damien thought. He and Hesseth had sailed through so much rough water in the *Golden Glory* that they were somewhat accustomed to it, but even so the last half-hour was difficult. Whatever power the child had drawn upon to summon up this storm, it had done its work blindly, with no attempt to control its course or its fury. If there hadn't been a sheltered port nearby when it struck, it probably would have killed them all.

The most unnerving thing about the incident was that the girl apparently knew nothing of what she had done. Whatever tidal forces she had wielded in her moment of terror, allowing her to call the storm, it had been purely unconscious effort. Which was all the more dangerous, he reflected. Ignorance and power were a dangerously volatile mixture. They were going to have to deal with that, and soon.

He looked over at Hesseth and said quietly, 'You'll have to train her. No one else can do it.'

She bared sharp teeth as she answered him, 'My people can only teach their blood-kin.'

He looked up at her. And waited.

At last she looked down at the girl who lay curled up on her side, her head on Hesseth's lap. With care she smoothed the tangled black hair, gently enough not to wake the girl.

'I'll try,' she promised.

Suddenly there was a thump on the hull, hard enough to shake the bench they were sitting on. For a moment Damien feared that they had hit a rock, and his whole body tensed as he prepared to grab the child and carry her abovedeck. Then there was another thump, somewhat softer than the first. And then a third. After a moment he recognized the sounds for what they were and leaned back, exhaling heavily.

'I take it we're secure.'

'Jenseny.' Hesseth shook the girl gently so that she would awaken. 'We made it. We're safe. Wake up, *kasa*.'

The large eyes fluttered open, bloodshot and tired. 'In Hellsport?' she whispered weakly. Her face was still a ghastly ashen hue.

'For what it's worth,' Damien told her. He patted the girl on the head with what he hoped was fatherly reassurance. 'Come on. Let's get out of this bucket.'

The port they'd chosen might have been sheltered, but one wouldn't know it from on board the ship; climbing up the galley stairs as they pitched and swayed was a trial in itself. The deck seemed somewhat more stable, but the difference was purely psychological. He could see from the way the long boat was rubbing against the pier that it was far from steady, despite its careful mooring. A cold rain had begun to fall, and Damien turned up his collar to keep it from seeping in at the neck.

'Well?' Moskovan joined them, wraped in an oilcloth slicker. 'What's the verdict? You want to wait this out and then move on to Freeshore? Or take your chances here?'

Damien looked at Tarrant, and hesitated.

'I should Know the city first—' the priest began.

The Hunter waved him short. 'I already did. There's no danger to us here. Not yet, anyway.'

Damien was aware of how hard those words must have been for him. It wasn't in the Neocount's character to say *I was wrong,* but that was damned close.

He looked out at the city, now sheathed in a curtain of rain. Impossible to see in the darkness. The lamps of the harbor were ghostly and inconstant, flickering like stars in the downpour.

'All right. We'll try it here.' He felt like a weight was lifted off his chest the minute he said it. No more sea travel, now. Not until they'd finished the job they'd come to do, or died trying. And in the latter case (Damien consoled himself) at least there'd be no more ships to worry about. That was something, anyway.

He dug several gold coins out of his pocket and offered them to Moskovan; in the face of what they had paid for this passage it wasn't much, but the gesture clearly pleased the man.

'Take care,' the smuggler warned them, taking the coins. 'The people here aren't overly fond of strangers.'

Yeah. That's the story of our life. He heard a bang as the gangplank was lowered, linking them to the pier. It looked far from stable. With a sigh he shouldered his pack and started toward it.

Just one more time, Vryce. Once you get your feet on solid ground, that's it for the duration.

God willing.

'Good luck,' Moskovan told them, as they made their way across the swaying gangplank. And then he added, cryptically, 'I hope he likes the child.'

Had they not been on a narrow bridge of wood over choppy

waters, trying to make their way in the freezing rain without slipping, Damien might have turned back to him. Not to question him: that would have been too obvious, too dangerous. But to see his face. To try to read some kind of meaning into his last comment. But the short walk was treacherous, and allowed no such distraction. And by the time they had gotten across and were safely on the pier Moskovan was gone, swallowed back into the bowels of the *Desert Queen*.

'Come on,' Tarrant urged, as the downpour worsened. 'This is no place to stand about.'

At last he nodded and turned back to his companions, and they began the long walk to land. Like all Ernan piers this one extended well out into the water, to make it useful in all depths of tide, and in the rain-lashed darkness the distance seemed endless. The storm winds battered them from the north, sometimes so powerfully that despite his best efforts Damien found himself staggering a step or two sideways as he walked; once he had to catch up the girl to keep her from being swept off the pier, into the angry breakers just beneath them.

Just a little bit more, he promised himself. Careful not to question just how long that little bit would take them. *Almost over*.

And then they were over land, making their way toward the myriad buildings that flanked the harbor. Temporary buildings, Damien noted, whose woven walls were lashed together with rope and whose roofs were plaited masses of reed, tarred over to make them waterproof. Such a structure could survive the worst earthquake, its pliant walls giving way to every tremor without snapping. Such a structure might survive stormy winds, if it was lashed firmly down to the ground beneath it. And such a structure could easily be replaced if a tsunami swept it away – which Damien suspected was the most important point of all. The sea wall might protect Hellsport from the majority of waves, but there was always the chance that some monster might wash over it. A good chance, from the look of it.

'Come on,' he muttered. 'Let's get to high ground, fast.'

Tarrant was carrying a lantern ahead of them, but its light was swallowed up by rain-drenched darkness so quickly that it was all but worthless. Damien took shelter under the eaves of one of the woven buildings long enough to light another. He wondered how far off dawn was. The Hunter might not like its killing light, but he would be grateful for it. When had they landed, about one or two a.m.? When did the sun rise in this latitude?

At last they found the narrow stairs that would allow them to ascend to the city proper, more than one hundred feet above the harbor itself. Lightning flashed, outlining buildings that were balanced high above them, well out of reach of tsunami or tidal flood. He thought he saw the braided steel ropes that would be used to raise and lower cargo up the cliff – and if necessary, he thought, boats as well. In the lightning's flash they seemed like serpents slithering down the rock face, gone to hunt some helpless thing now lost in the depths of night. He shivered and pressed himself close to the rock as he ascended the twisting staircase, so that the wind might not sweep him away. The girl was having a hard time and at last it was Tarrant who steadied her, his cold flesh making her cry out in surprise as he pressed her back, saving her from being blown away by one particularly violent gust.

'Almost there,' Damien muttered. For his benefit more than for the others. It was doubtful they could even hear him above the wind now, so furiously was it driven.

At last they reached the top and they paused there for a moment, catching their breath. Hesseth took advantage of the break to wrap a blanket about Jenseny's shoulders, shawl-style. It was meant more to conserve heat than to keep her dry; at this point, with all of them soaked to the skin, the latter would be a futile effort at best.

They moved on into the darkness, able to see no more than a yard or so ahead of them before the downpour cut their visibility short. The lamps were little more than sparks in a measureless blackness, about which they gathered like insects. The rain buffeted them in sheets, and more than once Jenseny needed a helping hand to keep going.

At last there were buildings. Small at first, but even those helped cut the wind somewhat. Damien's whole body ached from the effort of fighting the wind. They skirted the lee side of long warehouses, wading in ankle-deep water that was as cold as ice. At one point Tarrant signaled for them to stop and Damien did so, shivering as he used the opportunity to readjust the straps of his backpack. It was a new one that he had purchased back in Esperanova, and was not yet broken in; its stiff, unyielding straps rubbed the wet cloth against his body where he least needed discomfort. At last he slipped one arm out of its strap and used the other to sling it more loosely, satchel-style, over his shoulder. Better.

'There.' Tarrant pointed into the darkness. Though he couldn't see what the man was pointing to – didn't even know what he was looking for, for that matter – Damien was hardly in a mood to argue. They began to move again, splashing their way through the impromptu rivers that coursed down the street, stumbling as an unseen pothole or unnoticed ridge confounded their balance. Once the girl went down hard on her hands and knees in the water, and Damien had to help her up. It was hard to be sure of anything in the dark, but he thought she was crying. He hesitated only an instant, then lifted her up in his arms and held her tightly against his chest. Her own weight was slight, but her waterlogged clothing added considerably to the burden. Damien was just having second thoughts about his decision when he felt a hand on his other shoulder. Tarrant. The tall man placed a hand on the strap of his pack and waited for him to release it. After a minute he did so, shrugging out of it awkwardly while he maintained his grip on the girl. Much to his surprise the Hunter took it up, clearly meaning to carry it for him. It was a gesture so generous, so utterly unlike him, that for a moment Damien could do no more than stand there gaping while the rain poured down on them all. At last a sharp jab from Hesseth got him moving again, and he shifted his grip on the girl so that he could carry her more easily. He thought, as he moved, that he saw the Hunter smile. Slightly, very slightly. Hard to be sure, in the rain.

They passed through a squalid residential district, where homeless figures crouched shivering in doorways and refused to meet their eyes. Taking them for demons, no doubt. Who else would be walking about on a night like this? They made their way south as quickly as they could, keeping to the lee side of buildings whenever they were able. Jenseny shook in Damien's arms, but whether from tears or fear or simple cold he couldn't begin to tell. There'd be time enough later to sort that out, when they found some sort of shelter.

Won't do us any good to find a hotel, he thought grimly. *Can't afford to be noticed, and that would sure as hell do it. Besides, what manner of place would take in four strangers at this hour?* He didn't like to think that they would have to camp outdoors in this weather, but there didn't seem to be much of an alternative. Unless Tarrant's preternatural Sight could locate them a cave somewhere to serve as shelter. Or anything.

They followed the Hunter for what seemed like miles, until at last the man seemed to find what he was looking for. They had skirted what looked like the center of town, and were now far beyond the main clustering of houses and shops. Trees loomed high on either side of a muddy road, cutting the wind until it could almost be dealt with. Damien's limbs ached from the cold and the exertion, but he kept on moving. And he kept on carrying the child as well, though her weight made walking twice as hard. There was no way she could have gone on.

At last Tarrant turned from the road, following a path that led deep into the woods. Too tired to question him, Damien simply followed. He could see Hesseth beside, wearily keeping the pace. The narrow path was overgrown, and drowned grass squelched beneath their feet as they walked. Once he almost tripped, but the Hunter's chill grip steadied him. Hardly colder than his own skin, now. That was unnerving.

And then the path opened up to reveal a small clearing, inches deep in rainwater. In its center sat a primitive cabin, high enough on its log foundations that the groundwater hadn't flooded it. Yet. Without hesitation Tarrant walked up to the front door and lowered his lamp so that he might make out its details. There was a heavy padlock on it which he studied for a moment, then held it in his hand and silently conjured power. Silver-blue light flickered in and about the lock. He gave it a moment to do its work, then pulled back, hard. The lock's bar shattered like glass and fell in icy bits to his feet.

He kicked the door hard and it opened, granting access to a pitch-black space. As the lanterns were brought inside, Damien could make out details: rough walls, a coarsely-made table and chairs, two cots, a fireplace. Not much, but right now it looked like heaven. Despite his misgivings he moved inside, and lowered the girl gently to one of the cots. She collapsed on it trembling, her body limp as a rag doll.

He turned to find Tarrant setting their lanterns on the rough wooden mantel. Dust clouded up about the glass, stirred by his motion. Whoever owned this place, they hadn't cleaned it for a good long time.

He took a moment to catch his breath, then said what had to be said. 'This place belongs to someone.'

'Obviously.'

'They might come back—'

'They won't. Not right away. I don't know all the details, but my Working indicated that this place is only used in the summer. Which it isn't quite, yet.'

He looked about, and couldn't help but mutter, 'Breaking and entering?'

'Would you rather camp outside?'

He looked at the small girl shivering on the cot, and over at Hesseth; the *khrast*-woman looked equally miserable. 'No,' he said at last. 'I guess not. We can pay for anything we use.'

A faint smile flitted across the Hunter's face. 'If that makes you more comfortable.'

It was Hesseth who made them a fire, digging through her pack to reach the one dry square inch where her matches were stored, tightly wrapped in layers of waxed paper. Bless her for it. Soon the cabin's interior was glowing amber and orange from the flames, and though the heat of the fire was minimal at first Damien knew it would soon fill the small space.

Outside the wind whistled angrily; inside, the only sound was the crackle of the flames and the slow drip of water as it seeped down from their hair, their clothes, their possessions.

'You'll need to get the girl dry,' Tarrant told them. 'At her age children take sick easily. And she's never been outside before, which means her immune system is mostly untested; best not to subject it to too much stress.'

He moved toward the door then, as if to leave.

'You're going out?' Damien asked. Incredulous.

'It'll be dawn soon.' He looked out the window, as if searching for a hint of sunlight. If there was any, Damien couldn't make it out. 'I need shelter, too, priest.'

He moved as if to grasp the door handle.

'Gerald. Please.' When he said nothing in response, Damien added gently, 'Don't be an ass.'

The pale eyes narrowed.

'There's a trapdoor in the corner that must lead down to some kind of cellar. If that's flooded, we can easily cover the one window.' He nodded toward the thick glass, to the rain and the wind that shrieked beyond. 'There's no need to go outside in that mess.'

The Hunter hesitated. Water dripped from the hem of his tunic.

'We're all in this together,' Damien said quietly. 'Aren't we?'

Something flickered in the depths of Tarrant's eyes – some dark and secret emotion, that was gone too quickly for Damien to analyze it. When it was gone, the man's accustomed mask was back in place: perfectly controlled, utterly unreadable.

Slowly, Tarrant took his hand from the handle. Slowly, after a moment more, he stepped away from the door.

'Yes,' he said softly. As if savoring the words. 'We're all in this together, aren't we?'

Outside, the wind was still rising.

35

Damien dreamed. Not in cohesive images which held true to some internal narrative, but chaotic fragments, layered one over the other with no sense of unity. Images of a dark and sterile land where the earth was black and the trees were white and the sky burned crimson and orange overhead. Images of running, of terrible thirst, of a paralysis that came upon him muscle by muscle, limb by limb, until he could do no more than lie helplessly on the ground, his every breath a struggle for survival. And then there was rakhene laughter. Always that: gales of rakhene laughter, as cruel and as bloodthirsty as any he had heard in Hesseth's homeland. Sometimes there were crystals, too, glistening black columns like the citadel they had seen in Lema – the Master's citadel, which they had destroyed – only now there were thousands of them, more than thousands, large ones and small ones and carved ones and broken ones ... some of the carved ones were in the shape of skulls, but instead of empty sockets they had vast, glaring eyes. Faceted eyes, insect-bright, that reflected the fiery skies in a thousand molten bits. No need to ask where that image came from; he would never forget that baleful glare as long as he lived.

Maybe torture will loosen his tongue, the crystal skull urged. Bug-eyes glistening. *Certainly worth a try ...*

He awakened in a cold sweat, and for a moment couldn't remember where he was. Then it all came back to him: the rain, the cold, the frightened child in his arms. His shoulders throbbed painfully as he levered himself to a sitting position and his feet felt cold and sore, but at least everything was in working order. After more than a decade on the road you learned to be grateful for that and ignore the rest.

Outside the storm was still raging, and the light coming in through the one window was so feeble that Tarrant probably could have stayed upstairs without danger. *So much for traveling tonight,* he thought grimly. Hesseth had nurtured a fire in the small fire-place and its golden flames dispelled some of the gloom inside, but there were limits to what a mere fire could accomplish. As he eased himself gingerly onto his feet, hoping they would support him, he could feel the weight of the storm outside pressing against the walls and roof of the tiny cabin, and it was as if the pressure made their dimensions shrink. Suddenly the room seemed very dank and close, and it took considerable effort on his part to resist its depressive power.

Hesseth's voice broke into his reverie, a welcome distraction. 'You up to breakfast?'

He grunted assent and took in the rest of the room. The small table had been set with bowls and spoons and a pot of something steaming that smelled excruciatingly good. Beside it sat Jenseny, who had evidently just finished eating; her empty bowl had been set to one side so that she could concentrate all her attention on the little metal puzzles Tarrant had provided for her. As Damien approached the table, Hesseth produced another bowl and a ladle and spooned out a hefty portion of the steaming concoction. Some kind of grain-based porridge, he guessed. He didn't recognize the vegetables floating in it, nor did he care what they were. He'd have eaten swamp mud if it was hot enough.

The girl glanced up as he sat down opposite her, and cast him a fleeting, nervous smile. He tried to smile back, aware that between stubble and dried mud and rain-mussed hair he must look particularly gruesome. Hell, if she could face that in the morning, she could handle anything.

They let him eat in silence, Hesseth nursing a mug of some sweet juice she had heated over the fire. Like the grain and the vegetables it was not from their own stores but from among foodstuffs kept in the cabin. One more thing to pay for, Damien thought. Surely if they left a generous amount of money for the owner, he could manage not to feel guilty about all this. What man wouldn't happily trade a few tins of cereal and a can or two of vegetables for a handful of coins? He'd leave enough to assure fair payment and then some. Let Tarrant scorn him if he liked. Fair was fair.

'I had a dream,' he said at last, pushing the twice-emptied bowl away from him. It seemed to him that his words hung heavy in the silence, and that the air cooled somewhat for having contained them. He pushed back his chair a bit so that it was closer to the fire; the heat on his back was reassuring.

'Bad one?' Hesseth asked.

'Yeah.' The child had stopped her play and was watching him now. For a brief moment he thought of sending her elsewhere (but where? It wasn't like the cabin had another room), and then the total idiocy of that hit home. She had signed on to follow them into this sorcerous realm, knowing that they were facing death and worse. And even forgetting about that, look at where they had found her: among the Terata, sole witness to the true nature of that cursed tribe. And he, Damien, was going to protect her now by sending her away so she wouldn't hear about his nightmare? He remembered how she had cringed in the streets of Esperanova, how the pain and the suffering that clung to the streets of that city had come nigh onto over-whelming her. *She sees more horror in a walk down Main Street than most of us see in a lifetime ... and she's still hanging in there, despite it. How many other children her age could manage that? She's a lot tougher than she looks, and it's time we gave her credit for it.*

So he described his nightmare to both of them, both the images he'd seen and the emotions attending them. The latter was what was truly horrible about the experience: not the rakhene laughter, not the crystal skulls, not even the image of Calesta. It was his own feeling of utter helplessness as he lay upon that sterile plain, paralyzed by God alone knows what power.

Jenseny's eyes were wide as he described the scenario, and her toys lay forgotten on the table before her. Though she didn't interrupt Damien in any way, he could feel the tension building in her, and it didn't surprise him when, after he finished, she was the first one to speak.

'The Black Lands,' she breathed. 'Those are the Black Lands.'

Damien grimaced at the revelation; he would much have preferred to believe that his dream represented some symbolic vista, rather than an actual landscape. It was left for Hesseth to prompt the girl, 'Tell us about the Black Lands.'

The tidal power must have been strong then, for before she could begin to speak an image took form before her, hovering over the center of the table. A glistening black surface, that reflected the moonlight in ripples and whorls much like the surface of the sea. The image had barely become clear when it disappeared, too quickly for Damien or Hesseth to study it.

'He said ... the Prince lives in the Black Lands.' Her brow was furrowed tightly as she struggled to remember what her father had told her, so very long ago. Who had ever thought that she'd need to recall it all? 'He said the land there looks like the sea, or like a river, only it's black and it's frozen in place.' Again the image appeared before her, but this time only a flicker. She seemed not to notice it. 'He said . . . nothing grows there. He said it's a desert. And it's flat, so that the Prince can see everything.'

'No sneaking up on that bastard,' Damien muttered. Force of habit, assessing the enemy. The last thing he wanted to do this time around was go calling on the enemy face-to-face. Luck had been with them in Lema – not to mention forested mountains and a rakhene guide – but here, out on that open plain . . . they wouldn't stand a chance.

A man doesn't get that lucky twice, he thought grimly.

'Go on,' Hesseth urged.

'He said . . . the Prince lives in crystal. But not like a jewel, not like in his ring. He said that crystals can grow just like plants, and in the Black Lands there's a forest of them. That's where he lives. That's where he rules from.'

She looked up at him hopefully. Obviously she wasn't all that sure that the information she was providing was what they wanted. 'You're doing fine,' Damien told her, and he took one of her hands in his own and squeezed it. 'Go on.'

There was a flash of images in front of her: white trees, black earth, a strange knotted tube that turned inside out as they watched it. It took Damien a second to realize that the last was one of her puzzles.

'There's the Wasting,' she told them. Her voice was slowly growing stronger as she gained confidence in her narrative. 'The Prince put it between where humans live and where the rakh live, so that if one side gets angry it won't kill the other. He said he had to put it there because humans and rakh don't get along, and they always want to fight. But now it's hard for them to start a war, because no one can get through the Wasting without the Prince's help.'

'Why not?' Damien asked.

She said it with the simple candor of childhood. 'They die.'

'How?' Hesseth asked her.

The young brow furrowed tightly. At last she shook her head. 'I don't know. I don't think *he* knew. He just said that all things die in the Wasting, except things that normally live there. And . . . he said he saw it from a distance once and it was really weird, all black like the Prince's lands but it had white trees, only they had no leaves and he couldn't see anything else alive there . . .' She shook her head sharply, frustrated. 'I don't think the Prince told him anything about how it works.'

'Of course not,' Damien muttered. 'As far as he knew, the Protector might still turn against him. Why give a potential enemy more information than you have to?'

'It sounds pretty grim,' Hesseth muttered.

'Yeah,' he agreed. 'It does at that.'

'But necessary. I wondered how humans and rakh could live together—'

'And now we know. They don't.'

'They do in the Prince's house,' the girl told them. 'Humans and rakh work together there, and even though they don't like each other everybody behaves. Because the Prince is a human now, but he was rakh one time, so they don't fight because of him.' Her eyes, previously unfocused with the effort of remembering, fixed on them: first Damien, then Hesseth. 'Does that make sense?' she begged. 'I think that's what he said.'

Damien drew in a deep breath. 'Apparently the Prince . . . *transforms,* somehow. It must happen when he becomes young again; he can change his species or gender when he rejuvenates.'

'That's a strange kind of sorcery,' Hesseth mused.

'Not for one who rules in a place like this. Think about it. Is there any other way that a human could have earned the loyalty of a whole rakhene nation? Enough to keep them from tearing out the throats of their human neighbors?'

She snorted. 'Not likely.'

'My dad said the Prince is getting old now,' Jenseny offered. 'He said that means he's going to have to change soon.'

'So he does nothing to alter the aging process itself,' Damien mused. 'Just one gala transformation at the end of it.'

'Conserves energy,' Hesseth noted.

'But it's risky. Men have died playing that game,'

'Do other people do things like that?' Jenseny demanded.

Damien sighed. When he spoke at last, he chose his words with care. 'Lots of people would like to stay young,' he told her. *Or stay alive – like Tarrant – at any price.* 'Some people are skilled enough that they can manage it for a time.' He remembered Ciani, so very youthful at seventy years of age. Could she stay that way forever?

'Are you going to do that?' the child asked him.

'No,' he said softly. 'No. I'm not.'

'Why not?'

He shut his eyes for a moment, trying to come up with the proper words. How did one explain to a child what death was on this world, or what it would mean to his Church when he chose to die at his appointed time? 'Because we try not to use the fae just for ourselves,' he said finally. 'We only use it when it helps us to serve God.'

'Like back in the hotel?' she demanded.

Suddenly he felt very tired. Very old. He pressed her hand tightly in his, wishing that he had some better words to offer. 'Yes, Jenseny. Like back at the hotel. I believed that I was serving God by keeping us safe long enough to do His work here. And believe me, if I weren't convinced that there was some terrible evil here and that only we could fight it . . . then I never would have done what I did. Even if it meant that I might get hurt.'

He didn't dare look at Hesseth, but kept his eyes fixed on the girl. Despite his best efforts he could imagine the rakh-woman's expression: taut, disapproving. But much to his surprise she reached out across the table and placed her hand briefly atop his own, a gesture of reassurance if not approval.

'Your god demands a lot,' she said quietly.

From somewhere he managed to dredge up a smile. 'I never said it was easy.'

Afternoon watch: the girl and the *khrast* were asleep, curled up together on one of the cots. A bracing pot of tee, double-strength, hung over the fire. The rain outside was dying down, but the sky was still overcast.

Damien sat by the fire, nursing a cup of the hot, bitter liquid. The girl's questions had disturbed him deeply. Not because of what she said, or even how she said it. But the questions she asked struck deep at the root of who and what he was, a foundation already riddled with doubt.

Have I become too accepting, too complacent? Has the line between good and evil become so blurred in my mind that I no longer worry about where it is?

Long ago, on a dark grassy plain, the Hunter had told him what effect his presence would have on the priest. *For you I've become the most subtle creature of all: a civilized evil, genteel and seductive. An evil you endure because you need its service – even though that endurance plucks loose the underpinnings of your morality. An evil that causes you to question the very definitions of your identity, that blurs the line between dark and light until you're no longer sure which is which, or how the two are divided.* Had he done that? Had the Hunter's unquestioning acceptance of sorcery as a tool desensitized him to its dangers?

The issue was not one Working, he reminded himself, or even the sorcerous manipulation of another human being for a holy purpose. Every time that a man Worked the fae for his own private benefit it was another nail in humanity's coffin, a reinforcement of the patterns which were destroying them all. Where did you draw the line? When was *survival* a personal concern, and when was it service to God?

Once he had been sure. Now he was far less certain. And it had taken no more than a child's questioning to break down the barriers he had erected around his soul, forcing him to face his own doubts head-on. Forcing him to address his conscience.

He put his cup aside, setting it on the thick wooden table-top. And stared into the flames as if they could provide some answer. Golden fire, hot and clean. How long had it been since he'd felt truly clean? How long had it been since he'd felt sure of himself?

He closed his eyes slowly and sighed. The fire crackled softly before him.

Damn you, Tarrant. For everything. But most of all . . . for being right.

'Fact:' Tarrant pronounced. 'The Undying Prince appears to be the only figure in this region capable of altering the rakh the way we know they have altered. Fact: It was he who launched the invasion which resulted in the death of Protector Kierstaad, and the subsequent destruction of several villages.' Damien looked up sharply at that, but Tarrant refused to meet his eyes. How many scenes of brutal destruction had he visited when the Hunter left their company to feed in the Protectorates? They had never thought to ask him. Maybe they should have.

'Clearly,' he continued, 'Inasmuch as we have one enemy, the Undying Prince is it.'

'What about Calesta?' Damien asked him.

'No doubt the demon is allied to him, and serves his purpose. Which would make any direct assault exceedingly dangerous.'

'*Downright impossible,*' Damien reminded him. 'That's what you said before.'

The Hunter shrugged.

'What are our options?' Hesseth asked.

'For a band of four attacking an established monarch? Very limited.' He leaned back in his chair, steepling slender fingers before him. 'Assassination is the simplest solution, and it has distinct advantages. But with a Iezu for a bodyguard, he's not likely to give us an opening.'

'What else?' Damien demanded.

'Short of raising an army of our own – and Conjuring our own demonic patronage – we must work with what this country has to offer.'

'You mean look for someone local who can do the job.'

'Or help us to do it. Yes.'

'But if this Iezu is protecting him,' Hesseth pointed out, 'surely even a local couldn't get through.'

'Ideally, Calesta wouldn't recognize our agent as an enemy. But I wasn't even thinking of assassination. The Prince himself is a sorcerer of considerable power, and very probably an adept as well. Such men always incite envy, and they must be prepared for the violence that attends it.'

It took Damien a minute to realize what he was driving at. 'You're talking about an insurrection.'

The Hunter nodded. 'Just so.'

'A revolution?' Hesseth's tone was frankly incredulous. 'According to you, this country has been ruled by one man for centuries—'

'And there are always those who are restless, Mes rakh, and who await only the right opportunity to take the reins of power in their own hands. That's the human pattern. The more powerful a ruler is, the more likely it is that the seeds of his downfall are already taking root around him. We have only to find those seeds and nourish them.'

'If his enemies have been secretive all this time, they're hardly likely to come out in the open just because we need them.'

'Any sane man is secretive when he plans to overthrow a sorcerer,' Tarrant said evenly. 'And he would remain so despite our best arguments . . . unless he had a sorcerer of equal skill for an ally.'

'You mean you.'

The Hunter bowed his head in assent.

'But that still leaves Calesta,' Hesseth reminded them. 'Surely once an insurrection begins he'll use his power in the Prince's behalf – and these people will be no more immune to his illusions than you are. So what does that leave us? A whole army doomed to failure, instead of just us.'

'Precisely.' The Hunter's silver eyes glittered coldly. 'A whole army doomed to failure, *instead* of us.'

Damien breathed in sharply. 'A decoy.'

'I prefer to call it a distraction.'

'So that the Prince and his demons are watching them and not us,' Hesseth mused.

Damien's voice was very cold and tightly controlled. 'You're talking about *killing* these people. Sending them off to a war they can't win with the promise of your support – and then leaving them to die, while you attack another front.'

'If they want to free their land of its current ruler,' Tarrant responded coolly, 'then this would accomplish it. Many of these men are no doubt prepared to die in order to achieve that. Why should it matter how and when it happens, if in the end their goal is achieved?' When Damien said nothing, he added, 'Sometimes war requires a sacrifice.'

'Yeah,' he muttered. 'I know. I still don't like it.'

'If we were to do that,' Hesseth asked him, 'how would we start? How would we go about finding a group like that?'

'Ah,' he said softly. 'That is the sticking point.'

'Come on,' Damien snapped. 'With one Knowing—'

'I could interpret the tides of revolution in this land – and also announce our presence to the Prince like a thousand trumpets heralding an army. No, Reverend Vryce. We need to be circumspect in using the fae here. *Any* fae,' he added, and he looked pointedly at Jenseny.

The girl didn't quail as his cold gaze met hers, not in body nor in spirit. For all that the outside world still frightened her, she had come to terms with Tarrant's particular emanations. In that, Damien thought, she'd done better than most adults could dream of. Better than himself, sometimes.

'Jen.' Hesseth stroked her hand gently. 'Can you tell us anything? Something your father said, maybe, or something he showed you?'

She hesitated. 'Like what?'

'About people who weren't happy with the Prince. About places where the Prince might be in trouble.'

'Do you really expect her to know that?' Tarrant asked sharply.

'Her father came here because he was the Prince's enemy,' Damien reminded him. 'Whatever other reasons he might have given for the journey, basically he came here to scout out the Prince's situation – including possible weaknesses.' He reached out and squeezed Jenseny's shoulder in reassurance. 'Since he seems to have told his daughter everything else, why not that?'

'I think . . .' she said slowly. The words faded into silence as she struggled to remember. 'I think he said there were rakh who weren't happy.'

Hesseth exhaled noisily. 'I can believe that.'

'He said it was hard for them, because the Prince was like one of their kind. But also he wasn't.'

'Species bonding instinct at war with intellect,' Tarrant observed. Hesseth hissed softly.

'Do you know any names?' Damien asked softly. 'Did he ever talk about anyone in particular?'

'He saw a rakh city,' Jenseny said. Her eyes were unfocused, as if struggling to see something far, far away. 'The Prince took him on a tour. He said that he wanted to impress him with how good everything was. But my dad said that some of it wasn't good. He said he thought some of the rakh were angry, and they really wanted their own country. But they would never dare say anything.'

'Names,' Damien urged. 'Do you know any names?'

She bit her lower lip, concentrating. 'Tak,' she said at last. 'The city was Tak. And there was a guide, a rakh-woman . . . Suka, I think her name was. Suka . . . there was another part.'

'We need—' Damien began

'Shh.' It was Tarrant. 'Let her talk.'

'Suka . . . I can't remember.' Her hand, still covered by Hesseth's, had balled into a fist with the strain of remembering. 'And then there was another. Somebody important.' Damien could feel himself tense as she said that; it took effort not to press her for details, but to wait until she chose to offer them. 'He was strong, and really important. The way rakh-men are important, and women aren't.'

'Alpha male,' Tarrant provided.

Hesseth shot him a look that could kill. '*Prime* male,' she corrected him. Insisting on the title that her own people used, instead of the one that humans had created for studying animal behavior. And she was right, Damien mused. A people capable of overriding their inherited instincts deserved something better than a term used to describe dogs and horses.

'I think . . . his name was Kata something. Katas . . . *Katassah*.' Her hands unclenched as the memory came to her at last. 'That was it. Katassah.'

'A prime male,' Damien said softly.

'Which means that the others will obey him.'

'Which means that the others *might*,' Hesseth corrected.

'Tell us about this Katassah,' Damien urged.

The girl hesitated. 'My dad said that he was tall and strong and he liked to fight. All the rakh-men like to fight.'

'Assst!' Hesseth hissed. 'Tell me about it.'

'He acted like he liked the Prince, and maybe he really did, but my dad didn't think so. He didn't think any of the rakh really liked the Prince. He said that if there was a chance for the Prince to be overthrown, some rakh might go for it.'

'Including this Katassah?'

'I think so,' she said. 'But he wasn't really sure. It was something he said he just sensed, but he couldn't talk about it with anyone. Just a guess.'

There was silence about the small table. A sharp silence, heavy-laden with thought. At last it was Hesseth who spoke what they all were thinking.

'Dealing with the rakh,' she said quietly, 'means crossing the Wasting.'

'Yeah,' Damien muttered. It was not a concept he relished.

'Are we so sure they'd be willing to ally with us?' Tarrant challenged. 'A rakhene warrior who's dedicated himself to the overthrow of a human master is hardly going to welcome allies from that species.'

Damien looked at Hesseth, who reminded him, 'I'm not human.'

'What I meant—'

'You forget why I'm here,' she said evenly. Her voice was calm, but her eyes glittered darkly with remembered hatred. 'This man – this Prince – is transforming my people into demons. Worse: he's transforming them into monsters who *think* they're demons, who hunt and feed like the lowest of the faeborn, even to the extent of surrendering their lives to the sun.' She looked at Jenseny. 'Did these rakh go out in the sun? Did your father say?'

For a minute the girl was silent. 'He said they don't like the sun,' she said at last. 'But I don't think it hurts them. Not a lot.'

Hesseth hissed. 'So. What was finished in the west is only half-begun here. Maybe it's harder to alter a nation of a hundred thousand than it is a tribe of several dozen. Or maybe the woman who ruled there was more determined to make the transformation complete. Either way . . . what we saw there was a sign of things to come for these people. Why else would they be turning into . . . what Jenseny saw?' She turned to Tarrant, amber eyes flashing in the firelight. 'Do you think there is a rakh who wouldn't join us, once he understood that? Do you think any rakh would continue to serve the Prince once they saw where his power was leading?'

'I think there are always men who will serve a tyrant,' Tarrant said dryly, 'and your species is no exception. But the point is well taken.'

Silence fell once more, amid the golden flickering of flames. Amid thoughts of the Wasting, and its ruthless monarch.

'I don't see an alternative,' Damien said at last. 'Does anyone else?'

Hesseth looked pointedly at Tarrant. The tall man nodded slowly, his expression grim. 'No,' he said. 'There's no other way that presents itself here.' His tone was strange, but Damien chalked that up to the subject matter. Starting a war was no small thing.

'All right,' Damien said. 'But I want this understood. We'll go to the rakh cities, we'll find this Katassah, and we'll see if he wants to work with us. Agreed? And then we'll discuss what our options are. But I'm not agreeing to use him as a sacrificial cover. *Ever*. If we ally with him, then we ally. Period. All cards on the table.' He glared at Tarrant. 'Understood?'

The adept's voice was quiet, but his eyes were burning frost. 'You would doom us all for the sake of some abstract morality.'

'Maybe. We'll see. In the meantime, those are the conditions.' When Tarrant did not respond, again he pressed, 'Well? Agreed?'

'Your quest,' the Neocount said quietly. Very quietly. It was hard to say just where in his words the disdain was so evident, but it was. In his tone, perhaps. Or maybe in his expression. 'You call the shots.'

'Fine. That's it, then. On those terms.' He glanced out the window, at the darkness beyond. 'We'll wait another day to let the ground dry out a bit; if the weather stays this cold, that could make a big difference. I imagine in the Wasting it'll be even harder, with no real shelter—'

'And we don't know what traps that place will contain,' Tarrant reminded him. 'I don't imagine black land and ghostly trees will be the whole of it.'

'No.' A chill ran up Damien's spine, just thinking of the place. 'But we have my experience and Hesseth's senses, not to mention your own considerable power.'

'Yes,' the adept mused distantly. 'There is, of course, that.'

'And Jenseny's special vision,' he said, and he squeezed the girl's hand. To his surprise – and relief – he found that she wasn't trembling. Did she trust in them that much? Did she think they could protect her?

We don't know even what we're facing, he thought grimly. *We can hardly begin to prepare.*

But what the hell. He'd faced faeborn dangers before. Once with no more than a naked sword and a pair of socks.

From somewhere he managed to dredge up a smile.

'We'll make it,' he promised them.

36

In the realm of black ash
  In the citadel of black crystal
  Beneath skies that burned crimson at the edges
  The Prince waited.

Through the walls he could feel the messenger's approach. Softer than sound, subtler than vision, the man's movement was no more than a faint tinkling in the ancient rock. But that tinkling was magnified as it passed from column to column, from spire to spire, and by the time it reached the Prince's senses it was a clear message, replete with information.

He was, therefore, not surprised when at last it was not the messenger himself who approached him, but the captain of his guard. Like all his guards this man was rakh, and he served the Prince with a ferocity normally reserved for his own kind. That pleased the Undying. It also pleased him that in a realm where he ruled both humans and rakh, both species should be personally bound to his service. Oh, it hadn't been easy at first. Even before they had learned to hate humankind like their western brethren, these rakh had been loath to accept domination by an outsider. That was simple species survival instinct at play. But he had fought that battle on their own terms, and at last – on their own terms – won it. Now it was no longer necessary for him to adopt rakhene flesh in order to prove himself. And once the rakh had learned to accept his status as alpha male – regardless of the flesh he adopted, its species or its gender – they made excellent servants.

The captain bowed deeply. 'Highness.'

'You have news. From Moskovan?'

If the rakh was surprised by the Prince's knowledge, he gave no sign of it. 'The storm forced him into port by the cape.'

Ah, yes. The storm. That had been a surprise. He had Known it when it was still a fledgling squall way out in the ocean, and had been confident that it would never disturb his lands. He had even given his western ports some vague assurance to that effect. It had been distinctly irritating, therefore, to have the thing come to shore after all. But that was the way of weather-Working, and every adept understood it. You played your best cards out, and then Nature reshuffled the deck. Weather could be seduced, cajoled, even prodded . . . but never controlled. Never completely.

'His ship landed at Freeshore two days behind schedule,' the captain informed him. 'He apologizes that it did so without passengers. Apparently they chose to disembark at Hellsport.'

'Ah.' Briefly he considered his last communication with Gerald Tarrant, and wondered if he should have trusted in it. But no, there was no evidence of betrayal here. The company of travelers now moving through his lands consisted of four people, each with his own will and purpose. It was little surprise that in the face of such a tempest they'd had second thoughts and decided to travel over land. For Gerald Tarrant to defy such a consensus would only have focussed suspicion on him. No. It was better this way.

'Do you want me to dispatch some men to Hellsport?' the captain asked.

He shook his head sharply. 'By the time our men could reach Hellsport from here, they'll have been long gone. It would be a wasted effort.'

The current was in their favor, he reminded himself. He was experienced enough to understand what that meant. The minute he made a move it would be echoed by the earth-fae, whose ripples and signs would be carried swiftly north. He could Obscure such a trace, but not completely; if the travelers knew what to look for – and he strongly suspected they did – they could Know his every move.

'No,' he told the captain. 'Let them make their move. When they decide what they're going to do . . . then we'll deal with them.'

There'll be time enough, he thought. *Since Gerald Tarrant will give us warning.*

It was a pleasing thought.

37

When night fell they started off due south, toward the narrowest part of the Wasting. Soon the damp woods surrounding Hellsport gave way to a land bereft of trees or comfort, a rocky plain so cold and hostile that only a few scraggly bushes had managed to take root there. The animals which scurried quickly out of their way were tiny things, thin and nervous, that offered no threat to their supplies or to themselves. They hiked as long as they could and then camped for the day; a chill wind that swept in from the west was a solemn reminder that although they were not in the mountains proper, the land they were passing through was high enough in elevation that spring was unlikely to warm them.

It beats the rakhlands, Damien reminded himself. He remembered that icebound journey, and the unholy fire that awaited them at the end of it. God willing there would be no similar reception at the end of this one.

They took up their packs again promptly at sunset, waiting only for Tarrant to rejoin them before they resumed the long trek south. It was hard traveling – harder, in a way, than any which Damien had done before. The joint strains of looking after Jenseny and worrying about Tarrant – not to mention waiting for Tarrant to blow up *because* he was looking after Jenseny – frayed at his nerves constantly. So did the very real difficulties involved in bringing a small child with them. She could not match their pace. She could not equal their endurance. She could not do as they did, force their bodies to push on long after exhaustion had set in, because they had not yet found a site defensible enough to serve as a resting place. And yet she struggled to keep up with them and bore all her pains in silence, even when the blisters on her feet broke open along one particularly rough stretch of ground. If not for Tarrant's special senses, preternaturally attuned to the smell of human blood, they might never have known that anything was wrong at all.

He remembered that. He remembered the feel of her small feet in his hands, hot and swollen and sticky with blood. He remembered thinking that he was going to have to Heal her despite the risk or she simply couldn't go on, and he had expected Tarrant to argue with him. But when he had looked up at the Hunter, the man had simply nodded, his brow already furrowed in the concentration that presaged his Working. And while Tarrant Obscured, Damien Healed. Hopefully the Prince hadn't noticed it. Hopefully it hadn't served as a beacon to his power, giving away their position and their destination and – worst of all – their weakness.

But neither soldiers nor sorcery accosted them as they made their way through the Prince's lands, which meant that even if the Undying knew they had arrived, he did not yet know their exact position. Thank God for that. Or rather, more accurately, thank *Tarrant* for that. Without his constant Obscurings Damien had no doubt that the Prince would be breathing down their necks right now. He prayed that the adept's power would hold, and that the seismic tremors which occasionally interrupted his Workings would prove as much of a hindrance to the Prince's power as it did to his.

Day bled into day, night into night. The rocky wasteland gave way to broken hills, and that, in turn, to a damp, chill forest. There the leaves overhead shut out even the moonlight, so that they were forced to travel single file through tunnels of darkness with their lanterns held aloft, much as they had in the Terata's lands. Only here, of course, there were no horses. As he collapsed upon the chill earth at the end of one particularly hard night's hiking, Damien reflected that he had never appreciated that species quite so much as now. Or ever wanted to obtain a member of it quite so badly.

And then they came to it, and they saw it, and they felt its power. The Wasting.

It was vast. It was lifeless. It was utterly dark. A land as black as the thick night which enshrouded it, all but invisible from their vantage point. Valley bled into mountains bled into the night sky, and even the illumination of Prima's slender crescent failed to distinguish between them. In such a darkness it was impossible to make out any details of the land before them, or to estimate its dangers. It was *there,* black and forbidding; that was the sum total of their knowledge.

It had taken them more than an hour to get to where they might see even that much, climbing up a loose slope of broken rock and gravel that threatened to give way with every step. Hesseth had taken a bad fall near the top and, but for Damien's intervention, might have gone into a headlong tumble down the treacherous slope. Now, as she crouched upon the summit and studied the land before them, mouth parted slightly in rakhene fashion to drink in its scents, she said nothing of pain and asked for no Healing, though surely Damien's skills could have afforded her relief. Now, more than ever, they needed to refrain from casual Workings.

Damien stared down upon the night-shrouded land for a long time in silence, but if he had hoped that sheer persistence would render the region more visible he was clearly in for disappointment; his merely human eyes were incapable of piercing its cover. At last, frustrated, he turned to Tarrant. The adept's eyes, dilated to absorb the night, shone like black jewels against the ivory pallor of his skin as he stared out at the land before them. Loath to interrupt him, Damien waited. Once he thought he saw a deep violet flame spark in those depths, a glimmering of dark fae kindled by sheer force of will. It must pain him to conjure such a power in the moonlight, the priest reflected; that he did so meant that he was as uneasy as they about the nature of land before them.

At last the Hunter turned to acknowledge him; the violet sparks shivered into darkness, the darkness fading to a familiar silver scrutiny. He drew in a breath, as if preparing to speak, then hesitated. Choosing his words? At last he said quietly, 'No.' Only that.

'No what?' Hesseth demanded.

'No sorcery.' He turned to gaze upon the land again, his pale brow furrowing in perplexity. Silver eyes scanned an unseen horizon. 'No Workings, no Wardings . . . nothing.'

'Is that possible?'

The Hunter shook his head. Clearly this was not what he had expected.

'What about the Prince?' Hesseth asked. 'Is there any sign of his Working?'

'There wouldn't be,' Damien told her. 'Not unless he'd set some kind of trap.' He looked at Tarrant as he said that, but the adept made no response. 'Or unless he had managed to Know us. But he hasn't done that, has he?'

'Not to my knowledge,' the adept said quietly.

No sorcery. It seemed so unlikely that Damien could hardly credit it. Why would a sorcerer of the Prince's caliber go to all the work of setting up a buffer zone between two warring peoples and then not use his power to reinforce it? The thought was so incredible that Damien almost Worked his own sight then and there, to See the truth for himself. Maybe Tarrant had missed something, or misinterpreted a key element. That was possible, wasn't it? But even as he considered the move he knew it wasn't worth the risk. If there really was no active sorcery in this realm, then even a simple Working would stand out like a blazing beacon in the darkness. He couldn't even Work his vision without giving them all away.

'All right,' he said at last. Accepting the concept – for now. 'If there's no sorcery, at least that's one thing less to worry about.'

'Is it?' The Hunter asked sharply. 'A simple Warding would have left its mark on the currents here, or even an Obscuring. But there are other Workings that might not be as visible.' He turned back to Damien. 'You saw my Forest. I evolved each species in it with painstaking care, and set them loose in an environment which my power had nurtured. Generations later, when those altered creatures had hunted and mated and born their own young in a wholly natural manner, would my sorcerous mark still have been visible on them? I think not. And yet, they still served my purpose.' He nodded toward the black plain that awaited them. 'Knowing what we do of the Prince's power, I would suspect his techniques are . . . similar.'

'So, in other words, the fact that you can't see any sign of sorcery here doesn't mean that sorcery isn't involved.'

Tarrant nodded. 'Just so.'

'Well, that's just great.' He was remembering the Hunter's Forest and its warped inhabitants. It wasn't a pleasant memory. 'So much for an easy hike.' He turned to Hesseth. The rakh-woman's fur had risen along the back of her neck and her ears were flattened tightly against her head. 'You picking up anything?' he asked her.

She hesitated. 'A smell,' she said at last. 'Very faint. I'm not even sure of it.'

'What is it?'

She exhaled noisily and stood. Her ears were more erect now, but her expression was strained; it was clear that what she had smelled worried her. 'Dried blood,' she told them. 'Sun-bleached bone. Subtle scents, very faint . . . the kind of smells you would never notice if there were other scents to mask them, other living things surrounding—'

'Only here there aren't.'

She nodded.

He looked over at Jenseny. The girl sat hunched by Hesseth's side, thin arms clasped about her knees. Her wide, dark eyes were glazed with fear and exhaustion, but when she looked up at him there was something else there, too. Something so utterly trusting that his heart clenched in a knot just to see it.

Dear God, what have we brought her to? What are we doing here, all of us?

In a voice that was as steady as he could possibly make it, he said, 'All right. The night's still young. We can make good distance before dawn, then work out—'

'In the dark?' Jenseny demanded.

Startled, he looked out at the enemy's terrain and reconsidered. In his months with the Hunter he had grown accustomed to traveling in near darkness, to stumbling his way over roots and rocks with nothing more than a single lantern to guide him . . . but this place was different. What if darkness was part of this land's special power, and once they were within its grasp . . . He shuddered. No. Not this time. The child was right. This time they would wait for the daylight, so that they could at least see what they were walking into. They needed that much.

As if sensing his thoughts, the Hunter warned, 'You're talking about considerable delay.'

He nodded.

'If the Prince has figured out where we are—'

'Then we'd be his prisoners by now, and you know it. At the pace we've been forced to travel—' He stopped himself from going on, but it was already too late. The girl had turned away from him, and he thought he saw her trembling. Blaming herself for their delay, no doubt. Hating herself on their behalf. Damn his lack of diplomacy! Stiffly, awkwardly, he continued, 'Either your Obscurings worked and he isn't sure where we are, or else he's made other plans for dealing with us. Either way, I don't think a few hours here will hurt us.' Defiantly he added, 'I want to *see* this place.'

For a moment – a brief moment – he thought the Hunter was going to argue with him. But all he said was, 'As you wish, then.' Just that. Damien was struck with a sudden urge to strike him, to grab him by the shoulders and shake him, to shout at the top of his lungs, *Argue with me, dammit! Tell me I'm wrong! Tell me that I don't understand the dynamics of this place, or that my vision is too limited, or that we need to keep moving . . . anything!* He wanted the old Gerald Tarrant back, the one he understood. The arrogant, exasperating Neocount who had saved his life in the rakhlands even while threatening to destroy him. *That* Tarrant he knew how to deal with. *That* Tarrant he trusted.

What had changed the man? What *could* change such a man? He couldn't begin to fathom an answer.

'All right,' he muttered. Turning away, so that he need not meet Gerald Tarrant's eyes. 'We'll camp back there by the stream we passed—' and he pointed to the north, the way they had come, '—for the rest of the night. When the sun rises, we can take a look at what we're heading into. All right?'

He didn't wait for the Hunter's assent. He didn't dare meet his eyes. He began the treacherous descent with no further word, knowing that his companions would follow him. Hesseth, because she believed in him. Jenseny, because she needed them both. And Tarrant . . .

Tarrant . . .

Tarrant for his own reasons, he told himself. *As always.*
In this place, the thought seemed particularly chilling.

The dawn shed crimson light on the Prince's buffer zone, and the details that it illuminated were far from reassuring. Before them lay a twisted land, its hard black earth rippled and coiled like some swirling mudbath, its surface glistening in the harsh morning sunlight. Here and there a finger of rock jutted up from the ground, or a sun-baked dome blistered its surface, or a jagged crack, earth-quake-born, reminded the viewer that even here, in this desolate place, greater destruction was always possible. It was jarring, forbidding, desolate. A sampler of distortion.

It was their destination.

In the distance were Jenseny's trees, strange jagged blades of sun-bleached white that thrust their way up through the earth all along the blackened plain. Some grew in clusters, twining about each other with serpentine complexity. Others jutted up spear-straight from the dark earth, their slender trunks brilliant against the unbroken black of their surroundings. There was no sign of any leaf on them, or any flower, or any other sign of vegetative normalcy. With their bleached white trunks and their slender, twisted limbs they seemed almost skeletal in aspect, hands and arms and fingers reaching up from the black earth as if struggling toward the sun. It was a markedly unpleasant image, and one perfectly comple-mented by the aspect of the ground itself. In the distance the ripples of black earth appeared smooth, almost liquid, but where it lapped against the foot of their hill they could see that its surface was wrin-kled and pitted, scored with a network of tiny faults in much the way that an aged human face might be riddled by tiny wrinkles. In places these gave the mad swirlings an aspect not unlike that of living flesh: a serpent's coils resting in the sun, a tangle of intestines drying in the breeze. The combination of images gave Damien a sick, vertiginous feeling, and at last he turned away, to give his stomach a chance to settle.

'Assst!' The hissed exclamation was sharp and hostile. Glancing over at Hesseth, startled, Damien saw that the rakh-woman's fur was stiffly erect; the coarse bristle about her face banished any illusion of humanity which her altered features might otherwise have conjured.

'It's lava.' He forced the words out, imprinting the strange land with the ordered power of scientific nomenclature. 'Cooled lava flow. Perfectly normal.' He remembered seeing land like this in the Dividers, when he crossed the Fury Basin, and once before that in the desert north of Ganji. He had even seen trees like that once, trunks and limbs stripped bare by the heat of an eruption. *Perfectly natural,* he told himself. But though the shape of this land might have its origin in the natural balance of earth and fire, its aura was anything but wholesome. And he needed no Knowing to confirm that a man's hand, a Prince's will, was the source of its strangeness.

The crust could be thin in places, he thought. *Under our combined weight it might well give way, and then what? Cold tubes and tunnels if we're lucky, and if not* ... He had broken through the ceiling of an active lava tube once, and only barely managed to throw himself back rather than plummet down into it; the acrid fumes and raw heat that had blasted him in the face were sensations he would never forget. Was there a live volcano somewhere nearby? He searched the hills and mountains within sight for some characteristic sign. There was none. Which didn't mean that one of those mountains might not explode while they were passing by, or that some hidden vent might not vulk to life without warning, right beneath their feet. Volcanoes were notoriously unpredictable.

The Black Lands bordered on this region, he remembered suddenly. Was the Prince's stronghold also a lava plain of some kind? The name made it likely. If so, what did that say about the man who had chosen to make such a region his home?

If he's living this close to a volcano – any volcano – then he's a lunatic for sure. The woman in the rakhlands had built her home on an earthquake fault, he remembered. She had been quite insane, of course, and twice as dangerous for it. He prayed that the Undying Prince was more stable, for all their sakes; a crazy enemy was impossible to predict.

'Come on,' he whispered hoarsely. 'We've seen enough. Let's go back down.'

They had made their camp by a stream some two miles back, and although it was not a difficult journey once they had slid down the north side of the ridge, they hiked it in silence. Hesseth's fur was still erect, and periodically she hissed softly as she walked; clearly she had never seen such a landscape before, or considered its implications. After a while Jenseny began to come up with questions – mostly about volcanoes – but though he answered them thoroughly and honestly there were things in his experience he was careful not to tell her about. Like the cloud he had witnessed from a distance, that had descended without warning from Mount Kali and scalded nearly twenty thousand people to death. Like the molten boulders he'd had to dodge when he was searching for passage through the Dividers. Like the volcano-born tsunami he had once seen, a wall of water nearly three hundred feet high that had crashed into the shore by Herzog, swallowing half the town in minutes. Those were the kinds of images that would give a child nightmares, and he was careful not to share them with her. But it was humbling to consider the true power of Erna; compared to it even Tarrant's depredations were mere child's play, the Forest a mere amusement park.

But give him time, he thought dryly. *He's working on it.*

They ate a somber breakfast, a porridge of grain and local roots that Hesseth had concocted. There had been no game for many days now, which was just as well; he wasn't all that anxious to have her leave the camp in order to hunt. Fortunately he had purchased an assemblage of pills in Esperanova that should keep them nutritionally fit; he doled them as the tea brewed, vitamins and minerals and amino acids in thin gelatinous shells that should supplement the nutritive limitations, if not the boredom, of their fare. Hesseth made a face as she swallowed hers, as if to imply that her rakhene biology should be above such things. Jenseny watched her, then bravely gulped hers down.

All right, he thought. *Nobody's starving, anyway.*

'Let's see the maps,' he said.

Hesseth rummaged through her pack until she found the one they had consulted before, a crudely drawn rendering of the Prince's whole continent. The upper edge of the land mass, a ragged coast, was dotted with cities and towns whose names evoked a time of persecution and conflict. *Misery. Warsmith. Hellsport.* Farther south the names grew gentler, but the land was equally harsh, and most of the populated centers seemed to be on or near the coast. That was good news. He had cursed the emptiness of this land more than once in the last few days, but there was no denying the part it had played in helping them to travel undetected. As for the desert they were about to enter . . .

It stretched across the bulk of the continent, dividing the Prince's land cleanly in two. To its west a line of mountains served as stark sentinels of its border, denying access to the coast by any landbound route. To its east were more of the same, scattered mountains which coalesced into a vast continental spine, which continued down the eastern coast for hundreds of miles until at last it met and merged with the tip of the Antarctic land mass. Below the desert was a vast region with no cities marked, no roads, no borders: the rakhene sub-nation, shrouded in cartographic mystery. He frowned at that, knowing that it would make things all the harder for them once they got there.

One thing at a time, Vryce. First the Wasting. Then the rakh.

It was a vast area, nearly five hundred miles from east to west and two hundred across at its widest point. The western part, nearest the coast, was labeled *The Black Lands;* the rest was simply *Wasting.* There was no clear indication of where one region became the other, or what sort of barrier might divide them. Nor was there any indication of where the Prince's stronghold might be located. He stared at the map for some time, memorizing its details. At last he looked up at Jenseny.

'Your father went to the Black Lands.'

She nodded.

'Do you know how he got there?'

The tiny brow furrowed as she struggled to remember. 'He said . . . he took a boat to somewhere on the coast. Then the Prince's men picked him up in a different boat, and took him up the river.'

'Into the Black Lands?'

She nodded.

He studied the map again. There was indeed one path through

the western mountains, a narrow river that wound its way down from the desert plateau through nearly seventy miles of rocky territory before at last reaching the coast. He noted the port where it met the sea: *Freeshore*. That must have been where the Protector met his guides.

And where Tarrant wanted us to go, he remembered. He was suddenly very glad that he had nixed that plan.

'His stronghold, whatever it is, will be located on or near the river. That's good for him, since it guarantees both water and transportation. Not so good for us.'

'In what way?' Hesseth asked him.

He pointed to the northernmost tributary, a thin line of water that flowed through part of the Wasting. 'Normally we'd make for here; that would guarantee a source of water and maybe fresh food about two-thirds of the way through. But if the river's his main highway, it's a hell of a risk.'

'Tarrant will want to go that way,' she said quietly.

He felt something inside his gut knot up when she said that, something hard and tight and angry. Because she was right, God damn it. Even as his mouth opened to protest the thought, he knew she was right. Every time Tarrant had made a suggestion it had pointed in that direction, from his intended landing in Freeshore to a dozen tense discussions they'd had since. It was as if Tarrant wanted to bring them as close as possible to the Prince's territories – no, Damien thought, as if he was *drawn* to it, in much the same way that an insect might be drawn to a candleflame.

And suddenly it all came together, and he understood.

The Prince is a sorcerer of his own dark caliber. His equal, perhaps, or maybe even his better. When's the last time there was someone like that in his world? Was there ever?

He doesn't know how to deal with it. He's afraid and, at the same time, fascinated. He knows we can't afford a direct confrontation, yet he hungers for knowledge of the enemy. The concept was both reassuring and unnerving. Reassuring because it offered an explanation for the Hunter's bizarre behavior. Unnerving because it implied that Tarrant had lost his objectivity without even realizing it.

I wonder how much he's aware of the struggle going on inside him.

How much of it is conscious, and how much is masked by his unwillingness to look too deeply into his own soul.

'We'll take the safest route,' he promised Hesseth. Suddenly realizing that if the Hunter's judgment was impaired, the determination of what was *safe* and *unsafe* lay entirely in his hands. Hesseth didn't know enough of human sorcery to make the crucial judgments. The child didn't know enough of life.

Dear God, please help me. Not for my own sake, but for all the generations who have been and will be corrupted by the Wasting's creator. For the rakh and for the humans here, and for whatever future they might share. Help me to cleanse this land of his corrupt power forever, so that mankind may achieve its true potential without his interference.

He lowered his eyes. The heat of the fire warmed his face.

And help Tarrant get his shit together, he added. *For all our sakes.*

Night fell. Tarrant returned. He must have taken shelter not far from them, for the faeborn denizens of this desolate region had barely begun to gather about the campfire before he arrived; his presence, as usual, drove them off, or dissolved their wraithly essence, or maybe just absorbed their demonic substance into his own. Damien had never questioned the mechanics of it, was merely grateful to have the demonlings dispersed. One less threat to deal with.

They brought out the map again, and studied it together. Damien watched Tarrant closely as he considered the various options, and wished more than ever that he had some way of reading the man. But the pale face was stone-steady, impassive, and even when Tarrant looked up and met Damien's eyes, there was a mask in place that no mere human skill could penetrate.

'The river lies east, near the Black Lands,' he said, 'Going that way would mean added danger. But it also would provide a source of water, which might be scarce otherwise.'

He could almost hear Hesseth's soft indrawn hiss behind him. He didn't turn to her, but met the Hunter's pale gaze head on. 'We think it would be too dangerous.'

Seconds passed, silent and leaden. At last the Hunter turned away. 'Your expedition,' he said quietly. 'Your decision.'

Be glad for me, Hunter. Without me you would march right into the enemy's hands, without even knowing why.

'All right, then,' Damien muttered. 'Let's get going.'

They set off southward, canteens and water skins sloshing against their packs. Damien had purchased a dozen of the latter in Esperanova and last night they had filled them all, in anticipation of the long dry march ahead of them. This time Tarrant made no offer to shoulder the extra burden. Perhaps he meant to drive home the fact that mere human thirst was no longer of any concern to him.

But he must be weakening, Damien thought suddenly. There can't be prey in these lands for him, not enough to keep him at full strength. What can he find within an hour's flight of here – a hunter maybe, a lone forager, a handful of travelers at best. More likely he's gone hungry quite a few times, and that bodes ill for all of us.

Or was he feeding on Jenseny's fear? That would be quite a feast. He looked sharply at the girl, trying to sense any linkage between them, any trace of the Hunter's aura clinging to her own. But no, Tarrant feared her wild power too much to attempt such a thing. For better or worse, he would leave the girl alone.

The night was clear and all three moons were out when they regained their vantage point at the edge of the Wasting, but still the land itself was dark. Damien tried not to look at it as he half-climbed, half-slid down the crumbling ridge. The girl slipped once, but Tarrant caught her – and no, he saw nothing in the man's manner that would indicate a deeper, more predatory relationship. He felt something loosen up within his gut, to see that she was safe.

From him, anyway.

Carefully, warily, they entered the Prince's dark domain. The hard earth felt strange beneath their feet, and it took concentration not to stumble on the seemingly chaotic convolutions. Despite Tarrant's assurances regarding sorcery, Damien's every nerve was on edge, and it took all he had not to Work his sight and See the truth for himself. But the night was dark and the ground was unpredictable and it took all his concentration just to stay on his feet; he couldn't have Worked if he'd wanted to.

Half a mile into the wasteland they came to the first of the trees.

Tarrant paused to examine it, running a pale finger lightly along its bark. Damien brought the lantern close so that he and Hesseth might get a closer look; the girl stayed back, shivering, unwilling to approach the things her father had described so vividly.

'Is it alive?' Hesseth asked.

Tarrant nodded. 'Unquestionably. Its life processes are slow, mostly dormant . . . but it is alive.'

'It shouldn't be,' Damien muttered.

'No. Or rather, if it is alive, then other things should be. Land like this is fertile; once its hard surface begins to break down, many plant forms should take root. The fact that they haven't—'

'Nothing lives here but the trees,' the girl said from behind them. 'And one animal that eats them. That's what he told me.'

'Immune,' Tarrant mused, 'to whatever force the Prince created to safeguard this land. If we understood why those two species lived, perhaps we would know how to safeguard ourselves.' He caressed the tree's smooth bark slowly, as if searching for something, but at last with a soft curse turned away. Obviously he could uncover no clue in the tree itself.

They resumed walking. Deeper and deeper into the Wasting, until the darkness swallowed up the hills behind them and they were left walking on a blackened stone sea without any land in sight. Cold stone ripples passed beneath their boots, frozen wavelets, rigid whirlpools. The hard ground made their ankles ache and the constant need to study it as they walked – lest some crack or crevice surprise them – made Damien's head pound.

Then the texture of the earth beneath their feet changed, from the smooth flow of its southern border to a more broken, scrambled ground. After some discussion they decided to cross it rather than turn aside. But the footing was bad and the rocks were sharp and when they stumbled – which they did often – the rock fragments cut their knees and their hands, scoring deep into clothing and flesh alike. When they were finally on the other side of the broken region, they had to stop to clean and bind up their various wounds, and Hesseth brought out her healing ointment for all of them to use. It was bad enough that Damien thought perhaps he should dare a Healing, but when he looked up to get Tarrant's opinion on the matter, he saw the man staring toward the west, brow furrowed, as if he feared that some tendril of the Prince's power might be reaching out to them and was struggling to turn it aside. So with a shiver he simply rose up and shouldered his pack anew, aware that the aches and pains of their recent trial would be small enough suffering compared to what their enemy would put them through, if one careless Healing should draw his attention.

Two hours. Three. They stopped often, favoring Jenseny's young legs, but though her face was white and strained and a red trickle seeped from under the bandage on her knees, she never complained. Afraid that they would leave her behind, Damien thought. Afraid that if she became a burden they would no longer want her with them. To see a child live in fear like that tore at his heart, and more than once he reached out a comforting hand to pat her shoulder or stroke her hair or offer her a steadying arm as they climbed up the slope of a cracked black wavelet.

And then they saw the bones.

They didn't recognize them at first. The ghostly white trees were so ubiquitous that at first they thought the small white things on the ground were related to them; seedlings, perhaps, or root ends, or maybe random branches that had broken off and fallen. But as they drew closer, they could make out the edge of a rib cage etched in moonlight, fine white needles that had once been fingers, the staring sockets of an empty skull.

Bones. Animal bones. A whole skeleton, nearly undamaged. Damien knelt down by it and carefully tilted its jaw. Scavenger, he judged. No doubt it had wandered into this land in search of carrion, then had fallen prey to . . . what? He looked up at Tarrant.

'No sign of sorcery,' the adept whispered. He, too, knelt down by the small tiny skeleton and studied it. 'Nor any sign of violent death,' he said at last. He passed a hand over it, eyes shut, and breathed in deeply. 'Nor the scent of fear, or even its memory.'

Damien breathed in sharply. 'That's not good news.'

The Hunter's eyes opened. 'No,' he agreed.

'Can you Know it?'

'Of course.' The pale eyes glittered. 'The question is, is it worth the risk?'

Damien looked over at Hesseth. She nodded ever so slightly; her expression was strained. 'Go ahead,' he told Tarrant. Feeling his hand rise involuntarily to his sword grip as he voiced the words, an instinctive acknowledgment of the danger involved.

The Hunter closed his hand about the small skull, as if its texture might communicate some special message. For a moment he shut his eyes to close out distractions, then opened them again. His eyes were black.

'It came in search of food,' he told them, 'because it had found none in the surrounding lands. It wandered a long time on the black plain, searching for a promising scent. It found none. Nor was there any overt danger,' he added. 'At last, exhausted, it lay down to sleep. And died.'

'Just that?' Damien demanded.

The pale eyes met his. 'Just that.'

'And no sorcery?'

The Hunter shook his head.

'Shit.'

'Probably starved to death,' Hesseth offered. But she didn't sound like she believed it.

'The Prince didn't want it to live,' the child whispered. She wrapped her arms around herself and shivered.

'Disease?' Hesseth offered.

The Hunter considered – perhaps Worked – and then shook his head. No.

Damien balled his hands in frustration, longing for something to hit. Any kind of solid threat, that he could strike out at. 'So it died, all right? Maybe naturally. It was tired, it was hungry, sometimes animals just die.'

'You don't believe that,' the Hunter said quietly.

'So what now?' Hesseth demanded. 'Now there are bones. Does that change anything?' She stared defiantly at the two men. 'We know that the Wasting kills. We know most animals can't survive here. Is it such a surprise that there are bones?'

Damien knew her well enough to hear the edge of fear in her voice, and therefore he kept his voice carefully even as he responded, to calm her. 'You're right, of course. There's no point in wasting time here.' He looked up at Tarrant. 'Unless you think there's something more we can learn from it.'

The adept shook his head.

They continued onward, silent and uneasy. Their foot-steps grated on the coarse stone as they walked, and it seemed to Damien that a man many miles away might hear it. A soldier, waiting in ambush . . . he banished that thought, with effort. They had no way of knowing if the Prince had detected them, had sent out his men to intercept them. Hadn't Jenseny said that the Prince could enable his people to enter the black desert safely? It was something Damien tried not to think about. The flat plain with its lack of cover was less than an ideal battlefield, and he dreaded the thought of the Prince's servants confronting them there.

Nothing we can do except keep up the Obscurings and be ready to fight, he thought grimly.

There were more bones scattered throughout the black land, many more. Most of the skeletons they passed were whole, but some were missing a tail or a leg, and one was missing its skull. One had been broken apart, its pieces scattered across a good half-acre. Two were nestled together as if in peaceful sleep. That last was especially eerie, and as Tarrant dared another Knowing, Damien prayed that it would net him some kind of explanation that would help them avoid a similar fate. But like the first, these two had died peacefully, and their remains offered no useful information.

And then there was the human skeleton.

Unlike the animals it was clothed, in wisps of cloth that clung to its bones like weeds. There was a knife by its side, a can by its hip, the rusted remains of a belt buckle lying between its ribs. There were bits and pieces of other things as well, but they were so rotted and wind-torn and faded that it was impossible to make out what they were, or what purpose they had originally served.

Damien knelt down near the skull and examined it. Male, he decided, and he checked the pelvis to make sure. Yes, definitely male. Its owner had died leaning up against a cluster of trees and had fallen in between them; in the moonlight it was hard to distinguish bone from branches, and the ribs which splayed out about one tree base were nearly indistinguishable from the tangle of roots surrounding it.

He drew in a deep breath and felt himself tremble. Maybe up until that point he had thought they were safe. Maybe he had convinced himself that the Wasting had the power to claim smaller lives, but that men – intelligent men, wary men – were immune. Now that illusion shattered, and he was left standing naked and vulnerable before whatever strange force the Prince had conjured.

Then the Hunter said, in a low whisper, 'The stars are out.'

He looked up sharply at the sky. The stars were indeed out, a sprinkling of them overhead and a solid bank along the horizon. That meant that Corerise was less than three hours away, which meant, in turn, that the sun would rise soon. Too soon.

'You have to go.'

The Hunter nodded.

'Where? Do you know?'

'The land is riddled with cracks and crevices, and there should be empty spaces beneath the surface. I should be able to find safe shelter nearby.'

Damien looked up at him. He was remembering the night in the rakhlands when Tarrant had left them and had not returned. The night the enemy had taken him prisoner. 'Be careful.'

He nodded. 'Will you camp here?'

He looked down at the skeleton and shivered. 'No. Not here. We'll go south a while more, get away from . . . *this*.' He hesitated, embarrassed by his own discomfort. 'It doesn't make sense, I know—'

A faint smile creased the Hunter's lips. 'I understand.'

He didn't transform right away, but first crafted a careful Obscuring. A complex Obscuring, that must hide the awesome power of a shapechange. Only when it was done did he let the earth-fae claim him, and remake him, and give him the shape he needed to seek out a daylight shelter. Only then.

With a sigh Damien loosened his sword in his scabbard, ready to deal with any wraiths who might use these last few minutes of night to check out the strangers wandering through their realm. The faeborn would be hungry, in a place like this. Hungry and desperate. He didn't look forward to dealing with them.

'Come on,' he muttered. 'Let's find a good campsite and call it a night.'

And let's set up a damned good guard, he thought. *Because God alone knows when the thing that killed this man will come for us, or what form it will take.*

The weight of the night on his shoulders, Damien led his party onward.

38

Fire. Rising up out of the bowels of the earth, licking the walls of the cavern. Rising up into the canyons of the ceiling, lost in its whorls and crevices. Heat shimmering in the firelight, distorting outlines, distorting forms. A man's arm, shackled to an iron bar. An icy sword, blazing with silver power. A man — or a demon who had once been a man — confined to the fires of Hell while still alive, consumed by the unearthly flames even as he struggles to heal himself...

He tries to crawl forward, but the heat is too great to bear. Tries to reach out to this devil incarnate — his enemy, his companion — but the fire melts his flesh even as he struggles forward, and he knows that the moment is lost, the battle is over, the Enemy has won...

No! he screams. Refusing to accept it. His hands are gone now, charred to cinders, but he uses the stumps to pull himself forward, inch by inch, into the blazing heat...

Into the flames themselves, a white-hot silhouette...

Man's face, insect eyes

Faceted

Glittering

Laughing...

Damien awakened suddenly, his face hot with sweat, his whole body trembling. For a moment he could hardly gather his thoughts, or even remember where he was. It was as if each concept was mired in glue, and he had to slowly pry it loose before the next one would come.

I was dreaming.

Of the fire of the earth.
Of Tarrant's imprisonment.
Of Calesta.

When he had worked out that much, he shut his eyes and drew in a deep breath, exhausted. How much effort it took to think! His every fiber cried out for him to abandon the exercise, to drift in the shadows of ignorance, to rest . . . but he had traveled enough and experienced enough to recognize the danger in that, and so he fought it. His whole body shook as he struggled to remember who he was, where he was, what he was supposed to be doing. Every thought was a battle. It was as if some vital connection in his brain had been severed, or at least weakened; the simplest facts refused to come to him. Panic began to rise up inside him, and his pulse pounded like a drumbeat inside his head. What was wrong? What had happened? What had he been doing when it started? He sensed that the last question was vital to his survival, that he had to place himself in time and purpose immediately, because if he didn't—

If he didn't—

What?

He could feel the sweat trickling down his neck, cold now as it soaked into his collar. Where was he? What was he supposed to be doing? He struggled for a context. Images came to him, drifting in and out of the shadows like disembodied wraiths. He and Hesseth and the child . . . camping in the Wasting . . . tent erected, food shared . . . dawn's light bright over the hard earth . . . first watch established . . .

He gasped as it hit him. Suddenly, with the force of a blow.

First watch!

The child and the rakh-woman had gone to sleep, huddled in a nest of blankets. He had leaned his back against a tree and set himself to guard them, a process so familiar that it was now second nature to him. If any danger should approach, he would be armed and ready. He felt himself relax into the familiar watch-state, sleepless, alert . . .

And he had dreamed.

Fear knifed into him, cold and sharp. Never in all his years had he fallen asleep while on guard. Not even when he was traveling alone, when the only permissible sleep was garnered in restless snatches, too short to measure. Not even when exhaustion was a dead weight on his chest and he could barely keep his eyes open a moment longer – and yet he did, he did it because he had to, because you couldn't travel in this world without keeping your wits about you, there were too many things all too happy to feed on a sleeping man.

He had slept.

He had slept!

What the hell had happened?

He forced his eyes open and got to his feet, his hand already reaching for his sword. Or so he intended. But though his eyes did open and his right arm twitched, the rest of his body did not move. It was as if some vital link between mind and flesh had been severed, and his limbs would no longer respond to him.

He remembered his dream of the Black Lands, the terrible fear that had consumed him. It was nothing compared to what he felt now, the hot panic that blazed in his gut as he realized the full extent of his helplessness. Neither nature nor sorcery acted without a purpose, he reminded himself, which meant that if he was helpless there was something that *wanted* him to be helpless, something that would perhaps feed on his helplessness. Or on him.

Trapped in the confines of a crippled brain, Damien struggled to make his flesh respond to him. Each attempt was a trial, each thought a torment. It would be so much easier to give in, to rest, to let the shadows have him ... but there was no question of his giving in to that, none at all. He had done too much and seen too much for the concept even to tempt him. Thought by thought he forced his will out into the shell of his flesh, demanding that it respond to him. Thought by thought his demands dissipated into the shadows of his mind. He could feel his body trembling, feverish as he tried to work his will on an arm, a leg, *anything*. And that gave him hope. If he could feel his flesh, then surely he could control it! But effort after effort resulted in failure – devastating failure – and at last he lay panting, exhausted, caged within himself, unable to fight any more.

The fae.

Using it meant risk. Accessing it meant that the enemy might See them, might get a fix on them, might know how to reach them . . . but did he have a choice? It was that or die, he realized suddenly. Because whatever had taken control of him wasn't going to let go. And if he didn't Work soon, while he still had the strength, he might never get the chance to do so.

He envisioned the patterns of a Healing in his brain, felt the power coalesce in response. He didn't know if such a Working would help him, but it seemed the most likely course – and it was the strongest Working in his repertoire, which made it doubly appealing. The short prayer which he used to focus his intentions was normally muttered out of ritualistic habit, one part of a complex formula; this time he prayed it with all his soul, begging for response. *Give me the strength, God, to use this power. Guide me in my handling of it, so that my every use may be concurrent with Your Will.*

The power surged within him and he rode it down the avenues of thought, seeking the damage within him. There, a shadow; he burned it away, reveling in the smell of heat and ash which his senses supplied. There, bright thoughts mired in a bog; he set them free with a thrust of power, tasting their sharpness as he did so. Again and again he burned, cleansed, opened, freed – and each time he did so his thoughts came faster, his purpose was clearer, the power was easier to wield.

At last he felt that it was time. Eyes open, body braced, he tried to move an arm. For an instant his flesh failed to respond and he felt despair flood his soul – and then the flesh stirred, first faintly and then distinctly, as fingers, hand, and forearm came under his control. He used the arm to rise up, to support the weight of his torso as he forced that solid mass to respond to him as well. Pain lanced through him as his body left the ground, but he refused to relinquish his advantage. His legs were moving now, he had them under him, he was sitting upright and then rising, then standing unsteadily on the hard black earth—

He swayed and gasped for breath, reaching out to one of the white trees for support as he struggled to get his bearings. There was no enemy visible, thank God, although that didn't mean that none was around. Hesseth was sleeping soundly some ten yards away, Jenseny curled up against her side like a slumbering kitten. They both looked peaceful enough, but was that the result of true sleep or of drugged immobility? Try as he might, Damien could see nothing nearby that would account for his strange weakness, though even now he could feel the drag of it on his thoughts, the numbness of it in his body. There was no question in his mind that the minute he ceased to struggle the strange malaise would come upon him again, and this time it would consume him utterly.

He let go of the tree and headed toward Hesseth and the girl. Or tried to. But his body was weak, or else his control was lacking; he fell to the ground, hard, scraping his hands and bruising his knees on the black rock, his vision swimming as he focused downward on the place where he had been lying—

And for a moment he stopped breathing. Was still. Tried to focus on the ground before him, on the black expanse that had once been smooth and unbroken, which he had chosen for his watch-site.

It had changed.

With a trembling hand he reached out to touch the thing he had seen, to test its reality. His fingers made contact with a network of fibers that must have sprouted from the ground while he slept, root-like in form, their casing as hard and as white as the trees at his back.

The trees.

His heart pounding wildly, he struggled to his feet. He was seeing in his mind's eye the piles of bones they had passed, not sheltered by the bleached white trunks like he had thought but wrapped around them, *invaded by* them. And he knew what kind of creature would need to immobilize its prey, first lulling it to sleep and then invading its dreams, its mind, and at last its very flesh . . .

He fell to his knees by Hesseth's side, oblivious to the pain as his bruises hit the earth. He grabbed her by the shoulder and shook her violently, willing her to come awake. But for all his effort it was long seconds before her eyelids fluttered open, and even then the spark that was in them was dim and confused.

'You have to get up,' he told her. 'Our lives are in danger, Hesseth!' He shook her again, harder. Slowly her eyes came into focus, and she managed to nod. Thank God; whatever had gotten hold of him hadn't fully gotten control of her yet. As he helped her sit up, then helped her stand, he could sense the presence of the trees at his back. Hungry, so hungry. How long did they normally have to wait before some prey blundered by, some animal who had happened upon the black lava desert and then lost its way, until sleep – and death – at last claimed it? He tried not to think about it as he helped Hesseth get her balance, then looked at Jenseny. The girl hadn't moved in all this time, which was a dangerous sign; she had been shaken and jostled enough times by now to wake her ten times over.

It was Hesseth who took the girl by the shoulder and shook her – gently at first, then with greater and greater vigor as she failed to respond. 'Kasa!' she hissed. But the girl was unresponsive. Hesseth tried to pull her upright, but the girl's body wouldn't move that far. The rakh-woman looked at him, terrified. Damien grabbed the girl by the shoulders and pulled her toward him, but though she was limp enough and light enough, there was a point beyond which she would not move.

His heart cold with a sudden certainty of what he would find, he held her against him as he leaned down over her body, peering into the shadowed recess between flesh and blankets, a mere four inches of space. And yes, there it was. It had grown through the blankets and then into her flesh, rooting her to the ground. Feeding on her vitality, no doubt. Little wonder she hadn't woken up, despite all their efforts. If he didn't free her from the tree's embrace, she might never awaken again.

'Damien?'

He didn't answer. It was still hard to think clearly, and he needed all his strength to focus on the girl. Still holding her, he fashioned a Knowing, focusing it on the tangle of roots before him. His vision was augmented by the fae so that he could see it all: a network of roots that had insinuated itself throughout the lava, so fine that in places they were no more than threads. A network that waited, somnolent, until it sensed prey on the ground above. He traced it with his Sight as it passed through the earth, above the earth, into her flesh, saw it growing even as he watched—

And he cut it. Pulled forth his knife and severed the fine white threads, so that they no longer bound her to the earth. She cried out as he did so, and he had no doubt that it hurt like hell – but it would have hurt her even more had he delayed, he was sure of that. Quickly he rose, noting with horror that the fine white roots had pierced the blanket in more than one place; the whole ground beneath them must be coming alive even as they stood there.

'We have to get out of here,' he told Hesseth. Cradling the girl's limp body in his arms. Was that stuff still growing inside her, still feeding? Had it gotten inside him? 'Fast.'

She nodded her understanding. Her eyes were fixed upon the blanket's surface, and her expression was one of horror; she had figured it out, then. Good. She would know to watch for the roots while she gathered up their supplies, to leave behind anything that had been contaminated. God alone knew what these things required in order to reproduce, but he was willing to bet that a small clump of fibers, even one detached from its main body, could become a tree in time. *Would* become a tree in time, if it was rooted in something that would nourish it.

Like the fibers inside the girl?

He tried not to think about that. Tried not to think about the fact that the fibers might be inside him as well, and inside his rakhene companion. They didn't dare stop to check. It was too important that they get away from this area before the trees' influence grew stronger, before the unnatural exhaustion that still dogged their steps overcame their will and their survival instinct and turned them into sleeping foodstuffs for the hungry plants.

Hurriedly they gathered up their things, packing them hastily into bundles wrapped in spare clothing, bound in belts and scarves. Hesseth had to do most of the work herself; Damien was afraid to put the girl down for even a minute, afraid that once she made contact with the earth it would claim her again, maybe this time for good. *If it hasn't already,* he thought grimly, shouldering the dead weight of her unconscious form. Maybe it was his imagination, but it seemed to him that there were more and more white filaments rising up through the ground each moment that they delayed. He could feel the power of the trees beating against his brain, and once he nearly fell as a result of it. But the sheer horror of touching that ground, of lying down upon it again, was enough to keep him upright. He was acutely aware that if his nightmares had not awakened him when they did, they might all be plant food by now.

At last Hesseth was finished, and without a word he began walking quickly south. He was still too dazed to think about direction, and for now it didn't matter; the most important thing was to get away from this tree cluster, fast. Dimly he was aware of all the items they were leaving behind, blankets and clothing and some of their foodstuffs. Organic matter, all of it. No doubt it would serve as food for the hungry plants, allowing them to grow and spawn and spread . . . and hunt.

They walked. In the heat of the morning sun, which blazed livid orange to the east of them. Dry, exhausted, afraid to stop for either water or rest, they continued onward, struggling to make every footfall steady enough to bear their weight. Within minutes their camp and the trees that surrounded it were left behind, but the dark malaise that gripped their limbs refused to relinquish its hold on them; once or twice when they stopped to catch their breath, or when Damien paused to shift the weight of the girl on his shoulder so that he might bear her more easily, he felt that deadly sleepiness stir within him again, and he knew that if he stopped to rest for more than a minute he would drift away into sleep, long enough and deep enough for the local plant life to sense his presence and respond to it.

'Where?' Hesseth hissed. She looked out toward the horizon, where endless miles of basalt faded into the hot morning sky without visible juncture, a mirage of brilliance. 'Should we turn back?'

He thought of all the miles behind them, of how much ground they had covered the night before. 'Can't,' he whispered hoarsely. They would never make it, not in their current state. And if they did, what then? Their only chance of long-term survival lay in reaching the rakhene lands and making their case with that people. If they went back to the human lands – assuming they got there at all – they would spend their last days waiting for the Prince to find them. That land would not shelter them forever, nor would it support their mission.

'We go on,' he told her, and though fear flashed deep in her eyes she nodded, understanding. *We go on – because there is no other choice.*

Mile after mile the black desert stretched out before them; hour after hour they forced themselves to keep moving, keep moving, keep moving at any cost. Once when they stopped for a moment, to drink from their precious stores, Damien dared to sit down on a jagged outcropping of rock – and almost immediately he felt the trees' mind-numbing power engulf him, so suddenly and so forcefully that the cup he was drinking from dropped from his hand and the precious water spilled out upon the earth. It was a wonder he didn't drop Jenseny as he struggled to his feet, or when he turned to look back at the rock he had been sitting on. No white strands there, not yet. But he had no doubt that they were present, buried deep within the porous rock, wanting only the prolonged heat of his flesh or the spark of his life to start growing toward the surface.

Water. Walking. Food without taste, hurredly swallowed. More walking. The child was a hot weight on his shoulder, and his whole body ached from supporting her. Once or twice he shifted position, trying to find a more comfortable means of carrying her. Once Hesseth moved toward him as if she meant to take the child, but he waved her away. He gave himself reasons for that, like the fact that he was stronger and taller and more capable of bearing her for long periods of time . . . but he didn't really know the limits of either rakhene strength or rakhene endurance, and was aware that the two might well surpass his own. The truth was that as he walked he imagined he could sense the roots within her, still growing, and while he trusted himself to put up a good fight if they came through the surface of her flesh and tried to link up with his, he didn't know if Hesseth could handle it. And so he carried the girl through the endless miles, until his back and his legs and his feet burned with the pain of it, and tried not to think about what it would feel like when the slender roots invaded his flesh, tried not to think about how peaceful it would be when their power wrapped itself around his brain and cushioned him down in deep, numbing sleep . . .

'We need Tarrant,' he whispered hoarsely. Clinging to the name like a lifeline. Tarrant would be immune to the trees' power – or he would make himself immune, with much the same result. Tarrant would know how to excise the alien tendrils from the girl's flesh – and perhaps from their own – without killing them in the process. Tarrant would save them, as soon as night fell.

If they lived that long.

Hours passed, without rest or relief. They came to a crevice, earthquake-born, that turned them aside to the east for several miles. And then another, its tributary. The hard rock was brittle and seismic shock had taken its toll in this region; they tried to hold to a southward course, but sometimes it was impossible. Once they skirted a deep chasm whose rim led them directly into the sun; after nearly an hour of staggering toward that blinding disk, Damien's eyes were watering so badly that he could barely see. Still they kept moving. He didn't dare ask himself how long they could keep going, or what they hoped to accomplish. They could never reach the rakhlands by nightfall, and it was clear that this land offered no safe refuge. Time and time again they passed tree clusters that were littered with bones, and now that he knew what to look for he could clearly see what had taken place there. One tree, rooted in a human rib cage, rose up like a surgeon's scalpel just beside the sternum; another had cracked through a pelvis in its quest for further growth. They passed one skeleton that might have been rakhene, but neither he nor Hesseth wanted to stop to examine it. And what if it was, anyway? They knew the two peoples were enemies. Doubtless there had always been madmen of both species willing to brave the Prince's wasteland in search of vengeance or glory or some other gain. And doubtless they all had expired here, some taken in their dreams their first night in the Wasting, others struggling onward as Damien and Hesseth were now doing, until sheer exhaustion forced them to their knees and the Prince's creations claimed them at last.

There was no shelter. No hope. If they could make it until nightfall, then Tarrant might be able to help them, but if not . . . he didn't dare think about that. Not now. It sapped his strength, to fear like that.

And then they came over a rise and he heard Hesseth hiss sharply.

'Look,' she whispered. 'Look!'

They had been traveling due west for a while, and it was in that direction that she was pointing. The sun had begun to sink and was now directly ahead of them, which made it almost impossible to see; he blinked heavily, as if the moisture of his tears might somehow clear his vision. Black land, ripples and knots and whorls of it . . . what had she seen? A mound in the distance, somewhat taller than most, but that was no surprise; the vagaries of the lava flow had produced a number of swells, all of which served as host for at least one tree cluster. Yet it was clearly the mound she was pointing to. He stared numbly at it, trying to understand. At last, with an exasperated hiss, she grabbed him by the wrist and guided him on. The girl's weight jarred into his spine as he staggered westward, following her lead, wondering at her sudden spurt of energy.

And then they were walking on rock, only it wasn't basalt any more; it was rough and it was gray and he knew without Knowing it that it was granite, blessed granite – a granite island in the midst of the black lava sea, about which the magmal currents had parted so many eons ago, leaving it high and dry . . . *and safe*. Praise God, it was safe! No trees broke through its surface, though there were clusters enough about its boundaries. It stretched for hundreds of yards in each direction, and all those yards were utterly barren. Bereft of bones. Bereft of life.

It was sanctuary.

With a moan he fell to his knees, and he lowered the girl from his shoulder as gently as he could. Pain lanced through his spine as her weight finally left him, the agony of sudden relief. He could feel himself shaking – not quite in fear, not quite in joy, but in some strange admixture of the two that was totally overwhelming. And he succumbed to it. For the first time in long, tortured hours, he embraced the utter abandon of submission. Emotions engulfed him that he had been fighting off since morning; the weakness which he had fought for so long was at last allowed to take hold.

We made it, he thought. His heart was pounding, his body filmed with sweat. Thirst rasped hotly in the back of his throat; with shaking hands he managed to uncap his canteen long enough to take a drink without spilling anything. One precious mouthful, savored cool and sweet on his tongue. In the midst of this black desert he dared drink no more.

He looked out over their granite island, Hesseth's crumpled body, the girl's. 'We made it,' he whispered. To them. To no one.

Made it . . . to what?

'It's still alive,' the Hunter pronounced.

Damien pressed a hand to his head, as if somehow that could ease the pounding inside it. 'Can you help her?' he asked. 'Can you do anything?' He could hear the exhaustion in his own voice, knew that his weakness was painfully evident.

Night had come. Tarrant had been late. And Damien and Hesseth had spent a small eternity fighting off the faeborn scavengers that scoured the desert night for food. They were simple creatures, primitive in form, unschooled in demonic wiles and guises – but their simplicity made them no less deadly, and by the time Tarrant had arrived, the granite island was littered with the bodies of the fanged and toothed nightmares that the desert had thrown at them. One for each human who died here, Damien thought grimly. Or maybe more. Spawned by the terror of those whom the desert entrapped, given shape by their dying fears. It would be a slow death, to have one's flesh consumed by the trees; a man would have time enough to create a legion of monsters.

The Hunter leaned back on his heels and studied the girl. Stripped to the waist, she lay facedown on the bare rock before them, as still and unmoving as the trees themselves. Circular welts pockmarked the region between her scapulae and down to the right of her spine; here and there a white root was visible, pricking out from the swollen flesh.

'It's alive,' the Hunter mused aloud, 'without doubt. And still growing.'

'How far has it gotten?' Hesseth asked.

Tarrant hesitated; his gray eyes narrowed as he focussed his Sight on the girl. 'There are tendrils in her lungs, and at least one has pierced the heart. The other major organs seem to be unviolated . . . so far.'

'Can you kill it?' Damien asked sharply.

The pale eyes narrowed disdainfully. 'I can kill anything,' the Hunter assured him. 'But as for removing it from her system . . . that would leave wounds I cannot heal.'

'Like an opening in her heart.'

'Precisely.'

Damien shut his eyes and tried to think. His head throbbed painfully. 'Then we do it together,' he said at last. He couldn't imagine himself Working, not in his current state, and the thought of Working in concert with the Hunter was abhorrent to him at any time . . . but what other choice was there? The girl couldn't recover with a root system feeding on her vital organs.

A strange look came into the Neocount's eyes. 'I don't think that would be wise,' he said quietly.

'Yeah,' Damien agreed. 'And it won't be pleasant, that's for sure. But I don't see an alternative. Do you?' His expression dared the Hunter to state the obvious: that by killing the girl here and now they would be saved the necessity of such a trial.

But Tarrant, for once, did not rise to the bait. His lips tightened ever so slightly. A muscle tensed along the line of his jaw. He said nothing.

'Well?'

'I think it would be unwise,' he repeated.

Anger surged up in him, hot and sharp. 'Look. I won't kill her. I won't leave her behind. And I can't carry her for another day. That means she has to be healed, right? And if you can't do it alone and I can't do it alone, then we have to do it together, right?'

The Hunter turned away. Said nothing.

'Is it the act of Healing? Is that it? Are you afraid—'

'I would be killing a plant,' he said brusquely. 'Nothing more. The healing itself would be in your hands.'

'Then what's the problem? There's already a channel between us. Are you afraid of using it? Afraid that I might see something inside you so terrible—'

He stopped suddenly. He had seen the Hunter stiffen, and suddenly, with all the force of a thunderbolt, he understood. And the understanding left him speechless.

You're afraid, he thought. *Afraid I'll see something inside you that I shouldn't. Something you don't want me to know about.* The concept seemed incredible. They had experienced close contact before, once when the channel between them was first established and then later in the rakhlands, when the Hunter's soul took control of his. And Tarrant had fed on him for more than five midmonths on board *Golden Glory,* which was as intimate a contact as you could get. So what was he afraid of now? What new element was alive inside that dark and deranged soul that he didn't want Damien to see?

He looked at the Hunter standing there, so still, so alone, and he thought, *I don't know this man any more.*

'Look,' he said quietly. 'You do what you can. I'll move in and Heal her as soon as you're finished. If we're lucky, if we're fast . . .' *Then she won't bleed to death before I can fix her up,* he thought. 'All right?'

The Hunter nodded.

It was a nightmare Healing, and not one he would ever care to repeat. The network of fibers had invaded a good part of her body, and was still growing even as Tarrant focused his power on it. Damien Worked his sight so that he could watch the operation, but otherwise kept a respectful distance. He watched as the Hunter destroyed the network, strangling its life branch by branch, fiber by fiber. Watched as he degraded its substance, so that it might be broken down and absorbed by the fluids of the young girl's body. Watched as the slender branches dissolved into fluid, leaving pock-marks and scars wherever they had touched her flesh—

And he was Working then, quickly, before her flesh had a chance to react to those wounds. Closing up the wall of her heart where it had been ruptured, repairing the torn tissue in her lungs, sealing and cleansing and forcing cells to replicate themselves with feverish haste, before her fragile life could seep away. It seemed to him in that moment that he had never Healed so fast or so hard in all his experience.

When it was all over – at last – he sat back and drew in a deep breath, shaking. The girl was still asleep, but she seemed to be all right now. Physically, at least. God alone knew if that fragile spirit would respond to his ministrations and find its way back to the flesh that had housed it . . . but he had done what he could. The rest was in her hands.

'It would have been a mercy to leave her here,' the Hunter said quietly. 'To let her die.'

For once, Damien didn't respond in anger. Wiping the sweat from his brow with an unsteady hand, he gazed out at the desert before them. Miles upon miles of broken black landscape, that stood between them and their destination. Thousands upon thousands of deadly trees, and who knew how few islands like this one? Maybe a hundred such granite havens. Maybe a handful. Maybe only this one.

'Yeah,' he whispered. 'Maybe it would have been.' He looked up at Tarrant. 'How far did we get?'

'In miles traveled, a considerable distance. That's why it took me so long to find you. The distance is a monument to your stamina.'

'More like our desperation,' Hesseth muttered. She had the girl's head in her lap and was stroking her hair gently, oh so gently. Damien wondered if the child was even aware of it.

'On the other hand,' Tarrant continued, 'you hardly kept to a direct route.'

'There were a few minor obstacles—' Damien snapped.

'I wasn't criticizing. I was merely pointing out that in terms of passage south, you are hardly farther along now than you were when I left you at daybreak. Though considerably farther west.'

Damien lowered his head in exhaustion. For a moment it seemed like the whole of the desert was closing in on him, black and dry and deadly. For a moment he could hardly speak. Then: 'All right. We knew it wouldn't be easy.'

'*There's* an understatement,' Hesseth muttered.

'Clearly you can't travel tonight,' Tarrant observed.

He looked at the girl, at the rakh-woman. Considered his own state, drained and battered. 'No,' he muttered. 'Not tonight.'

'Which means waiting until dusk tomorrow, if you want me with you. Do you have enough water for that?'

He tried to remember how much they had drunk on that terrible journey. How much they had consumed at the end of it, half dead and not thinking straight. *Too much,* he thought grimly 'We'll make it. If there are no more surprises.'

'Do you want to count on that?'

Damien sighed heavily. 'You know an alternative?'

'There's always the river.'

He said it so calmly that for a minute Damien was at a loss to respond. Hadn't he said once that they shouldn't go to the river? For a moment he couldn't remember why.

At last it was Hesseth who protested, 'That means going farther west. Almost to the Black Lands themselves.'

'You asked me if there was an alternative,' he pointed out. 'Not how safe it was.'

'He knows where we are now,' Damien said. 'No way he could miss us, with all the Working we've done. What's the chance that your Obscurings will work for us now that his attention's fixed on us?'

'Practically none,' the Hunter admitted. 'That's in the nature of the art.'

'Great,' he muttered. 'Just great.'

He walked to the edge of the granite mound; lava coiled in ropy whorls near his feet. God, it was hard to think clearly.

'How about a misKnowing?' he asked at last.

The Hunter considered. 'Feed him the wrong information?'

'Would it work?'

'Possibly.' Not saying what they both were thinking: that it had been used against them in the rakhlands, and had almost cost them their lives. 'There are no guarantees, of course.'

There never are, Damien thought darkly.

He rubbed his head and tried to think. Was the power of the trees still affecting him, or was he just that tired? 'All right,' he said at last. 'It's our only chance. Let's do it.'

'You want me to lead him to believe that you're not going to the river?'

He closed his eyes. His head throbbed painfully. 'He won't believe that. Not if he knows what happened today. He'll know we've got to go for water . . . but that doesn't mean he has to know where we're coming in.' He looked up at Tarrant; in the moonlight the man's skin looked almost as pale as the trees. 'Would that work?'

'Perhaps.'

'No better than that?'

'The Prince isn't an amateur,' he said quietly. 'Any Working can be seen through, if one knows how to look.'

Damien looked at Hesseth. The rakh-woman hesitated, then nodded. 'All right,' he muttered. 'We'll do that. And then we'll pray.'

He started to take a step back toward Tarrant, but his legs were weak and his feet were unsteady and suddenly his knees folded and he was down, bruised legs striking the ground with numbing force. His upper body followed, and though he managed to get his arms out in front of him to keep from cracking his head open, his elbows hit the ground hard enough to send fresh pain shooting up his arms.

And then he was down, gasping. The granite island was spinning about him and the stars . . . they were streaks across the sky, throbbing in time to his pain.

Then: footsteps on rock. Soft-soled shoes. Gentle hands touching him and then a firmer, colder grip.

'Nothing's broken,' the Hunter assessed. 'Yet.'

'Thanks a lot,' he gasped.

The chill hand reached inside his collar, pressed against the side of his neck as if to test the pressure of his pulse. He could feel the channel that bound him to Tarrant come into focus, as if drawing power from the heat of his body; he let it, knowing that the Hunter was using it to examine him.

'He's tired.' The cold hand withdrew; the soft hands remained. 'Tired and dehydrated and bruised and cut up . . . but otherwise fine. He needs salt and water and sleep, in that order.'

The soft hands withdrew. The soft footsteps moved away.

For a moment there was silence.

'I'll stand guard,' Tarrant told him. There was the sound of someone rummaging through their packs. Hesseth? 'You just sleep.'

He could barely manage to shape coherent words. His tongue was hot and swollen. 'If the Prince attacks—'

'He won't. Not tonight.'

There was something being placed on his tongue, something small and salty. Then cool hands helped him rise up long enough to drink from the cup that was held to his lips, a cool arm braced against his back to support him. He took enough water to wash down the pill and then tried to stop, to conserve their precious stores, but the water remained at his lips and he swallowed and swallowed and at last it was all gone.

Gently the strong hands lowered him back down to the rock. There was something soft beneath his head, something folded up to serve as a pillow. The soft wool of a blanket settled down over him, shutting out the chill of the night.

'You're a stubborn man, Vryce.' The Hunter's tone was surprisingly gentle. 'But you have real courage. That's a rare attribute.'

He could hear the Hunter rising. He could sense him standing, gazing at him. Studying him, for God alone knew what purpose.

'Let's hope it'll be enough,' the adept said.

39

According to theologians, the Hell of the One God was a truly terrible place. It was so bad, they said, that if you tried to imagine all the terrible things that might exist in the universe, and then you put them all in one place, and then you multiplied them a thousand times over, the combination still wouldn't hold a candle to the horrors of Hell.

In short – Damien thought – Hell was probably worse than the Wasting.

But not by much.

He awoke soon after dawn, with a dry mouth and an aching head and a body that hurt in at least a dozen places. After a moment he dared to test it, and found that at least it moved when he wanted it to. After his last awakening, that seemed like little less than a miracle.

He managed to push off the blanket and get to his feet. It took his eyes a minute to adjust to the light: blinding yellow from the east, a cooler white from overhead. Around the Core the sky was an odd shade of green; he felt that he had seen it once before, but couldn't quite place the memory. His legs seemed strong enough, but his sense of balance felt precarious, and he stood where he was for a few long minutes, giving it time to settle in. When at last he felt that he could walk without falling he started back toward the center of the island, and looked for his companions.

The granite mound had a hump in its center and Hesseth was seated on it, her strange northern weapon cocked and ready by her side. Looking at her crouched there – long ears pricked forward, fur bristling slightly, eyes as golden as the Core itself – it was easy to forget her human attributes and see instead a predator, an alien, a creature to whom scent-cues and survival reflexes were as natural as they were to any four-legged hunter. He was suddenly very glad to have her there, and to have those reflexes on his side.

'Morning,' he managed, as he hiked up to join her. His mouth felt like he'd been eating rock dust all night. Ten yards across, maybe three feet up; it wasn't much of a vantage point, but it was the best the island had to offer.

She shot him a look that was half smile, half grimace. It took him a second to realize the reason for the latter.

'You see something?'

She exhaled noisily. 'Smell it.'

'Shit.' He flexed his arms in an easy, conservative stretch; they hurt like hell. 'Animal, rakh, or human?'

She shook her head. 'Not sure yet.'

Trouble. It could only mean trouble. God damn it, couldn't it have waited a day? Long enough for them to heal? 'If you had to guess, what?'

She hesitated. 'Animal. Maybe.' She faced into the wind again and drew in a deep breath, drawing it in through her nose and her mouth. Her neck fur bristled in the breeze. 'Shouldn't be here,' she said shortly. 'Nothing should.'

'Jenseny said there were animals in the Wasting.'

'Jenseny said they fed on the trees,' she reminded him. 'But I didn't see any sign of feeding on the trees we passed. None at all.'

He tried to remember, but revulsion welled up inside him at the mere thought. For a moment he swayed, wondering if he was going to be sick. 'No,' he muttered at last. 'I don't remember anything like that.' Was his fear of the trees that great, or was this some kind of defense mechanism his body had conjured, to keep them from getting hold of his mind again? Or had Tarrant whipped it up and glued it to his psyche while he was sleeping? *If so, he could have picked something a little more pleasant.*

With a sigh he turned in the direction she indicated and tried to detect any odd scent on the wind, but his merely human senses could not see or smell anything of consequence. At last frustrated, he looked about for the girl. 'How's the kid?'

'Alive. Just. I gave her some food about dawn. She seemed pretty shaken. I take it she had some rather fierce nightmares.'

Yeah. And I'll bet it wasn't just because of the trees. I had nightmares, too, the first time Tarrant Worked on me.

Hunger stirred in his belly, sharp and demanding. He looked back at the camp. 'She sleeping now?'

The rakh-woman nodded. 'Soundly, I think. Maybe for the first time all night.'

'I won't disturb her.'

He made his way down to the place where Hesseth had laid out their supplies; given her predilection for neat tents and carefully tended campfires, the jumbled blankets and scattered piles of supplies were mute testimony to her own exhaustion. The pile of food was all too small, Damien noted, the water skins too empty for comfort. He managed to find the vitamins with the first aid kit and downed two of them, wondering what their caloric value was. Could you survive on those alone if all other food ran out, or would you wind up poisoning yourself with some toxic dose of a trace mineral before they did you any good? He wasn't anxious to find out.

He ate as sparingly as he could, but even so their stock was noticeably depleted when he was finished. They must have left a feast behind when they fled from the trees. Damn it. He hoped there was game at the river, or at least some kind of edible plant life. They'd need something if they were going to make it to the rakhlands with their strength intact.

He looked out toward the east – the way that Hesseth was facing

– and thought, *At least if it's animal she's smelling, it might serve as game when it gets here.*

If we can kill it, he told himself soberly.

And: *If it doesn't kill us first.*

Shoe leather scraped on the rock behind him: it was Hesseth, coming down from her guard position.

'Joining me for breakfast?' he asked her.

'Hardly.' With a quick glance over her shoulder she stooped down, and with agile hands she began to place the food goods back in their pack. 'We've got problems.'

He capped the canteen in his hand and put it down. 'They getting close?'

She glanced up at him. 'Maybe.' Then down again, to the packages she was quickly storing. 'The scent's faded. It was coming straight at us and then it faded. Suddenly.'

'What do you make of it?'

'Something was upwind of us. Now it's not.' He knew her body language well enough to see the tension in her movements, to hear the tautness in her speech. 'Animals will do that. Hunting animals. When they get close to their prey, they position themselves downwind . . . or at least where the wind won't betray them.'

He felt something tighten inside him as the understanding came. 'Not the habits of a tree-eater.'

'No.'

She had finished with the dry goods now, and he helped her tie up the canteens and the water skins. The first aid kit was lying out on the rock; he closed that up and packed it, too.

'If they've been upwind of us up until now, then how would they know we're here?'

She looked at him. The was a spark of incredulity in her eyes, as if she couldn't understand why he would need to ask her that. 'The trail,' she said. 'They're following our trail.'

It hit him then. The trail they must have left behind them, paved in blood and sweat and fear. Not the kind of thing a man might follow easily, but it would stand out like a beacon to any predator.

Damn!

He stood. The wind ruffled his sweat-stiffened hair as he looked about the island, assessing their defensive options. Bad, he decided. Very bad. The low mound offered them a good enough vantage point but no shelter to speak of, and there was none within sight. *None within miles,* he thought, gazing out upon the flat wasteland surrounding them. In another time and place he might have noted the location of major tree-clusters and worked them into his defensive plans; in this time and place he would rather walk naked and unarmed into a den of ravenous meat eaters than ever approach one of those things again.

'Get the girl,' he said quietly.

He checked his weapons as Hesseth went to Jenseny, loading the projectile weapon Tarrant had left with them. Like the western springbolt it would launch a metal-tipped quarrel with good speed and reasonable accuracy; unlike a springbolt, it would only do so once before needing to be reloaded. Not a good situation if there was a whole pack of animals on the way, he thought grimly. Didn't the Neocount have a gun? He seemed to remember it at one point. Was it tucked into the pack Tarrant had left behind? He began to go look, then reconsidered. This was a hostile land, undeniably sorcerous in origin, controlled by an enemy adept who even now was focusing his attention on them . . . in short, if ever there was a situation asking for a misfire, this was it. No. He'd take his chances with the simpler weapons, and not give the Prince such an opening.

Then Hesseth was beside him, and the girl was with her. Eyes bloodshot, weaving slightly, she looked so small and so fragile that he could hardly believe she had made it this far. He'd known a lot of children who couldn't have.

'You okay?' he asked gently.

Her face was drawn and pale and there were deep circles under her eyes, but she nodded. From her movements he guessed that she still hurt badly – probably along her back, where the tree roots had pierced her flesh – but she obviously wasn't going to admit it. Still afraid, he thought. Still convinced that if she hurt too much or feared too much they might leave her behind. As if that was an option in this place.

Someday this will all be over, he promised her silently. *Someday*

*we'll be able to take you away from here and find you a real home,
where you can grow up in peace. Where you can be a real child again.*

'I'm going to Work,' he warned them.

He turned to the east and braced himself. Maybe it was foolish
to Work again, but the way he figured it the Prince already knew
where they were and what they were doing here, so he wasn't going
to make matters worse by crafting a Knowing in their defense. He
used a visual key, a linear pattern that he traced with his mind's
eye in order to focus his consciousness—

The Knowing took shape suddenly, brilliantly, before him. He saw
a scaled animal, obsidian black, whose long, low body flowed over
the ground with serpentine grace. The narrow head sported sharp
white teeth that glinted in the sunlight as it opened its mouth to take
in the smells of the region; its talons flexed on the hard black earth
as it caught the scent of blood. In the distance similar creatures were
moving silently, swiftly, their movements so perfectly coordinated that
it seemed as if some single will might have organized them. *As well it
might have,* Damien thought suddenly. How much sorcery would
it take to reach out from the Black Lands and take control of these
creatures? Very little, if they had been created for that purpose.

Suddenly cold, he turned to Hesseth. He didn't have to say
anything; the look on his face said it all.

'*Assst,*' she hissed. 'A pack?'

'Maybe worse,' he told her. 'Maybe a pack under somebody's
control.'

'How many?' she demanded.

The vision was gone now; he shut his eyes and tried to resurrect
it. 'At least a dozen,' he said finally. 'Maybe more.'

'Predators,' she mused. 'But how? There's no game here.'

'There's us,' he reminded her. 'And all the victims of the trees.
Maybe the roots don't use up all the meat. Maybe there's enough left
for scavengers.' *And sometimes living bodies, too, immobilized by the
power of the tree.* He remembered the skeletons that had been torn
apart, limbs and torso and head and tails each gone to provide an
individual meal. There would be other game, too, men and animals
not yet claimed by the trees' power but affected by it, who lacked
the strength to run and the clarity of thought to defend themselves . . .

Like we were last night. Like we might be again, once we leave this island.

'We can't defend ourselves here,' he heard himself saying. 'Not if they surround us.' There were species that did that, he knew. Pack instinct. Those were the most deadly hunters of all.

'Where can we go?'

He looked around helplessly, knowing what he would see. A grouping of trees here and there on the plain, one low dome of crusted lava. Otherwise: Flatness. Emptiness. A total and absolute lack of shelter, for God alone knew how many miles.

He felt panic rising inside him, drew in a deep breath as he struggled to fight it down. He had faced worse than this, hadn't he? He'd done it and come out on top. He would come out on top of this one, too.

'Undying Prince be damned,' he muttered. The man had made a crucial mistake. By forcing them to Work to defend themselves he might have managed to locate them, but now that they had given themselves away they had no more reason not to Work the fae. He drew in another deep breath, reaching out to take hold of the earth-currents. Not a Knowing this time, but a Locating. Something focused on the concept of *defensive ground,* something that would help them find a place where they could put their backs to a wall – so to speak – and face their enemy together.

'South,' he whispered, as the information came. 'Due south. Almost a mile.'

'What?'

'I don't know.' The Locating had faded as soon as its mission was accomplished; he didn't resurrect it. 'Some place where the terrain will favor us. Some place we can defend.'

She looked into his eyes. Deep into his eyes. 'That's a hell of a walk, isn't it?' And he knew what she meant. He knew what she was afraid of.

'The trees didn't attack us until we tried to rest,' he said quietly. Feeling his own gut tighten up at the thought of braving the trees' domain once more. 'If we keep moving, we should be all right.'

'You sure of that?'

He hesitated. 'We can't stay here,' he said at last. 'That means taking a chance. But it makes sense, doesn't it? If their power lies in sleep-inducement, it stands to reason they would wait until their victim's body had done half the work for them. Or at least given them some kind of opening.'

'Let's hope so,' she muttered.

They gathered up their things as quickly as they could. Damien took special care to see that the first aid supplies were easily accessible; there was no telling when or how quickly they might need them. Jenseny wanted to shoulder part of the burden, but when she hoisted up a blanket roll to her tiny shoulders Damien took it from her, and added it to his own. She was too small and too weak and too badly shaken by her recent experience; if they needed those small legs to keep up with them at a run, they'd better make sure she wasn't weighted down with anything.

'I can carry it,' she insisted, and he heard the fear in her voice. Not of the trees, he thought, or even of the Prince. Of her own uselessness, and the fact that it might cause her to be left behind.

'It's all right,' he whispered hoarsely, and he patted her shoulder in reassurance. 'You just keep up with us.'

They set out from the south end of the granite island, and if there was any difference between the hard gray rock they had rested on and the frozen lava beyond it, their feet couldn't feel it. Nevertheless, it was one of the hardest single steps Damien had ever taken. He could feel his whole body bracing itself for the onslaught of the trees, and he had to fight to make it move forward, to place even one foot on the ground which harbored that deadly species. But then he made contact and there was no assault, and he knew that the power the trees had gained over him had faded in the night. Or else been banished, by Tarrant's chill power and his own fledgeling efforts.

A mile. That would have meant maybe fifteen minutes for him alone, a little longer with Hesseth's shorter legs setting the pace. He didn't want to think about how long it would take with the small girl by their side. They pushed on as quickly as they dared. Sometimes when they walked too fast for her, Jenseny would break into a short run to try to keep up with them. That was all right. She could afford a brief jog here and there; they couldn't. At the end of this mile they would have to defend themselves against a pack of the Prince's pet killers, and if they didn't have their breath and their energy and their wits about them, then they could all kiss it good-bye together.

He stopped every few minutes to work an Obscuring; not because he thought that he could turn the hunters aside, but because he hoped that maybe he could slow them down. Maybe by casting out a false lead into the desert he could distract them from the true trail for a short time, and maybe – just maybe – it would take them a while to work their way back again. He could only hope. He had even tried to Work an illusion back on the granite isle, to make it seem as if they had never left, but he knew how hard it was to create an image so complete that an animal would believe it. And besides, when the beasts finally attacked, they would know the illusion for what it was and its power would fade instantly. Tarrant had the kind of skill it took to create an illusion that smelled right and tasted right and struggled properly as it died . . . but he would have needed a living creature to bind it to, in order to make that work. And Damien had seen enough simulacra die on their behalf that he couldn't have stomached another one. Not even to save their lives.

As for Hesseth, she made no offer to reinforce his Working with her own, by which he judged that the tidal power was simply not available. He deeply regretted that. As fleeting and unreliable as the tidal fae was, it was a type of power the Prince would have no experience with; Damien would have given anything to have it Obscuring them now. Perhaps it would become available later. He didn't imagine Hesseth would have any trouble Working it on their behalf this time. Though normally she could only protect her own family, he had traveled with her long enough and under intimate enough conditions that he might as well be her blood-kin. And as for the girl . . . he remembered a conversation he had half-heard one morning, as he rose up slowly from the depths of sleep to full consciousness.

Do you have any children? Jenseny had asked her.

It had taken her a long time to answer; when at last she did, her voice was strained. *I had one child,* she told her. *She was five years* old when I first went into the human lands. I left her with my kin for a longmonth, so that I might go.

What happened?

There was ... an accident. During an earthquake. It happens sometimes. A pause. I didn't even know until I got home. They didn't know how to tell me ... Her voice trailed off, thick with sorrow.

In a hushed whisper: *Will you have more children someday?*

There was a long silence before she answered. From the halting quality in her speech it was evident that she was struggling to find the right words, words that Jenseny would understand. *When the women of my species are ready to have children ... it's different than with humans. They can't think of anything else, they can't do anything else ... and humans would notice that. So when the khrast women want to leave the plains, they have to give that up. Forever. That's what I did.*

So you can't ever have children again?

No, kasa. Not ever. And she added, in a whisper, *But I have you.*

He had felt shamed, that morning. Shamed for having traveled with her so far, for knowing her so well, yet for never having asked such a basic question. Perhaps he had felt that if she had wanted to share her private life with him she would have, and it was not his place to pry. Of perhaps – more honestly – the memory of seeing a rakhene woman in heat still made him uncomfortable, and he had avoided any subject which might link such a display to his traveling companion. An unfair prejudice, perhaps, but a human one.

Periodically he turned back the way they had come and worked a quick Knowing. It was hard to manage against the current, and he could get only snippets of information. The animals had followed the false trail. They had abandoned it. They had found the true trail again and were tracking along it, losing time here and there to circumvent his Distractings, but always returning to the trail in the end. Clearly there was no hope of shaking this pursuit, and Damien prayed that he and his companions would reach their defensive post in time. If they were caught out in the open, they wouldn't stand a chance.

And then they came to a place where the ground fell away before their feet, into a chasm so deep and so shadowed that it was impossible to see the bottom of it. The walls of it were lined with black crystals, their edges gleaming like knives in the sunlight.

Twelve feet across, he judged. Too far to jump with any surety; certainly too far for Jenseny to leap across.

'Is this what you Located?' Hesseth asked sharply.

'Looks like it. Damn.' He shook his head as he gazed down into the depths of the abyss. 'Not what I would have preferred, that's for sure.'

'But better than open ground. Isn't it?'

Is it? 'Yeah.' He forced the words out. 'A little.'

Think, Vryce, think. There's got to be a way out of this mess.

'Can we get across?' Jenseny asked.

'Can't jump,' he muttered.

'What about the trees?' Hesseth asked. Pointing to one particularly stout specimen that was rooted several feet back from the chasm's lip.

He saw what she was driving at, and he didn't like it. He didn't like the thought of even going near one of those things again, much less cutting it down and manhandling it into position, and then trusting his life to it as they inched along its twisted trunk, over God alone knew how much empty space . . . but it might work. God damn it. It might save them, if they could get across before the animals reached them and then cast off their makeshift bridge, down into the chasm's depths.

He took a deep breath – a very deep breath – and started off toward the stocky tree. As he took his first step, a noise sounded to the north of them: a thin, wailing shriek that might have been the wind. Or a scream of pain. Or a hunting cry, voiced by an animal that had finally sighted its prey.

God, he prayed, *just give us time. That's all I ask. A few extra minutes to work with, so we can get ourselves out of here. Please, God. Just that.*

The tree Hesseth had spotted was tall and straight and its base was nearly as thick around as his thigh. He tried not to think about what manner of victim had nurtured it into such healthy growth, tried not to look for the bones that must surely be scattered about its base. Those things were irrelevant now. He reached for a nearby branch and bent it down, fighting the sickness that welled up inside him at the mere thought of touching the thing. But it might have been a normal tree for all that it affected him now, and the resiliency he noted as he tested its branch spoke well for the strength of its wood. Which was a damned good thing, he thought. Because twenty feet up it wasn't all that thick around, and he'd hate for it to break beneath their weight just when safety was within sight.

'All right!' he called back. 'We'll try it.'

He could hear the baying of the beasts now, the triumphant howls of hunters who were closing in on their prey. With a pounding heart he knelt down by the base of the tree and prepared himself for Working. No time for finesse now, or the delicate manipulations of a Knowing; he needed brute force, wielded with the Hunter's killing power. And he would summon that force for them here and now, if he had to draw on Tarrant's own power to do it.

Too determined to be afraid – at least for the moment – Damien plunged his will into the living wood. The shock of contact was almost unbearable, and it took all his strength and all his courage not to withdraw from it, not to try to save himself. If the tree's power had lapped at his conscousness before, now he was wholly immersed in it, and he shook body and soul as he fought to maintain control. The tree sucked him in, deep into its soul, deep into the source of its power, and even as he struggled with it he could sense the slender roots growing toward him, hairs so fine that the porous rock was hardly an obstacle, thin white fingers of death that were even now licking at the surface beneath his feet. It took a monumental effort not to think about them, not to back off and defend himself – but if he failed now, with this tree, then he might as well just give himself over to the pack and have it done with. And that knowledge gave him fresh strength, if not added courage.

He took hold of its substance, cell by cell. He insinuated his will into the very fibers of its being, in much the same way he would for a Healing. Then, instead of forcing the tree to grow, he forced it to die; instead of forcing the cells to bind tighter together, he ripped apart the very structure that bound them. It was a perfect reversal of the Healer's art: an un-Healing, an anti-Healing, an act that he would have found wholly repulsive had he not required it for survival. And the wood responded. Cells died, choked off by his power. Cell walls shattered and gave way, loosening their hold on their neighbors. Inch by inch he worked his way through the trunk of the white tree, cell by cell by endless cell . . .

And then it was done. He drew back, gasping for breath, and regarded his handiwork. The damage was barely visible on the outside of the trunk, but his Worked senses could see the wound scything through the living wood like a sword cut. Good enough. Now if he could only get the thing to fall right . . .

'They're coming,' Hesseth warned.

He didn't look. He couldn't afford to. If he couldn't get the tree in place by the time the pack attacked, then they were all doomed, and so he refused to spare the few seconds that looking would entail. Instead he moved to the north side of the tree and gathered all his power – not in the way he had been taught to do but the way that Tarrant did it, using the raw force of the currents to split the tree apart – and he pushed, he pushed for his life, he pushed with all the force of the earth-fae behind him, forcing the tree into a fall that would place it cleanly across the chasm and then using the earth-fae to see that it didn't break, it didn't bounce, it didn't skitter off to one side or the other and go plunging down into the depths. His whole body shook as the power surged through him, using his will as its focus. And then the tree began to fall. Slowly at first, as if fighting the fatal drop. Then smoothly, almost gracefully, its topmost branches sketching an arc through the air as it hurtled toward the ground. Damien found himself praying as he watched it fall, knowing that if even one of his Workings failed this might all be wasted effort.

The tree struck with a resounding crash, and all the ground around them shook. He could sense the force of the impact coalescing in the trunk, could feel it fighting to tear the wood apart. But it held. God be praised, it held. It shuddered once or twice and then settled into place, spanning the gap perfectly.

He looked back toward Hesseth – and saw movement in the distance, the glint of white light on ivory teeth, obsidian scales. 'Go!' he told her. 'Take the girl.' He saw that she had taken her shoes off so that her sharp claws might help her keep her balance. 'Now!'

'What about you—'

He glanced at the narrow bridge, felt fear tighten its grip on his heart. It was too thin, too thin; had he ever dreamed it would support him? 'If it's going to break, it'll do so under my weight. You get across first, then I'll follow.' When she hesitated, he snapped at her, 'Do it!'

She grabbed the girl's wrist and ran to the edge of the chasm. There she caught the girl up and scrambled to the upper side of the trunk. For a moment Damien's heart was in his throat as he watched, and then – as he witnessed the perfection of her rakhene balance, the anchoring power of those long, unsheathed talons – he knew she was going to make it. The rakh were designed for such excursions.

Not like humans, he thought grimly.

With a quick glance behind him to see how close the hunters were, he bolted for the makeshift bridge. He could hear claws clattering on the hard earth as the animals rushed to close in on him, could hear their growls of hunger and exultation as they ran those last few yards to claim their dinner. And then he was up on the trunk and he was moving south, out over the chasm's yawning mouth, trying not to look down or look back or, worst of all, think about the fact that any moment the trunk might crack and sent him plummeting down into those black, hungry depths . . . the tree shook beneath his feet as the animals grabbed hold of it and he realized with sudden terror that their claws would give them perfect purchase, that they could move along the twisted trunk as easily as Hesseth had, while he dared not slip so much as an inch. *Don't think about that. Don't.* He felt his hand go for his sword, but he forced himself to use it for balance instead. One step and then another, quickly but oh so carefully managed. There had been a kink halfway up the tree and he glanced down long enough to locate it, taking care that it didn't trip him. The wood was shaking beneath his feet; it seemed he could feel the animals' hot breath on his heels. His every instinct screamed for him to draw his sword, a knife, *anything* – but he knew that if the animals attacked him here, he had no hope of survival, none at all, and so he put all his energy into speed, into care, into hoping desperately that the slender end of the trunk would bear his weight . . .

And then he was across. He jumped to the ground so quickly that he stumbled and fell, tangling in the tree's upper branches as he went down. Had he been alone, that would have been the end of him, but even as one of the beasts lunged toward his leg, Hesseth met it head-on with a knife thrust that cut it open along the side of its neck, from the bottom of its jaw to the artery that coursed deep inside its flesh. Red blood spurted out onto the tree and the ground and the two of them, staining everything crimson. While Hesseth defended him against the next assailant, Damien struggled to his feet, and then his sword was drawn and he was cutting, thrusting, doing everything he could to keep the pack from completing their crossing. Sometimes one would get past him and Hesseth would have to bring it down, and once he heard her yowl shortly in pain as long claws raked her arm.

'The tree!' he yelled out. Hoping she understood. He looked desperately at the line of animals working their way across the bridge and saw a gap between two of them that was wider than most. Two animals down. He skewered the next that gained the ledge, and left its struggling, bloody form for Hesseth to dispatch. He thanked God for the length of his sword as he struck again, and for the advantage it gave him. He swung, and a black scaled body went hurtling down into the depths, screaming as it fell.

And then there was the gap in the rush of scaled bodies. Not much of one, but he knew in his gut that he wasn't going to get a better chance than this and so he took it. Throwing all his weight against the trunk he tried to dislodge it from its position on the ledge, trusting that Hesseth would see what he was doing and get the hell out of the way. For a moment there was extra weight as the rakh-woman scrambled over to his side, and then her strength was added to his and the trunk began to move, ever so slowly at first and then sliding along the hard black rock, farther and farther—

Pain stabbed suddenly into his shoulder and the weight of a large, hot animal slammed him sideways. The leading beast had dared a leap across the abyss and now it was on him, its sharp teeth swinging around mere inches from his throat. He couldn't bring his sword around in time but rammed its pommel into the black-scaled head again and again, trying to force it back. Hot, sour breath blasted him in the face as the animal struggled for access to his throat, where a single bite might dispatch him. As he fought, he prayed – not for himself, but for Hesseth. Prayed that she could push the tree over the edge by herself before the rest of the animals came across. Because if she couldn't, they were doomed. That simple. No single warrior, no matter how skilled, could fight off such an invasion.

Claws raked his stomach as he slammed the sword's pommel into the creature's eye, and for a moment he feared that the beast would eviscerate him; then the animal spasmed and he threw it off and managed to rise up despite his wounds. A quick slash through its neck satisfied him that the beast would be no more trouble, and though his stomach was cut badly and his clothes were splattered with blood, there were no vital pieces falling out of him and all his muscles worked, which was good enough for now.

Hesseth had managed to push the tree far enough that the bulk of it was now over the chasm, and she was struggling to get the topmost part over the edge so that the whole of it would fall. The child was beside her, gamely adding her pittance of strength to the effort, and rainbow sparks glittered about both their hands as the tidal fae manifested additional force. But though the tree was moving, there was now additional danger, for the sharp angle at which it now bridged the chasm permitted the leading animals to leap directly across to Hesseth.

He got there just in time. His sword stroke was desperate, undisciplined, but the sheer force of it knocked the creature off course and sent him slamming down into the chasm wall. There was a brief pause then, which Damien used to take up a better position beside Hesseth. Only seconds more and then the bridge would be gone, and all three of them would be safe . . .

It happened quickly. An animal leapt straight at him, forcing him to bring up his sword between them in order to defend himself. The beast impaled itself, but sheer velocity carried it forward, and the dead weight of its flesh slammed into him with stunning force. He was thrown back against the earth with a suddenness that drove the breath from his body, and his head banged the rock so hard that for a minute his vision deserted him, and all he could see were brilliant white stars in an endless sea of blackness. Then there were figures, hazy and indistinct, and he focused on them as he tried to struggle to his feet.

One of the beasts had gotten to Hesseth and they were locked in a death-grip atop the tree trunk, teeth and claws and silver knife flashing in the sunlight. He tried to stand, to go to her, but something was wrong with his balance and he fell, he fell hard, he fell down to his knees while the world swam in circles about him, fighting to orient himself. Dimly he was aware of Hesseth getting atop the beast, of the silver knife flashing again and again as it cut downward—

And the tree broke. With a crack like thunder its trunk split in two right near Hesseth. The part which had bridged the chasm went hurtling down into its depths, taking the rest of the animals with it. The shorter end hesitated for a second, counterweighted by Hesseth and the animal atop it, and then its balance point slipped over the edge and it, too, began to slide—

'Hesseth!'

—and she saw what was coming, she tried to get free, but the beast had hold of her and the branches were tangled about her and the sheer weight of it all dragged her off her feet—

'No!'

—and she reached out for something to hang onto, anything! but all her claws could find was the tree, branches and trunk all spattered with crimson, and then she went over—

—and down.

He lunged toward the lip of the chasm as she fell, trying to grab hold of her. Branches struck his face as the last limbs went sliding down into the chasm, slamming against the jagged black walls as it fell. For a moment rainbow power flashed in those lightless depths, and he thought that she had used the tidal fae to save herself. But then that was gone and there was only darkness, accompanied by the howls and the thrashing of dying beasts.

No. God, no. Not her. Please.

Pain was a fire in his stomach as he tried to focus on the earth-fae, enough to conjure light. His hands, slick with blood, gripped the edge of the chasm with spastic force as he spoke the key words over and over again. At last a faint light answered his summons, and as he felt the girl rush to the ledge by his side, as he heard her crying, the conjured light filled the chasm and let them see what had happened.

Bodies. Everywhere. Black, scaly bodies and broken tree limbs and pink flesh and rock . . . he searched desperately for Hesseth's body, at last found it sprawled across the viciously sharp outcropping which had stopped its fall. There was so much blood all over the place that it was impossible to see where her wounds were, but the sharp angle of her neck and the impossible bend in her back left no doubt about her fate. Grief welled up inside him with such raw force that he lost control of the light, and it faded. Into blackness. Into death.

'No!' the girl screamed. She jumped toward the chasm as if she would throw herself into it, but Damien grabbed her by the neck of her shirt and pulled her back. 'No!' She struggled blindly against his confining grasp, as if somehow by doing so she was also fighting Death. Bits of rainbow light swirled about her as she cried out to Hesseth, screaming words Damien didn't understand – rakhene words? – hysterical in her shock, in her grief. Numbly he let her rage. She was doing it for both of them, voicing the horror of this loss better than he ever could.

Hesseth. She was gone. The Wasting had killed her. She had been by his side for so long now that it seemed impossible that he would never see her again. Tears ran down his face as the loss of it – the terrible, fearsome loss of it – hit home. For a moment he envied Jenseny the freedom of childhood, which permitted her to rant and rave with total abandon; all he could do was lower his head, his whole body shaking, and let the tears come.

After a time the girl's struggles weakened, and she fell sobbing to her knees. He drew her to him then, gently, into his arms. She resisted at first, then clutched at him desperately, burying her face in his bloodied shirt and sobbing uncontrollably. Did she smell faintly of Hesseth? Was that possible? He lowered his face to her hair and for a long time just held her. The two of them alone in the Wasting.

In the end it was the pain in his shoulder and the hot cuts across his stomach that reminded him they needed to move. Softly, ever so softly, he whispered, 'Jenseny. We can't stay here.'

She drew back from him; her expression was fierce. 'We can't leave her!'

'Jenseny, please—'

'We can't leave her here!'

He held her out at arm's length, so that she was forced to look at him. 'Jenseny, listen to me. Hesseth is gone now.' He said it as gently as he could but, oh, how the words hurt! He could see her flinch as he voiced them and she shook her head wildly as if somehow that would make the fact untrue . . . but she knew. She knew. 'Her soul is free. All that's down there is empty flesh. The part you loved, the part that loved you . . . she's back with her people now. What you saw down there was just a . . . a container. She doesn't need it anymore.'

'She left,' the girl gasped hoarsely. 'She left us.'

'Oh, God.' He drew her to him and held her tightly, so tightly that there would be no room for grief or loneliness or any other source of darkness in that tiny, frightened soul. 'She didn't want to go, Jenseny. She was trying to protect us. She didn't want anything to hurt you, not for all the world.' He blinked fresh tears from his eyes as he stroked her hair gently, softly. 'She loved you so much,' he whispered.

Suddenly faintness welled up inside him. He forced himself to push the girl away and for a moment just sat there, trying not to lose consciousness. Then, when the world seemed steady once more, he pulled open his shirt front. Bloody strips parted to reveal a torso that had been ripped and torn in at least a dozen places; his chest and stomach were coated with blood, and his pants were soaked with it. As if in confirmation of the sight a fresh wave of pain washed over him, and its force was such that he nearly doubled over and vomited onto the lava.

'God.' He tried to work a Healing to close up the wounds, but the fae was slippery, blood-slick, and it defied him. He drew in a shaky breath and tried it again – and this time there was a response, he could feel the earth-power pricking his skin as the torn cells healed, the gashes filled in, the pain receded. When he was done, all that was left was an ache in his chest, a faint echo of the pain that had been. And an emptiness inside him that no mere Working could heal.

She was watching him with wide, frightened eyes. Calm at last, as if the sight of his wounds had scared her back to sanity. *She could have lost us both,* he thought. *Maybe that just hit her.*

'Come on,' he whispered. 'We have to get moving.'

He tried not to think about Hesseth as he helped the child to her feet. Tried not think about how vital and alive she had been a mere hour ago. How much she had gone through to come to this place only to be killed by beasts – by beasts! – at the very threshold of victory. He tried not to think about all those things, because when he did his eyes filled with tears and his throat grew tight and he found it hard to walk. And they had to keep walking no matter what, he and the child both. Otherwise the trees would have them.

Miles. Hours. He worked a Locating to find them another island, but no Working could bring it closer to them. Step by step he forced himself to keep moving, and when the girl grew too tired or frightened or numb with grief to walk they took a brief rest – never too long, lest the trees reach out to them – and they drank sparingly from their dwindling supply of water, and swallowed a few mouthfuls of dry food. It had no taste. The fact of Hesseth's death had leached all color from the world, all smells, all flavor. They marched on a black plain into a gray sky, and even when the tidal fae gathered around Jenseny to sketch a fleeting image of the rakh-woman before her eyes, its work was rendered in shades of slate and granite and mist.

It was well past noon when they reached their haven. This island was a sharp slab that thrust up through the lava flow at such a steep angle that they had to circle nearly all the way around it before they found a place where they could climb. On its south side the slab had shattered and fallen, leaving a pile of rubble that could serve as a functional, if precarious, staircase.

When at last they reached a resting spot – a wide ledge some ten feet down from the island's highest point – Damien felt the raw grief of the day's experience finally overwhelm him. He let it. The girl collapsed on the granite shelf – safely back from the edge, he saw to that – and sobbed wildly, giving vent to all the misery and the fear that she had been fighting for hours. He let her. He had seen enough grief in his time to know that this, too, was part of the healing. No wound could close until it had been properly drained.

At last, softly, he spoke her name.

At first she didn't seem to hear him. Then, seconds after he had spoken, she looked up at him. Her eyes were red and swollen and her whole face was wet with tears. Shaking, she wiped a sleeve across her nose as she looked at him, waiting to hear what he had to say.

'I'm going to say a prayer for Hesseth,' he told her. 'It's a very special prayer that we say when someone dies. Normally—' The words caught in his throat suddenly and for a moment he couldn't speak. 'Normally we say it when we bury people, but sometimes the people we love die when they're far away, or something happens to a body so that we can't get to it . . . like with Hesseth. So we just say it when we can, because God will hear it anywhere.' He gave that a minute to sink in, then told her, very softly, 'I'd like you to do it with me.'

For a moment she didn't answer. Then, in a hoarse whisper, she asked him, 'What is it?'

He drew in a deep breath, 'We tell God how much we loved Hesseth, and how sorry we are that she's gone. And then we talk about the good things she did, and how much she cared for all of us, and we ask God to please take care of her, and see that she gets back to her people, and to see that her soul is surrounded by the souls of those she loved . . . That's all,' he said hoarsely. 'It's just a . . . a way of saying good-bye.' He held out a hand to her. 'Come on. I'll lead you through it.'

She didn't move at first. The look in her eyes was strange, and at first Damien attributed it to her fear of his Church. For a brief moment he wondered if he had chosen badly, if the offer of healing he had intended might not hurt her more.

But then she whispered, with tears in her voice, 'After we do it for Hesseth, then we . . . can we please . . . say one for my father?'

'Oh, my God.' He pulled her to him, oh so gently, wary lest she reject the contact. But she came to him and she put her arms around him and she sobbed into the fabric of his shirt, shedding tears that had been kept inside for so long that they must have burned like fire as they flowed. 'Of course, Jen. Of course.' He kissed the top of her head. 'God forgive me for not having thought of it sooner. Of course we can.'

In the desert night, by the light of a single moon, they prayed for the souls of their loved ones.

40

The river was swollen fat from the spring tides, and its icy current easily submerged the various rocks and promontories which might be hazards in another season. The three boats slid over its surface with ease, reflections shimmering in the Corelight as the oars dipped quietly in unison, drew free of the water, dipped again.

They were using no steam tonight, nor any form of power that might make noise. If their quarry had been merely human, the captain might have chanced it, but one of the travelers was rakhene – and that kind could pick out the mechanical sound of a steam engine down a hundred miles of canyon, if they knew that their lives depended on it.

It was rare that he got to hunt his own kind. It was . . . intriguing.

They came to where the canyon turned, and then he signaled the three boats ashore. The thin leather gloves he wore made his hand seem almost human as it executed the command gesture, and the irony of it was not lost on him.

They dragged the boats ashore, beyond the reach of a sudden spring swell, and gathered about the captain. With minimal words and gestures he described the situation, their position, their intention.

One of them asked, 'Alive?'

'If possible,' he responded.

He opened the hood that protected his head and face from the sun and let it fall back on his shoulders. A cool breeze ruffled his mane and he breathed it in deeply, sifting it for scents. Nothing useful.

'Are you sure they'll land here?' one of the humans demanded. 'Shouldn't we have some kind of backup?'

He turned to face the man. There was no need to hiss a warning; his expression was enough. The man's color, already light in tint, went two shades paler.

'*His Highness* says they'll land here.' There was scorn in the captain's voice, and the absolute authority of one who has earned his position not only through civilized human channels, but by blood and by claw. 'Do you have a problem with that?'

'No, sir.' He shook his head vigorously. 'Of course not, sir.'

Deliberately, the captain turned away from him. 'All right,' he said. 'You know the plans. Take up your positions and be ready. Stay quiet. And remember: they have sorcery. Don't take chances.'

'Sir?'

Humans. It never ceased to amaze him how they needed everything spelled out for them.

'If they look like they're about to Work,' he told them, 'then kill them.'

And he added, just because they were human, 'Any questions?'

This time, there were none.

41

There was an earthquake soon after sunset. By the light of the Core they could see the twisted land rippling as the shock waves passed through it, the black earth heaving like a storm-tossed sea. And then, at last, all was quiet. New cracks surrounded the base of their island, but there was nothing they couldn't get across if they had to.

'Is he coming soon?' the girl asked.

Tarrant.

In Hesseth's absence he was their anchor, their key. Damien's Workings might net them a few helpful tips about dealing with their immediate environment, but it would take a man of Tarrant's power and experience to obtain what they must have now: exhaustive knowledge about a land few humans had ever seen, and a safe means of approaching a species hostile to their own. With Hesseth gone, he was their only hope.

'Soon,' Damien promised.

The local faeborn were beginning to gather about their mount, but they were few in number and lacked strength; evidently the more enterprising wraiths had made their bid for nourishment the night before. Unable to Banish them because of the earthquake-hot currents, Damien held the child close to him and watched as they flitted about the camp. Ghostlings, bloodsuckers, a single succubus. He watched the latter for a few seconds, marveling at the way she – it – responded to his scrutiny. Slowly the foggy form adopted all the features that he found desirable in women, and if he had responded even for a moment it would have taken that as an opening and attached itself to him faster than he could draw in a breath. But he knew all too well what it was and what it could do, and far from arousing his sexual interest it repelled him so thoroughly that at last the thing screeched in frustration and darted off into the night, no doubt to seek more cooperative prey. The rest kept their distance, circling warily about the ledge. Damien kept his hand on his sword, ready to deal with the more solid manifestations, and prayed that the subtler demonlings would make no move until the fae cooled off. Wouldn't that be the ultimate waste, to come all this way and fight so hard to get here, only to fry himself to a crisp in a single careless gesture—

Oh, my God.

For a moment he was unable to move, and barely able to think; if one of the ghostlings had attacked him then and there, that would have been it for him. Because a thought had just occurred to him that was so terrible, so absolutely devastating in its implications, that his mind could barely touch on it without opening a gateway to utter panic.

Tarrant.

Had awakened at sunset.

Had transformed himself in order to return to them.

Had *Worked*?

He remembered the earthquake which had so recently shaken their granite mount, rock shards tumbling down on them as the ground convulsed from horizon to horizon. And yet that physical upheaval was nothing compared to what preceded it. To the surge of earth-fae which flowed just ahead of it, swallowing everything in its path . . .

How alert was the Hunter when he first awoke? How careful? Did the deathlike trance release him so suddenly when sunset came that his mind was alert and functioning mere seconds later? Or was there, as with the living, a short period of dullness in which the brain struggled to throw off the bonds of sleep and get on with the business of living? Was that precisely disciplined soul so perfectly oriented that he would never think of transforming his flesh without first checking the currents for an earthquake's subtle warning signs? Or had he Worked his own flesh so many nights now, so fearlessly, that a glance at the earth-fae would seem enough? A token gesture without real concentration behind it—

'What is it?' Jenseny demanded. 'What's wrong?'

Shaking, he wrapped his arms around his chest and tried to believe that everything was all right. Because if Tarrant was gone, then there really was no hope for them. They might get through the desert, they might even find a willing ear or two among the rakh, but without Tarrant's power to back them up there was no way they could defeat a man like the Prince. Not a sorcerer who was so deeply entrenched here that even the plants served his will.

Oh, God, he thought, shivering. *Let him be all right. Please.*

'Nothing,' he managed, in answer to the girl's question. With childlike acuity she seemed to sense that he was lying to her, but with rare maturity she accepted his words at face value and did not press the point. Perhaps she was afraid to. Perhaps, after Hesseth's death, she had little stomach for bad news.

'Come on,' he muttered. 'Let's eat something.'

They went through the motions mechanically, silently. The dry food was tasteless to Damien, and the girl hardly picked at her portion. Another slight tremor shook the ridge as they washed the meal down with water – precious mouthfuls, carefully rationed – but the aftershock was of little consequence. Hopefully there would be no more of them as they traveled; Damien didn't relish the thought of the black earth rupturing beneath his feet.

When they had packed away the food and hooked the canteens to their packs, Damien took out his one spare shirt and pulled off the bloodstained one he was wearing. Neither was clean by any standard, but the new one was at least still in one piece; the other was so badly scored by claws that it pulled free of his body in strips, glued to his flesh by the blood and the sweat that had soaked into it. *Not a pretty sight,* he thought grimly as he packed away the ragged garment. Tarrant, with his usual hygienic chauvinism, would doubtless make some disparaging comment when he arrived.

If he arrived.

They watched together as the Core followed the sun into its western grave, the golden light turning amber and then blood-red as it was filtered through Erna's veil of volcanic dust and windborn ash. Still the Hunter did not return to them.

Tarrant, I need you. I need your knowledge, I need your insight, I even need your God-damned cynicism. Get back to us soon, will you please?

But Tarrant didn't come.

And in time, his heart as cold as ice, his brain a numb morass of confusion, he whispered to the girl, 'We're on our own.'

To do what? Confront the rakh?

Numbly he lowered himself to the lava plain, and helped her down beside him. Numbly they started off across the black earth, their movements mechanical, their conversation strained. Again and again Damien went over their situation in his mind. Again and again he didn't like what he saw.

You're on your own, Vryce.

The girl might help him somehow. She had been close to Hesseth, close enough to absorb some of her language and a number of her memories; Damien regretted now that he had respected their privacy too much to explore the parameters of that absorption. And Jenseny had power. Wild power, untamed power, but power nonetheless. A power the Prince could neither foresee nor dominate, if ever she could learn to wield it properly.

If.

The miles passed beneath their feet like an abstract painting, details blurred by the brushstrokes of a distracted mind. Occasionally Damien surfaced from his thoughts long enough to see a tree, an outcropping, a blistered dome. Most of it passed unnoticed by him as he trod the hard earth, careful always to set a pace that Jenseny's young legs could manage.

The river. That was the thing. They needed to reach the river first, and then all the rest would follow. Fresh water would renew them in body and spirit, and give them the strength to plan. If they were lucky, there would be some kind of food there, some plant or animal whose flesh could supplement their meager dried fare. And perhaps there would be time enough and safety enough for him to wash up a bit, so that when Tarrant arrived—

He stopped suddenly, unable to walk any farther. Emotion welled up in him with such force that it nearly drove him to his knees; only the knowledge that the trees were waiting for him to do just that kept him standing.

Tarrant was gone. There was no doubting it now, not after all these hours. First Hesseth, and then the Hunter . . . and the most painful part of all was that he couldn't begin to untangle his emotions, couldn't tell where the grief began or the anger ended or the pragmatism of their quest gave way to genuine caring . . . did he really care if Tarrant lived, beyond the practical advantages of their partnership? He abhorred what the man stood for so passionately that it was painful even to ask the question, and he dared not try to answer it.

I hope for his sake that he's dead. That would be far more merciful than the alternatives: To be incapacitated but not killed by the earthquake's power, so that he must wait out the centuries in a land bereft of food or healing. Or to be captured by the enemy, perhaps, while the earth-power still surged. After what he went through in the rakhlands, I think even he would prefer death to such an imprisonment.

'Are you all right?' the girl asked him.

He drew in a deep breath, then managed to nod. 'Yeah. I am now.' He caught up her hand in his – so small, her fingers, and her skin was so cold – and he squeezed it with all the love he could muster. 'I was just thinking. Trying to figure out where we're going . . .'

'The river,' the girl reminded him.

He chuckled – somewhat sadly – and squeezed her hand again. 'Yeah. The river. Thanks, kid.'

They didn't see it until they were nearly upon it.

The Wasting's one river had flowed long enough and hard enough to have eroded its way down through the layers of volcanic rock, down through the base rock beneath, carving out a steep canyon whose walls glistened in layers of black and gray and marbled white strata. Between those walls the current rushed westward, audible even from where they stood as it gushed over the rocks at its border. In the center it was deep enough that the water moved smoothly, swiftly, a silken black reflector that cast the moonlight back in a thousand shivering bits. After days in the desert, the smell of it was like something from another world.

For a moment he just stared at it. One moment. A luxury. Then, with a finger on his lips to warn the girl to silence, he worked a Knowing. Casting out a fine net, to trap the scent of danger. But though he directed his Working west and east and then both ways again, there was nothing upstream or downstream that seemed the least unnatural. Nor was there danger lurking hidden on either side of the canyon.

'Thank God,' he whispered. 'Tarrant pulled it off.'

'What?' the girl demanded.

'He was trying to make the Prince think that we were going somewhere else. Somewhere farther west along the river. I guess it worked.' He sighed heavily, feeling a weight lift from his chest at last. One weight among thousands. 'We're safe here, Jen. For a while at least.'

He led her along the edge of the canyon, searching the ground far below by Domina's light. At last he found a place where descent seemed possible and there was dry ground at the bottom, and after that it was easy. After days and nights of combating wraiths and nightmares and preternatural malaise, he welcomed the logistical challenge of simple rock climbing. Within minutes he had marked his path of descent, and soon after was rappelling downward with the child clutched tightly to his chest. It pleased him that the end of his rope had been looped about the trunk of a killer tree for support; let that species serve him now.

Water. He could feel it at his back even as he looked back up the way they had come, wondering if he should leave the rope where it was or yank it down to them. The water was more than a mere substance now, but also a symbol; in reaching it they had beaten the desert at its own game, at least for this leg of the journey. He breathed in its cool scent gratefully as he turned from the rope, leaving it in place for the moment.

He saw the girl moving toward the river and reached out quickly. 'Be careful,' he warned.

She looked at him with frightened eyes; he felt her tremble beneath his hand. 'Is something in there?' It was a reasonable question for one who had seen the Terata's warped creations, and before he answered he muttered the key to a Knowing under his breath. But the water held no secrets beneath its shimmering surface, and he assured her of the fact.

'The current's fast and the rocks'll be slippery ... and it'll be damned cold besides. Wait till the sun comes up, girl. It'll be safer then.'

It seemed to him that even as he spoke something flickered out on the river's surface. He recalled the sirens of the Sea of Dreams, the flickerings that had preceded their attack. His hand moved instinctively toward his sword, even as he told himself that it couldn't possibly be that, or anything like it. His Knowing would have detected such a threat.

Again the flicker. He could see it more clearly now, and no, it wasn't like the sirens. Those had been beautiful; this was repellent. A sliver of white that curled and uncurled beneath the surface, wormlike, reflecting the moonlight in broken bits. A tendril perhaps, attached to some larger whole? No, he told himself stubbornly. It couldn't be that. The Knowing would have revealed that.

But it bothered him. It bothered him so much that he didn't even dare turn back to look at the girl, to make sure that she was safe; he felt as though if he turned his back on the thing for a minute it would somehow manage to bridge the distance between them and do . . . what? He wasn't sure. But he felt in his gut that the thing was deadly, and that constant scrutiny was required. 'Stay with me,' he whispered, drawing his sword. 'Don't go near it.' Desperately he tried to study its shape despite the surface reflections that masked it, to figure out what the hell it was and what it was doing here before it could—

Before it—

What?

Too late, he realized what was happening. Too late he realized the pattern of his own thoughts, and what they were doing to him. Too late. Even as he tried to turn around – struggling against a tide of dread that demanded he watch the thing, *watch the thing!*, not take his eyes off it for a single instant – something struck him on the back of the head hard enough to send him reeling. The water was right before him and he splashed down into it, ice-cold liquid that drove the breath from his body in a startled gasp. Somehow he managed to keep hold of his sword. Somehow he managed to get his head above water before he breathed it in, and to ignore the blinding pain in his skull long enough to get to his feet and turn around—

There were a dozen of them, maybe more. Men in uniform, spread out with military precision along the narrow shore. One of them was holding Jenseny, and above the gloved hand which muffled her screams he could see her wide, terrified eyes pleading with him for help.

Tarrant had failed them. Or perhaps the earthquake had disabled him before he even had a chance to Work; perhaps the misKnowing was never even cast. Even so, there must have been a hell of an Obscuring guarding this company that Damien had never sensed its presence. Which meant there might be a Worker with them, and one of considerable power. If so . . . he tried not to think about that.

He tried to focus on what he could possibly do against such numbers, the one slim chance he had. With a desperate prayer in his heart he reached with his will down into the water at his feet, the icy current that hid the earth-fae from view—

'Don't try it,' a cool voice warned.

Startled, he looked for its source. A dark figure was moving among the soldiers, a figure cloaked in heavy wool that walked through the shadows with unhuman grace. The glint of buckles and clasps hinted at a uniform not unlike those which the other men were wearing, but with considerably more decoration. The voice was silken, with a trace of an accent that Damien didn't recognize.

'Don't,' the figure repeated. It was holding something up toward Damien, and with a chill the priest realized what it was. A pistol. 'If you Work – or even try to Work – I'll kill you on the spot. You understand me?'

Stiffly he nodded. Desperately he tried to think. There had to be a way out of this. *Had* to be. But as he looked at the soldiers spanning the shore, at the tall figure who so obviously commanded them, he could feel his heart sinking. There had to be a way out . . . but he couldn't see one for the life of him.

The figure nodded a command, and two of his men waded into the water toward Damien. For a brief instant he considered resistance, and then one of the men raised up a pistol of his own and trained it on Damien's face. Point blank. He stared down the cool steel barrel in utter despair, icy water swirling about his ankles as the other man yanked his sword from his hand, his knife from his belt, anything and everything that might be used aggressively from his person. If he had been stripped of his clothes in front of all these men, he could not possibly have felt more naked. Despair welled up inside him with numbing force. Was this it? Was this the end of everything they had fought for, suffered for, prayed for? He didn't want to accept that. He struggled not to believe it.

Roughly they hauled him back to shore, and forced him to his knees. His arms were jerked behind his back and manacles were snapped shut about his wrists; defeat engulfed him then, so powerfully that it nearly brought tears to his eyes. But he wouldn't give them the pleasure of seeing that. They had beaten him, bound him, stolen his dreams, but he would not give them his weakness as an added gift.

Slowly the cloaked figure approached him. As it did so, it passed from shadow into light, and Damien could see its features. Beside him he could hear Jenseny breathe in sharply, her struggles momentarily halted as she gazed upon the face of their captor.

Rakh.

A glorious, majestic rakh, with a thick silken mane that lifted in the breeze as he moved and eyes that glowed green in the moonlight. Not from Hesseth's own species, but a sibling race that had been transformed by the same power which remade hers. His face was marked with the bands and stripes of a jungle hunter, sable upon gold, and it gave his expression a fierceness that no human countenance could rival. His mane was not coarse and shaggy like those of the western rakh, but a thick ruff of silken fur that framed his head and shoulders in a corona of gold. Though his features were more naturally human than Hesseth's had been, the markings made him seem doubly bestial, and like war paint on a human face hinted at a ruthless, unforgiving nature.

'It's over,' the rakh said quietly.

Spoken in that way – so utterly calm, so perfectly confident – the words were like a spear thrust into Damien's heart. *It's over*. They had failed. It was finished.

He lowered his head in despair. *God, forgive me. We did our best. What more could we have done?*

'Get the boats,' the rakh instructed.

Three men ran off eastward along the narrow shore; moments later they rounded a promontory and disappeared.

'There should be three of them,' a familiar voice pronounced.

Startled, Damien twisted about. Despite the firm hand on his shoulder which kept him from moving too fast or too far, he was able to twist around far enough to see the tall, lean man who was approaching them now, his long silk tunic sweeping the rock wall at his side as he moved.

Gerald Tarrant.

'You bastard,' Damien whispered hoarsely. 'God damn you! You sold us out.'

'Where's your companion?' the rakh demanded from behind him.

He couldn't speak. He couldn't move. He could hardly breathe, so totally consumed by rage was he. Rage, and also despair; because if Tarrant was helping the enemy, Damien and his small ward didn't have a chance in hell of getting free. Not now, not ever.

With leisured grace the Neocount crossed the space between them. The soldiers carefully kept out of his way.

'Where's Mes Hesseth?' he demanded.

For a moment Damien couldn't speak. Then the words came, spiked with a burning hatred. 'What's the matter, you don't get paid as much for just two of us?'

He was struck on the head from behind, hard enough that for a moment his vision exploded in stars. 'Where is she?' the rakh demanded. His voice made it clear that he was ready to strike again if necessary.

'She's *dead,*' Damien choked out. He looked up at Tarrant, loathing the lack of reaction on that pale, arrogant face. Had Damien ever truly traveled with a creature that inhuman? Could he ever have really trusted him? 'God damn you!' he spat. 'She died for our cause.' The words were an accusation, and he poured as much scorn and venom into them as his voice could possibly contain.

'*Your* cause,' the Neocount said coolly. 'It hasn't been mine for some time now.'

'Where did she die?' the rakh demanded. 'When?'

The past seemed a blur; he struggled to remember. 'A day north. Maybe. There was a chasm . . .'

'I know the one,' the rakh said. 'I'll send men out there in the morning to confirm it.'

He remembered Hesseth's body, so lifeless, so broken. Thank God she had died before this moment. Thank God she didn't have to witness their defeat.

The boats were coming into sight now, three long canoelike structures that would seat two men across, three in the center. Two-thirds of the way back was a small metal housing that might contain some sort of engine or turbine, but its shape gave no hint as to its mechanical nature. The combined package was light enough and maneuverable enough that all three boats were easily brought to shore, and there a man held each in place, bracing it against the river current.

The rakh walked to the water's edge and knelt down by it, scooping up a mouthful of the ice-cold water into a pewter cup. When he had enough he stood again, and took out a small glass vial from a pocket in his uniform. This he unscrewed and upended over the cup; Damien saw a thin stream of white powder glisten in the moonlight.

He walked toward Damien, swirling the cup so that the powder and water might mix thoroughly. When he reached the priest, he held it out to him, close enough that he might touch his lips to its brim.

'Drink it,' he ordered.

His heart pounding wildly in fear, Damien asked, 'What is it?'

'It will make you temporarily incapable of Working. I trust you understand why that's necessary.'

He looked up at Tarrant, hoping for . . . what? Sympathy? Support? He'd sooner get it from a host of bloodsuckers than from that corrupted soul.

The cup was before him. The rakh commander was waiting. Fear was a garrote around Damien's heart.

'You can drink it,' the rakh said at last, 'or I can have you beaten into unconsciousness. Your choice.'

He saw Jenseny's eyes fixed on him, wide and terrified. For a moment that was all he could look at, all he could bear to see. Then he turned back to the rakh, shuddering, and nodded. The cup was brought to his lips and tilted up; bitter water, ice cold and algae tainted, filled his mouth and throat.

He swallowed.

Again.

When at last the cup was empty, it was removed from him. Trembling, Damien wondered what the potion's effect would be. Was there truly a substance that could rob man of his power to Work, without damaging his other faculties? He doubted it. Dear God, what had he gotten himself into?

They pulled him to his feet. Not gently and not slowly; he stumbled once as his legs unfolded, half frozen from their previous immersion. The wind was like ice on his body, its coldness trapped by the folds of soaking wet fabric. Hadn't he been in similar condition the last time a rakh had taken him prisoner? *Ernan tradition,* he thought wryly, as they pushed him toward the water once more. In another time and place it might almost have amused him.

They helped him board one of the canoe-things – no easy task with his hands bound behind his back – and then the rakh came over and clipped his shackles to a chain running along the seat. Worse and worse. He leaned back, shivering, not wanting to look at his captors, not willing to look at Tarrant. 'Don't hurt the girl,' he whispered hoarsely. He could hear his voice shaking. 'Please.'

The rakh didn't answer. On the shore one of the men had picked Jenseny up and was carrying her to a boat; when she saw it wasn't the same boat that Damien was in she started struggling, and such was the strength born of her desperation that she wriggled free of him and splashed down into ankle-deep water. He reached for her quickly, but by then she was gone, plunging through the ice-cold river with desperate strength, struggling to get to the priest before they grabbed hold of her again.

In the end it was the rakh who caught her, yanking her back just before she could reach Damien. She screamed and struggled and clawed and bit, but all to no avail; his species was accustomed to dealing with far more dangerous attacks from their children.

At last, exhausted, she hung whimpering in his grip, limp as a rag doll. One of the other men moved in to take her.

Damien met the rakh's eyes. 'What's the matter?' he challenged. 'Afraid that she might hurt you?'

The rakh hesitated, then looked at Tarrant. *Well,* Damien thought, *that's the end of it. After all the times that he's urged me to kill her, he's hardly about to indulge her now.*

But to his surprise Tarrant nodded. The rakh released Jenseny, and the girl splashed over to where Damien was. One of the men grabbed hold of the back of her shirt and lifted, and between that and her own efforts she was soon sitting crumpled in the bottom of the boat, her arms about Damien, sobbing into his chest.

'Chain her up?' one of the men asked.

'I don't think that'll be necessary,' the rakh said coldly. 'Our guest will answer for her behavior.' He shot a quick look of warning at Damien, then turned away to give orders to another man. Damien looked down at the girl.

'Shh,' he whispered to her. 'It's all right. We'll be all right.' It was such a lie he could hardly stomach it – and he was sure that she recognized it as such – but the moment seemed to demand a ritual reassurance.

If Tarrant told the Prince about her power, then it's only a question of time until they kill her. If not . . . then she may live long enough to see me killed first.

The rakh turned to Tarrant. 'You're welcome to join us.'

The Hunter shook his head. 'I'll be there tomorrow after sunfall. Tell his Highness to expect me.'

The rakh bowed his assent.

Damien's head felt fuzzy, and his thoughts were becoming muddled. Was that the drug? What must a potion do to a man's body in order to keep him from Working? How long would it last?

Dear God, I'm sorry. We tried our best. Forgive my many failures, I beg You. All that I did was done for love of You. Even my death. He sighed and shut his eyes. *Most of all my death.*

The boats were pushed into deep water and the current caught them up. Damien felt the thin hull bob as the last of the soldiers boarded, and then they were floating free. A few terse orders were voiced, after which the only sounds were the quiet dip and splash of oars and the near-hysterical sobs of the small, frightened child who clung to his chest.

Alone on the shore, impassive and aloof as always, Gerald Tarrant watched in silence as the river carried them away.

42

The rakh children were gone.

She had heard them scream when Hesseth fell – a shrill high-pitched keening that bespoke pain and fear and loss all in one sound – and then the noise was gone, and they were gone, and Hesseth was gone. Forever.

Jenseny shivered as she huddled close to the priest, partly from cold but mostly from fear. She had no one left in the world but him now, and it took no great stretch of intellect to realize that the chains on his wrists and the soldiers which surrounded him meant that he might soon be taken from her as well. She didn't know if she was more scared for herself or for him, but the combination of fears was overwhelming. All she could do was hold him, cling to him, press her face against his cold, wet chest, and pray. To his god, who believed in protecting children. Damien had said he wouldn't help them here, that he didn't do that kind of thing, but she wasn't so sure. When you really cared about someone, didn't you *want* to help them? Why would a god be different?

She could feel the priest's exhaustion as he leaned back against the engine housing, could sense his bone-deep weariness as the length of chain binding him tinkled and rattled into its new position. It wasn't just a tiredness of the flesh, like you felt when you had walked too far, or had gone too long without sleep, but a tiredness of the soul. She had never sensed anything like that in him before. She didn't think it was because of the long walks, or because of having to carry her so far, or even because of Hesseth's death. All those things were a price he had been willing to pay to get where he was going, to do what he felt he had to do. No, it was more than that. This tiredness was because he had been fighting hopelessness for so long, so very long, and now he was losing the battle. And she didn't know what to say or do to make it better, so she just stayed very quiet and held onto him and tried to keep him warm with her body, while the boats of the Undying Prince brought them closer and closer to the enemy's seat of power.

Black walls gave way to higher walls yet, speckled with rosettes of white and gray. She tried to focus on them as a way of fighting back the panic, but it welled up inside her anyway, sharp and hot and demanding. What was the Prince going to do with them, now that he had taken them prisoner? Each thing she thought of was more terrible than the last. It was clear that they had to get away from these people, but how? Once the Light flashed briefly and she tried to use it like Hesseth had taught her, to break through his chains, but she just wasn't strong enough, or maybe she didn't do it right. Or maybe it was like Hesseth had said, that the Light did its best work with minds and souls, and wasn't that good with inanimate objects. The failure filled her with frustration, and with anger. Tarrant had said that the Light was a kind of power, but what good did that do if she couldn't Work it?

The river meandered through the wasteland, twisting and turning as its current carried them westward. The walls were so high that Jenseny couldn't see the trees above them at all, not even when the moonlight was strongest. And then Domina — if that big moon was Domina — began to set, and sometimes the light would be lost behind a twist in the canyon. That was a very scary thing, when they were all in darkness except for the single great lantern at the head of each boat. Jenseny thought she could see things stirring along the edges of the water then, things that sometimes looked like white trees and sometimes animals and sometimes the Terata. Were those fear-things which they had made? Tarrant had explained that once, how the fae could make shapes out of fears and hopes and give them a life of their own. Did that mean she might see her father one day, reflected in the fae's dark substance? She huddled close to Damien, afraid of the thought. Tarrant said that all the fae-things fed on people, even when they looked like things you loved. What a horrifying concept, that your most precious dreams could be turned against you! How she longed to be in her own room again, where the love and order of her father's house had protected her from such nightmares!

Slowly, mile by mile, the canyon walls lowered. Equally slowly the river widened, until it was hard to see the far shore in the darkness. The nearer shoreline glistened like Tarrant's handful of gems had, only all white and silver and black, with no colors. She looked up at Damien to see if he was watching it, but he was gazing into the night with unfocused eyes, his brow furrowed as if in painful concentration. 'Are you all right?' she whispered. She made her voice as soft as it could be, so the soldiers wouldn't hear her. For a moment the priest's eyes turned her way, but they remained as glazed and unresponsive as before. He seemed to be trying to talk, but for a long time no words would come. 'Can't think,' he gasped at last; it was clear those two words were a triumph. 'The potion . . .' Then his strength failed him, or maybe it was just that the words deserted him; he sagged back against the engine housing and shut his eyes, shivering in the cold of the night.

'It'll be okay,' she promised him. Echoing his earlier words, hoping they would comfort him. 'We'll get through it okay.'

You can't be strong anymore, so I'll have to be strong for both of us.

She was hungry and she was thirsty and there was not much she could do about it. The soldiers had taken Damien's pack and that was where all the food was. She could scoop up water in her hand if she stretched down as far as possible, but she was afraid of drinking too much and then having to go to the bathroom. That would be incredibly embarrassing. She had gotten used to slipping off behind a rock or a bush to do her stuff, but there were no rocks or bushes here and she figured the soldiers would be quick to anger if she fouled their boat. What did *they* do when nature called?

'Water,' the priest whispered, and she cupped her hands and scooped some up – almost falling out of the boat in the process – and brought it up to his lips. He sipped a little, then nodded for her to spill back the rest. Evidently he didn't want to fill up his bladder too much either.

And then the three boats turned, bright oars managing the maneuver with practiced precision. That brought them into a cave that led from the river, and they were quickly swallowed up by its narrow confines. Lamplight glittered on a crystalline ceiling not ten feet from their heads; if one of the men had stood up, he could have reached up and touched it. She wondered what would happen if the river got higher. Maybe after a hard rain they couldn't use this route at all.

After a time, the walls opened up. The ceiling gave way to darkness, then to stars. They floated on the surface of a lake so black that it could hardly be distinguished from the land surrounding it. And then before them . . .

They rose up from the ground suddenly, magnificently, their manifold facets reflecting the moonlight with solar brilliance, their myriad surfaces like mirrors. Vast towers of crystal that soared toward the heavens, their peaked tips sharp against Domina's brilliance. Some were as wide as buildings and equally as solid; others were slender spines of glass, barely translucent, that jutted out from among their perpendicular brethren at sharp, arresting angles. Here and there a cluster of crystals, diamondlike, adhered to one of the mirror surfaces, or filled in the gap between two towers; here and there a spine had been broken by some mischance of nature and tiny crystals gathered in the wound like blood. It was a chaos of brilliance, of knife-sharp edges and night-black surfaces that flashed with light as the boats moved toward them, a field of living crystal so complex, so intertwined, that it was impossible to focus on any one form, or to trace a single outline to its end. Staring at it, Jenseny felt dizzy and breathless and afraid all at once, and at last she turned away from it.

'Rakhlands,' the priest whispered. No more than that. *Rakhlands*. She wished he had told her more about that journey, so that she could understand the reference.

Directly east of them, low on the horizon, the pale light of dawn was just beginning to compromise the night. Cool sparks played along the edges of the crystal towers where the newborn sunlight touched them, and one mirrored surface, angled perfectly to catch the dawn light, flashed a blue so bright that it hurt her eyes. Jenseny wondered what this place would look like in the sunlight. She wondered if they would live to see it.

The boats were brought to a gentle shore and there moored. Clearly the beach, like the lake it surrounded, had been deliberately sculpted; the land in this region was a wild mixture of swirling lava and crystalline growths, hardly suitable for a harbor. There were other boats nearby, Jenseny noted, some like the ones they were in and others much larger and much more complicated. None were tall, she noted. She guessed that was because of the cavern they had to sail through to get here.

When they had reached the beach, the soldiers at the front quickly disembarked, boots splashing in the water as they took up careful positions around their prisoners. They needn't have bothered. It was clear that Damien could hardly stand, and as two of the soldiers helped him from the boat he went down on his knees, hard; it was clear that their firm grip on his upper arms was the only thing keeping him upright at all.

She stayed by his side, trying to help him. One of the soldiers tried to push her away, but she clung to the priest's shirt, unwilling to leave his side for even an instant. From on shore the rakh captain snapped a sharp command, and the soldiers indulged her. Together, with effort, the men got Damien to shore. Together they forced him to his knees.

'The drug will wear off soon,' the rakh informed him. Jenseny heard the rattle of chain behind her, twisted around just in time to see shackles being fastened about the priest's ankles. A short length of chain connected them, enough to allow him to walk but not enough to run. Did they fear him that much? She looked up at the striped rakh, found his glistening green eyes fixed on her. They weren't afraid of him, she realized. Not at all. They were just being careful.

'Let's go,' he ordered, and the soldiers lifted Damien to his feet.

They were marched along a road of sorts, where the lava had been leveled and the crystals had been crushed and the result was a flat bed of black grit that crunched beneath their feet. Higher and higher the towers loomed as they approached, until the tallest of them seemed lost among the stars themselves. Would they be going inside them somehow? Jenseny wondered. Or was there some kind of space hidden in between them? As they passed into the shadow of the first of the great columns she saw Damien look up, not at the looming crystals but straight up at the sky – and she realized with a start that he was looking at the moon and the stars and the dawn because he thought that he might never see them again.

They passed between two crystal spires, into a space whose faceted walls reflected the soldiers' lamplight in flashes of molten gold. It was hard for her to see where she was going, and more than once Damien stumbled; the reflected light, constantly shifting, made it seem like walls existed that weren't really there, and once or twice a real wall was so shadowed that she nearly walked into it. The soldiers seemed to do well enough, but of course they were used to it; there was no doubt in her mind that a stranger would be trapped in this place like an insect in a spider's web, unable to move more than ten feet without walking into something.

And then they were going downward. Down past the crystal, down into the earth, on stairs that had been crudely carved from the black rock itself. It was hard going even for her, and she could feel the tension in Damien's body as he fought the length of chain about his ankles, struggling to descend safely. They seemed to go down forever, and only because she kept count of the lamps that the rakh captain lit as they passed did she have any idea of how far it was. Ten lamps, she counted. Probably ten turns on the rough stone staircase. Far enough that she didn't look forward to climbing back up.

At the bottom was a large chamber with lamps along the nearer side. The rakh lit those also as Damien struggled to catch his breath. Was that the drug weakening him, or had he gotten sick from being cold and wet for so long? She hoped it was the drug. Hadn't the rakh said that it would wear off soon?

Separating the two halves of the chamber was a wall of iron bars, the spaces between them narrow enough that not even Jenseny could squeeze through. With sudden panic she realized that they were going to lock them up down here and leave them. For how long? She would have begged them for an answer if she thought they would give her one. As it was, she had no choice but to allow herself to be maneuvered through the narrow gate, Damien right behind her. They unbound his hands, at least. Wasn't there some comfort in that?

'His Highness has instructed me to apologize for the nature of your accommodations,' the rakh said to Damien. The heavy iron gate was being swung closed again, and its lock fastened securely shut. Jenseny felt panic rising up inside her; she struggled not to let it show. 'But as a sorcerer yourself you understand the necessity for such an arrangement. We can hardly allow you free access to the earth-fae.'

With drug-dulled eyes Damien took in the details of their prison. Smooth floor, roughly carved walls, not much else. He seemed about to say something, but the words couldn't make it past his lips. At last Jenseny, sensing his intentions, whispered, 'We need water.'

There was silence. A long silence. Then, slowly, the rakh captain nodded. 'I'll have it brought.'

'And food,' she dared. 'We need that, too.'

A couple of the soldiers seemed to stiffen at her audacity, but the rakh was unperturbed. 'And food,' the rakh agreed.

'And blankets. We need blankets. And maybe . . . if you have some kind of clothing. Anything dry. *He* needs it,' she said defiantly.

The green eyes were fixed on her – searching, weighing, warning. 'Is that all?' he asked coldly.

'No,' she said. A little scared by her own defiance – but what choice did she have? She had to be brave enough for both of them now. 'We need something to . . . to *go* in,' she said clumsily. And then she added, to clarify, 'Unless you want us to pee on the floor.'

For a minute the rakh said nothing. An expression, ever so minimal, softened the harsh lines of his face. It might have been a smile.

'No,' he said quietly. 'We don't want you to pee on the floor, do we? I'll have something brought.'

He ushered the soldiers from the room. It seemed to Jenseny that they were less than thrilled about the prospect of climbing up all those stairs, but none of them complained. When the last of them had left the chamber, the rakh turned to Jenseny again, and nodded toward Damien. 'When the drug wears off, you may tell him that the Prince will deal with him tomorrow night. As soon as he has met with his *other* guest.'

He left them then, alone with the lamps and the bars and the chill of the underearth. Damien had collapsed onto the smooth stone floor and she knelt down by his side, wishing she knew how to help him. He was breathing heavily, hoarsely, and his forehead was flushed. There was a little bit of light in the chamber, so she could see just how bad he looked.

'Don't worry,' she whispered. Her small hand trembled as she stroked back his hair from his face, just like Hesseth used to do with her. 'We'll be okay. We will. I promise.'

43

Sunset. Slabs of crimson light flashing across crystal spires, deep purple clouds drifting like wraiths down glassy walls, stars reflected a thousand times over as the night unsheathed their brilliance. The Core's light, only half-swallowed by the distant mountains, adding the gold of fire to the tips of the towers, like a thousand glass candles all set alight in an instant. And with each moment, change. Darkness where there was brilliance. Blood-red light where there was shadow. The light of the heavens reflected, refracted, filtered, divided. A symphony of fire, now dying as night's embrace beckoned.

Tarrant watched it for a long time, though the sunlight made his eyes burn. How odd, that even after sunset it might still affect him so. There must be some special property to the crystal that enabled the solar fae to cling to its substance long after its carrier, mere light, had faded. How curious. He had never experimented with crystal himself, preferring the storage capacity of ice and silver and finely honed steel, but he knew there were those who swore by it. Even Erna's settlers had used tiny crystals in connection with their power sources . . . or so it was said. Who knew for sure?

When the last of the gold had faded, when there was nothing reflecting from the glistening towers but stars and a single sliver of moonlight, the Neocount of Merentha moved toward the citadel. Though there were no signs to direct him, nor servants to guide him, he had no trouble picking his way through the forest of false walls and faceted illusions that hid the entranceway to the Prince's palace. He saw by the light of the earth-fae, and that power did not cling to illusion; therefore the false walls were no more than ghosts, and the columns and spires that might otherwise cause him to be distracted were dismissed with no more attention than one might give to an errant wraith. At one point he even considered Banishing them just for the exercise, but that seemed poor etiquette for a guest of his stature, and so he let them stand.

Inside the citadel itself there were guards, but they let him pass without word. There were servants also, and perhaps they would have attended him had he required them to, but he chose instead to wrap himself in a Distracting so that they were not even aware of his passage. Voices shivered in the crystalline halls, reflecting down the labyrinthine hallways, and occasionally the sound of human laughter accompanied them, but he met no other people in the maze-like corridors. Whether in response to his will or that of the Prince – or both – the illusory walls proved more than efficient in isolating him from the inhabitants of the strange citadel.

Alone, unannounced, he at last reached what he presumed to be an audience chamber. Vast, multifaceted, it glimmered with falsehoods and illusions in an ever-changing array, ghostly columns winking in and out of sight as he gazed about its walls. There were rugs cast down on the floor, and they lent that surface a stability rare in this place; as he walked to the edge of the nearest, he noted threads of gold and silver and half a dozen other fine metals worked into its surface, along with a dusting of what might well be gemstones. Or were there crystal threads as well, nature's bounty drawn out and made flexible so that a man might walk upon them? As he set down his foot upon its thick pile, the nearest illusions faded, and a room took shape before him. Furniture in dark wood inlaid with gold, ivory fastenings, scarlet tassels. Silken cushions in the colors of the sunset. Gold silk spilled across a table, with polished silver goblets on its surface.

And two men.

One was a rakh, though not like any rakh that Tarrant had ever seen. His uniform and manner proclaimed him to be a guard of some kind, and Tarrant ignored him. The other was human, and familiar to him. He seemed older now than he had in his Sending, but perhaps that was just the inaccuracy of the fae interfering; it was hard for even an adept to send a perfect image across such distances.

'Neocount Merentha.' The Prince's eyes were a cool blue, Tarrant noted, his expression not hostile but guarded. 'What a rare honor it is to welcome such a guest. Your reputation precedes you.'

He bowed ever so slightly, a flawless blend of respect and wariness. Aware that his every move was being watched, his every expression studied and judged, he responded formally. 'The honor is mine, your Highness.'

'I regret that your journey here could not have been more pleasant.' He moved toward the table; ringed fingers closed about the stem of a goblet. 'May I offer you some refreshment to wash away the dust of the road?' He extended the cup toward him.

He came close enough that he might catch the scent which wafted forth from its contents, then accepted the cup from the Prince's hand. For an instant their fingers touched, and while a lesser man might have used such contact to probe his true intentions, the Prince's touch was utterly neutral. As was his, of course. They were both being infinitely careful.

He raised the goblet to his lips and breathed in its bouquet. Sweet and fresh and warm to the touch; body temperature? He took a ritual sip, bracing himself against the hunger it awakened, and then put the goblet down. Carefully steady, artfully disinterested.

'Weak vintage?' the Prince asked. Smiling slightly.

With studied nonchalance he shrugged. 'Disembodied blood is a convenience, not a pleasure. But I thank you for the thought.'

'I thought you might be hungry after days in my wasteland. But you wouldn't admit that in front of me, would you? Not even if you were starving.'

'Would you, in my place?'

'Hardly.' He chuckled. 'We're very much alike, you and I. If we can ever learn to trust each other enough to work together, it will be quite an alliance.'

'I'll admit that the potential intrigues me.'

'And the promise of godhood, eh? No small reward for a simple betrayal.'

'If you think it was simple,' the Hunter said quietly, 'then perhaps you don't know me as well as you think.'

The blue eyes sparkled coldly. 'You know I have the priest and the girl in custody.'

Tarrant shrugged.

'They mean nothing to you?'

'You know why I came here. You know what I want.'

For a moment he said nothing. Then: 'Calesta.'

'Calesta.'

The Prince's expression tightened. 'Calesta's been my servant for years. He helped me build this kingdom, and was instrumental in planning our invasion of the Church lands—'

'And the death by torture of several hundred humans.'

'Does that bother you?'

'I despise waste.'

'The Iezu aren't like other demons. They do their best work when you give them free rein. Who am I to complain about his methods, when I stand to gain so much from them? Or you, for that matter?'

'You intend to protect him, then?'

'I intend for you to be an honored guest here. Stay in my realm, see with your own eyes what part he plays here. I suspect that your feelings will change.'

'And if they don't?'

The Prince's gaze was intense. 'A Iezu is born every hour, it's said. A man like yourself . . . once in a lifetime. If that. I made my choice when I invited you here.'

He turned to the rakh and muttered. 'Go get her.' With military precision the maned guard bowed and left. The doorway was somewhere behind the prince, but Tarrant never saw it; one minute the rakh was yards away and the next he was gone, as though he had stepped into another dimension.

The Prince's gaze followed Tarrant's own; he smiled. 'The joy of this arrangement is that one can be fully protected without that protection being visible.'

'I never doubted that,' Tarrant assured him.

'It's all natural, you know.' He placed a loving hand on the nearest column, fingers stroking the glassy surface with obvious affection. 'I accelerated the process a million times over – redirected it a bit – but in the end it was Nature that did the work. A far more creative architect than man will ever be.'

'An exquisite piece of work,' the Hunter agreed. 'What about the volcanoes?'

'What about them?'

'You're sitting on a lava plain. Where I come from that's considered quite a risk. Or have you learned how to tame magma?'

The Prince chuckled. '*Taming* it is hardly necessary, Neocount. One need merely keep certain vents open, occasionally drain off a little gas here or there . . . it's little enough effort to see that the lava flows west instead of east, and does so in a civilized manner. Ah. But I forget.' His gaze was piercing. 'You have no dominion over fire, do you? Or anything that fire touches?'

Inwardly the Hunter stiffened; outwardly he managed – just barely – not to let it show. 'Don't underestimate me,' he warned. *Or bait me.*

The Prince smiled coldly. 'I have no intention of it.'

Footsteps approached. Crystal walls shifted. The rakh had returned, and with him was a woman. No, not a woman: a girl. Slender and dark and very frightened. Deliciously frightened.

'Permit me,' the Prince said, 'to offer you the hospitality of my house.' He walked to the girl's side and cupped a hand under her chin, turning her face toward Tarrant. Her eyes were wide, her lips trembling. 'As befits a guest of your station: the best my realm has to offer.'

For a moment he was still. Then, very slowly, he walked to where the girl stood. Her fear was like a fine wine, its bouquet intoxicating. Hunger welled up inside him with stunning force.

'I'm told you like them pale, but I'm afraid that's a rare commodity in these parts. All the rest should be proper.'

He put out a hand to touch her cheek, so very gently; terror flowed sweetly through the contact. It took everything he had not to shut his eyes and savor the sensation.

'She pleases?' the Prince asked.

'Very much so,' he whispered.

'You can hunt her in the Black Lands if you like. It lacks the conveniences of your own Forest, of course, but I think it will please you. Unless you would rather just take her here.'

He forced himself to release the girl's face; he could still feel her warmth on his fingertips. 'No,' he breathed. 'Let her run.'

The Prince nodded toward the rakh, who drew the girl away. She was clearly so frightened it was hard for her to walk, and her eyes were bright with tears. Exquisite.

When she was gone, when he and the Prince were alone once more, he said quietly, 'She's one of your people.' A question.

The monarch smiled. 'And you're my guest. And I feed my guests, Neocount, as their nature demands. Enjoy her. There are more where she came from – thousands more, if our alliance prospers. Not to mention all the innocents of the northern realms.' He chuckled darkly. 'All gods require their sacrifices, Neocount. Why should you be an exception?'

He could feel her presence calling to him from beyond the crystal walls. Sweet, so very sweet. How long had it been since he had last hunted? The deaths of invaders were nothing compared to this. The nightmares of a priest hardly served as appetizer.

'Go on,' the Prince said softly. 'Enjoy her. We can talk business tomorrow night. Or after. We have so much time, my friend. Endless time. Why rush things? Enjoy.'

Running. She was running. He could sense the motion, the fear. It awakened old instincts, too long denied. He burned to go after her, to take her, to kill.

First things first. Gestures. Ritual. He bowed in the way his era had taught, when kings and princes and their noble cohorts still roamed the planet in numbers enough that such gestures need be codified; the Prince's nod said that he understood the maneuver in all its subtle refinement.

The rakh had returned, and though he kept a respectful distance, Tarrant could sense him studying him. Assessing him as a possible threat? If so, he had his work cut out for him.

'Among men such as ourselves,' he said quietly – with only a hint of warning in his voice – 'a Knowing must be considered an invasion of privacy, and hence a hostile act. I would hate for anything like that to compromise our new-found fellowship, your Highness.'

'Indeed,' the Prince said coolly. 'I think we understand each other.' He nodded solemnly. 'Good hunting, Neocount.'

When he was gone – when the curtains of illusion had swung shut behind him, a barrier to sight and sound – the rakh asked, 'Do you trust him?'

'Trust isn't an issue,' the Prince said coolly.

'Will you Know him, then?'

He shook his head. 'You heard what he said. That would be tantamount to a declaration of war.'

'Then how can you make sure of him?'

He stroked the side of the silver goblet gently; the warmed blood within it trembled.

'There are other ways of getting information,' he assured his captain.

44

The drug was wearing off, at last. Damien could see again. The edges of his world were coming into focus, black and sharp and hostile. He could speak if he wanted to. Language was no longer disconnected from thought, so that every word was a struggle for meaning, every sentence a herculean effort. He could *think*.

With a moan he tried to sit up; to his amazement his body responded. It seemed a small eternity ago that the Prince's drug had robbed him of every mental capacity he held dear; in his more lucid moments he had feared that it would never wear off, that the prince had crippled him as one might cut off the claws from a hunting cat, or clip the wings of a captive bird. Only this was a hundred times, a thousand times more horrible. There was no way to keep a man from Working, he understood that now. All you could do was scramble his brain enough that any organized activity – including Working – was impossible.

Jenseny must have seen him stir, for she came to his side and tried to help him up. Not that she could have lifted his bulk, but the support was welcome. 'I'm okay,' he whispered hoarsely, and he put his arm around the girl. His wrists burned from where the shackles had cut into them, and instinctively he Worked his vision so that he could begin to Heal them. Or tried to. But there was barely enough power to transform his sight, so that he might see for himself how totally inadequate the currents were for his purpose. For any purpose.

'Underground?' he whispered.

'Pretty deep,' the girl told him. 'He said you'd understand why.'

'Who did?'

'The rakh.'

He struggled for memory, dimly recalled striped markings and a long, full mane. Green eyes, perhaps. Any more than that was unavailable, lost in the mists and veils that the drug had conjured. He wondered what other memories had been lost as well.

'Tell me about it,' he prompted her. 'Tell me what happened.'

She did so. As she talked, he studied the space they were in: the thick iron bars, the solid walls, the all but nonexistent earth-fae. No hope, not anywhere. The Prince knew who and what he was dealing with and he had planned their imprisonment well. Until someone unlocked that door, Damien and the girl weren't going anywhere.

'There's food,' Jenseny said. She seemed strangely proud, as if somehow the food was of her making, but he lacked the strength to question her about it. How long had he been trapped in that terrible half-sleep, his body starving while his mind struggled for control? Hunger, once acknowledged, was a sharp pain in his gut. He took the food she held out to him – sandwiches, no less! – and gratefully wolfed them down. Followed by clean water, which she also provided. Good enough, he thought. At least the bastard wasn't going to starve them.

'Is he going to kill us?' the girl asked him suddenly.

He looked down at her, reached out to stroke her hair gently with his hand. His hands and nails were encrusted with dirt, and his clothing likewise; Tarrant would have been disgusted. 'I don't know,' he said softly. 'Does it make you afraid, thinking that he might?'

She bit her lower lip as she considered. 'Would I be with my dad, then? Wherever he is,' she amended quickly. Not yet confident enough to assume him into the One God's heaven.

'I'm sure of it,' he whispered. They were words that had to be said; he wondered if they were true. What would happen to this precious child when the end came, where her soul was free to ride the currents of Erna? The One God took care of His Own, it was said, and she was hardly a member of His flock. What happened to those who embraced no god, who gave no thought to an after-life, but simply lived from birth to death in the best way they knew how? In a world where faith could create gods and demons, where prayers could sculpt heaven and hell, what happened to those who gave no thought to the moment after death, who made no provision for dying?

With a sigh he made his way over to a low pot set in a far corner of the cell, and, after ascertaining that it was indeed what he had guessed it to be, he relieved himself of the day's accumulated pressure. His urine was dark and murky and smelled strangely sour; he hoped to God that was due to the drug passing out of his system and not some more ominous sign. All he needed now was for his body to fail him.

And then he leaned against the rock wall and shut his eyes and thought, *Does it really matter? Does anything really matter any more?*

'Are you okay?' the girl asked.

Don't, something whispered inside him. *Don't give in to despair. When you do that, then he's won.*

'You mean he hasn't already?' he whispered.

'What?'

He drew in a deep breath, fighting to steady himself. Then he went back to her and sat down by her side. He took her hand in his – so small, so very small – and stroked it gently.

'Jenseny.' He said it quietly, very quietly. Was he afraid that someone might hear? There was no one within sight now, but what did that mean in a place like this? 'The fae that I use is too weak here; I can't do anything with it. What about the kind of fae that Hesseth was teaching you to use? Can you see that here?'

She hesitated. 'Sometimes. It was strong right after we came down here. There isn't too much now, but sometimes it changes fast. I never know.' She said that apologetically – as if somehow the shortcomings of the tidal power were her fault.

He squeezed her hand in reassurance. 'When it is strong, when you can use it . . . do you think you could Work this?' He didn't point to the bars of their prison – the real issue – but to the thin chain between his ankles. Metal was metal, and if she could use the tidal fae to alter his bonds, then maybe there was hope for the bars as well.

But she cast her eyes downward and said miserably, 'I tried. On the boat. Only I'm not good enough . . .'

'You just need practice,' he comforted. Thinking wryly, *And you may have a lot of time for that here*. 'Let me know the next time you feel there's enough to work with and we can try—'

Footsteps. He stopped speaking suddenly, hoping that whoever it was hadn't heard them. What would happen if the Prince found out about Jenseny's tidal sorcery? And for that matter, since Tarrant had sold them out, why the hell didn't he know already? *There* was a mystery worth examining!

The first figure to come into sight was a soldier, followed by three others. *They must think me capable of miracles,* he thought dryly, *if they imagine they need that kind of manpower*. Following them was the rakh from the river, his mane not hooded now but bared to the shoulder, golden highlights playing along the fur as he entered the chamber. The latter nodded toward the bars, and one of the soldiers took up station there. Armed, Damien noted. Another nod, and a pistol was drawn. The cold steel barrel pointed directly at his face.

'Come over to the bars,' the rakh commanded.

Slowly, heart pounding, he obeyed. The barrel was now little more than a yard from his face; even a born jinxer couldn't miss a shot like that.

'Turn around.'

He turned back toward Jenseny. She was crouched like a frightened animal, ready to bolt if threatened. Where? To what haven? Where could one find safety in this place?

'Put your hands between the bars,' the rakh commanded.

He felt his heart sink as he realized the purpose of all these directions. But what choice did he have? He extended his arms behind him, far enough that his hands slid between the bars. Cold steel shackles snapped shut about his wrists, pinning him in place. He tested them once to see how much slack they allowed him. Not much.

'He's secure,' the rakh announced.

Footsteps approached from behind. Damien tried to twist around, to see who was approaching, but the angle was wrong and the light was bad and all he could see was the sweep of crimson cloth as a tall, robed figure made its way toward his cell.

Then: a key rattled in the lock. The heavy door was swung aside. A man entered the cell, and took up position directly in front of Damien.

Oh, my God . . .

With one part of his mind he saw the body that stood before him: lean, aging, draped in a sleeveless robe of crimson silk that opened down the front to reveal a tighter, more tailored layer. He was fifty, maybe sixty, and the thin gold band that held back his hair betrayed graying temples, aging skin, a receding hairline.

Utterly familiar.

For a moment he was back in the rakhlands. Kneeling before the Master of Lema, his hands tied behind his back with simple rope (what he wouldn't give for that now!), at the mercy of her madness as a demon whispered behind her shoulder, *There is always torture*.

They were the same, she and this man. Not in body. Not in gender. Not even in their features, or any other physical attribute. But in their clothing – their bearing – even their expression! Watching him move was like watching *her* move; being bound before him was like reliving that awful day, when he waited in vain for the earth to move, to save him from her madness.

'Prince Iso Rashi,' the rakh announced. 'Sovereign Lord of Kilsea, Chataka, and the Black Lands.' And he added, 'Called the Undying.'

They didn't look at all alike. They couldn't be related – could they? The woman had left this region more than a century ago. Could two people be so very alike that after a century's isolation their taste in clothing would still develop identically? It was crazy. It was impossible.

It had happened.

'So,' the Prince said. His voice was a smooth baritone, even and disciplined. 'This is the soldier of God who would lay siege to my throne.'

He managed to shrug. 'I gave it my best.'

The expression that came across the Prince's face was eerily familiar; he wished he could forget where he had seen it before.

'So you did,' he said softly. 'And now that your efforts have been dispensed with, you can make up for the trouble you caused me by rendering a simple service.'

'I don't have a lot of choice, do I?'

'None at all,' the Prince assured him. 'But as for how much it hurts . . . that's up to you.'

He reached out to take Damien's face in his hands – and for a moment the situation was so much like what Damien had experienced in the rakhlands that panic overwhelmed him, and he tried to back away. But the bars at his back allowed no retreat, and the cool hands settled on his face with firm authority. Jenseny started to move toward them, but Damien saw her and warned her, 'No!' There was nothing she could do to help him now. 'Stay where you are! Don't interfere.'

'How very considerate of you,' the Prince murmured.

He tried to look away, but he couldn't. He tried to shut his eyes, but it was as if his lids had been glued open. The chill blue gaze of his captor drew him in, and its power skewered him like an insect on a mounting board. *Where the hell is he getting the power from?* Damien thought desperately. Then he felt the fire that was pressed against his cheek, the glowing ring that was pouring out tamed earth-fae to fuel the Prince's Binding. *Like Tarrant's sword,* Damien thought. Remembering all too well what that sword was like, and what it was capable of doing.

'Tell me about Gerald Tarrant,' the Prince commanded.

Images exploded in his brain, sight and sound and emotion all bound together into a blazing tapestry of memory. The Hunter in his forest. Ciani, helpless in his arms. Rakh dying in agony. Blood. Fear. Revulsion. He shook as the memories poured through him, all the emotion of a long, hard year packed into one terrifying instant. The boy that Tarrant killed. The women he tortured. The horror of knowing that they had to go in and rescue him, that there really was no choice, that the Hunter would live and thrive and feed because of Damien Vryce—

'No,' he gasped. 'Stop it, please!'

—and then this journey, this terrible doomed journey, the days and the nights and the battles and the horror and then that moment at the river, that terrible moment when all his hopes came crashing down and he looked at Tarrant and he knew – he *knew* – it was over, it was all over, their efforts were for nothing and all the dying was a waste, the Hunter had proven true to his nature at last and betrayed them to the enemy—

The power that held him released him suddenly and he slumped back against the bars. Weak and shaken, he shut his eyes. Though he heard the Prince step back from him, he had no strength to look up at him, and no desire. Though he heard the door swing open again, he didn't even look toward it. It was as if all the life had been wrung out of him along with his memories. It was an effort just to live.

And then the shackles were unlocked and taken from his wrists, and he was free to move. He fell to his knees on the hard stone floor, and felt the child run to his side. He hugged her hard, drawing strength from the contact.

'Thank you,' the Prince said from behind him. 'That was most informative.'

He refused to turn around. He refused to acknowledge the taunting words, spoken with an arrogance so like Tarrant's own. If he did, he would probably try to kill the man, despite the bars and the shackles and his obvious power. His need to strike at Tarrant was that strong, and at that moment the two seemed indistinguishable.

Damn you, Hunter! I trusted you. I did. How many others have you seduced into that fatal mistake over the ages? How many others wanted to believe that the Hunter's soul was still human, only to discover in the end that it was as cold and as ruthless as the Wasting?

From behind him the Prince was speaking. 'That'll be all, Katassah. No need to leave a guard down here.'

Katassah!

He twisted about suddenly, but they were already moving into the stairway's shadows. All he could see was the fleeting glint of lamplight on sable-striped fur, long golden strands masking the shoulders of a uniform.

And then they were gone and even that hope was gone – that fragile, nameless hope – and he slumped against the bars of his prison. Wishing he had known earlier. Wondering what the hell he could have done if he had.

'He called him Katassah,' the small girl whispered.

'Yeah.' He leaned back against the bars and shut his eyes. Desperate plans were flitting through his brain, but they all dissolved before they gained substance. 'Fat lot of good it does us now,' he muttered.

But deep inside, he wondered.

Dawn was coming.

A lone bird circled high in the darkness. Its talons were like rubies, its eyes as bright as diamonds. Its wingspan was broader than any bird's wingspan should be, and its feathers were tipped in cool silver unfire.

It banked low, took its bearings, then rose again. Seeking.

In the west a dull light glowed that was neither sun nor starshine. A faint red light that played along the ridge of one mountain, crowning its summit in blood. The bird flew toward it. As it came near the currents grew fierce, so much so that as it struggled to tame the winds to its purpose it must also fight to maintain its chosen form. Even a minute's relaxation in the vicinity of a volcano could prove fatal to a shapechanger.

It crossed over the ridge, and hot winds buffeted it from below. The coldfire on its wingtips died, and the feathers began to char and curl. It was struggling now as volcano-born thermals rose up from the ground with violent force, sometimes accompanied by a spray of molten rock or hair-fine ash.

At last it could fly no farther, and it landed. Earth-fae swirled hotly about its feet, almost too violent to tame; it took long minutes for it to mold the stuff to its will, to drain it of its intrinsic heat so that it might be Workable. At last, not without fear, it changed. Feathers gave way to flesh, talons to hands, down to clothing. Silken robes were cooked in the process, crisped to ash along the edges. The scabbard of the Worked sword was singed.

Gerald Tarrant looked down the long slope of the volcano, studying the deadly landscape. Not half a mile to the west of him the earth had been rent open, and lava poured red-hot down the mountainside; he could feel its heat on his face even from where he stood, and knew that he dared get no closer if he valued his life. Accompanying the lava was a flood of earth-fae so powerful that only a madman would try to Work it, and it established a current that flowed westward, toward the sea, away from the Prince's citadel.

Excellent, Tarrant thought.

The Prince had offered him accommodations in his palace, which Tarrant had politely refused. He wasn't about to spend his most vulnerable hours in the man's stronghold, alliance or no alliance. So he had put on his wings and headed west, toward the volcano. Let the Prince think that he had done it for privacy. Let him think that Tarrant had chosen this place because the fierce currents would disrupt any Seeing, any Knowing, any attempt on the Prince's part to discover his daytime hiding place. That was certainly part of the reason, but it was not all. And if the Prince ever knew the rest of it . . . then burning currents and molten rock would be the least of Gerald Tarrant's problems.

The ground trembled beneath him as he knelt on the black earth, and the smell of sulfur drifted to him on a hot breeze. The place reminded him of Mount Shaitan back home, a volatile crater whose outpouring fueled the Forest's currents. He had made a pilgrimage to it once, to tap that awesome power, and he knew just how deadly a volano's outpouring could be.

This time he had an alternative.

He put his hand about the hilt of his sword and drew it free of its sheath. Coldfire blazed furiously as it made contact with the hot power of the local currents, and a hiss like that of steam rose from its sharp steel edge. It was bright again, nearly as bright as it had been in the rakh-lands; he had been charging it night after night throughout their journey, molding the earth-fae with painstaking care until it suited his special need, then binding it to the steel until the whole length of the sword blazed with frigid power. It enabled him to Work when the currents were made deadly by earthquakes, or when he was deep underground where the earth-fae was feeble. It would enable him to Work safely now, even in this hostile environment.

One more tool, and then he was ready. He took it out of his pocket and opened it, laying it on the warm black earth before him. Memories clung to it like vapor, and for an instant he thought that the volatile currents would bring several of them to life. But all that manifested was a thin red fog, that twined about the handle in crimson filigree and left small drops, like blood, floating in the air.

Shutting the rest of the world out of his mind, he braced himself for Working. In all of his repertoire there was no harder task than what he was about to attempt here. It went against the very patterns of Nature, defied the very flow of reality. He had done it only once before, as an exercise, and even then he had not been wholly successful. This time, however, there was no room for error.

Carefully he wove power into the slender object, priming it to take the fae in the same way he had done to his sword so many centuries ago. That was easy enough. Next would come the Warding, a complex command that would enable the object to craft the fae itself, molding the currents, dodging magnetism, bending light . . .

An UnSeeing.

An Obscuring would have been far easier to establish, but that only decreased the chance of an object being noticed. A Distracting was more effective – he had used one against Damien and Jenseny at the river – but that was more suited to a single moment in time than a lasting need for secrecy. And a sorcerer might notice either of those Workings if he were alert for it, which the Prince most certainly was. No, this had to be the real thing. And that must affect not only the mind of the observer but reality itself, remaking the physical world so that nowhere was there even a shadow of its existence. True invisibility. Scholars had argued that it wasn't possible. He had argued that it was. And here, on this torrid ridge, he was about to bet his life on that assessment.

With care he molded the fae, weaving it about the small object as finely as a silk cocoon. Light, striking that barrier, would pass about its perimeter and then resume its course. Magnetic currents would be shielded from contact with the metal within before they were allowed to pass through. Heat and cold and conductivity and the currents, the winds, the tides . . . they must all be dealt with separately, for they all had their own special patterns. The only thing he left untouched was a narrow band of visible light; that would have to be dealt with on a more mundane level.

When at last he was done, he leaned back, exhausted, and studied his creation. Out here in the field it looked good, but if the Prince turned his attention upon it . . .

Then we'll find out if I'm right or not, he thought grimly. *The hard way.*

45

'Damn stairs,' the guard muttered. 'Don't know why he can't keep his prisoners on the ground floor this time, like all the others.'

He was less than thrilled about having drawn this duty, but he was hardly going to admit that to the captain. You didn't tell a rakh that you'd rather do sentry duty than walk a simple food tray down ten turns of stairs. He'd read you for a wimp in two seconds flat, and then there'd be some damn animal pecking-order bullshit and the next thing you knew you'd be hauling out garbage or waxing canoes or some such crap thing like that. No, better to just walk the vulking tray down the vulking stairs and try not to think about the climb back up.

He was about halfway down when a hand grasped his shoulder from behind. Startled, he turned around as fast as he could. Instinct said *go for your weapon*! but instinct also said *don't drop the tray*! and the result was that in his panic he nearly dropped them both.

'No need to be startled,' a cool voice assured him. The hand fell from his shoulder; his flesh was faintly chilled where it had grasped him.

The foreign Neocount. That's who it was. For a minute his testicles drew up in cold dread, because he'd heard what the man was and what he could do. Then he remembered what the captain had told him: that there were at least a thousand wards in the palace all fixed on this man, all waiting for the first time he used his power against the Prince. *Let him mutter even the first word of a Knowing,* the rakh had assured him, *and those wards will fry him to a cinder*. Which meant that he was safe, didn't it? Didn't hurting one of the palace guards count as hurting the Prince?

Then the smooth, perfectly manicured hands closed about the sides of the tray and he could feel its woven surface grow cool in his hands. For a moment he held onto it, thinking that the captain would give him hell if he let go – and then he looked into those eyes, those bottomless silver cold-as-ice eyes, and his hands lost all their strength.

'I'll deliver it,' the Neocount told him. 'You can go back up.'

He almost started to protest, but his voice failed him. At last, realizing that he was outgunned and outclassed and not about to start an argument with a sorcerer in a dark place like this where no one could hear him yell, he nodded his acquiescence. The Neocount's gaze released him and he shivered as the tall, cold figure passed him in the stairwell.

Oh, well, he thought. *I didn't want to climb the damned stairs anyway, right?*

Shaking, he went back up to tell his captain that the food had been delivered.

The light was dim, and in order to read by it Damien and Jenseny had to sit with their backs to the bars. Thus they were positioned now, with various piles of coins and cards and miscellaneous small items spread out between them. They were filthy, worn and bruised, and their attention was clearly fixed on the cards in their hands. Neither of them noticed Tarrant as he approached.

'Two,' the girl said, and she took two cards from her hand and put them on the floor. 'Give me two.'

The priest counted two cards off the deck and gave them to her. Evidently he had heard Tarrant move then, for after that he turned around—

And stared. Just long enough for Jenseny to turn around and see Tarrant and gasp. Just long enough for the Hunter to read the venom in his gaze. Then he turned back to the pile of items before him and picked up a coin. With studied disdain he cast it through the bars to the Hunter's feet; it rolled to a stop against his boot.

'You can leave it by the bars,' he said shortly. 'We'll get to it when we're done.'

He turned his back on the man then, and counted three cards for himself off the deck.

'Jen?'

'Two coins,' she said. She pushed them to the pile between them, where two other coins already lay.

He considered his cards, then added two coins of his own. 'I'll see you that, and raise you . . . a piece of chalk.'

'I'm out of chalk.' She dug a grimy hand down into her pocket, searching for any miniscule tidbits that previous searches had not revealed. At last she came up clutching something. She held it up into the light and asked, 'What is it?'

He studied the small bits of dark rock and rendered judgment. 'Lava.'

'What's it worth?'

He considered. 'Half a chalk each.'

Tarrant came forward as she counted off two pieces and added them to the pile of wagers. He put the tray down on the floor, right by the bars. 'I thought you would want to know what happened,' he said.

'I vulking well know what happened,' Damien muttered through gritted teeth. Then to the girl, 'What have you got?'

'Three Matrias.'

'Damn. Pair of sevens.' He watched as she pulled the booty over to her side, then cast another coin down between them. 'Your deal.'

'I thought you should understand—'

'I understand, all right!' He got to his feet in one sudden motion and turned to face the man; he felt as taut as a watchspring that had been overwound, about to snap. 'I understand that I fed you for *five vulking months* so you could get here and sell us out to the man we came to kill, that's what I understand! What did he offer you, anyway? A house of your own with some nifty crystal architecture, maybe a few girls to run around and bleed for you? What?'

'Immortality,' the Hunter said.

Stunned, Damien couldn't find his voice.

'The real thing.'

'God,' he whispered. He shut his eyes. 'No. I can't outbid that. Good God.'

'We didn't have a chance,' the Hunter told him. 'Not with a Iezu involved. I couldn't get within ten feet of the Prince without half a dozen wards attacking, and you . . . you wouldn't last a minute. The first time you even hinted at a threatening gesture your senses would be so warped by Iezu sorcery that you couldn't tell dream from reality, and then it would all be over. No contest at all.'

'Then you could have told me that!' he spat. 'When I asked you in Esperanova, you should have told me that. God damn it! I *trusted* you.'

'And I warned you not to,' the Hunter reminded him. 'Several times.'

'You could have told me!'

'I *did*. I told you there was almost no hope. I told you your only chance lay with one wild element – and it didn't come through, did it? That's hardly my fault.'

Damien's hands had clenched into fists by his sides; his knuckles were white with rage. 'Damn you,' he whispered hoarsely. 'Damn your infernal honesty!'

'I gave you the odds. You made your decision. Isn't it a little hypocritical to play the martyr now, priest?'

He might have answered – if he could have gotten words out

past the rage boiling up in his throat – but at that moment another person entered the chamber, and her presence startled him so much that words abandoned him.

She was slender. She was dark. She was beautiful, in the way that the Hunter preferred beauty: fragile, delicate, vulnerable. It was clear from the way she looked at Tarrant that she feared him, feared him terribly, and yet she approached him, drawn to his presence in the way a mesmerized skerrel might be drawn to a hungry snake. Every instinct in Damien's soul cried out for him to go to her, to help her, to shelter her from the Hunter's cruelty, but the chain binding his legs and the thick iron bars before him made any such movement impossible. Whatever Tarrant might do to this woman, Damien could do no more than stand and watch.

She looked at the priest, then at the Hunter, then quickly away. Her hand on the wall was trembling, and her voice shook slightly when she spoke. 'His Highness says to please come see him when you're finished here, he has some business he needs to discuss with you.' A bare whisper of a voice, so fraught with fear that Damien's heart ached to hear it. And for good reason, he thought; he could almost feel the Hunter's hunger reaching out to her, caressing her, savoring her terror—

'Leave her alone!' he choked out. Powerless words, futile sounds. There was nothing he could do if the Hunter chose to harm her. Nothing but watch, and hate.

Tarrant moved to where the woman stood. Though she drew back from him in terror, she made no move to get away. He lifted a long, slender hand to her hair, then stroked it; his finger passed down along the line of her throat, pausing gently to test the heat of her pulse. She moaned softly, but made no move to escape him. Her dark eyes glittered with fear.

'Tarrant. Please.' How he hated his helplessness! His hands closed tightly about the thick iron bars, but mere desperation couldn't bend them. 'She just came to bring you a message. Don't hurt her.'

The Hunter chuckled coldly. 'Our journey together is over now, priest. I no longer have to indulge your tedious morality.' He leaned down to the girl and kissed her gently on the forehead, a mockery of human affection; Damien saw the girl shiver violently. 'Sisa belongs to me. A gift from the Prince, to cement our alliance. A fitting tribute, don't you think?'

'You can't own a person,' Jenseny protested.

'Can't I?' the Hunter smiled. 'Last night I hunted her in the Black Lands. Tonight she lives only because I chose to spare her life. From this moment onward her every breath will be drawn in at my will – or extinguished at my command. That's ownership in my book, Mes Jenseny.'

He had to turn away. He couldn't watch it. Helplessness was a cold knot in his gut, a tide of sickness in his soul. 'Listen to yourself!' he said hoarsely. 'Look at what you're doing! That isn't the Gerald Tarrant I knew. What's happening to you?'

'Come now, priest, you would be the first to catalog my sins. What makes this woman different from a thousand others? My hunger hasn't changed. My techniques are hardly different.'

'You told me once about how you hunted when you were in the Forest. How you gave your victims a chance to escape you—'

'A chance so slim it was all but nonexistent.'

'But you gave it to them! Slim or not. You told them that if they could evade you for three nights you'd let them go free. Didn't you?' He waited for an answer, and when none came pressed on. 'You told me how you hunted them on foot, and how you wouldn't Work even if you wanted to because then they would have no chance at all. Remember that? Remember how you told me that at the end of three nights they would either die for your pleasure or be free of you forever, that that was part of the game?' He drew in a deep breath, struggling to make his voice steady. 'What you did to those women was *finite,* Tarrant. It tore them apart, but it *ended*. What you're doing here . . .' He couldn't look at the woman's face. It would bring tears to his eyes, to match those which were forming in hers. 'This place is corrupting you,' he whispered. 'First your loyalties, now your pleasures . . . what will you be when it's all finished? Immortal and independent? Or a slave of the Black Lands?'

'Maybe I have changed,' the Hunter said quietly. 'Maybe the freedom to cast off all fear of death has given me options that I lacked before. Or maybe . . . maybe you never really knew me as well as you thought. Maybe you saw what you wanted to see and no more. Only now the blinders have been removed.' He stroked the woman's hair possessively. 'Now the truth is uncovered,' he said. 'Now I can be what I was meant to be, what I might have been centuries ago had I not wasted half my energies in the paltry mechanisms of survival.

'Come,' he said to the woman, when he released her. 'I'm finished here. Let's go see your Prince.'

She went up the stairs ahead of him, one slender hand brushing the wall for support as she climbed. Damien watched until they were out of sight, then listened until the last of their footsteps echoed down the winding staircase, into silence. When the two were truly gone, he lowered his face into his hands, his shaking angry hands, and his whole body shook from rage. And sorrow. And fury, at his own helplessness.

After a time, Jenseny asked gently, 'You okay?'

He drew in a deep breath, tried to make his voice as steady as it could be. 'Yeah. I'm okay.' He lifted up his face from his hands; his eyes were wet. 'Deal the cards, all right?'

As she laid out the decorated cardboard rectangles, he remembered the food that Tarrant had brought, and after a moment he mastered his anger enough to reach through the bars to get it. There was no space large enough for the tray to pass through, so he had to collect it piece by piece: bread, cheese, meat, something wrapped in a napkin . . . the last thing struck him as odd, he couldn't remember anything like it coming down with previous trays. Maybe silverware, he thought as he unwrapped it. Maybe the Prince was going to trust them with a fork—

It was a knife.

Its handle was mother-of-pearl with a fine silver filigree. Its hilt had the crest of the Tarrant clan embedded in its center. The blade was as bright as sterling, and it glimmered with a light which was too cool to be reflected lamp-glow, too shadowless to be natural.

He stared at it, stunned. Coldfire. It had to be.

What the hell . . .

Jenseny crawled over to where he was and pulled his hand toward her so she could see. 'What is it?'

'It's his,' he breathed. He remembered it from Briand, drawing blood from a young boy's arm. From the Forest, slicing loose infected bandages from Senzei's stomach. From so many other places . . . 'His knife. Only it wasn't Worked back then . . .'

It was now, there was no doubt of it. And yet . . . if that light was the Hunter's coldfire, then he should be able to feel it through the cloth. He closed his hand about it – gently, lest he tempt the blade – but still he felt nothing. No cold. No evil. None of the sensations he had come to associate with Tarrant's power, or with the charged sword he carried.

'Is it now?' she asked.

He opened his hand again. The folds of the cloth were dark about the knife, yet the blade was bright. That was the unlight of coldfire, no question about it. He had seen it often enough to know.

'I think so,' he whispered. Thinking: Coldfire! He might be able to control it. No other man could. Even the Prince wouldn't dare attempt such a thing, not with a power that could suck the life out of him as surely as he drew a breath. The only reason Damien could was because of his link with Tarrant, the living channel between them. But to draw on that now . . . he had to fight off a wave of hatred and revulsion just to consider it. That lying, scheming bastard . . . but Tarrant had given them this. One chance. One slim, almost nonexistent hope.

The only hope we had, he realized suddenly. *The only possible chance he could see.*

'Why didn't he tell you about it?' Jenseny asked.

Even as he heard the words he realized the answer, and his hand closed reflexively about the knife. Wrapping it in its cotton shroud, hiding it from sight. 'Because the Prince doesn't trust him yet,' he told her. 'Because he watches him, always.'

As he might be watching us, even now.

'No,' he whispered. 'He thinks we're helpless. Tarrant's a possible threat; we're not.'

'What?'

He opened the cloth again and took up the knife to study it; after seeing that it was hinged, he folded the blade into its handle. Thus arranged it was slim and compact, and fitted easily within his hand. Or within a pocket. Or within a sleeve.

'We can't talk about this,' he told her. Very quietly. 'Because if we do, and someone is listening . . . then it's all over. You understand, Jenseny? Not a word.'

Eyes wide, she nodded. He wrapped the knife back up in its napkin, then slid it into his pants pocket. Later, when he was calmer, he would think of what to do with it. Where to keep it. How to use it.

A knife in the heart is as fatal to an adept as it is to a common man. Who had said that? Ciani? Or was it Tarrant? The memories were all muddled. God, he needed time to think. He needed time to plan.

'What should I do?' the girl whispered.

'Just play,' he told her. His mind was racing as he cast out a coin into the space between them, a northern half-cent. *No, Gerald Tarrant, I didn't know you.* He picked up his cards and spread them, sheltering them with his hands. *I didn't know you at all.*

In his pocket, the coldfire burned.

46

'Damien. Damien, wake up.'

Darkness faded into near-darkness, punctuated by lamp-fires. There were figures standing outside the bars, the glint of steel by their sides. Jenseny was shaking him.

'They say we have to go see the Prince,' she told him.

Slowly, painfully, he rose to his feet. His legs ached from cold and inaction and the short length of chain that bound them made it hard for him to get up. At last he stood, and faced the men who were waiting outside the cell. Six men in all, and the rakh who commanded them. Katassah.

'His Highness requests your presence,' the maned captain told him.

There was nothing to do but nod his comprehension and then step back while they unlocked the door. Three men came through it and took up position before him. 'Turn around,' the rakh ordered. He did. His arms were pulled back behind him, and cold steel bands were snapped shut about his wrists. They were linked by a shorter chain than the last time, he noted. The boys were being careful today.

'Bring him out,' the rakh commanded.

'What about me?' Jenseny demanded. She tried to go to Damien, but a guard held her back. 'You're not leaving me alone here!'

'You can come,' the rakh told her. 'But you have to wear this.' He held out something toward her, that shone in the lamplight. A metal band, half an inch in width and maybe ten, twelve inches around. There was a seal inscribed in a metal disk that hung from it; Damien couldn't make out the markings.

'What is it?' the priest asked.

'If you behave as you should, then it's merely a piece of jewelry. But if your behavior should in some way compromise the Prince's well-being . . . then let us say, the child would share his discomfort.' He gave Damien a few seconds for the implications of that to sink in, then asked, 'You understand?'

'Yeah,' he muttered. *You bastard*.

Jenseny was waiting for some kind of guidance from Damien; her eyes were wide and frightened. Did he have any right to involve her like this? he wondered desperately. He was probably going to get killed sometime soon. If he was lucky – very lucky – he might manage to take the Prince with him. Now, with this ward on Jenseny . . . killing the Prince would mean killing her.

Dear God, guide me. I have made the choice to sacrifice my own life, if necessary. Do I have the right to sacrifice hers?

At last he said, ever so gently, 'I don't think they'll let you come without it.' Guilt was a cold knot inside him, but there was nothing more he could say without giving himself away. Did she understand what it was she'd be agreeing to?

'Okay.' Her voice was barely a whisper. A guard took her by the arm and led her from the cell – a bit roughly, Damien thought – and then the rakh came over to her and fit the band around her neck. It snapped shut with a metallic click.

That done, the rakh ordered, 'Bring him out.'

They led Damien out of the cell, to where the rakh stood. Despite the chains binding his arms and his legs they held on to him while their leader studied him; Damien wondered just what it was they considered him capable of doing.

'You understand,' the rakh told him, 'that my orders are to kill you the instant you try anything. Not to wait, not to question, not to assess your true intentions ... just to kill you.'

He looked into those eyes, so green, so cold, and wondered what secrets they housed. What was it that the Protector had seen in this man, that he had considered him a possible ally? Whatever it was, Damien sure as hell couldn't make it out.

Kierstaad was an honored guest. That's a hell of a different vantage point than what I've got.

'You understand?' the rakh captain prompted.

'Yeah.' He nodded. 'I understand.'

'All right.' He turned to his men and signaled. 'Let's go.'

They were pushed toward the stairs and then up them. One of the men had grabbed hold of Jenseny's arm, but she wriggled free somehow and came running over to Damien; the rakh let her stay. He could feel her warmth by his side as he struggled to make the endless climb, and he wished he had some hope to offer her.

I haven't done you any great favor by bringing you here, he thought to her. *You would have been better off among the Terata*. But then he thought of how she was when they found her – filthy and frightened and living like an animal in the Terata's dungeon. *Now she's just filthy and frightened,* he thought wryly. Feeling the crust of sweat and dirt and dried blood flake from his own body as he walked. *I must smell like hell. Bet the rakh loves it*. It gave him a dry pleasure to think that the enemy – at least one of the enemy – was being made miserable by his presence. Not that this rakh – or any rakh – would ever admit that.

Halfway up he fell, his feet tangling in the short chain as he tried to go from one step to the next. He went down fast and hard and his knee hit the stair with a force that was audible. Pain lanced through his leg and he would have gone sliding downward if not for the grip of an alert guard on his arm. Another grabbed him from the opposite side and together they managed to get him back on his feet; he swayed as he stood between them, wincing from the pain.

The rakh came over to where they were and studied him, first his expression and then his feet. 'Take it off,' he said at last. Damien felt the shackles pull against his ankles as someone behind him unlocked them, and then he was free and the weight was gone and he could take a full step again. Thank God.

One down, he thought, as he started to climb again. His knee hurt like hell and he knew he could well have done it serious damage in his fall, but his gamble had proved worth the risk. The leg irons were off now, and while it was a small triumph it was nevertheless his first one in this place. And he had learned long ago that when things were really bad, so bad that it was all you could do to not think about the thousands of things that were going wrong, the best way to cope was to take one problem at a time and try to chip away at it. And so: one down.

He tried not to think about Tarrant's knife as they climbed the endless staircase. He tried not to feel its weight on his arm, its blade against his flesh. The guards hadn't seen it when they'd bound him, nor felt its stiffness when they grabbed his arms; was that due to Tarrant's Working, or the skill with which he had concealed it within his shirt sleeve? He wished he knew what the man had done to it. In truth, he couldn't feel it even when he tried, and he suspected that even if it cut his arm open to the bone he wouldn't be aware of it. It seemed to be protected by a strange kind of Obscuring, that allowed the eyes to see it but blocked all other senses. He wondered if he would be able to take hold of it when he needed to. Had Tarrant thought of that?

At last the stairs ended and they were standing in a gleaming crystal chamber. On all sides of them faceted walls glimmered and shone, their surfaces mercurial as they reflected light from some unseen source. He recognized the style, of course, and it chilled him in much the same way that the Prince's presence had. Because the Master of Lema's architecture might have been less grand, less magical, but it was inspired by the same design. Perhaps she had been attempting to copy the grandeur of this place, as she had copied the Prince's clothing. If so, she had fallen short. He had to half-shut his eyes as the guards led him forward, to close out the illusions that danced about him as he walked. Glittering walls like diamonds, waterfalls of light. How did they find their way around in this place? Was it some kind of Working they used, or were they just more accustomed to it?

I could never get used to it, he thought, as they led him through a sea of crystalline chaos. Jenseny kept a hand on his arm, and he could feel her trembling. Had her father described this place to her also? Or had he lacked the words to capture it?

And then the walls before them parted – or seemed to part – and they were standing in a vast room whose ceiling flickered with reflected lamplight, whose walls were spectral panels of shifting color. The room was filled with people – mostly guards – but it was the two figures seated directly opposite him that commanded Damien's attention. A perfectly matched pair, regal and arrogant.

The Undying Prince sat to the right, and his long fingers stroked the carved animal head of his chair's gilded arm as he studied Damien. Two guards stood behind him, and their manner made it clear that they were ready to move at a moment's notice to safe-guard their lord and master. It seemed to Damien that the man was older than when last they met – had it been only a day ago? – but that must have been a trick of the light, or the shadow that his princely crown now cast across his face. He was wearing red again, and the thick silk robe spilled like blood over the arms of his chair. So like the Master of Lema, he thought. It was an unnerving comparison.

To the left sat Gerald Tarrant, who sipped casually from a silver goblet as he studied Damien and Jenseny. This was not the dusty traveler who had ridden several hundred miles and then walked half that many, but a nobleman who had at last taken his place among his own kind. His outer robe was silk velvet, midnight blue in color, and the black tunic beneath was richly embroidered in gold. A coronet had been placed on his head so as to catch back his shoulder-length hair, and it made his eyes seem twice as bright, his gaze twice as piercing. By his side was the woman Damien had seen before, kneeling on the floor beside his chair; as the Hunter studied Damien he stroked a finger down the length of her hair, and though the priest saw her shiver she made no move to escape him.

'Reverend Vryce.' The Prince raised up a goblet as he spoke, as if toasting the priest's arrival. 'You claim to be a man of justice. Tell me, then: what judgment should I render to a man who has interfered with my army, disrupted my most vital project, invaded my lands, and plotted the overthrow of my government?'

Damien shrugged. 'How about some clean clothes and a bath?'

For a second the Prince's expression seemed to darken; then he glanced over at Tarrant and asked, 'Was he always like this?'

It seemed to Damien that the Hunter smiled slightly. 'Unfortunately.' He stroked the woman's hair absently as he drank from the cup and she shivered audibly with each new contact: a purring of terror. Her eyes were glazed and her lips slightly parted, and Damien knew that even as she sat there part of her was still in the Black Lands, running from a man so ruthless and so cruel that he would not even allow her the privacy of her own thoughts.

Regally arrogant, the prince rose from his golden chair and came toward Damien. As he did so, the priest slid one hand slowly up his sleeve, struggling to keep the rest of his body as still as possible while he did so. Thank God there were no guards directly behind him; he could only hope that the ones at his sides didn't notice the motion of his hands. In moments the Prince was close enough that Damien could see his face clearly and yes, he was older than before. Much older. There were lines on his face that hadn't been there the night before, and patches of skin that were just now discoloring. It took effort for Damien not to stare at the man, not to become so fascinated by the change in him that other concerns – like the knife – were forgotten.

Damn the knife! He couldn't feel it, not even by pressing down where the blade should be, risking a cut to his own skin. Whatever Tarrant had done to the thing to keep the Prince from sensing its presence, it was making it all but impossible for Damien to locate it.

He jerked back as the Prince drew up before him, trying to look fearful enough that the man would attribute his motion to a memory of what had been done to him the other night. In fact, it was meant to cover up the sound of his wrist chain as he slid one hand far up his other arm, scraping desperate fingers along the surface of his skin where he knew the knife should be, *must* be. And at last he found it. Not by feeling it between his fingers, like any normal instrument. He located it by the space that was left when his fingers closed, the gap between them which seemed to contain no more than air. That had to be it. He stepped back again as he pulled the slender instrument out from under its wrappings – or tried to, who could tell what was happening in that unfelt, unseen space? – and he saw one of the guards step forward, another take up his gun. That was it, then. That was as far as they would allow him to go.

'How old are you?' the Undying Prince asked him.

The question startled him so badly that he nearly lost hold of the knife. 'What?'

'I asked how old you were.'

For a moment he couldn't think, couldn't remember. The Prince waited. 'Thirty-four,' he said at last. Was he really that old? The number seemed too high, the age unreal. 'Why?' he demanded.

The Prince smiled; it was a strangely chilling expression. 'The Neocount has told me of your exploits. Tales of your strength, your endurance, your vitality . . . I wondered how much of that was left to you. Such qualities fade quickly once youth begins to wane.'

He had the knife free of its wrappings now, its grip firmly grasped in his right hand. 'I expect it'll fade rather fast sometime in the next few days,' he said dryly. His heart pounding as he fought to keep his voice steady.

The Prince nodded. 'I expect so.'

If he could have wished any one change into his life, he would have transformed the steel on his wrists to rope right then and there. Just that. But the substance which bound him wasn't anything that a mere knife could sever, and he could only pray that the power Tarrant had bound to the blade was sufficient to render the steel links brittle, as he had seen the coldfire do many times in the past. If not . . . then this was the end of it for both of them. Because the minute they moved him they'd see what he had in his hand, and it would take little Work for the Prince to decipher both its nature and its source.

He could feel Tarrant's eyes upon him, the silver gaze intense. *He risked it all,* he thought. *Everything, just to give me this one chance.* He flinched dramatically as the Prince drew closer to him, using the sound of his chains to cover his motion as he slipped the Worked blade between the links. Let the monarch think that he was responding to the threat inherent in his closeness; that excuse was as good as any.

Playing for time, he nodded toward Tarrant and asked harshly, 'What did you pay him for this?' Was that a chill creeping up along the steel links, toward his skin? Or simply wishful thinking?

The Prince turned halfway toward the Hunter, acknowledging him with a nod. 'His Excellency and I have an understanding. Among men of power such things are not a question of *purchase,* so much as mutual convenience.'

Time. He needed time. He forced himself to look at Tarrant, to make his voice into an instrument of venom and hate and spit out at the man, 'You killed Hesseth, you bastard! As surely as if you'd cut her throat with your own hands.'

Cold. He could feel it now. Cold on his wrists, where the thick steel pressed against his flesh. Ice on his fingertips, where the cold-fire licked as it worked. How long would it take to complete the job? How would he know when to chance movement? He'd only have one opportunity, and if he misjudged the timing . . . that didn't bear thinking about.

'Mes Hesseth forfeited her life when she committed herself to this journey,' Tarrant said coolly. He sipped from the goblet in his hand; another precious second passed. 'The mission was a mistake from start to finish, as you both should have realized.'

The Prince was turning away from him. Maybe it was only to give an order to one of his men; maybe it was to dismiss Damien from his presence. He would never get closer than this, Damien realized, or have a better shot at the man; it was now or never.

He pulled against his chains, hard. Praying as he had never prayed before, that the coldfire had done its work and the steel was brittle and it would give way before the violence of his motion. He saw the rakh starting forward, alerted by the motion, and the Prince was turning back toward him—

And there was a sound like breaking glass and then his hands were free, pain shooting up his arms as he brought them around, frozen shrapnel scattering across the silken carpet as the rakh lunged forward, the Prince fell back, the knife was an arc of silver fire as he brought it up toward the only possible target, the one single inch that he absolutely must strike—

Steel met flesh with a shower of icy sparks. Damien's momentum was such that even though the Prince brought up an arm in time to block his blow, it could not stop him; the point of the knife cut into the skin of the man's neck and through his flesh and deep into the artery that carried blood and life to his brain. Scarlet gushed hotly out of the wound as Damien ripped the blade back, and he prayed that in his last few seconds the Prince would be too shaken to Work the fae. Because if he wasn't, if he managed to close up the wound with his power . . . then they were all dead, he and Tarrant and Jenseny and all the millions up north who had been earmarked for destruction. The Prince would see to that.

The monarch's body jerked back suddenly, the motion knocking the knife out of Damien's hand. He saw it skitter across the rug as the Prince fell to his knees, lost sight of it against the fine silk pattern. No matter. He followed the bleeding monarch to the ground as he fell, prepared to tear out his throat with his bare hands if need be, the minute it looked like that ravaged skin was closing itself up. He heard voices, movements, weapons being drawn. Any moment now the men standing around might kill him, and the thought of death didn't upset him half as much as the fact that he might die with his work unfinished.

The scarlet stream was thinning now, and the Prince's face was a pasty white. Only seconds now, and the sorcerer would be beyond all saving. Only seconds.

It was then that Jenseny screamed.

Grief and horror and a terrible, numbing guilt all flooded Damien's soul, but he dared not turn back toward her. If the Prince healed himself in that one unguarded instant, then not only would she die but all that she'd helped them fight to accomplish would be lost forever. He couldn't let that happen. 'Forgive me,' he whispered, as he watched the last blood pulse out of the Prince's body. Knowing that even if she did forgive him, he could never forgive himself.

And then it was over.

And the room was silent.

And there was something so terribly *wrong* that he could taste it.

Why hadn't the guards moved? Why wasn't anyone *doing* anything? He dared a glance back toward where Jenseny was and saw her standing frozen with fear – not hurt, not dead, but utterly paralyzed by terror – her gaze fixed upon a figure who even now was approaching the corpse of the Prince, his shadow darkening the rivers of royal blood that played out along the carpet.

Katassah.

Damien stepped back quickly, expecting some kind of attack. There was none.

'You're a fool,' the rakh rasped.

His voice was different. His eyes had changed. They were still rakhene, still green . . . but there was something new in their depths that chilled Damien to the bone. Something all too familiar.

'And you,' the rakh said, turning to Tarrant, 'are a traitor.'

Comprehension flashed in the Hunter's eyes, and he moved quickly to draw his sword, to use the power stored within it. He wasn't fast enough. Even as the Worked steel cleared its sheath the rakh raised one hand in a Working gesture – and light blazed forth from all the walls, from the ceiling and floor, from every facet of every crystal in that vast room. Light as brilliant as sunlight, reflected and refracted a thousand times over until it filled the space with all the force of a new dawn. With a cry Tarrant fell back, stumbling over the chair behind him; the sword crashed to the floor by its arm. Damien started toward him, but the rakh grabbed him roughly by the arm and twisted it, forcing him down. By the time he could begin to rise up again, the Hunter had collapsed, beaten down by the raw power of the conjured light; his Worked blade smoked where it lay on the carpet, and it seemed that his skin was smoking as well. Strangely, madly, the woman he'd been torturing was trying to help him; in the end one of the guards had to pull her back so that the Hunter might be fully exposed to the killing light.

Guards held onto Damien as the rakh/Prince approached Tarrant's body. The Hunter had drawn up one arm to shield his face from the conjured light; the rakh kicked it away. 'You're not the only one with a storage system, you know.' He nodded toward one of his guards. 'Take him to the roof of the east tower,' he ordered. 'I've prepared it for him. See that he greets the dawn in suitable attire.'

With a sick heart Damien saw them gather up the Hunter's ravaged form and carry it away; Tarrant might have been dead already for all that he fought them. *I led you from fire into fire,* the priest thought. The rakh was coming back to him now, and the guards forced the priest to his knees to receive him.

'You can't kill me,' he said coldly. 'Not with your knives and not with your Workings. All you can do is force me to take another body before I'm ready, and that will hurt me a bit. But the pain is nothing permanent, I assure you – and in the end you'll answer for my discomfort.'

Damien looked for Jenseny, found her crouched down some ten feet away, shivering like a frightened animal. Had she Seen the change? What a horrifying thought! 'What happened to Katassah?' he demanded.

'Oh, he's still within this flesh. He just . . . *relinquished control* for the moment.' He brushed one hand down the front of his uniform, savoring the touch of its decorations. 'He's not too happy about the change in command, but that can't be helped. It's easier to claim a host when you know him well, and I was pressed for time. He'll have to understand.'

He nodded to the guards holding Damien, who pulled him to his feet. 'You destroyed the Terata,' he accused. 'That breeding-ground of adepts which I depended upon for rejuvenation. You destroyed them just when I was making arrangements to have a suitable youth brought to me . . . so I think it's only fitting that you take his place.' He reached out a hand to Damien, and though the priest jerked violently back the guards held him in place; sharp claws stroked down the side of his face, as if testing the resiliency of his skin. 'You're older than I would like, and it won't be ten years before deterioration begins . . . but look at that from the bright side. In ten years you'll be free again. You won't have to live in a body that moves without your willing it, or gaze out through eyes that are under another's control . . . by then you'll be grateful for what's left to you, priest. I guarantee it.'

'No.' It was Jenseny. 'No!' She started forward toward the rakh, but not fast enough; one of the guards tackled her roughly to the ground. 'No,' she sobbed. 'Don't do it!'

'Your little friend is loyal,' he noted. 'But never fear, there are compensations. You'll share an adept's vision for nearly a decade; there are men who would kill for a single year of that. Although admittedly, some don't cope too well when the vision is withdrawn.' Again the claws touched his face, this time not so gently; the contact made his skin crawl.

'Don't take him!' the girl yelled. 'Take me! I'll do it!'

The rakh smiled coldly. 'I took a woman for a host once,' he told them. 'I lived in her for nearly forty years. When I left her at last, her mind snapped; apparently the gender change combined with the loss of adeptitude was a little too much for her.' He bowed toward Jenseny, a mocking salute. 'So I thank you for the offer, little one. But I think I'll stick to my own sex this time. As well as my own species.'

He turned back to Damien, about to speak.

'You could see like I do!' the girl cried.

Damien realized in an instant what she meant, what she was doing. 'Jenseny, no!'

The rakh studied him for a moment, then turned back to the girl. 'And how is that, little one?'

'Don't,' Damien begged. Struggling in vain to get free, to go to her. 'Don't tell him!'

But she didn't listen, or else she just didn't care. 'I can see the tidal fae,' she said proudly.

The rakh was stunned. 'What?'

'I can see the tidal fae,' she repeated. Defiantly. 'And more than that. I can Work it a little. Hesseth said I could learn to Work it more, only we didn't have the time . . .' The last words were choked out as memory overcame her; she lowered her head, trembling. 'Only now she's gone,' she whispered.

'Is this true?' the rakh whispered. It was not so much a question addressed to her as a key to a Knowing; Damien could feel the fae gathering around him as he used it to test the truth of her words. 'Gods of Earth,' he whispered. 'You can.'

He walked over to her, knelt down by her side, put a hand to the side of her face. Though there was fear in her eyes, she did not back away. His fingers wiped a narrow path through the grime and the tears on her face and then fell back, releasing her.

'Why?' he demanded.

'Jenseny—' Damien began, but one of the guards struck him and he went down, hard.

'I don't want to be alone,' she said. 'And I don't want to be afraid any more. I'm tired of running and I want to have a place to live and I want the voices to stop. I think you know how to stop them. Don't you?'

'Maybe,' he said. 'Do you know what it is I do? Do you understand it?'

'Does that matter?' Damien demanded from where he lay. He was struck in the back and in the side; one blow landed right in his kidneys, and the pain nearly blinded him.

'I saw you move into that body,' she told the rakh. 'And I can see that he's still inside it, too. You're sharing it, aren't you? The two of you together. I could do that. You could use my eyes to see the tidal fae . . . and I wouldn't have to be alone any more.' She choked on those words, and the pain in her voice made Damien's heart lurch in sympathy. 'Not ever again,' she whispered.

The rakh stood. For a long time he just looked at her, assessing the situation. 'It would be hard to rule in such a body,' he said at last. 'But to see the tidal fae – to Work it! – that might be worth the inconvenience.'

He turned back toward Damien, who lay gasping on the carpet. 'Take them back down,' he commanded. 'I need time to think. I need—'

'Don't put me back with him!' the girl cried out. 'He'll try to stop me, try to talk me out of it . . . he might even hurt me if he thought I'd help you. Please, don't put us together.'

Oh, Jenseny. His eyes fell shut as despair filled his soul to bursting.

Please don't do this. He'll hurt you like no one else ever could, and you won't be able to get away from him. Not ever.

'All right,' the rakh agreed, and he told his guards, 'Take her to the west wing and watch her there. *He* can wait in his cell until I'm ready to deal with him.' The venom in his voice left no doubt as to what Damien's eventual fate would be.

Strong hands hauled him roughly to his feet; vomit welled up in his gut as pain shot through his back, and he struggled to keep it down. Spears of fire lanced through his left side with every step, and his feet were numb beneath him. How much damage had they done when they beat him? How long would he last if he couldn't Heal himself?

Down, down, down, they took him, down into the earth. Far beneath the crystal palace, whose walls still burned with the killing light. Miles beneath the place where Tarrant lay, his body left to catch the first rays of dawn. Down into the insulating depths where earth-fae was sparse and hope was nonexistent and pain was the only companion he had left.

Don't let him hurt her, God. Please. She's young and she's scared and she doesn't know what she's doing. Protect her, Lord, I beg of you.

Alone in the darkness, Damien Vryce wept.

47

Jenseny waited.

It was a small room they had brought her to, cluttered with furniture and wall hangings and so many scatter rugs that she could hardly see the crystal walls surrounding. That was all right with her. The Prince's architecture still burned with the false sunlight that had disabled Gerald Tarrant, and she couldn't look at it without sharing his pain, his terror, his despair.

Jenseny remembered.

That moment in the big room, that awful moment when the

Prince's essence had left one body and moved to the next: she couldn't get it out of her mind no matter how she tried. Not just because the change itself was terrifying. Not just because the image she had seen in that instant was so like the one that marked her father's killer: a slavering beast with blood on its jaws, hungry to devour its next victim. Hesseth had explained to her that the visions she saw didn't necessarily reveal what things really *were,* but their inner essence. So she understood that the Prince and her father's murderer might look the same because they both fed on death, and not because they really were the same kind of creature. That wasn't a problem.

It was what she had seen in the instant *after* that still chilled her soul. Snippets of a vision so bizarre that try as she might she couldn't explain it away. A white, shriveled form that might once have been human. A vast sea of green and brown mud, foul-smelling. Small things that fed on slime and rot and a wormlike creature that crawled along spongy flesh ... the images were so real that they were with her even now, and none of the techniques that Hesseth had taught her did anything at all to control them. Only knowledge would do that, she sensed: knowledge of what she had seen, and how it connected to the rest of this nightmare.

Jenseny feared.

This wasn't like running away from her father's house, when she knew that the creatures who had killed him were coming after her. There was a chance they might not catch her, after all. It wasn't like quivering beneath the onslaught of the solar fae, like she had that first day out. Even then she knew the sun would set in time. It wasn't even like cowering in the corner of a Terata dungeon, watching as malformed children and crippled adults beat members of their own tribe to death. Because even then she had prayed for freedom, and in some small corner of her soul she had dared to believe that somehow she might gain it. This fear was different. This was the kind of thing you felt when you had made a choice so terrible that you wanted to take it back more than anything in the world, but you knew you couldn't. It was like jumping off a cliff and then having to wait those terrible seconds while the ground rushed up at you, and maybe you wanted to change your mind now, but it was too late, too late, sometimes there's just no turning back . . .

The Light was still there; at least that was something. It wasn't strong but it was enduring, and that was a good sign. Hesseth had told her about something called a *soft tide,* when the tidal fae might last for hours. It wasn't nearly as powerful as a *hard tide,* which was when several planetary rhythms came together at once and their joint friction made the whole world glow, but it was much more reliable. And reliability was what she needed right now.

She wrapped her hands around her chest and shivered. *He'd* be coming soon. The hungry beast in a rakhene body, ready to abandon that furred flesh which he had claimed and move into hers. She wondered how Katassah would handle it when the Prince finally left him. Would he be like he was before, with a few hours of unclear memories? Would he be angry with the Prince for having used him like that, or grateful for having been able to serve him? Had he tried to fight the Prince in that first few seconds of possession, so that deep inside he might be hurt and afraid? *I'll know soon enough,* she thought unhappily. Wrapping her arms even tighter about her body, as if she could squeeze all the fear away.

A knock. She turned about quickly, just in time to see the heavy door swing open. It was the rakh guard, the Prince-thing.

He stepped into the room and gestured to the men behind him. 'Leave us,' he ordered, and they did. He pushed the door and it swung slowly shut, closing with a click as it finally met the frame.

She could see him as a man now, if she tried. His features kept shifting, maybe because he had taken so many bodies. Maybe she was seeing all of them at once.

'Mes Jenseny—' the Prince began.

'Kierstaad,' she said defiantly. 'My name is Kierstaad.'

The rakh eyes narrowed in irritation and for a moment she was afraid that he was angry enough to hurt her, but then she realized that she couldn't possibly be safer. In a very short while he would be living inside her body; surely he wouldn't want to lay claim to damaged property.

She thought suddenly of that *thing* moving inside her and for a moment she almost panicked. Did she have to do this? Wasn't there some other option?

No, an inner voice said gently. *No other option. Go on. Do it.*

'Mes Kierstaad,' he said. 'Does your offer still stand?'

She whispered it. 'Yes.'

'I'll need to have a look at your motivation first. Just to make sure there are no . . . surprises.'

She nodded. And shut her eyes. And concentrated oh so hard on everything she wanted him to know: how she really *was* tired and she really felt lost and she really was terrified of being alone, so much so that she would welcome him into her soul just to make that feeling go away. And she wanted to save Damien, she mourned for the loss of Hesseth, the voices followed her everywhere – everywhere! – and she wanted them to stop, she just wanted to be safe and warm and not be afraid any more, not ever afraid again. All those things were true, painfully true, and as his Knowing unearthed her feelings she felt tears come to her eyes, tears and a sorrow so intense that her whole body started shaking violently. Never mind that those weren't the *real* reasons she was doing this; if he believed them, then that was enough.

Evidently he was satisfied, for the next thing that happened was that the room was gone suddenly, along with its rugs and its furniture and its crystal light. She heard him moving toward her and she forced herself not to back away, not even when he reached out and touched her, not even when the power flowed from his flesh into hers—

From his flesh into hers—

Suddenly she Saw. Not the creature she had seen before, and not the man he pretended to be. She saw what he really was, the secret that was the core of his very existence. And the vision was so horrible that she almost tried to draw back from him, using the tidal fae to establish some kind of barrier between their souls so that no more visions could come. But he was inside her now and there was no turning back, not ever. Her eyes were his eyes.

She saw a space deep underground, a chamber fortified by so many quake wards that every inch of its inner surface was inscribed with signs of power. In the center of the room was a glass tank, and though the light cast by several of the wards was dim she could see it quite clearly, and smell its reek, and understand its purpose . . .

'No,' she gasped. 'No.'

Floating in the tank was a man. No, not a man any more. It had four limbs and one head and it wore a man's shape, but there the resemblance ended. The fingers were thick and white, and in the place of fingernails grew a dense brown fungus. The body was so bloated and its surface was so mottled with various growths and discolorations that it would have been a stretch of the imagination to call it human. The face . . . the face was a thing of pure nightmare, its hair and eyebrows long since rotted away, its eyes coated with thick brown sludge, its lips distended to serve as a gateway for the tiny finned creatures that used its mouth as home. All about the body there was movement: snails and slugs and tiny leggy things, all scrounging for the waste matter exuded by their host. There were plants to eat the leggy things and fish to eat the plants, a cycle of life so perfectly balanced that a little light and an occasional infusion of oxygen was all that was required to keep the tiny ecosystem alive.

My first body. The words were not spoken so much as placed in her mind; the taste of them was sour, the feel of them unclean. *Keeping it alive makes me all but invulnerable. And no man will ever find where it is buried.* She saw how the nutrients in the water were absorbed by that pliant flesh, so that the brain it housed might go on living year after year, century after century, sending out its spirit to claim more attractive bodies while it floated in the semi-darkness, slugs and snails for its nursemaids.

And then *it* was inside her. Unclean and loathsome, it slithered into her brain and coiled within like a serpent. She could feel its tendrils reaching out through her arms, her legs, all her extremities, and parts of her body began to twitch as it tested its control. Panic welled up inside her, and for an instant she nearly gave in to it. How easy it would be to go crazy now, to release her feeble grip on reality and slide down into madness for thirty years, forty years, until her body burned out and began to age and the Prince no longer wanted it. How easy . . .

Do it, he urged her. Hungry for a kind of control he could never have if she remained active in her flesh. *I'll give you dreams. I'll give you peace.*

She didn't give in, nor did she draw away. Instead she opened her eyes so that he might see as she did, to fully cement their bargain. Combined with his own abilities her vision was doubly powerful, and the brilliant, scintillating Light of the tidal fae filled the room almost to bursting. She could sense his shock as he shared her vision; she could taste his hunger as if it was her own. *Watch me,* she thought. *I can Work it.* As he gazed out in wonder through her eyes, she took up the tidal fae and wove it into pictures for him, beautiful pictures that stunned him with their power, pictures he could feel and taste as well as see

(and all the while she was taking out the object she had stolen, praying for him not to notice as she drew it from her pocket and opened it)

and she wove the tidal fae into a glimmering shell that contained them both, a vast knotwork of power that would support and enhance their union. He was too lost in wonder to question it. He was too busy reveling in his newfound potential to consider the implications of such a simple Working. *No man has ever Worked like this,* he thought to her. *Not even among the rakh.* While he explored the nooks and crannies of her mind, she wove and wove and wove with all her strength, using every skill that Hesseth had taught her and every ounce of power that the tides made available. Tidal power didn't work that well on material substance, the rakh-woman had told her, but in matters of spirit it was unequaled. She prayed it was so as she bound them together, forging a bond with her fledgling sorcery to support that which he had conjured, a bond which – she hoped – might never be broken.

Then she struck. Hard and fast, a single upswipe of her right arm that brought the knife – Tarrant's knife, rescued from the floor of the throne room when no one was looking – straight into her own throat, into that one special place (Damien had said) where the blood drew near the surface of the body as it carried life-giving oxygen to the brain. She struck fast and she struck hard, because she knew she would never get a second chance. And all the while she poured out her rage at this man, she drowned him in her hatred and her grief and her determination to destroy him, emotions she had been desperately holding in check up until now so that he wouldn't catch on to what she was really doing, but now that the act was done they poured out of her like a tidal wave.

You killed my father! she screamed silently. As the knife cut deep, deep in her throat, freeing the hot blood to gush down her neck, her chest, her arm. There was no fear in her now, only the fierce joy of triumph. *You killed Hesseth! You took away everything I had and now you'll do it to others, so many others! Only you won't, you won't, I figured out how to stop you!*

He was startled at first, then cocky, indignant – and then he tried to return to his other body, and he couldn't, and he got scared. He had thought that he could never be killed – certainly not by her! – but now he realized that wasn't true, she had thought of a way. She would drag him down into death along with her if it took every ounce of strength she had, every bit of power she could conjure. As he struggled to withdraw from her dying flesh, she gripped the tidal power with all her might, holding onto the rainbow tides and using them to reinforce her Binding, to hold onto him, to keep him from slipping free—

Earth-fae rose up from the ground beneath her with a roar, engulfing her in the flames of his fury. Blinded, she could no longer See; stunned, she couldn't Work. Even as she began the long slide down into the darkness of death she could feel him using his power to unravel the bond between them; he was starting to slip away from her, his spirit abandoning her bleeding flesh for a more dependable body. *No!* she screamed. *You can't go!* But he was going, and she was fading fast.

God, please. She prayed feverishly, desperately. *Help me!* Her vision was growing dim, as were her other senses; she could hardly feel the flames he had conjured anymore. *Please. For Hesseth and my dad and the children with the Terata and all the thousands he'll hurt, all the thousands who'll get eaten or worse if he goes free . . . please help me.* There was a ringing in her ears now, and the pulse of blood from her throat had weakened to a trickle.

'Please,' she whispered. As she fell to the ground, the soft ground, and darkness folded over her like a blanket. Soft, so soft. She struggled against it, but its power was numbing, suffocating. *Please, please don't let him go free . . .*

And Something answered. Something that cooled the flames around her until they vanished back into the currents which had given them birth, to flow like water around her supine body. Something that stilled her fears and soothed her hate and quieted the storms of her spirit. Something that reached out and touched the Prince's soul as well, filling his spirit with Its Presence. Peace. Quiet. Utter tranquillity. He recognized the danger and he fought it, fought it desperately, but it wasn't the kind of power a man could do battle with. His experience was in games of violence and domination, and those things had no power here. She felt his fear bleed out into the darkness – the soft, loving darkness – and slowly, gradually, his struggles ceased. It no longer mattered to him which body he was in, or whether his flesh was dying; his hunger for life had given way to something far more powerful. Slowly the tidal cocoon about them rewove itself, binding him to her flesh; slowly she slid down into the warm shadows of death, and he came with her.

Thank you. Voiceless words, silent peace. *Thank you.*

There were faces now, floating in a whirlpool of light. Hesseth. Her father. Her mother. All the rakhene children. She reached out for them, only to have them dissolve between her fingers like ghosts.

Come, they whispered, reforming just beyond her reach. *Time to move on. Come with us.*

She walked toward them. A bright figure led the way, a soldier whose armor gleamed golden like the Core, and whose crystal standard tinkled in the wind. She remembered him from a vision she'd had once, of thousands of bright knights preparing to give their lives for their faith. He held out a hand to her and she took it; the contact made her tingle.

Some things, he whispered, *are worth dying for.*

And then the whole world was filled with light, and there was only peace.

48

Well, Damien thought, this is what it's all come to.

The lamps had gone out maybe an hour ago. The darkness itself wasn't such a terrible thing – there was just enough fae in the cell that he could Work his sight to see by its dull glow – but the implication of that darkness was the final thread in a vast tapestry of despair. In his previous incarceration he had never been left without light. Men had come down those stairs at regular intervals to see that the wicks were trimmed and the fuel pots were full, so that the lamps might never go out. Now they were empty. And in a palace run with such clockwork precision, Damien could read no other meaning into that than the fact that he was meant to waste away in the darkness, to die at his own slow pace.

He tried to shift position, but pain stabbed through his back as he moved and he had to give it up. He had managed to gather enough fae to work a minimal Healing, enough to stop the internal bleeding, but the power in this underground cell simply wasn't strong enough for anything more than that. The pain was centered around his kidneys, where the worst blows had fallen, and he knew all too well just how bad that could be. How long would it be before he knew if there was fatal damage? What kind of dying would that entail? Maybe it was more merciful to let his system fill up with poisons, rather than die the slow death of starvation. Maybe he should be grateful.

There was a sound on the stairs. He looked up, startled, but saw only the dim glow of earth-fae as it trickled down over the stone. He listened so hard that it seemed his blood roared and his heart beat like a timpani, but even over those distractions he could still make out the sound of footsteps. Footsteps! They came toward him with excruciating slowness, echoing down the spiral stairwell. And then light, coming toward him like the dawn. Never mind that it was a single lamp. Never mind that the figure who carried it was cloaked, and the folds of his garments cast deep shadows on the cold stone walls. In this place a match flame would have seemed like the sun itself, and the light of a lantern was nothing short of miraculous.

He managed to rise to a sitting posture, though pain shot through his back as he did so. The figure approached the bars. The light of the lamp was blinding, and for a moment Damien couldn't make out any details of his visitor's face. At last the figure moved the lamp so that it was off to one side, and its light silhouetted rakhene features that Damien knew all too well.

For a long time Katassah just looked at him, as if trying to read something in his expression. It might have been a trick of the shadows, but his fur seemed strangely dull; a thin membrane had drawn across the inner corner of his eyes, making his expression twice as alien as usual.

'He's dead,' the rakh said quietly. His voice was strangely devoid of emotion, like that of a shock victim. 'She killed him.'

It took him a minute to realize what he meant, to accept that the rakh standing before him was exactly that, and not a sorcerer in disguise. The Prince was . . . dead? Then they had succeeded, he thought dully. The mastermind behind the atrocities of this region had been vanquished, and his works could now be undone. It seemed unreal, like something in a dream; he had trouble accepting it.

'Where's Jenseny?' he pleaded. 'Is she all right?'

The rakh said nothing. For a minute he just looked at Damien, and then he shook his head slowly. 'She took him with her,' he told Damien. 'Sacrificed herself so that he might die. All in the name of your god, priest. She bought into your myth and it saved her.'

He reached into his cloak and removed something from an inner pocket; Damien heard the jangle of keys. 'Under the circumstances I think it best that you leave here.' He seemed to fumble with the key ring, as though lacking the coordination to manipulate it. 'As soon as possible.' The key slid into place and turned; the door swung slowly open. He looked at Damien. 'Can you walk?'

He nodded and tried to get up, but pain shot through his back. Breathing heavily, he gritted his teeth and tried again. This time he got as far as a kneeling position. From there it was only one lurching twist and a gut-wrenching extension to a standing position. He reached out for the nearest bar and used it to steady himself; the lamplight was swimming in his vision. The rakh offered no aid and voiced no concern, but he waited patiently until Damien had released the bar and then said, 'Come with me.'

The Prince is dead, he thought. Waiting for the joy to come. But there was no room for it in his soul, not with so much grief already filling him. *Later,* he promised himself. *Later.*

Ten stairs. A hundred. Each one was a separate trial, an individual agony. More than once he had to stop and lean against the wall, fighting to catch his breath. The rakh said nothing, offered nothing, waited. At last, when they were close enough to the top that his Worked sight revealed enough earth-fae, he muttered, 'A minute. Please.' When the rakh stopped and turned to him he gathered up the precious power and patterned it into a Healing, a blessed Healing that poured through his broken flesh, cooling the fire of his pain. With desperate care he rewove broken blood vessels, mended shattered cells, prompted his body to clean out the pool of waste fluids that had accumulated in his wounded flesh. At last, satisfied that he had done the best he could possibly do, he let the Working fade and leaned against the cold stone wall, breathing heavily. Thank God the pain was fading quickly; that didn't always happen right after a Healing.

'All right,' he muttered. Pushing himself away from the wall at last, forcing himself to move again. For the first time since they had started their climb, he felt as if he might really make it. For the first time, it sank in that they had won.

No. *He* had won. Hesseth was dead, and Jenseny also, and as for Tarrant . . . how many hours had it been since the Prince had consigned him to the dawn? He wanted to ask, but he couldn't find the breath. At the top, he promised himself. He'd ask when they reached the top.

The stairwell was beginning to lighten, reflecting light from the palace above. The rakh drew up his hood to shield his face, and wrapped the cloak tightly around his body. *His people are sensitive to sunlight,* Damien remembered. Was he injured when the Prince conjured light to attack Tarrant? Was the Prince willing to accept that pain in order to guarantee his victory?

It could have been him in that situation, he realized. Hell, it almost was. What was that like, to have another mind controlling your arms, your legs, your eyes and hands, perhaps your very thoughts? It was too horrible to consider. Thank God Jenseny had died before the Prince had subjected her to that.

Two turns. Three. The light was brilliant now, and Katassah put up a hand to shade his eyes. Damien noted that the fur of his arm was matted and stained. With blood, it looked like. Whose? The rakh staggered then, and it was clear he was having trouble. Was he hurt also? If so—

'I can help you,' Damien offered. 'There's enough fae here for a Healing if you need one.' He reached out toward the rakh, intending it as a gesture of support, but the rakh snarled and backed off. Sharp white teeth were bared; the matted, stained fur of his mane bristled with aggressive vigor. Damien stepped back as far as he could, to where his back was against the inner wall; it didn't seem far enough. This was an animal display far beyond Hesseth's civilized snarlings, and he sensed that if he moved too fast or said the wrong thing those long, thin claws would slash his face to threads before he could draw another breath. Frozen, tense, he waited. At last the rakh seemed to shudder, and his claws resheathed. His lips closed over his sharp teeth, hiding them from sight. When he spoke, his voice was hoarse, and he clearly had to struggle to discipline it into human words.

'I'm . . . sorry.' The words were clearly hard for him; how often did he have to apologize? 'Human contact—'

'Hey.' Damien managed to force a smile to his face. It was stiff and awkward but he thought it communicated what it was meant to. 'I understand.'

Together they ascended into the light. After so many hours in darkness the brilliance of the palace was blinding; both he and the rakh paused at the topmost step, shading their eyes, struggling to adapt to it. 'He didn't care,' the rakh muttered. '*He* could see using the fae, and that was enough. He didn't care if the light damaged my eyes.'

'Sweet guy,' Damien muttered. 'Sorry I didn't get to know him better.' And then he dared, 'Speaking of light . . .'

The rakh understood. 'Your friend?'

Friend. What a bizarre word that was. What an alien, almost incomprehensible concept. Could one call the Hunter a friend? Would one ever *want* to?

'Yeah,' he muttered. 'Tarrant. Is he alive?'

The rakh hesitated. 'I think so. I went to him first when it happened, because time was such a factor.' He shook his head. 'I couldn't do anything. Maybe you can.'

'How much time is left?'

He glanced toward one of the walls, but if there was some kind of clock there Damien couldn't see it. 'Not much,' he muttered. 'I'll take you there. You can see for yourself.'

There were more stairs, crystal stairs that glowed with all the brilliance of the sun. It was clear that the light hurt Katassah's eyes, and more than once he stumbled. Was the whole damn palace Worked?

Two men came into sight. They looked startled to see Katassah there, but were far more surprised by Damien's presence. After a moment of confusion and hesitation they both bowed low to the rakh and then hurried away in pursuit of other business. Katassah stood still just long enough to accept their obeisance, then resumed the long climb by Damien's side.

'They don't know, do they?'

The rakh shook his head. 'No one knows. No one *will* know, until I tell them. Or until they guess.'

He would have asked him more about the Prince's death, but at that moment the stairs grew steep and uncomfortably narrow, and he decided that his attention was better spent on his footing. They climbed perhaps twenty feet that way, to a narrow tunnel which opened onto darkness—

And the night sky unfolded before them, in all its predawn glory. Overhead the heavens were as black as ink, with a spray of stars scattered across the east like drops of fire. Beneath that was a band of pale blue rising along the horizon, and it was bright enough already that the stars directly over it were nearly invisible. Damien had watched the sun rise often enough on this trip to know how little time they had left.

'Where is he?'

The rakh pointed. It was hard to make out shapes on the glowing rooftop, but he thought he saw a man-sized shadow in the direction indicated. Carefully but quickly he made his way over to where it lay; the walking was treacherous, and more than once he stumbled over one of the sharp crystalline growths that littered the roof of the palace. In the end he made his way more by feeling than by sight, to the place where the Hunter lay.

Gerald Tarrant had been bound, but not by chains. There were wards etched into the glassy surface beneath him, and the crystal substance of the palace roof had grown over his arms and legs in several places, binding him in arched fragments of a faceted cocoon that hugged his flesh tightly, cutting into it in several places. Whoever had brought him up here had torn his outer robes from his body, leaving only his leggings and boots and – ironically – his sigil necklace. *Prepared to meet the sun,* Damien thought grimly. He remembered what a moment's exposure had done to Tarrant in the rakhlands, and knew there was no hope of him surviving a longer immersion.

He knelt down by his body, noting the strain on the Hunter's face, the subtle tremors in his body. He was conscious, then, and struggling to overcome the pain the light was causing him long enough to free himself from his sorcerous bonds. But the light was too strong, too lasting; even Damien could feel its power, and he lacked the Hunter's sensitivity. The priest ran a hand over the nearest of the wards and worked a Knowing, but it netted him little real knowledge; whatever patterns had been used to grow those bonds were too subtle and complex for a man of Damien's skill to unravel it.

He glanced east, saw the sky just above the mountains brightening ominously. There wasn't much time.

'Can you unWork it?' the rakh asked.

He looked at the wards, at the Hunter's crystal bonds, at the

Hunter himself. *I should leave you here,* he thought. *The world would be a better place for your absence.* But somehow it didn't seem the time or the place to be making that decision.

'Do you have a sword?' he asked.

For a moment Katassah looked at him like he had gone crazy, but apparently he decided not to question the request. He reached inside the folds of his cloak and drew his own sword from its sheath: a short sword, narrow-bladed, which was meant to complement gunfire rather than replace it. Damien took it from him and noted the thick quillons, the heavy pommel. Good enough.

He chose a spot on one of the growths and brought the butt of the weapon down hard on the crystal, in the place where he judged it most likely to be weak. Chips flew as the steel pommel struck, but the formation held. He struck again. On the second blow a chunk of the arch broke loose and went flying, leaving a space just big enough for Tarrant's bare arm to be dragged through. In the east the stars were disappearing, swallowed up by the sun's early light. He moved quickly to another of the growths and struck at it, hard and fast. This one was a thick arch, and it took three blows for it to begin to shatter and five more before there was enough space to pull Tarrant's leg free. Katassah was helping now, pulling the man's limbs out of the way as soon as Damien made such action possible, and it was a damned good thing; the arches were growing back almost as fast as he could destroy them, and if Tarrant lay in one place for too long he might well have to do this all over again.

At last Tarrant was freed, and together they dragged his limp, death-cold body to the exit. Spears of white light crowned the eastern mountains in fire as they forced him into the narrow passageway, and as they fought to maneuver Tarrant's limp form down the stairs Damien imagined he could hear the solar fae striking the crystal spires behind them. They completed two turns down the staircase, then three, and Damien allowed himself a sigh of relief; the sunlight was behind them now, and while the conjured light inside the palace might cause Tarrant pain, he doubted it had the power to kill him.

The Healing Damien had Worked on himself might have helped ease the pain of his injuries somewhat, but it couldn't negate the strain of carrying a grown man across so much space; by the time they reached the stairs leading down to Damien's prison cell he could barely walk, and he had to lean against the wall for a long time gasping for breath. The rakh looked little better. But Damien was afraid that if Tarrant stayed in the light too long it might prove too much for him, and so he forced himself to move again, to drag the man's body downward, downward . . .

They stopped after the third turn, when the light in the stairwell was dim enough that a lamp's illumination would have been welcome. 'This is it,' Damien gasped. 'This is good enough.'

'Wouldn't he be better off at the bottom? It's darker there.'

Damien shook his head, 'He needs the earth-fae to heal himself. I think. And there isn't enough of it much farther down than this.'

He hoped he was right. He hoped the faint light which remained wasn't enough to cause further injury, or to keep the Hunter from healing. For now there was nothing more he could do for him, other than wait. The rest was in Tarrant's hands.

They set the body down on the wider part of a step; there was just enough room for it to lie securely. Kneeling down beside the Hunter, Damien studied his traveling companion with a practiced eye. The tremors had ceased; that was one good sign. And it seemed to him that the strain on Tarrant's face had eased somewhat; that was another. No, there was nothing more he could do here. Nothing more anyone could do.

He looked up at the rakh. How worn Katassah looked, how tired! In another time and place the captain might have tried to hide his infirmity, but here there was no point in dissembling. Damien knew what had happened to him. Damien understood. And more than any other man on the planet, Damien comprehended that the most damaging part of his experience was not the horror of bodily possession, or his sense of betrayal at his ruler's callousness, but the utter degradation of having a *human soul* inside his flesh. A wound like that would not heal easily, nor quickly. Damien understood.

'Is there anything I can do?' the rakh asked.

'Yeah.' He stood. The ache in his back was duller now, a mere vestige of pain; with a muttered key he Worked enough earth-fae to make sure that dragging Tarrant here hadn't damaged it anew. It was partly a safety precaution and partly a test of sorts; if he could Work the fae this far underground, it was a good bet that Tarrant could also. Given that power, the Hunter could heal himself.

He turned to the rakh and said softly, 'I'd like to see Jenseny.'

She lay on the couch where Katassah had placed her, one arm draped down so that its slender fingers brushed the floor, her eyes shut. There was blood all over the room, red and wet, and trickles of it had coursed down from the gash in her neck to stain the white couch crimson. Her coloring had gone from pale brown to an ashen gray, and the look on her face should have been one of fear and anguish. It wasn't. It was a look of utter contentment, such as men might dream of but never know. Of perfect and absolute peace.

Damien knelt down by her side, taking up her tiny hand in his own. It wasn't cold yet, not completely; he could still feel the echo of life beneath his fingertips, and it brought new tears to his eyes.

God, take care of her. She was gentle and loving and so very brave, and in the end she served You better than most would have the courage to do. Give her peace, I pray You, and reunite her with her loved ones. As he wiped his eyes he added, *And let her play with the rakh children now and then, if that's possible. She would like that.*

'How did it happen?' he asked.

Katassah had hung back at the door, unwilling to intrude upon the privacy of Damien's mourning; now that he had been addressed, he approached. 'He moved into her body and meant to take over. She held him there and took her life.'

'I wouldn't have thought she had that kind of power.'

The rakh's voice was full of awe. 'She called on those who did.'

He shut his eyes for a moment and drew in a slow breath; the fact of her death was finally sinking in. 'All right. At least it's over.'

'It isn't, I regret.' The new voice came from behind him. 'Not by a long shot.'

Katassah whipped about with the reflexes of a trained guard; Damien followed suit. The man leaning against the far wall was familiar to him, but for a moment he couldn't place the memory. A stout, bearded figure draped in black velvet and black fur, perhaps in deference to their mourning. Oddly decorated for this time and place, Damien thought. In the end it was the tastelessness of the man's jewelry, its utter inappropriateness for the occasion, that prompted him to remember.

'Karril,' he whispered. This was Tarrant's Iezu: the one who had healed Ciani, the one whom Senzei had consulted. Damien discovered to his surprise that the abhorrence he should feel for such a creature was absent. Had his recent experiences inured him to the concept of demonkind? Even the faeborn who did good deeds were still dangerous parasites.

'I came to warn you,' the demon said. As he stepped forward into the center of the room, the crystal walls lost their light, dimming to a comfortable glow. 'You need to go home, Damien Vryce, and you need to do it fast.'

He ignored the advice for the moment, focusing on a more important message. 'What did you mean, it isn't over?'

The demon seemed to hesitate, and looked around the room as if he expected to find someone listening. 'You'll find out when you go north,' he said finally. 'So I'm not telling you anything, really. Only what you would discover yourselves.'

'What is it?' Katassah demanded. His hand was on the brass grip of his pistol, a warning sign. 'What's happening?'

The demon turned to him. 'Your Prince was a pawn, Captain, nothing more. And now Calesta's game is played out. You forced his hand a hundred years early, but in the end that'll make little difference. You won the battle, but the war has just begun.'

Something cold tightened around Damien's heart. He had known that the death of the Prince was only the first step in healing this land, but something in the demon's tone warned him that the issue went far beyond that. 'Tell us what you mean,' he said sharply.

The demon looked pained. 'I can't. Not in detail. If I interfere in his affairs by helping you . . .' He drew in a deep breath and slowly exhaled it, trembling; the gesture was oddly melodramatic coming from a creature that didn't have to breathe. 'It's forbidden,' he said at last. 'But so is what he's done. To tamper with mankind's development . . . that's strictly forbidden. So which is the worse crime? Which is more likely to be punished?'

'Tamper how?' Katassah demanded, and Damien snapped, 'What the hell are you talking about?'

'Go north,' the demon said. 'You'll see. He used the Prince, he used the rakh, and now . . . I'm sorry,' he said to Katassah. 'Genuinely sorry. But you see, he can't feed on your people. So it really doesn't matter to him whether they live or die.' He looked at Damien and then quickly away, as though he feared to meet his gaze. 'Twelve centuries ago your ancestors came to this planet. There were only a few hundred of them then, few enough that when Casca made his grand sacrifice it shook this planet to its very roots. Now, with millions of humans on Erna, with thousands of them Working the fae, no one man can have that kind of influence. No single act can impress the fae so that its basic nature alters again. But a thousand men – a hundred thousand – might. A plan of action carried down through the centuries could.'

'That's Church philosophy,' Damien said sharply.

'Yes. And Calesta watched your Church develop. He learned from it, and from its founder. He took the lessons your Prophet taught him and applied them here, as a sort of grand experiment.' He shook his head, his expression somber. 'All too effectively, I'm afraid.'

'What is it he wants?' Katassah asked sharply. 'What's the goal?'

'A world that will respond to his hunger. A world with such an outpouring of the emotional energy he covets that the fae will absorb it, focus it, magnify it – until that in turn alters the very nature of humanity.'

'What does he feed on?' the priest demanded. He was trying to remember what Gerald Tarrant had told him about the Iezu. 'What aspect of mankind? Tell us.'

The demon stiffened, and for a moment Damien thought he would refuse to answer. But at last he said, very quietly, 'Calesta feeds on that spark of human life which delights in the pain of others. A universal sentiment, I'm afraid. Calesta grows stronger every time that spark is expressed.'

'It's far from universal,' Damien objected.

'Is it? Can you show me one man or woman who has never, *never* wished hurt upon another? Not as a child fleeing from bullies, not as a lover wronged by his or her companion, not even as a right-eous crusader setting out to save the world from those who would corrupt it? Have you never longed to see an enemy hurt, Reverend Vryce? Not the Prince, not Gerald Tarrant, not anyone?'

His lips tightened. He said nothing.

'*Go home,*' the demon urged. 'As soon as you can. You can't do anything to save this place – no one man can – but you can still save the people you love. Because he'll strike at them, I'm sure of that. He knows it'll be a year or more before you can get back to the west, and in that time he can do a lot to change things. If you stay away longer, if you give him that much more to work with . . . then the world you return to may not be the same as the one you left. Trust me.'

'Vengeance,' Katassah muttered. 'For interfering with his plans here.'

The demon nodded. 'I'm afraid so.'

'Why are you telling us this?' Damien asked suddenly. 'If you're not allowed to interfere with him, then why come here at all? What's in it for you?'

'I like humanity,' the demon told him. Smiling slightly. 'With all its quirks and its foibles and its insecurities intact. I enjoy them. Oh, I'd survive the change if Calesta had his way. Sadism is a form of pleasure, after all. But it wouldn't be nearly the same. Food without entertainment is nearly as bad as no food at all.' His expression darkened slightly, though the smile remained. 'Of course, I may yet pay for this indulgence. Who knows which transgressions the mother of the Iezu will tolerate, and which she'll punish? No one's ever dared to test her before now.' He shrugged, somewhat stiffly. 'I expect we'll know soon enough.'

With a formal bow he said to the rakh. 'I'm afraid your people have a long, hard battle ahead of them, Mer Captain. The Prince used his power to evolve your species to suit Calesta's need, and it will be a long time before those weaknesses breed out. But they will in time, if no human interferes. I'm sorry I can't help you more.'

'You've done enough by explaining things,' Katassah said tightly. 'Thank you.'

The demon turned back to Damien. His flesh was starting to fade, solid cells giving way to a more shadowy substance. The flicker of a lamp behind him could be seen through his black-robed torso. 'My family are symbiotes, not parasites,' he told the priest. 'And some of us are proud of that distinction. Be careful, Reverend Vryce. Be wary. Travel fast.' He was little more than than a veil of color now, fading out around the edges. '—And take care of Gerald Tarrant, will you? He seems to be getting himself into a lot of trouble these days.'

'I'll try,' the priest promised. A tight smile softened the lines of his face.

As they watched, the demon dissolved completely, his color and form fading into the very air that surrounded him. When he was finally gone, the illusion of darkness faded also, and the room was restored to its former painful brightness. Damien stared at the spot where he had been for a long time in silence, the demon's words echoing in his brain.

'Well, *shit,*' he said at last. 'That's just great.'

49

They left from Freeshore, on a merchant ship bribed to ply the northern seas for their purpose. It was Katassah who had paid for the journey, dispensing royal gold as if it was his own. Which it was, in a way. His men had seen the Prince take over his body, and until he informed them of the new state of things – or until he made some vital mistake that caused them to guess at it – the throne and the power were his for the asking. It would cost him dearly in the end, Damien knew. As the lights of Freeshore faded behind them and the gentle swells of the Novatlantic drew them northward, he remembered the rakhene captain as he had been at their departure: studiously proud, carefully arrogant, imitating with perfection the man whom he had served for half a lifetime. It was a masquerade that couldn't last, of course, no matter how well he played at it; in time his lack of sorcery would give him away, and the game would disintegrate from there. They would turn on him then, all the men and women who had served the Prince. He knew it would happen. And yet he wore the royal robes over his rakhene uniform and placed the Prince's crown on his head, risking that fate. Because – he explained – with Calesta's dark plan coming to fruition, he dared not leave his people leaderless.

There's the soul of a born ruler, Damien thought. *If only it could have been expressed under happier circumstances.*

They had taken a case of homing birds with them, and Damien released the first after a day at sea. *Found passage with the* Silver Siren, it said. *Proceeding as planned.* The rest of the birds would be saved for when they reached the northern kingdom, when they learned what havoc Calesta had wreaked there.

How isolated Katassah must feel, how very helpless, now that the Prince's power no longer served as a link between his people and their northern contacts! The crystalline palace was no longer the nerve center of an empire, but a tiny island of hope and fear nearly lost in the vastness of the black lava desert. Damien wished him well with all his heart, and prayed feverishly that his self-sacrifice would serve its intended purpose: to stabilize his divided nation against the threat of war, so that when the truth was at last made known the country might adapt and thrive, rather than dissolving into chaos.

The girl Sisa had come with them. When she had first shown up with her few belongings as the boats were loading, Damien had been aghast – no, furious – and he raged at Tarrant, declaring in no uncertain terms that he would not permit the man to bring her along for the sole purpose of feeding on her terror. To which the Hunter had replied, quite calmly, 'I must have food, Vryce, and you can't supply it any more. We've discussed that. As for the woman's motives ... I suggest that you ask her yourself.'

He did. And though she had claimed that she wanted to come with them, that Tarrant had in no way coerced her to make the trip, he found it hard to believe. Each time she glanced at the Hunter she trembled; each time conversation turned toward the Hunter and his needs she grew visibly paler. Had Tarrant found himself the perfect masochist, a woman who delighted in suffering? Damien doubted it. Not because such people couldn't exist – he had no doubt that they did – but because he couldn't imagine Tarrant taking any real pleasure in torturing one of them.

Why are you here? he asked her later that night, when chance left them alone together. *Why do you want to be with him?*

He thought for a moment that she wouldn't answer him. But though her eyes were cast low, there was fear in her voice, it was clear when she spoke that she trusted him. Slowly, hesitantly, she told him of the night that Tarrant had hunted her in the Black Lands, the night she had run like an animal in the desert night, fully expecting to die. But instead of killing her when he finally ran her down, the monster had offered her an alternative fate: *Survive my hunger, he said, and I will free you. Keep me alive for the months it will take us to reach my homeland, and I'll set you up as a rich woman in a land with no princes, no religious wars, no slavery*. And she had accepted. The challenge was all that was keeping her sane now, and the dream of success kept her going. So that she might suffer all the more, Damien thought. So that she might feed him. Like the women who ran from him in the Forest, convinced that three days of successful flight would buy them a lifetime of safety. How utterly consistent Tarrant was in his sadism, how perfectly ordered! Damien wondered if this woman would survive the test that so many had failed. He prayed for her sake that she would.

As for Tarrant . . .

He came to the place where Damien was standing, late in the second night of the voyage. There were no other people nearby and the sea was smooth and quiet. It was the kind of night in which two men might stand together companionably and watch the waves, thinking of the lands ahead and the trials yet to come. The kind of night in which a priest might turn to his dark companion and ask softly, *Why?* and expect to be answered with honesty.

For a long while the Hunter watched the sea, and Damien knew better than to press him. 'It was as I told you,' he said at last. 'We had no chance. No chance at all. Not with a Iezu involved, and a sorcerer of that caliber. I perceived that the only way to get near enough to strike was to allow ourselves to be taken by him, and thus I designed my subterfuge. I wanted to tell you,' he said, and his tone was one of rare sincerity. 'I wanted you to share in the choice. But it was already apparent to me that there was a real connection between the Prince and our adversary in the rakhlands, and I suspected their strategies would be the same. She Knew me, as you may recall, in order to determine what you would do; I guessed that he would proceed similarly. Which meant that you *couldn't* know, Reverend Vryce. The whole plan hinged on your ignorance. I'm sorry,' he said softly. Facing the night. Addressing the waves. 'I did try to make it easier on you. Tried to bring us in at Freeshore for an early capture, or arrange for a controlled ambush afterward. I wanted to spare you the hardships of the Wasting, but you fought me at every turn. I'm sorry.'

'That wasn't what I meant,' Damien said quietly.

The Hunter blinked. 'What then?'

'He offered you immortality. To use your own words, *the real thing*.' Damien shook his head. 'I know you, Gerald. Pretty well, I like to think. And I know what death means to you. I know that avoiding it is the focus of your very existence, and that nothing – not family, not ethical obligations, not even fear of divine judgment – is allowed to threaten that focus.' He looked at Tarrant, meeting the pale gaze head-on. 'So what happened? Why *didn't* you sell out? I'm grateful for it, mind you, I always will be – but I don't understand it. Not at all.'

Tarrant's expression tightened; after a moment he turned away, as if he feared what Damien might read in it. 'In my lifetime,' he said solemnly, 'I created only one thing of lasting value. One thing of such beauty and promise that long after I had committed my soul to darkness I still reveled in watching it grow, in seeing what turns it would take and what new paths would open up for it. Your Church, Reverend Vryce. My most precious creation. The immortality the Prince offered me was based upon its corruption. He would have taken my work and twisted it – destroyed it – reduced it to some neo-pagan drivel in order to harness its power for his own ends. And I couldn't stand by and let that happen. My vanity was too great in the end, my pride too all-conquering; to accept immortality on those terms. It would be like letting part of myself die in order that a lesser part might live. So you see,' he said quietly, 'it was that very offer which turned me against him.'

He turned away then, and left his place at the rail; perhaps he felt that in the wake of such a confession it was best to leave. But as he walked away from Damien, his footsteps as silent as the breeze in the sails, the priest said, 'Two things, Gerald.'

He turned back partway, startled. 'What?'

'You said you gave us one thing of value. But there were two. Have you forgotten? The Church of the Unification . . . and horses.' He smiled slightly. 'I know some who would even argue that the second was the more important creation in the long run.'

'Pagans,' he retorted, dismissing the thought. But it seemed to Damien that he, too, was smiling, and as he left the priest's company his step seemed lighter than it had in too many long, hard nights.

There's hope for you yet, Hunter.

North. Into warmer seas, brighter skies.

Into nightmare.

The Prince had died, and along with him a network of Wardings that supported the rakhene invasion. Now all of that was gone. Now the invaders, stripped of their protective coloration, were revealed for what they were: brutal imposters who had terrorized the land, using the Prince's illusions to mask their true identity while they put humanity to the sword.

No longer.

In every village where the *Silver Siren* stopped, in every city, in every Protectorate, the spirit of vengeance held sway. The luckiest rakh were simply slaughtered, their throats cut or their bodies gutted as hordes of humans descended on their strongholds. They had nowhere to run to, no way to hide. The Prince, being dead, could no longer protect them with his sorcery; Katassah, not knowing of their plight, could not send reinforcements. Quickly the humans learned their weaknesses, and the rakh who had once terrorized small human villages now cringed in terror as their victims rose up, their souls filled with fury, their hearts set on vengeance. And all the while Calesta fed, Calesta inspired, Calesta rejoiced, as a holocaust of epic proportions took root in the Church's most blessed lands.

Nightmare:

Rakhene bodies in Especia, flayed alive and staked out for the sun to torment. Rakhene heads adorning the gates of Tranquila. Rakhene claws worn as common adornment in Shalona. Everywhere there was rakhene suffering, rakhene pain . . . and more than that. Horribly, terribly more than that. Drunk with hatred, high on vengeance, the human mobs lost that fine sense of discretion which separated righteous indignation from blind destructiveness. In Infinita a human child who was sensitive to sunlight had been taken up and tortured to death; in Verdaza an adult suspected of sorcery had suffered a similar fate. Every man was suspect; every woman was vulnerable. Rumors circulated of impossible couplings, resulting in offspring which looked truly human but were loyal in spirit to their rakhene heritage. Children were torn from their parents and slaughtered for seeming rakhlike in their play; others were orphaned when a word or a sign hinted that their parents had tasted forbidden pleasures. All to cleanse the world of brutality, the killers claimed; all to make God's most favored land safe for human habitation.

No one man can save this place, Karril had said. Sick with horror at what he had witnessed, Damien found it easy to believe that. The very foundations of human society were beginning to crumble, and it wouldn't be long before such damage was done here that no one generation might save it. Did they understand what was happening to them? Did anyone even suspect? If so, that would probably be seen as a mark of the enemy's power. No doubt any churchman who tried to warn his fellows of the danger inherent in this course would be cut down in mid-speech, damned along with those he meant to save. In a time like this, who would dare to speak out?

In the Kierstaad Protectorate, where the rakh had razed whole villages, the cleansing had been thorough indeed. The once proud keep had been set afire so that only its stones remained, mute witness to the slaughter that had taken place within. Charred bones lay throughout the chambers and corridors, some skeletons missing hands or feet or even larger appendages; they had probably been crippled and left to die while the fire closed in on them. One balcony which overlooked the sea was carpeted in shards of glass, as though some fragile and beautiful thing had been systematically smashed; Damien remembered Jenseny's description of her mother's crystal garden and mourned for its loss.

They had brought her body with them, preserved by Tarrant's frigid power, to lay it in the ground of her homeland. But Damien couldn't leave her there, not in the midst of all that evil. So they went a mile or more down the coast, to a place where the trees were green and the ground cover was lush and no blood had been shed in recent history. And they laid her there, with a piece of her mother's crystal beside her and her father's gemstone in her hand. He said a prayer aloud over her grave, though no one else in the ship's small company shared his faith; let them see that his God was gentle at heart, that He cared about the welfare of a child's soul. It wasn't much in the face of all this horror, but right now it was the best he could do.

Rest in peace, precious child. God spared you sight of this slaughter, for which I will always be grateful. God spared you the knowledge of what kind of ugliness lies waiting in the human soul, wanting only the proper catalyst to bring it to life.

A familiar hand clasped his shoulder, strong and cold. In comfort? In warning? He nodded, and allowed himself to be led away. Toward the ship which would take them north. Toward the capital of this shadowed empire, and the men who might save it. If they could. If any men could.

Toward Mercia.

Sunset: the sky red and orange, with deep purple clouds hanging heavy at the horizon's edge. Overhead the Core, outlining shapes in molten gold. On the field of green a platform, lined in stone. On that platform, bound to a stake, a body.

Burning.

There were nearly fifty thousand people in the great square of Mercia, and only Tarrant's power made it possible for him and Damien to approach the platform unhindered. The breeze was blowing westward, but every so often it shifted and passed over them, carrying the sharp smell of burning, the pungent aroma of roasting flesh. Even Tarrant seemed sickened by it, or at least by its implications.

They were burning – had burned – their Matria.

It had happened in other cities, Damien knew. They had heard of it as they traveled up the shore, and once they had seen its gruesome aftermath. But never this. Never these thousands of people, so hungry for suffering. Never this palpable sense of corruption, so powerful that he could feel it Working the fae around him. So overwhelming that at times he felt he would surely choke on it.

A sudden movement by the platform caught his attention; beside him he felt Tarrant stiffen as a mounted figure robed in white and gold rode up to smoldering ashes. He was tall and regal and the horse he rode was one of Mels Lester's finest, a broad-shouldered stallion with a champagne coat whose glossy white mane and elegant tail rippled in the wind as it moved. It rode up to where the crumbled body smoked and then turned to face the crowd; the man on its back saluted the assembled with a motion that was half-religious, half-military in nature.

Toshida.

His power was tangible, his presence overwhelming. In a land where chaos and violence now held sway, he clearly controlled the reins of his city as surely and as firmly as he did the reins of his lustrous mount – and the crowd responded to him as obediently as that beast did. When he gestured for silence, they subsided; when he commanded attention, they listened; when he proclaimed Mercia's triumph over its adversaries, they cheered with a passion that was near hysteria in its intensity. The energy was the same as in the other cities, Damien noted, and every bit as volatile. But here it had a focus, a control. Here the hatred had been channeled, refined . . . *used*.

The spectacle was over at last. Slowly the crowd dispersed, as firemen saw to the safe removal of the still-smoldering debris. There would be parties aplenty tonight, as Mercia celebrated her freedom. None would question the fact that the Matria's death had freed them from rakhene domination. None would stop to consider that in dozens of cities up and down the coast, this burning would not have been a triumphal end but a dark beginning.

Damien looked at Tarrant; the Hunter said nothing, but nodded ever so slightly. As the crowd thinned out about them, they began to walk northward, and as they moved, the Hunter conjured an Obscuring that kept the masses looking elsewhere, moving elsewhere – in other words, out of their way. It took them little time to reach the Regent's Manor – or was it now the Patriarch's Manor? – and they had no trouble with the guards. The few who were allowed to notice them were carefully controlled, smoothly manipulated. Thus the two gained access to the building, the upper floors, Toshida's private wing. Thus they gained audience to the Patriarch himself.

'Your Holiness.' It was Tarrant who bowed first, a deep obeisance that acknowledged and glorified Toshida's new status. Damien followed suit. He could see the man's eyes glitter with pleasure as he accepted the offering. How long had he been waiting for this? Damien wondered. How great had his hunger become?

'I thought you might come here,' he said to Damien. 'Verdate. Although I will admit I expected you to travel with members of your expedition,' he nodded toward Tarrant, 'not locals.'

Tarrant smiled coldly. 'I came east on the *Golden Glory* along with Reverend Vryce. However, as I chose to disembark before the ship reached Mercia, I regret we haven't met yet. Sir Gerald Tarrant, Neocount of Merentha.' And again he bowed.

'Ah. No doubt you are the western sorcerer the Matrias warned us against.' He smiled tightly. 'I think I can say with some certainty that any enemy of theirs is welcome in my city.'

'Are all the Matrias dead?' Damien asked.

'Not quite all. Some have fled for the mountains, and will have to be tracked down. And they have their own citadel in the far north, where they train more of their kind; that has yet to be stormed. But give us time, Reverend Vryce. Only recently did we learn what the true situation was; day by day our knowledge grows.

Give us time, verdate, and soon all the human lands will be cleansed of their taint.'

Damien tried hard not to let that phrase turn his stomach; given what he had seen in the past weeks, it took considerable effort. 'We were hoping you could tell us what happened to the ship that brought us here.'

Toshida hesitated. There was something in his expression that warned Damien all was not well, so that when at last he said, 'The *Golden Glory* is gone,' it came as no real surprise.

'Left?' he asked. Knowing the real answer even as he asked.

'Wrecked. Off the shore of Almarand, in a squall. Most of the crew made it safely ashore, but the ship itself was destroyed, along with the cargo it was carrying. I'm sorry,' he said, and there seemed to be genuine regret in his voice.

'Captain Rozca? Pilot Maradez?'

A muscle along his jawline tensed. 'The captain is in Penitencia, negotiating for a replacement vessel. Rasya . . .'

Damien's heart sank. 'Drowned?'

He shook his head stiffly; his expression was strained. 'She made it ashore. Spent a week in Almarand, studying their old sea charts. Then she set off for Lural Protectorate, seeking some old log book that supposedly was stored there. An expeditional relic, I believe.'

'And?'

Toshida turned away. 'She was a stranger,' he said quietly. 'This is a bad time for strangers.'

Oh, my God. He pictured Rasya lost in an angry crowd, her height and her coloring and her accent branding her as an outsider, an unknown, a threat . . . he pictured her falling victim to one of the crowds he had seen and he trembled inside. *Not that. Please, God. Not her.*

'It happens,' Toshida said. Though he might have meant the words to be comforting, to Damien they sounded harsh. Inhuman. 'The price we pay, Reverend.'

'For what?'

'For freedom. For an end to tyranny. The land must be cleansed, and if in the end that cleansing causes pain—'

'God in heaven!' Damien exploded. 'Do you really buy that crap? I would have expected more of you than that, *Patriarch*.'

Toshida's expression darkened. 'Who are you to judge our ways? If the people need violence to heal, then let them have it. You can't expect emotion like that to stay bottled up forever; sooner or later it must express itself, and if that expression is uncontrolled—'

'And is this *controlled*? Is that what you call it?'

'They're killing rakh. I call that justice.'

'They killed Rasya!' His voice was shaking – with rage, with grief, with incredulity. 'And hundreds of others. *Thousands* of others. Anyone who gets in their way, or disagrees with their cause, or just plain isn't lucky—'

'That's the price we must pay, Reverend Vryce. Verda ben.'

'For what?'

'For unity.' His expression was hard. 'Or have you forgotten? The great tenet of the Church we both serve. Unity of faith. Unity of purpose. Unity of fate, at any cost—'

'No,' Tarrant interrupted. 'Not at any cost.'

Toshida turned on him. 'Will you teach me my own religion now? I was raised in the Church; I think I know the Prophet's teachings well enough.'

'You may know them,' Tarrant said coldly. 'But you clearly don't understand them.'

Toshida's eyes blazed with rage; his skin blushed copper with fury. 'How *dare* you! As if any outsider can ever understand the world we've built here, or what it takes to maintain it—'

'You want to see what it is you've built here?' The Hunter's anger was filling the room, chilling the air within it. Rage-wraiths flitted about his head, trembling in time to his speech. 'You want to see the precious world your religion of hate will foster? I'll show you!'

The room became a whirlpool of color, into which Toshida and Damien were sucked. The walls lost their substance, and the floors and ceiling also. Even gravity lost its hold; everything was sucked toward the center of the whirlwind, all matter and thought, all flesh and spirit, all hopes and fears and dreams—

And the future unfolded before them. Not one single timeline, pristine in its certainty. A wild, unfettered morass of futures, a chaos of raw possibility. Damien saw worlds in which Calesta's holocaust had swallowed up whole cities, whole regions, setting brother against brother in a war whose only purpose was to destroy life. He saw worlds in which the Church had become a tool of control, a vehicle of tyranny, and the Prophet's dream had been smothered in ritual brutality. World after world passed before his eyes, bloody and violent and hopeless and corrupt. He could see the corruption spreading out like waves, from the populace to the Church to the fae itself, until pollution flowed like a tide about the planet, fouling every soul it touched. Calesta's dream; Calesta's hunger. And in the midst of it all there was only one world with hope, only one vista in which any light shone. Only one world in which a man stood strong against the tide, a single man of vision and determination who could turn back the flood of corruption if he chose to, who could set his city on a new path, and through that city, his world. One new-made Patriarch, dark-skinned, triumphant—

There was a sudden cry – half anger, half anguish – and then the vision exploded like shattering crystal. Fragments of reality rained down on Damien as he struggled to get his bearings again, but for a long minute it was impossible; by the time he could make out the outline of the door it was already closing, and the figure that had passed through it had long since faded from sight.

'Gerald!' No thought for Toshida now; he bolted for the door himself, hoping to catch the Neocount in the hallway beyond. But the Hunter had moved quickly, or else he'd had a substantial lead; not until Damien had run from the building, startling half a dozen guards in the process, did he see Tarrant's lean form fleeing the Manor grounds, long legs covering the ground with feverish speed—

'Gerald! Stop!' He didn't know if the man could hear him, but it couldn't hurt to try. 'Please!' It had no effect. He pushed himself for as much speed as he could manage, trying to make up for Tarrant's natural advantage in height and endurance.

And at last, in a deserted district, he caught up with him, not because he was running faster, but because Tarrant had stopped. Fear showed starkly on that death-pale face; the silver eyes were bright with it.

'Do you know what I did back there?' he demanded. His voice was hoarse with terror. 'Do you understand?'

'You shared a Divining,' Damien told him. 'And if Toshida saw what I saw, then you may have saved this world. You've certainly saved this region—'

He stopped. No more words would come. Because suddenly, he understood. He *understood*.

'What I've done,' the Hunter whispered fiercely, 'is to commit suicide. Have you forgotten my pact? Have you forgotten the power that sustains me? There are conditions set on my existence, priest. And if in truth I inspired Toshida to lead this region away from its current course, then I just broke them all.'

For a moment Damien couldn't speak at all. 'You're still here,' he managed. 'You're still alive.'

The tortured face turned away from him. 'For how long?' Tarrant whispered. 'Until Toshida commits himself to change? Until that change begins to take effect? Where in that process is my life to be terminated? Nine hundred years of service, wiped out in one careless instant!' He shut his eyes. '*You* brought me to this, priest. You and your philosophy! You and your *human influence!* Are you happy now?' he demanded. 'Is this what you wanted? Will it please you to imagine me suffering in Hell while you plan your next campaign against Calesta?'

'If I did,' he said evenly, 'wouldn't that just feed the bastard more? Gerald. Please.' The Neocount had turned away; Damien could see his strong shoulders trembling. 'I don't relish the thought of fighting him alone. Quite frankly, without you I wouldn't last a minute.' As for the other question the Hunter's words had raised, he didn't dare face that. Not now. After months of praying that Gerald Tarrant would be brought to judgment for his many sins, that the world would be freed from his tyranny forever, he wasn't ready to admit that the thought of it actually coming to pass made him feel sick inside. Had his feelings toward the man changed so drastically in these last few months? If so, it was a dangerous development.

A shudder seemed to pass through that lean, tormented frame. 'Go find Rozca,' Tarrant whispered hoarsely. 'Help him get hold of a ship that can make the passage. Without our pilot we have little chance of surviving a journey, but make what arrangements you can. When they're done I'll know, and I'll come back to you. *If* I'm still alive.'

He began to walk away.

'Gerald—'

The Hunter turned back to him. His eyes were empty, black and cold and utterly without boundary; looking into them chilled Damien to the bone. 'I must be what I was meant to be,' he said coldly. Bits of his intentions were manifesting about him as he spoke, fueled by the raw power of his desperation; the images were filled with violence and pain. 'So don't look for me to return to Mercia until you're ready to leave here, Vryce. Because my only hope in surviving that passage – in surviving to *begin* that passage – lies in defining myself anew. In praying that the power which sustains me is capable of forgiveness . . . or at least of forgetfulness. *If* I please it.'

'Don't,' Damien whispered. Sick at heart as he realized what the Hunter intended. 'Don't do it!' But Tarrant wasn't listening to any arguments. Coldfire blazed up from the ground, engulfing his body in frigid power. His flesh melted, reformed, became a giant winged figure – not a bird this time, but something with a sleek black body and leathery wings, a creature out of nightmare realms – and then he was gone, rising up high into the sky so that he might survey his new hunting-ground.

Sick inside, Damien watched him fly until his black form faded into the distant night. Headed toward Paza Nova, perhaps, or Penitencia, or the Kierstaad Protectorate . . . anywhere there was fear. Anywhere there were unprotected souls to be harvested, so that the Hunter might cleanse his dark soul with the terror of innocents.

As he turned back toward Mercia's central district, as he numbly began to walk again, Damien tried hard not to think about how delighted Calesta would be when he learned of the Hunter's decision.

Epilogue

Darkness.

Not the simple blackness of Erna's night sky, with its absence of sun or stars. Not the insulating darkness of the ocean's floor, with miles of water filtering out each intrusive ray. Not even the total lightlessness of a cavern's interior, in which a man might put his hand before his face and not only fail to see it, but doubt that it even existed. Those were mere shadows compared to this, echoes of darkness that could be compromised by a single match, or lamp, or candleflame. This was a blackness that would swallow light, just as it swallowed life.

Things stirred in that blackness. Envies. Hates. Hungers. Echoes of the darkness in the human soul, now given independent life. Sometimes a few of them would coalesce, giving birth to entities as cold and as ruthless as the place was dark. Sometimes they would all scatter, and the only hint of consciousness in that black realm would be whispers of hate that wafted through the darkness like errant winds. Sometimes – rarely – all of them would gather together, and a Presence would take form whose nature was so powerful, so corrupt, so utterly maleficent, that if its existence had been stable it would have posed a threat to every living thing on Erna. Men who knew of it called it the Dark, the Evil, the Devourer, and they prayed to their various gods and demons that no man might ever give it a true name – for a human name has the power to endure, and that was the one power the Unnamed One lacked.

Into this darkness a stranger came. Though the body he wore was as black as night, it seemed brilliant as lampfire compared to the darkness surrounding him. For a moment he stood still, and the voices of that lost place whirled about him like some wild music, dismal and discordant.

Who is it
Who comes here
Who disturbs Us
Who
Who
Who

'My name is Calesta,' the demon announced. Several of the voices seemed to coalesce for an instant, and then their whisperings were separate once more. 'I seek an audience.'

Calesta?
Calesta
Manborn
Iezu
So hungry
Anger
Hate hate hate
What do you want, Iezu?

'You made a compact with a human.' Something flitted past his face, but he didn't flinch; the flesh he wore was only an illusion and he didn't fear for its safety. 'Nine centuries ago, with a man named Gerald Tarrant. Do you remember?'

Ah, yes
Blood
Hunger
Promises

The voices were becoming different now, as if all the disparate notes had been gathered up into one great chord. He sensed a presence circling him, studying him. *We remember. We feed.*

'He's betrayed that compact.'

Silence. Such utter silence that for a moment he wondered if the voices had left him.

What business is it of yours, Iezu? A different voice now, screeching and hateful. *Go back to manplaces. This compact is Ours.*

'He betrayed you!' the demon hissed. 'Don't you care? You gave him life on condition that he serve you and look what he did! Thousands will live because of him. Millions will know peace who otherwise would have suffered. A whole civilization has been jerked

back from the edge of ruin. By him! Doesn't that matter to you?
Don't you care?'

Compact is Ours

Ours

Ours!

Broken?

Conditions

Unlife

Broken

Ours!

The darkness stirred. In it a presence was gathering, so far
beyond the flitting voices in substance and power that they might
have been mere insects circling around it. Its voice, when it spoke,
was deep and resonant, and it reverberated throughout the
darkness.

Our compact with Gerald Tarrant is not a Iezu concern.

'I thought you would want to know what was happening.'

We find it offensive that you assume Our ignorance.

'He's still alive,' Calesta challenged.

That's Our concern, not yours.

'What about the compact? The agreement—'

We know the agreement. He knows the agreement.

'He defies you! He betrays everything that you gave him life for!'

*Are you concerned for Us, Iezu? Or simply driven by your own need
for vengeance? We will not become a tool of your kind.*

The demon stiffened. 'We share a common concern, you and I.
If you were to—'

We have nothing in common with the fleshborn.

The demon drew in a sharp breath; rage emanated from him
like wildfire. 'I'm no more fleshborn than you are,' he snarled.
'And if you're content to let Gerald Tarrant take advantage of you
– if you're content to have him *use* you – so be it. I thought you
might have a little more backbone than that, but evidently I was
mistaken.'

*Go home, man-thing. We will decide what to do with Gerald Tarrant
Ourselves.*

With an angry curse the demon dissolved his flesh, abandoning the darkness of that secret realm for the more comfortable blackness of the human soul. For a long time after his departure there was silence, as the various entities considered their exchange. Then, in voices that rippled one into another too quickly for the human ear to distinguish, a waterfall of sound:

Betrayed

Compact

Good service

Hunger

Blood

Betrayed

Promises

Life

Unlife

Betrayed

Betrayed

Betrayed

Vengeance?

Hunger

They began to coalesce once more, and a new thought took root. *This Iezu,* a voice mused, *does not know what he truly is.*

No, another voice agreed. *None of the Iezu do.*

Help him?

Destroy him?

Ignore him?

Wait, a deep voice recommended. *Watch. See if his own kind supports him. See if she takes sides.*

And Tarrant?

Something new stirred in the everlasting darkness. Something so powerful that the blackness became a fierce whirlpool, into which all the other voices were suddenly sucked. Something so malevolent, so utterly hostile, that the petty hates and envies of humankind were lost inside it, swallowed up by an Evil so vast that it fed on the very essence of life itself. It existed for only an instant, this Power, and then it began to break up again into its disparate elements. But the instant was long enough.

Tarrant, said the Devourer, *will have to answer to Me.*

The story continues in

Crown of Shadows . . .

PRIESTESS OF THE WHITE

Age of The Five: Book One

Trudi Canavan

When Auraya was chosen to become a priestess, she could never have believed that a mere ten years later she would be one of the White, the gods' most powerful servants.

Sadly, Auraya has little time to adapt to the exceptional powers gifted her by the gods. Mysterious black-clad sorcerers from the south plague the land, and rumours reach the White of an army being raised. Auraya and her new colleagues work tirelessly to seal alliances and unite the northern continent under their banner, but time is running out.

War comes to the lands of the White, and unless Auraya can master her new abilities, even the favour of the gods may not be enough to save them . . .

MYRREN'S GIFT

The Quickening Book One

Fiona McIntosh

When Wyl Thirsk, General of the Morgravian Legion, is forced to watch the torture of Myrren, a young woman accused of witchcraft, it seems little enough comfort to speed her passing. But Myrren is grateful for even this small mercy and promises Wyl a gift. He thanks her but dismisses the notion – what could this poor, doomed girl have to give him?

It is only years later that Wyl, shorn of his friends and allies, betrayed by his king, and forced to make an impossible choice, remembers the dying words of the young woman about to burn for the crime of witchcraft. As his enemy's sword draws closer, Wyl finally understands the meaning of Myrren's gift, and he wonders how one act of kindness could have unleashed such evil . . .